I0788197

RED RAIN

VOL.I: ANNIVERSARY EDITION

RED RAIN

VOL.1: ANNIVERSARY EDITION

RACHEL NEWHOUSE

WITH DAVID HARTUNG

ISBN-13: 978-1-957432-29-8

Cover Art by Clarissa Laurenda (Instagram: @fungzauu_)
Cover Layout by Shawn Jonas

This is a work of fiction. Any similarities to real people, living or dead, are merely coincidental.

Some titles previously published under the penname Aubrey Hansen.

rachelnewhouse.com

CONTENTS

RED RAIN

RED RAIN #1

RACHEL NEWHOUSE

OCTOBER 2075

1

It had been almost six months since anyone had died because they refused to go to school.

Today, Mr. Dass was determined to break that record.

"Mr. Dass, need I use force?"

"You will need to use a lot more than force if you expect me to move!"

I cringed. Commander Ambrose shook his head. "Mr. Dass, I ask nothing unusual. Your children have been attending our school since—"

"Since you made them!" the red-faced father bellowed. He held his daughter Mira close to him. His son Stanyard stood safely behind him, fiddling with a backpack.

"A fair point." The commander shifted and cast his gaze around the street. All along the row of solid concrete homes, families stood in their doorways and watched. The bus, painted red with the harsh black words ASSIMILATION SERVICES on the side, idled in the road. The handful of kids inside pressed their faces against the windows; two armed guards leaned against the door. The driver tapped a small electric pistol on the wheel impatiently. No one else moved.

I fingered the pouch strapped around my waist. After the Dasses', our house across the street was the next—and last—stop.

I felt hands slide over my shoulders. I glanced up into my father's sober face. He rubbed my shoulders gently as he watched Mr. Dass.

Commander Ambrose spoke again. "You realize, Mr. Dass, that you are a civil criminal and in violation of United policy."

"By choice," Mr. Dass spat back.

"In the interest of preparing the younger generation to rejoin the United as productive members of society, your children must attend our school to be—"

"Indoctrinated against everything we've ever taught them!"

That's a decent way of summing it up.

My dad stopped rubbing, but he kept his hands on my shoulders. His eyes were closed.

Commander Ambrose tipped his head to the side. "Exactly." He looked down at Mira, who gazed up at him with wide dark eyes. Mr. Dass gripped his daughter's arms, as though daring the commander to rip her from his grasp.

The commander did. In one swift movement, he grabbed Mira's shoulders and yanked her from her father. Mira screamed, but the commander didn't hurt her. He shoved her down the steps and swung at Mr. Dass as the infuriated man dived. Mr. Dass stumbled but quickly regained his footing.

"You beast!" he snarled. He backed up, shielding his remaining child. "Just try and take my son."

"Are you enjoying this? Is this some sort of game to you?" the commander threatened.

Some days I wonder. My father pinched my shoulders.

There was silence, except for Mr. Dass's ragged breathing. The commander glared, but Mr. Dass didn't move. Finally, the commander drew his gun from his side.

I instinctively pinched my eyes shut. Daddy muttered under his breath, "Lord, not today."

There was scuffling. I opened my eyes to see Stanyard squeeze out from behind his father and scamper down the steps, head lowered. Wordlessly, he grabbed Mira's arm and hauled her onto the bus.

The commander watched them go, then turned back to Mr. Dass. The father's face was no longer red, but white.

"Your children are learning," Commander Ambrose said coolly, sliding his gun back in its holster. "They are smarter than your generation." And with that, he turned and marched across the street—towards us.

My father twisted me around to face him. Holding my shoulders, he bent low and spoke in quick whispers. "Remember why we always homeschooled. Believe nothing they say without comparing it to the Bible. Save all questions for home—tell me everything. Remember me, Philadelphia. Remember your mother. Remember God."

I nodded rapidly, staring into his brown eyes. He kissed my forehead and let me go; I ran down the steps and fled for the bus. The commander moved aside, one foot on the bottom step, to let me pass. He looked up at my father.

"Well, Dr. Smyrna, coming around, are we? You used to be the troublesome one."

My father straightened and said nothing. He watched me find a seat in the back of the bus. I waved through the window until we were out of sight.

The bus turned the corner and rumbled through another lane of houses, exactly the same as the street before. The houses were two-story concrete boxes with only three windows on the front. All of them were identical on both sides of the blacktop road. There were no trees, no grass, no mailboxes. Nothing personal about the yards whatsoever.

The only difference was the front doors, which were alternating colors going up the row—red, blue, orange, purple, green—to help separate the houses at a glance. Each house also had a number burned into the concrete step and plated on the door. My house number was 79.

There used to be exactly 110 houses in the Street 17 Containment Camp when it was first built five years ago. Five years ago, Street 17 camp was full, as were Street 80 and Street 83 camps.

Now my camp was down to 64 houses, and not all of them were occupied. The unused streets had been demolished and the concrete wall moved up, fencing the remaining houses in more closely.

It must have cost a fortune to rebuild the wall every other year, but I guess it was worth it to remind us that they were slowly crushing us out.

The bus stalled in front of the energized metal gates. A sensor in the wall scanned the license plate and blinked approvingly. The gates rolled back into the wall; the bus chugged through and waited until the gates shut themselves again. Then, for about ten minutes, the bus drove through the Outside.

I was glad we still lived in the camp across town. I enjoyed, however short, my ride through the Outside every day; I could look out the window freely and watch the world and its people. The trees, the grass, the signs—colorful display windows and strolling crowds. Unlike the camp, the Outside changed, shifted, bore new colors and new faces. The brief glimpse on the bus ride over was a relief, an entertainment—a reminder of what used to be.

I glanced across the aisle. Stanyard and Mira shared a seat there. Stanyard was leaning with his forehead against the seat in front of him, eyes glazed. Mira twisted her hands together.

"I'm sorry," I said.

Stanyard nodded wordlessly. Mira looked up at me. "He didn't hurt me," she assured.

Cami twisted around in the seat in front of me and looked back. "I'm surprised your father didn't offer any objections, Phil."

"How could he, after that?" her brother Aid quipped from beside her. "The commander hasn't pulled his gun in almost a month."

"We talked about it, last night," I mused. "He said it wasn't worth the blood right now."

"Smart man," Stanyard muttered. He sat up and gazed out the window. Mira stared straight ahead.

We went to the same public school all the regular kids attended. I suppose they were hoping that we'd see our peers—with their learner's permits and after-school jobs and shiny devices with unrestricted internet access—and want to join them.

It certainly seemed to be working. Our bus used to be a lot more crowded.

Although we attended the rest of our classes with the regular kids, our morning homeroom was a special "remedial" class headed by a teacher who, in his opinion, wasn't getting paid nearly enough to supervise the indoctrination of some religious brats. It was his job each morning to lecture us about the freedoms we could have if we would just get with the program and sign over our right to religious expression.

He treated it as such a trivial thing, like we were giving up our right to choose what color of socks we wore. If we would simply succumb to a little conformity in the name of peace and equality, we could rejoin society with all the rights owed to us as full United citizens.

I never watched his face during his tirades; if I looked at something else, filled my mind with anything else, it made his voice sound smaller. I often looked at the projections on the wall, toyed with the cursor on my laptop, or prayed.

I never, ever looked out the windows. I never, ever looked at the Outside— the freedom I would gain if I followed my teacher's words.

The rest of the school day wasn't much better. Math was my favorite subject, although not because I was particularly good at it; they just seemed to waste less time trying to squeeze propaganda into trigonometry than they did with other subjects.

History was the worst. It was nothing like the stories my grandpa used to tell me; all of the glorious and inglorious escapades of humanity had been stripped and sanitized and manipulated. Every era now existed exclusively to demonstrate the need for the United.

According to our textbook, the United was humanity's greatest achievement. It was the solution to every war, every injustice, every inequality. The glories of the United were raved to us as our teachers reveled in the progress of the one-mind, one-body megacountry the world was slowly forming. Segments all over the globe were dropping their boundaries and cultural differences and assimilating into a homogenized body that was its own god.

And of course, it was stressed that religion was a major hindrance to progress in the United. A hindrance that must be assimilated or removed.

2

The bus was quiet on the way home. I sat by myself and thumbed through the Bible on my reader. I skimmed the virtual pages, picking up random verses.

My times are in your hands... deliver me... from those who pursue me...

I jumped when Cami slipped across the aisle and squeezed in next to me. I looked at her face and instantly knew what she was going to ask.

"Can you?"

I held out my hand. She pressed a tiny chip into my palm.

I closed my window and snapped the chip into my reader. The screen chirped.

Cami explained while I navigated my library to find the appropriate file. "The Marksens, the new people, had their data wiped."

"Weren't they caught transmitting?"

"Yeah. Apparently the father signed the file to keep his job, but the kids hadn't. Or something. But they lost all their data." She picked at the peeling vinyl bench with her fingernail. "Dad wanted me to ask you to do it."

I didn't need an explanation. I knew why I always made the copies, even though Cami's reader was perfectly capable. Everyone else stopped making copies after my mother died.

I suppose they stopped for the same reason my father kept doing it—and kept letting me do it. Even if his wife had died for violating the "no transmitting" law.

I suspected the commander knew what I was doing. After all, my device was continually connected to either the camp or school wifi. He could monitor my activity if he wanted to. I assumed he didn't care, not if I limited my distribution to my fellow inmates. We were all criminals anyway.

I knew he would care if he found out my dad was transmitting copies from work.

"Thanks," Cami said finally.

I nodded and tapped the screen. The progress bar seemed stuck at 15%. Usually it took about three seconds, five if my dinosaur of an electronic was feeling grumpy.

"Something wrong?" Cami asked, probably more worriedly than she intended.

"It's stuck. I'm going to try again." I canceled the transfer and backed out to the main menu. I clicked on the Bible folder and got a hideous beep. I shuddered and looked at the screen.

It said: *File not found.*

I frowned and backed out a few folders, then went in another way. This time, I couldn't even find the folder.

"What's wrong?"

"It's gone."

"What?"

"My Bible—the file. It's gone."

Cami snatched her reader out of her bag. She flicked it on and thumbed for a minute.

I squinted at her screen. "Bible" was missing from the alphabetical list of folders.

She stared at me dumbly.

I leaned forward and hissed across the aisle. "Mira!"

She glanced in my direction. Stanyard continued to stare out the window.

"Open your laptop."

"Why?"

"See if your Bible is still there."

"Why would it—"

"Just do it!" Cami squeaked. She chewed on a sprig of her hair.

Mira obeyed. Aid glanced back at us, frowning. He quickly opened a new window on his tablet.

"The file's gone," Mira reported.

"Can't find it." Aid tapped through more menus.

"I still have my study notes," Mira offered. Stanyard finally sat up and turned to face us.

"I'm missing some stuff for school, too," Aid said. "Some essays. The folder's there, but a few of the files are gone."

"Are you sure you downloaded them at school?" Stanyard questioned.

"Yeah." Aid flopped back in his seat and stared profoundly at his screen.

An idea hit me. I quickly scrolled through the menus, hoping. A second later I proved myself wrong. "It's not in trash, either."

"We'll have to recopy it from school tomorrow, I guess," Mira said.

"They don't have a Bible on the school's cloud," Cami reminded her.

"My dad does." I straightened. "I'll get a copy from him and upload it." Cami just nodded.

"Freaky glitch," Aid suggested. Stanyard scrunched his eyebrows.

A glitch... just a bug. I slid my reader into my pouch and smoothed the flap, praying. It was just a glitch.

RED RAIN

A glitch... just a bug. I slid my reader into my pouch and smoothed the flap, praying. It was just a glitch.

3

As soon as I got home, I checked the household desktop. The file was nowhere to be found.

I tried not to let that worry me. After all, my reader and the home computer both stored their data on the same cloud. If it was a glitch in the system, all the devices in the camp would be affected.

Cami came running to my house a half-hour later to confirm that fact.

I tried to make myself useful until Dad got home. He realized something was up the minute he walked in the door, so I told him.

He searched his work tablet. Nothing.

"I'll check at work," he said.

The next evening, he reported that all the copies he had on his work computer were gone. The ones he had uploaded to the United web were missing too. It was as if someone had gone through and deleted them all.

I prayed that didn't mean the government had found them.

Daddy said he'd ask around. For three days he searched, and for three days I tried to reestablish normalcy, half-expecting United officers to show up at the door citing Section 10.20.08 about the high crime of transmitting.

They never did. Daddy didn't find any Bibles, either. He looked at all the transmitting sites he knew of. All of them were down or blank.

On Friday, he finally brought something home. But it wasn't a Bible—it was a copy of an official statement by the United.

In it, they claimed they were not responsible for the virus and an investigation was being conducted.

The statement didn't say anything about the Bible. Daddy finally explained everything.

It was a virus. Someone had released a virus onto the United web that was attacking large chunks of data, permanently deleting or corrupting the information in seconds. It was miscellaneous data that had no apparent connection. Random entries missing from directories, blog posts and web pages that had vanished, sporadic issues deleted from magazine archives. And books. Thousands of books were wiped from the virtual libraries. The Bible was among them.

I wondered if that was intentional.

Daddy didn't think so. He said that if the United wanted to destroy all the Bibles as an attack on religion, they would have made a demonstration out of it. They would have deleted just the Bible and not crippled the entire system with a badly-programmed virus.

But who else would want to delete the Bible?

Perhaps it didn't matter. It was done. As near as they could tell, the virus had originated on a social media site, which meant that before anyone knew it existed, millions of devices had already contracted and spread it. And since every device was legally required to be connected to wifi through an approved carrier at all times, we could only assume the Bible was gone on every cloud from here to Mars.

Daddy said the Bible wasn't lost forever. It was hard to permanently erase data, he explained. They would find a copy burned on a chip, or maybe stored on a server that wasn't connected to wifi. Those were illegal, but surely they existed. Even the government itself probably had a copy on a secure database somewhere.

But I knew finding a copy wasn't the problem. The problem was distributing it. To share it, we'd have to upload it to the United web, and that was illegal. Would the United recall their "no transmitting" law to appease a bunch of criminals?

I doubted it.

4

I failed miserably at school all week. For the first few days, I woke up promptly at 6:30 for my Bible study—only to find I had nothing to study.

On Saturday, I stared at the list of files on my reader. On Sunday, I got up and tried to do something else, but I ended up on the kitchen floor in a sea of broken glass, weeping.

Monday was the worst. I sat at my desk and tried to reconstruct some verses from my study notes. For some reason mine hadn't been affected by the virus, though Cami had lost most of hers.

The exercise hurt more than it helped. I ended up with one page of verses, half of which I knew were paraphrases.

Daddy said I would remember more later, when I was in a clearer frame of mind.

I wondered if I would ever have a clear head again.

As soon as we walked into homeroom Tuesday, our teacher started herding us into a line. "Hurry up—the principal wants to see you."

He lined us up and inspected us. He sent Stanyard to wash his face and Cami to redo her ponytail. He gestured for Aid to stand up straight, then snapped his fingers in front of Mira's face to wipe the glazed look from her eyes. When he came to me, he tugged at the corners of his lips.

I forced a smile.

He returned it. "Respectable."

The principal divided us up and sent us into different meeting rooms. Mira and Stanyard went to Room 1, Cami and Aid to Room 2. I was sent alone to Room 3.

The principal shut the door behind me. At first I thought the room was empty, but someone suddenly stood up from a chair against the wall and walked towards me.

"Oh, Philadelphia, is it?"

Cropped blond hair bobbed around her face. Her lips were bright red and her cheeks were painted pink. She stopped in front of me and smiled broadly.

"Hello," I managed.

"Sweet voice!" she crooned. She rubbed her chin and examined me. "Hmm… They told me so much about you. You're better than they described!"

Better in what way?

She didn't explain. She just hugged me.

I wanted to pull away, but for some reason, I didn't. She squeezed me and then stepped back, arm around my shoulder. "I'm Mrs. Nolan. Delighted to finally meet you! Come, sit by me."

She led me across the room, and I did as I was told—stiffly.

"The school told me all about you. They described all the kids to us, but when I heard about 'Philadelphia,' I knew you were the one I wanted to meet. My husband agreed. You sounded perfect for us! Just the right age, calm disposition…"

I couldn't help it. "Perfect for us, ma'am?"

"Us—my husband and I. Just us, only kid is grown, so we have the spare bedroom, all ready for you. We're going to have it painted this weekend, unless you'd like navy walls? I was going to ask you what color you might like instead."

"Walls, ma'am?"

"I love how you call me 'ma'am'! Yes, walls. Bedroom walls. Your bedroom walls!" She grabbed her purse off the chair and fumbled with the zipper. "Do you want to see pictures? I have pictures of our street, the house… and the cat!"

"No, ma'am, I want to know why I need a bedroom."

She smiled. I decided she was enjoying the backwards conversation. "To sleep in, darling!"

I caught on. I was 16, old enough to work. Being assigned a job was not an unreasonable expectation. "That will be unnecessary, ma'am."

She laughed. "Oh, do you have other arrangements?"

"If I work for you, I will come home to the camp at night."

"Work? If you want a job, we can manage that later. There will be plenty of options available to you outside the home. I don't need a maid!"

"All assignments for unassimilated individuals must be approved by Commander Ambrose," I recited, for once finding solace in the rigidness of the law.

"When you're living in my house, that won't be necessary."

I looked her straight in the face. She stared back, coyness gone. Bluntly, "We want you to join our family."

I sank back in the chair.

"The school has been seeking loving United families to adopt the unassimilated children. We will take you into our family, make you ours, shelter you while you absorb into the real world…"

Assimilated or removed. Assimilated or removed.

"The officials talked to us, and we were eager to be a part of this program. I just loved your description! And now that I've met you, I know we'll manage beautifully. I'll bring Mr. Nolan by tomorrow—"

"I'm afraid I can't come, ma'am."

"Don't be so quick to pass it off! This is a unique program, sweetheart. We will ease you into reality, instead of dumping you on the street as an adult. You've had a difficult life away from the real world. This is your chance to come in, gently..."

"The real world won't accept me, ma'am. I won't sign the file."

"Is that it? I grieve for you, sweetheart."

She sighed. That was the end of the conversation for me, but it wasn't for her.

"They won't make you—I won't make you," she mused, looking elsewhere. "I don't want to force you into our family. But we want you, Philadelphia. We don't care about your past. We want to see you have a life before you—a real life! In the real world! We want you. Come out. Come out while you have open arms waiting for you."

I closed my eyes and thought of the open arms waiting for me at home.

When I opened my eyes, Mrs. Nolan was staring at me again. Her gaze was dark.

I got up and left unbidden.

She called to me when I reached the door. "You will have to sign the file eventually. You know you will. Take my offer while you can. Think about it, Philadelphia. Think about it."

I decided to never think of it again.

5

I wasn't able to talk to my friends until we were seated on the bus. I glanced across the aisle and instantly noticed how pale Aid's face was.

"Outsiders?" I suggested.

Aid nodded wordlessly.

"I hate them!" Cami screeched.

"Cam, hate's evil. That's what got us contained in a camp," Aid muttered.

Cami continued her tirade. "How could they! Assigning us families… I'm not going! I didn't listen to a word she said. Or he said."

"No one's going to make us go," Aid told her. "We'll tell Dad, and if they ask to see us again, we'll refuse."

Cami nodded, but her lip trembled.

I looked up the row at Mira and Stanyard. "You too?"

Mira nodded distantly.

"How were they?"

Mira shrugged. Stanyard wasn't listening.

"What about you, Philli?" Cami leaned across the aisle.

I looked out the window. "I wonder how much she knew about me before coming."

"Too much," was Aid's opinion.

"How was she?"

"Buttery." I thought. "Compromising."

*

"Daddy, you're home early," I declared as I walked in the door.

He pushed his computer away from him. "I've been home almost all day. I had a special meeting at the lab—that's it."

I sat down next to him at the table. "They had 'special meetings' today at school, too."

He noted my frown. "What is it, Phil?"

He stared at me quietly while I told him about Mrs. Nolan.

When I was done, he shook his head. "I'm sorry, Phil."

"I love you, Daddy."

"My meeting wasn't much more pleasant. I was told that I've received a commission to work on a special project—requested by name, they tell me."

I tipped my head. That sounded like good news.

Daddy got up and started to pace.

It wasn't good news.

"The assignment… is for a base on Mars."

I wasn't sure what to make of that.

"And you would not be permitted to come with me."

I looked up into his face. He was already staring at me.

"The commander says. 'Regulations.' The assignment is for me, not you."

"Where… would I go?"

"Nowhere." Daddy folded his arms behind his back. "I will not go, I will not take the commission. Philadelphia, I will not leave you." He drew a breath and added, "Not if I have a choice."

I looked away. My eyes fell on the picture frame hanging on the wall across the room. I got up and walked over to it. The image displayed a picture of Daddy and me; Daddy usually left that one up, because it didn't hurt to look at it.

I waved my hand in front of the sensor several times. The digital pictures scrolled slowly, dancing through a time-lapse. I stopped when I reached the picture I was looking for.

I stepped away, crossed my arms behind my back, and regarded the photo. In the plain metal frame sat a young man, fresh out of college. His thick dark hair stuck up in the front, and his lab coat was pulled around his shoulders. He stared calmly at the camera, not smiling—the smile was in his eyes. I knew; I had grown up with my older brother's eyes smiling on me.

"They sent Ephesus to Mars," I said aloud.

"Yes," my father replied.

"They didn't give him a choice."

"No."

I stared hard at the image of my brother's face, wishing the pixels could move. Finally I finished my thought.

"And he never came back."

It was several minutes before my father replied. "No," he said finally. And again, "No, he didn't."

6

When I arrived in my classroom Thursday morning, I was told to head straight to the principal's office. Without stopping to explain, the principal shoved me into a meeting room and shut the door behind me. Mrs. Nolan was waiting.

She sat on one of the boring metal chairs, fingering a tablet computer. She looked up at me and smiled warmly. "Ah, Philli, you're here."

I crossed my arms behind my back. I wasn't sure whether to sit, stand, or inform the lady that I didn't want to talk to her. What I really wanted to tell her was that she didn't have any right to use my nickname. But I knew my father would want me to be somewhat polite.

"I hope you're well, ma'am," I said, voice proper.

Her eyes twinkled. "'Ma'am,' again? You're such a sweet and well-behaved child. I love your mannerisms!" She gestured at the chair across from her. "Do sit down."

I gingerly did so, adjusting my skirt. I sat on my fingers to keep them from clenching. Mrs. Nolan leaned across and touched my knee.

"I wanted to talk to you about my offer."

"Thank you, ma'am, but I haven't changed my mind," I said quickly, trying to keep the terseness out of my voice.

"I know, sweetheart, but I had an idea that might prove satisfactory to you. What if you came and stayed at my house, just for a week? Then you could see the world, try life out here, you know? You might change your mind if you had a chance to experience it…"

"I'm sorry, ma'am, but I can't do that."

Mrs. Nolan was not deterred. She looked at me for a moment, then squeezed my knee. Her voice lost its butter; it was firm, but not hard. "You're scared, aren't you?"

I blinked. She held my gaze.

"You think coming outside will mean giving up your religion, don't you?"

"I have been informed that, to be fully assimilated, I must sign a file officially denying my right to expression of religion," I recited emotionlessly.

Mrs. Nolan nodded. "True enough, most of the time. But, darling, I have an offer for you."

I steeled my nerves. Each of her "offers" had been more disagreeable than the last.

"If you come to my house, you may keep your Bible. You may pray and worship however you like in your room, and no one will bother you."

I frowned. "Those found supporting and hiding observers of religion are subject to like punishment, ma'am."

Mrs. Nolan smiled coyly. "You underestimate the power of money, darling. Money can buy many things, and one of them is privacy. My husband is well spoken of with the commander; they have agreed on the terms. You do not need to sign the file to join our family—special exception just for you. Come with me, Philadelphia, and you can keep your Bible in peace." She leaned closer to me. "Come with me."

I scooted back on the chair. "I don't have a Bible anymore," I mumbled. "It was lost in the virus."

Mrs. Nolan straightened. "Then what do you have to lose?" She held me in her gaze.

Suddenly, I looked away.

She took her hand off my knee. I jumped up and ran for the door. Mrs. Nolan's voice called out to me. "Think about it, Philadelphia, think about it."

I hesitated, gripping the door handle. Then I yanked the door open and fled the room.

I slid through the principal's office before she could speak to me. I stumbled around the halls until I found a deserted side wing. Sinking down on the cold concrete, I hid my face and wept.

*

"What did the principal want you for, Philli?"

"Yeah, what's up? Did you do something wrong?"

I looked away, out at the barren school lot surrounded by electric fences. "I did nothing wrong."

Cami wouldn't accept that for an answer. She placed herself in my line of vision. "Your face is red," she informed me. "You've been crying. You were incredibly distant during class. Do you even realize you failed the quiz?"

I shrugged, clutching my reader to my chest. "I'll retake it tomorrow."

Mira joined the chase now. She pinched my arm. "Philli, what's wrong? You can trust us." She gestured at the kids gathered loosely around.

"Come on, Phil," Aid said, "tell us." The group murmured their agreement.

I wiggled out of Mira's grasp. "Mrs. Nolan wanted to talk to me again. That's all."

"Your Outsider?" Aid guessed.

"She's not mine. It was nothing important."

"Nothing important!" Cami squawked. "She must like you if she came back again. What did she want?"

"She just wanted to make sure I hadn't changed my mind," I said dismissively.

"And that made you cry?" Stanyard snorted.

"Stanyard, be respectful!" Aid snapped.

Stanyard backed away, shrugging carelessly. "I don't see what would have gotten Phil worked up, that's all."

"Well, Outsiders came to see you again today, too. What did they want, huh?" Cami planted her hands on her hips.

Stanyard looked away. "They just wanted to talk more." He shifted his backpack; it looked lumpier than usual.

"I doubt it!" Cami cried. "I had to take a laptop to the principal's office, and I saw you talking to her. You too, Mira." Cami turned on Mira. "What were you doing, huh? And why do you have two bags today?"

Mira wouldn't meet her gaze. She stepped in front of the extra duffle she had set next to her backpack, as though she could hide it.

"Ha, you're avoiding me! *Mira,*" Cami's voice changed to a begging wail, "what's up? Please?"

Mira shared a glance with her brother. Then she turned back to us and admitted, "We're going home with them today."

The group gasped. I couldn't find any air to gasp with; I just paled.

Mira scanned the group, and her fists tensed. "We're not going to do it anymore! We're leaving! We're not going to keep living stuffed away in a little hole until they decide to kill us. We accepted their offer, Stan and I. We agreed on it last night. They'll be here to pick us up any minute."

Stanyard nodded his consent. His face was hard.

"Then you… denied Him," I said flatly.

"We signed the file saying we wouldn't practice a religion anymore, yes." Mira shrugged as though it had no effect. "We figure they can't stop us from thinking about it, and that's what matters, right? It's a relationship, not a religion. The Bibles are gone, anyway."

"You… denied Him," I said again.

"It's the only way," Stanyard spat. "If you were smart, you'd do it too." His voice suddenly lowered, and he looked directly at me. "Take their offer while you still can, Phil—take it and run."

"But what about your parents?" Cami finally found her voice.

"We didn't tell them," Mira admitted. "I left a note this morning."

"This will kill your father, I can assure you," Aid declared.

"He's going to kill himself!" Stanyard shouted back. "He'll come out soon enough, when he realizes the truth."

I am the way, the truth... I watched them. Mira wouldn't look at me anymore.

A horn screeched. The bus pulled through the gates, followed by a little car. It was a normal silver four-door, driven by a normal mother and a normal father. The bus parked in its usual spot along the fence, but the car swerved up to us. The man and woman got out and walked towards our group.

"Mira? Stan?" the woman said hopefully. The brother and sister scooped up their baggage and walked towards the couple. The woman hugged and kissed them both. The man shook Stanyard's hand and patted his shoulder.

"Are you ready to go?" he asked.

The siblings nodded. "Yes, sir," Mira said.

"And thank you," Stanyard added.

The woman beamed. "It's our pleasure. Come on, our son is dying to meet you. Welcome home." The woman put her arm around Mira's shoulders and led her towards the car, chattering warmly. Mira did not look back.

The bus honked. The other kids fled towards its open doors; I stayed, rooted where I was.

Stanyard dropped his bag in the trunk and slammed it shut. He walked around to the backseat and stood with his hand on the door handle. I begged him to turn around; mentally I pleaded with him to change his mind. He abruptly glanced back at me, eyes filled with ice.

"Accept their offer while you still can." Then he got in the car and shut the door.

"Girl, if you're not going with them, you'd better come with us," the bus driver barked. I took one step backwards. The father looked up at me as he slid into the driver's seat.

"We'd take another," he said with a wink.

I turned and bolted for the bus doors.

7

Daddy wasn't home when I trudged off the bus. I waited for him in the living room until it was time to make dinner, but he never came. I managed to swallow a little something, then sat and fidgeted. Finally, at nearly 23:00, he opened the front door.

"Daddy!" I cried as soon as I heard the handle turn.

He didn't look at me as he slid around the door, locking it behind him. He kicked off his shoes and shrugged his lab coat from his shoulders. He dropped it across the back of the couch and then sat down, beckoning to me.

"Philli, we need to talk."

I sat down next to him. "Daddy, I know, it's Mira, and—"

My father shook his head. "No, Philli, I need to..." He looked into my face for the first time. "What's the matter? You're red."

I rubbed my arm across my cheek. "Did you have something you wanted to say first?"

"Yes," he said a little too quickly, then caught himself. "No, but it can... I think you had best tell me what's wrong."

I glanced at my white hands, wondering what to tell him first.

"Did something happen here, or was it at school?"

"At school," I replied, "and... Mira and Stanyard left." There, at least I was out with half of it.

"Left?" my father repeated, even though he knew what I meant.

"They went home with an Outsider family today," I said quietly.

My father pondered this before replying. "Of their own free will?"

"They agreed amongst themselves."

"And their parents?"

I shook my head. "They didn't tell them. We only found out after school while waiting for the bus."

My father groaned and sank back as far as the thin couch cushions would let him. He dragged his fingers through his hair, then held still for a minute. Eventually, he dropped his arms and looked back up at me. "Is that all?"

I swallowed. "No."

Daddy shifted so he was sitting up straight. "What else?"

I drew in a long breath. "Mrs. Nolan came to see me again."

Daddy let out his breath in a low sigh. "And what did she say?"

"She wanted to make sure I hadn't changed my mind... which I hadn't."

Daddy nodded.

"And... she offered me the chance to stay at her house for a week, just to 'try' it. I said no." I looked into Daddy's eyes for approval; there was none, less or more. "Aren't you glad I declined? Daddy?"

"What else?" he said, ignoring my question.

A clammy feeling rose up in my palms. I glanced down and dug my fingers into my skirt. "She... she said I could... She offered me the option to... keep my Christianity."

I looked up at his face suddenly; his expression was dead. I blundered through the rest of the tale.

"She said that her husband, who is important and rich or something, has spoken with the commander, Daddy, and they agreed that I could keep my faith... Daddy, she wouldn't make me sign the file. I could pray, worship—in the privacy of my room, and no one would bother me. Daddy, she offered me... freedom, Daddy, tolerance. She said I could go and not have to deny Christ!" My voice wobbled.

Daddy still said nothing. He blinked once. My jaw vibrated, but I forced the words out.

"And, Daddy... there's more. Daddy, I... I believed her. It sounded... so nice, so peaceful, a compromise, you know? With the Bibles already gone, there's no physical token, and if I don't have to sign the file..."

Daddy suddenly looked away. His crestfallen look broke my heart. My words gushed.

"Daddy, Daddy, I'm sorry! I know... I know it wasn't right, I know! I know she's just trying to convince me. Maybe she isn't lying, maybe she really won't make me sign the file, but, Daddy," I reached out to him, "I know she's just trying to get me to come. I know, it's compromise, and compromise is dangerous. Daddy, I know! I'm sorry! Daddy!"

He didn't turn to look at me. I shook in silence. When he didn't answer for a long minute, I dared to whisper, "Dad?"

He sighed. His voice was gently reassuring—not at all mad or disappointed. "I understand, Philli, I really do."

The quiver vanished from my nerves, leaving a watery feeling in their place. He thought for a minute before speaking again. "And... I'm glad you think that way."

"Daddy!" I screeched. My father, glad I was tempted by the Outside? I felt betrayed; never before had my father condoned anything from the Outside.

"I'm glad," he explained, still avoiding my eyes, "that you aren't repulsed by this family. I'm glad they like you. I'm glad they've offered you some tolerance. Because…" Finally he looked at me. "I want you to accept their offer, Phil."

"Daddy!" I wailed again, jolting upright. No other word could express my emotion. Now I felt betrayed—and abandoned.

"Philadelphia, it's the only way!" My father's voice rose to a terrified shout. He abruptly stood up and started pacing around the room. "I was informed today that, since I'm 'unassimilated,' I have no choice. I must accept the mission and go to Mars. I leave Monday morning. And you are not permitted to come with me."

He stopped pacing with his back to me. "I want you to send an email to your principal and tell her that you accept the Nolans' offer. You will stay with me for the rest of the week—you won't go to school tomorrow whatever they say—and join the family on Monday when I leave."

My father whipped around to face me. Helpless tears were streaming down his face. It took me a minute to realize silent rivers were coursing down my own cheeks too. "Don't apologize, Philli! *I'm* sorry! There's nothing I can do… nothing!"

I ran for him. He caught me in his arms and wailed openly. I could find no sound to utter—only bitter, drowning, ugly tears.

8

Monday morning found us standing on the step like we always did.

Only this time, we were alone on the street. Daddy's escort was scheduled to pick him up at 6, two hours before my bus would come.

For those two hours I would be completely alone. Two hours of interim, ripped from one family before being assimilated into another.

It was selfish, but I wished Daddy didn't have to leave until after I was gone. Then he could wave to me as I left, and we could pretend, just for a moment, that it was a normal school day and I'd be back in the evening.

But maybe that would have hurt even worse.

"Behave. Be polite," Daddy said after we'd nursed the silence for several minutes. "Obey the rules. Don't cause trouble."

I nodded, not trusting my voice to respond.

He kissed my forehead. "If I come back, I will find you." He was honest and used the word "if."

I hugged him and prayed, feeling tears and not caring whether they fell or not.

I wasn't unhappy that Commander Ambrose was fifteen minutes late. He finally drove up in a small armored car.

He got out and gestured with his pistol. "Get in." A guard emerged from the car and scooped Daddy's luggage off the sidewalk.

Daddy stooped to my eye level. "Remember me. Remember your mother. Remember God." We hugged one last time.

Then he picked up his carry-on and walked down the steps. The tears finally broke as a sob escaped my lips. I prayed louder, mentally scrambling for appropriate last words.

The commander interrupted the whirlwind. "Hurry up."

I glanced at Daddy, but the commander wasn't talking to him. He was looking at me.

Panic gripped my throat. No, it wasn't panic.

The commander repeated his order slowly. "Come on."

Daddy stopped and looked back at us. The commander jabbed his pistol at me. "Get in."

I slapped a hand over my mouth.

"You've been ordered to attend your father."

*

The world was oblivious of us. And it felt wonderful.

Masses of people crowded the port, joining lines and breaking them. Planes and transits crossed paths, bringing passengers from as far away as Neptune and as nearby as the city next over. A dizzying array of signs and status boards attempted to make sense of the mess.

Daddy and I pushed through the crowd. No one noticed us, no one bothered us. No one knew we were unassimilated—no one cared. We were simply passengers rushing to make our flight, just like everyone else.

The only person that paid us any mind was Commander Ambrose. He escorted us to our transit, armed with a pistol for show. He briskly stormed through the crowd, shoving people out of his way. Daddy ran to keep up with him.

I clutched Daddy's hand to keep from getting separated. That was the only thing I cared about.

We finally reached our terminal. A long line of people snaked out of the security gates—a splash of tourists, some businessmen, and a handful of regular people going up to populate.

There were more scientists than anything else. I wondered how many—if any—were going to our base.

I didn't know exactly where we were going. I doubted Daddy knew either. All Commander Ambrose had told us was that the governor of a base—he called him Dr. Nic—wanted Dad to work for him. And that was all the information Commander Ambrose thought was necessary. We would have to wait and find out more when we arrived.

But I didn't care what base we were going to. The only thing I cared about was that I was going with Daddy. We were together, and that was all I needed to know.

I wasn't sure what had changed. I highly doubted the commander had changed his mind out of pity. Commander Ambrose wouldn't say, just that it was an official order—from somebody.

But then again, everything was an "official order" with Commander Ambrose.

I didn't really care how it had come to pass. God can use whatever method He pleases to make things happen.

We cleared security and confirmed our tickets by pressing our thumbs to a scanner. The positive green light we received was comforting.

Commander Ambrose had a word with an officer, who gave us a frown and assisted us to the transit. Daddy glanced back once; I followed his gaze.

Commander Ambrose stood on the other side of security, arms crossed. He scowled until the crowd swallowed him up.

I turned around. I prayed that maybe, just maybe, I would never see him again.

The transit was like a plane bloated with air. The seats were farther apart, and the ceiling swooped high overhead like a bowl. The whole place seemed fancier, more luxurious—glitzy, shiny, well-padded—than the last airplane I had seen.

The officer led us down the carpeted main aisle and into a room filled with chairs. The seats weren't lined up in strict rows but rather scattered around in clusters with tables mixed in. A handful of passengers milled about, chattering and laughing like guests at a party.

Daddy and I sat near the door; the officer waited beside us. I watched the other passengers flow in and scatter; soon the room was filled with people. The final call for passengers echoed over the speakers. The officer told us the number of our cabin and informed us that another officer would "assist" us when we docked. Then he left.

We were free. For the next 59.5 hours, we were no different than any other passenger on the transit.

We were normal.

Somewhere deep beneath my feet, a rumble began to churn. A computerized voice over the speakers calmly instructed us through the basic rules of safety, then commanded everyone to take a seat while we launched. We obeyed. Every seat in the room was full, as far I could see.

The rumble surged. There were no seatbelts—I had a tiny fear that there should be something restraining me—but Daddy held my hand. The room went quiet briefly; chatter ceased while a high-pitched whir joined the rumble. A sound like air rushing down a huge tunnel streamed past the walls of the transit. I felt the ship turn, slightly.

Then the rumble and whir silenced to a muted grind. The speakers announced a successful take-off, and the noise of people erupted. The passengers resumed chatting and began to disperse.

We were flying.

We had left Earth.

And maybe, just maybe, we would never come back.

9

After the room thinned, Daddy got up to explore the accommodations. He left me with the instructions to stay put and be discreet. It was okay if I talked with people, told them my name and who my father was, and why we were going to Mars.

But I should tell no one that I was unassimilated.

He whispered in my ear, "'My father has received a scientific assignment on Mars' should be sufficient for most people. If they ask for more, they don't need to be answered. I assume the governor of the base already knows, but…" At this point, he sighed. "There's no reason to cause trouble and division where it isn't needed."

After he left, I moved to a more secluded spot in an empty circle of chairs. I climbed into the seat against the wall, tucking my legs under me. There were no windows, which I suppose was for the better. Earth would be shrinking so quickly, left far behind by our great speed, that the view probably would have been dizzying.

I slid my reader from its pouch. I rubbed the scratched case for a moment before turning it on. I watched the screen light up and spew off a random string of code that probably said, *"Good morning! My systems are in good shape and I'm waking up."*

As soon as the welcome screen flickered on, I remembered that I had nothing to read. All of my books had been stored on the camp's cloud, and I hadn't bothered to copy most of them over. Most of my books were from the United, things I only read because my teacher made me. But he couldn't make me read anything now, so why take the files with me?

I had copied over my Bible study notes. I wondered if it would be safe to paw through them and look for traces of verses. I voted against doing it in a public room—maybe when we got back to the cabins. I had a whole file of jumbled verses to organize in order when I had privacy.

Daddy had been compiling them. He wrote down a chunk every night. I had given up trying to think of many verses myself, but I reformatted the ones Daddy remembered, engraving them in my brain as I did so.

I imagined the phrases of Scripture forming across the screen, echoed by the comforting clack of keystrokes. The pages would fill...

But it would be a long time before we regenerated all 1,000 of them.

Or even 100 pages.

And then again, our devices would probably be monitored when we got to the base. Would typing up a file of verses count as transmitting? Commander Ambrose didn't care, but this Dr. Nic might.

The welcome screen sat waiting. I mindlessly clicked on the menu and watched the list of files generate.

Someone disturbed my solace. A 20-something gingerly eased into the chair across from me. She tucked her short blond curls behind her ears and glanced at me. I smiled but said nothing. It took a few seconds, but she smiled back—then looked elsewhere. I turned my attention back to my computer.

I stared at the meager list of files and debated about opening my email and typing instead.

I wished I could send an email to Cami. She and Aid were the only people I would truly miss from Earth—they were pretty much the only people left to miss.

But my message would have to clear the commander before Cami could read it. And, from my experience when Ephesus had been on Mars, I knew that the commander didn't bother to approve most messages.

Ephesus said, when we were able to call him once, that he sent a message every other day.

We only ever received about ten of them.

Maybe I could start keeping a journal of my experiences. It might be worth remembering.

Then again, Mars could be just like Earth. Just a concentration camp in the sky.

"That's a cute reader."

I jerked my head up. The 20-something was looking at me again.

"Thank you. It's kind of vintage."

She smiled. It was a small smile, but a nice one. She had gray eyes—soft gray—and a sprinkling of freckles across her cheeks. "Old is sometimes better."

"Are you going to Mars?" I asked.

"Only place this transit goes," she replied.

I frowned. She was looking away again. Maybe she didn't really want to talk to me.

I looked back at my screen and opened my email. The girl spoke again.

"Is this your first time?"

"Yes."

"Moving in or traveling?"

"Father's on scientific business."

She nodded. "I live on Mars. I was just on Earth briefly." She looked at me. "What base are you going to?"

Please don't ask too many questions. "I don't remember the coordinates."

She frowned. "Do you remember the governor or anything? Who is your father working with?"

I suppose that's not a huge secret. "A governor commissioned him. Dr. Nic, I believe."

Her face lit up. "Nic! So you're with Dr. Smyrna!"

Something inside me froze. She knew who I was! How much of our status, our history, did she know? How much had she told others? Was she going to ask questions I couldn't answer—or spread gossip I didn't want repeated?

But she already knew who we were. No harm in confirming the truth.

"That's my father."

She gave me a once-over, as if this revelation changed everything. "Nic mentioned you, but I didn't realize you were coming."

"Me neither, until this morning."

She smiled widely—a somehow reassuring gesture. "It's Philadelphia, right?"

"Yeah." I paused. "But I'm usually Phil or Philli."

She nodded. "It's a pretty name. I'm Cea."

"Nice to meet you." That was the truth, I thought.

Her eyes were sparkling now. "I'm glad to meet you, too. Nic should have told me we were on the same transit—I could have come and picked you up."

I'd just as soon you didn't… I'd rather you not see the prison I came from, if you don't already know.

She must have thought my silence was begging for more explanation. "You're coming to live at my base, #9.6.11. My brother summoned you."

10

When my father came to take me to lunch and received introductions, he gave me an amazed glance—*How you do make the most convenient friends!* He later told me that he was glad I had met someone from our base who had taken a liking to me.

Cea did seem quite friendly. She stayed with me the rest of the day. In fact, I spent most of the flight with her. She ate with us at all meals, soliciting Daddy's questions about the base. She was able to tell him a little more about his situation, but she said Dr. Nic would have to fill in the technical details.

In between times, Cea and I sat apart from the crowd in the main room, sometimes with Daddy and sometimes without. We talked, mostly about base #9.6.11. She sent me to the base's promotional website—only to find that most of the pages were down.

She sighed. "Virus."

I nodded understandingly.

She decided to recite the base's history from memory instead. It was a well-known base, having been founded on experimental technology. It continued to thrive on the new and emerging and was considered a testing ground for developing theories in space settlement. The base focused on sustaining and improving life on Mars—habitat construction, air quality, gravity replication, and the like. Labs on Earth would often commission the base to test their ideas, and the world's best scientists travelled there to put their technology to work in developing new methods.

That must be what Daddy had been commissioned to do. Daddy knew he had been called because of some success in the lab, but he wasn't sure what particular area of research Dr. Nic was interested in.

The base was rather large in size but small in population. It was a rambling structure of wide wings, with more constantly being added, all used to test different theories and equipment. Cea described the place as a maze of halls connecting huge, empty—or nearly empty—rooms, where an entire wing might be devoted to seeing how long a single plant could survive in a certain set of conditions.

She smiled coyly after this description.

We didn't talk much about ourselves. Cea asked about me, and I told her the basics—how old I was, my hobbies—no, my mother was dead—that kind of thing. But when I neatly refrained from discussing details about my social status, she caught on and stopped asking.

She didn't tell me much about herself either. Just that she lived with her brother, Dr. Nic, who had been the leader of the base for nine years, taking charge at the young age of 24…

At this she launched into a proud synopsis of her brother's prodigal successes on Mars, a safe course of discussion.

Cea sat next to us when all the passengers bunkered down for landing. As soon as we were released from our seats, she led us through the crowd like she knew where she was going.

I appreciated the sense of confidence. Mars was on the other side of the transit doors.

And I had no idea what to expect.

We stepped over the threshold into the docking station, and at first I couldn't see anything except swarms of people. Cea burrowed through the crowd and pointed to a waiting room off the side of the lobby, saying, "Wait here." Daddy took my hand and pulled me out of the crowd and into the waiting room. And there, with Daddy still gripping my hand, we both had our first look at Mars.

The sun, strangely small, was slanting far in the west. I had expected the horizon to be red, but the fading light had painted the sky blue-gray like a foggy morning in London. All around, the infamous red earth was descending into black as the shadows lengthened.

I could see for what felt like a long way. A rumbling string of black lumps, with an occasional glint catching the light, blocked the northern horizon—a metropolis. Other bases dotted the land here and there like shelled beetles. There was nothing in between the bases except thick stakes topped with flashing lights—the markers dividing the land, defining the coordinates of each base.

"This is what Ephesus saw," I said aloud.

Daddy let go of my hand to put his arm around my shoulder. He rubbed my arm slightly. "He liked it. The land—it was one thing he liked about going to Mars."

Was it the only thing? I would never know.

But I would soon make my own list of what I liked—and didn't like—about living on Mars.

Someone tapped Daddy on the shoulder. We turned to see a darkly-uniformed officer armed with a gun. He coughed.

"Dr. Smyrna and daughter?"

"Yes." My father straightened.

"Your escort."

"I believe they already have an escort." Cea walked out of the crowd, frowning. "Me."

The officer glanced back at her. "Are you traveling with them?"

"I'm going the same place they are."

"You have your own transportation arrangements, I assume? I have been instructed to see them to their base."

"I can see them there just fine, thank you." She eyed the officer nervously.

The officer almost smiled—a condescending sort of amusement. "I'm sorry, miss, but they're unassimilated. We have regulations."

I flinched. *Regulations, regulations...*

So much for being discreet about our situation around Cea. I looked up at her.

Her eyes were wide, face white.

The officer turned back to my father. "Other baggage?"

"Yes, two checked crates."

"Claim numbers."

My father brought up the numbers on his tablet. The man held up a communicator and instructed a fellow officer to pick up our belongings.

I glanced back at Cea. She had stepped a few paces away and was mumbling into a cellphone.

The officer lowered his communicator. With a jerk of his head, he started walking.

Cea stepped in front of him. She wordlessly held out her cellphone.

The officer eyed her. Cea just wiggled the device at him.

He cautiously took it and brought it to his ear. "Hello?" Pause. "Yes, sir." Pause. "Yes, sir." The exchange was repeated half a dozen times more, then the officer sighed. He handed the phone back to Cea.

She took it and slid it into her pocket. I thought the corner of her lip twitched.

"Other arrangements have been made. I will make sure the baggage is sent to the appropriate vehicle." Then without so much as a glance at us, he walked off.

Cea grinned. "Nic said otherwise." Turning to us, she waved her arm. "You're driving over with me."

11

Our ride was a bulky little thing, like an overgrown SUV with treads. It was painted a bright blue, almost unearthly—it stood out like alien life form amongst the dull dust and glint of metal.

A generous black man was loading our crates in the back. He turned around as we approached, and his face instantly exploded into a smile.

"Smyrna, Smyrna! So good to meet… You are Dr. Smyrna, aren't you?"

"I am."

The man pumped my father's hand. "Brilliant! So glad to make your acquaintance." He nodded, as if to confirm his statement. "I'm Arnold Sardis. Meet your fellow worker." He grinned, showing all teeth.

"Pleased to meet you. Are you a scientist?" my father asked.

"No, no… Well, not your kind of science, anyway. I'm a horticulturist—plant doctor! My job is to help keep plants alive in this place. Dr. Nic would kill them all without me." He laughed pleasantly.

He glanced down and spotted me. "Now, who's this?" He bent over to be more at my eye-level, planting his hands on his large knees.

"Philadelphia, sir," I replied politely.

"Oh? You must be the daughter! I didn't realize you were coming."

Most people weren't, it seems…

"Delightful news! So glad to have both of you." He grabbed my arm with both hands and shook it gleefully.

"We'd best be going," Cea said, taking my carry-on and dropping it in the trunk.

"Of course, of course. Come now, load up." Mr. Sardis sauntered over to the driver's seat and climbed in.

Cea closed the trunk and sat next to him. Daddy and I shared the middle, buckling into the sturdy and well-cushioned seats.

Mr. Sardis joined the lines of vehicles waiting to exit. We drove into a tunnel, where the gate behind us closed before the one in front of us opened. Our SUV rumbled down a ramp, and we were out in the open.

It was a relatively smooth ride—and a quiet one, with the engine gurgling lowly. I watched the multicolored ground pass beneath the treads.

The area around the docking bay was thickly inhabited by bases. Mr. Sardis wove around the bubbles and blocks, ducking under bridges that connected some of the metal homes. After a half-hour, however, the bases thinned, until there were only one or two dotting the horizon.

Another half-hour, and then we passed through a section of country where there were no bases at all—none. Endless red, quickly turning into the color of dried blood as the sun faded. Only the regular stakes, every kilometer, divided the sea in a rigid grid pattern.

Slowly, it rose on the horizon. At first, it looked like a tiny bug; as we drew closer, it seemed to grow before our eyes, sending out legs and multiplying. Rambling, glass glinting in the last shot of sunlight—it was base #9.6.11.

A wide hall with a curved glass roof ran down the center. The lower half of the base was fairly narrow, but the structure widened rapidly towards the north end. Wing built upon wing, sprawling out across the land—some rooms stuck out in the middle of nowhere, connected to the rest of the base by a snaking hallway. Some had windows, some had not; some were above ground, some half below. Dozens of shades—but all made out of metal.

At the far southern end, a docking bay bulged out. The gates opened to welcome us, and the SUV chugged up the ramp. The gate closed; there was a brief pause before a panel on the wall glowed green. Great doors slid open, letting in a flood of light from the rest of the base, and we all got out.

Someone stood in the hallway, beckoning to us. I couldn't see his face—the lights behind him were so much brighter than the ambiance in the bay. I shielded my eyes as Daddy took my hand and led me in.

"Dr. Smyrna!" It was a diplomatic voice, but not an unkind one. "You have made it at last."

I blinked, vision adjusting. Father let go of my hand to shake that of a man younger than himself.

He was only in his mid-30s, with a sophisticated little mustache under his nose. He had dusty blond hair like Cea, only his was straight and primly styled. His eyes were like Cea's too, only darker—almost bluish gray.

He smiled—again, a business-like smile, but a genuine one. "Dr. Nic, Governor," he explained.

"Honored to make your acquaintance," my father replied.

Dr. Nic's eyes sparkled. "The same, and more so. I've been awaiting your arrival. Your expertise is extremely coveted here."

"I appreciate the commission."

More so, 'I appreciate your allowing my daughter to accompany me...'

Dr. Nic glanced down at me. "So this is the daughter! What was your name again?"

"Philadelphia." I bobbed. It felt appropriate.

He liked it. He smiled. "You are welcome here."

That must have been the truth. Perhaps he had been the one to arrange my passage.

"I'm sure you're eager to see the base…"

"I'm sure you're eager to show it off," Cea quipped.

Dr. Nic rubbed his mustache. "So you met my sister, I hear."

"Phil found me." Cea shrugged.

"Did she? How convenient we have you along, then, Phil." He laughed. "Yes, I am eager to be the proud parent of my little kingdom. But! Some things must wait until morning. I'll show you to your rooms—rest well, please. Work must start immediately in the morning. No time to waste!"

He started walking. We followed. "Sardis, can you transfer the baggage?"

"I got it, I got it!"

We exited the receiving room and walked out into the main hall. Strips of lights glowed along the wall, and the glass-domed ceiling showed the darkening sky above. The hall stretched on, straight ahead, as far as I could see. All along the tunnel were doors, marked with numbers and letters above. Each door had a digital panel to the side.

Everything was made out of metal. Metal on the floor, metal on the ceiling, metal in the doors and the frames around the glass.

Dr. Nic walked a short distance up the main hall and turned off to the left. The big doors, marked with a number 5, opened automatically. Inside there was a foyer dotted with plants and two benches. Beneath the glass ceiling were two levels of smaller doors, marked with letters. There were six doors on each level, spaced erratically.

"F will be your quarters." Dr. Nic gestured to the door on the lower level, far right. "Let me set the lock."

He walked up to the darkened panel at the side of the door. He reached into his pocket and pulled out a chubby disc decorated with buttons. He held it close to the panel, and it snapped into place.

He pressed a button, and the door slid open with a beep. He removed the disc and gestured to my father and me. "Hold your hands over the panel. No need to touch it—just stretch your fingers out like that. One at a time, or it might mess the system up."

Father went first. A moment of orange, then a happy green circle flashed across the display. Dr. Nic nodded at me.

I slowly extended my fingers and held them over the black screen. The orange dash contemplated, then chirped. The green circle blinked, as if saying, *Welcome home, new resident!*

After a few seconds of silence, the door beeped again and slid shut. "The doors will open only for you now when they're locked," Dr. Nic explained. "There's instructions on the other side on how to lock it and all that."

My father tested the apparatus. He waved his hand over the sensor. The green circle appeared, and the doors reopened.

"No thumbprint scan?" he questioned.

"The panel is designed to scan DNA through the hand. Much more reliable than a face scan, more sanitary than a thumbprint. Just one of the many innovations we're pioneering up here." Dr. Nic smiled. "Well, go on then."

I followed Dad into the apartment. Inside was a cozy sitting room. Beyond, three doors—two on the right, and one in the back.

"Two bedrooms and a washroom. Should be sufficient. Let me know if you find the accommodations unsuitable," Dr. Nic said honestly.

My father walked into the middle of the room, gazing around at the smooth walls and flat ceiling. "No... no, they'll be just fine."

I cautiously approached his side.

Mr. Sardis came in, followed by an older, slender fellow. He was so pale, with gray hair and a white coat, that he looked like a piece of blank paper next to Mr. Sardis. They deposited our crates in the middle of the floor.

"Carnegie, my assistant," Dr. Nic gestured at the elderly man.

Carnegie took us in with his green eyes, as if measuring our competency. He nodded and left without a word. Mr. Sardis waved, smiled, and left right behind him.

Dr. Nic walked towards the door. "One of us will be along to collect you at 9, Doctor, and orient you."

Cea stood in the doorway to the hall. "I'll come get you about 9:30, Phil, and show you around."

Dr. Nic stopped and regarded his sister. "Excellent idea." His diplomatic smile returned.

He glanced back at us. "Welcome to Mars." He flicked his hand over the sensor and stood there smiling while the door closed. Cea watched from behind him.

Finally alone, I looked around the room. Neatly furnished, it looked cozier than our home on Earth. It was certainly artsier—a large digital frame on the wall scrolled through stunning images of the galaxy, while a few potted plants broke up the monotony of metal and plastic. Unlike the rest of the halls, a gray carpet softened the floor.

Daddy touched my shoulder.

"Was Ephesus's room like this?" I asked.

"I imagine so." He paused. "But now it's ours. Our home, Phil."

Home. Home was metal. So much metal.

But then again, on Earth I had been surrounded by concrete. I didn't suppose metal was much different.

I could only pray that metal would be more tolerant of Christians.

12

Before Daddy left in the morning, he told me to listen to Cea, to not get in anybody's way, and to generally behave. Mr. Sardis came to pick Daddy up—our hallway door was open, and we heard his whistling long before we saw him. He swaggered into the room, calling out boisterous greetings.

He had a little potted plant cupped in his hands—his skin was almost the same color as the rich dirt. He presented the tiny red blooms to me and said I ought to have a little color for my room.

Daddy smiled on while I thanked him.

I closed and locked the door after they left. While I waited for Cea, I sat on the couch and studied the sheet of instructions for the door so I would know how to get back in later.

Like Dr. Nic had said, the door worked by scanning DNA through the fingertips, making it easy to control access. There was an identical panel on the inside and outside of each door, and the sensors could be set from either side. Only Dr. Nic knew how to reset the system once the door had been programmed. When the door was locked, it would only open for the approved sets of DNA. When Cea came, I would have to open the door from the inside for her.

That made me wonder how Cea would announce her presence when she came. Would she knock—or was there a doorbell? Could I hear her through the metal door if she called? What would I do all day after Cea showed me around? Would it be easy to stay out of everyone's way? Most of the residents were scientists—were they set up to accommodate families, or was I the only tagalong? After all, my attendance had been an impromptu decision.

"Phil?"

I jumped when Cea called me—and so clear! Her voice was loud, though slightly electronic. I scanned the room as I got up and unlocked the door.

"Where is your voice coming from?" I asked as she came in.

"My mouth?"

"No, I mean, when the door's closed. I can hear you so clearly. Where..."

"Oh, there's a speaker at most doors." She gestured to the control panel mounted by the doorframe. "So you can contact those inside. Otherwise nobody would be able to hear anything around here. Just press the button marked 'call.'"

"Clever," I said, feeling anything but.

"If you want to talk back without opening the door, hit this orange button from the inside. It opens the communication two-way." She smiled. "Ready for breakfast?"

We didn't head straight to breakfast. Cea took me on a tour of the base between the docking bay and the cafeteria. She didn't take me down any halls, just showed me the gates and told me what was beyond—after she told me how to distinguish a gate from any other kind of door.

Gates were taller and marked with only numbers—1, 4, 23. Anything beyond a gate was a wing. Everything through Gate 19 was considered Wing 19, until you got to another gate, and so on. Within gates, doors were marked with letters and the wing number—1C, 4A, 23D. Some doors would open to halls with more doors, which would be marked with letters followed by decimals—1C.2, 4A.6, 23D.9.

I didn't ask what happened if you opened a door in a hall which led to another hall.

What I wanted to do was ask her was to repeat everything two or three more times. I felt lost just standing still in the middle of the main hallway. Was the system nonsensical, or was I simply too stupid to grasp it?

Maybe a little bit of both.

Thankfully, most of the halls at the southern end of the base were straightforward. The docking bay was marked simply DOCK. Agreeable. Cea told me that the main hall, with the glass dome ceiling, was considered Wing 1. If the call number of any room was preceded by a 1, it was off the main hall. We passed 1A, which was a meeting room, and 1B, which was an auditorium. Gate 2 lead to offices and general rooms, as did Gate 3 opposite. Gate 4 and 5, across from each other, were the main cabins.

I noticed that, so far, all the odd-numbered gates were on the left. I wondered if that was consistent throughout the base.

Probably not.

Just past the cabins were Gate 6, which led to a medical and sickbay, and Gate 7. Cea led me through the latter—the door opened automatically—and I smelled bread and heard running water.

The main cafeteria was straight ahead. The floor and walls were bright white, a sort of plastic instead of metal. The rounded glass ceiling let in streams of brilliant light, making the place almost blinding. The room was scattered with tables of various sizes, interspersed with plants. There were a few doors along the back wall—Cea said they were private dining rooms—and access to the kitchen, with a long buffet, was to the right.

The place was almost deserted already. Two white-coated scientists nodded at us as they left. A businessman lounged by himself in the back corner, chattering into his cellphone in what sounded like Mandarin. In the middle of the room, a dark-skinned woman was wiping the face of a chubby toddler. Both looked up and smiled at me, the toddler waving jam-covered fingers.

I waved back. Perhaps my father wasn't the only scientist who brought his family with him.

While we ate our selections from the healthful buffet, Cea ran down a loose schedule. I would normally eat breakfast and lunch by myself. I hoped that Daddy would sometimes be able to eat with me, but that would depend on his workload. Dinner, Cea said, was up to my father and me—but, in general, the scientists usually worked from 9:00-19:00.

Curfew was at midnight, unless one had a special pass. The base's systems, except for the dorms, went into hibernation mode from midnight until 5 to save power and allow for repairs. That's also when the base's clocks collectively rolled back 40 minutes to account for Mars' slightly longer rotation.

"Nic decided it was just easier this way," Cea explained with a wry grin. "So far, no one's complained about getting an extra 40 minutes of sleep every day."

Little else on base ran on an official schedule. Everyone plotted out the workday for themselves, depending on what project they were assigned to.

I wondered what I would find to fill my days.

As we were walking back to the dorms, Cea suggested an activity for the morning. "Want help unpacking?"

I thought of the crate waiting patiently on my bedroom floor. "Sure— thank you. Though, there isn't much."

I didn't want to think about the fact that I wouldn't have had *any* luggage had I not been packed to go to the Nolans'.

I let us back into my room. Cea glanced sideways at me. "Did you not bring most of your stuff?"

Oh, I brought it all… everything that didn't stay with the house because it belonged to the government…

"Or did you not have that much to bring?"

I looked away.

"I'm sorry…" Her voice reached out to me. "That was harsh. I was just wondering… if it's really like they say."

I looked back at her. "They who?"

"They… about Earth. About… the unassimilated concentration camps." She stared into my face, eyes wide and revealing. "Is it really… bad?"

"These are all the belongings I have. Everything else either belonged to the camp or was the school's." I took the lid off the metal crate and pulled out a stack of clothes.

Cea bent and took out a few shirts. "I've heard rumors... but most of the people here, they don't know. They don't care. 'That's Earth's business.' But I was curious... You don't have to talk about it if you don't want to."

"So you know?" I hit the button to open the mirrored closet doors.

"About?"

"About us... being Christians. That... we're not here of our own free will." I stared into the dark closet. Then I flipped on the light and spoke my mind. "Slaves."

"Don't you want to be here?" She followed me into the closet.

"Yes!" The exclamation was out of my mouth before I had time to think it—but I felt it.

"I knew," she responded. "Nic talked about having to go through the commander... Ambrose, is that his name?"

I nodded as I clipped a skirt on a hanger. "Does everyone else know?"

"I'm not sure... Why would they care?"

I didn't answer. I held the hanger up and let it snap onto the magnetic rod. *The same reason people on Earth care.*

I took the shirts from her. She walked back to the crate and changed the subject. "Where did you go to school?"

"Same high school as everyone else. We just had extra 'remedial' classes."

"Oh."

"They started making us go about five years ago. We homeschooled before that." I started hanging up shirts. "Speaking of school, I'm not sure if I should finish and get my diploma, or maybe take some higher-level courses... I was thinking some school might be a nice way to keep me occupied, out of trouble, you know?"

Cea was silent. I glanced over at her. She was bent over the crate, holding our digital picture frame in her hands.

The picture of Ephesus was still on the screen.

Cea frowned and squinted.

"That's my older brother," I explained.

She jerked her head up. Her face was colorless. "He's your brother?"

"Was." I looked down at the gray sweater in my hands. "He was sent to Mars on scientific business as well... But his transit home exploded."

"I know," Cea said quietly. She groaned and pinched the bridge of her nose. "Nic, you—" The next word she used was definitely not a term of endearment.

I stepped towards her. "What's the matter?" When she didn't answer right away, I abandoned the question in lieu of one that seemed more pertinent: "You knew my brother?"

She nodded and stood up. She held the frame close to the wall, and the magnets snapped into place. "I've met him." She gave the corner a tweak, adjusting the position. She regarded the image for a moment, then glanced back at me.

"This was the base he worked at."

13

No one said anything for a long time.

I stared, but not at Cea. I stared out my bedroom window at the dusty ground, the desert, the red—the view my brother saw.

"I'm sorry," Cea said at last. She let out a sigh and whispered again, "I'm sorry."

"Was this... was this his room? Did he... did he sleep in these cabins?" I walked into the middle of the floor, footsteps muted on the carpet—was that the sound my brother heard? Did he stand at that window, hang his coat in that closet?

"No. He slept in some dorms closer to the wing he was working in. It was a commissioned test... Well, I'm sure he told you about it."

I shook my head. "Only vaguely. He didn't know going in what his assignment was... and he... he wasn't able to write much."

"He wrote you all the time," she said incredulously. "Every other day, he'd turn in a half-hour early, saying he was writing home."

My mind spun with images of my brother, waving off fellow scientists, walking back to his room with a purposed air... in front of a computer, in the dark, typing furiously... only to pause, and blink...

"Didn't he tell you anything about his work?"

"He probably did. But we didn't get most of the messages."

She tipped her head to the side. I looked away, but I didn't see any reason not to tell her the truth.

"The commander has to approve all incoming and outgoing messages. Most of them, he doesn't."

Cea was silent. Her tone changed. "Do you... want to see his rooms?"

*

"Your brother's dorm was way back in Wing 88, right outside Wing 89."

We walked quickly down the hall. I listened to Cea's voice, but my eyes scanned the gates and doors as we passed, trying to grasp the numbers—12, 12C, 14… I had only gotten a tour up to Wing 7, and we'd left that behind a long time ago. We'd turned off the main hall into Wing 12, then through Wing 14, which jumped to Wing 27…

"89 was where his assignment was, and they were going nearly 'round the clock for a while. It was just easier to sleep over there. Or at least that was Nic's logic."

Cea shrugged. She waved her hand over the sensor for Gate 30 and waited for it to open.

"I guess it was that important. It was *the* test that year. Big dollars, famous scientists. Your brother was among them."

I'd never thought of my brother as "famous." How famous can an unassimilated get in the United? He had been wanted in the lab ever since he'd graduated from college—long hours, some months rarely home. Maybe that makes you "famous" in the science world, especially when you're so young.

"If I recall, Nic called him up here just for that test."

Just like Daddy. Was Daddy "famous" too?

We passed into the 40s. Through one hall, into the 50s… And there was Gate 88. Where were the 60s? 70s? Was there no logic to the numbers?

No logic from Earth, that was sure.

We passed through Gate 88 into a wing that was completely silent. We hadn't seen another human being for a while, but there was a different kind of stillness about this hall. All the doors were shut, keypads dark. The main hall was dimly lit with muted security lights instead of the brilliant beams of the rest of the base. The tunnel ended in blackness, as though it snaked on into nothingness and ceased to exist.

Cea walked down to the third door on the left and opened it. Then she stepped back and gestured at me.

I didn't hesitate. Why, I don't know—I felt like stalling, like avoiding it, like waiting a few more minutes. But my feet strode up to the doorway and stopped.

I looked in—and something in me died.

There was nothing in there. The lights were dark. The bed was stripped. Nothing was on the walls, the desk, the nightstand. Nothing. It was bare metal, a shell.

There were no pieces of my brother left. Nothing—nothing personal. It was as though he had never been there.

And for as much as I could get at him, he might as well have never been here.

"Not much, I suppose, but I thought you'd like to see it anyway. Poor substitute for his emails, though. I'm sure he described it to you in one of his notes."

"Why is it… empty?"

"Because no one's living in there anymore."

"But…" I turned around and pointed towards the end of the hall. "Why so… dark. So… unused?"

Cea followed my gaze. "Wing 89 is closed. The test is done."

"Why haven't they reused it?"

"The test failed. Badly. Some chemicals they were using… they think that's what caused the transit to explode." She looked into my face. "It didn't look good, for the science."

I stared into the blackness. Cea closed the door and started to walk back towards the gate.

I followed. "What happened… to his things?"

"What things?"

"Ephesus's things. His belongings. Where are they now?" I thought of the completely bare surfaces in the room.

She squinted. "I don't… know."

"They must have done something with them after he died. Did they save them? Are they still here somewhere?"

Cea shook her head faintly. Suddenly, she straightened, and realization hit her eyes. "Weren't they on the transit with him?"

My silence said everything. Somehow, I managed to keep walking.

We wove through a few halls before Cea spoke again. Her voice sounded far away, as though she were on the other side of a wall. "I'm sorry."

I watched the marked doors shift past. "I had no reason to expect anything. He's gone. All of him."

I paused. Why was I sharing my life's woes with Cea? Then again, what harm would it do to tell her? She had known Ephesus; she might—just maybe—even care.

"Being here… won't make him feel any closer. He's as far away as he's always been."

Unreachable. Always was, always will be, this side of heaven. He'd been dead ever since he left Earth.

Being here might just make it hurt even worse.

Cea walked a few steps ahead of me and held her hand over the sensor for a gate. It opened, and Dr. Nic appeared in the doorway like a picture in a frame.

"Well, I didn't even have to touch the sensor!"

"Oh, hi Nic."

He smiled that politically correct smile. He looked at his sister, who stared back—after a moment, she smiled. I thought I saw a bit of understanding, a flicker of sibling sympathy, pass between them.

It broke when Dr. Nic noticed me. "I was looking for you... Well, you have a buddy today! Making friends quickly, I see, sister?"

"Phil's a natural." Cea shrugged and stuffed her hands in her pockets.

Dr. Nic laughed. "Stop that. I'm glad, and you know it." Cea didn't respond, so he looked at me. "And what, might I ask, are you two girls doing?"

"She's showing me my—"

Cea spoke at the same time. "I'm just giving her the tour."

Dr. Nic nodded. "And how does our new colonist like the establishment?"

I blinked. "I've hardly had time to absorb it all."

"I'll take that as a good sign." He grinned, then coughed. "Well, Cea, I've been looking for you. I need you for a bit, if your buddy can spare you."

"I'll go find my father," I offered, hoping to be helpful.

Dr. Nic smiled approvingly. "He's on break. See you at dinner, Phil." He walked past me and opened another gate.

Cea trotted to match pace with him. "I'll catch you later!"

"Bye," I said, and watched the door close behind them.

It was only after the gate sealed shut that it occurred to me that going to find my father was easier said than done.

I looked up at the gate in front of me: Gate 69.

Wait a second. Hadn't we skipped the 60s on the way here? Had Cea taken a different route back?

I sighed, then shook my head. Surely there were multiple ways to get back to Wing 1. As long as I moved in the right direction, I'd eventually get there. In theory.

Straightening my shoulders, I opened Gate 69 and continued through. There was only one way to find out.

14

About an hour later, I had my answer.

I was lost. Utterly.

I hadn't seen a familiar gate number in at least half an hour. Sometimes I would find myself in the low numbers, and I felt like I was getting close—and then the next gate I would pass through would dump me back into the 80s. Once I even passed through a segment of the 90s.

It was as if I were going in circles, which was a reasonable assumption.

I sighed. What irked me most was the fact that I had not managed to pass another human being in all this time. Very few of the halls I had walked through contained anything more than doors.

I entered a wing with several gates and walked up to the closest one. At this point, it didn't really matter which one I tried.

I waved my hand over the sensor, and the panel released the most hideous sound I had ever heard. I almost screamed out of shock.

I dared to look down at the panel. An ugly red X glowed, with the words *Access Denied* flashing below it.

I stared at the words until the red faded away. Access denied?

The door wasn't set to accept me. Which meant I was most assuredly going in the wrong direction.

I moaned and tried another gate. Also locked. The next three ones I tried were locked as well. That sound was really starting to get on my nerves.

I cringed as I held my hand over the next gate, waiting for the beep. It didn't. It flashed green and opened agreeably.

I pushed loose hairs off my forehead and walked through, hoping for the best. The sight beyond made me stop and stare.

It was the strangest wing I had been in yet. It was massive—the size of a warehouse—but completely bare. There were only three gates in the entire place.

Two were on my side of the room—Gate 72, and Gate 73, which I had just come out of. Across the room was Gate 74.

I figured I might as well try the one across the room. Gate 72 probably led back the way I came, though there was no guarantee of that.

I held my breath while I tried the door. I let it out when the panel accepted me readily.

I walked through and immediately wondered if Gate 72 would have been a safer bet. The lights in Wing 74 were dim—had I run into another unused wing?

I shrugged. I was here. I might as well give it a go.

Wing 74 was lined with doors. I walked up to the first and tried it. *Access Denied.* Second and third doors were the same. After the fifth refusal, I began to worry.

I glanced around the hall and noticed something peculiar about the gates. They were unmarked. No numbers, no letters. Just bare doors.

Bare doors that, honestly, looked like nobody had been through them in years. Dust and debris gathered in the corners, and several of the access panels still had protective film on the screen. If it weren't for the fact that the middle of the hall was swept clean, I would have thought the wing hadn't been used in a decade.

I suddenly felt the urge to speak aloud. It was just too creepy being in a hall of unmarked doors without evidence of a single soul.

"All these halls!" was the only thing I could think of to say.

My voice reverberated off the metal, and I instantly regretted speaking. The echo was surreal. I glanced back over my shoulder and waited until the silence returned. This time, it was welcome.

I drew in a deep breath and kept walking. If I got in here, I could get out. At the very least, if I didn't find a door that opened, I would go back out of Gate 74.

Yes. A reasonable plan.

I continued down the hall. The ambiance of the lighting began to unnerve me; moving constantly in and out of shadow was disturbing. I tried more unmarked doors, all locked. A few at least looked like they had been used recently, but they still didn't let me in. Just as I was beginning to wonder if I'd reached the point where I'd better turn back, a door opened for me.

I almost shrieked in relief. After all the red X's, the green circle was the most comforting thing I'd ever seen.

I passed through the door—and found myself in that empty wing again. I frowned and glanced back at the door.

Gate 74. Again.

I sighed. Well, at least I was out. And I knew which way *not* to go.

I went back through the gate I had come in by—at least, I hoped it was the same gate. I found myself in a wing with several more gates, and I picked the smallest number. Maybe if I kept doing that, I would eventually end up at Wing 1.

The door opened before I could touch the panel, and I almost screamed for the third time in an hour. Then I promptly wanted to collapse in relief—Dr. Nic and Cea were standing on the other side of the door.

It felt cheap, but I had to say it: "I am so glad you're here! I—"

"What are you doing back here?" Dr. Nic's voice was more of a snarl than a question.

"Lost," I confessed readily. "You left me, and I tried to get back to Wing 1, and I—"

"You should not be back here," he interrupted me again. Cea glanced between us.

"Don't I know it." I sighed, then looked up pathetically. "I don't suppose you know the way back?"

Cea stepped up and took charge. "Of course. I'm sorry, Phil, I shouldn't have left you alone. I should have given you directions or something. It's my fault." She glanced sideways at her brother.

Dr. Nic's scowl melted into his diplomatic smile. He actually laughed. "Of course! I should have thought of that. Just stay with Cea and don't go wandering around. It's not safe."

Cea abruptly started walking. I called over my shoulder as I ran to keep up with her. "I won't, I promise!"

His smile faded. "Good." He stood still and watched us until the gate closed.

15

I had to run to keep pace with Cea. She didn't slow down until we were back in the 30s.

"I'm sorry, Cea, I didn't mean to make trouble."

Cea abruptly reduced her pace to a casual walk, as if she suddenly realized she was running. I almost bumped into her. "It's okay." She let out her breath, and her voice returned to normal. "You didn't mean it."

"I didn't mess anything up, I don't think." I struggled to steady my breathing after the sprint. "I didn't see any rooms with equipment or people, so I'm pretty sure I didn't disturb anything."

"Where did you go?" Cea opened a door, and there was Wing 1. I was so glad to see the sky shimmering above the glass dome.

"Everywhere and nowhere. I passed so many numbers that I don't remember any at all—except Wing 74. That was weird."

"What?" Cea stopped and looked at me. "Where?"

I thought, making sure I had my numbers correct. "Wing 74. It was way in the back. Well, it felt like it was way in the back. It was weird, because all the doors weren't marked."

"Unmarked doors...?" She squinted. "I'm not aware of a hall with unmarked doors. Are you sure?"

I nodded. "Positive."

Cea's face was set in a disturbing frown. "Let's go check." She started walking again.

"Go check?" I repeated.

Cea walked a few paces down the hall and opened the door for Room 1C. She ushered me inside and locked the door behind us.

The room was almost completely bare. There were a few chairs inside the door and a computer terminal in the back corner. The walls were blank and windowless. A section of the ceiling in the far right corner was dotted with black sensor eyes.

I pointed. "What's that on the ceiling?"

"You'll see." Cea walked over to the terminal and waved her hand in front of the screen. A menu appeared. "Do you remember what time it was when I left you?"

I struggled to remember the last time I had touched base with a clock. "It was about an hour ago, I think."

Cea typed on the keypad. There was the faint sound of static, and suddenly a holographic copy of me was standing in the room!

Cea laughed when I jumped. "Sorry, I should have warned you. It's the security tape. Watch."

I did. It was a ghostly version of me—faded and slightly transparent. But the colors were correct, and I moved as though real. The sound was real. I listened as my footsteps and my ghost walked towards the far corner of the room. Gate 69 could be seen behind me.

My ghost walked off the edge of the projection. Cea touched the computer screen, and the background shifted to the next camera's viewpoint. My replica walked into view again, stepping out of thin air on the edge of the image. The hologram formed under the square of black-dotted ceiling; when my ghost reached the edge of the sensors, it vanished.

Cea switched viewpoints again. She tucked a curl of hair behind her ear and rapidly pawed through menus. "It's hard to track a moving body, because you have to keep switching cameras, but it works."

We traced my ghost as it wandered the maze, twisting through random doors. I felt lost again.

"You were going in the right direction up until this point. This is where you took a wrong turn." Cea walked into the hologram and pointed at a door marked Gate 45. "You should have gone here."

"Oh," I said as my replica took Gate 43 on the other side of the room.

Cea backed out of the hologram and stood beside me. We watched my image try random doors, cringing at the horrible beep of denial.

Cea frowned. "You got way out of course, girl. There's nothing down that hall."

"Nothing for me, anyway! None of the doors would let me in."

"Why did you keep trying them?" She walked back to the terminal.

"Um… I figured the doors closer to Wing 1 were set to accept me. So if the door opened, I was going in the right direction."

I hoped Cea would laugh at my incompetence. Not surprisingly, she didn't.

I jumped and pointed. "There it is! Gate 74. That's the gate that leads to a hall with unmarked doors… and none of them would open."

My ghost walked up to Gate 74. Cea straightened. Her eyes narrowed. My hologram waved its hand, then sighed with relief as the panel flashed green. It walked into the hall and disappeared out of range.

The image abruptly went blank. I glanced back at Cea. She rapidly tapped the screen. "You walked out of range of our security cameras."

"But there were more halls beyond Gate 74... lots of them! None of the doors would open, and none of them were marked."

"How did you get out?" Cea's eyes were wide.

I shrugged. "I made a big circle... When I finally found a door that would open, it was Gate 74 again."

Cea shook her head and turned back to the terminal. "I don't know where you went, Phil."

"Why are there no cameras beyond Gate 74?"

"I've never been back there... maybe it's unused." She paused. "Or unfinished. Since the doors aren't marked or anything."

I remembered the dusty corners around the doors. Maybe it was construction debris.

Cea shrugged. "I'll have to ask Nic—I don't know." She went back to scrolling. "I wouldn't worry about it. You won't have to go back there again—there's nothing back there."

She continued typing. I regarded the bare room, the empty stage. Slowly, "Cea... are all the security records on that computer?"

"Most of them," she replied. "Anything that's public."

"How far... do they go back?"

"Since the cameras were put in." The terminal beeped at her.

"Are there... any records from when..." I stopped.

She looked up at me. "From what?"

"Ephesus?" I whispered. I turned to face her. "Do you have any records from when Ephesus was here?"

She regarded me. Compassion flickered across her gray eyes. "Yes."

"Can... you?"

"Do you want to see them?" she asked.

I looked down at the floor and battled. "Yes, I do."

Without a word, Cea turned and touched the screen. She thumbed through several menus, then dropped her arm. I waited.

The image snapped into place, but at first I couldn't see anyone. It was a meeting room somewhere, with a vacant table in the middle. I bit my lip.

Voices echoed somewhere off the recording. I heard him, jumbled amongst other men. I tensed my nerves as he walked into view.

There he was, perpetual lab coat and all. He walked to the table and leaned on his knuckles. The other men gathered around. One laid a tablet on the table, and they began discussing the chart displayed on it.

I had no idea what Ephesus was saying. I couldn't grasp the words—technical gibberish—but I didn't care. All I wanted was his voice.

It matched the memories in my head perfectly. Some secret fear in me died.

I took a step towards him. I took another step—I was standing right beside him. He felt real. Thin but real. I reached out my finger to tap his arm.

My hand went right through.

I cupped my palm and brought back air. I stared at my fingers, as though hoping something would materialize on them.

I looked back up at Ephesus. The tears in my eyes made his image blur.

"Do you want me to shut it off?" Cea asked carefully.

I backed out of the hologram. "No… no."

We both watched in silence as the men finished their meeting. Ephesus left, and the recording continued to display a blank room. Cea shut the hologram off.

"You can look through the files," she said, walking away from the computer. "You can watch whatever's on file. If it's on that computer, it's public."

I took her place before the terminal. "Do you have… the day he died?"

"Some. A couple of the records were removed to investigate the accident. But… I wouldn't recommend watching that day."

I drew a breath and nodded. The computer screen displayed a form field and a "browse" button.

"If you know what you're looking for, enter the specs and it will pull up the exact recording. But you have to know which camera you want."

I shook my head and hit "browse," then "search by date."

Cea walked away. She paused in the doorway. "Phil… be careful."

I looked up at her. "Thank you."

She stared back at me. Then she left.

I entered 2073 into the year field, then August. I wanted to see when Ephesus arrived on base for the first time. What day was it?

Something in the corner of the screen caught my eye: "History."

I opened the menu. The most recent entry was dated 2074—the meeting. The entry before it was for this morning, not long ago.

I tapped it. I wanted to see Gate 74 again.

The computer screeched, a sound akin to *Access Denied.* I swallowed.

A red-bordered message appeared on the screen. I blinked to make sure it was real.

Error: File not found.

16

After two hours, I was miserable.

I thought looking at recordings of Ephesus would ease the pain by filling the gap in my memory, allowing me to relive time we had been separated.

Instead, they tore the bandage off an old wound by reminding me that I had missed, been completely left out of, the last days of my brother's life.

Most of the recordings were mundane, of him in meetings, or walking down the hall, or toying with some scientific gadgetry. Those didn't bother me.

The ones that hit me were the few rare recordings that caught him reclining in a lounge, or sitting by himself in the cafeteria—of him being relaxed. Because whenever he was relaxed, whenever he could not distract his mind with work, I saw the oft-buried emotion surface in his eyes. I could see the brotherliness, the confusion, the loneliness, the thoughtfulness. The pain.

It was then that I could tell he had missed me just as much as I'd missed him.

Once, the tape caught him reading his Bible during lunch. The highlighted text filled the screen of his laptop while he added yet another note to the overflowing sidebar. I had once sat beside him on the couch while he wrote those notes.

That was when I turned the recording off and cried.

I didn't feel like eating lunch after that. I sat in our dorms and prayed, wondering if Daddy would come anytime soon.

He didn't, but Cea did.

"Phil?"

I briefly glanced at the monitor, wondering if I wanted to employ the two-way communication feature. I decided against it and let her in.

"You weren't at lunch and I…" She trailed off.

I turned away to face the digital picture frame. "I'm all right," I answered her question before she could ask it. "Physically."

"Ephesus?"

"Yes."

"I'm sorry."

"You warned me." I let out my breath.

She was silent for a moment. "You should go eat something. They're still serving lunch for another half-hour."

"Okay," I said in ambiguous consent.

I expected the cafeteria to be empty, but it wasn't. Mr. Sardis occupied a table with the woman and toddler I'd seen at breakfast—presumably his wife and son. They were laughing and playing with the boy, copying his silly noises.

I scooped up a little food and sat on the opposite side of the room. I was glad Cea hadn't insisted on sitting with me.

I stirred my food for at least three minutes before eating any of it, turning my selections into one homogenous mush. I didn't even notice the horrible taste, probably because my mind was still choking on grief over Ephesus.

The image of him highlighting a verse in his digital Bible repeatedly came back to me. I wanted to know what he had been reading. I wanted to know what he had highlighted—what verse had struck him and encouraged him. Because I needed that same touch.

I needed that Bible.

But his computer was reduced to ashes, scattered on the four winds of empty space, along with him and the entire transit. If only his scheduled flight had been one transit sooner, or if only his baggage had gotten put on the wrong transit...

It hit me so hard I nearly gagged on my obliterated potatoes.

His baggage hadn't been on the transit with him. Or, at least, not all of it.

He was only coming back for a visit. Not specifically to visit us, of course— the United wasn't that kind—but to do some research-whatever in the lab. He should only have taken enough baggage to last him a week.

Granted, my brother didn't have that many belongings. He probably took most of his clothes.

Would he have left his computer behind? If he did, would it have the Bible on it? He probably took his personal laptop, but he had more than one computer for work. He'd copied the Bible to his personal laptop before leaving, I remembered that. Maybe he transferred the file to his other work laptops, too. He had an encrypted app on his phone; it wouldn't surprise me if he'd put a copy of the file on all his devices.

And if he did, that laptop might be shut off, tucked away in storage somewhere, safe from the virus. With a Bible resting on its hard drive.

It was a stretch. If the computers were for work, the lab probably took them back. But the rest of his goods, whatever wasn't on the transit, had to be somewhere.

And at this point, I would do anything to get my hands on even the tiniest piece of him.

A scraping chair broke my reverie. Mrs. Sardis and her son were leaving. She smiled as she passed my table; the little boy waved.

"Hi," he called.

"Hi!" I replied. The happy tone of my voice was genuine.

I stood up. Mr. Sardis still sat alone, munching on his dessert. Maybe he would know.

I walked over to his table. He turned, grinned, and swallowed his mouthful.

"Hello again, Philli!" he burst out. He sure picked up on my nickname quickly. "Enjoying yourself?"

"Yes," I said, which may or may not have been the truth. "I have a question."

"Fantastic! I might know the answer." He winked and took another bite.

I searched for a way to clearly phrase my question. "If I were looking for some baggage, where would it be?"

"Did I forget some of your luggage?" He licked frosting off his lips and looked properly horrified.

"No…" I chewed my jaw. How much did I want to explain? Did it really matter? If Cea knew about Ephesus, Mr. Sardis probably did too.

"I'm looking for some baggage my brother left behind."

"You've got a brother? You really need to be more open about your family relationships. First a surprise daughter, now you're telling me you have a brother!"

I sighed. Might as well take the plunge. "Ephesus Smyrna. He worked here a few years ago. The… transit exploded."

The smile died from his eyes, and his big voice dropped to a tiny whisper. "Oh."

"Do you know where they put his stuff?" I asked hopefully.

He scrunched his face. "What stuff? Didn't he have all his baggage with him?"

"No!" I protested, a little too loudly. "He was just coming back for a visit. He should have left some things behind. Where would they have put it?"

"I… don't know." He abruptly leaned back and ran a hand through his hair. After a second, he straightened and looked at me carefully. "What do you want?"

"Well, anything, really, but especially his old laptop or something."

"Why?"

"He… might have some books stored on it."

"What books?"

I hesitated. Did I really want to tell the man I was looking for a book that was illegal to distribute back on Earth? What else was I going to tell him? *"I was really hoping for some study notes from the lab"* probably wouldn't work.

"I was hoping to find… his Bible." My voice dropped at the end of the sentence.

Mr. Sardis stared. "Why do you need his?"

I felt my palms go clammy. "I… didn't you hear about the virus? Didn't it wipe the systems up here?"

Hope surged. Maybe Mars hadn't been affected. Maybe everything was still here. Maybe…

"Ah… yes," Mr. Sardis stuttered. "But… well… hmm." He propped his elbow on the table and thought a minute. Then he shoved his chair back.

"Wait right here," he said, gesturing with his finger for emphasis.

I did, quite literally, too baffled to go anywhere else. He came back about ten minutes later, waving a reader very similar to my own.

He presented it to me with a grin. "Here you go!"

The metal felt warm in my hands. I squinted at the screen, almost afraid to look—and there it was. A folder labeled "Bible," with each book arranged in order.

I was so elated I almost forgot to ask. But common sense—and disbelief—caught up. "Where did you get this?"

Mr. Sardis popped his jaw. "Erm… Nic made back-ups."

"*Dr. Nic* made back-ups?"

"Yeah. For Cea, I think it was."

For Cea? I couldn't help but remind him, "Doesn't he know transmitting is illegal?"

"Of course. That's why he made copies when the law went into effect. Just in case." Mr. Sardis winked.

I didn't find that comforting. Something wasn't snapping into place. "But… isn't he a Unionist?" That sounded stupid, so I clarified. "Aren't all the colonies up here subject to United policy, too?"

Mr. Sardis laughed. "Well, we would be, if they enforced it." He sauntered back to his chair. "You see, Philli, the United doesn't ask a lot of questions. Not if you've signed the file."

He scooped up his trash. "Don't ask, don't tell. And if they do ask, still don't tell. If you tell the officials what they want to hear, they won't come sticking their noses in your business. Sign the file, submit your annual report, and they think you're being well-behaved Unionists."

I looked down at the screen in my hands. *We figured they can't stop us from thinking about it, and that's what matters, right? It's a relationship, not a religion.*

Mr. Sardis walked towards the cafeteria doors. I followed in a daze. "What do they know!" he boomed. "Up here, I can sing hymns from the rooftop if I want, as long as I shut up when we have official visitors."

If you come to my house, you may keep your Bible. You may pray and worship however you like in your room, and no one will bother you.

Come with me. Come with me.

"Yup, I'm one of you. A Christian! But that's our little secret." He chuckled as he dumped his trash. "So, will that do you?"

"I... yes. Yes, thank you very much." All other thoughts evaporated from my head as I realized what I was holding. I quickly picked a random book and opened it to make sure the words were still there.

See, I have placed before you an open door that no one can shut...

"Ah... one thing," Mr. Sardis added. He rubbed his chin. "Don't connect that to the wifi."

"Doesn't it...?"

"Not automatically. You'd have to go in and add the network."

That's illegal. I looked up at him, but I didn't say it.

He shrugged. "It's old. Been around for a while."

I studied the metal case. It looked newer than my reader. Certainly had more buttons.

"But... shouldn't we send this... to everyone? So they can have the Bible, too?"

"Isn't transmitting illegal?"

I looked down. *That hasn't stopped me before...*

He laid his hand on my shoulder. "Maybe later—once we're sure the virus has been fixed. If we do it now, the virus could corrupt it and we'll just lose it."

That made sense. I looked into his face again. "Thank you."

His brilliant grin returned. "You are welcome, Philli. Anytime you need anything, just ask. There's no need to be shy around us. Up here, we accept you for who you are. That's Dr. Nic's vision. You can worship whom you will. Just keep it down when we've got company, okay?"

He winked, patted my shoulder, and left.

17

I stood for a long time in the hall, just staring at the random page of Revelation I'd opened. My thoughts were a garbled mess of Mr. Sardis's words and streams of Scripture. Eventually, I switched to a different page and began to read.

I probably would have stood there for hours had Cea not stumbled across me.

"What are you doing?"

I almost responded "reading," then caught myself. I held out the reader to show her. "Mr. Sardis copied it for me."

"Where did he… Why did you need one?"

"The virus wiped all the copies on Earth," I reminded her.

She stared blankly. I waited for some explanation, some excuse for why Dr. Nic had copies of illegal books lying around. She shook her head and looked away. "You should have said something."

"How was I supposed to know that…" I sighed and tried to organize my thoughts. "I didn't know if Mars would be… like Earth. If the rules were the same. If Dr. Nic would be like…"

"Nic is *not* like that Ambrose character," Cea snapped. I felt bad for asking.

"Is he a Christian?" I ventured.

"No… sadly." Cea's shoulders drooped.

"Are you?" I looked into her face.

She lifted her gaze to meet mine. "Yes."

"Why didn't you tell me?"

"You didn't ask." She shrugged and abruptly started walking.

I skipped to catch up with her. "You didn't say anything when I mentioned coming from a camp."

"Can you blame me for not wanting to admit that I should be in a camp right now?"

"No," was my ready response. Then, "Why aren't you?"

At this, she smiled and turned to face me. The light in her eyes was comforting. "Nic. That's why he came up here. He's always working to make life better—why else would he specialize in experimental technology? One day he's going to cut us off from the United so everyone can worship in peace, to whomever they worship."

The glint in her eyes turned from comforting to disturbing. "How's he going to do that?" I said carefully.

"By becoming more powerful than they are. That's the only way to cut yourself off from a monster and keep them from assimilating you back in."

Assimilated or removed. "How will he be more powerful?"

Cea opened her mouth, then stopped. Her smile faded as though she realized she had gone too far. "That's... the pet project."

"A secret," I guessed.

"Yeah." She sighed, then shook her head. "But you're not involved. In the meantime, Nic's doing the best he can. As governor, he can make sure we have space to worship, as long as we behave when the United calls."

She laid her hand over the reader screen. "We want you here, Philli. Nic wants everyone to have freedom. You're safe here."

She looked into my face. "Just do what Nic says and you'll be fine."

I looked down at the verses peeking out from behind her hand. *Take their offer while you still can. Take it and run!*

I looked up again. "I want to show this to my father. When will he get off work?"

Cea smiled, gaze returning to normal. "I saw Nic and a few others wandering around the halls just now. I think they're on break."

She turned and pointed. "If you head straight up that way, Gate 34 is on your right. Go through that, then Gate 38. Last I saw them, they were working around meeting room 38D. Just don't go anywhere else and you'll be fine."

"I hope so," I said with a lack of conviction. "But thank you." I started walking in the direction she indicated.

"It will be fine, Phil," she called after me, first loudly, then softly. "It will be fine."

18

I tried to force all other thoughts out of my head as I walked, just concentrating on remembering the directions. 34 on the right, then 38, then 38D. I could remember that.

Remembering on the way over wasn't necessarily the problem. Remembering on the way back could be a different story.

I let out my breath. *Please don't let me get lost again, Lord. I just need to talk to Daddy.* My thoughts perked up as I passed through Gate 34, which was on the right like Cea said it would be. *He'll be so excited to see these, and then I can tell him about...*

My thoughts drooped down again. Daddy didn't know about Ephesus yet. I would have to tell him about seeing Ephesus's room, getting lost, watching all the tapes, talking to Mr. Sardis, and...

This could be a long conversation. Some of this might have to wait until after dinner.

I entered Wing 38. Meeting room 38D was right ahead of me, and the door was shut. No one was in the hall.

I hope they're still down here... and they're not busy! Mustering up my nerves, I walked up to the door and pressed the call button.

There was a moment of silence. *Well, you have to say something!* "Dad... Dr. Smyrna?"

Silence. Static and mumblings. Grumpily, "Who is it?"

Dr. Nic's voice. His terseness made me fumble. "Me... Phil. Philadelphia. Is my father there?"

"Yes." Silence.

"May I speak to him please?"

His response was difficult to hear. "And it can't wait?"

No, actually... "Well, Cea thought he was on break, and I didn't catch him at lunch." *Sorry to involve you, Cea!*

Bitter mutters. He said something—was it directed at me? I couldn't distinguish it. I stood on my toes and leaned my ear closer to the speaker.

I slipped, and my hand brushed the sensor.

I gave a small scream and stumbled back, clutching the reader to keep from dropping it, as the door hissed open. The panel glowed green cheekily.

The men's heated conversation stopped. All the white-coated figures turned and glared at me.

"You are not allowed in here," Dr. Nic informed me thoroughly.

Carnegie frowned. "How did you..."

"It was an accident!" *That's what they all say...* "I bumped the sensor, it..." I shook my finger at the panel.

Dr. Nic strode into the hall and watched as the green circle faded away.

Carnegie crowded behind him. "But she doesn't have access..."

Dr. Nic muttered, "I'm beginning to think that fact is irrelevant."

"Curses," Carnegie spat, and offered a few examples.

The other scientists hovered and murmured, gazing curiously at me. My father calmly emerged from the crowd.

"Phil." He tapped my arm.

"Daddy, I'm sorry... I need to talk to you." I tipped the reader to show him the screen.

His eyes went wide. Lowering his voice, he spoke quickly. "It will have to wait until we're done here." He looked back at the meeting room and frowned.

Somehow I got the impression that he would have gladly abandoned the meeting to talk to me.

"Well, little miss who defies all security systems." Dr. Nic turned away from the panel and crossed his arms.

"Perhaps she should work in security. She might be a genius waiting to happen," Carnegie said without amusement.

The men whispered amongst themselves. Daddy knotted his eyebrows together and glanced at me. *What did you do?* I shrugged honestly.

Dr. Nic tossed his hair and spoke up. "Is there anything else we can do for you?"

I shook my head quickly. "It can wait until you're done. I'm sorry to interrupt—I didn't know you were in a meeting."

My father let go of my arm. I turned.

"In the future, Philadelphia..." Dr. Nic called after me.

I stopped but couldn't bring myself to look back at him.

"You will not bother your father during working hours."

One of the men objected to this. "Heavens, Nic, she interrupted one meeting by accident. What's the crime? You don't mind if my wife visits me during the day."

"Regulations," Dr. Nic snapped. I cringed.

Daddy stared. He said nothing.

"And…" Dr. Nic held me back still. "You will not come around here in the 30s again, do you understand? This is private space for work of which you are not a part."

I ran.

"Tell Cea I will speak with her in half an hour!" he yelled.

I couldn't bring myself to respond. I darted through Gate 38 and fled.

*

I nearly collided with Cea as I crashed back down the hall towards the dorms.

"Did you find him?" she said, sidestepping to avoid me.

I stopped and panted. "No… yes. They were in a meeting. It will have to wait."

She eyed me. "Sit down." She gestured into a nearby office.

I collapsed in the nearest chair. She shut the door behind us.

"Why were you running?" She walked over and sat behind the desk.

"It felt emotionally appropriate." I drew a long breath and steadied my voice. "Nic said he will speak with you in a half-hour."

Cea frowned, but her eyes were not accusing. "What happened?"

"I accidentally interrupted their meeting."

"How did you manage to do that? Didn't you just use the call button?"

"I did, but… I bumped the sensor, and the door opened." I singed red. "It wasn't supposed to let me in, I gather."

Cea was silent.

"He told me not to go back there, in the 30s…"

"He who?"

"Nic. And he said not to bother my father during work hours anymore."

Cea stared into my eyes. "I'm sorry."

"Regulations," I muttered.

She sighed. "Well, I wouldn't worry about it. You won't have to go back there again."

That was the second time today she'd said that. I stiffened and sat up. "I don't think he really cares about me wandering the halls in the 30s."

She turned to face the computer screen. I kept talking.

"I think he's worried about me accidentally opening doors that were not meant to open for me." I paused. "Like Gate 74."

Cea abruptly started typing on the computer.

"Cea, please…"

She stopped typing, but she didn't look at me. I got up and stood in front of the desk.

"Gate 74 wasn't supposed to let me in, was it?"

She covered her face with her hand, but she answered. "No."

"Does it have to do with Daddy's work?"

"No… not yet anyway. Your father is not allowed in Wing 74 either. Few people are." She looked up at me finally. "Please leave it that way."

I thought a minute. "It's the pet project," I declared.

She swiveled the chair to face the wall, then whispered, "Yes."

She suddenly twirled the chair back around. "Just leave it be, Phil. Please stay away."

"I will."

"Thank you." She sighed.

"Then maybe you can tell me something else."

She looked at me out of the corner of her eye with mixed hopefulness and dread.

"Where are Ephesus's things?"

"Weren't they on the—"

"No. He was just coming back for a visit. A week, two weeks tops. He should have left some stuff behind."

"Didn't… didn't the United send them back to you after his death?"

I could tell by the look in her eyes that she didn't believe her own words. "The United is not that kind."

She stared directly into my face, perhaps unintentionally.

"What did you do with them?" I repeated. I realized how harsh my voice sounded. "Please. It's all I have left of him."

"I… can't tell you."

I wasn't sure whether that meant "I don't know" or "I'm not allowed to say." I was beginning to believe it was the latter.

I searched her gray eyes. They pleaded with me. She wasn't telling me everything, that I knew.

But what she was telling me—it was the truth.

"I'm going to my room."

She nodded. I walked to the door.

She called out to me, voice hushed. "Phil… I'm sorry."

I left.

19

After dinner, I gave my father a detailed synopsis of the day. I wasn't entirely surprised when he said the same thing as Cea.

"Don't go snooping around the halls. Just leave it be."

"I didn't mean to cause trouble."

"I know," he sighed, voice reassuring, "but we must avoid trouble if we can help it. Christians do not need trouble, even in a tolerant place."

"I'm sorry, Dad. I'll stay close to the dorms tomorrow. I'm going to look through more of the security records."

He frowned. "Do you think you can handle more of… him?" His phrasing was awkward.

"I'll manage. I'm going to see if I can find out what they did with his baggage." I looked at him for silent approval.

He pondered before giving it. "Perhaps they destroyed the leftovers."

"If they did, no one will give me a straight answer." My eyes pleaded with him to understand.

He did. He shook his head. "It's a touchy subject. I guess I don't blame them. If I had a tragedy like that on my hands… it wouldn't be my favorite thing to talk about."

That hadn't occurred to me. "Do you think Dr. Nic just doesn't want to remember?"

My father contorted his eyebrows. "I'm… still trying to figure Dr. Nic out. He's… confusing."

I slid closer to him on the couch. "Was work okay?"

"Not entirely," was the somewhat unexpected answer. He sighed wearily.

"What's wrong?"

"Nothing—yet. Nothing I can discuss." He looked down at me. "And you know that when I withhold information from you, it's not to hurt you."

I snuggled close to him. He rubbed my back in silence for a moment.

After a while, I asked again, "May I look at the security tapes and try to find out what happened to his stuff?"

"Yes," he consented, "you may."

*

I didn't catch Cea at breakfast, which was just as well. I wasn't sure I wanted to talk with her. Honestly, I wasn't sure I wanted to tell her what I was doing.

No one was using the security room when I went in. I had several uninterrupted hours to work, during which I did nothing but flip between cameras.

I had a good plan for figuring out what happened to my brother's stuff. I would find the camera that was stationed outside his dorm and watch all the recordings surrounding the day of the accident. Then I would see for sure how much baggage he carried out when he left, and what happened when people went in to clean the room later.

There were only two catches to my plan. The first was that the recordings with the information I needed could have been removed. Cea said some of them had been taken off to investigate the accident.

But I wouldn't know for sure until I watched all the available recordings. To do that I had to figure out which camera corresponded to that hall.

That was the second catch.

I had no idea what numbers I was looking for. Was there even a camera in that hall? It didn't help that I couldn't remember what wing the dorms had been in.

Cea knew, but I wasn't going to ask her right now.

Discouraged or otherwise, I decided to try. After all, I didn't have anything better to do.

After an hour of searching, it occurred to me that I might not even know the hall when I saw it. They all looked the same.

Then I had an idea. I brought up yesterday's records and scrolled through random cameras until I saw myself.

Cea and I were walking out of my room after unpacking. Perfect.

I kept one eye on the display generated in the corner of the room as I pawed through menus. I used guess and check to follow our trail, switching cameras madly in an attempt to keep up.

I managed not to lose track of my ghostly self, and my efforts were rewarded. I sighed aloud with relief when the recording showed Cea opening the door to my brother's dorm and stepping back to give me space. The camera angle was perfect—you could see straight down the hall towards the main door, monitoring everyone that came in and out.

I turned back to the computer and searched for the numbers. Camera 88.3. That didn't sound hard to remember, but I'd better write it down just in case.

I scanned the computer desk, oblivious of my own voice playing over the recording. There was not a single scrap of paper in the room.

I reached down and felt my pouch for my reader. Empty. I must have left it in my room. I sighed.

Leaving the recording running, I ran across the hall to our dorms and fetched it. I opened a blank file and typed with my thumbs as I walked. Not watching where I was going, I collided straight into someone standing in the hallway.

I moaned and mentally told myself I should be smart enough not to walk and write at the same time. I looked up and panicked.

Dr. Nic glared down at me.

"What are you doing?" His voice was unnervingly loud.

"Looking at the recordings," I said hastily, scrambling up.

"For?"

"For?" I repeated dumbly.

"For what?" He was outright shouting now. "What are you looking for?"

"For… for Ephesus."

"Ephesus!"

"My… my brother, sir. He was my brother." My voice hushed, partly because his loudness was scaring me.

"Your brother." He growled and turned away. He didn't seem surprised to hear this information.

I swallowed and waited. He ran a hand through his hair.

"What about your brother?"

Why was that the automatic response? Why, when I spoke of my brother, did everyone demand an explanation? He was my brother—wasn't that enough? Wasn't I entitled to know everything?

I closed my eyes and prayed, hard.

My silence was too long for Dr. Nic. He turned around, glare settling on me again. "What do you want to know?"

"I wanted… I wanted to know what happened to his stuff."

"His stuff?" It was Dr. Nic's turn to repeat me dumbly.

"His things—his baggage. Whatever he left behind when he came back to Earth for a visit. I want his leftover things. They belong to my family and no one will tell me where they are!"

I spoke too quickly—and too harshly. "Do not talk back to me," Dr. Nic spat with venom. "What happened to the baggage after the accident is none of your concern. Your brother's business and his doings here are none of your concern."

It's his assignment, not yours. I took a step backwards.

Dr. Nic turned to the door. "Do not mess with the recordings again." He reached into his pocket and pulled out that disc-gadget.

I sucked in my breath. "But Cea—"

"Cea is not in charge. I am." He snapped the disc on the panel and punched a button.

The panel beeped unhappily. Dr. Nic removed the disc and waved his hand over the sensor. A pause, another beep, and the doors shut, locked for good.

Dr. Nic turned to me again, voice strangely calm. "I expect you will refrain from any further snooping. You have been far too inquisitive for having been here less than 48 hours."

At first I couldn't think of anything to say. My breath rose in my throat, and my volume rose with it. "I was just asking about my brother! He's my brother! And you took him away!"

"I took him away?" His mustache twitched.

"You're the one that requested him, weren't you? You didn't give him a choice! You didn't give my father a choice, either." I took two more steps backwards.

"No," he said without regret. "I'm also the one that called for you."

I froze.

"The commander didn't want to let you come. Said it was against 'regulations.' But I didn't think it was right to leave a young girl in the hands of strangers. Your brother was an adult," he cut off my excuses before I could think them, "you're a minor. And you have nobody. I didn't think that was right."

I backed away. He advanced and narrowed the gap. "If you don't want to be here, you don't have to stay. I could... send you back to Earth." The threat was calm, flat like a sheet of razor-sharp ice.

I sucked in several gasps. "I'm... sorry. I'm sorry."

He was smiling again, but it wasn't an encouraging smile. I didn't feel like he was forgiving me for my disrespectfulness—I felt like he was accepting my surrender.

"It's all right," he said, and he sounded reasonably truthful about it. "Just stay out of my way." His smile deepened, eyes glittering. "Just keep your head down, Philadelphia, and no one will know the difference."

I turned and ran for the dorms.

20

I went to lunch, but only because I didn't want anyone to worry. After pretending to eat, I went back to the dorms and huddled on the couch, praying. Or trying to.

A knock on the door interrupted my stewing.

I forced myself to get up and hit the call button. "Who is it?" I said, making a mental list of people I was willing to talk to right now.

"Cea." The line fuzzed with her breath.

She wasn't on the list, but I answered anyway. "Come in."

She did—and shut the door again.

She regarded the keypad. "Lock it, please."

I stood up. "Why?"

"So no one else comes in."

I didn't move towards the panel. "Why?"

"Ephesus."

I walked over and tapped the keys to lock the door.

I turned towards her. She was staring at me, eyes narrowed.

"How intelligent are you?" Her voice was bitter.

"What?"

"I suppose how patient and trusting are you might be a more accurate question."

"Define trust."

"If I... tell you something... about your brother. About Ephesus. Are you... will you wait... with the questions? Can you trust me until I can explain more? Will you do as I say and not try to figure it out yourself?"

I stared at her. Her eyes softened; her voice faded.

"Can you take it one step at a time?"

*

"There are two rules."

I ran to keep up with her. Cea was walking briskly, but aimlessly—or so it seemed. She'd weave down a hall, then turn, then turn again. North for a few halls, then south again. If she was trying to get me lost, she'd succeeded five minutes ago.

"First rule is... you must never speak of anything you hear or see today—anything—with anyone."

How cliché! My heart sank. I couldn't go along with this, not if I couldn't...

"Except your father."

I looked up at her. She kept walking, but she gazed into my eyes.

"You may speak of it with your father—but only your father! And only in your private quarters. Mention it anywhere else, and it could end up on a public security tape."

She turned away from me and picked up the pace.

"The other rule... you must never go where I am about to take you. Not by yourself. Never come near it. If someone mentions it, act like it doesn't exist. Never, ever come back without me. And don't ask me to come! I will bring you when it's safe, and that will be few and far between."

Her voice cracked. "This is going to be hard, Phil. I'm warning you, this is not going to be easy on you—or your father."

I stared up the hall ahead of us. "Where are we going?"

It was a moment before she replied.

"Wing 74."

21

Wing 74. "The pet project."

"Yes."

"Which I'm not supposed to know about."

"Yes."

"What does that have to do with—"

"Some questions must wait for later!"

She halted at a junction and glanced up the halls. Silence.

She outright ran. I followed as fast as I could. Our boots seemed loud—so loud. Why did that make me nervous?

The halls began to look vaguely familiar—or did they? Then we entered that unsettling wing, that open space with nothing but Gate 72 and 73.

And 74.

Cea strode across the hall towards Gate 74. She held up her hand—then stopped. She looked back at me.

"Go ahead."

I nervously obeyed. Cea waited. Did the system pause on purpose? Then it flashed green.

Cea shoved me in and whisked me down the hall.

"Most of these doors are locked, but one day they'll hook to a maze of new halls. Only one door works right now. A."

"It's not marked," I said as she stopped in front of a gate. I glanced back up the hall and counted the doors—6th down.

"Not from this side."

She opened the door. I already knew that it wouldn't work for me—I tried all the doors the first time I came down Wing 74.

That did not explain why Gate 74 opened for me in the first place.

I subconsciously expected the depths of Wing 74 to be something fantastical. It ought to be—I had every right to expect something extraordinary.

But somehow I wasn't surprised to find that the hall on the other side of the door was… normal.

It looked like the rest of the base.

I glanced at the door as it closed behind us. It was indeed marked *A*.

I didn't get a tour. Cea shoved me into the first door on the right. It was a meeting room, an unfinished one. The walls and ceiling were sealed in and half of a bench was bolted to the back wall. The keypad was dark; Cea dragged the door almost shut with her hands.

"Wait here." And she was off running again.

I stumbled over to the bench and sat down, gripping it with my fingers. The only light came in a sharp shaft through the crack in the door. I scooted down the bench until I was completely in darkness. For some reason, I didn't want to sit in the only shade of light.

Cea soon returned with a second set of footsteps. Her voice was sharp. "You have twenty minutes—use it wisely. I have to get her back and edit the security tapes before Nic returns."

She shoved the door open and manually flicked on the light.

And there he stood.

Dark fluffy hair, absorbent eyes, flat face that only loosely concealed a smile. Unbuttoned lab coat, brown pants, clomping shoes with a scuff on the toe. Not a piece of him was missing.

I knew instantly that I was looking at Ephesus. I never doubted that.

But I utterly doubted that he was real.

Cea threw a quick glance at us and was gone, leaving the door cracked only a millimeter.

"Use it wisely," she said again. Her footsteps retreated.

I stared at him. His eyes were large, but his face was calm—as though his eyes were just widened to take me in faster. He didn't seem that surprised to see me here.

He couldn't be real.

"Philli," he said, "Philadelphia."

A perfect recording.

I stood up. "Why."

"Why what?"

"Why all this trouble… for a hologram?"

"A hologram?"

I stepped towards him. "A hologram. A recording. Robot?" I tipped my head back and looked into his face. "You're not real."

His eyes blurred, though his face did not move. He extended his hand. "Try it."

I remembered touching his hologram in the security tape—and having my fist go right through. This version looked thicker.

I gazed at his hand. Slowly, I brought mine down.

Our palms contacted.

I drew my hand back and did it again. He caught and pinched my hand this time.

I looked into his eyes again. "You're dead," I whispered, but my tiny voice testified to the truth.

"I'm alive."

"You're alive," I repeated. One gasping breath, one shake—one moment of elated terror. Then I screamed.

"Ephesus!"

"Philli!" His voice was a teary wail, and it was the most beautiful sound in the world.

He hugged me. He swept me up in his arms and held me, kissed me, sat down in the middle of the floor and cradled me, muttering in my ear.

He wasn't dead.

That one fact ignited a hundred questions, some I had already been asking myself. But the one answer was worth them all.

Ephesus was alive.

Like Cea said, some questions could wait.

22

But Ephesus didn't make me wait long.

"It's okay..." he sat me down on the floor across from him, "if you ask questions now."

"What... what can you tell me?" I started.

"What did Cea tell you?"

"Nothing. She just asked... if she told me something about my brother... could I save the questions for later? One step at a time. She made me promise..."

"What?"

"...never to tell anyone..."

"Never. No one."

"...except Daddy..."

He leaned forward, dark eyes brewing. "Tell him everything."

"...and only in our private quarters."

"Never breathe a word of it in the halls—anywhere. The tapes. They hear everything."

"And... never come back here again." I blinked. "I see what she meant now. About it being hard."

He gripped my shoulders. "No—never! Not without her. She's the only one that can make sure it's safe. Not even for me, Phil, never come close. Never tread near Wing 74. Pretend like it doesn't exist. If anyone mentions it, act like you know nothing."

He shook me. "I'll be here. Don't worry about me. I'm safe."

"Are you?" I gazed into his eyes.

He returned the challenge. "I am—honestly. All this time I've never been hurt and never lacked anything. Nic... he's not that bad, most days. Really, Philli, I'm safe. I'm comfortable and I'm thinking of you. Now I can pray... and know you're praying for me, too."

"Have you been...?"

"Every day. Or almost."

"Did you know I was here?"

"Yes." He looked away. "When you wandered into Wing 74 yesterday... I saw the security tape. You were... so close. So... far."

I touched his knee. "You're locked in here, aren't you?"

His head bobbed in a barely perceptible nod.

"Why?"

"Mainly, so no one knows I'm here."

"So everyone believes you're dead?"

"Exactly."

"The transfer...?"

"Staged. No one was on it."

"The other passengers?"

"All down here, plus a few others."

"Doing...?"

"Working. For Nic."

"The pet project."

"That's what Cea calls it."

"It must be a secret."

"The defining factor."

"Illegal?"

"Effectively. The United didn't like it, told him to stop. That's why he had to move it underground... and 'kill' scientists to stock the lab." He sighed.

"What is it?" I dared to ask.

"I... don't want to give you the details."

I searched his face. "Don't want to?"

"I don't want to even think the details, let alone scar you with them."

"What?" I repeated, a little taken aback by his harsh tone.

"I don't want to try and explain it right now." He turned away.

I thought of a gentle conversation changer. "I don't understand most of the lab gibberish anyway."

He smiled, that surge of warmth I had missed for so many years. His voice softened. "I love you, Philadelphia."

I hugged him again. "I love you, too."

Footsteps approached down the hall. Ephesus held me at arm's length and spoke quickly.

"Tell Dad everything—everything! Make sure he knows. Make sure he knows! I'm alive—I'm okay. And I love him. Tell him I love him!"

I nodded. Cea grunted, and the door grated open. We stood up; Ephesus kissed my forehead. I squeezed him around the waist.

"I'm sorry, but we've got to clear. Ephesus, get back to work. Remember— speak of this to no one. Make no notes anywhere, not even on your personal computer. There must be no record of this event anywhere on the base. I've got the security tapes."

Ephesus nodded and breezed out of the room. He paused in the hall and glanced back.

"Cea… thank you."

She looked at him, then glanced down. "You're welcome." She grabbed my hand. "Phil, quickly."

I threw one glance back as she hauled me through Gate A.

Ephesus caught it—and smiled.

I smiled back.

*

I didn't speak until we had fled into the 60s, which seemed far enough away to me.

"Thank… you…" I gasped, for she insisted on running.

"No more!" was her harsh reply.

I silenced until we reached Wing 45. Then I ventured an indirect question.

"When will my father return?"

I wondered if she caught the implications. "He and Nic should be getting back in about an—"

"We docked half an hour ago."

I yelled. However, I had every right, as I suddenly ran into him.

Dr. Nic watched me tumble to the floor. "That is the second time you've run into me today, Philadelphia."

"I'm sorry, sir. I… don't watch where I'm going." I hoped I looked startled—not frightened.

He did frighten me. More every time I saw him. More every time I learned something new about him.

Cea tried not to pant. "Sorry, Nic, I started it."

He looked at her. "And since when does my controlled sister run anywhere?"

She crossed her arms. "We were having fun."

"Doing what? I thought I told you no more snooping." The latter sentence was directed at me with a scowl.

Cea came to my defense. "We weren't snooping. It's exploring."

I cringed at how juvenile that sounded. Cea, to her credit, continued seamlessly. "She's with me. And I know where to go."

I knew that actually meant *"I know where not to go."*

He looked down at me.

What do you want me to say? "'Exploring' is what she calls it. I have no idea where we are."

He was not amused. "Wing 45. Four gates straight that way is the main hall. Your quarters are on the other side."

I took that as a hint.

I stood up. "Thank you, Cea. I'm going to find my father."

She nodded and forced a smile. I copied, hoping it was natural. "I'll see you after dinner," she said.

I wondered if that was a promise. I waved and ran off.

Dr. Nic spoke before I was out of earshot.

"Do you want them to stay together?"

"Yeah?"

"Then act accordingly."

He stomped off. Cea stayed. She looked up and saw me, hesitating there. At first her gaze was white, wide—then it narrowed into a bitter glare.

I fled.

✱

Needless to say, I shocked my father on a number of levels with my report after dinner. It was a wonder he could understand it at all—I kept mixing up the events, and my voice wobbled between a tearful sob and an excited shriek.

I finally reached the end and drew a long breath. "And he wanted me to tell you that he loves you. Both of us."

My father echoed the sigh. His shoulders quivered. For a second, he turned away from me and didn't say anything. I hugged him.

"God… brought him back. All that time… God was saving him." I heard the tears in his voice.

I sat back and found his hand. "Cea said she'll take you to visit him as soon as she can."

Daddy pushed crumpled hair off his forehead with his other hand. "I think Dr. Nic will be arranging a meeting soon enough."

"Dr. Nic? But he doesn't want…"

Daddy looked into my face and declared bluntly, "He wants me to join the project."

I realized I wasn't breathing and took a quick gasp. "The pet project?"

My father nodded. "It's the sole reason he called me up here. He thinks my lab expertise is the missing piece to completing a certain phase. Something about Red Rain."

"He... already told you about it? But it's a secret. No one's supposed to know."

"No one's supposed to *tell*."

"But if he doesn't have you locked up, couldn't you tell?"

"I guess he figures I won't. Not when he could send my daughter back to Earth on the next flight."

I waited, eyes wide.

"I, unlike the average Unionist, have nothing to gain from alerting the authorities. If I ruin Nic's project, I go back to Earth to be persecuted. If I stay, I live in tolerance. All my family is up here."

"Which was not the case with Ephesus a few years ago." I connected the dots.

My father squeezed my hand. I rested my head against his shoulder for a moment before looking back into his face.

"Do you want to join?"

"I want to stay," he said emphatically. "I don't know if I want to join. I need to hear more about the project. I'm not sure what I'm dealing with."

"Ephesus doesn't like it," I offered, remembering my brother's cryptic harshness.

"Would you be pleasantly disposed to a project if you'd been kidnapped and forced to work on it?"

"Um... no."

"Nic hasn't given me many details yet. I know it's chemical-related, but what the chemicals are for I haven't figured out. We'll have to talk more. I have a few days, at least."

He tipped my chin up. "This information is confidential. Some of the other scientists don't know about the project, I gather. Tell no one."

"Except Ephesus."

I watched the tears pool in the corners of his eyes. "Tell him everything," he whispered.

I hugged him and allowed myself to release the tears I'd been bottling all afternoon.

23

After the adventure of my first two days at the base, I was amazed that the next two days were completely uneventful. I actually succeeded in "keeping my head down." No one gave me suspicious glances—not even Nic—and I didn't stumble through any more locked doors.

I didn't receive any new information, either. Daddy didn't speak any more of his work, and Cea didn't mention Ephesus or Wing 74 at all. Even though I thought of my brother constantly, I managed not to ask—and I found that he was right. It was comforting to remember that he was only a few halls away.

I filled my days by catching up on my Bible study and writing a long email to Cami—Cea promised to help me get it through the commander. Even though I had to resist the urge to tell her about Ephesus, I found letter-writing to be very distracting. I was caught completely off-guard when Cea came in and announced I could spend a half-hour with Ephesus.

I didn't object.

"I'm sorry I can't get your dad down here. It's a lot harder, because after-hours is usually when Nic is in Wing 74. But that might soon be a non-issue." Her voice perked up, causing me to look at her. She was smiling happily.

Suspicion prevented me from smiling. She must have taken that as a prompt to explain. "I hear—don't quote me on this—that Nic wants your dad to work with Ephesus. That means you'll all get to live here, and we won't have to hide anymore. You can stay."

I didn't think I should tell her what my dad and I had discussed. "We want to," I whispered.

She paused to let me open Gate 74 again. It still worked.

"Who has access to this door?" I asked as we went through.

Cea wrinkled her brow. "Nic, Carnegie, myself... I think all the scientists that are down here have access too, because they helped build it before it was locked off."

She opened Gate A. "Only Nic, Carnegie, and I have access to this one, though. A couple of other scientists know, but they don't have access. Nic has to take them down."

Cea led me to the left this time, to a door across the hall labeled LAB 1. She waved her hand over the sensor, and it refused her. She pressed the call button. "Ephesus, it's me."

"Sorry," came the response, and the door opened. My brother stood there, balancing three test tubes in his hands. He spotted me and beamed. "Philli!" Then he frowned and glanced at Cea. "Cea, she can't be in a lab. Nic reviews all the records—"

"It's fine," Cea assured him, shoving me in. "Nic took the camera for this lab down for repairs this morning. You're clear. But you only have about 30 minutes."

She turned to go, then glanced back and smiled. "Have fun. Don't blow anything up."

I stared after her until she disappeared down a hall, wondering if I should let that admonition concern me.

"Close the door and hit lock, just in case. If someone stumbles by... at least that buys us a minute." My brother staggered over to a table and deposited his tubes.

"Who will be able to get in when it's locked?"

"Just me and Dr. Nic. Who, I suppose, is the person we are most worried about... Lock it anyway."

I did as I was told. I turned around and watched my brother carefully arrange his tubes in a holder. The table was cluttered nearly to the overflowing with a multicolored chaos of glass and chemicals.

He wiped his hands on his coat and came to hug me. "It's good to see you again, and so soon. Cea's in a good mood today."

"What did she mean about 'not blowing anything up'?"

Ephesus turned and gestured at the table. "Because in this room we have the components for a bomb."

There was something about that information that irked me to the core.

"Bomb?" I finally squeaked.

Ephesus sighed and ran a hand through his hair. "Yeah. Big ones. Not all of the pieces are here, but you could create a... disturbance, which we don't need."

I decided to stay a safe distance away from the table. I followed him carefully and watched from a few feet away as he went back to work.

"Does Dr. Nic's plan include bombs?"

Ephesus nodded. "Several. And that's only part of it. Nic wants to have multiple options available."

"Options?"

"So if bombing Earth full of holes doesn't work, he can try something else to get them to back off."

"Them?"

"The United." He paused and glanced back at me. "Has Cea told you anything?"

"Only that Nic wants to break from…" I halted. Everything snapped together. Painfully. *One day he's going to cut us off from the United… By becoming more powerful than they are. That's the only way to cut yourself off from a monster and keep them from assimilating you back in.*

Ephesus looked into my eyes and nodded to confirm my fears.

I swallowed. "And then what?"

"Utopia. In theory. He wants political freedom, which includes religious freedom. Or so he claims." He turned back to the table. "I'll believe it when I see it. And I hope I don't have to see it."

"Why?" For some reason, I felt bad that the first thought that ran through my head was: *Don't we want to break from the United? Don't we want religious freedom?*

"Because I don't want to see what happens when Nic uses this stuff." Ephesus poured two tubes together and watched the liquid change color. "The bombs are a rather small and inconsequential part of his plan, in the grand scheme of things."

He looked up at the ceiling. "That's why I'm working on bombs and not something… worse."

I decided now was a good time to update him on the developments. "Nic wants Dad to join the project."

Ephesus nearly dropped the glass bottle he was holding. "What?" He whipped around.

"He told Daddy about it. Not all of the details, but a lot of the technical stuff."

"Why?" Ephesus looked as confused as I had felt when Daddy told me.

"Things are different with Daddy. He doesn't have anything to gain by alerting the United. All his family is up here."

Ephesus took a step back and braced himself against the edge of the table. He cradled his forehead with his other hand.

"If he says no, he gets sent back to Earth," I offered. "Or… I get sent back to Earth."

"I know." Ephesus looked up again. "Why does he want Dad?"

"He thinks Daddy has the last piece to the project. Something about Red Rain?"

"No," Ephesus breathed, so quietly I wasn't sure if I heard him right.

"No what?"

"No!" He lunged, making the table rock. He grabbed my shoulders. I nearly fell over with the force, but he didn't seem to notice.

"No! No! Tell him *no!*"

"Him who?" I tried to keep calm.

"Dad! Tell him no! Tell him not to accept. He can't accept."

"But, Ephesus, why—"

"Philli," his voice cut in and forced me to focus on him. "Do you know what acid rain is?"

"Well, yes, but—"

"Can you imagine that... with an intensity that can melt metal?"

"What?"

Ephesus let go of me. He turned around to gaze at the table of chemicals. "Red Rain. It's the last phase of Nic's project. It's a concentration of chemicals that can turn normal precipitation—even, in some places, just high humidity—into an acid strong enough to melt metal, let alone scald and kill living beings. It's those chemicals... and the methods to distribute them as gases. To *subtly* distribute them."

I didn't say anything. I didn't know what to say.

Ephesus's voice hardened. "Tell Dad he doesn't want to join the project. Tell Dad he doesn't want to join the project, unless he wants to be responsible for raining fire and brimstone on half of Earth. Tell him he doesn't want to join unless he wants my *guilt*."

He choked off and covered his face with his hands.

I stepped closer to him. "Did you... work on..."

"Yes. When I first came here, I did a bit of work, not knowing what it was. When I learned more, I tried to stop it. I was the one that got the United curious. I was the one that made Nic take it underground."

I felt a strange sense of warmth at that statement. "I'm proud of you," I said honestly.

He gave a sort of chuckled snort. "Yeah. Nic said he'd send me back to Earth—I told him I wanted to go. I had family down there. So he sent me. Only... my transit 'exploded.'"

"He wouldn't let you go. Did you know too much?"

"Yes, but I still haven't decided whether it's because I knew too much about the project or because he needed my brains, as arrogant as that sounds. Thankfully, I didn't have the knowledge necessary to advance Red Rain, so I got moved to another phase. I agreed to work on another phase, as long as it wasn't Red Rain." He let out his breath. "I wish I hadn't agreed."

"What would he have done?"

Ephesus shrugged. "I don't know. Killing me—for real—wouldn't have gained him anything. But what else was I supposed to do? There's no point in turning back now. This phase is almost done."

"Have you been working on this for two years?" I gazed at the table.

"No. I did some bombs, some guns…" He gestured casually. "My first project was a virus."

"What?" The word came out in a strangled gasp.

"Computer virus," he replied. "Nic wanted something that could wipe out Earth's data, to cripple them digitally if we had to. Another scientist and I did it."

I looked for something—anything—to grip. My hand found the pouch around my waist. I felt both readers thump against me.

"We switched it up, though. We set it so that the virus would only delete data that contained the letters 'Nic,' with a capital."

Ephesus actually grinned. "Nic's not good at coding, so he can't tell. We figured we'd delete a few books and web pages about Nicolas's, but at least Earth wouldn't lose enough data to send them back to the Dark Age."

He looked back at me. "I wouldn't do that to Earth. I wouldn't do that to you."

I was surprised to find that my breath was still coming in regular gasps. I touched my forehead, trying to process.

Ephesus squinted at me. "What's wrong, Phil? Are you all right?"

"You… wrote the virus," was the only thing I could think of to say. Perhaps it was the only thing that needed to be said.

He shrugged.

"Why?" I looked into his eyes, searching for logic, an explanation—an apology.

I didn't find any. "Nic won't have to use it," Ephesus said. "Once Earth hears of Red Rain, they'll cower in terror. Nic might have to demonstrate a little, but… He wouldn't bomb the unassimilated camps. Not intentionally, because of Cea. The virus won't be necessary. None of this will be necessary if he doesn't complete Red Rain. He won't try anything early."

I felt hot and flushed. I rubbed my cheeks. "Yes, he will."

He shook his head. "Don't worry, he won't. Trust me. I know Nic."

"He already did." I took a step back.

His face softened. "What's wrong, Phil?" He stepped towards me, but I kept the distance between us. I almost sighed aloud when Cea's voice echoed through the speaker.

"I'm sorry, Phil, but we've got to go. Nic changed his schedule."

I ran for the door and waved my hand over the sensor. I knew it would open.

As the doors parted, I stole a glance back at Ephesus. He stared, dumbfounded.

I didn't wait for Cea to say anything and raced across the hall to Gate A. If she noticed my impatience, she didn't question it. She walked up beside me and opened the gate.

"Phil, wait!" Ephesus darted to the doorway of Lab 1.

I stopped but didn't turn around.

He drew in a breath—then let it out. He finally spoke, a little quietly. "Tell Dad. Tell him not… to."

"He won't," I said confidently. Then I strode through the doors and left him behind.

It wasn't until we were a few wings away that I realized I might have forfeited my last chance to say goodbye.

I managed to hold it back until we reached Wing 1. Cea asked questions, but I didn't answer. She finally left me alone in the dorms.

And then I cried.

24

I was eating lunch with Cea when he came for me. He sent Carnegie.

"The doctor will see you."

I stood up, even though I didn't want to. He glared down at me, eyes glinting like polished steel.

Cea burst into tears.

Carnegie grabbed my arm and dragged me out of the room. "I'm sorry! I'm sorry!" Cea wailed at no one in particular.

"Assimilated or removed!" Carnegie shot back.

He hauled me across the base. I expected him to take me to Dr. Nic's office, but he didn't. He wound down to the very tip of the base, to the docking bay.

A little treaded car was parked in the wing. The doors were open.

Dr. Nic stood in the middle of the room, arms crossed. A suitcase—mine— sat at his feet.

"No," I said.

"Yes," was his reply. "Get in."

I wasn't sure if I walked, or if Carnegie shoved me. I neared the open doors and suddenly stopped, bracing my hands against the side of the car.

The inside of the vehicle was empty.

"Daddy," I breathed.

I heard groaning. I glanced over my shoulder. Gate 74 stood there, open.

Daddy lay inside, crumpled against one of those unmarked doors. He held his head and mumbled.

Ephesus stood over him, gripping his shoulders.

"No, Daddy!" I ran for him.

Gate 74 began to shut.

I heard a familiar voice—not Dr. Nic's, or Carnegie's—behind my head. "It's his assignment, not yours! Regulations!"

Ephesus saw me. "Philli!" he screamed.

Daddy had no voice. He looked up—our eyes met through the shrinking crack between the doors.

I screamed.

I slammed into the door just as it sealed shut. I quickly turned and flapped my hand over the sensor.

Access denied.

I whipped around. "No, please!"

Dr. Nic wasn't there anymore. Carnegie was walking away, cackling, "System fixed!"

Someone else stood next to my suitcase.

Commander Ambrose.

"Regulations!" he snarled. "Regulations!" He waved his pistol at me.

Assimilated or removed. Assimilated or removed.

"Come on, honey, we missed you."

I pinched my eyes shut. "No, you didn't!"

But it wasn't the commander speaking. It was a buttery voice, a happy voice. A compromising voice.

Mrs. Nolan emerged from the car.

"Come on, darling, we've been waiting for you." She beckoned to me. "We still want you. Join our family. Join our family."

"I don't want to!" I clenched my fists and backed away. I ran into someone else—a large someone.

He scooped me up in his arms.

"No!" I shrieked. I fought—but could only hit air.

"Shh," Mrs. Nolan stroked my hair, "it's just my husband."

I looked into his face. He gazed back. Soft blondish hair, eyes so calm, so relaxed, so... relaxed...

"You've made the right choice, daughter."

"You're not my dad," I hissed. I wanted to yell—but my voice came out in a whisper. I could hardly hear it. Could anyone else hear it?

Commander Ambrose answered me. "He is now. Take it or leave it."

Take it while you still can! Take their offer and run!

I couldn't resist. I felt as if I were floating.

He set me down in a seat inside the car. He moved where I couldn't see him. I felt alone. No, there was someone next to me.

Cea.

She sat, twisting white hands. Tear streaks ran down her cheeks. A duffel lay between her feet.

"Cea!" I cried.

She noticed me. Her eyes widened. "Phil! Philadelphia!"

She stood up. I reached for her—she was right there, but our hands didn't touch. Her voice rose in panic.

"Phil! Philadelphia! Phil! *Philli!*"

Suddenly, I hit the floor.

Everything was dark—and so hot! I groped—and felt a rug beneath my fingers.

I froze, forcing my gasping breaths to steady. Cea was still calling my name, but more calmly. Her voice warbled over a speaker.

The speaker at the door of our apartment.

I scrambled up—and tripped. A blanket tangled my feet—the throw blanket from the couch. I struggled away and stood, panting, in the middle of the room. Sweat ran down my neck.

"Phil? Philadelphia? Are you in there? Phil!"

I stumbled over to the door. I flicked on the lights and jammed the thermostat as cold as it would go.

I blindly waved my hand to open the door and sank to my knees.

Cea came in, took one look, and quickly shut the door behind her. "Phil!" She knelt beside me.

I quivered on the floor, listening to the fans churn wildly, letting the cold air swoop down my arms. It felt chilled, frozen—and I relished it.

Cea waited a moment. "What's wrong?"

"Why are you here?"

"I wondered why you weren't at breakfast." She paused. "It's after 10."

I moaned.

"Phil, what's wrong?"

"Nothing, everything… yes… no. Part of it. You're not on a transfer to go back to Earth."

"Me? Why would I…"

"I don't know. That part didn't make sense. Most of the rest did. Too much sense. Too… plausible." I shivered.

"Why were you sleeping on the couch?"

That was an excellent question. I concentrated, and the memories returned. "I was up with Dad before he went to work. I guess I dozed off."

Cea pinched a damp tangle of my hair between her fingers. "Are you sure you're not ill?"

"Reasonably."

She let go of my hair. Slowly, she stood up.

"Wash up and come down to get something to eat."

✳

For once, the cafeteria was actually deserted. Not a single soul was there. The buffet had already been taken down, but Cea ordered a little something for me.

Despite myself, I figured I had ignored enough of my meals lately in favor of emotional trauma. It wasn't healthy. I ate everything Cea gave me even though I didn't have any pleasure in it.

Cea waited until I was nearly done before speaking. "I'm sorry. These past few days…" She sighed. "It's mostly my fault."

"No," I said emphatically. "I'm glad you were honest with me. You're the only one outside my family who has been in a very long time."

I took a sip of water before continuing. "Thank you. Without you, I would have never seen Ephesus again."

She stared at me. "You're… welcome," she said finally.

Abruptly, her eyes lit up. "But I have good news." She glanced around and lowered her voice. "Nic is settling the job details with your father today. If all goes well, your father will be able to see your brother, and then you can visit whenever you want. There won't be any more secrets. You'll just have to act surprised when Nic takes you to see Ephesus for the first time." She winked.

I swallowed, then finished my piece of toast before replying. I needed the time to formulate my thoughts.

Cea frowned at my silence. I wiped my lips and looked up at her. "My father isn't taking the job."

"What?" she said, more of a gasp than a word.

"My father will not accept the position. He will not work on 'Red Rain.' It goes against his ethics—our ethics."

"But…" Her face crashed. She closed her eyes, drew a breath, and looked at me again. She spoke quickly but calmly.

"I know. I know how it looks. I hate it, it's the worst part of Nic's operation. That's why I'm not down there, helping."

Apparently Nic wouldn't force his own sister to work, but he'd kidnap a dozen scientists and forge their deaths.

"But I promise you—he won't have to use it. He just has to prove to the United that he could beat them in a war, so they'll stay away. Then he can expand the base, open the doors to colonists, and establish a new world—on Mars!—with religious freedom. It will be like America in the old millennium. It will be perfect."

"Perfect?" I ate my last forkful of eggs.

"I won't have to worry anymore—you won't have to worry anymore. We won't have to play 'perfect obedient Unionists.'"

"I never have been a very model Unionist," I mused, more to myself than to her.

"Philli…" She reached out to me. "Please. Just give him a chance. It's the only way we'll break from the United and find freedom. If we don't do something, it will just get worse."

Evildoers and impostors will go from bad to worse, deceiving and being deceived... "Dr. Nic's already made it worse."

"What? How?" She frowned.

"The virus. He made that. My brother made that."

"Oh." She paused, and I thought I'd made my point. Then she stiffened and rattled off again. "That was an accident. He was testing it on a private cloud, and something went wrong. It didn't do what it was supposed to, and it got onto a wifi-connected device. He has to fix it."

Fix it? So he can release it again and do worse damage?

"But he said he'll repair the damage. He's got back-ups of a lot of the lost lost data on Wing 74's cloud."

"When?"

"After his plan is done. After everyone knows about Red Rain and he doesn't have to explain why he's got a system totally disconnected from the United's surveillance."

I arranged my trash on my empty plate in a weird pattern. "After he's desecrated half of Earth with chemical warfare."

"He won't have to use Red Rain."

"He didn't have to use the virus." I stood up.

She didn't follow at first. "It's the only way. The United is too big for any other method to work. Can you think of another way?"

I pondered that as I stacked my empty dishes. "No."

Cea's shoulders relaxed slightly.

"But that doesn't mean I'm going to choose the wrong way."

She didn't say anything. She didn't move at all, not even blink.

I looked her in the eyes again. "Daddy and I prayed about it. He's going to refuse the commission. He will not work on Red Rain."

"That's the only reason Nic called him up here," Cea declared.

"I know."

Her voice grew bitter. "He will probably send you back to Earth."

"I know."

"You'll never see Ephesus again."

I turned away. *Not if I can pull this off.*

She must have thought my lack of response was consent. "Nic won't let him go. He's still dead."

He knows too much. So do I.

She pushed harder. "If you try something, he might kill Ephesus for real."

Not if we're careful. Not if God helps us. God, please! I closed my eyes and rehearsed my daddy's warning. *"Yes, you may, but don't try it until I know how Dr. Nic will react. He does have weapons."*

Cea stood up and walked towards me. "Please give Nic a chance. Please reconsider."

"We won't." I turned around to face Cea again. "Please, let me see Ephesus. Now. As soon as possible."

She stared. I couldn't read her expression. "One last time," I pleaded.

She squinted. I wondered if she could tell that *I* was now the one keeping secrets.

Whether she knew or not, she relented. "Okay. I'll make it happen. Wait in your dorms until it's safe."

She started walking away.

"Cea," I called after her. She paused. "Thank you."

She glanced over her shoulder, gaze soft. "You're welcome." Then she left.

I pinched my eyes shut and prayed. *Please, God... we have one chance.* One chance.

I reached into my pouch. Both readers were there, ready.

25

Ephesus was working in Lab 1 again. I didn't wait for him to set down what he was holding before I hugged him from behind.

"Philli!" He stumbled forward and dropped something on the floor.

"I don't know how long you have," Cea said from the doorway. "Nic will be busy as long as he's talking with your father. But if your father refuses the job… the meeting could be short."

I lifted my head and looked at her. "Thank you again."

She didn't say anything. She just nodded and fled.

I ran over to the door and locked it behind her. I turned around to find Ephesus squinting at me.

"The door. Yesterday. You didn't have access," he declared bluntly.

I beamed. "No, but you do. And I'm your sister. By blood." I held up my palm.

He stepped forward and pressed his larger fingers against mine. Slowly, he smiled.

I walked over to the table and pulled the two readers out of my pocket.

Ephesus sighed. "Phil…" he said, voice heavy. "I'm sorry. I… asked Nic about the virus."

I set my personal reader on the table and turned the one from Mr. Sardis on.

"He wants me to fix it. I won't do it, this time."

"You won't have to. Not if you give me evidence." I thrust the device at him.

He skeptically took it. "What?"

"Give me some files. Something techy and revealing. If Dr. Nic sends us back to Earth, I'll have evidence to show the United and prove there's something up here they should investigate." I looked into his face.

He stared, then beamed. He looked down at the device and started toggling menus. "Is he saying no?"

"He's saying no. If Dad doesn't get to see you…"

"You can tell him that I love him," he smiled and typed on the reader's pad, "and I'll be here when the United calls."

The device beeped. He looked down at it and frowned. "Where did you get this?"

"Mr. Sardis gave it to me. Because... I didn't have a Bible." I clasped my hands behind my back.

"It's connected to Wing 74's private wifi. It can access all of the base-level data."

I wasn't sure if I should feel stupid for not realizing that earlier, or perturbed that I had been carrying the secrets for chemical warfare around in my pocket. "Well... that's terrifying."

"I'm not surprised you didn't notice. I doubt the range on the wifi is very far."

I thought for a moment. "What if we just connected it to the public wifi and copied over some files?"

Ephesus shook his head. "All of Wing 74's devices are specially coded to make connecting to a new network very difficult. The access codes are Nic's heavily-guarded secret, for obvious reasons."

My spirits fell again, only to surge back up with a rush of adrenaline. The cycle was getting vicious. "We can use this." I snatched my personal reader off the table. "This is just a regular device. Can we download something I can copy over?"

Ephesus didn't respond. He was frowning.

"Ephesus?"

He shushed me harshly. Cautiously, he set the reader on the table and eased over to the door. He listened for a second, then reached up and hit the call button.

Dr. Nic's voice blared over the speaker, muddled with Carnegie's.

And then I heard Dad.

I choked. Ephesus stuck his arm out, and I instinctively stopped breathing. I forced myself to hold still, panicked prayers spiraling through my head.

"I question the wisdom of kidnapping," my father grunted. I relished how calm his voice was, even though I could sense the tension.

"It worked the first time, didn't it?" Dr. Nic returned.

Daddy didn't respond.

"You're welcome to admit it any time you like. You know. And I know who told you." Dr. Nic cursed. A few other voices I didn't recognize muttered along with him.

My father drew in a long breath and lowered his voice. "Just because it worked once doesn't mean it will work again. I don't think the United will buy another transit explosion."

He snarled in pain. Ephesus clenched his fists. I shut my eyes—and reached down to slide my reader back in my pouch.

"I'm creative. As soon as I find your brat of a daughter..."

I opened my eyes.

"I won't work on the project," Daddy interrupted. "Dead or alive."

Ephesus mouthed a prayer.

"I gathered that," Dr. Nic said coolly. "But you know too much."

There was scuffling. Daddy grunted. "Put him where Ephesus won't find him. Then search the base. I need to know where that rebel is before she realizes her father isn't coming back from his meeting. Be... discreet."

He embellished with a few swear words, but I didn't hear the rest. Ephesus punched the call button and whipped around, talking in hushed tones.

"We have one shot. We have to get you where Nic won't find you—if we can give him a chase, it'll buy us some time. Then—"

"Can we download some files to my reader? If we can get something up online, somewhere, it will alert the United."

He pondered that for a second, a split second too long. Before he could respond, the door whooshed open. Dr. Nic strode in, talking.

"Ephesus! I need—"

He glanced up and halted, for a brief second looking as shocked as we were. I stared back like a deer caught in headlights. Ephesus put a hand to his forehead as if to stabilize.

The tension shattered. Dr. Nic jerked upright and demanded, "How did you get in here?" He sounded a mix of enraged and curious.

I opened my mouth, then changed my mind. I stiffened and said with as much sass as I could muster, "I defy security."

He growled and looked on the verge of hitting me—or whatever was within reach. He drew his arm back.

Ephesus seemed to snap back to reality. "Don't touch her!" He lunged forward.

Dr. Nic turned and caught him in the shoulders. Ephesus crashed backwards, ramming his head on the table.

"You're in luck." Dr. Nic grabbed my arm and hauled me out of the room. "If the two of you behave, I'll pretend to kill you," he pinched my arm, "and your father, and you can stay here. If you pull stunts, legally dead won't be enough."

Ephesus staggered back to his feet. "Philli..."

Dr. Nic ignored him. He dragged me across the hall and shoved me into the half-finished meeting room.

I landed in a heap on the floor in the darkness. Dr. Nic toggled a few switches, and the lights flickered on. The panel glowed to life.

I sat up and stared at him. He crossed his arms calmly. "You have two choices. You can wait here for a few hours and live in peace with your father and brother for the rest of your life. Or you can make a ruckus and force me to decide how many of you I need to kill."

He took a step backwards, out of the room. He reached into the pocket of his lab coat and removed the reprogramming disc.

He set it on the panel and hit one button. The doors slid shut as he fiddled with a few other buttons.

The thought came to me so fast I barely had time to react. I jumped up and ran to the door just as it shut. Dr. Nic didn't notice. I stuck my hand over the inside panel and held it there.

The system chirped. A green circle glowed beneath my hand, as if winking conspiratorially. *The system can be set from either side of the door...*

I closed my eyes and praised God.

Shouts erupted in the hall. I hit the call button out of curiosity—it worked.

"Let her go!" Ephesus yelled.

"If you want me to kill her, I'd be happy to oblige."

There was silence. Dr. Nic continued. "I let you work on another phase; I can do the same with your father."

My whirlwind of thoughts crashed to a stop.

"No one has to die. You can stay and not have to work on Red Rain. All you have to do is be quiet for a few hours while I clean up your mess, and then it will be done."

I waited for Ephesus's response. He didn't give any. Dr. Nic grunted, "Smart choice. Carnegie!" Their footsteps retreated down the hall.

The speaker was silent for a minute. Two. Three. Now was my chance—my only chance.

I gazed at the panel. *You can wait here for a few hours and live in peace with your father and brother for the rest of your life.*

You can stay and not have to work on Red Rain.

All you have to do is be quiet...

I prayed—then waved my hand over the sensor.

26

The door opened willingly. I glanced in both directions and then stepped out into the halls, praising God.

I was out!

I locked the door behind me for good measure. I took two steps down the hall and spotted Gate A to my left. I stopped, stared at the letter, and moaned.

Well, I was halfway out. I was out of the room, but I wasn't out of Wing 74. And I wasn't going to be able to jump the system on that door.

I pinched my temples until I could feel the blood pounding beneath my fingers. This wasn't going to get me anywhere! I was just making things worse!

My nerves calmed in answer to prayer. No, it wasn't pointless. I still had my reader.

I needed to find a computer. One simple enough I could operate.

Like another reader.

I turned and ran for Lab 1. The door was open but the lights were off. My boot squeaked on the floor—and another footstep promptly answered it. Two voices approached down the hall—Dr. Nic and Carnegie.

I slapped my hand over my mouth to stifle a squeak. I skipped across the hall, hoping my footsteps were too faint to hear, and ducked around the door into the lab.

I knelt in the shadows under a table and pressed myself against the wall. I prayed they were just passing by. I closed my eyes so I could hear their voices better.

They were talking about me.

They weren't just passing by.

"I'm impressed with her boldness, actually," Carnegie said.

Dr. Nic sounded anything but impressed. "You'd think unassimilated would be more discreet and compliant." The footsteps stopped.

A pause. I cringed, waiting for the whoosh of the door and Dr. Nic's curses of anger.

I heard neither. Instead I heard a hideous, horrendous beep I knew all too well.

Access denied.

Something surged up my throat until it hurt. I opened my eyes.

Dr. Nic did swear. "What's wrong with this thing?"

Another beep. Another muttered breath. I eased towards the door.

"Didn't you set it?" Carnegie asked.

No... I did.

"Just now, when I locked her in." A third beep.

Hold your hands over the panel. One at a time, or it might mess the system up...

"I think that girl curses security systems wherever she goes." Carnegie sounded mildly amused.

Dr. Nic was far from it. For the third time, the only word to leave his mouth was foul. "I'll have to reset it." Footsteps retreated.

The disc. I stuck my head around the door in time to see Dr. Nic storm down the hallway.

Carnegie followed him at a more relaxed pace. "Didn't you just have it?"

"I left it on the desk!" They disappeared around the corner.

I jumped with excitement—literally. My foot smacked an empty glass bottle, sending it spiraling. I grabbed it just before it fell.

I shuddered. That would have been bad. Dr. Nic would have come running.

It hit me, like two magnets snapping together. With a million thoughts running through my head, I stood up too quickly.

I rammed my head on the underside of the table. Thankfully there was no glass on *top* of the table, and the only noise I produced was a faint thud.

I rubbed my hair, all the thoughts gone from my head except one. *Thank you, Lord.*

I eased out from under the table and stood up. The reader from Mr. Sardis was abandoned on the table in the middle of the room. I slid it in my pouch with my other reader and then shook the table. It shifted; it wasn't bolted to the floor. That would do.

I gazed at the chaos on the table. The various chemicals glowed surreal shades in the indirect light. *Not all the pieces are here, but you could create a disturbance.* Just what I needed.

But it wasn't enough. I glanced behind me and saw a closed door in the side wall.

I tried it. It opened. My brother must have had access.

Beyond was another lab, also deserted, with a door back to the hall. I opened it and looked around.

Carnegie's voice echoed, signaling their return. I backed into the shadows and watched them approach.

Dr. Nic, scowling bitterly, held out his hand. My heart leaped to see the reprogramming disc in his palm.

Everything was there. Everything was perfectly planned. But certainly not on account of any brilliance of mine.

I slid quickly along the wall, staying in the shadows, back into Lab 1. I stood next to the table, gripping it with both hands. I prayed for a burst of masculine strength.

I looked boldly out the door. It didn't matter if Dr. Nic glanced over his shoulder and saw me now. He'd be looking over his shoulder in a minute anyway.

The men stopped in front of the door. Dr. Nic reached out and held the disc over the panel.

I closed my eyes. When I heard the magnet click in place, I heaved.

Either the table was lighter than I expected, or God answered my prayer. Probably both. The table flew faster than I intended, causing me to jerk back with a little shriek.

Not that anyone but me could hear the shriek. The symphony of clattering metal and shattering glass was dazzling.

I cringed and threw my hands over my head instinctively—then remembered to run. I tripped over a pan and nearly fell through the door into the adjoining lab.

I was around the corner just in time. I heard Carnegie's unfinished "What the…" from the doorway.

Dr. Nic started yelling. "Argh… stop it!" Something crackled and sizzled. I took advantage of the noise to skip quickly out the door and into the hall.

The disc was waiting patiently for me on the panel. I snatched it and ran to Gate A. I didn't dare look back.

I snapped the disc onto the panel and raised my hand—then stopped.

How was I supposed to work this thing?

Panic and stupidity seized me—then bravery slapped it into silence. *You can do this. Just think. It can't be that hard. God, help me!*

I looked at the round device. It didn't have that many buttons. *This can't be that hard, this can't be that hard…*

The men's shouting disrupted my concentration. "Too late!" Carnegie screeched.

Dr. Nic hollered back, probably involuntarily. "Run!" They both obeyed. Frozen still, I looked back and watched them scramble out of the doorway.

Carnegie ran down the hall without looking in my direction. But Dr. Nic backed away slowly, staring into the room. I heard the crackling and sizzling grow louder now.

I knew what was going to happen a split second before he did it. The despair in my heart expected it.

Dr. Nic turned his head slightly and spotted me.

He whipped fully around in a blink. I couldn't move.

"You!" he snarled, which was what I expected him to say.

What I wasn't expecting was a sudden explosion to rock the lab, spewing a cloud of white smoke out into the hallway.

Suddenly I couldn't see Dr. Nic anymore. And he couldn't see me.

God had this more perfectly planned than I thought.

The smoke alarm went off, sending a wail and flashing lights coursing down the hall. No time to revel in perfection.

Coughing, I fanned smoke out of my face and hit a random button on the disc. Adrenaline was making my hand shake too much for me to be more precise.

Dr. Nic hacked. Someone—more than one someone?—shouted. But my ear was focused on the noise the panel was making.

It beeped. Then the doors slid open.

I glanced over my shoulder and saw Dr. Nic's hand emerge from the smoke like a monster rising from the grave. I snatched the disc and ran.

The doors eased shut behind me—too slowly. I saw Dr. Nic stand up, still coughing, just before the crack sealed. I waved my hand over the sensor and hoped that locked the door. I didn't wait to see.

I stumbled out of Gate 74 and locked it, too. I collapsed right where I was. I didn't have time to spare.

I yanked the readers out of my pouch and dropped the disc in their place. I tossed the reader from Mr. Sardis on the floor while it warmed up. I flipped mine over and pried the data chip out of the back.

The welcome screen on the Wing 74 device glowed. I picked it up and opened the main menu. Ephesus was right—a conglomeration of cryptic folders appeared.

I didn't have time to copy them all. What was most telltale?

I involuntarily grinned. Sliding the data chip in, I selected "Bible" and copied it. I picked a few other random important-looking folders.

The transfer bar filled quickly, but I was in such a rush that I almost yanked the chip out before the process was finished.

I shoved the chip in my reader and watched the bar climb again—slowly this time. My aged device choked at 30%.

"Please, God, please!" Then I remembered—getting them onto my device was only half the battle. They had to be where someone would see them.

I couldn't think of any websites I could access quickly enough. Nothing that was obvious. A United official had to see these files—now. How could I get ahold of a United official directly?

I smirked and opened my email. I started typing "Ambrose" and the system fed the appropriate address into the "to" field.

I tried to think of an eye-catching subject line. He had to read it, not glaze over and delete it like he did with most emails from criminals.

It came to me. *Subject: transmitting site*

Footsteps approached from the hall ahead. Friend or foe, I wasn't taking the risk.

No time to get cutesy with the message body. I typed: *Found a private database with Bibles and secret research. Send help. Philadelphia Smyrna*

I switched to the other window and found the copying finished. Praising God, I attached the files to the email and started the process all over again.

Gate 73 ahead of me opened. I looked up to see Cea enter. "Phil? What are you doing out here? How did..."

I looked back down at the screen. The last file began to load.

"What are you doing? What's going on?" She was on top of me.

Done. I hit send, and it went.

"Phil? Philli!"

I looked up at her. For an answer, I pulled the reprogram disc out of my pocket and held it up.

She gasped.

"It's over," I said. "It's over."

It truly was over.

Because two seconds later, a muffled explosion rocked the hall from behind. I instinctively dropped the reader and covered my head.

Two more explosions fired, the blast reverberating off the metal halls. Cea screamed and dropped to the ground.

Metal popped and cracked. I peered through my arms to see the walls buckle.

I heard the sound of electricity sparking. Cea screamed again, and I turned towards her—only to be knocked flat by something hitting my head. Glass shattered around me. I saw bright white, then darkness.

27

When I woke up, I didn't know where I was. It was too bright, too sterile. Nowhere I could remember being recently.

Fear, then panic, seized me. Something must have gone wrong. *Nic caught me again! Or... the explosion. The explosion went off, and I'm in the hospital, and everyone else is probably dead, and...*

Then I saw someone I recognized leaning over the bed. All other emotions left in favor of joy. "Ephesus!" I screeched and sat up.

He made a random noise of reproof and pushed me back. "Stay."

"Where's Dad? Are you okay?"

"Not so loud. I'm fine. Dad's talking with the officials."

I absorbed that information. My voice quieted. "You called them?"

"We didn't have to. They came with orders from Commander Ambrose."

I smiled and praised God.

Ephesus squeezed my hand. "I'm proud of you. That was quite the stunt."

"I didn't mean for it to blow up." The worry in my voice was real.

"What did you do?"

"Turned over the table in Lab 1."

He cringed. "I told you I was making a bomb."

"You said all the pieces weren't there!"

"Thankfully. Otherwise you would have killed all of us."

I pinched my eyes shut. *God had it all planned...*

I thought of something and sat up straight again. "Nic?"

Ephesus stared at me for a moment. "He'll heal. He was far enough away."

I closed my eyes and let out my breath. *Thank you, Lord.*

Ephesus gently pushed me down again. "You were pushing it, though. That close to the explosion, had you not been near an outside wall..."

I reached up and touched my neck. I felt a bandage across the back of it. "What happened?"

"Light fixture. A few cuts from the glass. It could have been a lot worse."

I flexed my arm and counted the small scrapes. "It would have been worth it."

Ephesus was quiet for a moment. "You ended Red Rain."

He stood up. "Rest. As soon as you're well enough, we're taking the first transit back to Earth."

He left, shutting off the light. I watched the low security lighting flicker on around the baseboards. I smiled into the darkness.

We were going home. All of us.

*

Daddy made me stay in bed until the morning, then we got up to pack. I was surprised to find the base nearly evacuated. Two United officials guarded the dorms, and the rest of Wing 1 past the cafeteria was blocked off.

Red Rain—and all of Nic's operations—were over for good.

I was surprised when Mr. Sardis bumbled in to pick up our crates. He didn't look at us, just scooped up the luggage and hustled out.

"Sir!" I called after him. He stopped but didn't turn around.

I glanced at my father, then ventured, "Are you… coming on our flight?"

He shrugged. "I signed the file years ago."

He looked at me out of the corner of his eye, then left. My face fell. Daddy rubbed my shoulder.

We were waiting near the dock for our ride when I saw Cea. She breezed past the hallway and didn't glance in our direction.

"Cea!" I cried. She didn't stop.

I pounded to catch up with her. She ignored me. I squeezed past her in the hall and halted right in front of her, forcing her to stop.

She wouldn't look at me. I wasn't sure if I wanted to make eye contact. "I'm sorry," I said.

"You didn't mean for it to blow up." Her tone was cryptic, neither forgiving nor accusing.

"Nic?" I dared to ask.

"When he gets out of the hospital he'll have a home in jail." She pushed past me.

I didn't try to stop her. "Thank you," I called loud enough to be heard. She hesitated at the turn. "For being honest."

She left.

Commander Ambrose was neither pleased nor displeased to see us back, though to his credit he pretended not to be surprised by Ephesus's return from the dead.

Our neighbors at the camp were a different story. I couldn't remember the last time a new arrival in camp had been a cause for celebration.

I was surprised at how happy I was to go to school again, to ride on the bus with Cami and Aid and listen to my teacher's rants. Daddy still waited for the bus with me, only this time Ephesus stood with us.

The only thing that was missing was Mr. Dass's arguments. He didn't come out of his house much anymore. Cami said they hadn't heard a word from Mira or Stanyard since they left.

I made a note to pray for them more often. Their names went right below Cea's.

It was on the bus ride to school that Cami reminded me what I had left behind on Mars.

"Do you still have the file?"

I gasped and reached for my pouch—then remembered it wasn't there. I hadn't put it on because I didn't have anything to go in it.

I'd left both readers on the floor in the wreckage by Wing 74. I hadn't been allowed to go back and collect them.

I abruptly grinned. I knew who had a copy. "Ephesus has one on his computer."

I bombarded him as soon as I came home from school. He stared at me for a long moment before shaking his head.

"What?"

"They confiscated all the computers from Wing 74 for evidence."

I covered my face. Ephesus reached out and touched my shoulder. "Didn't you send a copy to Commander Ambrose?"

I looked up at him and smiled.

Daddy transferred our query the next day. The response he got was "no transmitting."

I cried into his shoulder when he told me. Ephesus spoke up. "Someone will upload a copy sooner or later. I'm helping them patch the virus."

"God will find a way," Dad repeated.

I sat up. "He preserved the Bible through the virus." I looked at Ephesus.

He smiled sadly. "With Wing 74."

Daddy squeezed my hand. "With Wing 74."

28

A few days later, the bus dropped me off on the wrong street. It couldn't go down my row because Ambrose's car was blocking the road.

I jumped off the bus, listening to the driver complain about conflicting schedules. As the bus drove away, I walked down the sidewalk and tried to see what the commotion was.

A guard carried a crate up the steps of one of the vacant houses. New people.

I ventured closer to the house, looking for the unfamiliar faces and wondering if they'd want to be greeted. Sometimes new convicts didn't want to talk to anyone for weeks.

Commander Ambrose was talking with someone on the sidewalk. The guard came out of the house and climbed into the car. Nodding curtly, Ambrose followed in suit, leaving the new resident alone on the sidewalk.

I recognized her.

"Cea!" I ran for her—then stopped, confusion overtaking my joy.

She turned in my direction and stared stoically at me.

I crept closer. "Are you…?"

"I came to return what's yours."

"And you had to bring all your belongings with you?"

I could see the smile tugging at her lips now. She reached into her bag and pulled something out.

My reader. She pressed it upside down in my hand. I stared at the scuffed case for a minute before flipping it over and looking at the screen.

It was on. Revelation was loaded.

I know your deeds. See, I have placed before you an open door that no one can shut. I know that you have little strength, yet you have kept my word and have not denied my name.

I threw my arms out and hugged her.

"Thank you," she whispered in my ear.

I stood at arm's length. "Welcome home."

She smiled.

PROJECT 74

RED RAIN #1.5
ANNIVERSARY EDITION

RACHEL NEWHOUSE

AUGUST 2073

1

Since when was it legal to kill a student because they refused to get on the bus?

I stood with my little sister on the front step and watched the commander herd the neighbors' kids onto the bus at gunpoint. Government schooling had been mandatory since my father was in middle school, but it never used to be this *dramatic.* I remembered getting pulled out of class once or twice in high school; whenever the curriculum got particularly heinous, my father made me play hooky as a form of protest. We'd gotten fined and had derogatory marks put on our files, and I think Dad spent a night in jail once, but I'd never worried that I might get shot.

Today, I wondered if our neighbors were about to lose another child—if only because Commander Ambrose had no concept of gun safety. He kept his fat finger on the trigger as he bullied the family next door. It wouldn't be the first time he'd shot someone by accident.

I winced at the memory and turned away. Now I knew why my parents had risked imprisonment to homeschool my little sister. Up until a few years ago, they had skirted the law, using Dad's multiple PhDs and Mom's special education degree to convince the government they were private tutoring.

Of course, the government closed that loophole when they rounded up the unassimilated and put them in camps.

I scanned the row of tiny concrete homes and wondered when it had gotten this bad. My family had been sentenced to Street 17 Containment Camp three years ago for refusing to sign the file and assimilate into the United. I was in college at the time, and there were already so many regulations on campus that turning it into a prison had been a short trip. They'd put a tracking chip in my arm and a lock on my dorm room door and called it good.

I hadn't spent much time in the containment camp—only coming "home" on school breaks—but it didn't used to be this inhumane. It was a prison, sure, but when the camps were first opened, community backlash put the place under constant scrutiny. There were enough advocacy groups and regulations to keep unstable people like Ambrose in check.

But eventually, the outside world forgot about us, and those safeguards were taken away. Now Ambrose could satisfy his addiction to power by tormenting middle schoolers with a loaded weapon, and he couldn't even be prosecuted for it.

It made me sick to think that, starting today, my little sister would have to deal with him alone.

She found my hand. "When are you coming back?" she said, even though she'd asked me the same question at breakfast, and the night before. No doubt she was hoping for a different answer.

I wished I had a different answer to give her. I had been summoned to Mars on scientific business; my transit left this afternoon. Under any other circumstances, I would have been thrilled. Going to Mars was a dream come true, and working for Dr. Nic, a prestigious scientist whose awards spoke for themselves, was a privilege. When I first got the notice, I'd shouted so loud that my lab partner dropped a beaker full of chemicals and almost burned herself.

And then I'd learned that my father would also be away on business.

He was currently stationed in China, working on some hippie smog reduction experiment so the government could check their "environmentally conscious" box for the year. He'd be there until the project was complete, which could be months. Until they released him, my teenaged sister would be coming home to an empty house surrounded by a concrete wall with a sniper tower.

I squeezed her hand. "My contract is for three months. If we complete the project, they'll send me home then," I said with an optimism I knew was unfounded. Science had no regard for deadlines.

She just nodded. "Will you call?"

"Every day." *If Ambrose will let the call through.* "Unless I pull some all-nighters so I can get done faster. If I only sleep for four hours a night, I'll finish the project in half the time."

She squinted up at me. "That doesn't sound healthy."

I winked. "It worked in college."

She grinned and started to reply—but Ambrose interrupted.

"Philadelphia!" he screeched as if he'd just caught her committing a crime.

She flinched and washed white.

He planted his foot on our bottom step. His gun was mercifully holstered. "Why are you still standing there? Didn't you hear me call your name?"

If he had, I hadn't heard him, but that fact was irrelevant to Ambrose. "Bus, now, or I'll count you tardy," he ordered, leering so close I could see the spittle on his lips.

"Y-yessir," Philadelphia stuttered. She let go of my hand and grabbed her backpack.

I gripped her shoulder and held her back. "Was that necessary?" I snarled at Ambrose. "Being late to school isn't a crime."

"Actually, it is," Philadelphia mumbled.

Ambrose snorted. "Don't you have your own business to attend to, Ephesus? I heard you get to go on a special trip. They really shouldn't let people like you go to Mars—but I signed the waiver. You're welcome."

I gritted my teeth.

He surveyed me, eyes tracking up and down as if searching for the crack in my armor. "If you're worried about your little sister," he sneered, savoring every word, "I'll make sure she gets home safely."

I tightened my grip on Philadelphia's shoulder.

He noticed. "Do you have an objection, Mr. Smyrna?"

I did. I glared at him, and for a brief moment, I contemplated punching him. I considered knocking him down and taking his gun. I thought about grabbing my sister's hand and making a break for it—anything to get us out of this place.

I jumped when Philadelphia's icy fingers brushed mine. She patted my hand and offered a smile. "It's okay," she said in a voice intended to be brave. "Daddy told me not to cause trouble."

The objections leapt to my tongue—but then I remembered why. Why my father hadn't complained about his assignment even though he'd be gone for months. Why he sent my sister to school even though it went against everything we believed. Why he let the commander have his way even though Ambrose was insane, wicked, and cruel.

Our mother had caused trouble once, and the commander had offered no mercy.

It's not worth it, my father would have said.

I let go of Philadelphia's shoulder.

She shrugged on her backpack and scampered down the steps, eyes on the sidewalk. It was only after she reached the bus that I realized we hadn't said goodbye.

"Philli, wait!" I shouted, lunging forward.

She paused on the step and glanced back. The commander reached for his holster.

I ignored him, instead finding my sister's gaze. "I'll be back in three months," I declared with all the strength and conviction I knew she needed.

She nodded, but the look in her eyes told me she didn't believe me.

I forced a smile. "I promise."

FEBRUARY 2074

2

I lied.

I wasn't back in three months. Or six. If Nic had his way, I wouldn't be going back to Earth, ever.

"I'm renewing your contract for another year," he declared. He swiped his signature on his tablet like a judge banging a gavel.

"A year?" I yelped. My shout echoed painfully around Nic's cramped office, causing his eyebrow to twitch, but I didn't care. "I am on a three-month contract. You are supposed to reevaluate my employment every quarter."

"Well, now you're on a one-year contract, so I can do a fourth of the paperwork. Work smarter, not harder." He tossed his tablet on the desk.

I grabbed it and squinted at the fine print to make sure he wasn't lying to me—something I suspected he did frequently. For once, however, he wasn't being sarcastic: My commission to Mars had been extended for another year.

And, of course, Ambrose had already approved it.

I threw the device back at him. "I don't want to stay."

"That's hyperbole." He turned to face his computer, as if this conversation were boring him out of his mind. "And I didn't ask."

I grunted; he was right on both accounts. As an unassimilated scientist, I was essentially a convict working on probation, which meant I had no say in my employment. I could and would be reassigned at the discretion of the government.

And I didn't *want* to leave Mars. I loved Mars, and apparently my enthusiasm was obvious even to Nic. Everything about this planet fascinated me—the blue sunsets, the untwinkling stars, the yellowed horizon that was permanently cloaked in a shroud of dust. The weak gravity and thin atmosphere made even the most basic science exciting; it was like I was learning everything for the first time as I discovered how physics and chemistry operated on this alien planet.

Working on Base #9.6.11 would have been a dream come true—if my family weren't trapped in a prison on Earth.

"You're right." I mimicked his sarcasm, hoping that would help him translate. "I love my job, and you're the best boss I've ever had. But my family is on Earth."

"They're not going anywhere," he intoned with all the compassion of a concrete wall.

"I wouldn't bet on it," I muttered. Last I'd heard, my family was still in Street 17 Containment Camp, but Dad had gotten several derogatory marks on his file for accidentally violating a new regulation at work. He'd had his pay docked and spent a few nights in solitary—a relative slap on the wrist.

It was only a matter of time before those derogatory marks added up to a worse punishment.

"Look, you don't understand." I let some of the concern into my voice, even though Nic seemed impervious to normal human emotions. "My dad—"

Nic sighed so hard he was in danger of bruising a rib. "You know, Ephesus, if you spent as much time worrying about your work as you do worrying about your perfectly capable adult father, the project would be done by now."

"The project would be done by now if you would tell me what it is we're making!" I shot back.

I would be more amicable to my contract being extended if I knew I was working towards an attainable goal. But despite the fact that Nic kept me obsessively busy, often requiring overtime and unrealistic deadlines, I still had no idea what we were trying to accomplish.

Every Monday, he handed me another stack of assignments that read like they were written by a badly programmed AI. There were seemingly pointless experiments to run, fantastical simulations to program, and broken chemical equations to salvage—most of which had no solutions. The parameters were completely different each time, as if Nic had a manic case of ADHD and couldn't decide which project to focus on.

To make matters even stranger, most of the hypothetical equations were designed to function in Earth's atmosphere—making me wonder why Nic was on Mars at all. If he wanted to create a chemical compound that functioned on Earth, he should just commission a terrestrial lab to do it, instead of spending millions of dollars replicating Earth's physics in a testing chamber on Mars.

I'd suggested as much, but he'd just told me to get back to work and mind my own business, using much less friendly language. No matter how many times I badgered him, he refused to give me any details about his plans. As far as he was concerned, I was just a lab rat being used to generate data—as were the other scientists on the station. There were rumors of a "pet project" being developed in Wing 74, one of the unfinished sectors of the base, but everyone I'd talked to claimed to know nothing. Most didn't even know where that wing was.

I wasn't about to waste another year of my life crunching numbers for a crass mad scientist who changed projects more often than he changed lab coats.

I took a deep breath. "Listen," I tried one more time, "just tell me what it is you're trying to do, and I'll make it happen." *Or prove it's not possible.*

"Love the energy," he said without looking up from his monitor, "but your assignment is that stack of simulations that's due on Friday. And I don't see any updates in my inbox." He clicked his mouse and refreshed his screen several times.

The aggressive clicking snapped what little patience I had left. "And what if I don't want to run your stupid simulations?"

He must have seen that coming, because he delivered his next line smoothly like a backhanded slap. "Then you'd better sign the file and assimilate so you can legally refuse me without getting shot."

My comeback died in my throat. *You're no better than Ambrose.*

"Luckily for you, though, I've had three cups of coffee today, so I'll settle for putting a warning on your file and assigning you to lab cleanup duty for a week. You can thank me after you've cooled off." He grabbed his nearly empty mug and took a swig to emphasize.

There was no point in responding. I shoved my chair back and stormed to the door. I flapped my hand over the sensor, and it had the audacity to refuse me, screeching and flashing up an ugly red *X*.

"Forgot I locked that," Nic mumbled. He tapped his screen, and the door opened.

I growled and strode into the hall. I would have slammed the door behind me had it not been hydraulic.

I hurried past the other offices and back to Wing 1. It was almost noon, and the distant sun was high overhead, filling the glass-domed hallway with muted light. The wing bustled with activity; laughter and clattering dishes came from the cafeteria up ahead, and clusters of scientists and businessmen chattered loudly as they trickled down the hallway in search of food. Mr. Sardis—a horticulturist and one of the nicest people on the station—waved and called out to me as he approached.

I gave him a half-smile and quickly turned the corner in the other direction. I wasn't about to sit at a table and pretend everything was all right. I needed to walk this off, or I was in danger of blowing something up.

I stopped at the first door I came to and checked to see if it opened for me. The doors on the station were controlled by sensors that scanned DNA through the user's fingertips—one of the many experimental projects Nic had his hand in. I only had access to about half of the sprawling base, but it was still more than enough surface area to get lost in.

Which was exactly what I wanted to do right now.

A green circle appeared on the panel as the doors opened. I marched through and continued down the hall, not caring where I was going. Was I really stuck here for another year? What was I going to tell Philadelphia? Would I even be able to call her?

I'd barely spoken to my family since I'd left. I sent emails religiously, but I knew most of them weren't getting past the censors—and that was one thing I *couldn't* blame Nic for. Even though it was his job to monitor all my outgoing emails, he'd made it abundantly clear that he had no time for such things and approved most messages without reading them. Ambrose, unfortunately, had too much time on his hands and delighted in manually censoring every email. I knew from past experience that he deleted most of them to give himself a power rush every morning.

It had been even harder to get a call through. Ambrose insisted on personally supervising the conversation, which meant we were at the mercy of his schedule. The last time we'd been allowed to have a video conference, my dad wasn't even home. Ambrose had dragged Phil into his office and sat brooding in the background the entire call. She'd looked more like she was getting interrogated than talking to her big brother.

At this rate, it would be weeks before I could even tell my family that my contract had been extended. Although, knowing Ambrose, he might have already broken the news to them, just to gloat.

I walked through another random door and doubled back in the opposite direction. *God, why is this happening?* I demanded of the heavens. I'd been searching high and low for an answer to that question since I'd arrived and hadn't gotten one.

Just like I didn't have an answer for why my family was in prison in the first place.

I halted as the conviction rolled over me. I knew exactly why my family was in prison—because they refused to sign the file denying all national, racial, and religious identities. The United, a global megacountry, had been formed to prevent another world war, and the government's solution to nuclear apocalypse was to force everyone to be the same. Their glittery propaganda claimed that if we didn't have religious and racial lines dividing us, we'd live in harmony.

The reality was that the government now had the power to eliminate anything that resisted its control. Including, but definitely not limited to, Christianity.

We were unassimilated for a reason. But being unassimilated had its perks—like being able to talk to God without shame.

I sighed and resumed walking, struggling to open a conversation with the One I knew was still listening.

"God, I need You." I spoke aloud to force my thoughts to focus. "I don't know what to do. I don't want to be here for another year. I'm worried about Phil. She's living in that camp alone, and Dad's not home half the time. Who's going to protect her?"

The answer wafted back almost before I finished the sentence. *God will.*

I groaned. I knew that, of course—but it didn't make me feel any better. "I know, but... she *needs* me. I have to be there."

The words felt cheap as they echoed down the bare corridor. This wasn't just about Philadelphia, and I knew that. Even if I did go back to Earth, I wouldn't be able to protect her. There was no guarantee I'd be home any more than Dad was, and there was nothing I could do to stop Ambrose. The government would continue to abuse my family whether I was there or not.

And maybe—maybe that was what I was really afraid of.

I stopped in the middle of the hall and looked at the ceiling. "God, I'm worried that... something's going to happen while I'm gone, and I won't get to say goodbye. Just like with... Mom."

Grief sucked the air out of my chest, but at the same time, I felt the wave of peace that told me I was finally being honest with myself—and the Lord.

I was still in school when my mother died. My father didn't call me until late that evening, after Mom had been dead for nearly twelve hours. By then, he'd had time to pack his emotions in a box and shove it under the bed. His voice was rote as he relayed the story to me, lines clearly rehearsed. He didn't let me share his grief, and by the time I was able to go home on leave, it was as if Mom had never been there. Even Philadelphia had dried her tears as she and Dad built a new routine to fill the void Mom had left.

A routine that didn't include room for me.

And that was what I feared most: That the longer I was on Mars, the longer we went between phone calls, the more my family would forget me. My father would find other friends to talk chemistry with; my sister would grow into a young woman until I would barely recognize her. They would build a life that didn't involve me, and by the time I would be able to go home, it would be almost impossible to pretend we were a family.

I knew they weren't doing it on purpose. My sister, especially, needed a mentor, and if I wasn't there, someone else would have to fill that gap.

But I wanted to be the one she looked up to.

I continued walking, finally finding the clarity to tell the Lord what I really needed to say. "I want to go home."

I opened another door and found myself in a large corridor littered with construction debris. I strode across the dusty floor to the gate on the other side.

"I'm tired of being stuck on a different planet and not even being able to make a phone call. I'm lonely, and I miss my family. I want to talk to my dad, and I want to be involved in my sister's life."

I stopped in front of the door and glared at my hazy reflection on the shiny metal. "I want to go home," I repeated. "I don't want to be here. But if Nic has his way, I'm going to be working here until I'm forty. So, if there's a way out of this—I need Your wisdom."

I stopped and gave Him room to answer. The wing grew unnaturally silent as I waited. There were no people or machines in sight; even the omnipresent whir of the air purifiers and gravity augmenters seemed quieter here. I closed my eyes and searched for the release in the Spirit—but it never came.

I grimaced. I knew what that meant: I was asking the wrong question.

I knew what question I should be asking. And it was the one question I didn't want an answer to.

"Unless…" I barely got the word past the fear in my throat. "You want me to be here."

The air came back into the room, and I had my answer. I braced myself against the door as my soul broke.

What if God *did* want me to stay on Mars? I had to admit that theory made a lot more sense than most of the other explanations I'd concocted. Nic had gone through a herculean effort to bring me here. He'd sought me out amongst thousands of candidates and went through reams of red tape to get my transfer approved. That was a lot of investment for someone who hated paperwork, especially when there had to be hundreds of Union scientists more qualified than me. It made no sense for him to pick me—unless God was the one that put the idea in his head.

And if God wanted me here, then He'd bring me home safely when it was time—and my family would be there waiting for me.

I took a breath and found my courage. "Well, if You want me here, then show me what You want me to do."

I swiped my hand over the door panel—and it rejected me.

I leaned back and read the numbers over the door: Wing 74.

The pet project.

I looked down at the red *X* as it faded away. If God called me up here, it definitely wasn't to run random experiments for Nic while he lied through his teeth about what he was developing. There were too many missing pieces, too many unanswered questions, for this to be a mundane science project. Something was wrong with Nic and Wing 74.

And it was time for me to find out what.

I stepped back and looked around. The wing was unlike any other area of the base that I'd been in. It was a huge room, the size of a small warehouse, but completely empty. Gate 74 was the only door on this side; the rest of the wall was blank. Across the room was Gate 73, which I'd just come out of, and Gate 72, which wasn't even finished. The doors hadn't been installed yet, and a sheet of plastic hung over the opening. Other construction paraphernalia was scattered around the room; a stack of ceiling tiles was shoved against the wall next to Gate 74, the torn plastic overwrap drifting across the floor.

I tapped the sensor panel next to the gate. Clearly, I didn't have access to this door, but maybe the settings would have useful information.

There was a connections menu, which told me what network the gate was on as well as the serial number of the scanner. I took a picture on my phone, then switched to the activity log. A quick skim revealed that Nic, his assistant Carnegie, and a few names I didn't recognize visited this wing several times a day.

As if reinforcing the point, distant voices echoed from Wing 72. The plastic over the unfinished gate fluttered in warning.

I turned and ran for Gate 73. The last thing I needed was for Nic to catch me snooping around his pet project. He would definitely assume the worst after the argument we just had.

I barely made it. I heard the plastic being thrown aside just as Gate 73 slid shut behind me. I hit the call button on the access panel, opening two-way communication, and listened.

It was Nic. He was having a vehement conversation on the phone with someone. Thankfully, whatever they were discussing was distracting enough, and he hadn't noticed me. His voice faded as he crossed the room, then disappeared.

I shut off the call and hurried away. I didn't want to chance running into anyone else. I had no idea who all was involved in Nic's project, and until I knew who I could trust, I would just as soon not answer any incriminating questions.

I waited until I'd passed through several gates before reopening my conversation with the Lord. "All right, Jesus," I sighed, "how are we doing this?"

I pulled my phone out of my pocket and swiped through menus. I couldn't open Gate 74, which either meant I needed to hack in remotely—or find a different door. Was there another gate into that wing?

"Is there a construction entrance or something?" I muttered aloud, hoping for confirmation from the Spirit.

I got an answer, but it wasn't from the Lord.

"Who are you talking to?"

I looked up, but not fast enough. Someone blocked the hall, and there was no time to stop. I crashed into them, sending us both to the ground.

"Ephesus!" they complained with a grunt—and I recognized the voice.

"Cea! I'm so sorry!" I stuffed my phone in my lab coat and scrambled up to offer her my hand.

She accepted the help. "Are you lost again?" she said with a laugh that told me she wasn't upset.

I grinned at the memory. I'd met Cea, Nic's younger sister, during my first day of work on base. I was running late and couldn't find the lab. She'd been helpful and friendly and *beautiful*—the exact opposite of her brother. I'd been lonely and maybe a tiny bit desperate, so I'd decided to take a gamble and asked her to have dinner with me, right then and there.

Turned out, Cea was also a betting woman, and I had absolutely no regrets.

"Actually, yes," I answered her question. I looked down at her and counted the cute freckles that were smattered across her heart-shaped face. "But it was intentional this time, I promise."

She smirked, making her gray eyes sparkle. "Well, let me know if there's anything I can do to help."

"Oh, you're helping." Cea had helped me more than she knew. I wasn't sure I would have made it through six months of Nic's suffocating mismanagement had it not been for the private dinners, long talks, and stolen glances I'd shared with Cea.

Of all the reasons I loved Mars, Cea was on top of the list.

I abruptly realized I was still holding her hand. I loosened my grip—then changed my mind. I squeezed her fingers and pulled her closer.

She winked and didn't resist. "So, who were you talking to?"

"The Lord," I admitted, knowing she was one of the few people on base who would understand.

"Am I interrupting?"

I pretended to ponder that. "I'll allow it."

She rolled her eyes and started to say something else—then frowned. "You're sweating."

I flicked my other hand across my forehead and found she was right. "I was walking," I said by way of explanation. "Aggressively."

"Why?"

"It seemed more responsible than going to the lab and dumping random chemicals together just to watch them explode."

She searched my face, concern overriding her features. "What's wrong?"

I sighed. "Nic extended my contract for another year."

She started to respond, then changed her mind. She bit her lip and looked down, looking royally embarrassed.

"What?" I prodded.

"Well, the first thought I had wasn't very supportive."

I arched an eyebrow.

She flushed and confessed, "I'm trying not to be excited that you have to hang out with me for another year."

I chuckled as some hope came back into my soul. "You're right, this job does come with employee benefits."

She met my eyes again. "I'm sorry, Ephesus. I know you want to go home to your family." And then, without warning, she threw her arms around my neck and grasped me in a hug.

I jerked in surprise—then, very carefully, I returned the affection. "I feel better already," I murmured into her hair.

She snorted but didn't let go.

I held her gently, letting the warmth of her slender frame put a bandage on the wound. "It wouldn't bother me so much if I knew why Nic wanted me in the first place," I muttered, allowing myself to vent my frustration.

She stiffened, and I knew the moment was over.

She pulled away, leaving a cold draft in her place. "I'm sure it's because you're the best in your field."

It was framed as a compliment, but I knew it wasn't. "Cea," I sighed, "you know that's not true."

That was perhaps the most confusing thing about this whole ordeal: I wasn't qualified. I was a competent chemist; if I'd been in the habit of bragging, I would have even claimed I was a genius one. I'd been at the top of my class, won multiple awards, and even earned the prestige of assisting on several government projects.

But that didn't change the fact that I was barely out of college and only had a few years' practical lab experience. I was nothing like my father, whose accolades outnumbered even Nic's. If Nic had bent over backwards to commission my father, I would have understood. But me? Why was I so important to him?

"There's hundreds of chemists with more experience than me—including, notably, your brother," I continued the thought aloud, prodding for Cea's reaction.

She fidgeted with her blonde curls. Unlike most people on base, Cea never lied to me. She was always open and honest and shared her true opinion—except when it came to her brother's work. She never talked about him and always avoided going near the labs. Whenever I complained about Nic's pedantic assignments, she swiftly changed the subject.

If Cea knew what was going on in Wing 74, she wouldn't tell me.

Instead, she did what she always did when she couldn't lie: She avoided the question. "I don't know," she mumbled, looking elsewhere. "He doesn't involve me in his projects."

I believed that to be true, but I suspected it was because Cea *chose* not to be involved.

She glanced behind her, as if abruptly realizing how close we were to Wing 74. She grabbed my hand and tugged on my arm. "We shouldn't be back here. Come on, let's go get lunch."

I allowed myself to be led down the hall. I knew from experience that pushing her wouldn't work; she avoided the topic of "the pet project" almost as religiously as Nic himself.

It didn't take a master's degree to see why: She was scared. Whatever was going on in Wing 74, Cea was terrified of it.

Or, perhaps, of her brother.

I tightened my grip on her hand and matched pace with her. *All the more reason why I have to stop him.*

4

It wasn't until late that night that I was able to start investigating. I didn't want to arouse Nic's suspicions, so I went back to work and put on a good show. I finished over half of my assignments for the week in one shift, mostly just to spite him.

He responded immediately to my email and told me to stop overcompensating.

Unfortunately, he wasn't kidding when he said he condemned me to cleanup duty, so I was stuck in the lab after hours sanitizing beakers and mopping the floor. By then, Cea was waiting for me. We shared a late dinner, and our table discussion, as always, evolved into an intimate dialog that lasted until curfew. It was only after the lights dimmed, taking the base into power-saving mode, that we put a period on our conversation.

I hurried through the darkened halls back to my dorm. Technically, I could get punished for being out after curfew, but Nic usually couldn't be bothered. His assistant Carnegie, however, was vicious; he'd fined me more than once for being out even five minutes past my bedtime.

Thankfully, Carnegie was off-base on vacation, which presumably meant no one was watching the logs. That meant I had the perfect window to do some digging.

I locked myself in my dorm and spent the next several hours scrubbing the base's servers on my laptop. Even though chemistry was my profession, I was also a decent programmer, mostly out of necessity. Being an unassimilated criminal in a surveillance state meant that if I wanted any semblance of freedom, I had to outsmart the algorithm. Over the years, I'd become adept at hacking and modifying devices so I could transmit illegal Bibles, listen to old sermons, and pray without every electronic in my house recording the conversation and reporting it to the government.

I'd been able to hack my way out of trouble multiple times. Maybe now that skill would help me undermine Nic.

I worked well past midnight breaking into every network, database, cloud, and server I could find. It wasn't as difficult as it should have been. Nic wasn't a programmer, and it showed. His digital infrastructure was almost as idiosyncratic as the man himself. There were dozens of outdated programs, redundant servers, and unpatched vulnerabilities that even a mediocre hacker could have exploited. I even found some systems that were still using the default administrator credentials. I could tell someone—probably Carnegie—had tried to mitigate the mess, but the only way to fully secure the base's infrastructure would have been to factory reset it and start over.

Unfortunately, despite the fact that Nic basically left the door open for me, all of this information told me nothing. I quickly discovered that Nic wasn't being fully compliant with the law, but there was nothing particularly insidious on the database. I found several experiments that violated federal regulations and evidence of massive tax fraud. There was also a media archive with a bunch of banned music and books—including, much to my surprise, several versions of the Bible.

I stared at the file list and tried to assimilate this information with the scientist I thought I knew. For someone who had threatened to *shoot* me for not complying with the law, Nic dabbled in a surprising amount of criminal activity. I knew he was weirdly permissive about the oddest things; after all, his sister openly practiced Christianity, and it didn't seem to bother him. But transmitting the Bible could get him executed.

After all, that's what happened to my mother.

I drummed my fingers on the side of my long-empty coffee cup. None of this evidence, while intriguing, had anything to do with chemistry. It also didn't explain why Nic had an entire wing under lock and key. What was he doing that required a dedicated sector?

I brought up a schematic of the base and navigated around, trying to find Wing 74. After twenty minutes of squinting and scrolling, I reached an astounding conclusion.

Wing 74 didn't exist.

At least, not officially. With some digging, I was able to find a few references to it—mostly in emails and other internal messages that had accidentally found their way onto public databases. But according to the official paperwork, Wing 74 wasn't on the map.

You'd think it would have been hard to hide an entire wing, but it really wasn't, not with the way the base was laid out. Base #9.6.11 was old by Martian standards, one of the first science stations founded in the region. The original structure had been small, and previous governors had continually added onto it as technology expanded. Every time a new facility was needed, they simply built a hallway and tacked a new wing onto an existing one, resulting in a layout that looked like a maze from a children's activity book.

As near as I could figure by comparing the official schematic to aerial shots of the base, Wing 74 was on the north end of the station. It creatively borrowed space from the surrounding sectors so that you couldn't tell at first glance there was a whole wing missing. With the ways the halls twisted and turned, it would have been very easy to drop a few airlocks and seal the wing off entirely. The layout was either accidental genius or sinister design.

But even more impressive was the fact that I couldn't find any *digital* evidence the wing existed. It was one thing to erase a room off the map. It was an entirely different matter to hide that room from the computer—especially on a space station, where the ability to breathe depended on a constant flow of electricity.

Nic must not have been the one who wired Wing 74's infrastructure, because whoever it was knew what they were doing. I combed through every system that was easily accessible—electricity, the environmental controls, water. All the resources had been creatively allocated so that it wasn't obvious they were keeping an extra wing online.

I also couldn't find evidence of any internal servers. The wing was a dead zone; there was absolutely no communication going in or out. If there were any devices in Wing 74, they were on an extremely secure local network, and I wouldn't have been surprised to find there was a dampening field covering the entire sector.

Whatever this "pet project" was, Nic had gone to great lengths to make it private. And if the government ever came snooping, he could easily lock the wing down and pretend it didn't exist.

He must be doing something worse than copying a few Bibles and Linkin Park albums.

Unfortunately, the lack of digital activity meant my hacking skills couldn't help me. I wouldn't be able to break into the wing from a computer. If I wanted to find out the truth, I was going to have to unlock the door.

Without combing every single hall—something that would be difficult for me to do with my limited security clearance—I couldn't guarantee there wasn't another way into Wing 74, but it certainly looked like Gate 74 was the main entry point. And I knew I didn't have access to that door.

I glanced at the security panel on my dorm door—and got an idea.

I rooted around in my desk drawer until I found the right cable, then grabbed my laptop and knelt next to the door. With a bit of fiddling, I was able to pry the sensor off the wall, exposing the wiring beneath. I patched my laptop in, sat cross-legged on the floor, and opened the code for the sensor.

As I suspected, the door locks communicated on a wireless network. The sensor compared the user's credentials to the database, where each unique DNA could be coded with an individualized set of permissions. I ran a couple of commands and easily pulled up my user data. According to the code, I had Level 5 security clearance, meaning I could access any doors with Level 5 permissions or lower. Unfortunately, that only gave me access to most of the common rooms.

I'd also been granted access to a couple dozen individual doors. Judging by the names, that included my dorm room, several labs, some supply closets, and the like. That meant there were two ways to control access on the base: by permissions group, or by manually adding individual doors to a specific user.

Of course, altering user permissions required a Level 1 security clearance. There were only two users in that group: Nic and Carnegie.

It might be possible to conduct a privilege escalation attack and promote my user to Level 1, but that was stretching the limits of my ability. It would also take time, which I didn't have. Carnegie would be back in the next few days, and it would be a lot harder to sneak around while he was on base. I had to act now if I wanted a chance of going undetected. My best bet would be to crack Nic's password and use his own credentials against him.

And *that* was hacking I knew how to do.

5

My plan worked.

Just like the other hacking I'd done tonight, cracking Nic's credentials was deplorably easy. His password was only seven characters long, and I'd found so many reused and default passwords on the other databases that I had several hints as to what his phrase might be. It still took the rest of the night, but just after 4am, I got in.

It took some homework to figure out what permissions I needed. Gate 74 was on the name network as several other doors in that sector; anyone with Level 3 or higher security clearance could open it. I knew escalating my security level was more likely to get noticed, so I manually added myself to Gate 74, then edited the change log to cover my tracks. It wasn't bulletproof; if someone dug into the code, they could still figure out that Nic's credentials had been used to alter my permissions. But at least now there wasn't a notification on the homepage.

However, getting through Gate 74 was only half the battle. I had no idea what doors I would need to access beyond that point, and the user permissions for that wing were a mess. According to the activity log, at least a dozen other people besides Nic and Carnegie worked out of that wing, but most of their permissions had been manually coded, only giving them access to specific doors. I finally found a permissions group that, as best as I could figure, would give me access to the entire wing. I added myself and hoped Nic wasn't paying too close attention to how many users were in that group.

By the time I'd finished scrubbing the change log, it was nearly 6am. I stole a scant hour of sleep, then stumbled down to breakfast and tried to pretend that everything was normal. Mercifully, Cea had morning plans and didn't join me. I knew she would notice the circles under my eyes, and if she asked questions, I wasn't sure I could lie to her.

Working ahead on my assignments yesterday turned out to be a blessing. For one thing, I was too exhausted to do genuine work. For another, I needed to figure out the best time to break into Wing 74. I had to do it soon; I didn't want to bet on my hacking going unnoticed for long.

But figuring out Nic's schedule was like trying to corral a dust storm. I logged into his calendar (using yet another default password) and watched him cancel and reschedule meetings at least three times before lunch.

It took me an inordinate amount of time to realize that this wasn't something I could control—so, I turned to the One who could. I spent the afternoon reorganizing a supply closet and muttering prayers under my breath. My lab partners probably thought I was crazy, but it kept my eyes open and my heart rate down.

Then, about 3pm, God answered my prayer in the most ironic way possible: through the government.

Nic got a call from the officials summoning him to a mandatory meeting. From the sound of it, he hadn't filed some paperwork correctly, and now he had to appear in court and do penance. I only found out about it because he was so ticked off that he was storming through the halls, complaining loudly enough for the entire base to hear him. I overheard him cursing about how the magistrate's office was in another quadrant, and it was over six hours away, which meant he had to leave tonight, and knew I had my chance.

As soon as his transfer left the docking bay, I grabbed my phone and navigated the halls back to Wing 74. I took a different route through Wing 72. The hall was unfinished, which meant there were no cameras to record my movements.

I approached the sheet of plastic that covered the doorway and listened. It was a few minutes before five; first shift was about to end. Based on the door log activity, a small group of people had been working in Wing 74 over the past few months—construction crew, I guessed. They normally got off at five, and then the wing would be quiet after hours except for Nic and Carnegie, neither of whom were currently on base. My hope was that if I accessed the door around shift change, the activity was less likely to get noticed before I had time to scrub the log.

Several sheets of metal were propped against the wall near the end of Wing 72. I ducked behind them and waited, hidden in the shadows. I forced myself to take even breaths, even though it did nothing to calm my nerves. Three, five, ten minutes passed. The only movement came from the torn plastic overwrap on the stack of ceiling tiles, which was dragging across the floor in an unseen draft.

And then, at precisely 5:01, Gate 74 opened. Half a dozen construction workers in greasy coveralls exited, carousing amongst themselves. I held my breath as they walked towards me. The last one through the door tripped on the plastic overwrap. He cussed and kicked it behind him, then raced to catch up with the others.

Most of them vanished through Gate 73, but two walked right past me. Thankfully, they were both absorbed in their devices and didn't even glance in my direction. I waited until they were out of sight, then scrambled up and ran across the corridor.

I was shocked to find that Gate 74 stood open. The hydraulics started to close—then caught on the tangle of plastic and bounced back open. I slipped through and kicked the plastic out of the way, praising God for the happenstance. That was one less instance I had to scrub from the activity log.

The doors drifted shut, plunging the hall into near darkness. The vestibule clearly wasn't finished; of the half a dozen doors that lined the hall, only one was online, its security panel glowing faintly like the light at the end of a tunnel. Judging by the way the hall curved, I suspected the corridor looped around in a circle, but I knew I didn't have time to explore. I ran up to the working door, flapped my hand over the sensor, and braced myself.

It opened without complaint.

Murmuring a prayer of thanks, I stepped through and glanced up at the letter above the door: *A.* Then I turned and scanned the hall, waiting for my eyes to adjust to the dim security lighting.

Somewhat to my disappointment, Wing 74 looked exactly like the rest of the base. If anything, it was a bit outdated, making me wonder if it was part of the original layout. There were patches of rust in the seams on the metal walls, and several of the doors still had numeric keypads instead of fancy scanners.

Nic was clearly in the process of upgrading the facilities. The air reeked of sealant and freshly fabricated plastic. The meeting room to the right of Gate A was completely gutted, and several panels had been removed from the wall in the entryway, exposing a briar patch of wires and insulation. It looked like they were installing new door scanners for the rooms across the hall. The signs above the doors read LAB 1, 2, and 3.

I decided to start there. I had no idea what I was looking for, and a lab was as good a bet as any. More importantly, the fewer digital logs I could leave, the better.

After pausing to make sure I was alone—the corridor was silent except for the grind of a nearby generator—I walked up to Lab 1 and dragged the door open with my hands. I debated about closing the door behind me but decided it was more important to leave myself a quick exit.

The weak security lighting barely made a dent in the darkness. I didn't dare turn the fluorescents on, so I pulled out my phone and used the flashlight, dimming it to the lowest setting. I scanned the worktables cluttered with lab paraphernalia; the sharpened instruments and shiny flasks glittered in the half-light, making the place look like the set of a horror movie.

A giant whiteboard covered one wall. A complex chemical equation was scribbled across the length of it. I passed the flashlight over the messy writing and tried to interpret the symbols. Several portions had been aggressively crossed out and rewritten with a red pen, making the entire whiteboard look like it was dripping in blood.

I swallowed a lump of unease. *What are you making, Nic?*

I spun around and shone the light across the rest of the room, looking for anything useful. *There*—in the far corner was a computer terminal. I ran to it and tapped the screen. It brightened, revealing a desktop cluttered with programs and tantalizing files.

I shut my flashlight off and dropped my phone in my pocket. Bracing myself against the desk, I steeled my nerves with one final prayer, then opened the file explorer.

I flipped through the documents, scanning the contents as fast as I could. At first, everything was Greek, the notes a disorganized mess. But, slowly, pieces began to look familiar. There was the simulation I coded last Friday; those were the results from the experiment my lab partner and I ran last month. Every bit of data I had generated since coming to Mars was there— along with several papers I had written in college.

I frowned. A quick skim of the other documents in the folder revealed that Nic had scalped a great deal of my work. There were reports from my government projects, articles I'd written for scientific journals, even my test scores and college transcripts. My entire life's work was on this database.

I gripped the edge of the desk as every muscle in my body tightened. I was right; Nic was using me. And it wasn't an accident. He'd clearly been stalking me for a while and had chosen me specifically based on my scientific achievements. He *needed* me.

But for what? What was he trying to do?

I swiped through menus, looking for a report, a proposal, anything. My panic grew with each stroke. There were impact reports for explosives, corrosion tests for hideously strong acids, and even a fallout prediction for a nuclear weapon. There were plans for a missile that could bring down a spaceship and artillery shells designed to deliver chemical warfare. But worst was a map of Earth, several cities hashed out in red as someone plotted a path of destruction that would leave no room for escape.

I tasted bile as my vision briefly blurred out of focus. Whatever Nic was planning, he didn't expect anyone to survive.

I searched faster, oaths and prayers competing for bandwidth in my head. The further I dug, the more sinister the material got. The apocalypse flashed beneath my fingers like an old movie as I uncovered Nic's plot to light the world on fire.

And then, finally, I found it. *The pet project.*

It was a presentation, clearly styled to bewitch some sponsor. I stared at the title, emblazoned on the screen in an irreverent font:

RED RAIN

I skimmed the proposal, and suddenly, everything made sense. The corrosion tests, the artillery shells, the fallout predictions: Nic was planning to bomb Earth with a chemical superweapon.

The concept was cruelly simple. Red Rain was just that—rain. It was a manufactured acid rain with an intensity that could melt metal. But what made the project wickedly horrifying was how he was planning on distributing the weapon. He intended to disperse the chemical in gaseous form. If successful, he could bathe an entire city in the compound before anyone knew what was happening.

Then, as soon as it started to rain, it would be too late. When any source of water mixed with the gas, it would condense into liquid fire capable of wiping entire cities off the map. In some regions, all it would take was high humidity to unleash the angel of death.

I stumbled back from the computer as the truth wrapped its claws around my throat. Nic wanted to destroy Earth.

And he was using *my* research to do it.

"Oh God," I gasped aloud, "what do I—"

I didn't get to finish the question.

"You really shouldn't work in the dark. It's bad for your eyesight."

The lights flicked on. I whipped around.

It was Nic.

6

He filled the doorway. In his hand was the wad of plastic that had been an accomplice to my crimes.

"I knew this thing would be a tripping hazard." He wadded it up and stuffed it in the nearest trash can.

I stood there, frozen. There was nowhere to run, even though my panicked heart was definitely trying. There was a second door out of the lab, but I was under no delusion that I'd get very far.

Nic didn't seem to be in a hurry, either. He walked across the room and claimed a coffee mug he'd abandoned on a worktable. Then he faced the whiteboard. "Since you're here, can you look at this equation for me? My math is off." He pointed at a diagram in the corner.

The request was made politely, which was somehow all the more sinister. "Sure," I said hesitantly, not sure how else to respond. Keeping one eye on him, I approached the board and scanned the scribbles. It was immediately obvious where he'd gone wrong. I grabbed a marker off the tray and annotated his equation.

"Brilliant. Well," he turned towards me, "what do you think?"

I backed up, putting a few steps between us. "About what?"

"About all the data you just hacked into." He gestured behind me at the computer terminal.

I glanced over my shoulder. "You're not mad?"

"Of course, I'm not mad," he intoned. "It's my own fault for not including at least one numeral, uppercase letter, lowercase letter, and several Egyptian hieroglyphics in my password."

I turned back to face him. "How'd you find out so quickly?"

"I didn't," he confessed. "Carnegie did."

I shivered as every hair on my arm prickled. "I thought he was on vacation."

"You and me both. But he's got the security software on his phone, and he noticed the unusual activity for Gate A and called me."

"Don't you have to be in court?" I ventured.

"Carnegie will have to take care of it. I have bigger problems."

There was no anger in his voice, but the arch of his eyebrows was threatening enough. I swallowed.

He leaned against the worktable and continued. "So, I drive all the way back here to figure out why my door locks are magically not working. Lo and behold, you now have access to this entire wing—and I'm the one who gave you the permissions." He paused his explanation to take a sip of coffee. "Didn't take a genius to figure out what happened after that."

I was suddenly glad I'd taken the time to edit the change log and cover the evidence of the other hacking I'd done—not that it would do me any good now.

"Well, no harm done." Nic slammed his now-empty mug down on the table. "I was going to invite you to join the project anyway. How would you like a promotion?"

"What—you were?" I exclaimed.

"Of course. I was going to wait until Carnegie got back, so sadly my introductory PowerPoint isn't ready. I'll have to improvise with dramatic hand gestures." He demonstrated.

I just gaped at him. He sounded completely unaffected by the whole situation, and the nonchalance was terrifying. Yesterday, he'd threatened to *shoot* me when I defied his orders. Now I'd broken into his secret project, and he couldn't even be bothered to raise his voice.

"I don't understand," I managed.

He sighed. "Your lack of wit disturbs me. Do you really think I called you up here just to run a bunch of petty experiments?"

"You were pretty enthusiastic about those experiments yesterday," I reminded him.

"Let me spell it out: I was testing you. I had to make sure you were the man for the job."

"Which job?" But as soon as I said it, I knew.

No, I can't.

"Red Rain." He spread his hands. "I think you can give me Red Rain."

I won't. "You're insane," I shot back.

"Am I?" he returned, the question cool, suggestive.

It's not possible... But even as I tried to formulate a refusal, my analytical mind began running through the implications. Red Rain was fantastical, but it wasn't improbable. The difficulty would be in stabilizing the compound so that it wouldn't evaporate before it could be deployed. I thought of several common equations I could use as a starting point and imagined which chemicals I would employ for the base.

My hands went numb when I realized what was happening.

Nic was right. I was the man for the job.

He smiled. "Welcome to Project 74, Mr. Smyrna."

"No," I snapped, loud enough to put a period on my racing thoughts. "I won't do it."

Nic looked merely annoyed. "And what do you think happens if you refuse?"

"You shoot me." I folded my arms, trying and failing to mimic his disinterest.

He snorted. "Tempting, but it's too much paperwork. I'll just send you back to Earth and let Ambrose do it."

Relief washed over me. I would rather deal with a clumsy politician like Ambrose than gamble with a mad scientist like Nic. "Excellent," I chirped. "I'll pack my bags."

For once, my comeback seemed to stump Nic. He squinted like he didn't believe what he was hearing. "You *want* to face Ambrose?"

"Better him than you," I snapped.

He leaned back. "I find that vaguely offensive."

"You should. You're no better than they are." I let some of the holy terror into my voice, believing for one rabid moment that I could reach him. "I read the reports. If you use Red Rain, you'll be just as evil as the United."

If not worse.

He shrugged. "If I'm no better than they are, then why not me?"

I could think of several reasons, but he spoke before I could. "At least I won't kill you for something so pedantic as religion."

The arguments died on my tongue.

"You've met my sister. Does it look like I'm taking my job of anti-religion enforcer very seriously?"

I thought of the illegal Bibles saved on the server—and wondered.

His gaze searched me. "Did she tell you about our parents?"

She hadn't. I'd asked once, but when Cea had referred to them definitively in the past tense, I'd done the math and stopped asking.

There was no affection in Nic's voice as he relayed, "They used to be just like you. Religious, stubborn, and getting in all kinds of trouble for it. I tried to convince my dad to join me for his own safety, but he wouldn't."

I wonder why.

"Cea didn't want to either, but she was underage, so CPS ruled in my favor."

I'd never once considered that Cea had been *forced* to come to Mars, but suddenly, everything made wicked sense. Her anxiety, her fear of her brother, the way she avoided talking about the pet project—Cea did know what was going on. And she was terrified.

I clenched my fists.

"I think she still hates me for it," Nic muttered, sounding almost amused. "But when time was up and the government finally had enough of our parents, do you know where she was? Up here, safe, with me."

She's not safe. No one is safe here.

"I could do the same for you."

I looked up.

"That's who you're worried about, isn't it?" he said. His voice was authentic, without any hint of malice—almost as if he actually cared. "Your little sister. What's her name? Philadelphia?"

"Leave my sister out of this," I growled.

"You and I both know she's not safe down there," he continued. "It's only a matter of time."

My heart jammed its way up my throat when I realized he was right. It was only a matter of time before my family ended up like Nic's parents.

And I wouldn't be there to save them.

"If you work for me for a year, I can sign a paper verifying that you're an upstanding citizen, and you can take custody of her. She can come live here."

I sucked in a breath—too hard. "You'd do that for me?"

"With my fingers crossed behind my back, but yes."

Hope raced through me—and then vanished when I realized what he was suggesting. "And take her away from our father?" I snarled.

"It'll happen eventually. Better you than someone else."

I wanted to refute him but couldn't. If something happened to our father—if he got one too many marks on his file—my little sister would go into the system. The state would ship her off to a group home or worse, and I would never see her again.

Dad would understand. If he knew I could protect Philadelphia, he would tell me to take her in a heartbeat.

"And I'm sure I can come up with a job for your father," Nic added, as if reading my mind.

I met his eyes.

He stared back, honest and willing. "All I ask is that you work on the project. Help me build Red Rain, and your whole family can live here. They won't even have to sign the file."

My gaze drifted to the whiteboard, where the broken chemical equation was scrawled in blood. I could see what it was now; I could string the elements together in my mind and imagine how it would form a chain reaction of misery. Red Rain would bring death.

Or would it?

"It's too late for my family," Nic whispered from somewhere in my peripheral. For the first time since I'd met him, his voice carried a weight close to regret. "But it's not too late for yours."

I could save them.

The silence hung in the lab, growing heavier by the minute until it felt like there was no air left in the room. Nic finally moved and disturbed the fog.

"I don't expect an answer tonight. Get some dinner, sleep on it. We'll talk tomorrow."

He walked towards the door, and I knew I had no choice but to follow. He led me out of Wing 74, locked the gate behind us, and then left me alone in the hall.

I stood for a long time, staring at the metal numbers above the door and cycling the same question over and over and over.

Is it worth it?

7

The question followed me, nipping at my heels like a dog, as I trudged back to the cafeteria. I wasn't hungry, but I didn't know what else to do besides go through the motions. I swallowed a tasteless dinner, turned in my belated lab reports for the day, and took a shower. All the while, I scraped at my conscience, searching for any semblance of peace.

Was this the right thing to do? I didn't want to work for Nic. He was evil—but so was the United. If I refused, my family would stay in prison. If I agreed, I could buy them some tolerance. I didn't trust Nic, but he let his sister and several other residents practice their religion on base without interference. I had every reason to believe that if I gave him what he wanted, he'd live up to his end of the bargain and grant my family their freedom.

But what if he succeeded? What if Red Rain *was* possible? Nic hadn't exactly explained what he planned to do with the weapon, but the simulations I'd seen on the computer sent a clear message. Nic intended to go to war against the United—and if he had Red Rain, he would win.

Earth would burn if Nic got Red Rain, and it was only a matter of time before he acquired the formula. If I didn't give it to him, he'd find someone who would. But if I agreed to help him, I could move my family to Mars, where at least they'd be on the winning side of the war.

Of course, if I developed the formula, I'd be responsible for starting that war.

I stood and stared out the window of my dorm room at the unblinking stars. Wasn't war coming? The United would have to end, someday, somehow. Someone would have to challenge their bureaucratic wickedness. Why not me? Why not now? I didn't want to fight Earth—but wouldn't it be worth it to save my family?

And in the meantime, Nic was offering something the United never would: tolerance. If we moved to Mars, I could own a Bible without worrying that I might end up like my mother. My sister wouldn't have to go to school at gunpoint; my dad wouldn't have to spend any more nights in solitary. Most importantly, we could stay together. We wouldn't truly be free, not while Nic was in charge, but we'd have security.

A weight filled my lungs when I realized where I'd gone wrong. The United had offered "security" once, too. It had promised to end war, abolish poverty, and eradicate inequality. It had sold the people on a future free of borders—and the people had bought in, exchanging their personal identities for a piece of paper that granted them temporary relief.

If I helped Nic, I would be buying into the same lie. I would be passing the baton to the next dictator—only this regime would have the ability to destroy a planet. I knew that once Nic had power, he would sacrifice everything to keep it. And if he was willing to rain acid on Earth, there was no telling what he'd do to me and my family if we ever got in his way.

I pinched my eyes shut and leaned my forehead against the cold glass as fear rolled through me. I knew what I had to do.

It's not worth it.

Unfortunately, I knew refusing the job wouldn't be enough. I doubted Nic would be so stupid as to send me home—I knew too much. He'd kill me and then find another scientist to do the work.

I pushed away from the window and started pacing tight circles around the cramped room. There had to be another way. I wasn't just going to waltz into Nic's office, tell him off, and then let him use my body for target practice. I was going to find a way out of this—and bring him down with me.

I stiffened as resolve replaced the fear in my blood. *This* was why I had been sent to Mars: To stop Nic and save Earth from Red Rain.

But how? As much as I hated to admit it, alerting the United was the safest bet. If there was one thing the government loved to do, it was crush dissidents. If they found out about Red Rain, they would burn Nic at the stake and destroy his research.

Unfortunately, reaching someone would be easier said than done. Thanks to my unassimilated status, all my outgoing communication was censored. If I made an outbound call, Nic would know immediately. I couldn't leave the base, and it would take days for an email to reach someone, if the message was even approved.

I halted in the middle of the rug when I remembered there was one United official who was guaranteed to see my email.

Ambrose.

It was risky. Nic—and presumably Carnegie—had access to all my communication. If Nic realized what I'd done, he'd kill me and bury the evidence before investigators could get here. But Carnegie was gone at least until tomorrow, and Nic had been vocal about the fact that he didn't have time to censor my emails. I suspected he had his program set to auto-approve every message. If that was the case, I just might be able to get an email through before he noticed.

I strode to my desk and booted up my laptop. I opened my email and discovered a notification informing me that the message I'd sent my family a few days ago had been rejected. For once, I wasn't upset. The fact that Ambrose was so religious about his job just might be my saving grace.

It took me the better part of an hour to craft the message. I struggled to figure out a subject line that would catch Ambrose's attention while hopefully deferring Nic's. I then crammed as much detail as I could into the body of the message without using proper names—like "Red Rain" and "Wing 74"—that might trip the base's algorithm. If Nic caught on and locked down the wing before help arrived, I wanted them to know where to look.

I hesitated with my finger over the send button. There was no guarantee this would work. But if it did, I could save a planet *and* my family.

It would have been worth it.

I closed my eyes and took a minute to pray for favor. Then I hit send.

The status of the email changed from "draft" to "pending approval." I refreshed the dashboard, waiting. One minute passed, two. I refreshed the page again.

A bright green checkbox appeared as the status updated to "sent."

I praised God.

I went back to pacing and praying, forcing myself to stay awake. Every fifteen minutes, I stopped and refreshed the dashboard.

A few hours later, just before midnight, Ambrose opened my message.

✻

I didn't mean to sleep. I knew I should have stayed awake and kept guard, watching the server for any sign that Nic was onto me. I probably shouldn't even have been in my room, where I was cornered with only one way out.

But getting only one hour of sleep the night before was dulling my reactions. I don't even remember lying down.

All I remember was jerking awake when a sweaty hand clamped over my mouth.

I flung my eyes open but couldn't see anything around the flashing colors. Someone pressed their weight on me, pinning me down. I felt something sharp and metallic prick my neck—and then adrenaline kicked in.

I lunged, flinging my entire body into my attacker. They stumbled back and crashed into the nightstand. The lamp tumbled to the floor and shattered.

My attacker cursed. And that's when I recognized the voice.

Nic.

He stood between me and the open door, his frame weakly backlit by the security lighting in the hallway. I couldn't see his face in the shadows, but his shoulders were heaving.

A loaded syringe was in his hand.

Gingerly, I stood up.

He cursed again. "You just don't know how to follow orders, do you?"

My heart was in my throat, but I spoke around it. "Decided to start doing your job and censor my emails, I take it."

He twisted the syringe in his fingers. "You didn't even give my proposal any thought," he accused, sounding genuinely offended. "I told you to sleep on it."

I exhaled a prayer and inhaled a rush of courage. "I didn't need to sleep on it."

He growled—then seemed to change his mind. He slid the syringe back in the pocket of his lab coat. "Well, then let me help you get some rest."

He withdrew his hand from his pocket and pulled out an electric pistol, warmed up and ready to fire.

I instinctively put my hands up as my vision flashed black.

"Don't worry," he crooned before I could speak, "it's set on stun." And then he fired.

I shouted, but it was too late. All I registered was a flash of blue before a wall of pain hit me like a tidal wave. I tried to breathe but couldn't; all the air was sucked from my chest as my nerves iced over. The room spun, and I felt my legs give way.

I hit the ground. Then, darkness.

8

I woke in the same place I started: my bed.

It took several minutes for me to feel anything but residual pain. But as the static faded from my nerves and my vision cleared, I looked around and realized I was still in my dorm.

At least, the room was almost identical to my old dorm. The walls were painted the same gentle gray, and the sheets were made of the same industrial cotton. The bed, nightstand, and chair were all in the exact same position. Even my phone and laptop were charging on the desk, right where I left them.

The only difference was there were no windows. The only light came from the muted security lighting around the baseboards.

I sat up and fumbled for the bedside lamp. The sudden brightness set my head spinning again. I groaned and closed my eyes, waiting for my body to repossess itself.

The throbbing finally stopped. I opened my eyes and gave myself a once-over. I realized I felt fine except for an ache in my ribs.

I lifted my shirt and found a large bandage. I peeled back the edge and grimaced; a vicious red welt snaked across my chest, making it look like I'd been struck with a whip. The wound was peppered with festering black blisters that glistened under the slimy burn cream.

I shuddered and put the bandage back in place. I guess Nic wasn't kidding when he said his weapon was set on stun.

I cautiously stood up. When gravity behaved like I expected it to, I walked over to the desk and picked up my phone.

I was surprised to find that it was online. I didn't recognize the network name, but I had full bars.

I opened the web browser and searched for a random site. It immediately coughed up an error about "no internet access." I switched to my contacts and called my father; the only answer I got was a dial tone.

I grunted and slid the phone in my pocket. Whatever network I was connected to must be internal.

As soon as the thought crossed my mind, I knew where I was.

I ran to the door and flapped my hand over the sensor, expecting the worst—but it opened without complaint. I stepped out into the hall and glanced around. The corridor was brightly lit and lined with more dorm room doors, all closed. At the end of the hall to the left was a gate marked *D*. I walked over and tried to open it. I wasn't terribly surprised when it refused me.

I doubled back in the opposite direction and followed the hall around the corner. The next gate I found was *B*, and it let me through.

Suddenly, the place looked familiar. There was the cafeteria, Labs 2 and 3, the unfinished meeting room to the right of the entryway—and Gate A.

This was Wing 74.

I laid my hand on the sensor for Gate A. It screeched at me and flashed up that cruel red *X*.

My throat closed as the claustrophobia washed in. *You're trapped.*

"Of course, I removed your access to that door."

I whipped around. The door to Lab 1 was open, and Nic stood at one of the worktables, mixing a beaker of chemicals. He held up the glass and squinted at it. "I'm not stupid, although I realize my lax behavior for the past twenty-four hours has sent the opposite message."

I walked over to the lab. I stopped just inside the door and noted that they'd finished installing the new sensors—making me wonder how long I'd been out. "Have you been waiting here all day for me to come to?"

He snorted so hard his safety glasses fogged. "No. Believe it or not, I have other things to do besides watch your soap opera of a life."

The desire to punch him in the face tingled down my arms, but I knew I should get answers before I drew blood. "You found time to start censoring my emails, though," I prompted.

He yanked his gloves and safety glasses off. "Hardly. You'll be very pleased to know that it was a total surprise when your friends from the government called."

That information did delight me, although the pleasure was short-lived. "And what did you tell them?"

"What they needed to hear. That you were insubordinate and rebellious, and I suspected you were trying to take over the base. So, I sent you home to be prosecuted, and you died on the way."

The last statement was delivered with so little inflection that I was sure he must be exaggerating. "I'm sorry, what?"

He walked over to the sink and washed his hands. "I told you I would send you back to Earth, so I did." He raised his voice to be heard over the running water. "Only problem is, your private transit exploded shortly after takeoff. A design flaw in the hyperdrive, I'm told."

"What?" I screeched again. "You *faked* my death?" *He's joking. He has to be.*

"Look, I'm sorry if that's a lame way to go, but I needed a good story for why I didn't have a body. I was short on time, and thanks to your little stunt last night, I didn't get any sleep. A transit explosion was the best I could come up with." He shut the faucet off and shook his hands.

"You can't be serious," I scoffed. "No one will buy that story."

"The district warden did." Nic dried his hands on the hem of his lab coat, taking care to wipe each finger individually. "He already signed off on the incident form."

The world caved in around me, as if all the gravity in the room had suddenly crashed down on my shoulders. "You're serious," I repeated, this time quietly.

"I am." He finally turned to face me. All the pretense evaporated from his voice, leaving only malice. "You are officially deceased, and your file has been updated."

"Show me," I snarled.

Nic must have expected that response, because he merely gestured at the computer terminal. I stormed over and stabbed the screen.

My personnel file was loaded. At the top, in bloody red letters, was the word "DECEASED."

Just like my mom's file.

The room pitched as I processed the implications. I braced myself against the nearest worktable. "Then my family… thinks I'm dead."

"Depends on how fast the government processes the paperwork, but yes."

I thought of the anguished phone call, the rigid hopelessness in my father's voice as he told me my mother was gone, and almost vomited. "God, no," I whispered, and even I didn't know if that was a prayer or not.

Nic picked up a coffee mug. "This isn't how I wanted to start my week either, but here we are."

I gripped the table so hard the metal edge cut into my fingers. I couldn't let my family go through that pain a second time—I *wouldn't*. "You can't do this!" I slurred.

"Already did." He swirled the contents of his mug. "Welcome to Project 74, Mr. Smyrna."

Rage exploded in my chest. "I am *not* working for you!" *Does he really think I'm that stupid?*

"I'm not sure what part of 'you're dead' you didn't understand, but let me see if I can dumb this down." He crossed one arm over his chest and leaned against the sink. "You're legally dead. That means no one's looking for you, and you don't have a say in your employment anymore. The upside is I don't have to *literally* kill you, so take that into consideration."

I slammed my fist onto the table, jostling several beakers. I wasn't taking *anything* into consideration. There was no way I was going to stay locked in here like a lab rat while my family mourned my gruesome death. I had to get out of here. But how—

I stared at the glittering jars of chemicals on the table as the vibrations faded away. A quick scan of the labels told me I had the components for an explosion—a big one.

Slowly, I reached down and grabbed the table with both hands.

"Although if you flip that table, I guess it will be a moot point."

I jerked my head up.

Nic nursed his mug. "I already filled out the paperwork. If you want to make it official, that's your prerogative."

He was right. If I took him out, I was going with him.

"You also won't be seeing your family again."

I glared at him. He shrugged. "Just making sure you have all of the available data."

I looked back down at the table.

Is it worth it?

Nic didn't seem too concerned about my answer. He took a sip of coffee and waited, looking altogether bored by the prospect of death.

I struggled to find something, anything to say as my conviction wavered. *God, what do I do?*

The answer didn't come fast enough for Nic. "Are you going to flip that table?" he prodded. "Because if not, I've got a 10 o'clock meeting that should have been an email."

I let go.

He grunted and pushed away from the sink. "Look, since I already went to the trouble of forging your death, I'm willing to give you a second chance. Give me Red Rain, and as soon as the project is complete, you can leave."

"Really?" I meant the question to be incredulous, but it came out sounding weak, desperate.

"Why not?" he returned. "One undead scientist will be the least of the government's problems after I declare war."

He had a point. There would be no reason to hide anything once he revealed Red Rain.

Which was exactly why I couldn't give it to him, dead or not.

He strode to the door before I could find the words to argue. "In case you're wondering, I fixed the door permissions for this wing. You can go anywhere in Halls B, C, and E, but no further." He paused in the doorway and glanced back. "And yes, I also changed my password."

I stared at him. Vaguely, I wondered if he'd noticed that I'd also manually added myself to Gate 74. He might not, since I'd edited the change log after I altered the permissions. He may have just assumed I got through the door while it was already open.

Not that it mattered. I couldn't get to Gate 74 if I was stuck behind Gate A. *Unless…*

"Take the rest of the week off," Nic said. It wasn't a suggestion. "We'll talk on Monday." He stepped out into the hall and closed the door behind him.

I stared at the panel until the screen went dark. He was right; flipping over a random table of chemicals wasn't my smartest idea, especially if I wanted to live to see my family again.

But maybe there was another way out.

9

"What are you doing?"

I reacted, closing the program and slamming my laptop shut in a motion that was anything but casual. I whipped around—and realized who it was.

"Cea." I let out my breath and tried to put the brakes on my heart rate. *If it had been anybody else...*

She stood behind me in the darkened hall, her frame silhouetted by the dim security lighting. "What are you doing?" she repeated.

"Nothing," I fudged, even though it was an obvious lie. It was 2 in the morning, and I was kneeling in a back hallway of Wing 74 with my laptop wired into the security panel for a door. I was obviously doing something.

But for the first time since I'd met her, I wasn't going to tell Cea the truth. I didn't want her involved in case I failed. Nic would kill me—for real this time—if he found out what I was doing, and I wanted Cea to have culpable deniability.

Unfortunately for me, Cea wasn't gullible. I couldn't see her expression in the shadows, but I could hear the suspicion in her voice. "Were you trying to—"

"There's been power failures in this hallway," I cut her off. I spoke loudly for the benefit of any cameras that might be within range. "The lights keep flickering on and off. I couldn't sleep so... I decided to try my hand at it." I enunciated the words slowly, prompting her to take the bait.

She didn't. The doubt in her voice cracked, replaced by genuine fear. "Ephesus, no, please. Don't do this."

What else am I supposed to do? I couldn't stay here and give Nic the keys to the apocalypse. And since blowing up a lab would be a suicide run, I'd decided to try what I was best at: hacking.

Unfortunately, it had only taken a day of digging to prove what I already knew: Wing 74 was on an extremely secure local network. Not even Nic had remote access to it, and none of the servers connected to the rest of the base. The only universal systems I'd discovered so far were the environmental controls and the door locks.

Since tampering with the environmental controls was more dangerous than blowing up a lab, I decided to focus on the door locks. I'd been able to hack into Wing 74; surely, I could hack out. Nic had changed his password and added an extra layer of authentication that would make it extremely difficult for me to compromise his credentials, but there had to be another way. Unless he reset my permissions for the rest of the base, the main Gate 74 should still open for me. If I could figure out how to override the access on Gate A, I could get out. I'd been copying code from the sensor on a door to my laptop when Cea found me.

I took a deep breath and started unplugging my cables from the wall. "This doesn't involve you, Cea," I said, even though that was another lie. Nic was her brother; she was more involved than she wanted to admit. "Just walk away."

"No, Ephesus, please, listen to me. If Nic finds out…" She glanced behind her, as if expecting her brother to materialize out of the shadows.

She didn't have to finish the sentence; I was aware of the risks. "I know, and I don't care."

"But I do."

I stopped and looked up at her.

She knelt beside me. "Ephesus, if they find out what you're doing, they *will* kill you. Carnegie thinks Nic should have killed you already. If you try something, I'm not going to be able to convince him—"

"What do you mean?" I turned around to face her, then rephrased the question. "What did you do?"

She gnawed on her lip, as if realizing she'd gone too far. She weighed her choices and mercifully decided to let me in on her secret. "I talked Nic out of killing you."

I sat in silence as I struggled to reboot my universe around that revelation.

She fidgeted with her curls, her eyes still hidden in the darkness. "After you tried to alert the authorities, Carnegie wanted to kill you. They were going to do it, but I happened to hear them shouting in the hall and… I convinced Nic to forge the paperwork instead."

The fact that Cea had begged for my life—and Nic, the soulless scientist, had allowed it—shed new light on both characters. But even more disconcerting was the realization that Cea, the one person I cared about on this planet, had been involved in faking my death and lying to my family.

I struggled to find a center of gravity to fix my emotions on, then realized there was only one solution. I had to do what I'd promised I'd always do: Tell Cea the truth.

Jesus, help me.

I scooped both her hands in mine. "Thank you for saving me."

She just nodded, her gaze on the floor.

I pulled her closer. "But we both know that what Nic's doing isn't right."

She still didn't respond, and I felt her body tense—making me wonder if, in fact, she *didn't* know that.

"Cea." I tugged on her hand. "This is wrong. Red Rain is wrong. Tell me you agree."

"I…" she croaked, barely managing to get the first word out. "I don't… I don't know anymore."

I weighed my tone of voice. "You think it was right for him to kidnap me and lie to my family?"

"No," she snipped immediately, giving me some hope.

I rubbed her fingers. "Then you must know that the rest of this is wrong. Bombing Earth—that's not the solution."

"But what else can we do?" she cried, still refusing to concede.

I could think of several alternatives, but that was irrelevant. She knew better. She could have stopped her brother a dozen times before now, and she hadn't, even though she clearly hated what he was doing. Why? What could I say that would get her to see the truth about her brother—and herself?

"This isn't justice, Cea," I started. "What Nic's doing—it won't save people. It will kill them. It won't bring freedom, and it won't create tolerance for people like us. If Nic succeeds, the world will be worse off than it started—and we'll have helped him get there."

She didn't argue, her fingers limp in mine.

I leaned forward, allowing hope to build in my voice. "There is another way. We don't have to do this. *You* don't have to do this. You can help me get out of here."

I cupped her chin and forced her to look at me. She stared back, her eyes a swirling galaxy of confusion.

"Laodicea." I parsed her full name out. "This is not you."

She looked at me, and for a brief moment, I knew she saw what I saw.

And then she closed her eyes.

"Ephesus," she sighed. Her tone walled up even as tears threatened to seep through the cracks. "You don't understand."

But I did understand; she had no idea how well I understood what she was going through. "But I do—"

"No." She slapped a period on my arguments. "You don't understand what you're up against. You don't know what Nic's like. I do—I've lived with him for six years."

And that's exactly why you are the way you are.

I struggled with how to tell her that—how to make her see that her brother was controlling her. But she didn't give me a chance to find the words. "This isn't a joke to him. He's spent years building this project, and he's not going to let you ruin it."

As she talked, her words gained speed and venom. For an eerie moment, she sounded exactly like Nic.

She barreled on. "He's got weapons, and he will use them. He will kill you to protect his project, and I can't... I can't lose you!"

Her anger crumbled like a house of cards. All the fear and pain came pouring out as she collapsed in my arms, sobbing. "I can't lose you!" she screamed, her voice jagged like broken glass. "You're the only good thing in my life, and if Nic kills you, it will be my fault, and I can't, I can't..."

I pulled her into my lap and held her tightly, wishing I could suffocate the sound of her tears. Each shattered cry scraped at my soul and exposed the only emotion that could keep me in this place.

I love her.

"What... what do you want me to do?" I whispered in her ear.

"Please don't fight him," she cried, gasping out each word in between sobs. "Please, just give it time. We'll... we'll figure something out. Maybe... maybe it won't work. Maybe the project will fail. He has to let you go sometime. He promised you could come back when he's ready."

Nic had told me as much. In a bitter irony, I knew he would keep that promise. I could come back from the grave—if I kept my head down and let him have his way.

But if I fought him and lost, I wouldn't see my family *or* Cea again.

Cea sucked in air and struggled to control her tears. "Please, Ephesus. I can't lose you. Not like this. Promise me you won't push him."

I stared over her head at the long shadows in Wing 74—the prison I would be calling home if I agreed.

Is it worth it?

Cea wasn't comforted by my silence. She grabbed my shirt like I was the only thing keeping her head above water. "Please, Ephesus. Do it for me."

Those four words slammed into my conscience like nails on a coffin. I thought of my father, stripped down to a shell of a man after my mother's death, and knew what he would do, if he were here.

It's not worth it.

I closed my eyes, swallowed my heart, and made my decision. "Okay," I said, even as anguish welled up my throat. "I'll do it for you."

Cea relaxed, her dead weight sagging in my arms. "Thank you," she whispered, and fought down another sniff.

I held her to me, rocking us both as I waited for the world to settle around the terrifying promise I'd just made. "I'll wait," I repeated. "I'll wait for you."

10

Monday morning found me standing in front of Nic's office in Wing 74.

Habit carried me there more than willpower did. Every Monday for the last six months, I had presented myself at Nic's office to receive my assignments for the week.

Apparently, that's what I would be doing every Monday for the foreseeable future.

I reached for the call button, but regret weighed me down like a millstone. *Is this what I want?*

No, it wasn't. I'd spent all night wrestling with that ugly truth. As soon as Cea had gone to bed, leaving me alone in the dark hallway, the claustrophobia had swept back in like high tide. I couldn't give up. I couldn't become a prisoner. I couldn't—*wouldn't*—give Nic Red Rain.

But maybe... there was another option.

The idea had come to me just after dawn. I'd tossed and turned in my bed for at least two hours. When that failed, I'd taken to the halls. I'd wandered aimlessly, doubling back and forth until I was as lost outside as I was inside.

I kept walking until the daylight fluorescents turned on, signaling the end of curfew. That's when I surrendered and made my way back to the cafeteria in search of coffee.

The door to Lab 1 was open as I passed. I stared at the familiar cacophony of equipment and jarred chemicals—and wondered.

I tried to pray as I muddled my food in the abandoned cafeteria. The silence in the Spirit was worse than the silence in the halls. But then, I was almost more afraid of getting an answer.

I knew why I'd been sent to Mars. And I'd failed.

Finally, at precisely 9am, I went to find Nic. I'd been standing outside his door for at least five minutes, trying to find the courage to open it.

I took a deep breath, even though the gesture brought me neither oxygen nor peace. I'd made a promise to Cea and my sister. Until I got a better idea, this plan might be the only hope I had of living to see both of them again—without losing myself in the process.

Of course, it was all dependent on whether Nic was in a compromising mood this morning.

I cringed and pressed the call button.

He answered before the ring even finished. "Come in, Ephesus."

I swiped my hand over the panel and let myself in. He sat behind the desk, fingers tented in a gesture too fake to be threatening. His coffee cup was almost empty and he had no work open on his computer, making me wonder how long he'd been sitting there, waiting for me to knock.

I stared, suddenly questioning my resolve. *Is this the right thing to do?*

"When I said 'come in,' I meant walk *through* the door," Nic coached.

I grunted and stepped into the office, barely catching the door before it shut again.

I stopped in front of his desk. He gave me approximately thirty seconds to find my own words before he got bored. "Is there something you want to tell me?"

"Yeah." I sighed and centered my gravity on the one fact I knew to be true: "I won't work on Red Rain."

He blinked. He didn't seem surprised or angry. If anything, he was disappointed.

"Mondays," he groaned. He stretched across the desk to grab a carafe and started refilling his mug. "Ephesus, you know—"

I interrupted him before he could launch into his rehearsed threats. "But I will work on something else."

He froze, as if that idea had never occurred to him. He almost overfilled his mug and caught himself just in time.

I pressed on, building an argument for myself as much as for him. "I'm not going to work on Red Rain. I can't—won't—give you a weapon like that. But I know you have other projects. Assign me to something else. Surely, you have something that could use my expertise. My resume speaks for itself."

I coated the last sentence with pride and desperately hoped it was still true.

He still hadn't moved, brow furrowed in concentration. Slowly, he shifted his eyes from the wall to my face.

I returned his stare and made one final plea, using a language I knew he could translate: sarcasm.

"Unless all of your projects are apocalyptic doomsday devices."

He leaned back in his chair. I saw him studying me and knew he was weighing my life in the balance—deciding whether my free labor was worth the cost of keeping me alive.

After a long minute of silence, he bent over and opened a drawer. He withdrew an overstuffed manilla folder and tossed it on the desk. "Take your pick."

I picked up the folder and riffled through the papers. The folder was loaded with project concepts, some no more than fantastical doodles scribbled in the margins of scrap paper. There were, of course, plenty of gruesome weapons, but not everything was designed to kill. There were stun bombs, EMPs—and a computer virus.

I squinted at the notes that had clearly been written by someone with no programming experience—probably Nic. The concept was intriguing: A computer virus that could erase all data from any device it infected. It was far-fetched, to be sure, but if it was possible, this virus would be the ultimate weapon against a totalitarian government. You could collapse an entire infrastructure in minutes, all without firing a single shot.

It was the perfect project for someone like me.

I slammed the folder shut. "I'll have my proposal on your desk by Friday."

"Excellent," Nic said. He went back to his computer without another word.

I shoved the folder under my arm and turned to go. I made it to the doorway before the doubts caught up. "Do you mean it?" I called over my shoulder.

"Mean what?" he replied tiredly.

I glanced back. "That I can go home once you're ready to launch."

"Once I'm ready to launch, you can walk right out those doors. I'll even buy you a transit ticket." He didn't look up, but the honesty in his voice was cruel. "But I still think you'll want to bring your family up here."

I didn't want to admit that he was right. If Nic succeeded, Mars would be the only safe place in the galaxy.

I left, closing the door behind me.

I wandered back to Hall B, struggling to wade through the emptiness that settled over my soul like the dust on the horizon. My emotions felt frozen in place, like someone had cut the power line. Was this how my dad felt after Mom died?

I stopped in front of Gate A and looked up at the cold metal letter above the door. Had my family already gotten the call? The United was infamously slow when it came to paperwork, but Nic may have expedited the report to cover his tracks. And knowing Ambrose, this was a message he would be glad to deliver.

I winced. Ambrose would relay the news with all the tact of a police scanner. And how would my family react? I knew Dad would bury his feelings just like he had with Mom, putting on a blank face for my sister's benefit, but Philadelphia would have no such reservations. I remembered how she had sobbed into the phone after Mom died, begging me over and over to tell her it wasn't true even though we both knew it was.

Would she grieve that much for me? Or would it be easier for her to accept because I'd been away at college for so long?

The realization wormed its way into my stomach. Maybe it was for the best that I hadn't been home much over the past few years. Maybe my absence was a mercy all along.

Maybe she was better off without me.

I slammed my fist into the door. "I'm sorry, Philli."

I stood there, my forehead pressed to the cold metal, for several minutes. Then I took a deep breath, stuffed the emotion where I couldn't find it, and continued down the hall.

CROOK Q

RED RAIN #2

RACHEL NEWHOUSE

MAY 2076

1

I was graduating, and my teacher couldn't be more disappointed.

At most schools, graduating means you have succeeded. The virtual diploma signifies your achievement and grants you acceptance and opportunities in life. Teachers will do everything to ensure their students pass the final test.

For my class, however, graduating means we have failed. The virtual diploma demotes us to unteachable savages, and our teachers will do everything they can to ensure we drop out as soon as possible.

Today I graduate. Today I officially become a failure, an inmate who went through years of government schooling and still refused to sign the file. A Christian who survived hundreds of hours of conditioning, belittling, and propagandizing and still won't deny her religion.

Unassimilated. Reprobate. Criminal without any rights of citizenship.

Those were the terms my homeroom teacher hurled at me as he tried to dissuade me from accepting my diploma. It took all my willpower not to smile at him.

I was mildly surprised when he kept his tirade brief. I guess he finally understood that if I hadn't succumbed after being in his high school class for four years, another fifteen minutes of lecturing wouldn't make a difference.

"The principal will see you," he finished with a dismissive wave of his hand. He ungracefully flopped down in his chair and looked entirely fed-up, clearly wondering how all *his* years of schooling had condemned him to this moment.

I indulged in a cheeky smirk as I skipped out of the classroom and down the hall.

I composed myself as I came within sight of the principal's closed door. A pinch of fear wiped the smile off my face.

I desperately hoped the principal just wanted to talk to me. Sometimes being sent to the office meant someone else was here to see me—like Mrs. Nolan.

Banishing memories of the buttery voice from my head, I straightened my shoulders and rapped on the door.

"Come in, Philadelphia."

I offered up a quick prayer as I pushed the door open and stepped inside.

The principal was sitting with her hands folded on the desk, staring straight at me. I wondered how long she had been posed like that, waiting for my arrival.

"Decided to graduate, have you?" she declared.

She didn't sound as frustrated about it as my homeroom teacher—probably because she wasn't surprised.

"Yes, ma'am," I replied.

"Sit down."

I obeyed, and she shoved a tablet computer across the desk towards me. "You need to sign this file indicating that you have been offered remedial services through our institution and have voluntarily refused them." She tapped the legal document displayed on the screen. "You're acknowledging that, due to your unassimilated status at graduation, you will not be receiving a full high school diploma and are not entitled to the rights and privileges associated with one, although your academic record will still be posted to your file for future reference."

I thought it was delightfully ironic that I had to sign a file stating that I refused to sign the other file—the file that said I agreed to submit to United regulations as an assimilated citizen, which included denial of any and all religious, racial, and national identities. I suppose, since they couldn't get me to sign *that* file, they would get me to sign another, just for formality's sake.

I couldn't keep the smile off my face as I picked up the stylus and wrote my signature as tidily as possible.

The principal typed on her keyboard, and another legal document appeared on the tablet. "And this is your consent to be submitted for consideration in our Assisted Employment Program."

I squinted at the fine print on the document, waiting for her to explain before I signed.

"As an unassimilated citizen, you are eligible to be employed in select fields under the supervision of the United. Inclusion in the program also makes you eligible for opportunities for higher education and specialized training. Please note, however, that unassimilated citizens have far fewer opportunities for employment and education than citizens with full rights."

I looked up to find her gazing down her nose at me. I knew that was the final prod—one last opportunity to sign the file, join the Outside, and get a real job.

"No thank you, ma'am," I replied.

She didn't even blink. Turning back to her screen, she continued to recite: "If admitted, you will be assigned a job at the United's discretion. Your position and hours will be regulated by the government, and you will serve under the supervision of certified employers. You will not earn monetary compensation, but you may receive extra credit on your account for the purchase of necessary items, as deemed appropriate by the government based on your performance."

I went ahead and signed the file as she talked. I knew from experience that the employment program wasn't as horrible as she made it sound. Daddy had been working through the program since we had been contained, and he said it was like working a regular job, except that all your paychecks were in the form of credit to use through the United's approved catalog. But since the unassimilated could only own approved items anyway, that didn't seem like a huge sacrifice.

"Now, we need to fill out your application. Have you ever held any kind of job before?"

I set the stylus down and frowned at her. Didn't the United already have that information on file? They had been in complete control of my entire life for the past five years and had a pretty good hold on it before that; the government would know if I had ever held a job.

But I knew better than to answer sarcastically; Daddy said sarcasm wasn't respectful. "No, ma'am."

She nodded and clicked her mouse. "Have you had any special training for any particular fields?"

She ought to have known the answer to that, too—unassimilated citizens couldn't get any education except through the government. "No."

She clicked another box on the application. "And in what fields do your family members work?"

"My father and brother are scientists," I said, hoping she wouldn't ask me what branch of science. I could never keep them straight. "But I've never assisted them professionally," I added.

She nodded and typed a bit. "Well, you're a clean slate, then!"

I didn't like the perky tone of her voice. She made it sound like I was a mindless drone the United could program however they wanted.

Sadly, that was probably the case.

The principal submitted the application and spun her chair back around to face me. "You're all set! You're dismissed." She sounded so nonchalant about it, like a dental receptionist happily sending a patient off with clean teeth.

"Thank you, ma'am," I said as I rose. "And goodbye."

She didn't respond to that as I slipped out the door.

I slinked back to my classroom. I walked in to hear our teacher lecturing the few remaining unassimilated students about their duties as citizens, admonishing them not to be a deplorable failure like me. My friends Cami and Aid shared a gleeful glance and then winked in my direction.

As I sat down, the teacher wrinkled his nose at me like I was a species of pest that refused to be exterminated.

"Remember your former students, Mira and Stanyard. They accepted the wonderful opportunity the United offered them and went on to enjoy productive lives as free members of society," he said, staring at me as though he knew the comment would hurt me the most.

Cami and Aid stopped smirking. I hung my head and didn't look up again until the bell rang.

Lieutenant Clint picked us up from school in a United van. He was the new supervisor of our containment camp, having replaced Commander Ambrose who had been abruptly transferred a few months ago. One of the first things he had done upon taking control was to file a complaint that a full-size bus staffed with three armed guards was too much expense for the handful of elementary and high school students who still resided in our camp. Apparently his supervisors were more interested in saving money than they were in making a statement, because they had allowed him to start transporting us by himself in an unarmored van.

I liked the new arrangement. I had always enjoyed our brief sojourn across the Outside every day, but I enjoyed it even more now that our ride didn't turn heads, as the overgrown bus with the condemning words ASSIMILATION SERVICES splayed on the side had.

Being the oldest and therefore presumably bravest, I volunteered to sit shotgun next to the lieutenant. Normally he did not talk to us except to take a headcount or impart United announcements, but today he glanced at me as he navigated the harried late-afternoon traffic.

"Are you officially graduated now?"

"Yes," I replied, tensing and waiting to see if he would be scornful.

"Did you apply to the employment program?"

"Yes."

He nodded and turned back to face the road. "Good. I'll see what I can do to arrange for a job for you."

"Thank you," I said, mostly as a way to close the conversation. I wasn't sure how I felt about the lieutenant taking a personal interest in me. If Commander Ambrose had arranged a job for me, I would have been very wary that it was part of some scheme to get me—or my father—to sign. But Lieutenant Clint had so far shown himself to be more realistic, if not disinterested.

But why was he offering to arrange a job for me when he had not yet secured one for my father?

Maybe today was the day. Maybe today he had found something, and my father and brother would meet me at the door with excited smiles. Or better yet, maybe today they wouldn't be home to meet me at all, having gone for orientation at their new job.

That line of thought was the only way I could justify feeling disappointed when Daddy opened the door to meet me as I approached the step of our concrete home.

"Congratulations on your graduation," he said with a smile—the first proud smile I had received all day, and the only one I needed.

I beamed and hugged him. He returned the affection with a kiss on the top of my head.

"No news?" I prodded as we went inside.

He shook his head but retained a chipper tone. "Nothing today, but we have some new leads."

"What he means is none of the labs in this region want us, so Clint is going to ask all the labs in the neighboring districts," my brother Ephesus quipped from the kitchen. We came around the corner to find him sitting at the table, scowling at his laptop.

"Let's not talk about that tonight," Daddy said firmly. "We have a graduation to celebrate." He squeezed my shoulders, and I grinned.

Ephesus flashed a quick smile at me but kept talking. "I can't imagine the United will approve our transfer to another camp, though, and I desperately hope they'd consider commuting too much of an expense. We'd never be home if we had to commute that far."

I didn't like the idea of transferring, or of my only family being gone any more than they had to, but where else could they go for work? "Have you reapplied to the chemical research lab?" I said with weak hope. "Maybe now that the investigation with Dr. Nic has been completed, they'll let you back in…"

Ephesus was shaking his head despondently before I even finished.

"But the lab always wanted you before," I pouted, flopping down next to him. I thought of the long hours and special assignments that had kept them away so often in the past. What had changed?

"That was before we worked on Red Rain," Ephesus snapped.

"But it wasn't your project! You were… working against your will," I fumbled, not sure how to say it without offending him—or bringing back painful memories.

"Yeah, and I think that's the only reason they're not prosecuting me as an insurrectionist like they did with Nic." Ephesus crossed his arms and glanced away, but not before I saw the flicker of guilt in his eyes.

Daddy sat down with us at the table and touched Ephesus's shoulder. "We should just be grateful that no further trouble came from it."

Ephesus relaxed and unfolded his arms, but he didn't turn to look at us.

"But what about you?" I asked, looking imploringly at Daddy. "You didn't work on the project."

Daddy's expression was calm. "I was still involved."

Even though I knew he was being sensible, I couldn't copy his complacency. "But you were on the United's side! You turned Dr. Nic in."

"No, I didn't. You did."

I stared at him.

A proud smile lifted his lips as he said, "You're the one that stalled Dr. Nic and called the authorities."

"Yeah," Ephesus piped up, "you're the good little Unionist. If there's anyone they'll be fond of, it's you."

I glanced at him, and he winked. I couldn't bring myself to smile back, even though I knew he was teasing. I didn't like comparing myself to a compliant Unionist.

"Does that mean they'll probably give me a job?" I asked, turning back to Daddy. The United had never given me any recognition for turning in Dr. Nic except to question me briefly about the events. Was it possible my involvement had made a favorable mark on my file?

Daddy reached across the table and found my hand. "I don't know. But I do know that you'll be rewarded for your work one day, even if it isn't by the United." He squeezed my hand and smiled.

I smiled back.

We celebrated my graduation with the only thing we had available to us—food. Ephesus, unable to work with his beloved chemicals in the lab, had turned to mixing spices as a way to keep his hands busy. While I was gone at school, he had turned out a rather impressive dinner and a darling little frosted cake, which we enjoyed with much laughter around the table.

After dinner, Ephesus excused himself to his bedroom, gleefully saying he had to "wrap gifts." He returned with a cloth draped over his hand just as Daddy and I were finishing up the dishes. "Your graduation present, dear sister," he declared, yanking the cloth off with more flourish than was necessary. My beloved old reader lay on his palm.

Apprehension damped my excitement. "What did you do to it?"

"Look at your Bible study notes and see," he said with a grin.

Taking the warm device in my hands, I quickly navigated the menus to my study folder. My jumbled note documents had been replaced by an application titled "Study Reflections." With a sideways glance at my brother, I opened it and discovered all my notes had been filed and organized into one program.

"Now your study notes are all in one place, and you can search through them. And look, you can sort them by passage, or date, or keyword..." Unable to contain his excitement any longer, Ephesus leaned over my shoulder and pawed through options so rapidly I couldn't keep up with him.

"Wow," I managed, which was usually the only thing I could find to say in response to my brother's expert programming.

Knowing that was a genuine compliment coming from me, Ephesus stood back with a grin. "It's a gift from Cea and me."

"'Cea *and* me'?" I repeated, looking up at him.

He nodded eagerly. "We made it together," he said with a strange smile I didn't know how to interpret.

I glanced sideways at Daddy, but his face held no particular expression. "So *that's* what you two have been working on for the past few weeks," I edged casually, thinking of all the times I had come home to find Ephesus and Cea bent over the computer with their heads together. Sometimes she came in the evening and stayed unduly late into the night.

Ephesus shrugged. "Some of it," he said, and offered no further explanation.

"What else do you suppose they've been working on?" I asked Daddy after Ephesus had wandered off a little while later.

"I don't know," Daddy said with just the slightest hint of concern.

Glancing around to make sure Ephesus wasn't within earshot, I voiced the thought I had been harboring for several weeks. "Do you think there's... something going on between them?"

"I don't *think* so..." Daddy's eyebrows knotted together in a disgruntled expression I found more amusing than worrisome. I couldn't help but smile.

He shook his head and rose from the table. "Come on. I have something for you, too."

I followed him up to his bedroom. I stood back and watched while he got down on the floor—an action which looked surprisingly painful—and dragged something out from the farthest corner under the bed.

I involuntarily gasped when I recognized the small purple carry-on. *Mama's suitcase.*

Daddy hoisted it onto the bed with a sigh. "This was hers," he said, even though I didn't need to be told. "It was the suitcase she brought when we were first taken to the camp."

I remembered that day. It was almost six years ago now, when the soldiers forced us to pack and move into the concentration camps. One suitcase per person had been the rule. My mother had been the wisest packer; there were still things I regretted not bringing with me, and others I wish I had left behind.

Daddy unzipped the suitcase. "Everything that's left of hers I saved in here." I dared to step closer and look over his shoulder.

He opened the flap to reveal a meticulously-packed stack of clothes interspersed with other personal items. He took the objects out one by one, arranging them on the bed. I reached out to gingerly finger a floral skirt, remembering how it had looked fluttering around Mama's ankles as she danced about the kitchen.

"I want you to have everything." Daddy's voice was hushed, but his sudden declaration still startled me.

I turned to face him. "Me?"

His eyes were on the suitcase as he nodded. "Some of it might fit you now. Here, try these on." He pulled a pair of shoes from the bottom of the suitcase and set them on the floor.

It was a pair of black suede flats, simple yet pretty. I stared at them for a moment before I pulled my socks off and gingerly slipped my pale feet into them. They fit like Cinderella's glass slippers.

I looked up into my father's face. He was staring at me, but with an expression that made me wonder if he wasn't really seeing *me* anymore.

"You really do look just like her," he commented, more to himself than to me.

I waited. Surely he hadn't given me all this just because I could wear some of it.

He sighed, voice returning to normal. "I was going to save this for your eighteenth birthday, but I think today is a more appropriate occasion."

He looked into my face, eyes clearly focused on me now. "Today, in the eyes of the United, you became an adult. Up until now you have been under the authority of your parents and your teachers. We have raised you, and the United has attempted to train you. You have been given a foundation, tools, and beliefs with which to design your future."

He paused and laid his hands on my shoulders. "Now it is up to you to decide what to build."

I studied his expression, waiting.

"From today on, your identity is your own. Your circumstances do not dictate what path you choose for yourself. The United respects that and hopes you will use that opportunity to join their ranks."

I snorted. Daddy smiled, but he nudged my chin and forced me to look back up at him. "I, too, respect your freedom."

I frowned. Daddy's eyes were full of loving severity as he continued. "I have given you a choice just like the United has. I cannot make that choice for you. Even while you are living with me under my roof, I cannot force you to accept my beliefs as your own."

A pressure, a feeling close to grief, filled my heart, even though I couldn't explain why. The warmth in Daddy's voice only made it heavier. "It has given me great joy to see you follow God's path this far, to make the right choices even without my encouragement. But from here on out your choices will become even more important. Your life will no longer be regulated by school and the constant oversight of your teachers. You will have freedom and opportunities, and you will have to decide what to do with those opportunities. And one day..."

He hesitated, and pain clogged his voice and clouded his eyes. "And... there may be times when I am not with you. The decision is always yours, but the time may come when I am not even able to give you counsel. If you get a job, you will be out in the world, faced with temptation, and I won't be within arm's reach. There might not be anyone you can turn to."

The pressure in my heart started to make my eyes burn. Daddy's eyes were openly watering as he pulled me into a tight hug. "I love you, Philadelphia," he whispered in my ear. "I love the beautiful young lady you have become. But only you can decide to continue to grow up and become a strong woman like your mother."

Like my mother. How I wanted that! How I wanted to be brave like her, so brave that I would die for my beliefs—and so godly that everyone would remember me as a beacon of hope, a reminder of why we kept fighting.

I took a deep breath, suddenly finding the courage to voice a proposition I had been praying over for weeks. Standing back from my father, I declared in the most mature voice I could muster, "Daddy, I want to transmit."

His first reaction was a confused frown. "You already give copies to your friends. There isn't much else you can do from camp."

"I know, but if I get a job in the Outside, there could be an opportunity for me to transmit from work. Just like you used to. Just like… Mama." I looked up into his face.

He regarded me with a sad but dry expression, the expression of hardened grief. "You know your mother died for that," he said, which was what I had expected him to say.

"I know." I could still remember the exact words he'd said to me when I came home from school that day. His voice had been calculated, as if he had spent all day preparing what to say.

"They came to investigate charges of transmitting Bibles through the internet. She was brave and honest and wouldn't deny it." I'd interrupted his prepared speech and demanded to know what they'd done with her. He'd been forced to admit very plainly: *"They took her away. They said she'll be executed."*

I denied it. For three weeks I hotly insisted that she couldn't be dead. Daddy quietly insisted that she was. My young, grieved mind found a million ways to refute his statement. How would he know? They *said* they were going to execute her, but what if they didn't? What if she was pardoned? What if she escaped?

I spent three weeks waiting for her to come home, and three weeks begging the guards, my teachers, and even Commander Ambrose for information. I even went behind Daddy's back to ask the neighbors what they saw, hoping they would contradict my father's claim.

Everyone told me she was gone. But it wasn't until I found traces of blood splatter on the wall in the entryway that I truly believed it. There were only a few drops, as though my father had tried to clean it up, but I knew what it was.

Then I understood how my father could be so resigned. He had seen her die. They hadn't taken her away to be executed; they had executed her right then and there, shot her for confessing to transmitting.

After that I stopped asking questions about Mama's death. But I didn't stop transmitting, copying Bibles to give to my fellow inmates when they needed them. Father hadn't stopped either; he had continued to transmit onto the internet from work until he lost his job.

And I wanted to continue the task for him.

He sighed again, an almost wistful sigh this time. He stroked a hand through my hair, his eyes glazing over again. "I'll think about it," he said finally.

Shaking his head to clear the fog from his expression, he straightened and forcibly brightened his voice. "Now, you run along downstairs and have fun. It's your day to celebrate."

I scrunched my nose. Exactly what did he expect me to have fun doing?

A knowing smile tugged at his lips. "Go downstairs and you'll see."

I obeyed, giving him one last smile over my shoulder.

I skipped downstairs and nearly collided with my surprise—Cea, who was standing in the entryway talking to Ephesus.

"There's our special graduate!" she declared, turning around with a grin. "Congrats on surviving the system, girl."

I chuckled. "Thanks."

She brushed her cropped blond hair behind her ears. "How about a sleepover at my place?"

"A sleepover?" I repeated.

"Yeah! You know… Haven't you ever had a slumber party?"

I gave her a look that clearly said I hadn't.

She gaped at me. "You *are* sheltered."

Ephesus came to my defense. "It's not like there's anyone to party with around here. A sleepover isn't much of an event if it's just across the street."

"Oh, you're no fun." Cea flapped her hand at him. "Come on, grab your jammies and toothbrush. I've got Cami over too, and it will be just us girls all night."

I was still unsure about the whole concept. "Well, I have to ask my dad…" I turned around to find him standing at the bottom of the stairs, holding out my duffel.

"All packed," he said with an encouraging smile. "Have fun."

I couldn't help but laugh as I took the bag from him. "Guess I don't really have a choice, then."

"Nope!" Cea chirped, grabbing my arm. "Come on!" Then she dragged me out the door and across the street before I could even give my family a proper goodbye.

Cami was already there, in her pajamas and nearly buried in a pile of blankets and pillows in front of Cea's TV. "Philli!" she called in greeting, bouncing on a pillow. "Isn't it awesome? We're going to watch a movie! Cea even made popcorn!"

"A movie?" I said, trying to hide the skepticism in my voice. Ever since the United had started regulating media, most movies had ceased to be worth watching.

"Yup!" Cea said, clearly sharing Cami's excitement. "Ephesus finally figured out how to hack the DRM lock on the disc drive of my laptop so it can read old discs."

"Your laptop can play uncensored discs?" I cried with no small amount of alarm. "That's—"

"Yeah, and your reader has an illegal Bible on it," she returned.

I snapped my mouth shut.

She glanced back at me as she untangled some cords. "Your dad said it was okay."

At that, I relinquished and permitted myself to change into my pajamas and join Cami on the floor.

Cea hooked her laptop up to the TV and then showed us her secret collection. I didn't recognize any of the titles, so I let Cea pick which movie to watch. It ended up being a cute animated story about a clownfish who went on a great search to find his son after the little fish was caught by some divers. I liked it; the daddy fish reminded me of my father. He, too, would do anything to keep our little family together, now that Mama was gone.

Cami was practically out before the movie finished, but Cea and I were still wide awake. Cea let me look at the other discs before she put them away; I couldn't resist the urge to twirl one around my fingers and watch the dim light reflect off the shiny surface.

It had been a long time since I'd seen a disc. Grandpa used to have a whole collection of vintage movies on various disc formats, all in the original cases. I remembered sitting in front of the shelf, reading the titles and looking at the little pictures on the spines. I used to imagine what the story was about based on the picture. I hadn't seen any of Grandpa's movies; it was a collection and not for touching.

That just made it all the more tragic when the United had raided his house and seized his collection, snapping all the discs in half and tossing them in a dumpster.

"How did you smuggle these into camp?" I asked.

"Mostly in books," she replied, not looking up from her laptop screen. "I had more at the base. I brought them up before the United started collecting uncensored media, and they never bothered to come looking on Mars."

I nodded and tucked the disc carefully back in between the pages of an old dictionary. I fingered the spine for a moment before I dared to ask, "Have you heard anything about Nic yet?"

"No," was the sad reply. "Nothing."

"Have you asked the lieutenant if he can find out for you, since you're family?" I suggested hopefully.

Cea shook her head. "I did, and even he couldn't find any information. It's bizarre… It's not like it's confidential. It's like Nic never existed."

I frowned. Cea turned around to face me. "I can't find anything in the news, not even on the Martian sites, about his arrest. There's nothing linking him to the virus. His file hasn't had any new entries since he was granted governorship of the base. Even my file only says I was sentenced to containment because it was discovered I did not have the necessary paperwork and I refused to sign. That's a lie," she added rather indignantly. "I had signed the papers years ago. I chose to turn myself in."

My mind scrambled for the logic behind it all. "What about my file?"

She shook her head. "Nothing. Your file has remained unchanged since you were contained. The only thing that has been added is your school grades."

So they didn't make note of the fact that I turned Dr. Nic in. This upset me, but not because I wasn't getting credit for my good deed. There was something more, but I couldn't put my finger on it.

"Ephesus has hacked the camp's internet restrictions and managed to access some of the government criminal databases, but even he can't find any mentions of Nic or Red Rain or anything. It's like… it's like they don't want anyone to know what he did."

"Why?" I asked what we both were thinking. "Why wouldn't they make a big deal out of having arrested him? That's what they usually do with rebels. Make a spectacle out of their punishment to scare everyone else away from trying."

Cea shrugged. "The only thing I can think of is maybe they didn't want people to know how close he came to succeeding."

I nodded, shivering a little at the thought. Dr. Nic was good. He'd convinced the United—and my family—that my brother was dead, maintained a secret server of dangerous research, and released a virus that had wiped a significant chunk of Earth's data. And even if Red Rain remained unfinished, he had built a startling array of other weapons without ever arousing the United's suspicion.

Cea turned back to her computer. "Ephesus will keep digging. But we're beginning to wonder if they've given Nic a code name to conceal the records."

She resumed typing. I took my hair out of its ponytail and twisted it around my fingers, debating how hard I wanted to push the subject. "Is that what you two have been working on? Hacking around the internet controls?"

"Some of it," she replied without looking up. "We're working on a few other projects too."

"Like what?" I asked, hoping I sounded curious and not accusatory.

"Stuff for the future." She kept typing.

I wrinkled my nose in confusion. "The future?"

She finally looked at me. "You don't expect us to stay in this camp forever, do you?"

I stared at her. No one had ever asked me that, except the United, who excepted me to deny my religion and join their order.

And Stanyard and Mira. They had said something like that to me before they left. I remembered Mira's painful voice shrieking angrily at me. *We're not going to do it anymore! We're leaving! We're not going to keep living stuffed away in a little hole until they decide to kill us.*

I swallowed. What choice did we have but to stay here? The only other option was to join them.

Cea frowned. "There are other options, Phil." Her voice was condescending. "We don't have to sit quietly here and play their game. Ephesus and I won't."

I wasn't sure how to respond to that. Thankfully she didn't expect an answer and returned to her typing.

I buried my chin in my pillow, trying to fight the dread that filled my stomach. I wasn't even sure what was upsetting me. Maybe it was the accusation in Cea's voice. Maybe it was my worry over what other "options" she and Ephesus might be working on.

What did she expect us to do? Staying in the camp meant we got to keep practicing our religion without interference. Maybe it wouldn't last, but in the meantime, where else could we go? Breaking out of the camp would put us on the run and in danger of our lives, unless we intended to fight back to maintain our independence—like Dr. Nic had.

And I didn't like that idea at all.

3

The knock came during dinner.

I think all three of us jumped. It was rare for us to get visitors, especially late at night. The fact that they were knocking—pounding, more like it—rather than using our obnoxious doorbell made it even stranger. We were so surprised that all three of us stood up and went to see who it was.

Ephesus answered the door. He had barely pulled it open before three armed guards shoved their way inside.

"May I help you?" Ephesus yelped indignantly, stumbling back.

The soldiers spread themselves in the entryway and halted. "We have orders to take two unassimilated citizens into special custody," the captain of the group declared.

I gasped, a sound which seemed gratingly loud in the sudden silence. For a moment it seemed the only thing moving in the entire room was my panicked heart.

Special custody... two unassimilated...

"What?" Ephesus yelled, more as an exclamation of shock than a question.

Dear God, no.

The captain ignored him. He scanned the room, his eyes coming to rest just above my head. I knew in my heart that he was looking at Daddy, who was standing behind me.

Please no...

I didn't have time to finish the prayer before the captain confirmed my fears. "You're under arrest."

God, no! Please don't take my father and brother away. Not again!

I whipped around to look at Daddy, silently begging him to tell me it wasn't true. Shock and fear briefly flashed across his eyes, but he let it out with a sigh. Straightening, he said with brave calmness, "Will you allow us to gather a few belongings first?"

The captain nodded. "Ten minutes."

Daddy turned towards the stairs. I yearned to cry out after him, but I couldn't find any words.

Ephesus stayed where he was and sputtered, "What is the meaning of this?"

The captain finally looked at him. "The reasons for her arrest are confidential."

Silence again iced over the room. This time my heart stopped altogether.

"Her?" Ephesus repeated.

Daddy stopped at the bottom of the stairs and glanced back.

"Yes," the captain said slowly, as if he didn't understand what the confusion was. "She's the one under arrest."

The statement was accompanied by a flick of his hand at me.

I gasped again, the sound catching in my throat like I was gagging. I slapped my hand over my mouth, afraid a worse sound would escape.

The captain glared at me. "Ten minutes. Hurry up."

Ephesus shook himself and resumed sputtering. "But what did she do?"

"That's confidential," the captain repeated with condescending patience.

Ephesus continued to argue, but I couldn't understand what he was saying. My head spun. *What... why... where...* I couldn't even formulate a complete question.

"Daddy," I managed. I turned towards him, groping for an explanation.

Wordlessly he grabbed my hand and hauled me up the stairs. He pulled me into my room and shut the door behind us.

Turning to me, he started talking swiftly but clearly. "I don't know what they want you for, but we'll find out. Don't worry—special custody doesn't mean anything."

My head and heart were throbbing too much for me to obey the admonition not to worry, but I did my best to focus on his instructions around the whirlwind.

He strode to the closet and fetched Mama's purple suitcase. I wished he had grabbed my old duffel instead—something about using Mama's suitcase made it seem more serious, more final—as if we were both silently agreeing that this was something I wouldn't come back from. But I couldn't find the words to voice my pathetic fears.

He started moving methodically around the room, scooping items into the case with purpose. "It just means something's come up that the United wants to look into. That's how they are—if there's any suspicion, they take people into special custody until they can investigate. They probably just want to talk to you. Just answer their questions honestly and it will be okay. You've already been contained for being unassimilated; you can't have done anything that will warrant a punishment worse than a warning and getting sent back here."

"But I haven't done anything at all!" I cried, some of my panicked thoughts escaping. "They haven't even given me a job yet!"

He glanced back at me as he moved into the Jack-and-Jill bathroom. "I know. But that probably means there's nothing wrong and they'll send you back here."

As much as I tried to absorb his calm demeanor, I did not find words such as "probably" to be comforting. What if there was something wrong? Something I couldn't deny?

"Hopefully it won't take long." At this, even Daddy's confidence wavered; I could hear it in his voice. He looked down and shoveled the contents of my bathroom drawer into the bag. "But if there's a wait, you'll have your belongings. Your belongings will have to be inspected by security, though. You'll speed up the process if you don't take any suspicious items—no electronics."

I involuntarily glanced towards my reader, which lay on the nightstand. *But my Bible…*

"Don't worry," he said again, and I still couldn't take it to heart. "It's not like being put in prison. You'll probably be taken to something like an apartment building where you'll wait until the local officials can see you."

Being confined in solitude, ripped from my family without any explanation, sounded a lot like prison to me.

"This should tide you over." He zipped the suitcase shut and dropped it on the bed, then walked over to me.

I looked up at him, searching for something more. Some reassurance, some admonition, some token of wisdom. Something that would give me his confidence, his peace. He had been in this kind of situation before; he knew exactly what to say, what to do, when to bend, and when to stand firm. I wanted to be like him. I wanted to do the right thing—so that no one would get hurt.

Daddy suddenly seemed at a loss for words too. He gazed at me for a moment, the kind of loving stare that indicated he was studying me, pondering thoughts that only fathers know.

I wanted to say goodbye—I wanted him to say goodbye—but I knew that neither of us could come up with the words.

Finally, Daddy scooped my jacket off my desk chair and held it up. I numbly slid into it. It did nothing to warm the chill tingling down my arms.

"Behave. Be polite." Daddy absentmindedly zipped my coat as he talked. "Obey the rules. Don't cause trouble."

I swallowed. I remembered the last time he had recited that exact same list—when we were standing on the porch waiting for Commander Ambrose to take Daddy to the airport. The day Daddy was supposed to be flying to Mars on business, forced to leave me behind. The day I was supposed to go live with the Nolans, not knowing if I would ever see my father again.

Tears suddenly shot to my eyes.

"Oh, Philli." Daddy reached out and pulled me into a hug. I tried to dam the tears, to trust, to pray, but the brokenhearted tone of his voice only made me panic more. I sobbed and grabbed him around the neck.

"Oh, Philadelphia," he said again. "I'm sorry." He kissed my cheek and stroked my hair, pressing my face against his chest. I let myself sob, tears and prayers spilling freely.

Suddenly I felt him stiffen, and he jerked away. "Come on."

His tone had changed to one of hard determination. I stared in confusion as he grabbed my arm with one hand and my bag with the other. He dragged me out of the room and down the stairs. I stumbled along behind, sniffing to swallow the tears.

Ephesus's urgent voice reached us from the front room. "Can't you tell us anything, off the record?"

"Nothing happens off the record," was the blunt reply.

"But she hasn't done anything wrong! She's always been compliant."

With a wince, I realized that he wasn't being completely truthful. I wasn't violent, but I wasn't always compliant. I was a transmitter. I copied illegal Bibles. Was that what they wanted me for? Had Commander Clint decided to crack down on my distribution and charge me with transmitting?

Were they going to execute me just like they'd done with Mama?

Ephesus's voice was getting dangerously heated, like a chemical reaction about to explode. "She's the one that told you about Red Rain! She could have let Nic scald you to death, but she decided to turn him in even though she knew you'd send her back to a concentration camp! How can you say—"

"Sirs," my father interrupted, stepping into the room.

The group of soldiers turned their faces and guns towards us. The captain nodded and beckoned at me, but Daddy stepped between us.

"Please," he said, "allow me to accompany her."

I stiffened, hope sending a jolt up my spine. I squeezed Daddy's hand, praying desperately.

The captain drew his eyebrows together, as if unsure what to make of that request. Daddy continued, "I will gladly join her wherever she is being sent."

Ephesus glanced between us, then raised his hand. "I could go also."

I shook my head at him. As much as I didn't want to choose between them, this was a time I needed Daddy.

The captain shook his head. "That's against regulations. Come on." He reached towards me.

Daddy shoved me further behind him. "Please, she's a minor." Daddy's voice was rising in panic, and his words became less formal. "Whatever you want her for, I'll come with her. I will take whatever punishment—"

"No." The captain's voice took on a commanding edge I knew all too well. "She's the one under arrest, not you."

It's his assignment, not yours. Regulations. Another sob escaped my throat unbidden.

Suddenly I was in Daddy's arms again. He kissed me and muttered quickly in my ear, "I love you. Remember me. Remember your mother. Remember God."

The blood was pounding in my ears so hard I could barely hear him. I opened my arms to hug him, but someone else grabbed my hand. A soldier yanked me so fast I stumbled backwards. Another gripped my other arm, hauled me up, and shoved me towards the door.

"Philli!" Ephesus cried.

I turned towards him, but there were soldiers on all sides of me. I opened my mouth to call out to him, but the soldiers pushed me forward again. I tripped on the threshold and crashed down the front steps. I yelled as my leg scraped on the concrete. I landed on my knees on the sidewalk.

"Careful!" someone barked.

Soldiers tromped down the steps. I sensed them around me, but I couldn't move. I just knelt there, pain and blood coursing from my torn shin.

An arm appeared in my peripheral vision. I looked up to see a guard bending over me with his hand outstretched. As much as I didn't want to go with him, instinct made me reach out and accept his offer of help.

He pulled me to my feet and straightened into the light of the streetlamp, allowing me to make out his face. He was young, not that much older or taller than myself, with a tidy red-orange goatee. "Are you all right?" he said in a bright voice, not seeming at all impatient.

"Yeah," I said. It was a lie, I realized as I put pressure on my scraped leg, but I appreciated the kind question. "Thank you."

He nodded and, still holding onto my arm, guided me towards the windowless van idling on the street. I was glad to be walking rather than dragged, so I went willingly.

He was just about to help me step up into the back of the van when the captain approached. "Blindfold her," he ordered without ceremony.

"But why?" I cried, all the terror resurging in my mind.

"The general doesn't want her and the other prisoner to meet," the captain said, more to the guard holding my arm than to me. He held up a strip of black cloth.

I shied. The young guard holding my arm didn't move, but he didn't reach out to take the cloth, either. "In that case, sir, perhaps she should sit up with us in the cab, and the other can ride in the back. Then they won't hear each other's voices."

I turned and looked back at him in surprise. Was he showing me mercy?

The captain considered that for a moment, then retracted his hand and put the cloth in his pocket. "Fine. But keep a gun trained on her."

He turned and walked across the street. I tried to see which house he was going to, but my escort tugged on my arm and pulled me around to the front of the van. "This way."

He opened the door and spotted me while I climbed into the back seat of the cab. There was no one else in the cab except for a surly driver who spared only two seconds to glance over his shoulder at me before returning his attention to his phone.

The young guard hopped into the front seat beside him with the careless agility of a teenager climbing into his friend's pickup for a joyride. Shutting the door, he tossed his gun, which he evidently had no intention of pointing at me, on the dashboard and propped his boots up beside it.

Leaning back against the seat, he turned his head to face me. "Jayde," he offered. "Is Philli short for something?"

"Philadelphia," I replied.

"That's a long one," he said with an amused puff of breath. I just waited, wondering how far his friendliness would go.

He propped his arm on the back of the seat. "So what are you in for?"

I swallowed. "I don't know…"

"I mean, here in a camp," he quickly clarified. "Are you in for religious reasons?"

"Oh, yes," I said, relieved at the change of conversation.

He nodded. "Thought so. This place is too low security for anything else. But don't tell anyone I told you that; they'll accuse me of helping you escape." He guffawed and jabbed the driver in the shoulder. The driver only responded with an eye roll.

I stared at him, not at all sure what to make of the conversation. If our camp was low security, what did high security look like? Were they taking me somewhere with higher security? Why? I had never tried to escape.

"So what religion are you?" he continued his casual query.

"Christian," I said, wondering what that term would mean to him.

"Figures," he responded shortly. I couldn't tell if he sounded annoyed, bored, or completely disinterested.

Before I could ask what he meant by that, shouting outside interrupted us. The van rocked roughly.

Jayde turned around in his seat and picked up his gun. "Guess they got the other one."

I winced, hoping the other prisoner wasn't being treated roughly. Who were they? There weren't that many people left in camp. Who could it be? What had they done? Why didn't the officials want us to meet each other? Did they suspect us of being in crime together?

An order was shouted outside, and Jayde buckled his seatbelt. "Let's go," he said.

The driver reluctantly pocketed his device and started the engine. I hastily found my seatbelt and buckled it.

The van lurched to an ungraceful start and lumbered out of the camp. I scooted up to the window and watched, taking in the scenery like I had done while riding to and from school. It had been a long time since I had seen the city at night, and gazing in childlike wonder at the passing lights distracted me from the fact that we were driving *away* from camp and not towards it.

It did not take long for us to reach our destination. Daddy was right—the place did look like an apartment building. It was an altogether boring structure that blended in perfectly with the other shapeless high rises on the street. The only visible sign was the generic United seal with the words "Office No. 32.8" emblazoned in metal above the door.

Despite the unassuming appearance of the building, I still caught myself swallowing repeatedly in fear as we drove down the ramp into the parking garage below.

As soon as we stopped, Jayde jumped out and opened the door for me. I stepped down and looked towards the back of the van, hoping to catch a glance of the other prisoner.

Jayde seemed to have been ordered to prevent exactly that, however, and pulled me away at such an angle to keep me from being able to see in the back of the van.

He led me to an elevator which took us up an alarming number of floors. I began to feel dizzy, though whether from the height or the dread accumulating in my mind, I couldn't tell.

Finally the elevator stopped. The doors opened to reveal a long, sterile, gray-painted hall, lined further than I could see with numbered doors.

Hefty body scanners stood guard on either side of the elevator doors. Jayde instructed me to walk through them slowly. After a second of irate buzzing, the scanners flashed a bright, welcoming green.

I found the irony of that absolutely sickening.

Jayde led me to the third door on the right. He opened it with a flick of his fingers across the security panel.

The room beyond was dark, but thankfully Jayde stepped in ahead of me and turned the lights on. *It's just like an apartment. Nothing scary about a dorm room,* I reminded myself. Taking a deep breath, I willingly stepped into the room.

My heart sank at the sight of it. The room was small, and worse, it was bare. It had a low cot, a rickety card table with two chairs, a narrow bathroom, and an even narrower locker. There were no windows, and everything was made out of cold, hard metal.

Metal. So much metal.

"I can't bring your baggage up tonight. It has to be approved by security," Jayde said from behind me, sounding apologetic.

My heart sank even further.

"If you need anything, press the star button and it will alert a guard."

I didn't answer. Jayde didn't seem to expect a response and stepped back, closing the door.

The familiar beep and *woosh* of air struck my nerves. I spun around and stared at the panel by the door. It looked exactly like the technology they'd had in the base on Mars—technology I had been able to circumvent.

I ran to the door and pressed my hand over the sensor.

The hideous beep pierced my ears, making them ring.

Access denied.

I stumbled backwards and tripped over the cot. Sitting down hard, I stared at the red *X* until it faded away.

The ringing in my ears subsided, leaving me completely alone in the silence. I dropped back on the cot and pulled my knees up. And then I allowed myself to cry.

4

A buzzing stirred me from my sleep. I laid still for a moment, blinking the haze out of my eyes. The lights were on full blast. Why was I sleeping with the lights on?

The buzzing continued erratically, like someone was ringing a doorbell repeatedly. I lifted my head and looked around, then remembered. It *was* a doorbell—the doorbell to my tiny cell.

I groaned and wondered if prisoners were allowed to ignore their doorbells. Figuring I'd better not push boundaries on the first day, I dragged myself out of bed.

I yelped as soon as I stood up. My right leg burned. I lifted my skirt and realized my shin was clotted with a delightfully large scab. I'd forgotten about scraping my leg on the concrete last night.

Sighing, I stepped forward—and tripped over the chair. I crashed into the door, narrowly managing to miss hitting buttons on the control panel. I growled, feeling more annoyed at my own clumsiness than anything else.

Shaking my head to clear it, I reached up and pushed the call button. "Who is it?"

"Jayde," was the answer from a male voice. Then, as if realizing that name meant nothing to me, he added, "The guard from last night."

After a moment's thought, I was able to recall his face, and while I was glad it was him and not some surly guard who didn't even know my name, I still wasn't sure I was up for another friendly chat with him. I leaned my head against the door, trying to think of a way to ask what he wanted without being rude. Daddy said be polite, and I didn't want to get in trouble for being snappy.

Thankfully, Jayde volunteered the information. "I came to see if you needed anything."

I straightened. "What time is it?"

"Umm…" There was a pause. "8:30," he answered finally. "Can I get you anything?"

"Umm…" It was my turn to stall. I glanced around the room, trying to decide what I even wanted. "Some breakfast would be nice," I decided.

"It's already on its way. Anything else?"

"Not really…" I shifted my weight and winced as the tender skin on my leg stretched. "Actually, I think I'm going to need a bandage for my leg."

"Oh, they forgot to look at that last night?" He let out a low whistle. I wondered if someone was going to get in trouble for the oversight. "I'll get the nurse. Be right back."

I would have thanked him, but his footsteps were already pounding down the hall. I shut off the call and turned back to the room. I took a minute to straighten the blanket on the cot and tidy my appearance as best I could without my toiletries. I didn't want to look like a prisoner that had been sleeping in the king's dungeon for a week. Hopefully the officers would approve my baggage soon.

My doorbell buzzed ten minutes later. I went to open it, then remembered I couldn't. Cringing, I pressed the call button and said, "Come in."

I backed out of the way as the door opened. Jayde appeared with a breakfast tray in one hand and my suitcase in the other. "Here's your breakfast." He set the tray down on the table. "And your baggage has been cleared. Everything was fine." He tossed my bag on the chair.

"Thank you," I said, mentally directing the same at God.

A second set of footsteps approached the open door. "Here's the nurse," Jayde said.

Before I could turn, a voice I remembered all too clearly rang out.

"Oh, Philadelphia, sweetheart!"

I wasn't sure whether to cringe or gasp in shock. I managed to turn my head and look at her.

Mrs. Nolan looked exactly like she had on the day she'd come to visit me at school, wanting me to come live with her. Her hair was cropped and perfectly styled, and her cheeks were painted a doll-like shade of pink. The only difference was that she was wearing a prim white uniform with a shiny name badge instead of casual jeans and a t-shirt.

She looked almost as shocked as I felt. She stared at me for several minutes like I was a ghost from her past. Then all at once she started gushing, voice as buttery as ever.

"Oh, you poor thing! Whatever are you doing here? Did they hurt you? Oh, sweetheart." She dropped her supply bag and bustled towards me. I involuntarily stepped back.

Jayde glanced between us. "Do you need any assistance?" he asked Mrs. Nolan.

"Oh no, she won't be any trouble at all. She's such a sweet and polite dear, aren't you?" Mrs. Nolan crooned.

Jayde arched his eyebrows and looked at me. I almost begged him to stay behind for *my* sake.

Smirking with obvious amusement, Jayde turned to go. "Call if you need anything," he said as he shut the door behind him.

I turned around just in time to see Mrs. Nolan come at me with a hug. "Oh darling, it's so good to see you again."

I couldn't return the sentiment, but I didn't refuse her hug. She squeezed me and then held me at arm's length. "Are you all right? What did they do to you?"

"I'm fine, ma'am, really," I said, hoping my sincerity would deter any further mothering. "I just tripped and scraped my leg on the way in." I lifted my skirt to show her.

She gasped. "Oh, look at that… Sit down." Her voice suddenly changed to one of authority, which I found much more comforting than her squeal. I obeyed, and she fetched her medical bag from the floor.

"We'll get that cleaned up." She pulled a sterile wipe out of her bag and started cleaning the wound. I was surprised at how swiftly and gently her hands worked.

She continued to interrogate me as she treated my injury, but her voice was less urgent than before. "How did you get here, sweetheart?"

"They took me last night," I answered. How else did one get into prison?

"What did you do?" She glanced up at me sideways as she fished some antibiotic cream out of her bag.

I blinked a few times. "I… don't know," I managed finally. "They wouldn't tell me. They just said I was under arrest and had to be taken into special custody."

Mrs. Nolan pouted. "That's just like them, the beasts. Terrifying innocent little girls for no reason."

I watched her rub the cream onto my leg. I wasn't going to tell her that one of the most terrifying things the United had ever done was try to send me to live with her.

She started wrapping my leg with a white bandage. "You don't deserve this. You'd never hurt anybody. I bet this is all a big mistake and it will be cleared up soon."

I had to admit that I found her words somewhat comforting. The United had a "shoot first, ask questions later" policy when it came to arresting people. There was a chance they were acting on suspicions and would soon figure out I wasn't a threat. But I was already in a concentration camp—what would drive them to put me under special custody?

As soon as Mrs. Nolan finished securing the bandage, her motherly fussing returned, and she took it upon herself to get me cleaned up. She made me wash my face, brush my teeth, style my hair, and change into an outfit she selected from my baggage. All the while she took the liberty of putting my belongings away in the little locker of my cell. I didn't like her interference at all, but I wasn't sure I was in a position to refuse her. I knew Daddy would want me to be lenient, at any rate.

She had just finished tidying the room to her satisfaction when the doorbell rang again. She opened it to reveal Jayde and two other guards, all armed.

"The captain has summoned you," he said, leaning over to look at me around Mrs. Nolan's plump frame.

Mixed fear and hope fluttered through my stomach. Maybe they would finally tell me what I had done wrong.

I stepped forward, but Mrs. Nolan blocked the doorway. "Oh heavens!" she blustered. I noted that was a rather odd expression for an Outsider, who was supposed to have no religion, to use. "You didn't even let the poor girl finish her breakfast."

I glanced back at the untouched meal and sighed.

Jayde scrunched his brow in a look that said, *"What have you been doing all this time?"* I shrugged helplessly.

Jayde shook his head. "He will see her now," he said firmly.

I nodded in consent, but Mrs. Nolan wagged her head, making her cropped hair flop about. "Don't give me that. You already terrorized the poor girl by dragging her here in the middle of the night—let her have something to eat! She's not going anywhere."

"He will see her—" Jayde started to repeat.

"No, she needs to eat. Doctor's orders." Mrs. Nolan flapped her hands at him. "You tell him I said that."

I gazed at her in wonder. I'd never seen an Outsider stand up to a soldier like that—and I'd never had anyone defend me in front of the United.

For the first time in my life, I thanked God for letting Mrs. Nolan take an interest in me.

To my surprise, Jayde backed away. "I'll tell him," he said, almost condescendingly. I assumed that meant he was going to blame Mrs. Nolan and let her face off with the captain. I swallowed and hoped neither of us was going to get in trouble for it.

As soon as the guards walked away, Mrs. Nolan turned back to me. "Never mind them. Now you eat up, every last bite. You need your strength."

"Yes, ma'am," I said with grateful obedience.

She beamed at me with her porcelain smile. "I wish I could stay, dear, but I need to go check on someone else. I think they came in with you last night— poor thing."

I stiffened. "Do you know who it is?"

"You haven't met them?" she said with an innocent frown, but thankfully she didn't wait for an answer. "I don't know, but I'm going to go find out!" She grinned and scooped up her medical bag.

A thought raced through my mind. I swallowed and ventured, "Will you… come back and visit me later?"

Her expression melted into one of deplorable pity. "Of course, darling."

She wrapped me in another hug. I forced myself to return it, feeling wickedly manipulative.

After Mrs. Nolan left, I sat down and ate hastily. I didn't want to bank on the captain listening to Mrs. Nolan and waiting for me to finish.

Surprisingly, Mrs. Nolan's orders were heeded, and the guards didn't come back for fifteen minutes. By that time, though, I had begun to regret eating before going to see the captain—the butterflies in my stomach made it difficult to even swallow.

Jayde led the way, with the other two guards following behind me. I tried to pretend that they weren't there and instead focused on Jayde, who walked with a lax confidence that I found somewhat comforting.

Jayde took us back to the elevator and up several more flights to a floor that looked vastly different than the one my cell was on. Instead of bland halls that looked horribly institutional, this floor was classy. It had wood-paneled walls, plush carpet, and potted plants interspersed between the gold-numbered doors. The wall on the right was entirely glass, allowing a brilliant view of the city. I squinted in the sudden onslaught of unfiltered daylight.

Jayde walked up to a door halfway down the hall and paged the occupants. Without waiting for a response, he said, "I've brought her, sir."

For an answer, the door beeped and opened. I found that welcome somewhat unsettling.

I took a gulp of air, trying one last time to swallow my queasiness, and bravely strode into the room without being bidden. Jayde followed me inside.

It was an unbelievably posh office. It was dominated by an intimidatingly large desk, behind which sat an equally intimidating, although not particularly large, man.

"You two are dismissed," he called out into the hall. The other two guards left with an obedient nod. Jayde closed and locked the door behind them. He took up station to the side of the door. Three military officers stood guard in the shadowy corners of the room.

The man behind the desk didn't move, probably because he was already sitting with precise posture. He wore a tailored and evidently expensive suit. He didn't look like a military officer, but he was clearly rich, which meant he almost assuredly had to be a United official of some kind. The decor of the room certainly reminded me of a politician's office.

"Sit, Philadelphia," he commanded in an unerringly calm voice.

I obeyed hastily, taking the closest chair. I suddenly felt clumsy compared to the man's perfect movements. I folded my hands in my lap in a vain attempt to maintain some delicacy.

"Thank you for your cooperation thus far," the politician said. He sounded genuine in his praise, but I wasn't sure how to respond to that.

He shifted ever so slightly to reach forward and stroke his fingers across the tablet lying on the desk in front of him. I heard a quiet tinkle and knew I was being recorded. I tried not to let that fact disturb me; the United was always recording everything no matter where you went.

"I need you to answer some questions for me," he said.

A breath of relief rushed into me as I recalled Daddy's words. *They probably just want to talk to you. Just answer their questions honestly and it will be okay.* I nodded and sat up a little straighter.

I could have imagined it, but I thought the man smiled at this. Folding his hands on the desk, he began, "I need you to tell us everything you know about the project called 'Red Rain.'"

My heart skipped at the familiar but near-forgotten name. Red Rain? Dr. Nic's pet project? Was that what this was all about?

Of course. It all made sense now. That's why Dr. Nic's arrest still hadn't been published in the news. They were investigating his operations and wanted to know more about my involvement. Why they had waited this long to question me I didn't know, but who knows how much bureaucratic paperwork they had to sort through on this case.

Regardless, Red Rain wasn't my crime. I was just a witness. Which meant I had nothing to worry about.

Feeling more confident, I replied, "What about it?"

"You were the one that discovered Dr. Nic's secret operations, were you not?" the politician asked.

"Discovered" didn't seem like an appropriate term. "Stumbled across it accidentally" would have been a more accurate description of my contribution. "I found his secret labs and was able to alert the United, yes."

"Yes, I know all about that." The man definitely smiled that time. "But while you were investigating his secret labs, what did you find out about his operation?"

"Well, I found he had forged the deaths of several scientists and was forcing them to work," I started, trying to figure out what there was to tell. Hadn't we reported this all to the United when they arrived on the scene? "And I know he had a—"

"No," the politician cut me off, "I mean, what did you find out about Red Rain? What do you know about the project itself?"

I unintentionally gaped at him. Why were they asking *me* about Red Rain? Couldn't they have found out everything they wanted from the computers—or squeezed it out of Dr. Nic himself?

A shiver passed up my spine at the thought, but even more disturbing was the fact that the United would press me for information about the project at all. What did they expect me to know?

Suddenly nothing made sense anymore.

"Were you able to find out anything about how Red Rain works?" the man pressed.

I audibly stuttered. "It… the project wasn't finished. It didn't… It doesn't work. That's why Dr. Nic requested my father, but Dad never worked on it," I added the last bit hastily, hoping I didn't just incriminate him.

"Yes, I know about your father's involvement." I didn't like how the man inflected the word "involvement." "But I'm wondering about your brother. He worked on the project the entire time he was stationed on Mars, did he not?"

"Yes, but he didn't have the knowledge to complete it. That's why—"

"I know that," the man cut me off again, and he was starting to sound somewhat annoyed. "But he worked on it a great deal and should have at least understood the theory behind it. What did he tell you about it?"

Why don't you just ask him? As much as I hated to think of Ephesus being interrogated, it would make much more sense for them to ask someone who actually worked on it than to harass me.

"Philadelphia," the man prodded me in my silence. "Tell me everything."

It was an order. The slightly benevolent tone of his voice made it even more threatening.

"He said…" I pinched my eyes shut, taking a moment to recall what Ephesus had said to me—and to pray for strength. Ephesus's exact words came back to me, and I found comfort in remembering the tone of his voice. *Philli, do you know what acid rain is?*

"Red Rain was supposed to be a concentration of chemicals that could turn normal precipitation—or even just high humidity—into an acid rain strong enough to melt metal. It was supposed to be distributed as a gas for subtlety." I took a deep breath and waited, hoping that had satisfied them.

The politician frowned at me. After a moment of silence, he seemed to pick up on the fact that I wasn't going to say any more and concluded, "That's all he told you?"

I nodded.

The man's frown deepened. "He didn't try to explain to you how it worked?" He sounded so incredulous that it made me feel stupid.

"No? I... don't really understand the technical gibberish," I managed, voice growing meek. I hunched my shoulders, wishing I could curl into a little ball to show them I was harmless. It scared me to not be able to give them what they wanted.

The politician's polished demeanor broke when he sighed and slumped back in the chair. He muttered something under his breath which I loosely translated into *"Figures."*

One of the military officers standing behind the desk spoke for the first time. "I told you she wouldn't be of any help."

I sat up straight again. That voice was familiar.

The politician's professional expression was replaced by a look of unrestrained annoyance. "All leads are worth following."

"Of course they are," the officer responded. I *did* know that voice. And it wasn't a voice I had wanted to hear ever again. "Which is why I told you she'd be very useful for other reasons."

Oh yes, it was him. I knew it before he stepped forward, bringing his face into the direct light of the desk lamp.

Former Commander Ambrose—he looked as if he had gained a few extra badges on his uniform since I last saw him—didn't greet me with anything more than a condescending smile, which was just as well. I couldn't have found the words to respond had he spoken to me.

The situation was making progressively less sense, but it was managing to get progressively more frightening.

"Watch what you say, Ambrose," the politician returned coldly. "You're on record." Somehow I got the impression that he was more worried about what I heard than what went on the recording.

Commander Ambrose smirked—a little too gleefully for my tastes—but remained silent.

The politician sighed and turned back to me. "Thank you for your cooperation," he said again, much more dryly than before. "We may have more questions for you later." He nodded at Jayde. "You may take her back."

Jayde nodded and stepped forward, but I instinctively stuck out a hand. "Wait. But why..." I faltered when I realized I didn't know quite what I was asking. I swallowed and forced myself to be pitifully blunt. "Am I still in custody?"

"Yes?" the politician replied with one raised eyebrow.

"But..." A million objections came to mind, but the politician's cold stare shot them all down before I could open my mouth. "I... I don't know anything about Red Rain. I can't help you," I managed pleadingly.

"We still may have more questions for you later," was the blanket response. "Go."

Jayde laid a hand on my arm. Desperation welled up in my head. I looked to Commander Ambrose as a last resort.

The look of bitter pleasure on his face told me everything I needed to know.

Jayde tugged on my arm. I didn't have the will to move, but I didn't have any motivation to resist, either. I allowed him to pull me to my feet and out the door.

The politician wordlessly watched me leave.

Jayde was considerate enough not to say anything as he took me back to my cell. I was in shock and walked over to sit on the cot without objection.

The beep of the door locking stirred me from my stupor. I shivered as the sense of cold aloneness overtook me again.

I didn't know what to make of this. I had done what Daddy suggested. I hadn't caused trouble. I was polite. I answered their questions. And yet that still wasn't enough.

I had been prepared for cruel opposition and harsh threats. I was ready for the United to coerce or intimidate me into fitting their mold. I had expected the officials to lay their unbending demands on me.

I was not prepared for them to have no demands at all.

5

Mrs. Nolan did come back to visit me as she'd promised. She came the next morning when Jayde brought my breakfast and promptly resumed her mothering, making sure everything in the room, myself included, was still to her satisfaction.

When Jayde saw that Mrs. Nolan would be busy for a while, he left us alone, which was exactly what I'd hoped he'd do.

As soon as the door shut and I was sure Jayde was out of earshot, I asked, "Did you visit the other inmate?"

"Oh yes!" Mrs. Nolan said, not looking up from her work. She was applying some ointment to my scrape which, according to her, had scabbed "beautifully." "Not much of a talker, but she seems like a nice girl. Cute hair."

Girl? There weren't that many women left at camp. I prayed desperately it wasn't Cami.

As I suspected, Mrs. Nolan readily provided the information. "What was her name?" She cocked her head to the side. "Something short... oh yes, Cea. Unusual name, but rather sweet if you ask me. A unique name can be so attractive for a woman."

I involuntarily sucked in my breath. Mrs. Nolan looked up worriedly. "Is your leg still hurting, sweetie?"

"Oh, it just stings a little," I fudged, forcing a smile for her benefit. She returned the gesture and carried on chattering about her impression of Cea.

I wasn't listening. My mind was scrambling for clues. There had to be a reason both Cea and I were taken at the same time. One unprovoked arrest could be chalked up to the United's paranoia, but two in the same night was more than coincidental. If we had been accused of a specific crime, they surely would have told me by now. There was something else afoot, and whatever it was, somehow Cea and I were both involved.

I recalled the questions the politician had asked me yesterday. Cea had been involved in Red Rain as well, and she might even know some useful details about how it worked. But, then again, I remembered Cea telling me herself that she hated that phase of Nic's project, which is why she hadn't volunteered to help. She might not know any more than I did.

And all of this didn't explain why the United was interrogating us and not the scientists who created it.

There had to be more behind the United's motivation for arresting us, but they certainly weren't eager to give me any details. Over the course of the next three days, the politician didn't have any more questions for me. I didn't receive any contact from the officials. No word about the charges laid against me or any idea of when I'd be released. I asked if I could call home and was denied. The only visitors I received were Mrs. Nolan and routine check-ins by a guard, usually Jayde.

Mercifully, they didn't make me spend those entire three days locked in my cell with nothing to do. I'm sure I would have gone nearly insane before the end of the first day otherwise.

Jayde took me out for several hours each day. I wondered whether he had orders to do so or was simply doing it out of compassion. I didn't ask, but I was immensely grateful for the mercy.

It turned out there were several nice facilities in the building that I was allowed to use under supervision. I preferred the library best of all; even though it was all censored media, I could still amuse myself for a great while wandering the rows and hunting through the rare collection of physical books.

But even with the novelty of real paper to distract me, I quickly grew stir crazy. After three days I was not only deplorably homesick and lonely but also becoming quite worried—worried that I'd be stuck here for a very long time while the United administration crawled at its usual snail's pace. As best I could figure, I was an asset—albeit not a very useful one—to an investigation of some kind, and that meant I could be detained until the investigation was completed. Which could be indefinitely.

The thought of waiting in custody until the United managed to slog through its paperwork didn't appeal to me. I was desperate enough that, on the third day, I asked Jayde to take a message to his superiors for me. The message was either not delivered or not answered. I tried again in the morning. Still no response. By the end of the fourth day, I flat-out asked Jayde if he knew what was happening. He said no, which either meant he was just following orders in the dark, or that his orders were to keep me in the dark.

The next day, I pushed my time and wandered around the library as long as Jayde would let me. Walking peacefully back to my cell was requiring increasingly more willpower, and I wasn't sure how much more willpower I possessed.

My insistence on wandering around the library in circles proved to be providence—just as I was about to give up and go back to my cell to cry in frustration, I came around the corner to find the politician pulling a volume off the shelf.

It was definitely the same politician who had met with me the first day; even when he was casually flipping through books, he carried himself with undeniable poise. His commanding presence still frightened me, but not enough that I was deterred from walking up to him and saying, "Sir."

His controlled demeanor broke briefly as he jumped, evidently startled to find me at his elbow. His gaze quickly narrowed into a frown. "What are you doing out here?" he demanded.

Jayde was beside us in a moment. "I'm watching her, sir. I had assumed she would be allowed out of her cell for exercise."

The politician glanced at him. "Fine," he said dismissively. He snatched another book off the shelf and walked away.

"Wait!" I called. Jayde shushed me, but I ignored him and ran after the politician.

"Please, sir," I said, darting up beside him and struggling to be seen. "I just wanted to ask you if you knew when I might be able to go home."

"Not my decision," was the brisk response, and he walked faster.

I tried to keep up. "But please, sir, it's been days, and nobody's said anything to me."

"The department will let you know when we have further questions for you."

"But sir!" I cried again, not sure what else to say. "I didn't do anything!"

He didn't even respond this time.

"Miss Smyrna," Jayde said warningly from behind me.

"Please," I begged, taking one last shot. "I just want to see my father! At least let me contact—"

The politician dropped his books on the circulation desk with a startling thump. "Philadelphia," he said in his coldly calculated voice that cut off all argument, "the United has determined that you need to be in custody, and there you will remain until the officials decide otherwise." He glanced back at me. "I would also like to remind you that this is a library, and appropriate voices should be used."

Jayde grabbed my arm before I could even think of anything to say.

He dragged me out of the library and hustled me down the hall. I stumbled along, the frustrated tears I had been holding abruptly revealing themselves.

"It's not fair!" I cried, my voice cracking in a sob. I sounded pathetic. Why was I complaining in front of Jayde? He wouldn't care. But then, what did it matter if he heard me? "I didn't *do* anything. I just want to go home!"

"Hey, stop it," Jayde snapped, yanking on my arm.

I winced. Guess I was wrong. He *did* care. I snapped my mouth shut and did my best to dam another sob.

"I said stop!" he yelled again, this time shoving me roughly.

"Jayde!" I cried, annoyed. I wasn't doing anything!

"That's *enough*!" And faster than I could blink, he had me slammed against the wall, pinning me down with his arm.

"Don't you ever try that again," he snarled.

My heart was beating so fast I couldn't respond. What had I done? Jayde's face was so close to mine I was afraid to even draw a breath.

And then I realized that this position also allowed Jayde to put his mouth discretely close to my ear.

"This is off the record," he said, suddenly talking in a nearly unintelligible whisper. "But you're not here because of anything you've done."

I swallowed and waited.

"You and that other girl are here because of a project they want some scientists to work on."

What scientists? Even as the thought passed across my consciousness, I felt stupid for missing the obvious. They wanted my father and brother, of course.

"I don't know what the project is, but they've taken the scientists to a lab across town, and—"

"Is this young man harassing you, Philli?"

Both Jayde and I jumped and turned to see Commander Ambrose approaching us at a stroll. The sight of his cruel expression made me remember what he had said that first day. *Which is why I told you she'd be very useful for other reasons.*

Suddenly everything made sense. True, hard, brutal sense.

Looking at the rich anticipation in Ambrose's eyes, I briefly wondered if I would have rather stayed in blissful ignorance.

"Everything's under control, sir," Jayde said in a voice that was entirely unfazed.

"Oh, I wasn't worried about you," Commander Ambrose crowed benevolently. "I have no doubt that a strong man like you could handle her."

Both Jayde and I were equally put out by that statement.

"I'm more worried about her causing trouble. She's a stubborn one." He actually had the audacity to wink at me.

It took all my willpower not to make a sassy face at him. I had to keep up the act.

Turning to Jayde, I said very meekly, "It won't happen again, sir."

He nodded briskly. "Good. Come along." He grabbed my arm and guided me down the hall, giving Commander Ambrose a respectful nod as he passed.

I couldn't resist a stolen glance back at Ambrose. He was grinning.

Jayde didn't talk as he led me back to my room, which was just as well. My mind was spinning, rapidly snapping the pieces together.

We were hostages, Cea and I. A bargaining chip to force my father and brother to comply with the United's wishes. I couldn't guess what the United wanted them for, but if the United felt the need to use hostages to intimidate them into complying, it must be serious. And more than likely it was something immoral, unethical, and dangerous.

But if they wanted to coerce my father and brother, why did they need Cea? Was there really more going on between Ephesus and Cea than I realized? How had the United found out?

Unanswered questions still burned in the back of my mind, but I shoved them aside. Only one thing was important right now.

I had to talk to Cea. And I knew who could help arrange a meeting.

6

As usual, Mrs. Nolan visited me during breakfast the next morning.

"Looks like you're healing well," she said with proud satisfaction. "Just don't pick at the scab."

I slowly laid the groundwork for my proposition. "How is Cea doing?"

Mrs. Nolan scrunched her nose in concerned thought. "Better. She had a few nasty scrapes and bruises when she came in, but I think she's feeling mostly herself again."

I poked at my breakfast, as if that reinforced my casualness. "Yeah… she must be feeling pretty lonely, though."

"Oh, no doubt, poor thing!" Mrs. Nolan fussed as she remade my bed for the second time.

"I mean, being in prison, and hurt, without any family or friends to visit you…"

Mrs. Nolan made a *tsk, tsk* noise as she bustled about the room doing her routine maintenance.

"I mean, it's been bad enough for me, and I'm not hurt…"

"I know, sweetheart."

She still didn't pick up on it. I decided to be blunt. "I guess… I would just really like to visit her."

Mrs. Nolan stopped. I held my breath, praying, and waited to see how she would take it.

"You know what," she declared after a moment, "a visit is just what you two need!"

Hope surged through my veins. *Yes, thank you!*

"I'll make it happen. Doctor's orders." She smiled. I returned the gesture.

Mrs. Nolan's influence worked wonders yet again—although I wouldn't have been surprised if Jayde had a hand in it as well—and at lunchtime she came to get me. She took me up a floor to a place where the hallway bowed out in a little glass-walled sitting area. A few tables and chairs were scattered around, and one was topped with a dainty little lunch for two.

I guess Mrs. Nolan took the whole "visit" idea seriously.

I thanked her profusely for more reasons than one and sat down to wait. Within a few minutes Cea came up, escorted by Jayde. I was glad it was him; at least I could trust him to keep his distance.

Sure enough, he led Cea to the table and then walked across the hall to the nearest bench—far enough away that he couldn't hear us if we talked softly.

I wasn't really interested in eating, but I knew it would look suspicious if I didn't touch my food. I said grace, using the time to pray for guidance, and took a bite before starting.

Cea stared at me until I looked up, then said with loaded casualness, "That nurse seems to like you."

"She's nice," I replied with a shrug. "He's friendly, too." I gestured with my shoulder at Jayde.

Cea glanced at him, then turned her attention back to me. "Does he talk to you at all? My guard won't even say hello."

After throwing a look around the hall to make sure we were alone, I forewent the cryptic talk and lowered my voice to a whisper. "He said it's not because of anything we've done."

"Figured that much out myself," Cea replied dryly.

"He said it's because the United wants to make some scientists work on a project. I assume he means my father and brother."

"Ephesus," she breathed, and there was more than one emotion attached to the name.

I took the handy opportunity to voice my suspicions. "But if it's my family they want, I don't know why they need you."

Somewhat to my disappointment, Cea did not divulge her affections. She furrowed her brow for an awkwardly long moment, long enough for inspiration to hit her. She jerked her head up, eyes wide like she'd been punched. "Nic. They've got Nic."

It was my turn to stare in uncomfortable silence. Suddenly Dr. Nic's apparent disappearance from the records made sense. The United had kept him and his unlawful genius to themselves.

Cea's gears were still churning. "But what..." She trailed off and nibbled on her sandwich. I copied her and pretended to eat.

She set her sandwich down and looked back up at me. "Did the rich guy meet with you too?"

I nodded, trying to chew my mouthful quickly.

"What did he ask you about?"

I swallowed a bite of fruit. "Red Rain..." I started to say.

I almost didn't get all the way through the name. Hearing it out loud, suddenly I understood. I knew what was going on.

The look on Cea's face confirmed it.

"But why?" I gasped, mostly because I hoped it wasn't true.

"Why not?" she returned. "Why wouldn't a tyrannical government want a weapon that could desecrate its resistance?"

That's why there was no mention of Dr. Nic or his project in the news. The United wanted Red Rain for themselves.

And they were going to force my father and brother to help Dr. Nic create it.

Dear God, no.

"We have to get out of here," Cea hissed.

"What?" I said loudly, still not thinking clearly.

Cea cast a nervous look at Jayde. He glanced up at us briefly but then returned his attention to his handheld device.

Cea leaned in closer. "We can't let them use us as hostages. We have to escape before they can pull that card."

Escape? The word made my chest instantly cramp in dread. How did she expect us to break out of here? By beating up the guards?

No, there had to be a better way. "It won't work," I said confidently. "My father won't work on the project, no matter what."

"The fewer bargaining chips the United has, the better. I'm not taking chances with this," she returned. "We're getting out of here as soon as we can."

"But—" I started, my mind racing through a million objections and concerns.

"Phil." Cea reached out and touched my hand. "Trust me. I know what we're dealing with, and I know that we can't let the United have Red Rain. Think about what they would do with it."

I didn't need to think about it. They would do what Dr. Nic had been planning to do with it, only they wouldn't show any discretion about who they bombed. Dr. Nic had intended to use Red Rain to defend his haven; the United would use it to destroy all havens.

Cea squeezed my hand. "I'll make the call as soon as I can."

"Call?" I questioned.

"I've got a phone I can use to call some friends." She said it with absolutely no regard for how phenomenal a feat that was. "But I'll only be able to use it once before the United recognizes the device, so we'll have to time it right. Do you think that nurse would arrange another lunch if you asked her?"

"Yes," I said. My mind was spinning over everything, but Mrs. Nolan's affection for me was one thing I could be confident of.

"Okay," Cea said, sounding encouraged. "I'll let you know by sending a message through her."

I closed my eyes and took a deep breath, trying to muster a comparable amount of courage. *It will be all right. With Mrs. Nolan's cooperation, we can get out of our cells. Then we just need to distract Jayde and slip out a back door. You can do this.*

"I need you to take this."

I looked up to see Cea slowly unzipping her jacket. A small pistol was tucked into her belt.

I couldn't bite back a gasp.

"You'll need it." She carefully slipped the pistol out and held it down out of sight below the table.

"How did you even get that in here?" I squeaked.

She looked up into my face. "It's not metal. Besides, I gave the guards something else to think about on the way in."

I frowned at her. Looking closely, I could see the ghosts of healing cuts and bruises on her face and arms, and I remembered what Mrs. Nolan had said. My eyes widened.

"Here." She extended her hand beneath the table. "It's loaded. I've got one for myself, and between us that should be enough bullets."

I didn't make a move to take it. "Enough bullets for what?" I said, even though I genuinely didn't want the answer.

"Enough to get us out of here."

I stared at her. Did she want us to shoot our way out of here like terrorists? I couldn't. I *wouldn't*. My father would never approve.

"I-I don't know how to shoot," I fudged, even though that wasn't entirely true. I remembered learning gun safety with Grandpa as a child. But that was before the United started using guns to keep us in concentration camps.

"It's easy," she said callously. "Just press the red button on the back to turn it on. It does everything else automatically; you just have to pull the trigger."

She tapped me on the knee with the hilt. I squirmed back. She frowned at me impatiently. "Hurry, take it before someone sees!"

I instinctively threw a glance at Jayde. At that exact moment, he looked up at me.

He didn't even lift his head; he just shifted slightly and caught my gaze out of the corner of his eye.

We looked at each other for a split second. A split second in which he had the opportunity to turn away and pretend he never saw anything.

He didn't take it.

"Hey, drop that gun!" he ordered, rising.

Cea didn't obey. Instead she stood up, switched the pistol on, and fired.

I screamed. Thankfully she missed Jayde, instead puncturing the wall behind him. Jayde threw us one scowling look before taking off at a run.

"Guess I'm making that call now." With a furious look, she turned and forced the gun into my hands. "Now you've got one less bullet. Pay attention!"

I held the weapon away from me. "But I—"

"Just do as I say and we'll make it out of here! Come on!" She took off in the direction Jayde went.

I didn't have any choice but to follow. I wasn't about to stand there and get caught with a gun in my hands.

I ran after her, struggling not to fall behind. "But the elevator is back the other way!"

"Exactly! This way!" She turned around a corner.

I followed her as she twisted through random side halls, ending up in a deserted corner by a janitorial storage room. She halted just outside the door to the stairwell.

"They'll be expecting us to head straight for the doors. If we throw them off it will give us a minute's headway." She reached down and slid a cellphone out of her shoe as she talked. It was dated slim touchscreen, one of those smartphones from the 2020s. She slid her fingers across the screen and dialed.

I wondered if the thing would even work. But after only a brief pause, the call connected.

"Hi," Cea said. "I'd like to order pizza to be delivered."

It took my mind a moment to even process what she was saying. *Did she just...?*

"Yes. Two medium house specialties, please. With drinks."

She did. "Cea—"

She shushed me harshly. "Yes. That's for Caesar. Deliver to 1217 North 13th Street, please. Thank you."

She hung up. I suddenly had significantly less hope in our escape.

"What in the world was that?" I screeched, trying not to panic and failing significantly.

"Just trust me." She switched the cellphone for her other pistol and turned it on. I remembered I was holding a gun and hastily slipped it into the pocket of my jacket. Hopefully I wouldn't accidentally shoot myself or something.

She walked up to the stairwell door and peered through the window. "Coast clear, at least on this floor. Now, listen. We have to go quietly and not too fast. That way, if someone on another floor happens to see us, we won't look immediately suspicious."

She pushed the door open slowly and stepped through. I followed, wondering if the rapid beating of my heart was enough to make someone suspicious.

We started down the stairs. I focused on watching where I put my feet, struggling not to trip or make too much noise. *Just keep moving. All the way to the bottom. Don't panic. You can slip out the back way and everything will be—*

"They're down here!"

Oh dear God.

Cea had already broken into a run and was nearly half a floor ahead of me. "They're several floors back! We can make it ahead of them!"

I grabbed the railing and ran, but my feet suddenly seemed to want to tangle with each other. I couldn't move fast enough. Cea slipped further ahead while the shouts behind me grew closer. "Stop! Stop right there!"

A little voice inside me echoed them. *Stop. Just stop right here and sit. They won't hurt you if you don't fight back.*

Cea paused at the foot of the stairs to wait for me to catch up. "Come *on*, Phil!"

I jumped two steps to the last landing. I glanced at the door just in time to see a guard approaching from the hall. He was nearly at the door. "Cea, there's more in the hall!"

"Shoot the door panel!" she yelled.

"What?" I shouted back.

She didn't wait for me to figure it out. She took aim from where she was and shot at the security panel by the door. I screamed and instinctively dropped to the floor as pieces of glass flew. Cea fired three more times, shredding the inner electronics.

I shielded my face with a shriek as sparks and smoke spewed from the panel. Cea's voice cut through the ringing in my ears. "Keep going, Phil!"

I stumbled to my feet, coughing and trying to fan the smoke out of my face. I heard cursing from the other side of the door, and then something banged against it. Once, twice, three times, and then the door groaned open, revealing a guard with his gun pointed at me.

Before I could react, a shot fired from below. The guard slumped over and hit the ground with a thud, almost before the moan escaped his mouth.

I grabbed my throat as I watched in mesmerized horror. *He's... he's... she didn't!*

"Philli, *now!*"

I gagged. Lurching forward, I stumbled down the last flight of stairs and nearly fell into Cea.

"Cea, that guard back there, he's..."

She wasn't even listening. She fired several more times back in the direction I had come from. I slapped my hands over my ears as I heard several more guards meet their demise.

Without a word Cea grabbed my arm and yanked me through the door to the parking ramp. Kicking the door shut, she blasted that security panel to pieces too.

"That should slow them." Her gun clicked dully. "I'm out. Where's your gun?"

I just shook my head rapidly, my hands still over my ears.

"Phil, stop it. Come on." She took off at a run again.

I looked up to see where she was going. For a brief moment, hope fluttered through my shaky heart. The parking garage seemed deserted.

Please, God, no more guards. No more shooting.

But then I saw them—guards coming down the stairs at the opposite end of the lot.

Before I could get the words out to warn Cea, one of the guards yelled, and the place erupted in shouts and barked orders. More guards poured down the stairwell and surged towards us, weaving between the parked vehicles like an army of rats.

I stared at the approaching danger, at first too disheartened to even process the situation. Distant yelling from behind reminded me that going back was not an option. *Dead end.*

Cea froze, then spun around to face me. "Philli!" she yelled. "Your gun!"

I jerked out of my stupor. I hastily pulled the lethal weapon out of my pocket and fiddled with the button. The gun hummed to life, vibrating in my hands. I fitted it in my palm and put my feet apart, just like Grandpa had taught me. And then I looked up at the army of approaching guards.

I stopped. What was I doing?

"Come on, Phil!"

Did she expect me to blast through them? Did she expect me to kill?

"Shoot!" she shrieked.

She did. She expected me to gun them down, one by one, cutting through them like underbrush blocking the path.

"Shoot, Philli, now!" she continued to holler, panic making her voice nearly unintelligible. *"Shoot!"*

I focused my eyes on the nearest guard. His iron-gray hair betrayed his age. He looked about as old as my father.

Daddy...

I let the gun slip from my hands. I heard it bounce on the floor.

Cea continued to shriek at me. I wasn't listening. I sagged against the nearest support beam, suddenly aware of my exhaustion. The will to stand left me as the adrenaline drained from my nerves.

Cea dove for the gun, but the first guard reached us at the same moment. He lurched forward and kicked Cea squarely under the chin. She dropped to the ground with a cry, blood splattering from her lips.

I screamed, a new kind of panic surging through me. "No, please don't hurt—"

I didn't get to finish my plea. Someone grabbed me and cuffed my hands behind my back in one swift motion. Before I could even turn my head, they spun me around and shoved me into someone who gripped me with powerful hands.

I looked up to see a captain of some sort glaring down at me. "What is the meaning of this?" he snarled, punctuating the threat by giving me a hard shake.

I wasn't sure he actually expected an answer to that question, but I knew I couldn't come up with a sensible one. I stared at him, blood pounding in my ears.

"Captain!" My heart plummeted at the sound of the familiar voice. It was Jayde.

He didn't even look at me. "The commander wants them transferred to headquarters immediately for questioning and punishment." He held out a communicator with a message displayed on the screen as proof.

I didn't even try to read what it said. The word "punishment" swirled around in my head, crowding out all other thoughts with dark fear.

The captain drew his eyebrows together in a scowl. "Blindfold them," he snapped, shoving me towards Jayde.

This time Jayde did not object.

He did as he was told, dragged me a few steps to the right, and then threw me like unwanted luggage. I hit the floor of a vehicle hard. Blotches of color flashed across the darkness in front of my face. I heard Cea hit the ground beside me with a grunt. What sounded like van doors slammed behind us.

Heated talking continued outside the van for a moment, which was silenced by a harsh order. The vehicle rocked as the cabin doors slammed, and then the engine roared to life. The heavy vibration ground right beneath my head, giving me a debilitating headache on top of everything else.

The van surged forward roughly, sending me skidding to the side. I tried to hold steady until the van dipped up the exit ramp and turned, where the driving leveled out. Then I collapsed on the ground, letting my every joint go limp.

Cea groaned. "Philli?" she mumbled, so hoarsely that I wasn't sure she was really talking to me. Either way, I didn't answer. I didn't want to talk.

Another groan and some shuffling. It sounded like she was trying to sit up. "Philli?" she said again, more clearly. "It will be all right."

For an answer, I turned my face to the wall and sobbed.

I didn't care what she thought, or if the guards heard me. I didn't care about facing my punishment bravely, not when I'd brought it on myself.

There had been no reason to cause trouble; no one was getting hurt. If we had complied, waited quietly in special custody until the United realized bargaining wouldn't work, we all would have survived. But now several guards were injured, probably dead, and we were going to be punished. We had gained nothing—only caused more pain.

My father would be horrified when he found out.

If he ever found out. My chances of being returned home to him were slim now, and I knew it. If I had just waited out my confinement quietly, they probably would have sent me home. Now I'd be lucky if they just stuck me in a higher-security prison.

And what would become of my father? How would our stunt affect him and Ephesus? Would they be in trouble because the hostages had tried to escape? What would the United do to them now?

I couldn't bear to think of the possibilities. I couldn't bear to think that I had caused my father pain.

Please, God, I begged, even though I felt like I didn't deserve to ask anything of Him. *Don't let them—*

The van lurched around a corner, throwing me into the wall. The resulting pain was an almost welcome diversion. Before I even had time to regain my bearings, the van swerved again, dealing me another blow. This time, darkness mercifully washed over my mind, and I knew nothing more.

7

I woke up to darkness. It took me only a fraction of a second to realize it was dark because I was still blindfolded.

I lay still, letting the unwanted memory flow back to me. With it came an ache in nearly every joint and bone—and the realization that I was no longer handcuffed.

I stiffened, involuntarily clenching my hands into fists. Why would they let me go? I must be in a secured room. Had they locked me alone in a cell to await my punishment?

I couldn't think of anything more horrible.

But at least I didn't have to wait in the dark. If they'd removed the handcuffs, they obviously couldn't stop me from taking the blindfold off.

I sat up gingerly, groaning a little under my breath as dizziness and pain assaulted me. I waited for my head to clear, then reached up and felt for the knot in the cloth.

A voice called out, making me suddenly realize I wasn't alone.

"You might not want to do that just yet."

I stopped, but not because of the admonition. I knew that voice. And it wasn't Cea's.

"Don't torment her. The United did enough of that." *That* was Cea.

"I just don't want to startle her," the other person said again. His voice sounded exactly like I remembered it—cool and even, almost disinterested, forcibly propped up with a hint of arrogance. But it couldn't be him. Why would he be here?

"As if waking up blindfolded isn't startling enough," Cea returned.

"Probably less startling than waking up and seeing me," he replied without any sarcasm. I had to admit that he was right, but my shock was quickly giving way to hope—hope that he might still be a friend.

I yanked the blindfold off and gasped out his name in the same breath. "Stanyard."

He sat across from me with his arms folded on his knees. Wherever we were was dark, with only one electric lantern illuminating the room, but there was enough light for me to make out his features. He hadn't changed one bit; he even wore the same calm, slightly moody stare.

I wondered if that meant his opinions hadn't changed, either.

Questions welled up inside me, but none seemed as important as: "What are you doing here?"

"Glad to see me, huh?" he returned, his subtle, wry smile showing itself. Cea, who was sitting nearby, chuckled. I flushed, realizing that hadn't been a very friendly greeting.

"I'm saving your skin, that's what," he declared, leaning his chin on his arms.

That statement made me pause to take in my surroundings. I quickly realized we weren't in a prison or a government building of any kind. It looked like we were in a cellar—stained concrete walls, crates and junk scattered around, and a damp, musty smell hanging in the air.

"Welcome to my basement," Stanyard said without ceremony, confirming my suspicions.

I turned back to him. "But how—"

"You have Jayde to thank," he answered my unfinished question. "I just took you in and stashed you out of sight."

"Jayde?" I exclaimed. "But he…" I couldn't bring myself to say it out loud. *He betrayed me. But was it really betrayal? He was just doing his job. He's a government agent, not my friend.*

"That's what it's supposed to look like," Stanyard said, as if reading my thoughts. "That order to take you to headquarters for punishment? It was fake."

Cea grinned deviously, confirming his statement.

My eyes widened in a combination of amazement and alarm. "Will he be blamed if they find out?"

"Not if he's smart and does his job right," Stanyard retorted. "If he follows the steps, it will look on paper as though your van was hijacked by rebels, and the fake order will be attributed to someone hacking the system from the outside."

I didn't know what to say. I didn't even know how to swallow it all. "So he's… you're…" I groped, begging for an explanation.

"Yup. We're both members of the underground. Augustine at your service." Stanyard extended his hand jauntily.

"And I'm Caesar," Cea chirped.

I gaped at her. *Augustine? Caesar?* Who makes up names like that? "That… doesn't sound anything like you," I managed.

"That's the point of code names," Stanyard quipped.

I glared at him. They were starting to sound like little kids playing superheroes. Was he even being serious?

"What?" he returned in response to my look. "Do you expect us to go around using our real names? You know as well as I do that the United listens to everything."

Suddenly everything began to make at least some sense in my head. I glanced at Cea. "So when you made that call…"

"Yes, I was passing a call for help to the underground."

"Underground?" I repeated.

"What else would you call it?" Stanyard said. "It's not exactly formal. It's just a network of communication amongst people who are willing to help."

"Are they all Christians?" I asked, struggling to put the last pieces of the puzzle together.

"No. Some are just citizens who are fed up with the United. Like Jayde." Stanyard paused, his voice sobering suddenly. "And me."

I saw that as an opportunity to broach the more personal questions burning in my heart. "So you're still legally part of the Outside?"

"Technically," he replied without enthusiasm. "My standing is hanging by a thread, but I've managed to hold onto my job."

"Job?" I asked out of pure curiosity.

"Pizza delivery," he explained, smiling somewhat. "My 'day job' is running a little pizza shop above ground."

"So that's why Cea ordered pizza," I declared.

Cea winked. "Best deep-crust in town."

Stanyard laughed. "Yes. Running the shop feeds me and also keeps the United off my tail. As long as the shop appears to be following regulations on paper, they don't snoop into what I'm really doing with my business. This is the second-level basement under the shop. On their map, the building only has one basement, where I live."

I could only nod in wonder. I wasn't sure what to say, but I wanted to hear more. I wanted to hear everything. "What's it like?"

"What, sleeping in a basement?" he replied, his dry smirk returning.

"No… Living. In the Outside."

He finally locked eyes with me. After sharing a long stare, he admitted in a husky voice, "Horrible."

"What? Really?" I exclaimed.

Stanyard shushed me harshly. Snapping my mouth shut, I inwardly scolded myself for being so surprised. It was the Outside, ruled by godless people who wanted all citizens to deny their religion. Of course it would be horrible to live there. That's what we had been raised to believe, told to repeat in our minds to keep ourselves from temptation. You didn't want to join the Outside. No one did.

And yet, I knew that none of us, even the adults, truly believed that. We all believed—hoped, perhaps—that the Outside was something better. That there was more to life beyond the walls of the concentration camps. That out there, somewhere, existed freedom.

Stanyard glanced around the basement, dark eyes flashing with worry. "Keep it down," he hissed, voice a whisper for emphasis. "This basement doesn't exist, remember. I've got the TV on loud in my room, but you can't take chances."

I bit my tongue, suddenly afraid to make any sound, and waited for more explanation.

When he turned back to me, his expression was filled with an emotion I hadn't seen from him in a long time—fear. "You can't breathe out here. There's too many ways to make a mistake and arouse their suspicion."

"All the regulations?" I ventured in a suitably quiet voice.

He gave a little snort. "They don't even follow their own standards. It's whatever pleases them at any given moment. If it makes a government official or your neighbor worry, it's against the law, and you're out."

"Your neighbor?" I frowned.

"Backbiters," he said, voice heavy. "I've never seen a culture so self-centered. The government isn't actually as omnipresent as some make it out to be. They have access to all your data, but they don't have time to monitor it. But the people you pass on the street… They can report you at any time. And they will. Some do it to keep from being accused of harboring you should you turn out to be doing something illegal. Others do it to get on an official's good side, or to keep the United off of their own tail. Even members of the underground do it to each other to shift the blame. I've had to fend off the United's dogs a few times myself."

"That's the main reason Nic settled on Mars. Things are a lot less tedious when your nearest neighbor is twenty miles away and has to don a spacesuit to come spy on you," Cea contributed.

Stanyard sighed and leaned his chin on his arms again. "I don't mind playing mind games with the government," he said candidly, "but I hate having to treat everyone around me like a traitor. You can't trust anyone."

You can trust me, I wanted to say, but didn't.

"Trouble is," Stanyard continued, leaning back against the wall, "the United doesn't exactly ask for proof of wrongdoing before locking you up. I've done some time in 'special custody' waiting for stuff to blow over."

"Tell us about it," Cea groused.

"How have you managed this long?" I asked with more than a small amount of admiration.

He shrugged. "You learn the tricks of staying low. Everyone else, even the officials, are just trying to get by. If you make their lives easier by doing what's expected of you and not getting in their way, they'll leave you alone. You become part of the scenery. Play the part of a well-oiled gear and the system won't kick you out."

"Just play by the rules," I muttered, to which he nodded. *Just like life in the camp*, I thought, the realization settling in. The game truly was the same, assimilated or not. Play by the rules and nobody gets hurt.

"Well, I need to be getting back," Stanyard said suddenly. His voice was falsely cheerful, which I knew was his way of ending the conversation. "Can't stay away too long, or someone might worry."

He stood up and walked past me. I turned to see a ladder bolted to the wall. "Do you think they're watching you in your room?" I stood up to follow him but nearly fell back down when I realized how stiff my legs were. I ungracefully braced myself against the wall.

He glanced over his shoulder. "Not directly. But I can't take chances. One careless step could put us all in danger."

I nodded numbly, suddenly burdened by all the risks he was taking to hide us after we'd been dumped on his doorstep without warning. "Thank you," I said, hoping he understood.

He nodded and grabbed the ladder, stepping up on the first rung.

"Wait!" I cried, suddenly finding the courage to ask the question I had been holding back. I dreaded the answer, but I wanted to hear it from him. "Where's Mira?"

He stared at me. The sadness in his expression clearly answered my question.

He stepped back off the ladder. "She left," he related in a quiet tone. "Ran away from our host family and married a soldier before she was even of legal age. She hasn't written me in months. I'm not sure where she is."

I involuntarily clenched my skirt in my fingers. Wailing questions swirled through my head, fueled by pain and betrayal. *Why would she do that? How could she leave her own brother?* Looking into Stanyard's face, I knew he had spent many long nights torturing himself with the same unanswerable questions.

"Why did you never write me?" I asked abruptly. "I mean us. Back at camp."

"I couldn't," he said with a careless shrug. "Former unassimilated can't contact those that are still noncompliant. Even the underground couldn't get my emails through. Once you leave, you can't even speak of those left behind.

The United acts as if the camps and their inhabitants don't exist. I guess it's part of their policy to keep us from going back."

"Why didn't you come back?" The painful question slipped off my tongue before I could stop it.

His eyes darkened defensively. I expected him to snap at me, but he didn't. What he did say was worse.

"Come back to what?" His voice was cold and utterly dry.

Come back home. To your father. To your friends. To God. To me. So many responses swirled around in my head, but I couldn't find the courage to say any of them. This time, I was the one who looked away.

I heard Stanyard climbing the ladder. "I'll be back in the morning," he said in his normal tone. "Stay down here and remember to be quiet."

I glanced up in time to see him disappear through the hole in the ceiling. The door closed after him, and there was the sound of something heavy being dragged on top. I felt like something heavy had been dropped on my heart, too.

"I wish we were back on Mars," Cea suddenly declared, thankfully disturbing my thoughts.

"Yeah," was all I could say, thinking of my brief visit to the base. If it weren't for Dr. Nic's obsession with apocalyptic weapons, it would have been wonderful. No one had been afraid to breathe up there, even us unassimilated. We had all wanted to stay.

But I was a fool for thinking the rest of the Outside was like that. The only reason Dr. Nic had been able to build his own little kingdom without United interference was because the base had been so remote.

I jolted out of my moody daze when I remembered what else was at stake. I turned to Cea. "What about my family, and Nic? Are they going to be... all right?" There was more I wanted to ask—namely, *"Will we ever see them again?"*—but I couldn't bring myself to phrase it so bluntly.

She gazed at me. I recognized her expression as the look of an adult who's struggling to decide how honest to be with a child. "We'll just have to trust Augustine and the others," she settled for finally.

"But what can they do about it? Are they going to—"

"Just wait and see," she said firmly, making it very clear that she didn't want to say any more. "You need to rest."'

I indulged in a childish pout. "I just woke up."

Her lips twitched with amused affection. "Being knocked cold doesn't count as sleeping. Lie down and try to rest." She gestured over to the corner, where a few blankets and pillows were stacked.

I relinquished with a sigh and did as I was told, curling up against the wall between some crates. Having boxes around me made me feel safer and less cold.

Before long, Cea dimmed the electric lantern and laid down on her own makeshift bed. I assumed she fell asleep because of the thick silence that settled soon after.

Still wide awake, I listened hard into the darkness, trying to grasp any sound from above. Nothing. Of course Stanyard had probably fallen asleep, but it would have given me great comfort to hear his footsteps on the floor, to know that there was someone out there. To know that we weren't completely alone, shut in a dark basement like fugitive criminals.

I shivered. We *were* fugitive criminals. Even if the United believed the van hijacking story, they would know we were still on the run. Whether or not they would bother searching for us I couldn't guess. Maybe we weren't worth it. But we would still be wanted, and we couldn't show our faces above ground without risking getting caught. We couldn't even turn ourselves in at the camp; Commander Clint would know what we had done.

My throat and chest tightened at the realization. We couldn't go home. Not ever.

Clutching the blanket in my stiff fingers, I sobbed into the darkness.

8

I didn't sleep all night. Therefore, I was wide awake when muffled voices broke the silence several hours later.

After my brain roused enough to process that noise was coming from the room above and that there was more than one voice talking, I realized I should be worried. Only Stanyard was supposed to be up there. Who else could there be?

I was too groggy to process the terrible possibilities, much less do anything about them, so I sat with my arms around my knees and listened while the heavy object over the hatch was dragged away. They hadn't even opened the door all the way before I could hear the voices clearly enough to identify them. All my worry vanished, along with the remembrance that I was supposed to keep my voice down.

"Daddy!" I shrieked, scrambling up so fast I tripped.

Stanyard shushed me from above, but I willfully ignored him. All my attention was focused on the familiar pair of Oxford shoes and long white lab coat descending the ladder. I darted over and grabbed him around the waist before he had even stepped off the last rung.

The man didn't return my hug. "Glad to see me, Philadelphia? I wish I could say the same of you."

I gave a muted squeal of terror and jerked back. Stanyard shushed me again, and this time I was too stunned to make another sound. I looked up into the stoic face of Dr. Nic, half-expecting him to fly into a rage.

Thankfully, Cea spared me further embarrassment by grasping her brother in a hug and pulling him away. My dad was the next one down the ladder.

"Philli," he said, expressing all his emotion in that loving name.

"Daddy," I said, much more quietly, but no less joyfully. I threw myself into his arms, fighting the sudden urge to cry.

"Oh Philli, I'm so glad to see you." He smoothed his hands over my hair and kissed my head, then held me away from him. "Are you all right?"

"I… I think so," I managed, the events of the past few days suddenly swirling through my head. Now I would have to tell him what I'd done.

"What happened?" Ephesus joined us and scrutinized me with a frown. "Did you not sleep at all?"

I flushed a little. My face must look terrible. "No… I got knocked out on the way in, and now I'm not tired, I guess."

My father sucked in his breath sharply. Dr. Nic piped up helpfully from across the room. "You know they used to say that sleeping after a concussion can kill you."

I gaped at him in horror. Was he serious? What if I had—

"Leave her alone," Ephesus snapped.

"It's just an urban legend," Nic returned. "No medical truth to it."

Ephesus ignored him. He laid a hand on both Daddy and me. "Come on, let's talk over here."

Daddy guided me over to the corner, and we all sat down in a circle. Ephesus gave my shoulder a squeeze, and then Daddy took both of my hands in his.

"Now, tell me what happened."

I took a deep breath and obeyed. I told him everything, every detail. I watched his expression as I talked. He didn't interrupt, only rubbed my hands encouragingly, but I could see the emotions flickering across his eyes—slowly, like a lagging video feed. And they were exactly what I had expected to see: worry, fear, shock, then grief. Finally, disappointment.

I finished with a sigh. "I'm sorry, Daddy."

"Don't be sorry," Ephesus said quickly. "You did what you had to. I'm proud of you two." He touched my arm.

I glanced at Daddy. He didn't look proud, but he didn't scold me, either. "I'm sorry we put you through that," he said with a sigh.

"It's not your fault," I said, almost indignantly.

He smiled, a strangely sad sort of smile that I wasn't sure how to interpret. "Never mind," he said, patting my hand. "It's over now."

I realized they hadn't told me their side of the story. "How did you get here?"

"We broke out and Augustine picked us up," Ephesus answered.

"How did you break out? Break out from where?" I asked slowly, wondering if I even wanted to know.

Ephesus smirked triumphantly. "Just some secured lab across town. Some computer hacking did wonders on the security systems."

"Yeah, and your bombs helped too," Dr. Nic chirped. Clearly he was listening to our conversation.

"Bombs?" I squeaked, and then suddenly had the feeling that we'd had this conversation before. "The same bombs you were—"

"Yes," Ephesus replied, voice sour with a grudge. "Apparently the United salvaged all my work from Mars and gave it to Dr. Nic to play with."

"Well, it turned out to be useful, didn't it?" Dr. Nic returned. "We'd have never made it out of there otherwise."

Guns. Bombs. And not just any bombs. The horrendously destructive bombs Dr. Nic had been creating to threaten Earth. And now the United had it all.

"Never mind," my father said again, more sternly this time. "It's over."

"Dad," Ephesus protested. "She deserves to know."

"I don't want to talk about it," Daddy outright snapped. Then he sighed, as if he realized how prickly his voice sounded. "What's done is done, but it's behind us now. The important part is that we all made it out alive, and we're together."

"You're right," Ephesus said with a little sigh of his own. "I'm sorry. I'm glad you're safe, Phil. Come here." He opened his arms for a hug.

I accepted it and squeezed him around the neck. After a moment, I whispered, "It didn't work, did it?"

"What?" Ephesus asked, setting me away from him.

"The United keeping us as hostages. Did they threaten you with us?"

Ephesus glanced at Daddy. I followed his gaze. "Yes, they told us that's why they had you in custody. I suspect that's why they arrested you before bringing us to the lab," Daddy said.

"What did they say they'd do to us?" I asked, feeling morbidly curious.

Daddy shook his head, his eyes suddenly looking everywhere but into my own. "They wouldn't say. Just that there would be trouble if we didn't make progress."

"What did you do?" I slid back over to him and found his hand, eager to hear his side of the tale.

Daddy didn't answer for a long moment. Ephesus spoke first. "*I* worked on hacking the computer and finding an escape route."

I looked up at him with a frown, disturbed by the sharpness of his voice. He was scowling furiously at our father.

I turned to Dad, worry rising in my chest. "Daddy, what happened?"

Daddy squeezed my hand. "I did work on it a little."

"A little?" Dr. Nic objected. "Old man, you nearly had it!"

"Shut *up*," Ephesus snapped, and he sounded like he meant it.

My heart was in my throat. "Daddy, you *worked* on it?"

He finally met my gaze. "It was the only way. If they didn't see progress, there would have been trouble for all of us."

The only way? The only option was to surrender and give the United a lethal weapon?

"I didn't finish it," Daddy continued. "We couldn't make it work. I highly doubt it will ever be operational."

That was good news. It should comfort me to know that the United still didn't have Red Rain.

But somehow it didn't make me feel any better.

"It did buy us enough time to escape," Ephesus inserted, trying to sound encouraging. "Now their game's up."

And the United had won. Their bargaining chip had worked.

"They won't get Red Rain from us now. Will they?" Ephesus gripped Daddy's shoulder.

Daddy laid his hand on top of Ephesus's and looked into his son's face. "No. It's over, and we're all safe. There's nothing else they can do to us now."

Safe for how long? We were all fugitives. We would always be fugitives.

Daddy squeezed my hand again, distracting me. "I brought something for you." He retracted his hand to reach into his coat pocket.

I looked up to see him pull out my reader. Sudden joy shoved all other thoughts aside. "But how did you..."

"I brought it with me when they took us to the lab." He laid it in my lap.

I untangled the power cord and clasped the device in my hands, savoring the familiar feel of the buttons.

"I kept it with me because I knew I'd find you eventually, and I wanted to be able to give it to you." Daddy touched my face, causing me to look back at him. "It will be all right. I'm sorry it came to this, but we're together now."

"And we'll stay together," Ephesus echoed. "No matter what."

I threw my arms around Daddy and hugged him. He was right; everything would be okay. I had my family and my Bible. Maybe we couldn't go back to camp, but we could make a home somewhere else—together.

The nightmare was finally over.

9

I heard it.

I couldn't see it, but I could hear it—the sharp hiss of air, like steam escaping from a canister.

I had to find it and turn it off. There wasn't much time; already thunder was grumbling in the darkening sky, indicating the impending rain.

I ran down the street. Stanyard fell in beside me.

"It's too late!" he shouted, voice almost lost under another thunder strike. "There's enough in the air already that half the city will be destroyed."

"Then we can save the other half!" I shouted back.

He didn't respond, and his footsteps faded from beside me. Maybe he ran down another street to search there. I couldn't tell; the clouds above had grown so dark I could barely see.

But I didn't need to see. I just listened, straining to catch the unmistakable hiss over the whistling wind.

I followed the sound around a corner. And there, in a plaza at the center of town, was the container.

It was massive, blocking the road like a beached submarine. The metal side was peppered with valves, all of which were cranked fully open. The shriek of invisible gas pumping into the air made my ears ring.

I grimaced and tried to focus around the thrumming in my head. I stumbled over to the canister, hacking in the cloud of gas, and felt my hand along one of the valves. There had to be a way to shut them off!

I looked around. There—in the building across the street was a control room. I could see the dashboard of levers and knobs through the windows.

A lightning strike suddenly crashed somewhere close—too close. The flare of white light blinded me, and I nearly stumbled with the impact of the thunder. I staggered forward, blinking the colored spots out of my eyes. The storm was upon me, but if I could get inside the control room, I'd be safe.

I let adrenaline work for me as I ran over and yanked on the door handle for all I was worth.

It didn't open.

I slammed my body into the glass, panic replacing the adrenaline. "Let me in!" I wailed, even though I knew nobody was inside.

I was wrong. I heard a muffled voice from the other side of the glass. "It's too late, Miss Philadelphia."

I looked up. It was Dr. Nic's voice, but I didn't see him. Someone else was inside the control room.

"Daddy!" I shrieked.

He didn't answer, but I doubted he could hear me. He was bracing himself against the dashboard, head hanging. His eyes looked so tired and bloodshot that I was worried he was going to pass out. What had they done to him?

Never mind that. He could let me in, and we could shut off the machine. "Daddy, Daddy!" I banged on the glass.

Daddy glanced at me, but someone abruptly stepped between us. Dr. Nic stood at the door and gazed down at me, arms crossed in a stance I knew all too well. I took one step back instinctively.

"It's too late," he repeated.

I believed him. He wouldn't shut off the machine, but surely he wouldn't leave me out here in the rain! "Let me in!" I cried, yanking on the door handle for emphasis.

"So you can shut down my operation again? I don't think so." His tone wasn't triumphant, but the disconnected calmness in his voice was even more disturbing.

I stared at him. *He wouldn't. He wouldn't!*

"No, please! Let me in! Please! Daddy!" I pressed my face against the glass, struggling to get a glimpse of my father. "Daddy!"

Daddy walked up and touched Dr. Nic's arm, looking at him pleadingly. Dr. Nic shrugged him off. "She had her chance. If she had joined the project when she had the opportunity, she would be in here with you."

Joined the project? I looked to Daddy. He would never join Dr. Nic's project!

Daddy wasn't looking at me. He gazed at the floor as he turned and trudged back to the control panel.

No.

Then it started to rain. I knew not because I felt the drops—but because I *heard* them. A crackling sizzle somewhere across the street. First softly, then louder. Then a scream.

I looked over my shoulder. The street behind me was wet, not with water, but with a bubbling, steaming pool of bright orange-red acid. More drops fell from the sky like dripping blood.

And the wind was blowing towards me.

I turned and pounded my fists into the glass. "Daddy, let me in!"

He wasn't listening. He was bent over the control panel, sliding a dial.

"Daddy, how could you?" I whimpered. Betrayal flooded me, followed by hope. "Daddy, shut it off! Shut it off!" I raised my voice as loud as I could. "Shut it off!"

He looked up at me, eyes so sunken it looked like he was nearly dead. "Philadelphia, it's the only way," he said, so quietly I could barely hear him.

"Daddy!" I wailed, not sure what else to utter. "Daddy, Daddy, *Daddy!*"

I heard the sizzling acid creep up behind me like a vat of quicksand. I rammed myself into the door—my fists, my elbows, anything, as hard as I could—willing the glass to break. I prepared myself for the sharp pain of broken glass cutting my skin, and it came. Pain seared up my arms, and I screamed.

But the glass hadn't broken. I looked down to see the vile red liquid dripping off my arm, leaving a horrible burn.

More splashed against my face, my hands, my legs. I screamed again and again as the horrible sensation of scalding wetness drowned my senses.

I crumbled to the floor, my sense of touch quickly leaving me. There was nowhere to run.

No one could escape Red Rain.

"Philli, Philli!"

"Ephesus?" I gasped, unable to place the voice. "Stanyard?"

"Philli, it's me. Daddy."

It was him. His voice sounded like he was right by my head, but I couldn't see him; I couldn't see anything but darkness and splashes of red. Had he opened the door for me?

"Daddy…" I whimpered, not having the strength to speak any louder.

"Philli," he said again. This time his voice was so loud and clear I jumped. He touched my arm, and my sense of feeling came back.

And I felt no pain.

At first, I felt nothing. Then, cold stiffness came to my bones; I was lying on something hard and unforgiving. A blanket was draped over me. And Daddy was shaking my shoulder.

"Philadelphia." I looked up into his concerned face. "What's wrong?"

It took me a minute to figure out the answer to that question. I blinked, and the darkened ceiling above Daddy's head came into focus, causing me to remember where I was.

I let out a sigh and relaxed against the concrete. "Nightmares."

Daddy rubbed my shoulder. "About?" he prodded.

I glanced back up at him. He looked almost as tired as he had in the nightmare.

I cringed as the events of the dream came back to me in full color. I should tell him. He would want to know.

But I didn't want to. How could I tell him he had become a nightmare to me?

I avoided his gaze, curling back up under the blanket. "Just… everything that's been going on," I fudged.

He grunted in understanding and rubbed my shoulder consolingly. His fingers felt cold. I shivered and hoped he couldn't tell.

I was grateful when the hatch to the basement opened and Stanyard called down to us, distracting my father from further conversation.

My gratefulness vanished when I realized Stanyard was yelling in panic.

"Come on! We need to run, *now!*"

He was loud enough that he roused Ephesus and Cea from their sleep. Ephesus mumbled something generic, but Cea was upright and alert in a heartbeat. "Where's Nic?"

I think that's when we all realized Nic was no longer in the basement. And given the fact that Stanyard had ordered us not to leave the room, I think I subconsciously understood what was going on.

Stanyard confirmed my suspicions when he snapped at Cea, "Your brother decided it was a good idea to hack some government sites on the public wifi where everyone could see him. And judging by the sites he hacked, I don't think the United will have any trouble figuring out it's him."

Ephesus had fully woken by this time and joined us in collectively staring at Stanyard in disbelief. Even Cea couldn't find anything to say.

Stanyard jumped down the ladder and dropped his voice to an authoritative whisper. "We need to move immediately. Nic's hacking no doubt raised huge red flags in the United's system, so it won't take them long to investigate it and track the internet usage to here. I need you all out of here by the time they get here—if they find anything amiss, we're *all* done for."

By the time he finished, we were all standing. Ephesus and Cea were already scrambling for belongings.

"Where are we going?" Daddy asked with firm calmness.

"A rendezvous point across town. We just need to get you off the premises while the United looks around. Hopefully when they don't find you or the computer here they'll assume you were just passing through and using the area wifi. If they pin me with harboring you, I don't know what I'll do."

My heart lurched. "Where are you going?"

Stanyard looked at me. "I'm going with you. You need to use my car, and it will look suspicious if I'm here but my car's gone. The shop doesn't open until 11, so I have a few hours' window before they'll expect me to be back."

"We're ready." Ephesus stepped up with a bag slung over his shoulder, looking fully prepared. "How many will fit in your car?"

Stanyard opened his mouth, but Daddy interrupted him. "All of us." Stanyard turned to him with a frown, but Daddy returned the look with one of parental authority. "We're staying together."

The frustration burned darkly in Stanyard's eyes as he snapped, "Then some of you will be going without seat belts. Let's go." Without another word, he turned around and scrambled up the ladder. Cea followed him without hesitation.

"Philli."

I turned and brushed arms with Ephesus as he leaned close to me. He pressed something cold and small into my hands.

"Keep this on you," he said in a voice designed to prevent overhearing, even though the only other person in the room was Daddy.

I flipped the device between my fingers; it was an old flash drive. "What's this?"

"It's some of my files," he said. "If something happens, they'll definitely take my bag." He shifted the duffle protectively. "I don't want all my work in one place."

The foreboding implications of his words should have disturbed me, but adrenaline was clouding my ability to think of anything but the present. Images of spies hiding knives and guns in their shoes came to me, and I slid the drive inside my sock and wedged it down into my sneaker. I felt silly copying what I'd seen on TV, but Ephesus smiled encouragingly.

Daddy laid a hand on my shoulder. "Are you ready?"

I threw a glance around the room, startled by the question. What did I have to prepare? I hadn't brought anything with me when we broke out of the apartment complex.

I pressed my hands against my pocket to make sure my reader was still there. "I'm ready," I said with as much brave confidence as I could muster, even though my heart was starting to flutter rapidly.

He nodded and gestured for me to climb up the ladder ahead of him.

I stole a quick glance at Stanyard's bedroom—if you could call it that—as we ran through the upper basement. The stairs took us to the hallway behind the shop, which was cluttered with teetering stacks of supplies.

"You can't go into the shop," Stanyard warned in a whisper, standing in the hallway as if to block the way. "Regulations require security cameras to be placed in all businesses. I managed to block the one in the hallway with supplies." He pointed towards the exterior door. "Wait in the garage. Keep quiet and stay below the windows. I'm going to make it look like I went grocery shopping." He turned and darted off down the hallway.

Daddy took my hand and led me towards the door. We stepped into the garage just in time to hear Cea slap her brother in the face.

A brief bitter argument ensued, but Ephesus stepped between them. "Hey, save it for when you don't have to whisper."

Cea scowled like a bulldog but remained silent. Dr. Nic looked merely annoyed and not nearly concerned enough for the severity of the situation.

The door slammed seconds later, and Stanyard came out jangling keys. "Everyone in. Who's volunteering to ride in the trunk?"

I wondered if that was sarcastic, but Cea instantly responded, "Nic and I will." I was even more surprised when Nic didn't argue.

Stanyard popped the hatch on his green car. "Okay. The rest of you will have to get down on the floor. If they watch the security cameras to see when I leave, they can't see that there's anyone else with me in the vehicle."

Guess we're all going without seat belts. I glanced at Daddy in alarm. He didn't look happy about it either, but he didn't object and guided me towards the car.

Ephesus managed to fit creatively on the floor in front of the passenger's seat. I got in next and curled up on the floor behind the driver's seat. Daddy got in from the other side and laid down with his arms over me protectively. I squeezed his hand, but it didn't make me feel any more secure.

Stanyard slammed the trunk and climbed in the driver's seat. My stomach lurched as the car rocked and rumbled noisily to life. My uneasiness was not at all abated by the fact that Stanyard's car was obviously and audibly a clunker.

Stanyard paused for a split second to adjust the controls. I couldn't see him from my position, but I heard him take in a breath and let it out. "Hang on tight," he said by way of warning.

I heard the garage door groaning open. Stanyard pulled the car out slowly. I gasped and braced my hands against the seat as the car lurched down the incline of the driveway.

Stanyard braked at the street and flicked his turn signal on. He let it click irritatingly for what seemed like an unusually long time. Was the road that busy? I couldn't hear much traffic.

"Coast clear?" Ephesus ventured after a moment.

Stanyard swore for an answer.

Daddy and I both stiffened. "What?" Ephesus hissed.

"Either Nic was on the computer longer than I realized, or the United really wants him back. Three squad cars approaching." He drummed his fingers on the steering wheel before abruptly switching the signal off and turning. "I wonder what the chance of them chasing me is if I pull out slowly?" he remarked with dry amusement.

I swallowed and held my breath to keep my stomach down as we turned onto the road. For a few seconds, the ride was smooth as Stanyard casually accelerated.

And then I heard glass shattering.

I screamed and covered my head as a few pieces of glass flew. Someone else yelled, and the car swerved. I looked up to see a spiderweb spreading through the glass of the rear window.

"Well, that answers that question!" Stanyard muttered, and slammed on the gas.

I shrieked as the car revved forward, shoving me into Stanyard's seat. Daddy shook my shoulder. "Get up and buckle your seat belt, now."

I struggled to obey, but Stanyard shouted back at us. "You're less likely to get shot if you stay down there!"

"Stay down, Dad," Ephesus urged us from the front.

I curled into a ball, pressing myself flat against the floor. I felt Daddy lay down on top of me, shielding my head with his chest.

The car continued to race forward, faster and faster. I could just barely hear sirens over the groan of the engine laboring furiously.

The car suddenly wrenched around a corner. I involuntarily cried out in fear at the violent motion. *Please don't crash. We'll all lose if you crash.*

"Where are we going now?" Ephesus yelled.

"Still the rendezvous point, if we can lose them!" Stanyard returned, sounding like he was talking through gritted teeth. "Looks like I'll just be staying with you all."

My heart shriveled in grief. *What are we going to do now?* I slid my hands over my face, even though I couldn't see much of anything anyway.

The car swerved again. "Drive safely!" my dad urged, echoing my thoughts.

"Not an option!" Stanyard fired back.

"Can you try losing them on the freeway?" Ephesus suggested.

"Not enough traffic this early in the morning." Stanyard braked roughly before making what felt like an almost 180-degree turn.

"Try the—whoa!" Ephesus broke off in a yell.

"Ephesus, are you all right?" my father shouted.

"Yeah," he replied, although his voice was noticeably shaken. "They're still firing."

I heard the shots firing outside the car. I could only hope they weren't peppering the trunk with bullet holes.

"We could try that back street. Park the car behind a business and let them blaze past."

"Can't—they sent a car down the side street. Saw them."

"You have to get where they can't see you turn—this street is too wide open."

"I know that! But I can't turn here!"

They continued to bicker, voices deteriorating into chaos. I covered my ears. *Please, God, please.* I struggled to take deep breaths. It didn't help that I could feel my father's chest shaking.

"Here! Turn here!" Ephesus yelled.

Stanyard did. And then we crashed.

Everything happened all at once. The car lurched so hard I lost my sense of direction. My father's weight pressed down on me as he fell. Several people yelled. I think I screamed. Above it all I could hear the hideously distinct sound of metal crunching. Glass shattered.

And then everything became abruptly still. For an eerie moment, nothing moved, and there was no sound except for the distant wailing of sirens.

Then my father groaned and struggled to sit up. "Philli?" He shook my shoulder. "Philli, are you all right?"

I wasn't even sure how to answer the question. I slowly lifted my head and looked around. "I… think so."

I became aware of Stanyard muttering in the front. I turned to see Ephesus slumped into the passenger seat, hands pressed against his bloody face.

"Ephesus!" I shrieked.

"Son!" Daddy echoed my cry. He started to rise, then turned and pressed a hand on my shoulder. "Stay here. We're waiting for the officers to arrive. I'm not letting either of you get hurt anymore." He sat up and threw his door open.

The meaning of his words sank into me. "We're turning ourselves in? But what about Stanyard and Cea?"

"Don't move!" was the firm reply. He scrambled out of the car and opened the passenger door, bending over Ephesus.

I sat up and looked around for Stanyard. He was struggling to force the driver's door open; it was jammed against a dumpster. With several swift kicks he managed to get the door open just enough for him to squeeze through. He jumped out and yanked my door open.

"Let's go! We can escape on foot through the alleys. They can't take their cars down here, so we still have a chance of losing them."

I scrambled up and looked out. It appeared as though we had raced around the corner into an alley and hit a dumpster. I could hear the sirens still approaching us from the main road, but the alley was a clear shot. We could easily run.

But just as I grabbed the door to step out, I heard Daddy's voice behind me and halted.

No. We were not running again. Daddy said—

Before I could even finish the thought, Stanyard's urgent cry countered it. "Come on, Phil! We have to go, now!"

"Philli, come over here!" Daddy called. His voice sounded so distant and squeaky.

Stanyard held out his hand to me.

"Philadelphia!"

We could stop running. We could end this game of cat and mouse.

"Phil, if you don't come now I'll leave you behind!"

Or we could escape and perhaps never have to play this game again.

I reached out and grasped Stanyard's hand.

I was a second too late.

A shot fired somewhere in my peripheral. I had barely registered the noise before pain ripped through my leg.

I screamed and stumbled forward, falling out of the car. My head hit the ground so hard I could barely feel the sensation of the concrete scraping my face and my arms.

I saw Stanyard standing over me and was able to remember that I had to get up *now*. I tried to sit up and abruptly realized what had happened when I found my right leg was completely numb and immobile.

I had been hit by a stun shot. Now I *couldn't* run. I looked to Stanyard in a panic.

He kept his word. He turned around and ran, leaving me behind.

"Stanyard!" I cried, wheezing and nearly choking. All the wind had been knocked out of me. Stanyard disappeared around a building without looking back.

I slumped back on the ground, my clouded emotions suddenly venting themselves as tears. I heard shouts and sirens and orders from all directions, but it seemed like an inordinately long time before an officer bothered to come around the car and pick me up. Somehow that made the wound burn all the worse.

The officer scooped me up in his arms without a word. He was big and strong, and that made me feel all the more pitiful. *You're a fool. Such a fool!* I started to cry.

"Philadelphia!" My father was beside us. His hands were cuffed, but he didn't seem to mind as he reached up and stroked my forehead. "Are you all right? What were you doing?"

His tone was more condescending than concerned, like he was disappointed I had even considered making a break for it.

I sobbed harder.

"Philli, Philli." Daddy's tone changed to the one of gentle love I so craved, though I could barely hear it around the buzzing in my head. "It will be all right. I'm here." He kissed the top of my head and then found my hand.

I squeezed his hand and struggled to dam my emotions. It would be all right, I told myself. As long as we went quietly, everything would be fine. No more running. No more secrets and guns and bloodshed. And our family would be together again.

That's what was most important, I reminded myself. I needed to be with my family, no matter where that took me. This wasn't about escaping or finding freedom. This was about keeping my family together. That's what Daddy would say.

And yet, glancing back down the alley where Stanyard had fled, I couldn't help but wonder if I had my priorities wrong.

10

I was wrong.

Turning ourselves in didn't do any good. Daddy and I weren't even able to stay together. As soon as we reached the station, they split us up, because of course male and female prisoners had to be separated.

They put me in a holding cell and did just that—hold me. They didn't even bother to search me, make me sign paperwork, or give me a prison uniform. They just shoved me in, closed the door, and walked away.

They didn't allow me to send a message to my father. They never even told me how Ephesus was doing or how bad his injuries were. They just left me alone in my cell, which was even tinier and more deplorable than the one at the apartment complex, to wait until they gave me my sentence.

There wouldn't be a trial. I had forfeited that formality long ago by refusing to sign the file. Not that there was anything to stand trial on; there was no denying what I had done. I had been condemned since I broke out of the apartment building. Now it was just a matter of the officials deciding what to do with me.

I knew being sent quietly back to camp was no longer an option, but I didn't know what other options existed. I didn't want to imagine the possibilities and, in a way, I wasn't sure it mattered what they did to me. I had already lost the only thing that was important to me—the privilege to live with my family. Where I was sent now hardly made a difference.

At the moment, it looked like they wouldn't bother to send me anywhere and would just leave me to suffer in prison until they were motivated to process my paperwork; it had been three days without a word of contact from the officials.

I spent those days crying bitterly off and on. It was over. Surrendering had ended the game of cat and mouse, but it ended with the cat eating the mouse. I was a fool to think it would ever be any other way.

It was a great mercy when, on the fourth day, the United sent a guard down to talk to me.

"You have been sentenced to prison for life," he said without any other greeting. This was hardly news to me; I had been in one form of prison or another for the past five years.

"You are being transferred to the facility on Rott immediately," he continued. The name meant nothing to me, but what was one prison from another?

The guard pressed his thumb on the keypad and opened the door to my cell. I guess he meant "immediately" literally.

I stood up and followed him without a word. I didn't need to do anything to get ready. I had nothing except for the clothes on my back—and my reader, which I had managed to keep concealed in my pocket.

The guard led me through the sterile white halls to a little visiting room, where another guard met us at the door. "You have been permitted to see your father," he informed me.

I jolted out of my stupor with a sudden resurgence of hope. Maybe Daddy was coming with me. Maybe God had given us a way to be together after all.

"Ten minutes," the guard warned, and pushed the door open.

I ran through it. "Daddy!" I cried.

He was the only one in the room. He sat at the far end of a bare conference table, one hand cuffed to the metal chair. He didn't call out as I approached, but as soon as I was beside him he put his free arm around me and kissed me on the head.

"Philadelphia," he whispered.

I knelt by his chair. "I've been sentenced to Rott," I said, talking quickly to make the most of the time.

He stroked my hair. "I know. They told me."

I looked into his face. "Are you coming with me?"

He shook his head. "I haven't received my sentence yet."

The hope started to drain from my heart, making it beat faster. "Maybe they'll send you and Ephesus there too," I said, still grasping at the chance, "and then we can be together."

"I doubt it," was his quiet reply.

I doubt it? What kind of response was that? "Why wouldn't they send you to prison too?"

He just shrugged.

I struggled to maintain a calm tone of voice. "Daddy, we have to hope. God kept us together when you were sent to Mars—He can keep us together now." I grasped his free hand between both of mine. "Try asking them. Maybe they will because we're family."

"You know they won't listen, Philadelphia," he said with a sigh.

I knew it was true, but what did it hurt to try? It was our only chance. "Dad, please. Just ask them. It's our only hope—I'm not going to be coming back from Rott."

"I know," he replied.

I know? Was that all he could say? I looked up into his face, searching for more.

He pulled his hand out of my grasp and reached up to touch my cheek. He studied me for a long moment before he whispered, "I'm sorry, Philadelphia. There's nothing I can do. Nothing."

I remembered the last time he had said those words to me: When he told me that he was being sent to a base on Mars, and I was not permitted to accompany him. When he was sending me to live with complete strangers because he didn't know if he would ever be back. When we had no choice but to allow the United to split us apart.

I didn't want to believe that this was the same situation. I didn't want to admit that the only option was to say goodbye.

Daddy stroked my cheek. "It will be all right."

I didn't believe him this time. It wouldn't be all right. Not now. Not ever.

"Behave. Be polite."

No. Not this again. I won't do this again!

"Just do as they say. Go with them quietly and they'll go easier on you."

No, they wouldn't. They never had. Surrendering never worked. Surrendering got us contained in a camp, and now it had brought us here.

I wouldn't surrender again while they tore my family apart for good.

"No, Daddy, we can't do this. I won't leave you!"

"We don't have a choice."

"Daddy, please! We have to do something!" I stood up and grabbed his arm. "Just ask them! Just try for once, please!"

"Philli—"

"I'm not going quietly!" I declared, fairly shrieking. "I'm not going to just stand by and let them rip us apart again. We have to *do* something. Please, Daddy, help me!" I yanked on his arm, begging him to move, to stand, to do something, anything. "Daddy, please!"

"Hey!" One of the guards grabbed my arm and pulled me back. "That's enough. Time's up."

"No!" I screamed, struggling against him in every way I knew how.

I managed to land a good kick on his shin. With a growl he shoved me to the floor, causing me to ram my chin on the tile.

"Behave," he ordered from above.

I pushed myself to my knees, wiping a smear of blood off my lips. "No," I said, this time coldly collected. *Not this time.* I took a deep breath and rose.

"I won't go," I said calmly. I stepped in front of Daddy's chair, shielding him. "We're a family. Splitting us isn't right, and you know it."

"Girl—" the guard started to warn me, but I cut him off.

"Think about what you're doing! You're breaking apart a family and sending a woman off to prison alone. How is that right? How is that a fair punishment for what I've done?"

Both of the guards stepped towards me, as if I would find that threatening. "You have been sentenced—" one started.

"I'm not asking what your superiors told you—I'm asking if you think this is right! If you have to send us to prison, why can't you send us both to the same place? What will that hurt? How's that any different than keeping him locked up here? All I'm asking is that you put in a word—"

"Philli," Daddy interrupted, the softness of his tone causing me to stop and turn to face him.

He stared into my eyes and said, "Just go. Please. Before you get hurt."

Just go. Not "Goodbye." Not "I love you." Not even "I'm sorry."

Just go.

I, for my part, could find nothing to say.

The guards took advantage of my sudden silence and dragged me away. Daddy watched me go. I searched his eyes for the reassurance his words had lacked, but his expression wasn't teary. It wasn't even shocked. It was just tired. Tired and weary.

It wasn't until after the door had slammed and locked between us that my own emotions began to flow again. Tears blurred my vision as the guards continued to shove me down the hall. I didn't care. I didn't need to watch where I was going, so I kept my head down and allowed myself to be led along.

The guards started bickering. Something about transporting me. I only started listening when a voice I knew joined the conversation.

"That's already been arranged."

Recognition made me look up and focus on the face. Shock briefly dried my tears.

Commander Ambrose stood over me. The cold, professional expression I was used to seeing him wear had been replaced by an unreservedly delighted sneer.

My nerves snapped out of their grief when I realized things could still get worse. Much worse.

"I will be escorting her to Rott personally," he chirped. He hooked his arm with mine and swept me down the hall. Had he not been pinching my arm deliberately, one would have thought by his tones and actions that he was talking me out on a date.

The very idea made my stomach reel.

He led me out of the building to a waiting car. He opened the passenger door with a flourish. "Won't you sit up with me so we can have a chat?"

My utter disgust was making me feel defiant, so I quickly slipped into the back seat, opening the door for myself and slamming it resolutely.

I instantly regretted my decision when, not seconds later, a guard opened the opposite door and deposited a handcuffed Dr. Nic in the backseat.

Suddenly sitting shotgun with Commander Ambrose seemed like a good option.

Dr. Nic glared at Commander Ambrose so viciously that the arch of his eyebrows looked downright painful. After a moment of concentrated hatred, he seemed to realize there was someone beside him and glanced sideways. When he spotted me, his gaze focused into a look that was far worse than the one he had just given Ambrose.

I wished he would come right out and say, *"You just turned this into pure torture for me."* It would have taken far less effort than contorting his face the way he was.

Unfortunately, despite my best attempts, I was probably giving him the same look.

A glance at Commander Ambrose's grin in the review mirror confirmed that he had planned it this way.

This *was* torture. Specialized torture devised just for me, simply because Commander Ambrose had a grudge and enough political weight to achieve vengeance. His personal agenda was probably the only reason I was getting sent to Rott while my family was left behind.

Grief nipped at my cheeks. I sucked in my breath and turned to face the window. I forced thoughts of my family out of my mind and instead brooded over the injustice. I raved inwardly about how this was all Commander Ambrose's fault because he hated me, elaborating on how absurd and unfair this all was. They weren't very charitable thoughts, but they kept me from succumbing to fear. I was sure my dad would agree—

No. My dad had no expectations on my behavior anymore. As far as he was concerned, I had flown the nest.

I was on my own.

11

Mercifully, Ambrose was content to savor his victory in silence as he drove us to our destination. I had assumed mutual distaste would keep Dr. Nic and me from attempting any small talk, but to my surprise, he was the first to break the silence.

"It's an island," he declared after about fifteen minutes.

"What is?" I said, venturing a glance at him. He seemed to have cooled off considerably; his livid scowl had been replaced by a frown of cold boredom as he stared out the window at the nondescript highway.

"Rott," he replied. "The prison. It's an island." He paused, then added, "I've been there," as if he had anticipated my next question.

He didn't offer any more information, and even this revelation quickly became redundant. As soon as we came in sight of a military dock filled with various United ships, I made the intelligent deduction that our prison must involve water.

Being surrounded by open sea was certainly as effective a containment method as any.

Several guards approached the car and helped Commander Ambrose escort us to a waiting ship. Ambrose led the way, brandishing his badge at all the nearby officials, although none of them were asking for it. I realized in retrospect how idiotic he looked: a pompous, over-decorated commander leading a sorry parade, as though capturing a few riffraff criminals was something to be proud of.

Aside from Ambrose's gleeful display, there was very little ceremony to our boarding. We were led up the gangplank, checked off on a ledger, and shoved over to a corner where Ambrose kept a needlessly close eye on us until the ship launched. My heart lurched with the deck when the ship detached from the dock, but I was more worried about Ambrose's constant stare than the receding shoreline.

I kept waiting for something to happen—for them to handcuff me, or put a tracking device on me, or lead us off to cells. This was a prison ship, wasn't it?

Instead, the opposite happened. As soon as the ship had chugged far enough out to sea that swimming back to land wasn't a feasible option, Commander Ambrose approached Dr. Nic. Dr. Nic's eyes flitted defensively as he watched Commander Ambrose's every move, but he didn't flinch as the bulky guard leaned over him. With an annoying beep from a handheld device, Dr. Nic's handcuffs dropped off.

Commander Ambrose stepped back and gestured at the open deck. "Enjoy your voyage," he said, still too gleeful to be considered sane. "You can go below deck in the main hold, or you can savor the view."

Without waiting to see what our choice was, he sauntered off and disappeared into an officer's cabin.

I stayed still for a long minute, still stunned with confusion. Were they not afraid that we might try to escape?

Only when I heard a cold splash on the water, followed by callous laughter and shouts of *"First!"* from the guards, did I realize that their intent was quite the opposite: If we wanted to jump overboard, we were quite welcome to.

"Tempting," Dr. Nic muttered, "but I'd rather not go out freezing. I'm going below deck out of the wind."

I'm not sure why he was telling me, especially when he didn't wait for a response before walking away. I didn't follow him.

I stayed on deck all night. I'm sure sitting out in the cold wind, being sprayed by the occasional stray wave, did not help my vain pursuit of sleep. But I didn't want to go below deck. Somehow it seemed safer to stay up top, in sight of the security lights and the night watch, than to go down below in the open hold with all the other prisoners.

Finding sleep down there would have been impossible, anyway. Might as well stay on deck, where I had found a somewhat sheltered spot between some shipping containers and a ventilation pipe.

Sleep never came, but I didn't bother looking for it. I wished I could have read my Bible, but I was worried the glow of the screen would arouse the suspicion of the guards. So I spent most of the night with my knees pulled up to my chest, my hands pressed against my reader in my pocket.

Watching the sunrise was a bittersweet affair. On one hand, I thanked God for the return of the daylight to brighten the deck and warm the air. On the other hand, the sunshine also brought the other prisoners back to the surface.

I ignored the call for first meal. I wasn't keen on giving away my position. The rations probably weren't worth the effort, anyway. I stayed curled up in my hidey-hole, hoping to go unnoticed and ignored.

When no one approached me for the better part of the morning, I decided to risk taking out my reader. What good was having it if I was never able to read it? I kept the screen light down and my knees pulled up, hopefully shielding the device from any nosy passerby.

I opened the bookmark to the Bible passage I had been studying last. At first I spent more time fugitively glancing around than reading, but the lull of the text soon pulled me in. Settling back, I glazed through the chapters, idly swiping my finger across the screen to turn the pages. I wasn't studying the passages; the deeper meaning was lost on me as I devoured the book like one might scarf down a novel for pleasure. I wasn't looking for prophetic instruction this time; I just wanted the comfort of the familiar text. It was like having a friend sitting next to me in companionable silence; just looking at the words on the screen reminded me that the book—and its Author—were still near.

I became so absorbed in the rhythm that I didn't notice someone approaching until they stopped in front of me and blocked the sunlight. Startled, I jerked my head up and nearly collided with the chin of Commander Ambrose.

For a split second I was frozen in fear, partially because of the close proximity of his face to mine. But the hot foulness of his breath soon made me squirm and struggle to pull away. I tried to slide my reader into my pocket, but that second lost in fear was a second too long. Ambrose already had his hand around my wrist.

"What's this? Smuggling electronics?" he jeered with an annoying perk to his voice. He had clearly gotten plenty of sleep.

"It's mine!" I cried fruitlessly as he easily yanked the device from my grasp.

He straightened and squinted at the screen. His face lit up with that delighted sneer I had seen one too many times in the past twenty-four hours. "Oh," he crooned, "contraband."

I snarled, more out of anger than fear. "Give it back! Please," I added, briefly wondering if pleading would work on him.

He started walking away. "You know, this book is illegal to own."

I scrambled up and trotted after him, trying not to panic. "Not for unassimilated," I reminded him, hoping to hit on whatever fragment of mercy had caused him to allow us to keep our Bibles at camp. But somehow I knew that fragment of mercy didn't exist anymore, if it ever had.

He stopped by the deck railing and looked down at me. "You're not unassimilated anymore," he spat. "You're worse than that. The unassimilated are still part of the system. You've been thrown out with the trash."

I couldn't come up with a reply, partially because I knew he was right.

"That means you have no rights," Ambrose continued with unmasked glee, "and certainly no rights to own something like this." He dangled the reader above my head and wiggled it tauntingly.

I gazed at it helplessly, all the resistance gone from my system. "Please," I whispered, "just let me keep it."

He closed his large fist around the device. "And what will you do in exchange?"

I shifted my gaze to his face. Is that what this was all about? Had he truly dropped so low?

But what could I do about it? I might as well play his petty games if it meant I could keep my Bible.

"Anything," I said with total honesty.

He grinned wildly. "Tempting," he said, "but I can't think of anything I want from you." And in one swift motion, he turned and hurled my reader into the sea.

I think I screamed an objection. I could never remember. My mind wasn't on whatever pitiful exclamations may have left my mouth as I lunged forward, propelled by the desperate hope that I could catch it.

I slammed into the deck railing with my stomach and had to grab the bar with both hands to keep from falling overboard. All the wind knocked out of me, I couldn't even cry as I watched my reader hit the water with a fatal splash and sink out of sight.

I stared at the waves for several moments, vainly hoping to see it bob back to the surface. But I knew it wouldn't float. As hard as it was to process, I knew my reader was gone—and with it my only hope of ever owning a Bible again.

Ambrose approached me from behind, talking. I had no idea what he said because my mind was suddenly overcome with a ravenous thought. In one instinctive motion, I turned and punched him in the gut.

He grunted and jerked back, glaring at me with unmasked shock. I was just as surprised as he was. My hand tingled from the impact and my mind from the realization of what I had done. Then, for a very brief moment, it felt good.

That moment ended when Ambrose punched me back.

I stumbled backwards but managed to retain my balance. His next strike seemed perfectly timed to send me to the ground.

No sooner had I hit the deck then he kicked me. Twice. Three times. My head was spinning so violently I couldn't do anything but squeeze out a whimpered cry, the breath again knocked from my chest.

Ambrose paused for a moment to leer over me and issue threats. I couldn't remember his exact words, but I got the gist. *That's what happens when you sass me, girl.*

I coughed, struggling to get my breath back. Reprimands swirled around in my head, as if spoken by my father's voice. *Stop fighting. You'll only get hurt.*

Tears shot to my eyes and quickly dropped to the deck.

"Hey!"

Both Ambrose and I looked up to see Nic leaning on the deck railing nearby. He stroked his mustache casually. "I'm curious, Ambrose," he said cheerfully. "Did the United train you to hit women, or are you just that vile on your own?"

Both Ambrose and I stared at him. Was he defending me, or just enjoying the spectacle? I struggled to sit up.

Dr. Nic pushed himself off the railing and sauntered towards Ambrose. "I'll admit to being a little impressed, though. I mean, you had the guts to hit a woman in front of all these men," he gave a broad gesture at the prisoners and guards loitering around the deck, "whose protective instincts might flare up at any moment. Even I don't have the courage to do that."

Commander Ambrose gave a short laugh. It was short because Nic punched him in the stomach and cut him off.

Ambrose sputtered indignantly, but his return strike was almost immediate. But Nic's lean and swift form seemed to have an advantage over Ambrose's hefty one, and in the ensuing scuffle he managed to deal at least twice as many hits as he took.

I watched in speechless wonder. I had no idea Dr. Nic could fight like that. I was even more surprised that he would employ his skills in my defense.

I doubted either of them were getting hurt that much, but when blood spurted from Ambrose's lip, he decided he'd had enough. He roared and lunged forward, slamming all his body weight into Dr. Nic like a charging bull. Nic lost his balance and fell backwards on the deck with a grunt.

Ambrose shook himself and stomped towards Nic as he struggled to rise. Suddenly I worried that the fight was about to get ugly—if not lethal.

"Stop!" I cried before I could catch myself, but a shrill whistle blast outshouted me.

I turned to see a captain and several guards jog towards us. "Ambrose!" the captain barked. "What is the meaning of this?"

Ambrose stopped and turned to him. He seemed to struggle for a reply, long enough that Nic spoke first. "Oh, just having a friendly duel in defense of a lady," he chirped, sitting up and brushing himself off. "All in good fun."

The captain abruptly seemed to realize I was there, kneeling on the floor with my arm around my stomach. I could tell by the way his eyes widened and then darkened that he understood the situation.

"They were causing a ruckus, sir," Ambrose offered, voice noticeably shaky.

"I've no doubt about that," the captain quipped. "But that's what tasers are for. You know the regulations."

Before Ambrose could sputter out a defense, the captain added, "Or were they too much for you and your only option was to defend yourself with your fists?"

The look on Commander Ambrose's face was priceless. It took all my willpower not to smile.

Dr. Nic seemed to have no such reservations as he stood up, grinning delightedly as if he'd planned it this way all along.

The captain straightened, his voice returning to its normal bark. "Quarters, Ambrose."

"But—" he protested, looking and sounding like a child being sent to the corner.

"Did you not tell me yourself that your job is not to guard the prisoners?" the captain cut him off calmly. "So since you cannot do your job until we reach Rott, it would do me a great favor if you would stay below deck and stop interfering with my guards' work."

It was phrased as a polite suggestion, but the captain's tone and expression indicated it was anything but. Offering up no argument except a smoldering stare, Commander Ambrose turned and marched across the deck.

The captain turned back to us. "Now, what do you have to say for yourselves?"

"She started it," Nic said with a shrug.

I shot a pained glare in his direction. Now was not a good time for jokes. My glare turned into an honest grimace as I struggled to rise. I gasped and braced myself against the railing.

The captain grunted. "It seems I'll need to separate you from the other prisoners, girl. Someone is going to get hurt—most likely you, it would seem."

I looked up at him worriedly. Did he honestly think I had done something to provoke Ambrose? Was he going to punish me now?

The captain glanced at the guards behind him. "Lock her in one of the unused quarters and prohibit anyone from visiting her without my permission. That should prevent further... incidents."

"Yes, sir." One of the guards came over to assist me to my feet. "You, come with me."

I didn't dare resist as he took my arm and led me across the deck. It wasn't until we reached the door to the stairwell that I realized what the captain had done for me.

I glanced over my shoulder, but the captain had already walked away. Dr. Nic was still there, leaning against the deck railing with his arms crossed, watching me.

Had he planned it this way? Had he done this—for me?

I recalled the images of him punching Commander Ambrose in the face. I didn't have the courage to shout with all the guards listening, so I simply mouthed the words *"Thank you."*

He answered me with a nod.

12

Rott was, in fact, an island, and that was really all that could be said about it.

It was a formless floating mass of land that had been razed of all vegetation. There was barely even any sand on the shore. Mismatched concrete and stone buildings crowded for space as though they were afraid they were going to fall off the edge into the ocean. There was no fence or barbed wire; again, it seemed like swimming with the fish was always a viable option.

The only thing that distinguished it as a prison was the four guard towers stationed at each perpendicular of the island. We passed under the shadow of one as we were herded off the boat and into the yard. I glanced up at the glass-walled balcony three stories above me and caught a glimpse of a lone guard idling at the controls. He was not that much older than me, with dirty blond hair he hadn't bothered to comb. He was watching the offloading prisoners with, of all expressions, a raised eyebrow.

"That's Tower."

"I can see it's a tower," I returned without looking. I knew it was Dr. Nic beside me.

"No, that's his name. The guard."

"Really?"

He shrugged.

"Is he a friend?"

Nic paused and looked up. The two men stared at each other for a good ten seconds, but if any emotion was exchanged, I missed it.

Nic looked away and continued walking. "I don't think friends will help us much in here."

I decided to resume ignoring him.

The captain shuttled us into the barracks, which was the first building on the right. I was relieved to find that all of the buildings and their subsequent halls were clearly labeled. My new quarters were marked Cell #3.8—third floor, eighth cell from the elevator. None of the prisoners had any security clearance; all doors had to be unlocked by a guard.

At least I wouldn't be getting lost in prison.

My cell wasn't that much different than the one back on the mainland. If it weren't for the irritated sound of the restless sea echoing through the drafty building, I could have imagined I was back on the shore.

As a mercy to us both, Nic was contained on another floor. However, if I was hoping my confinement would lead to some alone time, I was sorely mistaken.

Not ten minutes after I got settled in, Commander Ambrose sauntered up to my floor, again dragging Dr. Nic behind him. I assumed Nic was as frustrated as I was, but he didn't bother to belie his irritation. He just looked grossly overtired.

"I'm here to assign you to your new jobs," Commander Ambrose crooned. He seemed to have recovered from his scolding on the ship and was back to exuberantly enjoying his vacation.

Working for Commander Ambrose sounded like cruel and unusual punishment, but perhaps doing menial work was better than scratching off the days on the wall in my cell. In either case, I decided to follow Nic's example and not betray my ragged emotions as I followed the commander down the hall.

He led us to the building at the center of the island. Even though it was the plainest and ugliest building—if that were possible—it appeared to be the most important. Ambrose had to flag us through multiple layers of security—armed guards at the door, metal detectors, even a secretary—before we descended on a dimly-lit elevator to the heart of the building.

"I'm one of the few people who has full access to this building," he reminded us at least twice. "They won't let you in without me—so don't be late for your shifts."

He resumed that self-important grin he had been practicing so much lately. I thought about asking him what would happen if I were late, but I decided not to push it on my first day at work.

The elevator stopped three floors down. As if relishing the reveal, the doors groaned open slowly, allowing our eyes to adjust to the sudden brilliance of a million fluorescent lights. They dangled from the ceiling like tired stars, illuminating an absolutely monstrous factory.

The thunder of noise hit me almost as hard as the smell of grease and sulfur. The elevator dumped out onto a railed ledge overlooking it all. Without thinking, I walked up to the edge and leaned over, taking everything in at once. Below me, dozens of machines worked overtime to the tune of hissing steam and clanking gears. Across the room, two massive holding tanks like barn silos were bolted to the wall. From their sides spawned a writhing network of pipes and gauges that crawled across the ceiling, accessible only by the swaying network of catwalks and service ladders that dangled by rusty chains.

My head spun just looking at it. It wasn't until Commander Ambrose spoke that I realized I had closed my eyes.

"You'll be working over there." He pointed across a narrow walkway that jutted out over the factory. It led to an alcove in front of the holding tanks, where the mess of gauges and dials could be accessed. From this distance, the whole platform seemed to sway, but that might have been my stomach reeling in protest.

"But I can't—" I squeaked, afraid I might vomit if I raised my voice.

"Not you," Commander Ambrose snorted. "That job's for him. I don't trust you with the equipment."

I was so relieved that I didn't even notice his heavy-handed insult.

Dr. Nic didn't seem bothered by his assignment, but he did have the gumption to ask: "What is this factory making?"

Commander Ambrose didn't respond right away, a sign that should have concerned me had I not been more focused on trying to swallow back nausea. As it was, his answer caught me off guard and nearly made me hurl from the impact.

"I'm surprised you don't recognize it," he sneered, as if the ugly tangle of machines gave any indication of their purpose. "We're making Red Rain."

13

Before replying, I spent a good five minutes genuinely contemplating the feasibility of building a boat and attempting to row towards the mainland, whatever direction that was in. I would rather attempt an improbable escape than help produce the superweapon I had worked so hard to destroy.

"Wow," Dr. Nic whispered. To his credit, he sounded—perhaps for the first time in his life—regretful. "I guess the old man really did have it."

I wanted to punch him, but strangely, I wasn't sure he deserved it. Yes, Red Rain had been his idea. But this time, he wasn't responsible for forcing my father to work on the project. The United had played their hand, and my father had folded.

My father had completed Red Rain, and there was no one else that could be blamed for that.

But as much as I wanted to cry or scream or *kill something*, my first concern was getting out of this factory. The United may have the formula for Red Rain, but they couldn't make me produce it. If they wanted to churn out a whole factory of that vile stuff, they could do it themselves.

I may be a prisoner. They may have taken everything from me. But I still had my dignity, and they would have to kill me before I worked on Red Rain.

Commander Ambrose graciously listened to my tirade for several minutes. It wasn't until halfway through that I realized I was even using real words, not just seething and screaming internally like I thought I was.

"And your options are...?" he asked when he got bored enough to interrupt.

That was an excellent question, and I would have loved to know what my options were. What was he going to do? Confine me to my cell? Threaten me? Was I worth the trouble?

I glanced around the factory. Out of the corner of my eye, I spotted a control room off to the left and up a short flight of stairs. The room was dark except for a wide dashboard glittering with a dozen displays. All around the factory there were computer terminals, gauges, dials, and control switches—

more than enough ways for a rebellious girl like me to tamper with the operation.

I took a deep breath. If they wanted me to slave 9-5 in this factory pushing paperwork or mopping floors, so be it. That was plenty of time for me to become familiar with the controls—and figure out a way to stall production.

Not wanting to arouse Ambrose's suspicion by resigning too early, I fired another question at him. "Why me?"

He raised his eyebrow.

"If you wanted to rub your victory in *his* face," I gestured at Dr. Nic, "I get it. But why me? Why didn't you drag Cea and Ephesus and my father here so you could gloat over all of us?"

He hesitated, as if he never expected he'd have to answer for his personal vendettas. Perhaps there truly was no reason he'd picked me other than pure hatred.

As if realizing I couldn't be fooled, he settled for a cold smile and a haughty, "There were… regulations preventing getting your father and brother here."

I crossed my arms and remained silent.

Claiming the victory, he turned away and started walking towards the control room. "Come along, I'll show you what your job is."

Leaving Dr. Nic languishing by the railing, I followed the commander up the steps. With a swipe of his card, he ushered me into the cramped room and flicked on the light.

The room thrummed with the grinding of motherboards and hard drives. It was so crowded with file cabinets and server racks that there was barely room enough for both of us to maneuver around the desk chair. Most of the equipment was brand new, glittering in shiny black, except for a surprisingly ancient laser printer in scratched cream. It was lazily spitting out paper with a content hum, like an old granny clicking away at her knitting.

"Your job is to file all the reports that print out." He gestured at the stack of paper rapidly piling up on the printer's tray.

I picked up the stack and riffled through it, wondering if any of the information would be useful. Almost immediately, the printer dispensed another five sheets in rapid succession.

"How often does it print reports?" I asked.

"Every fifteen minutes for general production, plus reports of any abnormality."

I glanced at him suspiciously. Why would the United want to keep such detailed reports in hard copy? They no doubt had access to all of this information digitally. It's not like they were going to ask Ambrose to mail his paperwork to them in a manila envelope.

An ear-piercing beep interrupted our staring contest. "Oh," he piped, "you'll also have to reload the paper."

I sighed and pulled open the paper drawer on the printer. As stupid as it was—I was beginning to suspect Ambrose was wasting paper for the sole purpose of having me do menial work in his presence—I wasn't going to complain when my "job" gave me full access to the control room *and* all of their classified reports.

I half-listened while Commander Ambrose explained the organization of the file cabinets to me. I impatiently waited for him to stop talking so I could start exploring the office and reading the reports.

I didn't have any time to waste. We had to stop production before any product was shipped back to the mainland.

Why my internal dialog thought there was a "we," I'll never know. When I approached Dr. Nic at dinner, he made it very clear that he intended to be utterly useless.

"It's too late," he muttered as he aggressively stirred his colorless food.

"No, it's not. They can't have had the factory operational for more than a few days," I reasoned, doing the math in my head. "There's no way they've already shipped a boatload back to the mainland."

"Not that," he whined, as if frustrated by my stupidity. "I mean it's too late—just, how do you propose destroying something that eats metal?"

"Why are you eating metal for lunch? The rations aren't *that* bad, except on pizza day."

I jumped, although more so because the stranger's voice was extremely loud than because I was startled. I looked up to see a curious pair of men grinning at me. They looked incredibly alike, as though they were related, but there were just enough differences between them that it made me go cross-eyed. They were both short, but one was a fraction of an inch taller. They both had white hair, but one had more gray than the other. I could have also sworn their eyes were slightly different shades of grey, but at that point I realized I was staring.

Neither of them seemed to mind, because they were both doing the same thing right back at me. "Oh, you brought a lady friend back with you! How nice!" the slightly taller one chirped.

"Dowe, she's too young for him. Don't be disgusting." The other jabbed him in the ribs.

"You're right. She could definitely do better, John."

They both paused and rubbed their chins with one hand, as if assessing potential suitors in their mind. I decided I'd better put a quick stop to their train of thought before I got set up on a blind date with a prisoner, so I spoke up, "You're John... and Dowe?" I tried not to grimace at the irony of the names.

They nodded eagerly.

"And you thought 'Tower' was a weird name," Dr. Nic muttered.

"So how you doing, Q? I didn't expect you back so soon." John and Dowe sat at the table next to us.

Nic looked up and stared them straight in the eyes. "But you did expect me back."

They shrugged and started eating.

"'Q'?" I ventured.

Nic rolled his eyes. "I wasn't going to keep going by Prisoner 120518."

"Are you... friends?" I glanced around the table at my unlikely group of prison mates.

Dr. Nic looked genuinely bored. "What did I tell you about friends?"

Dowe slapped his hands on the table so violently that our canteens sloshed. "Whatever he told you was wrong! We are definitely your friends, so don't listen to this stick-in-the-mud."

"Yeah!" John agreed. "We're way more fun than he is, anyway."

That last statement definitely wasn't a lie, so I decided to let it slide for the time being.

I looked back at Dr. Nic. "Should I tell... them?"

"Pretty sure we're not the only people on the island who know what that factory is making," he replied dryly. Then without offering further comment, he picked up his dishes, stood up, and walked away.

He didn't look at me as he passed, but I could read the expression on his face. I could tell by the look in his eyes that he truly *didn't* care what I did. He had given up, surrendered himself and his precious pet project to the hands of the United. He looked as tired as my father used to.

The thought made my heart sick in more ways than one, so I shoved it aside. Never mind Nic. If he was content to slave in a factory of his own design, let him. But I wouldn't. I wouldn't let the United have Red Rain if there was anything I could do to stop it.

But Dr. Nic had a point. How *could* you destroy something that ate metal?

John and Dowe didn't have any helpful advice to offer, even after I explained the situation to them as best I could. "Does it burn? We could burn it."

"It's a gas. You can't burn gases."

"Yes you can! Like those vintage gas stoves!"

"Not that kind of gas!"

I excused myself as soon as I politely could and locked myself in my cell. I spent the night curled up on the cot, trying to think of ways to destroy Red Rain. I didn't know how to create it, but perhaps I could think of a way to destroy it. After all, I had destroyed Dr. Nic's operations once before.

Of course, I hadn't exactly destroyed anything important then—if I had, we wouldn't be in this mess. And besides, I didn't have any tables of random chemicals I could turn over to create a makeshift bomb.

I growled and rubbed my forehead. There had to be a way! I had full access to the factory, albeit during working hours. There had to be *something* I could do to stop it.

I wished Ephesus were here. He would know how to destroy something he helped create.

A sudden wave of homesickness washed over me at the thought of my brother. What had they done to him? Had he even heard where I'd been sent?

Taking a deep breath to dam the rising tears, I closed my eyes and leaned back against the cold wall, trying to keep my thoughts on the task at hand. If Ephesus were in my place, what would he try first?

He'd hack the computer, of course. The thought made me smile at the same time it made my heart sink in despair. I could probably tamper with the computer if Ambrose left me in the control room unsupervised, but it wouldn't do me any good. Almost everything was probably password-protected, and I wouldn't know what to look for even if it wasn't. I only knew how to manage simple devices like readers and flash drives.

Flash drives! With a rush of recognition that made me sit up faster than was healthy, I remembered the flash drive Ephesus had passed to me before we got caught. It was still tucked down the side of my shoe, safe and sound—because I hadn't exactly had a reason to take my shoes off and put my feet up the past few days.

I fished it out of my sweaty sock and held it up to the bleary light. It was definitely Ephesus's drive; the initials "E.S." written in permanent marker were still faintly visible. It was a dated unlocked model he had used in school before the United had started confiscating unapproved electronics. Somehow he had managed to smuggle it into camp and had used it to store files off the cloud. He and Cea had been using it for their recent projects. I wondered what was stored on there now.

Perhaps it was time to find out.

14

"Wowee, an unlocked drive! We could really use one of those!" John crowed when I showed it to him and Dowe the next morning.

"Yeah," Dowe said, fingering it admiringly. "We need a place to store our covert files. Can we borrow it?"

"We'll be careful with it!"

"We're always careful with other people's stuff!"

"Actually, I need to figure out what's on it. My brother passed it to me before we were transported," I replied.

"Ooh, a secret message from the mainland!"

"We have just the translation device. That old laptop should work. The screen's almost history, though."

"That's because you dropped it down shaft 9. You should have taken the elevator."

"It was an undercover operation! I couldn't take the elevator! Someone might have *seen* me!"

I hated to interrupt them, but I only had a few minutes before Commander Ambrose would expect me to be down in the factory for work. "Can I borrow this laptop for a minute?"

They were right; the laptop was about ready to give up the ghost. But the USB port was still intact, and I could see enough of the screen to read the file list that popped up. I scanned the titles; regretfully, most of them meant nothing to me.

A file from the bottom of the list did catch my eye, though—it was named "Sans Nic (fixed)." I thought that was a funny name, so I clicked on it. The file extension was unusual, too.

A big warning box engulfed the screen. I read the text aloud in wonder: "'This file may contain viruses or other programs that may be harmful to your computer. Are you sure you want to run?'"

"Whoa Nellie, don't open that!" John or Dowe yelped from behind me.

"Yeah, don't destroy this laptop! It's the last one we have left!"

"We do have a couple tablets, though. And half a desktop."

"This is still the last *laptop*."

"True."

I ignored them as I pondered the warning. Why would the computer call the file out as a virus?

I canceled the action and clicked on a different file out of curiosity. It opened without complaint.

I looked back at the corrupted file, pondering the name. *Sans Nic... without Nic... a virus without Nic...*

I stopped. That was it. A virus without Nic. A virus that *removed* Nic.

We switched it up, though. We set it so that the virus would only delete data that contained the letters 'Nic,' with a capital.

This was the data virus my brother had coded for Nic back on Mars. He'd sabotaged it so that it would only delete data that contained Nic's name.

But now, judging by the file name, it had been fixed. That must have been one of the projects my brother and Cea had been working on back at camp. Now the virus would do what it was originally intended to do—completely wipe all data from all systems it infected.

Suddenly, I knew how we'd destroy Red Rain.

15

Dr. Nic and I didn't speak when we both showed up for work, which was just as well. From my perch in the control room, I watched him unenthusiastically monitor the gauges on the machines and briefly wondered if it would be better to leave him out of my plan. But as much as I questioned his dedication, I knew that he understood Red Rain better than I did, and it would probably be wise to get an expert opinion before I attempted to sabotage a factory full of lethal chemicals.

As we exited the elevator at the end of our shift, I cowered in the back corner so Ambrose would get off first. Letting him get a few paces ahead, I whispered to Dr. Nic, "Meet me at Tower's place after dinner."

Not waiting for his response, I skipped ahead of him and ran to mess hall to avoid Ambrose's suspicion.

After hastily scarfing down my food, I went above ground and asked Tower if he would keep watch while we met behind his building. I hadn't bothered to ask for his cooperation beforehand, partially because I had come up with the plan on the spot, and partially because now was as good a time as any to figure out whether or not Tower was an ally. As I had hoped, Tower agreed. He didn't ask what we were going to be talking about, so I didn't volunteer the information.

I promptly sat down in the shadows behind the building and waited. There was no reason to go anywhere else. Besides, I needed time to think—and pray. I needed to plan what to say if Dr. Nic showed up or, more importantly, what to do if he didn't show up, which was more likely.

I was extremely encouraged—and a little bit flattered—when he actually came.

I didn't wait for him to ask what I wanted. I stood up and declared in a low tone, "We need to destroy Red Rain."

He raised one eyebrow in a bored gesture of disbelief but said nothing. I took the opportunity to keep talking. "I have to try. I won't just stand by and watch while they destroy the world. I can't..."

I stopped. No. This wasn't about me, my emotions, or my opinions. This was about doing what was right. And if we were going to pull it off, Dr. Nic and I needed to be in it together.

" *We* can't let them do that," I rephrased, emphasizing the inclusive word.

He didn't take the bait. "Why don't you just destroy it yourself? You've done it once before," he cut dryly.

I struggled not to get frustrated and instead returned his sarcasm in kind. "There aren't any tables of chemicals I can turn over," I said with equal sass. "And I need your help."

"Why?" he demanded. His tone was still condescending, but I sensed a little bit of curiosity in his expression.

"Because I'm no good with computers," I said with total honesty, hoping that would be enough to pique his interest.

"You seem to do just fine hacking security systems."

"Only because I stole a device *you* invented."

"I'm impressed that you'll admit to stealing." He was still using the same dry tone, but he straightened and watched me as I talked.

"We need to hack the computer in Ambrose's control room." I figured I had enough of his interest to cut to the point. "From there we can wipe their data and shut down the operation."

"Even if... even *after* I hack into the computer, it will be incredibly difficult to erase the data such that it's irretrievable. It is almost impossible to permanently delete information from a computer."

I was immensely pleased to hear him discussing the situation with rationality. "I know. But this will do it for you." I drew my brother's flash drive from my pocket and held it up.

He gazed at it. "What good will that do? That has all the Red Rain files on it too, you know."

"What?" I gasped.

"I transferred the complete research files from the lab before we escaped," he said with utter calmness. "I'm sure the United added a bit after we left, but I could easily figure it out from your father's notes."

Horror swept over me as I realized I had been guarding the complete formula for Red Rain in my shoe, but Nic continued talking. "But how is that going to help us destroy their operation?"

I clenched the drive, resisting the urge to run to the shore and throw it into the sea. "It also contains my brother's virus."

After a few seconds of dull staring, recognition flashed across Dr. Nic's eyes. "The data virus."

"Yes," I said, watching his face to see his reaction. "He and Cea fixed it."

Dr. Nic's expression brightened in surprise, but he quickly covered it with a scowl. "So the little twerp *did* know how to code it properly."

I gracefully ignored the slander on my brother's name and kept talking. "Yes, and if you upload it to the computer in the control room, it will completely wipe their systems."

I waited for him to commit or argue. When he did neither, I added, "Hopefully it's a closed system so nothing else will be affected."

Thoughtfulness cloaked Dr. Nic's voice again. "Yes, no doubt it's a very secured private system, but if we're lucky the gates won't be too hard to crack. They must have some way they're transmitting progress reports back to the mainland. If we can find out how, hopefully we can use that access to open a two-way door."

He looked up at me and explained, "Wiping the control system in the factory won't be enough. The United will have copies of the research on their mainland computers. Even if we destroy the factory, they can rebuild it. If we want to stop them from producing Red Rain, we need to wipe all their systems."

Panic rose in my throat as his voice gained velocity. "If we're going to do this, we have to do it right. We need to hack through the computer and upload the virus to the internet, wiping everything. We have to erase Red Rain from their systems for good!"

Tower shushed him from above. Dr. Nic ducked his head and lowered his voice, but his tone retained its vehemence. "We have to use the virus as it was originally intended."

"But that will erase everything!" I blurted the obvious, unable to contain it. "The Bibles—"

"Then why did your brother create the virus?" Dr. Nic challenged. "He didn't have to rewrite it. Why would he code it and keep it on hand, if it wasn't for a situation like this? We have to use it."

He reached for the drive. I retracted my hand.

Dr. Nic grunted and clenched his fist like he might force the drive from me. He raised his arm, then stopped. He lifted his head and gazed at me.

And he waited.

I pressed the drive against my heart. It was my choice. My choice whether or not to use the virus. My choice whether or not to trust Nic.

After thinking a quick prayer, I held the drive out.

His hand closed around it, and our eyes met. Respect briefly flashed across his face. I nodded and lowered my arm, closing the deal.

"This still won't be enough," he said lowly. "We have to destroy the product they've already made."

"Why?"

"For one, there's enough in there already to desecrate a small country. I did the calculations during my shift today. And two, there's a risk they can reconstruct the formula from a completed sample. We have to destroy their reserves so there's no trace left."

I agreed, but that didn't make the feat any less daunting. "How are we supposed to destroy something that can eat metal?" I threw his own words back at him.

He stopped and stared profoundly at the wall above my head. I let his brain work in silence for several moments.

My patience was rewarded when he mumbled, "We let it burn."

"What?"

Realization brightened his eyes as he explained, "We drain the vats. If we can release the acid and get it to condense, Red Rain will burn through the floor and destroy itself."

Let Red Rain destroy itself. We both reveled in the brilliant irony of that for a moment before Dr. Nic continued. "We'll need to get Ambrose out of the factory during working hours when all the systems are open and online."

"How?" I said, hoping his genius mind would work wonders again.

"How about a distraction?" a cheerful voice joined the conversation.

I gave a small shriek as John and Dowe materialized out of the shadows. "Tower!" Dr. Nic hissed up at the guard's window.

"I didn't think they were a problem," came the reply.

The pair sauntered over to us. "How about a distraction?" John repeated.

"A big one," Dowe clarified.

"We could do a demonstration!"

"Those are always fun!"

"We could make it like a talent show, and Philli here can help us. I bet she can put on a real good distraction!"

Dowe slapped his partner. "Don't be a fool! We don't want a woman getting tangled up in a demonstration. This could get messy."

"We need it to be messy," Dr. Nic inserted, stepping up. He glanced between the men and nodded encouragingly. "Really messy. 'All guards on deck' messy."

The matching grins on John's and Dowe's faces indicated that they were catching on. "Oh, I think we and a couple dozen of our prison buddies can handle that," John sneered.

"Let's ask Art," Dowe suggested.

"And Marty. And that guy who calls himself 24... What's his real name again?"

"I think it's Cloud."

"How's that a real name? You sure the guy ain't duping us with a double-double alias?"

The pair continued chattering. I turned back to Dr. Nic. "Commander Ambrose always locks the control room door when he leaves," I offered, my mind suddenly racing through all the possible hitches to our plan. "What if he takes the time to lock it?"

"If that happens, you can figure out a way to circumvent the lock." It wasn't a question.

I didn't argue. "When should we do it?"

"Tomorrow," Tower suddenly inserted into the conversation. I looked up to see him leaning out his window. "A ship is coming at noon to transport the first batch of Red Rain. If you want to keep the reserves out of the hands of the United, you need to destroy it before that ship comes."

I glanced at Dr. Nic. The despondent look on his face set all my worries whirling into a tornado in my stomach. "Tomorrow is my floor's 'day off.' We're all forcibly confined to our quarters. For lack of a better phrase, I'll be locked in my room." It was a fitting expression; he looked about as grumpy and pathetic as a disobedient child in timeout.

I grappled for encouraging words, but no immediate solution came to mind. Even with my knack for breaking through locked doors, I knew that getting onto his floor would be nearly impossible. Someone with access would have to let Nic out of his room.

I glanced up at Tower's window. He was still leaning there, gazing at me. I wondered if he too was weighing in his mind whether or not he was truly on our side.

After a moment, he slid back inside his tower, but his voice came floating down to us. "I'll make it happen." With that, he slammed his window shut, cutting off my opportunity to thank him.

I turned back to Dr. Nic. He nodded. "We have less than 18 hours," he said, taking a deep breath. "Better get back to our cells before we arouse suspicion for being up here."

"Good point," John agreed with a yawn. "See you tomorrow."

"Don't let the bed bugs bite!" Dowe added by way of goodbye.

The two sauntered off without being bidden. Not in a rush to get back to my cell, I took a deep breath of the cold night air and savored the silence as an opportunity to pray.

I watched as Dr. Nic walked on ahead of me. After a moment, I realized I wasn't just praying about tomorrow.

16

I went to work as normal in the morning. At least, I tried to pretend it was business as usual. I had only been at this job two days; what did "acting casual" even look like? What kind of behavior did Commander Ambrose expect from me? Despondency? Bitterness? Fear?

Fear was easy to fake. I flinched at the commander's every move, always worried I had made a wrong step and aroused his suspicion. He did seem to notice that I was acting jumpy, but if anything, he appeared to be amused by it. For once, I wasn't bothered by his condescending pleasure. As long as he was smiling cruelly at me like he always did, I could assume I was safe from suspicion.

Thankfully, John and Dowe were punctual—and successful—and at precisely 10:15 Commander Ambrose's communicator beeped shrilly.

"What?" he answered in a dry tone with obviously no regard for the person on the other end.

"Ambrose, we need you topside immediately. The prisoners started a riot and it's getting… sticky." The guard's awkward tone of voice made me wonder if he was using that word literally. I wouldn't have put it past John and Dowe.

"That's not my job," was Ambrose's completely uninterested reply.

"The captain's called all guards on deck."

"I'm not a guard. I'm here to oversee production, not herd prisoners. Take care of your own charges."

I gave up pretending to ignore the discussion and watched, inadvertently crumpling the papers I held in my hands. I hadn't bargained on Commander Ambrose's self-authority. What if he refused to obey orders?

Heated talking came through in the background of the line. With a small cough, the guard responded, "The captain says it's topside or mainland."

I tried not to grin. I really did like this captain.

Commander Ambrose surrendered with an exasperated sigh. Clicking off his communicator, he shoved his chair back and stood up. "Get out," he commanded with a flick of his finger at me.

My panic resurged. I had been so focused on not tripping up that I'd neglected to think of a plan to get back into the office should Ambrose lock it. "But sir," I protested, "I have to finish filing these papers!" I held them out to him for emphasis, then realized I'd crumpled several. I hastily smoothed the stack.

He growled. "Fine. Don't touch the computer, or I will know about it when I look at the task log. I'll be right back." He stormed out. I watched him disappear into the elevator and finally released my pent-up breath in a prayer of thanks.

I could only hope that Commander Ambrose *wouldn't* be right back.

Now all I had to do was wait for Dr. Nic to arrive.

Waiting turned out to be harder than pretending to act casual. At least when I was "acting casual" I had something to distract myself from thinking of all the things that could go wrong. I actually ended up filing the crumpled papers properly, just to give myself something productive to do besides worry.

I was so relieved when Dr. Nic arrived that I nearly ran to him with open arms.

Without pausing to greet me, he shoved a bundle of cloth into my hands. "These are the dials and switches on the tank control panels you need to change, and the numbers you need to change them to," he gushed, evidently out of breath.

I untangled the cloth and held it up. It was a shirt of Nic's—a dirty one at that. I wrinkled my nose and glanced up at him.

He shrugged. "Tower had a marker but no paper."

I turned the shirt around to find a mess of numbers and diagrams scribbled on the back in permanent marker.

"This is a diagram of the control panels on the side of the holding tanks. If you flip these switches, it will drain all the product from the factory into the two main holding tanks and seal them off." He gestured at some of the markings on the shirt, then pointed out across the factory to where the two huge tanks extended up the wall.

"Then if you move these dials to the right numbers, it will begin to chill the gas to the point of condensing. Then all we have to do is puncture the bottom of the holding tanks, and the liquid acid will drain safely out the bottom."

I wasn't sure there was a truly "safe" way to drain lethal acid, but, glancing across the factory, I saw what he meant. If we punctured the bottom of the holding tanks while the acid was in liquid form, it would drain down into the factory below, where it would destroy the unwanted equipment and— hopefully—nothing else.

I nodded. "Got it."

"Wait until I give the signal. I have to shut down production first, and then the tanks have to fill completely before we can close them off and condense the gas. Don't touch anything until I tell you to." He turned and ran for the control room without waiting for confirmation.

I headed towards the holding tanks—then remembered they could only be accessed by the narrow catwalk that extended over the machinery. Shuddering, I stared straight ahead and charged across the catwalk as fast as I could force myself, trying to ignore the groan of the working machinery below me.

With another shiver, I ducked onto the platform where the control access was mounted. The massive motors on the side of the tanks extended over the controls, forming a rather cramped alcove. As I squatted on the platform, I understood why Commander Ambrose had assigned Dr. Nic to work here—it must have been torture for someone as tall as Nic to work in so narrow a space for hours on end.

I spread the shirt on the ground and studied it, trying to find the appropriate switches and dials. Dr. Nic's rushed handwriting took some work to decipher, but I found all the right routing switches. The first step was to adjust a dial so that the product from the factory would flow into the tank at full speed.

I laid my hand on the dial, waiting for the signal. I rehearsed the steps in my head. Tank it, condense it, then puncture the tanks and...

I stopped, the full implications of our plan hitting me. Puncture the tanks? We were about to puncture two-story-high tanks filled with a shipload of dangerous chemicals—with the intent of flooding the entire factory with enough acid to melt it into the ground.

That was an extremely violent act of rebellion if there ever was one.

My father's last instructions echoed through my head. *Just do as they say. Go with them quietly and they'll go easier on you.*

Go quietly.

No one has to die. You can stay and not have to work on Red Rain. All you have to do is be quiet for a few hours while I clean up your mess, and then it will be done.

I closed my eyes, remembering those words. Remembering the screech of the security panel denying access. Remembering the crash of metal and glass tubes on the floor. Remembering the explosion. Remembering the voice that cursed me.

And now that same voice shouted at me. "Now, Phil!"

I cranked the first dial for all I was worth.

17

I sat back on my haunches and surveyed the flashing control panel. As near as I could figure, I had rerouted the flow of chemicals correctly. Now I had to wait for the tanks to fill before I could seal them off and start condensing the gas. I had a pretty good guess which display would tell me when the tanks were full, but Dr. Nic had said he would give the signal. For lack of anything else to do to speed the process along, I watched the numbers on the display climb.

They climbed steadily at first, then suddenly jumped. I watched with slightly worried amusement as the numbers on the display spun in a nearly indistinguishable blur.

Abruptly, the display froze. The ominous number 99999—completely maxed out—filled every slot on the display board.

I chewed my lip. Did that mean the tanks were full? Was it time?

I became aware of a high-pitched whirring coming from the factory equipment below me. I crawled to the edge of the alcove and glanced towards the control room, looking for a signal from Dr. Nic. I could just see his bobbing head bent over the computers.

The whirring grew louder, enough to make my ears tingle. I summoned the courage to look over the edge of the platform at the tangled mess of pipes and tanks below.

Nothing seemed amiss, but I could hear the moan and grumble of machines laboring heavily. Hadn't Dr. Nic shut down production? Shouldn't the machines be quiet? I sensed a slight tremble through the floor; was that normal?

Before I could decide, one of the pipes below me cracked and split open.

I shrieked and threw myself to the floor. I heard more metal breaking and clattering to the ground. I curled into a ball and shielded myself, expecting lethal acid to spray everywhere, but suddenly there was silence.

I cautiously sat up and looked over the edge. The network of pipes was split in multiple places, but nothing poured out of the broken ends. After a moment of listening carefully, I detected the soft hiss of air escaping from somewhere.

And then I remembered. Red Rain was still in gas form. A gas that was now leaking out all over the factory.

I forced myself to breathe normally. I hated to think I was inhaling the stuff, but I knew it couldn't hurt me... right? Could it condense inside me? Could it burn me from the inside out?

I struggled to slow my heart rate, but Dr. Nic's panicked shout sent it racing again.

"Phil, get out of there!"

I turned towards the control room. He had stepped out of the door and was leaning over the railing, waving his arms at me. "The entire system is failing!"

I stood up, my heart flooding with despair. It was my fault; I must have set the dials wrong—

Dr. Nic unwittingly assuaged my guilt. "The virus sent the system into overdrive. You need to get out of there! It thinks the factory is on fire and it's going to—"

He was drowned out by the sudden wail of sirens.

Warning lights started flashing from every direction. And then the emergency sprinklers turned on.

Miraculously, I had the presence of mind to dive backwards as water showered over the factory. With an almost indistinguishable hiss, it met the gases in the air and instantly turned into bright orange-red acid.

I screamed and put my hands over my face, bracing myself for the burns. It took me several seconds to realize nothing was happening. Looking up, I realized the tank motors over the alcove shielded me from the shower.

Pressing myself flat against the tanks, I looked out across the factory. Red Rain showered over the catwalk, cutting off my escape. There was no way for me to reach the exit without entering the downpour.

The exit! There was an emergency panel by the elevator door; the sprinklers could be shut off from there. Dr. Nic could reach the door; the control room and the path to the exit were out of the range of the sprinklers.

Dr. Nic was still shouting at me. Disregarding whatever he was saying, I leaned forward as far as I dared and yelled back, "The emergency panel by the door! Shut off the sprinklers!"

Thankfully he could hear me over the sirens. He glanced towards the exit. I shouted again for emphasis. "Shut them off! Hurry!"

"Just hang on!" he shouted back. "I need to grab the drive! Don't move!"

He darted back into the control room before I could protest. I tried not to feel insulted. He was leaving me here, surrounded by a shower of scalding chemicals, while he went back for the flash drive? What did he even need the drive for? We had uploaded the virus; our job was done.

Then I remembered what else was on the flash drive. The original files for Red Rain. Dr. Nic's copy, which presumably hadn't been affected by the virus.

The realization made my head spin with anger and betrayal. I wanted to scream, but I didn't know what to say. I was crushed by the overwhelming feeling that I had failed. All this meant nothing if Dr. Nic still had a copy of the research.

He had tricked me. I told myself I shouldn't be surprised, but that wasn't true. I was surprised. I had believed him; I had trusted him. And that made it hurt all the worse.

Unable to go anywhere, I clutched my knees to my chest and rocked from side to side, struggling between equally vicious urges to seethe and cry.

The sound of metal crashing nearby startled me out of my thoughts. I turned to see a gaping hole in the catwalk. An entire section was missing from the middle.

It took me a moment to process what was happening. Red Rain was eating away at the metal. Even as I watched, a weakened seam snapped, sending another piece of the catwalk tumbling down to the factory below.

Now I really was trapped.

Despair briefly flooded me, but I fought it back with prayer and common sense. There *had* to be another way off this platform. Surely they had built a second access to the control panel in case of emergency.

I got to my knees and looked around the alcove. There, sandwiched in the narrow space between the tank motors, was a service ladder that led upwards.

I crawled forward and traced the ladder's path. It went up the wall between the tanks, just barely out of reach of the sprinklers. I couldn't see what was above the tanks, but it was my only option.

I stood up, wedged myself between the motors, and struggled to hoist myself onto the ladder. Ironically, it probably would have been easier for someone taller than me, but I managed to get my feet onto the first rung by pushing off of the control panel.

I paused to take a deep breath and adjust my grip. Then I started climbing. It was more strenuous than I imagined, but I focused on finding a steady rhythm. One hand, one foot, next hand, next foot, always testing my grip. I kept breathing deeply in between moves, trying to ignore the sound of the self-destructing factory below me.

As I neared the top, I saw that pipes extended out of the top of the tanks and ran along the ceiling. Presumably that was how they transferred the product from the factory to the ship for transport. Another narrow service catwalk, hanging by steel chains from the ceiling, followed the pipes. It hung just above the network of emergency sprinklers, making it safely out of reach of the hazardous shower.

Praising God, I carefully climbed off the ladder onto the catwalk. The pathway bounced and swayed under my weight. I shrieked and dropped to my knees, causing the catwalk to swing all the more. Swallowing a sudden onset of nausea, I closed my eyes and waited for the movement to subside. *Just go slowly. It will be all right.*

I didn't have the guts to try and stand, so I crawled, trying to make as little motion as possible. The catwalk still bounced, making my stomach and heart bounce with it, but I kept moving forward steadily. I could see a ladder at the other end—my escape to safety.

After getting halfway across the factory, I made the mistake of glancing down. The pipes for the sprinklers were affixed to the underside of the catwalk, and I could see the showers of acid rain right below me. I could have reached out and touched the lethal liquid.

The thought made me shudder, so I quickly looked back up and focused my eyes on the ladder ahead.

The sirens and lights still continued full blast, but I had already begun to tune out the monotony. In the self-imposed silence, I perceived the sound of something gurgling through the pipes above my head. I looked up and saw that there were boxes spaced periodically along the pipeline. The boxes were wet with condensation, and I heard the faint sound of fans whirring.

Cooling containers. They must be shipping the product in liquid form; while dangerous, it would be far more space efficient. These pipes must condense the gas as it flowed up to the shipping yard on the surface. That was why the cooling containers had condensation on them.

No sooner had I processed the thought than I realized the condensation was also turning into acid and eating away at the exterior of the containers. And I knew full well that the exterior was not formulated to resist corrosion.

I saw it coming and had time to scramble backwards before a crack split in the cooling container above my head. A stream of Red Rain gushed out and poured over the catwalk in front of me. It was a narrow stream, but it was enough to block the way. I could only watch in despair as the acid ate away at my last chance of escape.

The metal of the catwalk was thin, and it took only moments before the acid had eaten completely through it—and the chains supporting it. Before I had time to react, the chains snapped, and the section of catwalk dropped from beneath my feet.

I screamed and scrabbled for any handhold, managing to grab another chain. For a perilous moment, I dangled by one hand over the imploding factory. The broken sprinkler line beneath me continued to spray water from both ends, sending Red Rain flying in all directions. A few drops grazed my leg.

I wanted to scream as the tiny burns peppered my skin, but I didn't have enough breath. The world spun and blurred, and I could hardly grasp what was happening. *Oh, God, help!* was the only thought I could gasp out.

He answered by giving me the strength to reach my other hand up and grasp the chain. Even though my body was writhing in pain, I managed to haul myself back onto the catwalk. The remaining sections swayed wildly, but their chains were still intact—for now.

Clarity rushed to my head as I was able to process the situation. I couldn't reach the ladder to the exit. The other ladder only led back to the control platform, where the catwalk was also washed out. There was nowhere to run, and it was only a matter of time before Red Rain corroded the other chains and sent me plummeting into the remains of the factory below, where the acid was rapidly pooling.

I was going to die.

My heart buckled in surrender. I gasped for breath, my mind spinning out of control. Reality slipped from my grasp. The world washed out around me, my head too dizzy to focus. My ears rang with a strange sound—a subtle, rhythmic beep. It was much more calming than the hissing and crackling of Red Rain as it devoured metal, so I focused on it. I closed my eyes and concentrated on it, trying to identify it.

And then I remembered. The beeping of electrical equipment. The sterile scent of sheets. The austere white lighting in the medical bay. And my brother's worried tone.

You were pushing it, though. That close to the explosion, had you not been near an outside wall…

My own voice answered him. *It would have been worth it.*

I took a deep breath. The repulsive scent of Red Rain and corroded metal filled my nostrils, but I didn't fear it. I opened my eyes and looked down at the red sea below me.

"It was worth it."

18

Somewhere across the factory, another chain snapped. I closed my eyes, choosing not to look at the ones closest to me. I didn't want to watch the acid drip and tick off the countdown to my own death.

The factory continued to scream in agony below. Machines hissed and ground as metal cracked and split. The sirens continued unabated, just in case anyone was questioning the ongoing state of emergency.

Despite the din, I was still startled when a human voice yelled at me. "Philadelphia!"

I looked down. Far below, Nic was inching along the outer wall, trying to stay out of the spray as he made his way towards the door.

I sat up. I could think of many colorful words I wanted to shout at him—most of which he had probably inadvertently taught me. None of them seemed sufficient to convey the anger I was suddenly feeling towards him. I settled for the woefully inadequate, "You idiot!"

If he heard me, he accepted the accusation without objection. "I'm coming!"

"Ten minutes too late!" I screeched.

This time, he simply ignored me.

I pinched my eyes shut. It was hopeless; both of the walkways were washed out. What was he going to do?

Suddenly, with a deep-throated purr echoing from somewhere beyond the walls, the factory grew strangely silent. I opened my eyes to see Dr. Nic cranking the levers on the emergency panels. He shut the sprinklers off, followed by most of the power. The water dried, taking the sound of sizzling acid with it. The factory shuddered to a halt and groaned in relief as the machines ceased their endless whirring.

I let out my frustrations in a salty breath. Words could—and would—be exchanged later. But if it was a choice between taking my anger to the grave and accepting an improbable rescue from my unlikely ally, I would swallow my emotions in favor of hoping we might actually make it out of here alive.

Nic walked to the edge of the platform and surveyed the damage. About a third of the catwalk remained on his end—almost enough to reach beneath me, but not quite.

Nic looked down. I followed his gaze to the puddles of Red Rain shimmering on the factory floor. They were bubbling and gurgling but gradually receding as they melted through the concrete floor and soaked into the rocky dirt below.

"Just hang on!" he shouted unhelpfully. "As soon as a path clears, we'll get you down!"

It wasn't a bad plan, but that didn't stop the anger from nipping at my consciousness. I took deep breaths, coaching myself internally. As long as my perch held, everything would be fine.

As if objecting to my optimism, another chain snapped.

I looked around wildly before remembering that sudden motions caused the catwalk to sway. I clung to the chain in panic, then regretted my actions as I felt the chain loosen and start to give way.

Despite the shuddering of the catwalk, I had the sense to let go of the chain and push myself backwards into the middle of the pathway. The chain held, but it was little consolation. I watched in abject horror as a trail of Red Rain dripped from a now-silent fan and dribbled down one of the few remaining chains supporting my section of catwalk.

It was clear from the groaning and shuddering of the other chains that they wouldn't support my weight once one of them snapped.

"Did you hear me, Phil?" Nic called.

"I don't think we have time to wait!" I shrieked. "These chains aren't going to hold!"

For once, Nic seemed to take my concerns seriously. Even from this distance, I could see the panic coloring his face.

Before he could offer any helpful suggestions, another voice joined the chaos. "What have you done?"

The door slammed open—or, I imagine Commander Ambrose would have slammed the doors open had they not been elevator doors. To his credit, he at least had the respect to pause and survey our work before saying anything more.

"What did you expect? You left *her* alone unsupervised," Dr. Nic chirped. I couldn't tell if his sarcasm was genuine or an attempt to deflect Ambrose's rage.

In either case, his humor didn't land. With a warning snarl, Ambrose lunged at Nic, throwing him backwards into the already weakened railing. Nic's lanky frame nearly flipped right over the edge. He hardly had time to find his footing before Ambrose threw a solid punch in his face.

"Don't!" I screamed. I could tell by the look in Ambrose's eyes that this fight was going to end quickly. I had seen him grow lethal on the ship—and there was no one to stop him now.

Dr. Nic dodged the next punch but couldn't avoid the kick that swiftly followed. With a groan even I could hear, he buckled over and retreated three steps. Ambrose charged at him shoulder-first like a bull. Nic sidestepped into the only space available—the catwalk.

Realizing he'd cornered his prey, Ambrose grinned and slowed his approach. "I hope you enjoyed your little act of rebellion," he sneered. He advanced and forced Nic to back down the narrow walkway.

For once, Nic didn't answer.

"Because once you're out of the picture," Ambrose jabbed Nic's shoulder, "we'll just rebuild and pick up right where we left off."

"I know you will," Nic coughed, "after you finish repairing all the damage from the virus I just released on your perfect little United internet."

Ambrose cocked his head in confusion. Nic took a deep breath and straightened to his full height. "You really do have a great upload speed, especially for being so far out in the ocean."

I caught myself smiling with pride—a feeling that evaporated when Ambrose howled. With the speed of a viper, he backhanded Nic.

I squealed. "Please, stop!"

Nic slid three more steps backwards—to the end of the catwalk. He twisted around, scanning the wreckage of the factory below him.

I realized that he could make the jump—if there weren't puddles of acid everywhere.

The commander closed the gap. I sat up on my knees, straining to be heard. "Ambrose! Please, don't do this!"

He hesitated long enough to cast a venomous look in my direction. "Don't think you aren't next, darling."

And then he lunged at Nic.

I screamed—and then nearly choked on the sound as my heart leapt to my throat. With the agility of a lynx, Nic ducked. Ambrose, too slow and heavy to stop his forward motion, tumbled over him. Nic swiped at his legs and easily set him flying over the edge.

Ambrose didn't even have time to yell before he landed—face-first in a puddle of Red Rain.

I wanted to scream again—but at that moment, a chain snapped.

The catwalk plunged backwards as the far corner gave away. Thrown to my hands and knees, I scrabbled at the platform, my palms tearing and bleeding on the rough metal, searching for a handhold.

"Nic!" I squeaked out.

If he answered me, I couldn't hear him. Like violin strings taunting my demise, the other three chains quivered and groaned. Then without further ado, the chain behind me broke. The platform swung down like a trapdoor, gracelessly hurling me into the factory below.

I plummeted backwards towards the ground. I lost all breath to cry out as the wind rushed around me like waves cocooning a drowning ship. Eerily suspended in air, my voice gone and my vision blurred, I hung in a moment of unearthly silence as my last thought crystalized.

Goodbye, Daddy.

And then I hit the ground.

At first, my landing seemed strangely soft—and then my neck snapped backwards and hit hard concrete, finally sending me into permanent darkness.

19

I could hear long before I could see. Noises murmured in my mind, murky and unclear like they came through water. For a while, I felt like I was floating, unable to feel anything except for the vague sense of motion around me.

My consciousness pushed back against the waves. *Let me out!*

The darkness slowly melted into light—blinding, burning light. My sense of smell returned, bringing with it the taste of salt, ash, and blood. I was grateful—because without the sulfuric stench, I probably would have thought I was dead.

As it was, I was still a little disappointed when the world came into focus and the first person I saw was Dr. Nic.

A voice somewhere behind me murmured, "She'll be all right."

And then, like a puzzle snapping together, consciousness rushed at me. The first thing I became aware of was the *grinding* headache I had. Then I saw the noonday sky above me, punctured by the misshapen buildings of Rott. I heard guards barking orders, a distant siren, and the sea slapping against the shore like it didn't care.

I managed to push past the pain to formulate a clear thought. *You made it. You're alive.*

Thank you, Jesus.

I put out my palms and felt beneath me. I was lying on a rough medical cot of some kind. Gripping the sides with as much strength as I could muster, I started to rise.

Nic's palm met my shoulder and shoved me back. "Don't you *dare.*"

His voice cracked. Startled, I squinted and focused on his face. He was glaring at me so intently that at first I thought he must be angry. His expression was so strange, almost disconcerting in a way—not because it was hard to read, but because I had never seen him look that way at anyone, much less me, before.

He looked worried. And then, maybe just a little bit relieved.

I smiled.

Tower disrupted the moment by stepping into my line of vision. "Sounds like you two had fun down there." He squatted next to my cot.

No longer distracted by sentimentality, I was again accosted by the magnitude of my headache. "Yeah, and I have the hangover to prove it." I paused, acknowledging the gaps in my memory. "What happened?"

Tower's unkempt eyebrows shot up, almost disappearing into his shaggy bangs. "I was hoping you would fill in the details. What exactly did you do to the computers?"

"Wasn't that a gem?" Nic inserted, still sounding a bit salty about the virus. "*I* came up with the original concept for that—"

"No," I interrupted. The pain was making it very difficult to string thoughts together, and I was losing patience. "I mean, how did I survive? I fell. I remember hitting the ground." I blinked, for the first time appreciating the miracle. *How am I still alive?*

Tower deferred to Nic with a sideways glance. I followed his gaze. "Nic, did you…"

He avoided my eyes. "Something broke your fall."

"Mostly," Tower added. "You did get a nasty concussion."

"We are going to need to get you checked out," Nic agreed. "That's your second head injury in a week."

I grunted, frustrated. What did any of that matter? "Fine, whatever. But how did you—"

"It doesn't matter."

"But Nic—"

He cut me off with another harsh glare. This time, he was clearly angry. "When are you going to learn that not all unanswered questions are bad omens? Sometimes it's okay to leave a door shut."

I opened my mouth, grappling for a protest, but found none. Even though I didn't know why, I decided to take his advice—just this once.

Diffusing the tension with a sigh, Tower said, "So, about the computers…"

"Did it work?" I exclaimed, a little too excitedly. I winced as my skull throbbed.

"If you mean every computer on the island is loading a blue screen of death, then yes, it worked."

My heart warmed. *Good job, brother. I hope Cea is proud.*

I flinched as I remembered one missing detail. "What about… Ambrose?"

This time, even Tower refused to look at me. "I'm pretty sure the fall killed him first," Nic said, as if that was any consolation. I shuddered and tried to offer up a prayer, but could come up with no words.

All around us, the din of military orders and general chaos continued. I became aware of a familiar voice approaching out of the crowd and turned to see the captain striding towards us, flanked by at least six other heavily armed officers.

Tower hastily stood up. "Well, you two are going to jail for a very long time."

"Thank God," Nic muttered—and, surprisingly, he didn't sound sarcastic about it.

With another nod at me, Tower melded into the crowd.

The captain stopped next to me and leaned over, blocking out the sky with his imposing shadow. "I'm impressed," he said in a tone as dry as sand. "You're the first convicted 'terrorist' the United has sent me that has actually managed to perpetrate an act of terrorism."

I cringed. "Thanks?"

Dr. Nic stood up, matching the captain in height. "What, did our reputation not precede us?"

The captain ignored the comment. "Care to explain to me why my computers seemed to have been wiped of their data, young man?"

Nic nodded smartly. "It would be my pleasure."

The captain flicked his head, and two of the guards flanked Nic and handcuffed him. He seemed entirely unbothered by it all.

The captain looked down at me. "Take her to the infirmary, and put her under guard. I don't want any more incidents until they're shipped back to the mainland for trial."

"Trial?" I gasped.

The captain eyed me condescendingly. "I only deal with convicted criminals. Since you two have taken it upon yourselves to commit a new crime, you'll have to answer to the United for that."

My head spun, although whether from confusion or the developing brain injury, it was hard to tell. Of course our little stunt wouldn't go unnoticed. The United was going to want all the details about the virus we had unleashed—and then what? Would they kill us? Send us back to prison? Would this affect Ephesus? Cea? My father? Where were they?

I pinched my eyes shut, partially to quell the pain and partially to hide the tears that spontaneously formed.

"Hey." The gentle reprimand tapped my ear. I looked up to find Dr. Nic gazing at me again. "It will be all right."

Before he could elaborate on that sentiment, the guards prodded his shoulder and pushed him across the yard. Dr. Nic went without resistance or another glance at me.

My skull was throbbing so much that I hardly noticed when two of the other guards lifted my cot and started carrying me across the yard. I covered my face with my hands to block out the harsh sun, focusing instead on taking slow breaths.

I wasn't quite ready to trust Dr. Nic with much of anything. But I supposed, given the circumstances, I could follow his lead and let things go for a few hours.

Besides, I knew he was right, even if for different reasons. Come what may, things would work out for good.

20

I underestimated the United's eagerness to interrogate us. I was only in the infirmary for a few hours, doted on by a nurse who seemed more interested in pressing me for all the gossipy details about our crime than he was in examining my injuries, before a helicopter arrived to ferry us back to the mainland.

Deemed "fit to travel" by the useless nurse, I was handcuffed and crammed onto the stuffy helicopter with a chained Nic and several armed guards. Nic seemed in good spirits and cast several grins in my direction. I decided it was not a good idea to risk conversation while my forearm was pressed against a holstered gun, so I didn't ask him what he was so stupidly happy about.

Despite the unease in the air, I was nevertheless comforted by the sight of the mainland bleeding into the horizon. I had no idea if this was the same port we had taken off from, and I didn't recognize any of the geography, so we could have been halfway down the coast for all I knew. But it didn't matter—it was still one step closer to my family.

If I was honest with myself, I didn't have any hope that our escapades would inspire the government to reunite us. If anything, they probably realized I was a danger regardless of where I was imprisoned, and solitary confinement and maximum security were likely in my future, if they even kept me alive.

But for some reason, the prospect didn't bother me. I had no idea where my family was or what had been done with them. But as the helicopter lowered itself onto the green earth, I reminded myself: My family was on this soil, somewhere. And that was enough for now.

Our new ride was a train, of all things—and an old one at that. Its metal cars were washed-out shades of green and orange, and its squeaking wheels were so rusted they looked like they might be fused to the tracks. We were hustled to a car at the rear and roughly loaded in like cattle. One guard accompanied us. The door was dragged shut with a screech that plunged my headache to a new level of pain.

A single battery-powered lantern illuminated the dusty interior. They hadn't even bothered to clean out the abandoned crates and dusty tarps left over from the car's shipping days.

The rest of our escort wandered away, their shouts fading from outside the train. Figuring our sole escort wouldn't be too bothered by conversation, I ventured, "Where did they find this old piece of junk?"

Nic shrugged.

"Most of the electric trains aren't working. Something about the navigation system being screwy," the guard offered. I shared an excited glance with Nic. *So the virus did make it back to the mainland.* I shivered with the realization.

If the guard understood the implications, he didn't betray any interest. With a callous pop of his bubble gum, he tossed a pair of keys over his shoulder and walked away. "It'll be a bumpy ride—might want to find something to hang on to." He wandered over to the corner and began amusing himself with a pocket knife.

"Thanks," Nic said. He knelt and fetched the keys from the floor, then gestured at me.

I dumbly held my hands out. "What's going on…?" I said in a half-whisper, wondering if I should have already picked up on the hints.

My handcuffs dropped to the floor. I hastily freed Nic as he explained, "This train is about to get hijacked in…"

"Thirty minutes," the guard offered.

Nic nodded.

"Again?" I exclaimed, the weight of his words hitting me.

"It worked last time, didn't it?"

I had no answer for that. "But how did you—"

"As much as I don't want to admit it, I owe John and Dowe more than a few favors—starting with a new laptop, for some reason."

I squinted. I knew I had underestimated those two, apparently in more ways than one.

"And where will we go after we get 'hijacked'?"

"Depends on who's nearby," Nic replied, seemingly unconcerned with the uncertainty of it all. "But our first step will be to get new prints taken."

"New prints?"

Dr. Nic stretched, popping the joints in his neck. "The most important thing the virus did was screw up databases—including databases of criminal files. They no doubt have offline backups of much of the information, but it will take time to get that restored. Until then, we have a narrow opportunity where it will be very easy for certain gifted individuals to falsify personnel files."

He looked up at me. "If this goes well, by the time they get the systems back online, our fingerprints will be associated with new names and new files."

A new name? But what will I call myself? How will I find my family if they also wipe their files and change their names? My broken mind struggled to jump through the hoops, but it kept tripping over one seemingly obvious roadblock.

"You mean… they can get the systems back online?"

"Eventually. What can't be restored will be replaced."

"But the virus…"

"Nothing is perfect. I'm confident we wreaked havoc in their top-level systems, because that computer on Rott was connected to one of their major government servers. It was their big project of the year, and that will be their downfall. But there will always be alternate connections, private servers, and good firewalls. They didn't lose everything—but they have much bigger problems to solve than some missing criminal files."

"But that means…" I couldn't formulate the words, partially because my head hurt and partially because I didn't want to say them out loud for fear they might be true. "They might still have Red Rain."

Nic didn't say anything at first, which was just as well. The train's engine roared to life, sending a rumble reverberating through the cars. The noise grew louder and louder, punctuated by several sharp screeches of the whistle. Despite having several minutes of warning, it still startled me when the train jerked forward, sending me sprawling on the floor.

"I told you to find a handhold," the guard admonished.

Pulling myself to a seating position, I found a handle near the door and stabilized myself against the wall. I watched the shifting light seeping through the cracks in the boards as we pulled out of the station, the train picking up speed with slow determination. Eventually, it seemed to find its rhythm, and despite the grinding of the wheels and the soft shake of the car back and forth, the noise became bearable.

I looked to Dr. Nic, expecting an answer.

He met my gaze boldly. "It's possible."

My heart shattered, although I somehow managed to avoid crying out with the anguish I felt.

"But that's why you need this."

He drew his hand from his pocket and held out a slender object. I gasped when I recognized it in the weak light. *My brother's flash drive.*

"But you—" My voice turned accusatory once I remembered what else was on that drive.

"I deleted Red Rain," he assured me. "That's why it took me so long. I know that's not an excuse, but I had to make sure it was gone."

The fact that he continued to hold my gaze told me he was being honest. He was right—it wasn't an excuse. But somehow I didn't have the energy to be mad.

"But the rest of your brother's work should still be on here. It's hard to know, because that virus is incredibly thorough and deadly, but I think everything is intact."

He pressed it into my open palm. "Keep it. You will need it. If not for Red Rain, then for something else. The rebellion will need weapons. We 'terrorists' lost a lot of work today too—we're going to have to start somewhere."

He paused, as if contemplating his own words. "We may no longer be fighting with chemicals, but we still have to win a war."

I closed my fist around the drive. "Thanks."

By way of reply, he smiled.

The remainder of the ride passed in silence. I was far too consumed with attempting to process my spiraling thoughts—as best I could around my receding headache—to solicit any more conversation.

As promised, in about half an hour the train began to slow. Our guard stood up and walked over to the door. "You might want to stand back," he advised me.

Scrambling backwards to the middle of the car, I watched in horror as the guard callously dragged the door open. With the force of a tornado, heavy wind gushed into the cabin, bringing with it the furious noise of the train laboring across the tracks. I squatted close to the ground, hoping my low profile would prevent me from getting blown away.

The guard leaned precariously out the door and looked around. "There's the drop site—that rooftop around the bend."

"Rooftop?" I screeched, unable to contain my rising panic any longer.

The only consolation I got was another annoying pop of his bubble gum. "Yup. You're going to have to jump, tuck, and roll."

Having—literally—nothing else to hang onto at this point, I looked to Nic in a desperate grab for assurance. He shrugged. "It's a hijacking. The train isn't exactly going to stop and let us off."

I pinched my eyes shut, fighting a premature wave of nausea. *Oh dear Lord, help us.*

"Hey," he urged, "how is this any scarier than blowing up a whole factory of chemicals?"

I glared at him—mainly because I knew he was right.

"Here she comes," the guard warned.

Standing up slowly, I took a brave step towards the door—and stumbled as the train lurched around a bend. With a scream I fell forward and slammed into the broad side of the door. Thankfully it held.

"Be careful," Nic said, sounding a mix of concerned and sarcastic.

Taking deep breaths, I found the door handle and used it to pull myself over to the opening. Muttering prayers, I swallowed and dared to open my eyes.

The world rushed past so quickly it was just a blinding whirl of color. We were on elevated tracks, racing at least two stories above the ground.

Oh God, I can't do this… I forced myself to hold steady, trying to match the rhythm of my breaths with the clacking of the train. *Just one jump, and you can start a new life.*

It took a minute of coaching, but the scenery slowly came back into focus. City buildings began to punctuate the countryside as we rapidly approached a sprawling town.

Nic appeared beside me. "It won't be a far jump. The tracks run right between the buildings. You can do it."

I have to.

Despite his candor, I could tell Dr. Nic was also bracing himself for the leap. "Just try not to hit your head again, okay?" he offered, his joviality cracking somewhat.

I was about to answer when the thought rushed past me, almost as fast and fleeting as the wind grinding against the train.

You should learn to program.

I felt the flash drive shifting in my shoe. Being able to manipulate computers had gotten my father and brother out of trouble and into favored jobs more than once. Dr. Nic had built an entire colony with a carefully-programmed private server. And I had just witnessed the chaos a well-designed computer virus could deal to the United.

The rebellion will need weapons.

Shouts ricocheted off the tracks ahead. The train careened around a curve, and I could see figures swarming on a low, flat-topped building about a half-mile ahead.

"Brace yourself!" Nic hollered, almost a second too late. The brakes kicked in, drowning out all conversation with a high-pitched screech as the train lurched violently.

I gripped the door with both hands. My heart was racing, but, for the first time in several weeks, it wasn't from fear.

We have to start somewhere.

The rooftop loomed closer. I could hear yelling over the scream of the brakes and vaguely understood that Nic was giving me instructions. I stepped back and prepared to run, one last thought solidifying in my mind and filling my legs with courage.

I may not be a scientist. I didn't know how to handle guns, and I definitely didn't want to design weapons of mass destruction.

But I could still fight.

The train leveled in front of the long building. A group of strangers hovered with open arms ready to receive us. Nic shouted at me.

"I'm coming, Daddy," I said aloud.

And then I jumped.

PRISONER 120518

RED RAIN #2.5

RACHEL NEWHOUSE
& DAVID HARTUNG

MAY 2076

1

Rott was an island, and that was really all that could be said about it.

Like most prisons, it was a tasteless mass of concrete. The guard towers and cramped barracks had long since crowded out most of the sand from the shore, their barnacle-crusted foundations disappearing into the water with high tide. There was no need for a barbed wire fence—the open waters of the frigid North Atlantic had the same effect. Cold wind whipped mercilessly across the yard at all hours, and the only thing that disrupted the monotony was the occasional silhouette of a passing ship.

I had been shuffled between five prisons in so many months, but this reassignment had a finality about it. Maybe it was the location—a dead-end in the middle of the ocean—maybe it was the name. I'd like to think the name was a sadistic pun, but the United had literally never done anything clever during its illustrious tyranny, so I assumed the name was just a happy accident.

Still, the island definitely seemed like a place where you left things to decompose. I was confident that's what the government intended to do with me.

They assigned me the number 120518 because it was convenient; the patch for the jumpsuit had just been sent up from the morgue, and the secretary hadn't put it away yet.

I immediately donned a nickname, because I was told that's what all the prisoners did. I chose Quetzalcoatl. The name had no significance, except that it was as far removed from my real name as possible, and I enjoyed watching the secretary suffer when she tried to spell it.

It didn't matter what they called me. Personally, I had zero intentions of learning anybody's name, real or assumed, on this island. Anytime someone was so rude as to introduce themselves, I made a concentrated effort to purge their name from my mind as soon as they walked away. I didn't want to know anyone, and I didn't want anyone to know me. I wasn't here to make friends.

The only person whose name I retained was Tower. He was a guard. You can guess where he was stationed.

I'd asked him for the time once while taking a lap around the yard, and he had the audacity to introduce himself. Since he was one of the few reliable sources of time, I decided to let it slide.

I took laps because I had nothing better to do. There was plenty of activity on the island; most of the prisoners had been assigned to a nearly-complete construction project in the middle of the yard. Based on the random bits of machinery that were continually getting delivered, I assumed it was a factory, but I hadn't bothered to ask. I hadn't been assigned to work on it; in fact, I hadn't been assigned a job at all.

I wasn't sure if my unemployment was error or slight, but I was in no rush to correct their mistake. I figured if I took laps and acted like I had somewhere to be, no one would pay me any mind. So far, it was working.

My incarceration went swimmingly until my 29th day on Rott. That's when everything went to hell. Never mind it was a short trip.

It was a bright, but not in any way cheery, day, and I was getting another lap in before dinner. I had just passed under Tower's station when I heard the shout.

"42."

I jumped, mainly because this was the first time he had initiated a conversation. I glanced up at the control booth that sat atop the three-story tower. The window was open, and I could see him sitting there, but he wasn't looking at me. His eyes were molded to his binoculars, as they often were, and he was watching something across the yard.

"I'm sorry?" I called back.

"42," he repeated. "That's how many laps you've taken today."

"Were you counting?"

Without taking his eyes away from the scopes, he held one arm out. It was covered with tally marks checked in black permanent ink.

"That's weird, and I want to unsee that."

He shrugged.

"Why are we having this conversation?" I demanded.

"I just thought you should know they're looking for you."

A chilly breeze brushed my arms—but then again, that was the only kind of breeze they had around here. "They who?"

"I don't know, I can't read nametags from here. They're meeting with the big boss right now."

"How do you know they're looking for me?"

"Who else would they be looking for? You're the only criminal on this island worth the title."

"Thanks for the compliment, but this all sounds like a lot of conjecture. The United had me in prison for months on the mainland and barely talked to me. I don't think they're looking for me now."

He swiveled his binoculars to the other side of the yard. "All I'm saying is, you might want to lay low during dinner—and avoid government officials."

"I make a habit of it," I muttered, and resumed walking. "Stop me when I get to 50 laps."

Dinner was called before I completed my 46th lap. As I always did, I waited until almost everyone else had gone before joining the back of the line. My theory was that everyone would have already picked their seats by the time I got to the mess hall, and I could choose the most abandoned table.

Tonight, however, I was not so lucky. No sooner had I sat down than two old men got up from their table and came to join me.

I was appalled. Sure, there was no rule forbidding people from changing tables—I had just never seen anyone on this island exude that much effort.

"Hey Q! It's your buddy John!" the first one said.

"And Dowe!" the second echoed. "Remember us?"

I groaned. I *did* remember them, and that was the problem. This was the third time these fools had tried to introduce themselves to me, and the repetition was making it hard for me to block them from my memory.

It didn't help that their appearance was also very memorable, in a downright creepy way. John and Dowe were almost identical in height, hair, and weight, so much so that from across the yard you would swear they were twins. But when you got up close, you could spot just enough differences to know that they couldn't be related. Yet, they were joined at the hip and completed each other's sentences in a way that amplified their obnoxiousness.

"Much to my dismay," I returned. "But *you* seem to have forgotten that my name is not Q."

"Yeah, I'm not saying that," John retorted. "It takes too long."

"Sorry I'm such a test of patience."

"It's fine, he could use the practice." Dowe drained the last of his water and thumped his canteen on the table. "We've been looking for you, Q."

Tower's warning flashed through my mind. I eyed the curious pair, but I couldn't imagine them as government agents. Firstly, they were ancient. Secondly, they were dumb. Not in the inept, hive-mind way most United officials were—no, John and Dowe were *actually* stupid. I was sure some of it was an act, but the fact that they never broke character was disconcerting.

Best case scenario, they were harmless mental cases. Still, I would take any excuse to avoid them.

"I'm sorry, but my mom always told me never to talk to strangers."

"Don't worry, I left our big white van at home."

"Correction, you drove our big white van into the ocean six months ago."

"We can still get to it! It's stuck on a rock or something like ten yards out. I think we should turn it into a party space and rent it."

"What, so people can picnic on the roof?"

"Yeah!"

"I like the way you think."

"That's the entrepreneurial spirit," I inserted, hoping the interruption would derail the conversation permanently.

"We'll give you a cut if you advertise, Q."

"No thanks," I stood up and gathered my dishes, even though I hadn't had a chance to take a bite. "I've already got a job."

"So I heard."

I looked up sharply, but not quickly enough to see which one had spoken. "What did you hear?"

"Nothing definitive," Dowe answered. "But just in case, we wanted to cover our bases and make sure we got to you first."

Maybe Tower *was* talking about these two.

"I'm not interested," I snapped.

"Take it easy—we just wanted to give you this." Dowe pulled a crumpled piece of paper out of his pocket and tossed it at me.

I smoothed it out. It was a coupon for free pizza delivery. Expired, of course.

"Order whatever you want, on the house," John beamed.

"But it only works on the mainland," Dowe clarified. "Overseas shipping is too expensive."

"I'll save it for when I go on vacation." I crumpled it back up and dropped it on my tray.

"Hey, don't throw that away! It cost us an arm and a leg!"

"Yeah, Bob and Fred would be mortified."

"Dare I ask who Bob and Fred are?"

"When you see guys missing an arm and a leg, you'll know." Dowe held my gaze, dead-serious.

With the tips of my fingers, I gingerly picked up the coupon and stuffed it in the pocket of my jumpsuit, intending to throw it away or forget about it, whichever came first. "Well, thanks for the invigorating intellectual discussion, but I need to go…"

"Right, right. Hey, are you going to eat that?" Without waiting for an answer, John pulled my tray to himself and dug in.

"Nah, lost my appetite."

Neither of them appreciated the implications of that statement, so I left them to it and went to finish my laps.

"That's 50!" Tower called down to me. I saw him make another tally mark on his arm.

"Seriously, stop doing that."

"Who's the prisoner and who's the guard in this relationship?" He picked up his binoculars.

"Touché." I stopped beneath his tower. "By the way, you were right about them."

There was a pause. "Them?"

"John and Dowe," I clarified. "They found me. Again. I can't get rid of them."

He snorted. "I wasn't talking about them. They're friends."

"Well, that explains everything. So who *were* you talking about?"

He lowered his binoculars, revealing sunken raccoon eyes that were nearly hidden under a mess of unkept dark hair. "I was talking about Ambrose."

2

I immediately turned around and walked away.

"Where are you going?" Tower shouted after me.

"Following your advice—avoiding government officials."

Ambrose was a name I knew. I had seen it dozens of times in the form of a rubber stamp at the bottom of paperwork. Back when I had been the governor of a research base, Ambrose had been the supervisor of two scientists I wanted to recruit, which meant my transfer requests had to go through him. He had been a piece of red tape then—the all-powerful government figure whose hand I had to kiss if I wanted my paperwork approved.

We'd met in the flesh only once. He had been so gracious as to visit me in my first prison and lord his accomplishments over me. He claimed responsibility for putting me behind bars. I was quick to correct him and remind him that a Christian teenager—one of the many unassimilated, socially noncompliant reprobates his perfect government was supposed to be filtering out—was the one who turned me in. Ambrose just happened to be the recipient of her email and seized the profits. Credit where credit is due.

I could tell he wanted to kill me in exchange for my helpful fact-checking, but that would have required filing an incident report. I knew from experience how much paperwork that involved, and he decided I wasn't worth it.

I would have made the same choice, in his shoes.

I hadn't seen him since then. In fact, I hadn't seen much of anyone. Despite the fact that I'd been months away from staging a massive terrorist attack against the United, they hadn't been very interested in questioning me. You'd think they'd want to know how I'd almost managed to free *the entire planet of Mars* from United control, but apparently they didn't care, as long as I'd failed.

Which meant there was no good reason for him to track me all the way out here in the middle of the ocean.

I thought about giving him a chase—I could probably lose him in the unfinished factory for a few hours—but thought better of it. It was only a matter of time before they sent guards to haul me in, and if they discovered I wasn't in my cell after curfew, Ambrose would probably get to beat me free of charge.

I made it back to my cell just before the door automatically locked, signaling curfew. I turned out the light, slid the cover across the barred window of the door, and sat down at the desk to wait. I'm not sure why the cell had a desk—I hadn't seen a single book or piece of paper on the entire island—but sitting at the empty desk was slightly less dehumanizing than curling up on the weak cot that was too short for my lanky frame.

It wasn't ten minutes later that I heard heavy footsteps and winded breaths enter the corridor. He stopped outside my cell, blocking out the silver of light that crept in under the door.

"Let's talk," he said by way of introduction.

Let's not. I decided to ignore him, mostly just to see what he'd do.

"120518, I know you're in there."

What a Sherlock.

"Open the window."

Nah. I crossed my leg, leaned back in the chair, and waited.

He grunted and cussed. I heard keys rattle, then a swipe of a card in the door. It rejected him with a beep.

I couldn't resist a laugh into the darkness. They hadn't even given him access privileges.

He heard me and swore again. "Open up!"

"You want me to open the door from the inside? That's not how prisons work."

"Do it or I kill you."

"What kind of threat is that? You can't shoot me through the door, unless they gave you one of the good guns, but I don't think you have the clearance."

He mumbled into his communicator.

I lazily stood up and strolled to the door. "How pathetic. You have me in prison on the mainland for months—months!—and hardly say a word to me. Now you swim across the Atlantic to track me down, and you can't even get the door open."

I slid the cover back from the window, revealing an electric pistol aimed at the bars. I was right—it wouldn't have punctured the steel door. It was a child's weapon, really, perfectly suited to the childish man.

I put my hands up. "Please, go ahead. Shoot me. I've been waiting six months for one of you to have the courage."

He spat at me, but the spittle just landed on the handle of his own gun. He grimaced and wiped his hand on his pants.

"What do you want?" I asked. "It's past my bedtime."

He composed himself and put on a smile. "How are you liking Rott, 'Q'?" he slithered, lines clearly rehearsed.

"Don't even try. If you think I'm going to play that song and dance, you're wrong. Just tell me what you want so I can make a show of pondering your offer before slamming this shut in your face." I kept my hand on the window for emphasis.

"You're no fun. At least the Christians put on a good show."

"Then why don't you go back to supervising them, Ambrose? Go back to your cute little concentration camp with a cushy office and a dozen underlings to do your bidding. Go back to watching a bunch of spineless martyrs who don't have the gumption to scale a six-foot wall. Take the easy paycheck, you deserve it."

He was less bothered by that statement than I expected—probably because it was all true, and he didn't mind admitting it. "Maybe when I retire. Right now, though, I've received a better offer."

"Wonderful. I hope your promotion takes you far away from me."

"That is the only downside to this position—it dictates that you and I will be working very closely for the next few months."

"That tells me everything I need to know—I'm not interested, and goodbye."

I slid the window shut. He gave a startled noise I took some pleasure in.

"If you don't..." He swallowed the threat and reinstated his professionalism. "You haven't even heard the employee benefits yet."

"There's nothing you could offer me that would justify those working conditions."

He chuckled. "Really? There's nothing you want? Nothing at all that I could tempt you with? What *do* you want? Money? A state-of-the-art lab? Your own island?"

"I'd consider my own planet. If you offered me Mars, I'd probably play ball, but anything less than that—not interested."

"Your own planet, huh? I think that can be arranged."

"Oh really."

"Well, maybe not a whole planet but—"

"You're lying? How did I know."

"—I think we could spare a moon."

I walked back to the desk. He kept talking, his voice slightly muffled through the door. "We could set you up on a nice, deserted moon. Give you all the supplies you need to build your own self-sufficient base. Send a few scientists with you to keep you company. We couldn't give you interstellar travel, of course—you've proven you're not trustworthy with it—but we could abandon you to the stars to be the ruler of your own little kingdom."

I stopped, folded my arms, and waited for him to go away.

"That's what you want, isn't it? To be in control. To be free from government regulations and run your own life. To be alone."

I looked to the ceiling. "That last part is spot-on. Can I go to bed now?"

"I have the power. I know the people. I've been authorized to offer you whatever you want, if you'll just do one little project for me."

"And what project is that? What could I possibly offer you that would be worth such a price?"

He savored the moment a beat too long. "Red Rain," he cooed. "You could give us Red Rain, Dr. Nic."

3

My blood ran like fire and ice through my veins. I wasn't sure which reaction was more appropriate—abject horror, or unbridled rage. Mostly, I was annoyed that I hadn't seen it coming.

Of course the United wanted my beautiful weapon. Any overbearing government worth their salt would love to have it. It was genius—a compound of gases that, when combined with normal precipitation, condensed into an acid strong enough to melt metal. It was *the* perfect weapon.

Sadly, I had never been able to complete it; if I had, I wouldn't be in this mess. I would have beaten the United into submission, cut my base on Mars off from their control, and lived happily ever after. But the scientists who were supposed to be helping me design Red Rain got cold feet and turned it over to the government—or rather, their daughter did. She'd ratted me out to Ambrose, who'd been all too happy to alert the higher-ups and take the credit.

Now the United had all the research for my world-ending weapon—and probably all of my other inventions, too. I wondered what Philadelphia, with her self-righteous, cowardly morality, would think if she realized what she'd done when she involved Ambrose.

The emotions continued to vacillate in my mind, but I had no intention of wasting any of them on a subject as undeserving as Ambrose. "Well, that answers that question," I snapped, loud enough to be heard through the door. "No."

He struggled with a comeback for a minute. "You won't get a better offer."

"I also won't get a worse one."

"I can give you everything!" he screeched, stamping his foot like a toddler.

I stormed back to the door and scraped the window open. "Are you stupid? You can give me nothing."

He looked confused. "But the moon—"

"Do you know me so little? The moon means nothing to me if you have Red Rain. You can offer the whole galaxy and I still won't give you my weapon."

He was finally catching up. "Why do you care? We can't use it against you—not if you're on the moon."

I huffed. "I trust you about as far as I can throw you—but that's not what I'm worried about."

He guffawed. "So you're the altruistic one now, are you? Did prison give you a change of heart? Are you afraid some Christians are going to get hurt?"

"Don't bother me with morals. I just don't want you to have it."

"But why?" It was a genuine question. "Within a year you could be living on your own moon, completely free from our control. No rules. No red tape. No government looking over your shoulder or monitoring your phone calls. Why do you care what happens down here?"

He had a point—and to be fair, I didn't care. That had always been my plan: Cut myself off from Earth and leave the United to wallow in its tyranny until the heat death of the universe. I really didn't care what the United did to win its war; it would continue to commit atrocities with or without my weapon. But that didn't mean I was going to give it to them.

"Why, doctor?" Ambrose demanded. "Why won't you give me Red Rain?"

"Because I hate you," I said, and smiled.

He snarled. "Don't make me resort to threats."

"I think you're already past that stage—and threats of what? Will you finally kill me?"

"I'll put the paperwork in tonight."

"Great, I'll wait five years for it to be approved."

"Or I could just leave you here."

"You were going to do that anyway."

He grunted. I put my face to the bars, locking eyes with him to make sure I was understood. "You have nothing on me. If I refuse you, I go back to taking laps around the yard and pretend this conversation never happened."

He stepped back and eyed me over his nose—or he would have, had I not been a good five inches taller than him. "We'll see about that," he snapped, and turned to leave.

I waited until he had disappeared in the elevator before slamming the window shut in relief. I flopped back in the desk chair, exhausted. I had done more talking today than the last six months of my imprisonment combined, and not a single word had been intellectually stimulating.

I rolled Ambrose's threats around in my mind. If you weeded past the bravado, he had a point. He would be back, and he would bring the big guns. If the United was motivated enough to ship him across the ocean to find me, he wouldn't leave without a fight. He would try every trick in the book, and despite my nonchalance, I knew none of them would be pleasant.

Ambrose would do everything he could to make my life hell—and then, just maybe, he would be motivated to end it. And what if he didn't? What if I got my wish—to wander endlessly around this island until Tower tattooed his entire body with tally marks? Is that the best I could do?

I had no intention of giving the United Red Rain, and I was under no delusion that they'd give me the moon even if I did. But if I took their deal, they'd at least have to set me up in a lab somewhere. And maybe, just maybe, I could find a way to escape that didn't involve hitching a ride on a shark.

The longer I ran the numbers, the more I realized I didn't have anything to lose. If I failed, they would just kill me or send me back here, and I'd be no worse off than when I started. But at least, if I was on the mainland, I'd have a chance of getting the upper hand.

I liked those odds.

4

After breakfast, I started taking my laps like normal. I wanted to make Ambrose find me; I wasn't going to crawl to him sniveling.

It took him long enough. Lunch came and went, and I was a good twenty-five laps in for the day before he intercepted me.

"All right, Nic, let's talk. You want a planet? I've been authorized to consider it. You get us Red Rain, and we'll talk about Mars."

I was shocked. I had expected him to lead with threats, not more bribery. But I accepted it with a shrug. "Okay. Want to get coffee sometime?"

He jerked back. "What?"

"So we can talk details—it's too cold to be standing out here in this wind."

He wasn't there yet. "You… you want to talk?"

"Do I want to talk to you? No. Am I willing to? Yes."

He fumbled for a comeback and settled for honesty. "I'm… surprised, doctor."

"No one's more surprised than me. What can I say? Your speech yesterday—very convincing."

"You're kidding."

"About you being a convincing speaker? Of course I'm kidding. About being willing to negotiate? That's a genuine offer."

He squinted at me. "I don't trust you."

"Nor I you, but it seems we have found something in common—which, I hear, is the first step to friendship."

He bellowed a full-throated laugh. "That's rich."

"Like chocolate. Now. Shall we talk?"

He calmed himself. "I'm listening."

I had my list prepared. "I want a lab in North America, fully outfitted. I don't want to work with any Unionists, not even a secretary. I work my own way at my own pace—I don't want to hear anything about red tape or 'unapproved substances' or any of your other pomp and circumstance."

"Done," he said without batting an eyelash.

Those were the easy requests. "And I want my old assistant—Carnegie."

I didn't have to clarify who I meant. Ambrose's eyes flickered—he knew him. "I... I can't do that," he stuttered.

His nervousness was palpable, and that was deeply concerning. "Why not? He's a frail old man—he's no use to you."

Ambrose composed himself and plastered a cruel smile on his face. "Let's just say he's permanently unavailable."

I caught up. "Did you help him get there, or did he spare you the trouble?"

"It was a combined effort—made the paperwork much simpler."

"How considerate of him." I shook off the inconvenient emotion that threatened to invade my consciousness. "Fine. Then I'll work alone."

"As you wish."

"And one last thing."

He arched an eyebrow.

"I don't want to do any paperwork. Not a single report. I'll give you the work, but I'm not feeding your obsession with bureaucracy. I'll do the science, and I'll give you my progress updates verbally. If you make me do *any* kind of paperwork—and I mean any—the deal's off."

"You want me to put that in a contract?"

"Not if I have to sign it."

He grinned with the pent-up wickedness of a lifetime wasted on political ambition. "I'll see if I can pull some strings."

He started walking away. "Pack your bags, doctor. Our ship leaves in an hour."

I waited until he was out of sight before I resumed my walk. I had nothing to pack, and I was hoping that if I kept going in circles I could avoid John and Dowe. I was not interested in a goodbye.

There was one person I couldn't avoid, though, no matter where I went on the island. I kept my eyes straight ahead as I passed under Tower's post.

I heard his window open. "Hey, Q."

I reluctantly paused and looked up. Tower was staring into his binoculars, eyes elsewhere, but his voice floated down to me clearly. "A word of advice?"

"I collect them."

"If you reach a dead end—order pizza."

I remembered the expired coupon and came to the sad realization that Tower, John, and Dowe were just three peas in a pod. I continued walking. "I'll be sure to tell them who referred me."

✳

It took more than an hour for our ship to leave—I'm sure something was wrong with the paperwork. Then came the idyllic two-day boat ride, during which Ambrose invested way too much energy in guarding me like he actually had to earn his paycheck. I'm sure he knew it was unnecessary; a pair of cuffs and a locked door would have done the job. Evidently he was trying to entertain himself, so I let him have it. He'd be out of my hair soon enough.

The boat ride was followed by a short trip up the East Coast in a helicopter. They blindfolded me when we neared the city so I wouldn't recognize it, not that it particularly mattered to me. I was herded into a van, which drove for another thirty minutes. Finally I was guided through a parking garage, up an elevator, and down a hall. There was a beep and a whoosh of a door being opened. Ambrose kicked me through, and then he finally removed the blindfold.

"Welcome home, doctor."

I glanced around the entryway, but there was nothing to see. "Save it for when you give me the moon."

He cackled. "I think you'll find the amenities sufficient. All of the research from your computers on Mars has been transferred to the databases. If you're missing anything essential, just put in a request through any computer terminal."

"What did I tell you about paperwork?"

He smiled. "I'll make sure to put your requests through on priority."

"Thank you for your attention to this matter."

He stepped out the door. "Get some rest. We'll touch base in the morning."

The door slid shut behind him, and I admired the control panel for it—it looked similar to the prototype door control system I had been testing on Mars. Of course, that system had its flaws—one of which ended up being my undoing.

I pushed the thought out of my mind and went to explore the amenities. It was nothing like my base on Mars, where I had unlimited space to build whatever facilities I needed, but it wasn't shabby. The United did have plenty of money, and apparently they were willing to throw some at this project.

The main lab was the first door down the hall to the left. It was well-stocked with the latest equipment, three computer stations, a gigantic digital whiteboard, and a sealed testing chamber.

A smaller, secondary lab was on the right, followed by the dorms. There were four small rooms attached to a combined bathroom/laundry room.

I opened the final door and found myself in a common room. It was connected to the main lab by a door, so you could easily walk back and forth from work to play. The room was cluttered with a recreational computer terminal, a couch, and a few tables and chairs. A small kitchenette was built into one wall, and the other was embedded with a vending machine. You could place an order for whatever you wanted, and it would be piped up from the cafeteria on another floor.

I patted my lean stomach, remembering the tar and plastic that had been considered "food" on Rott. Clearly, bargaining with Ambrose had its perks.

I walked over and tapped the screen, displaying a shockingly short menu of options. My disappointment fell as I tabbed through the dinner choices and realized I would not be dining on steak anytime soon.

No matter. I tabbed over to the drinks. As long as they had—

"Curse you, Ambrose." There was no coffee on the list.

I better get started on that escape plan right away.

5

I spent the first day looking through the data the United had stolen from me. It only took about ten minutes to determine that they'd copied my entire database; everything was exactly as I left it, except for a few paltry additions no doubt contributed by some inept United scientists.

Still, I wasted a whole day looking through it. The more time I could buy myself by pretending to be busy, the better.

The second day I wasted trying to hack onto another network. All the computers in the lab were connected to the same wifi. It could access the censored United internet, which was basically useless to me. United science was almost as bad as United politics, which meant, if I were going to do any real research, I needed to get onto some illegal sites.

More importantly, I was sure that the United was remotely monitoring everything that went on in the lab. It wasn't that hard for them; it was their wifi, and they had plenty of programs that did most of the work for them. If I had any hope of escaping, I needed to get onto another signal where I could speak a bit more freely.

Not that I had any idea who I would contact. Carnegie, my first choice, was dead. My other associates on Mars had likely fallen to similar fates, but even if they hadn't, none of them had the resources needed to truly help me. That left me with a few wealthy investors who might still owe me a favor for allowing them to conduct unsanctioned experiments on Mars. But wealth was a fickle thing, and now that I had none, they might not be so willing to honor their debts.

Although, at the rate I was going, it might not matter. Even though I found dozens of other wifi signals within range, I couldn't get onto any of them. I invested two whole days into the endeavor and had nothing to show for my efforts. Either the connections were very secure, or I was completely incompetent when it came to coding.

I knew the answer, not that I would have admitted it to anyone but myself. I'd almost blown my entire operation once by prematurely releasing a badly-coded computer virus. There had been two problems with that experiment. One, I didn't know enough about code to notice that the scientist behind it had intentionally written it wrong. And two, I'd been too dumb to realize that the network I was testing it on wasn't fully secure.

Thankfully, Carnegie had been around to help me clean up the mess. But that was a luxury I'd never have again.

I was moping over a boring dinner—pasta with plain tomato sauce (there wasn't an option to order cheese)—when the phone rang.

It wasn't a phone, per se—it was a communications program on the computer. A pop-up engulfed the screen, accompanied by a dorky ring that was probably a lame attempt at nostalgia.

I walked over to the terminal. I didn't recognize the number, and there was no profile picture—just an icon of the United's seal.

I rolled my eyes and accepted the call. "Good evening, Ambrose."

"Good guess, but this isn't Ambrose," a calm, calculated male voice answered.

"Well that just made my evening. To whom do I have the pleasure of speaking?"

"You can call me Thames, and trust me, there is absolutely no pleasure in our relationship."

"Suit yourself." I took another bite of pasta and spoke around it. "So how can I help you?"

"I'm a simple man—give me Red Rain, and I'll dance."

"Sounds great, but if you're expecting me to have it completed after only being here three days, then you need to learn a thing or two about science."

He snorted. "I know we can be demanding chaps up here in the office, but I'm not that stupid."

"Excellent. We'll get on fine, then—it's the stupid ones I can't stand."

"I'll do my best to meet your approval. In the meantime, give me your progress so far."

I chewed and swallowed another bite before answering. "I've started."

"That so? Because I haven't seen a single change to the database, and I don't believe you've been granted paper privileges."

The pasta landed like a lump of coal in the pit of my stomach. "There's a whiteboard..."

He sighed. "Doctor, I don't enjoy these conversations any more than you do, so I'm going to make it easy on both of us and keep it simple. Either you start working, and you work hard, or I'll kill you."

"I think I liked Ambrose better—at least he had the decency to banter a bit before he issued the death threats."

"Perhaps that's why Ambrose is still working for me, instead of the other way around. In any case, I'll check on you tomorrow evening. I hope you have a better story for me then."

He hung up without ceremony. I aggressively stirred my pasta around my plate. "Oh don't you worry, I will," I mumbled to the empty room.

The next day, I did my best to work without working. I modified databases, fiddled with equations, and ran simulations—all of which I'd run before on Mars. The results were all the same, but at least it generated a fresh wave of data to satisfy Thames.

When he called that evening, I did my best to sell the work I had done. This was a skill I was actually quite good at. When you're soliciting investors for a project that is entirely theoretical, you have to be able to sell a concept rather than a product. Each test and simulation can represent a golden breakthrough if you stage it right.

Thames seemed to buy my advertising. He left me with another threat to get me through the day, then hung up. I spent the next day fudging, and we repeated this song and dance for two weeks.

While my pointless tests were running, I continued to scour the internet, looking for any lifeline. I looked up my old investors; unsurprisingly, all of them had changed their contact information after the government busted my base. I looked for information on my sister Cea but found nothing current. I tried looking up Thames and discovered he was fairly high up the political food chain—which meant literally every scrap of information on him was classified.

I knew they could see all of my internet activity, but at this point, I wasn't sure it mattered. I was getting nowhere.

It was also becoming increasingly harder to fake work. I had already put nearly a decade of my life into this project, and that was coming back to bite me. I had been working for years to come up with the formula for Red Rain, which meant there was literally nothing I had not tried. I had run every test and every simulation and used every program known to mankind. I had hundreds, if not thousands, of failed chemical sequences. And, unfortunately, being in prison hadn't made me any smarter—all the problems that had stumped me before continued to perplex me. I was no closer to completing my weapon than I ever was.

All this meant that there was only so much work I could fake, so many tests I could repeat, before it became obvious even to a non-scientist that I was copying and pasting.

I could tell by the way my conversations with Thames were getting shorter and shorter and his voice was getting colder and colder that I was reaching the end of the line with him. But I knew I was done for when he called twice in one day.

"Back so soon? You must really love me." I was attempting attitude, but the words came out limp.

"Don't worry, I won't keep you. I don't want to take up your evening."

"How considerate. I was just about to watch one of your inane censored TV shows. I really love the part where everyone's stupid."

"Same. Anyway, I just called to tell you—we have your sister in a concentration camp."

He said it like a threat, but I didn't take it as one. "Which is where she should be, according to your hierarchy. She is too religious for your tastes—and mine, most of the time."

"She doesn't have to stay there."

"You could send her to Rott—tell her I'll meet up with her when you get tired of dealing with me."

"I mean I could kill her, Nic."

"I knew what you meant," I muttered, but my boisterous sarcasm died halfway through the sentence. It was a cheap shot on Thames's part, but well-aimed. I had never been under any delusions that Cea was safe with the United, but I had never intended to use her as my scapegoat.

Thames was content to let me ponder that threat in silence for a moment. I weighed the odds. It had only been two weeks, and Thames was already resorting to his trump card. That meant I didn't have a lot of time before he put me—and Cea, apparently—on the chopping block. In the meantime, I was no closer to figuring a way out of here.

If I was going to get out of this alive, I needed to buy myself more time. That meant Thames had to see real progress, which was something I couldn't give him.

But I knew someone who could.

It was time to pull out *my* trump card: Blame somebody else.

But for that to work, I knew I had to sell it. You can't just cast blame around like confetti; if you wanted it to stick, you had to prime the wall.

"Listen, Thames. I'm going to tell you something that will blow your mind."

"Please don't."

"The truth."

The line went silent. I modulated my voice to make it sound like I'd had a change of heart. "I can't complete Red Rain."

"Really? What finally gave it away? The two weeks of crushing failure?"

I laughed. "I knew before I even set foot in this lab."

He didn't respond.

"Don't you get it?" I jeered. "I knew I couldn't complete the formula. I've known that for years. I just wanted to get off that putrid island. I figured I could string you along for a while until I figured out a way to escape… but I see you don't have that kind of patience."

"You expect me to believe that?" he spat in a way that suggested he might.

"No." I let the silence bake for a beat. "But you might, if I gave you the man who *could* complete the formula."

"If you were lonely and wanted a roommate, you could have just said something. Who is it?"

With a smile he sadly couldn't see, I whispered, "Smyrna."

"The girl?" he sputtered.

The girl? You mean Philadelphia? It was so absurd that I cackled. Since when had that obnoxious brat become the most famous member of her family?

Although, when I considered it, it made some sense. After all, she was the one who had cozied up to the government and dropped the hint about my project. She had probably become a household name around the office.

The memory of her stupid doe-eyes caused my fists to tighten, but I kept the bitterness out of my voice as I continued to lead Thames along. "Yes, of course I mean Phil—she's a chemical genius, didn't you know? No, you moron, I mean the old man. Dr. Thomas Smyrna. If you want this project complete, he's the one you want."

"Prove it."

That was easy. "Why do you think I summoned him to Mars? Do you know how much that cost? How much red tape I had to hurdle? You politicians do not make it easy to reassign unassimilated. You think I would go through all that trouble if I didn't think he could do it?"

"You said the same thing about Ephesus once."

"Ephesus and I had a labor dispute. He probably could have done it, but he didn't like my benefits package." With a dry chuckle, I realized how true that was. I cleared my throat. "However, I don't think you'll have that problem."

"Fine," he said after a pause. "I'll bring him in. But you're not going anywhere until I have a complete formula. I don't care who does the work—just make it happen, or I'll kill all of you."

"I'd expect nothing less," I said, and hung up.

6

I tried to tidy up the place—and myself—before going to bed. I knew I was essentially a caged lab rat, but at least I didn't have to look like one. As far as the old man was concerned, I ran this lab, and I was very comfortable doing it.

Thames, for all his flaws, wasn't a procrastinator, and my victim was delivered early the next morning. I heard the commotion coming down the hall and staged myself right inside the door. My lab coat was freshly bleached, and I had my mug posed in my hand. The effect would have been better had there been something other than water in the cup, but the old man would probably be too flabbergasted to notice anyway.

I put on my most commanding smile as the door slid open. "Welcome to the… what are *you* doing here?"

Ephesus stood in the hall. He had apparently not come willingly; two burly guards were at his elbow. He threw both of them off to lunge at me.

There was nowhere to run in the narrow entryway, so he succeeded in slamming me against the wall. I dropped my cup, spilling the contents all over my coat. "Good thing that wasn't coffee," I hissed at him.

In typical Smyrna fashion, he wasn't listening. His hands were cuffed, but that didn't stop him from putting them around my throat.

"What are you doing here? Answer me!" he screeched as he attempted to throttle me.

I drew my knee back and kicked him where it hurt. He stumbled backward into the guards, who were kind enough to restrain him.

"This is my lab," I huffed. "And I asked you first."

His face twisted, like he couldn't decide whether being confused or angry was more important. "What do you mean? You called me here!"

"I did no such thing! I haven't needed you in two years, and you know it."

He did know it, which shut him up, at least for the moment.

"It's your father I want."

"I'm here." He emerged from the hall. He wasn't cuffed, which said volumes about the situation. "Care to explain what's going on?"

"You and I are here to work. Him?" I jabbed a finger at his son. "I have no idea." I gestured at the guards. "Take him back. He'll only get in the way."

They shrugged. "Thames's orders."

I groaned. "Of course they are."

The guards released Ephesus's cuffs and unceremoniously dropped him on the floor, then promptly left, locking the door behind them. Ephesus took a moment to orient himself before springing back into action.

"All right, you, let's finish this."

I cast a bored look at Smyrna. "Control your son. What a disgrace."

"Enough, both of you," he said in a voice that indicated he hadn't slept all night. He certainly looked like he hadn't slept in a week, or maybe a year. "Before anybody throws any punches, I think we need to hear the full story. What's going on? Why are you here?"

"Yeah, how are you still alive?" Ephesus brushed himself off. "I figured they would have executed you."

"Ephesus," Smyrna scolded.

I laughed. "Too much paperwork. Prison is a much easier legal process. And I was rather enjoying the reprieve—until they realized they couldn't survive without my genius."

"Spare me."

"What can I say? They saw how brilliant Red Rain was and demanded to have it for themselves."

They responded with stunned silence, and I realized that may not have been the best way to introduce the project.

"You've got to be kidding me," Ephesus exclaimed, and the look in his eyes said that he hoped it really was a joke.

Smyrna muttered something that was a cross between an oath and a prayer.

"I wish I was, young man, but I'm afraid the terms are very simple: Either we collectively put our genius together and give them the completed formula for Red Rain, or we die." I shrugged.

Ephesus balled his fists, but Smyrna put his hand up. His eyes locked with mine. "Show me."

I led them to the main lab. Smyrna sat down in front of a computer terminal and started riffling through the databases. His son read over his shoulder.

"It's all here," Ephesus breathed after a minute. "Every bomb and gun I ever created for you—it's all here. And you gave it all to *them!*"

"I didn't 'give' them anything. They stole it."

He wasn't interested in the semantics. He screamed, a primal yell of pure rage. He drew his arm back, but for once, his fist wasn't aimed at me. He turned to the nearest wall and slammed his entire body weight into the plaster—one, two, three times.

"Ephesus," the old man tried.

Ephesus gave another punch, weakly this time, then leaned his head against the wall. "This is all my fault."

"That's a bit of a stretch," I said.

He traced his finger around the hole he'd created in the drywall. "I never should have bargained with you. I never should have made *anything* for you. I should have made you kill me."

I shrugged. "Probably."

Smyrna frowned at me. "What did they tell you? What do they want?"

"Red Rain, obviously." I took the other desk chair. "Apparently when they raided my base, they decided to keep my work for themselves. Philadelphia did them a favor, really."

Ephesus turned. "Leave my sister out of this!"

"She's already involved," Smyrna said, so quietly I was lucky to hear him. He shared a heavy-handed look with Ephesus.

The kid washed white.

"What?" I said, suddenly very concerned that there was something I should know. I hated that feeling.

"Conveniently, Phil was taken into 'special custody' last night," Ephesus snapped. "Now I know why." The anger returned to his eyes, but they burned a different shade of black now.

"I don't know anything about that," I scoffed, even though I definitely did. As I suspected, Thames *did* know how to assemble a good "employee benefits" package.

Smyrna turned back to me. "What other demands did they give you? Any deadlines?"

"You know how they are—it's all blood and death and totalitarianism. They haven't set a deadline, but Thames's patience only lasted about two weeks with me, so I'd personally recommend 'sooner' rather than 'later.'"

"This 'Thames' character—he's in charge?" Ephesus asked.

I turned the chair to face him. "His one claim to fame."

"Let me guess." Ephesus crossed his arms. "He called your bluff—you don't know how to complete Red Rain—so you threw us under the bus to buy yourself some time."

I grinned. "That's why I always liked you, Ephesus—you're smart. You know, in another lifetime, we could have been great friends."

"Thanks, but I don't plan on seeing you in the next lifetime."

Smyrna looked appalled. I thought it was hilarious. Where had this Ephesus been all my life? "Guess we'll have to get all our male bonding done in this lifetime, then."

He rolled his eyes. "I really hate you."

"Tell me something I don't know."

"I'm not working on Red Rain."

"Again, I'm waiting…"

He ignored me. He strode over to his father and leaned on the desk. "Dad, you stall them. Fiddle with the formula and make it look like you're making progress—buy me a few days. I'll hack around in the computer and see what I can find out. We need to get out of here before this Thames guy gets bored."

"I like this plan," I said, not that they'd asked.

Smyrna tentatively laid his hands on the keyboard. "But what about Philadelphia? If Thames thinks we're planning something, she'll take the fall."

Ephesus searched his father's face. "I'll see if I can figure out where they're keeping her," he said, which didn't answer the question.

"You," he straightened and turned to face me, "are going to help me hack out of here."

"I thought you'd never ask. I know just the place to start." I stood up and gestured with my arm, and he followed me to the common room.

"The vending machine? Are you serious?" he muttered when I gestured to the cursed object.

I tapped the screen. "It's locked to a limited—and entirely tasteless— menu. I want you to hack it so we can order whatever we want."

Ephesus sighed, but the sound was more tired than angry. For a flicker of a moment, he looked uncannily like his father. "Can't you take anything seriously? Is that a function your brain possesses?"

"You can't order coffee."

He blinked. "I'll get right on it."

7

Smyrna also got "right on it." Out of sheer boredom, I went to check on him a few hours later and found that he had completely reorganized and recategorized the entire Red Rain database. All of the backups the inept government officials had carelessly copied were now properly synced and labeled. When I approached, he was converting some of my redundant lab test results into a usable report.

"Slow up, old man," I said with as much genuine appreciation as I dared give him, "or they'll expect this kind of pace all the time."

"How *do* you work like this?" He gestured at the computer.

"That's just it—I wasn't working."

He arched one eyebrow and resumed typing.

"But… my real databases are almost as bad. That's why I needed Carnegie."

"No wonder you never finished the project," he muttered.

"Hey, I don't need that level of violence from you, old timer." I leaned against the desk and watched him work for a minute. "So, what do you think?"

"About what?" he said without looking up.

"The data. My idea." I jabbed my finger at the diagnostics he had pulled up. "Red Rain. Can it be done?"

"You asked me that once before."

"And you never gave me a straight answer—your daughter quite rudely interrupted us with her theatrics."

He almost smiled.

"So? What do you think?"

He paused mid-keystroke and stared at the screen. I could tell by the way his eyes were flickering back and forth that he was reading, processing.

I leaned over and tapped the monitor, navigating to a new folder. I pulled up a different report and enlarged it, then sat back and waited.

I had been through this process dozens of times. Each time I invited a new scientist to join the project, I showed them the data and asked for their verdict. Their answer determined whether or not they would be allowed access. As they studied the data, I watched their faces, searching not only for intelligence but also for faith.

Ah, faith—such a double-edged sword. Faith in religion was a stumbling block. Faith in the government was a death sentence. But faith in science—it was essential. I needed them to believe in the project. I needed them to believe it could be done. If I saw doubt and rejection in a scientist's eyes, I disqualified them from the project, no matter how brilliant their test scores.

That was why I had liked Ephesus, at first—he believed everything could be done until proven otherwise. To his credit, I don't think he ever stopped believing in Red Rain. In fact, it was his faith in the project that was his undoing—he *did* believe it could be done, and that scared him.

I expected the father to be much the same way. Still, I was more than a little gratified when I saw that telltale flicker of curiosity burn in his eyes.

It extinguished when he leaned back and sighed. "In theory, I suppose," he said after he took a painfully long moment to filter his thoughts. He glanced at me. "But I won't do it for you."

I stood up. "I wasn't asking."

I returned to the common area to find Ephesus rebooting the vending machine. He glanced over his shoulder and beckoned to me. "Here, try it now."

I grabbed an abandoned mug from the table and set it on the dispenser. I tapped the screen and was delighted when a whole menu of options popped up. I found coffee, selected the blackest setting, and hit dispense.

Both Ephesus and I held our breaths. After a minute of contemplation, the machine gurgled, and a stream of freshly brewed coffee sizzled into the cup.

Ephesus muttered congratulations to himself. I waited until the mug filled, then took a swig, welcoming the burn on my tongue. As the life-giving fluid rushed through my veins, I contemplated nirvana and wondered if this was what it felt like to be a normal, balanced human.

"You know what your problem is, Ephesus?"

He spared me a sideways glance as he screwed the access panel back on.

"You never should have gone into engineering. Hacking is clearly your true calling."

He acknowledged the truth of that with a half-smile. "Well, hopefully I'm good enough to hack our way out of here." He fetched a clean mug and made a cup of coffee for himself, although his had more cream and sugar than I thought healthy.

I sat down at the table and waited for him to join me. He took a swig and then leveled his gaze on me. "So what really happened? Have you been in prison this whole time?"

"No, I've actually been on vacation in the Bahamas."

"You should have worked on your tan—you look paler than usual."

"First of all, I don't tan, I burn. Second of all, of course I've been in prison. What else were they going to do with me?"

He shrugged. "Which prison?"

"What's it to you?"

He spread his hands. "I'm just trying to figure out what's going on. And I'm morbidly curious."

"Well, I wish I could give you all the gory details of their torture routine, but in reality, it was quite dull. It's an island, and absolutely no one of import was imprisoned there."

"Such humility."

"You know, I think I liked you better when you were too scared to talk back to me."

"The good old days. But how did you get here?"

"Ambrose found me," I said with no ceremony at all, and waited for his reaction.

His eyes flared. "Ambrose! So he guards a prison island now?"

"No, apparently he's a big shot under Thames." I sipped my coffee. "My guess? He got a promotion because he tipped them off about Red Rain after your sister alerted him."

Mentioning Philadelphia was unnecessary—I just added it to annoy him, which it did. However, he didn't argue. "So what do you know about Thames?"

"Absolutely nothing. I haven't even met him. We've only spoken on the phone."

"Mysterious," Ephesus muttered, which it kind of was.

"He's got money and influence, so I'm guessing he's either a politician or has bought a few off, and I suppose that's really all we need to know about him."

Ephesus nodded and swirled his coffee around in his cup. "And what about this lab? What do you know about the building? Do other people work here? How busy is it?"

"Again, absolutely nothing," I admitted. "They blindfolded me on the way in—something about a grand reveal."

"I hope someone brought confetti." He leaned back in his chair. "They brought us in the back of a van. This place isn't very far from camp—we were only driving for maybe 20-30 minutes."

That was important information; the proximity to the camp probably meant Ambrose and Thames had a preexisting professional relationship. However, I wasn't sure this revelation helped us at all.

Although, if we were close to the concentration camps, that meant we were also close to Cea—a prospect I hadn't considered before.

"They brought us through a parking garage and then up an elevator—so we're up at least a couple stories," Ephesus continued. "What we need to find out is how many other people work in this building, and what the security's like. That's how we'll know the best way to break out of here."

"Your best bet is to try and hack onto another wifi connection. There are several nearby."

"Have you been able to get onto any of them?"

It was asked without malice, but I ignored the question. "If you can see what kind of activity there is on the other networks, that should tell you how busy the building is."

He searched me for a moment, then decided it wasn't worth the effort. "I'll see what I can do. Meanwhile, I need you to try and build a bomb."

A comeback leapt to my tongue immediately, but it took me several beats to comprehend what he was implying. "Why would I need to build a bomb? You've already designed dozens."

"I'm well aware—I need you to construct a prototype of one. I'm sure you can scrouge up enough material in this lab to string something together."

"I'm sure," I returned, "but why?"

"First, it'll buy us some time if it looks like you're doing actual work. Maybe if they see you doing something constructive, they'll assume we've 'seen the light' and are being compliant. Second..." He let out a courage-rallying breath. "I'm sure we're going to need it."

"I'm sure we will."

I drained the last of my coffee contemplatively. When I lowered my cup, I found him gawking at me. "What? Is my mustache not even?"

"I mean, kinda," he said, "but I was expecting you to argue."

"It is?" I reached up and felt it with both hands. "Cheap razor..."

"Nic."

I met his gaze. "It's not rocket science. I don't want to die. And if busting out with you is my best chance at life—and, to my dismay, I think it's my only chance, based on all the available data—then, well: Whatever you say, captain."

He hummed contemplatively and stood up. "I can accept that."

"I strongly recommend that you do—because it's also *your* only chance of getting out of here alive."

He left me with a cold-hearted glare as he walked out of the room.

8

For the next two days, our strange little threesome hummed with harmony. I stayed out of everyone's way and made a bomb—two of them in fact. The first one was a dud (thankfully I didn't set off the smoke alarms), but the second would suffice.

It was harder than I would have expected. Despite being in a lab full of chemicals, I had to jerry-rig some obscure ingredients—several of which I got off the vending machine—to make anything even remotely explosive. It was almost like Thames had planned it that way, but I wasn't sure he deserved that much credit.

Ephesus, meanwhile, hacked onto several of the other wifi networks. It took him the rest of the day to do it, which made me feel slightly less incompetent—but only slightly.

He quickly determined that the building we were in was very busy, nearly around the clock, but not with other lab work. Most of the activity seemed to be mundane office traffic—computers, cellphones, and even a live printer that used real paper.

What was strange was how highly secured everything was. Ephesus claimed he was having trouble hacking into any of the devices or shared databases on the networks. He spent the whole second day trying and failing. And since he had no trouble admitting defeat—unlike myself—I knew he was being completely honest.

It wasn't difficult to connect the dots. Clearly we were in a government building of some kind. For a government that demanded uninhibited access to all its citizens' information, they sure did know how to keep their own stuff secure.

Ephesus also failed to find out any information about Philadelphia. I personally wasn't worried. I knew how the United operated; as long as Smyrna continued to make progress, they would gladly sit on their hands and wait. Phil was probably languishing in a cell somewhere, bored out of her mind but completely unharmed.

Out of curiosity, I had Ephesus run a search on Cea. Her record claimed she was still at the containment camp—but then again, so did Phil's.

Smyrna, for his part, was putting on a great show for anyone who might be watching the computer log. In two days he did an astounding amount of work without actually accomplishing anything. Every byte of data on Red Rain was converted and reformatted and converted again. He created tables, repositories, and even a pie chart. Currently he was working on putting together a formal scientific paper about the project. Anyone who wasn't a scientist would easily believe that great progress was being made.

The phone was pleasantly silent; it wasn't until after lunch on the third day that Thames decided to check in.

I was close to a terminal, having dropped into the lab to keep Smyrna company, so I answered. "I thought you'd forgotten about me, Thames."

"Put Smyrna on the line," he demanded without any kind of greeting.

At the mention of his name, Smyrna looked up from the monitor.

I took a chug from my third cup of coffee for the day. "Wow, so I'm not the favorite child anymore. I see how it is."

"Put Smyrna on the line," he repeated, "or I'll send a technician up there to 'fix' the vending machine."

I swallowed my mouthful very slowly.

Smyrna rolled his desk chair over to the terminal. "I'm here."

"Let me know when Nic has left the room."

Smyrna looked up at me. I raised my hands in surrender. "Fine, I'll text you later."

I walked out into the hall, shut the door behind me, and stubbornly leaned against the wall to wait.

Ephesus found me a few minutes later and questioned me with a raised eyebrow.

I jabbed my finger at the lab. "Thames wanted to have a one-on-one with your father."

All of his features darkened. He strode up to the door and tried it, only to find it locked.

We waited there together, Ephesus tensed like a tiger ready to strike, for another five minutes. Finally, the doors parted, revealing the old man leaning on the frame. He looked winded, like the conversation had taken everything out of him.

"Dad!" Ephesus was in his face. "What happened? Are you all right?"

"Thames just wanted an update," he replied, ignoring the latter question.

"And?" I prompted.

His eyes met mine, but his expression was uncategorizable.

"Dad, what did he tell you?"

"I'm supposed to tell you—" his gaze shifted to Ephesus and back again, "—both of you that he has Cea in solitary."

I wasn't sure which was more disturbing—this revelation, or the fact that Ephesus was exponentially more distraught about it than I was. "Cea! She was the other arrest. Oh no…"

"It's his funeral," I huffed. "Cea has probably made him regret that choice several times already."

Neither seemed consoled by this nugget of humor.

Ephesus kicked his feelings aside and turned his attention back to his father. "What else did he say?"

Smyrna shook his head.

"Dad."

"He asked about progress—"

"Dad," Ephesus grunted, "there's no way he called just to tell you about Cea."

"Agreed," I said, laying on the pressure. "And, to my chagrin, I must remind you that whatever he told you affects all of us."

Smyrna's eyes snapped to mine again. This time, his expression was clearly one of anger and hate.

"Dad," Ephesus tried one more time, "what is it?"

"Well, we already knew he had Philli," he snapped, the bitterness in his voice still matching the expression on his face. He turned to his son, then immediately looked down and away, as if regretting that decision.

"We should get back to work," he mumbled. "And watch what you say—if Thames knows about the vending machine, he probably knows about other things."

He stood back and shut the door to the lab before either of us could ask any more clarifying questions.

Ephesus turned to me with a raised eyebrow. I decided to answer the easy question first. "He threatened to take away my coffee." I contemplated the bottom of my empty cup. "And, I'm no psychologist, but based purely on your father's uncharacteristic display of emotion, I suspect he threatened to take away some other things, too."

"I'll talk to him later," Ephesus said, and I wondered if he actually would. "In the meantime, we'd better iron out the kinks in our escape plan."

I followed him to the common area. He turned on the cafeteria computer and pulled up a blueprint.

"I found this schematic of the building. It's back from when the construction project was originally approved, so it's probably not completely current, but close enough."

I glanced at it; it was a typical office layout, with an elevator on either side of the building and stairwells on the opposite ends.

"Unfortunately, according to these plans, the only floors that could accommodate a lab this size are fifth and ninth—which means blowing a hole in the wall and jumping for it is not an ideal option."

"Good, because I don't like that plan anyway. Any other ideas?"

"Well, the good news is I think I found a way to unlock all the doors at once."

I blinked. "Run that by me again."

"It's not as miraculous as you think. Because this building isn't normally used as a prison, it has the typical safety features of a public building—namely, if the fire alarm goes off, all doors immediately unlock so that everyone can have free access to the emergency exits."

"So what's the problem? Anyone can set off a smoke alarm."

"Yes, but there's a delay. The smoke alarm will run for a few minutes— then, if no one yells 'I'm just cooking!' it will assume there's a fire and enact the emergency protocols throughout the building."

"Okay," I said, chagrined that I was clearly missing the obvious flaw.

"I guarantee you, if we set off the smoke alarm on this floor, all the guards will come running."

"As they should," I admitted. I thought for a minute. "So let's blow them up with one of my bombs."

Ephesus cracked a smile. "Precisely. I think we should lure them into this room and plant a bomb on that wall." He turned and pointed to the far corner. "An explosion should create more than enough cover for us to slip out one of these doors."

He was right—the common room had two entrances, one to the lab and one to the hall. No matter which door the guards came in, we wouldn't be cornered.

"I'm sold. When do we leave? I'm free next Tuesday."

"I think we should do it after-hours—the fewer people that can respond, the better. But *when* is not really the issue."

I lifted an eyebrow and waited.

"The issue is where do we go after we get out."

"I recommend far away from here."

"Agreed, but as soon as we break out, we'll be wanted criminals. We're not going to be able to show our faces anywhere within a 30-mile radius, and if they flag our prints, we won't be able to use computers at all. We need a place we can go, preferably off the grid, while we try to find our sisters."

He had a point—and I was fresh out of off-the-grid sanctuaries at the moment. "Too bad we don't have access to a remote scientific base on a distant planet."

He glared at me but continued. "I have some ideas, but I need more time. Trouble is I can't just 'make a call' from any of these computers—I'm sure they can track all the internet usage in this building, even on the other networks. I have to find another way to contact my friends."

"But you do have friends," I clarified.

He let out his breath. "I hope so."

"Must be nice."

"You should try it sometime."

"Maybe when I have more free time." I got up to refill my coffee. "So what do we do?"

"I think we have a few days. They just threatened us—they'll give us some time to comply before they up the ante. As long as Dad continues to fake progress, I don't think they'll pull the trigger." He paused. "But in the meantime, another bomb wouldn't hurt."

I took a slow drag of coffee. "They never do."

Ephesus locked himself in the secondary lab and emerged only for dinner. I took over the common room and started building another bomb on the kitchen counter.

It proved much harder than the first two, primarily because several of the ingredients I needed were no longer available on the vending machine. Was the kitchen merely out of stock, or had the ingredients been intentionally removed? If Thames knew what I was doing, you think he would have sent someone to dispose of the bomb I already made.

I tried not to think too much of it and instead put my PhD in chemical engineering to the test as I tried to concoct another explosive equation. It was past midnight when I finally felt ready to make a prototype.

I opened the door to the adjoining lab and walked in. I started rooting through the scientific paraphernalia on the table, tossing what I didn't need on the floor.

"What do you need?"

I'm not pleased to report that the sudden declaration made me jump. I hadn't realized Smyrna was still in the lab. He was standing in front of the digital whiteboard, a red marker in his hand. He turned his head only slightly to acknowledge me.

"I could ask you the same question. Have you left this lab at all today? Do you need water? Food? A potty break?"

He looked like he needed all three—plus a shower and a week of sleep. The dark circles turned his face into a raccoon's, and his eyes looked like they had been murdered. They were bloodshot beyond recognition and swam with either fatigue or tears—maybe both.

"Seriously, old man, you need a break."

"I'm fine," he snapped. "I need to finish this."

"What's the rush? The United doesn't expect you to work 24/7. There's always tomorrow."

"Not always. Are you done?" His eyes shifted to my armload of gadgetry.

I passive-aggressively grabbed three more things—even though I didn't need them—and retreated back to the common room.

My bomb was a flop. Thankfully it didn't misfire; it failed to ignite at all, and the only explosion was the eruption of curses I let out. By then, it was almost 2 AM, so I gave up and went to bed.

Ephesus had long since been asleep. If Smyrna ever came to bed, I didn't hear him, and his dorm was empty when I got up.

Ephesus made a brief appearance to get breakfast before returning to his work. I reworked my chemical equation, and by mid-afternoon I was ready to make another prototype.

This one also failed to ignite, but the problem was one I thought I could solve. I needed another tool from the lab.

This time, I opened the door and looked in before entering. Somewhat to my surprise, Smyrna wasn't around. There was an abandoned plate and cup on the desk, so he had at least stopped to eat at some point. Maybe he had finally given up and gone to the bedroom to pass out.

It wasn't hard to tell where he had left off: The whiteboard, which was nearly ten feet long, was completely covered in scribbles. Several markers lay uncapped on the tray.

I walked over to it. What could he have been working on that was so urgent? He was only supposed to be faking work, and the whole idea of fake work was that there wasn't a deadline.

I scanned the board, and at first, I had no idea what I was looking at. It was a chemical equation, but his work was a mess of notes and half-finished sequences and revisions on the above—some numbers crudely hashed out and rewritten two or three times.

What was this for? Had he simply barfed random engineering nonsense onto the board to make it look like he was busy? There's no way that would have kept him up all night.

I took a step back so I could see the whole picture. I started in the corner of the board and read the entire sequence, then read it again, and again. Bits and pieces started to look familiar. I recognized the components and strung the chain reaction together in my mind. I combined the molecules and visualized the compound forming—and suddenly, I knew what I was looking at.

This was the formula for Red Rain.

The *real* formula. Not a dummy equation strung together to put on a façade of progress—this was functional science. Smyrna had done it. He had finished Red Rain.

Well, almost finished. The formula needed some polishing; the equations needed to be condensed and simplified, and the sequence wasn't quite complete. But this was further than I'd ever gotten, and I was confident that, given enough time, Smyrna could complete the project.

A decade of aspirations culminated in one wild, drunken burst of elation. My project was a success. Every hope I'd left to die on the sand at Rott came rushing back—cutting myself off from the United, defending my own planet, kicking the government where it hurt. I could do it. I could still win.

Except for one problem: This was a government lab, which meant the United now had Red Rain, too.

I cussed and examined the whiteboard. A quick browse of the settings menu showed that it wasn't wifi-enabled; it was, essentially, a big piece of scrap paper.

I let out my breath in relief. That meant Smyrna's scribbles weren't synced to any databases. I needed to download the screen capture to something portable, then erase the board before anyone else got ahold of it.

I ran to the desk and started rifling through the computer paraphernalia. There had to be some device I could use. Maybe Ephesus could hack one of the tablets and take it off the wifi so it couldn't be monitored.

Just then, the phone rang.

It took three rings for me to compose myself. I hastily answered and hoped my voice sounded as disinterested as usual. "The renowned Dr. Nic speaking."

"Where's Smyrna?"

I hesitated, then realized the truth was the safest answer. "I actually have no idea. I think he finally took a much-needed siesta. He was up *all* night working for you. You'd be so proud." I laid that last part on thick, hoping the implication of progress would satisfy him.

"Oh I know," he replied. "He told me."

My blood ran cold.

Thames didn't wait for a reaction. "Tell him my representative will be there at five to review the report."

There was a beat, but Thames kept talking before I could fully appreciate how my world had just ended. "By the way," he added, "I owe you an apology, doctor. You were telling the truth about the old man."

He hung up before I could thank him for his humility.

I stumbled back from the monitor. I dug my hands in my hair, taking a few strands out by the roots, and swore over and over and over into the empty room. It did nothing to relieve the tension.

Thames knew about Red Rain. Smyrna must have called him late last night. And how he was sending someone to retrieve the data.

It wasn't supposed to be this way. Smyrna was supposed to take the fall for my failure—receive the brunt of Thames's anger, die if he had to. He wasn't supposed to *give* them my weapon.

I'd rather die than let the United have Red Rain. Which meant we had to move, and now.

I wiped my palms on my coat. Returning to the desk, I started hurling devices on the floor until I found one I could use: An orange flash drive. Ephesus's initials were written on the scuffed surface. It was old, which meant it was unlocked—just what I needed.

I jammed it in the computer and copied over anything I thought I might need. Then I took it to the whiteboard, plugged it in, and saved the contents of the screen to the drive. After double- and triple-checking to make sure it had copied, I used my hand to hastily wipe the board clean.

Putting the drive in my pocket, I opened the door to the common area and looked in. Neither Ephesus nor the old man was there.

I stepped out into the hall. The door to the bathroom was open, and I heard the dryer running. I walked in and saw Ephesus leaning over the washer.

"Ephesus! We need to—are you doing my laundry?"

He turned, holding my old prison jumpsuit in his hands. "I needed to wash my clothes, and your stuff was in the way."

He flushed beet red, but in his defense, he had a point. I didn't have that many clothes, but I had somehow managed to scatter *all* of them around the bathroom.

"Well, had I known you were willing to do laundry, I would have been nicer to you on Mars."

"I'm a pretty good baker, too." He coughed and held out his hand. "Where did you get this?"

It was the expired pizza coupon, now even more crumpled than before.

"Just a souvenir from Rott. You can throw it away."

He flattened it and held it up to the light. "Who gave this to you?"

"John and Dowe. Yeah, I know how it sounds."

He jerked his head to face me.

"What? Do you know them?"

He shrugged. "Doesn't everybody know a John Dowe?" He folded the coupon and pocketed it. "Do you want this jumpsuit washed or should I throw it away?"

"As much as I'd like it pressed and mended, we don't have time. There's a problem."

He gave me his full attention.

"Your father just completed Red Rain."

"You're lying," he retorted without hesitation.

"You're right—it's not 100% complete. But he's getting close—give him another few days and he'll be there."

Ephesus's eyes tracked mine.

"He was up late last night working. Now I know why. Whatever Thames said to him yesterday, it must have been convincing."

Satisfied I was telling the truth, Ephesus paled. He opened his mouth, ready to spew a wad of objections and exclamations, then changed his mind. He strode towards the door. "I need to talk to him."

"Save it." I put out my arm and caught him. "We don't have time. We need to get out of here, now."

"Now? Now's like the worst time. It's four o'clock—everyone is still in the building, and it's rush hour out there."

"You want the United to have Red Rain? Because that's what happens if we stay here. Thames is sending a representative at five to review the data."

Ephesus immediately changed gears. "Then our best bet is to make as much disturbance as possible. How big is your bomb?"

"Big enough. We need to wipe the computers—and clear the recycling bin. I don't want them to have any trace of your father's research. I deleted the whiteboard already."

"I'll take care of it." It was said with unequivocal confidence, so I didn't question it. "Get everything ready. I'll meet you in the common room."

He strode out the door without waiting for an affirmative.

I fetched my homemade bomb from its hiding place and ran to the common room. I planted it in the trash can near the door. Then I calibrated the detonator, locked the safety, and put it in my chest pocket.

I went to the vending machine and ordered the most sugary confection I could find. It ended up being these abominable, brightly-colored marshmallow puffs. Even the smell gave me cavities.

While the dispenser was popping them out, I found wire and a battery in the lab to create a makeshift lighter. Then I tipped two of the tables over to form a shield. I used the third table as a stool. I stacked three chairs in a pyramid on top of it and placed the bowl of marshmallows on the seat, putting it as close to the smoke detector as possible.

Smyrna walked in just as I was completing this balancing act. "What are you doing?"

"Preparing a sacrifice to my god."

"Which one?"

"Self-preservation."

Ephesus joined us, a duffle slung over his shoulder. He was cramming several tablets and gadgets from the lab inside. "Nic, where is my flash dri— Dad!"

The old man turned and met eyes with his son. The two wordlessly volleyed emotions back and forth, none of which were pleasant.

I broke it up when I pulled the flash drive out of my pocket and tossed it to Ephesus.

He caught it and, conveniently, didn't question why I had it. He strode to the computer terminal. "Is everything ready?"

I waved the detonator at him.

Smyrna looked between us. "Will someone please tell me what's going on?" he demanded, even though the inflection in his voice indicated he was catching up.

"We're getting out of here," Ephesus cast over his shoulder without looking, "before they realize what you've done."

Smyrna didn't argue. "But how?"

Ephesus plugged the drive into the terminal. He opened the menu and tabbed through the folders. I wondered if he would notice the new additions, but his focused glare never wavered. He found whatever he was looking for and dragged it to the desktop. Then he yanked the drive out, dropped it in his duffle, and zipped it shut. I smiled.

"I need to make a call," he explained, the information directed primarily at me. "If the United eavesdrops on it, they'll know we're up to something. I need you ready to fire as soon as I hang up."

I nodded and held up my homemade lighter.

Understanding flooded Smyrna's eyes with terror. "But what about Phil? If you pull anything, Thames will—"

"You should have thought of her last night if you cared about her safety," Ephesus snarled. He keyed a number into the com app.

"No, you don't understand. Thames said—Ephesus, listen to me." He strode to his son's side and grabbed his arm. Ephesus shrugged him off and hit dial.

The line rang once, twice, three times. "Ephesus, please," Smyrna begged. "Don't do this. I—"

He stopped when the line picked up.

"4th Street Pizza Parlor, how may I help you," a teenage voice droned.

Both Smyrna and I froze.

"Hi, yeah, I'd like to order three house specialties, please. No drinks."

"Carry out or dine in?"

I swore, hopefully loud enough for the kid to hear. "Are you mad?"

Ephesus shushed me. "Do you offer curbside?"

"Sure. Address?"

Ephesus gave it to him.

Smyrna squinted. "Is that..."

Ephesus thanked the kid and hung up. Immediately his hands started flying across the monitor as he opened a program I didn't recognize and typed rapid commands. "Light it up."

"Are you going to tell us what that was all about?" I demanded.

He didn't. "Light it up. Now." The terminal screeched at him.

"Son, are you sure—"

"Do you all want to get out of here alive?" he fairly shouted. "I said, light it up!" He turned to glare at me, his finger posed over a red button on the screen. I couldn't read what it said from this distance.

"Well, I'm about to regret some life choices," I muttered. I ignited the lighter and threw it into the bowl of marshmallows. Instantly the sugar flared into flame.

Ephesus watched the smoke pool along the ceiling. "Dad, get behind the table."

The old man hesitated. I jumped down from the table and demonstrated for him, crouching behind the overturned tables. He reluctantly followed suit.

Ephesus stayed where he was. The minute ticked on, the smoke spreading at the speed of molasses. I was coughing long before the smoke detector kicked in.

Finally, it decided to come to work and erupted with a shriek. I plugged my ears and waited. The smoke thickened. When the detector realized nothing was being done about the situation, the beep changed pitch. Then the sprinklers turned on.

Smyrna flinched and covered his head. Ephesus stayed where he was, even as the water began to run down his face. He was listening.

I filtered past the sirens and spraying water. A fire alarm somewhere else in the building kicked in. Faint shouting. Then, the beep of a door opening, pounding footsteps, and a yelled demand to know "what was going on here."

The door to the common room whooshed open, revealing three guards. Ephesus punched the button on the terminal and shouted, "Now, Nic!"

All three drew their guns. Ephesus dove behind the table. I let the guards take two steps into the room, then released the detonator.

The original plan had been to plant the bomb on the opposite wall. It would provide a distraction, but no one would get blown up in the process.

I altered the plan when I planted the bomb by the door. Those guards definitely wouldn't be chasing after us now.

Smyrna screeched something, but I couldn't filter the words past the ringing in my ears. Ephesus had the dignity to admire the carnage for a split second, then he grabbed his father's arm and hauled him to his feet. "Let's go!"

I followed as he shoved his father through the door to the lab. The old man slipped on the wet tile floor and nearly brought Ephesus down with him. I grasped his other arm and pulled them both out into the hall.

The panel for the main door was beeping erratically, the display flickering on and off like the power was shorting out. "Is that what the emergency protocol is supposed to do?" I shouted at Ephesus.

He shook sopping dark hair out of his eyes. "I don't know!" He waved his hand over the sensor. The panel gave a glitched moan, and the doors slid open halfway.

I pushed the old man out ahead of me. Ephesus squeezed through behind us. Out in the hall, chaos continued to reign. Emergency lights pulsed, and multiple sirens competed for dominance. Every panel on every door was having a similar episode. I was definitely going to have a migraine after this.

"This way!" Ephesus took off down the hall, shoes squishing on the soaked carpet. It wasn't hard to find the exit: Every emergency exit sign was flashing like a fire truck. Ephesus led us to the nearest stairwell, which was packed with businessmen and secretaries fleeing from the upper floors.

Ephesus adjusted the duffle on his shoulder. "All right, act normal and slightly panicked."

"Done," I said.

Smyrna was a bit past the "slightly panicked" stage, but he offered no objection.

Ephesus opened the door, and we merged with the river of people. We flowed as a unit out onto the street, where the rest of the office staff huddled. I struggled to catch snatches of conversation, looking for signs that anyone suspected us.

"What happened?" "Did someone get laid off and pull the fire alarm?" "My makeup is ruined!" "Do you have the time? My phone is locked up." "Is there something wrong with the internet?"

Ephesus followed a group of businessmen headed towards the nearest bus stop. At the curb, a beat-up green sedan idled in a no-parking zone. A teenager with dark hair and antagonistic eyes stood on the sidewalk, holding three pizza boxes.

He glanced down at the receipt. "Three house specials?"

Smyrna gaped. "Stanyard—"

Ephesus gripped his wrist to silence him. "I think you have the wrong address, man. I can give you directions."

"Cool, cool." The kid dropped the pizza boxes in the passenger seat and walked back around to the driver's side.

Ephesus opened the rear door, and we all piled in without a word.

The kid put his blinker on, waiting for a break in traffic. I saw flashing lights in the rearview mirror and opened my mouth to warn him—but it was only a fire truck. It blared its horn, and the kid was all too happy to run a red light to get out of its way.

I waited until we were a few blocks away before glancing back. The scene was a mess, but no one was running after the car waving their arms.

I broke out laughing. Smyrna nearly jumped out of his skin. I patted him consolingly on the shoulder. "I've been waiting months to laugh like that."

Ephesus shot me a look, then leaned towards the front. "Hey, thanks."

The kid gave him a thumbs up. He reached over and flipped one of the pizza boxes open. "Anyone hungry? These are getting cold."

"I am," I said. I leaned forward and grabbed a slice. I nibbled on the rubbery cheese. "Guess John and Dowe weren't kidding about that coupon."

Ephesus grinned and also took a slice.

Smyrna composed himself. "Stanyard? Is that you?"

The kid looked at him in the review mirror. "Hello, Mr. Smyrna." It wasn't said sarcastically.

I cocked an eyebrow at Ephesus. "Friend from camp," he explained.

"Saint Augustine, delivering it hot and fresh." He checked his blind spot, then glanced at me. "So you're Cea's brother."

It was the first time in a long time that I'd been identified by my familial relations—instead of my scientific or criminal achievements—and I didn't know how to respond.

Ephesus made up the difference. "Cea? Is she all right?"

This seemed to snap the old man back to reality. "Philadelphia! Do you know where she is? What have they done with her? Is she safe?" he demanded in rapid succession at a volume much too loud for the close confines of the car.

Stanyard put his hand up. "Hey, calm down, it's okay. They're both fine. They're already at my place."

Smyrna melted into the seat, seeming to lose all his structural integrity. He covered his face with his hands.

Ephesus touched his father's knee. "It's going to be fine. Everything's going to be fine."

I glanced at the duffle at his feet and smiled. "I think you're right."

10

Of all the things I'd contemplated doing to Philadelphia when I found her, hugging was never on the list.

After taking several detours to make sure we weren't being followed, Stanyard drove us to a pizza shop—he was really going all out with this façade—and herded us into a secret basement beneath the building. I was the first down the ladder, and apparently Phil was so elated to see someone in a lab coat that she hugged me without pausing to make a proper identification.

Frankly, she was lucky that my brain was occupied with solving other, more pressing problems. If I'd had more mental energy, I would have prepared a much more appropriate greeting for her.

Not that Ephesus would have let me fulfill my revenge fantasies, but at least I could have gotten a swipe in. The endorphin rush would have been worth it.

For the time being, though, I had to settle for savoring her utter mortification when she realized who she was hugging.

"Glad to see me, Philadelphia? I wish I could say the same of you."

She squeaked. But before I could lord the moment over her, Cea pulled me into the corner and buried me in a hug.

This was a hug I was expecting. But it was no less awkward.

I let her squeeze all of her fear, rage, and aggression out in a rib-bruising embrace. She wasn't making any sound, but I could feel her arms shaking. Once I thought she'd calmed down enough to attempt conversation, I reached up and patted her greasy curls.

"Hey sis."

She sighed in response.

Across the room, the Smyrnas were having a much more verbal reunion. "I'm so glad to see you." "Are you all right?" "What happened?"

"I got knocked out on the way in," Phil confessed.

I glanced over and was mildly gratified to see that she did indeed look like death. "You know they used to say that sleeping after a concussion can kill you."

She gaped at me in horror. Toying with her really was too easy.

"Leave her alone," Ephesus snapped. His muscles tightened in a warning.

I snorted with amusement. "It's just an urban legend. No medical truth to it."

He ignored me and herded his family into the opposite corner where they could pretend to have privacy. Cea tugged on my arm, and I allowed myself to be pulled to the floor next to her, even though I kept my ear tuned to the Smyrnas' conversation.

I turned to look into my sister's eyes for the first time. She was studying me, absorbing me. I waited. I'd learned in childhood that it was more efficient to let Cea talk first.

"You're alive," she said when she was ready.

"Somewhat to my surprise."

"What happened?"

"They sent me to prison," I summarized, not interested in getting graphic. "And when they got tired of banging their heads against the wall trying to make Red Rain work, they fished me out."

"You agreed to give them Red Rain?"

It was impossible to tell how accusatory she was being, but there was definitely more disdain in her voice than I was willing to deflect. "I had absolutely no intention of giving them the formula. You and I both know that I don't possess the knowledge to complete the project, much to my eternal shame."

"So you dragged Ephesus back into it?" Her bitterness was unveiled now. She glanced over her shoulder at him. I followed her gaze.

"Yes," he was saying, also with palpable bitterness, "apparently the United salvaged all my work from Mars and gave it to Dr. Nic to play with."

I answered them both together. "Well, it turned out to be useful, didn't it? We'd have never made it out of there otherwise."

"Never mind," Smyrna inserted, trying and failing to be the parental authority in the room.

Cea returned her glare to me. "You didn't have to get him—them—involved!"

"The United would have had his bombs with or without his person; they had the plans."

I was right, which, as usual, only made her angrier. "Then why'd you do it? Why drag them into this? Why—"

"Because I didn't want to die."

That was the unadulterated truth, which shut her up immediately.

"That's right—I didn't want to die. Is that what I should have done? Bravely volunteered to be executed? Stayed on Rott for the rest of my life? Is that what you want?"

She didn't answer, because there was no answer to that.

I took two slow breaths, counting to ten as I did so. When I spoke again, my voice was soft and brotherly, just how I knew she liked it. "They were going to kill me, Cea, so I thought I'd explore some other options. At least together we had a better chance of escaping."

I added that last bit for her benefit, to help her reconcile her disjointed morals. I knew that if I could help her reach some sort of ethical resolution, we could end the conversation. All she needed was an explanation she could justify, no matter how untrue it was.

I knew that wasn't the reason I had thrown the Smyrnas under the bus. I had no grand designs of becoming allies and staging a brave escape—that was all Ephesus's doing. My plan had simply been to buy myself time. I had every intention of using both of them as scapegoats until I could find a way out.

What I hadn't planned on was the old man completing the formula.

Cea continued to be silent, so I shifted my attention back to the Smyrnas.

"What did you do?" Phil was asking her father. She held his hand and gazed up at him with the purest trust.

She *was* such a stupid little girl.

Smyrna didn't respond. Ephesus did. "*I* worked on hacking the computer and finding an escape route."

His scowl could have set the room on fire.

Phil's peace cracked, and it was beautiful. "Daddy, what happened?"

He weakly squeezed her hand. "I did work on it a little."

"A little?" I yelped, quite involuntarily. "Old man, you nearly had it!"

"Shut *up*," Ephesus snapped, and for once, I thought he might actually follow up on the threat.

The betrayal snuffed the light out of Phil's eyes like a candle. I could see it; I wondered if the old man could. "Daddy, you *worked* on it?"

He met her gaze, but not bravely. "It was the only way. If they didn't see progress, there would have been trouble for all of us."

He wasn't wrong, but Phil was not consoled in the slightest.

"I didn't finish it," he continued. "We couldn't make it work. I highly doubt it will ever be operational."

I opted not to tell them that the near-complete formula was sitting right at their feet, on a flash drive in Ephesus's duffle.

But I wondered what Phil would say if she knew.

11

Sleep was a waste of time.

However, I had no intention of sharing my most productive hours with anyone else, so I lay down and pretended to doze, hoping the others would ignore me and follow suit.

Cea lay awake for an annoyingly long time. I knew she was staring at me, but I couldn't tell if it was because she didn't trust me or because she was contemplating the great mysteries of our relationship. Eventually, however, exhaustion did its work, and her breathing settled.

Phil was the next to drop off, although judging by the sweat beading on her forehead, I wondered how long it would last. Her father and brother stayed up talking, evidentially fooled into thinking I was asleep. I watched them through nearly-closed eyelids.

"You lied to her," Ephesus said, too calmly. It was a fact, not an accusation.

The old man was silent.

"About Red Rain," his son continued. "It does work—you almost perfected it. Nic told me."

"I know," was the breathed reply.

"Why did you tell her it would never be operational?"

"She's been through enough." Smyrna reached down and laid his hand on his daughter's shoulder. She flinched in her sleep.

"And it's not over yet. If the government realizes how close you came to finishing it, they'll come after you."

My eyes flung open in the dark. I swore, thankfully not out loud.

The old man responded with a sigh.

"I tried to wipe the computers before we left, but I have no way of knowing what kind of backups they've got going, or how much they saw on the cameras."

"You did your best." Smyrna stiffly patted his son's shoulder. He conveniently didn't mention that he'd already talked to Thames and told the man everything he wanted to know.

Ephesus studied his father, clearly struggling with all the things he probably should be saying. After a painful beat, he deferred with a cowardly, "Let's get some sleep."

Smyrna didn't object. I was grateful. I needed them to drop off so I could get on a computer.

My mind whirled while I waited for them to settle down. Ephesus was right; if Thames truly comprehended how close Smyrna had come, he would hunt him down. And if he caught him, I had no doubt that the old man would complete the formula for him—in exchange for his daughter's life, of course.

If I wanted to be the only one with Red Rain, I had to get away—and I had to take the Smyrnas with me.

The thought gave me absolutely no joy at all, but it was a small price to pay for getting my life back. The question was: Where could we go?

I had an idea, but I needed to do some research. Thankfully, I knew Ephesus had stolen a tablet from the lab.

I waited until I was confident everyone had passed into a deeper state of sleep, then slowly stood up. They'd left the lantern on in the middle of the room, so I had no problems finding Ephesus's duffle. What was problematic, however, was unzipping it without making an obscene amount of noise.

Philadelphia whimpered. I glanced at her, but she was clearly deep into a REM cycle. Her subconscious was torturing her more than I ever could.

I successfully extracted the tablet from the duffle and started up the ladder. I paused beneath the door and listened for Stanyard. I heard what sounded like a TV and a fan running. I pushed on the door gently and was gratified to find that he hadn't replaced the box of junk that had been covering it before.

I lifted the door just enough to look into the room. He was passed out on the bed, fully clothed, in a position that clearly said he hadn't intended to fall asleep. I wondered if some substance had helped him get there.

Between the blaring TV and the creaky fan, there was enough white noise to cover me as I slipped out and closed the door behind me. I quickly climbed the stairs, which were thankfully concrete and didn't squeak, and went out into the garage. I figured I was least likely to be heard—or seen by security cameras—there.

Through the windows in the garage door, I could see that early morning light was already beginning to bleed into the horizon. I sat on a non-greasy patch of concrete and fired up the tablet. I opened the connections menu and found that the shop had public wifi, as all businesses did. The United tried to make it easy for people to connect to the web—one of the perks of allowing the government to spy on all your devices was unlimited data and abundant free hotspots.

It was amazing how many people considered that a fair trade.

I accepted the terms and conditions and logged on. They had no idea who this tablet belonged to—as long as I didn't do anything terribly stupid, I shouldn't raise any red flags.

I opened a browser and pulled up the promotional website for Base #9.6.11.

While the page struggled to load—the signal was a bit weak in the garage—I scolded myself for wishful thinking. Returning to the base on Mars was hugely impractical, if for no other reason than forging interplanetary travel tickets was a nightmare. It could be done, but it would probably cost about the same to buy an abandoned warehouse. If I wanted to set up operations somewhere, I was better off going to the slums or a farm in the middle of the country.

Still, the thought was so deliciously tempting. I had everything I needed—my greatest weapon, plans for numerous bombs and guns, and the scientists who knew how to make it all work. If I could just get back to my castle, I could make it as though the last year never happened.

The page finally loaded, and I was shocked to find that it was untouched.

It was pristine, in fact. All the links worked, and someone had even updated the "current projects" page recently. Most notably, there was absolutely no mention of a government crackdown.

I was still listed as governor. My own poised smile in my staff photo mocked me from the bio page. Myself and I shared a stare as I contemplated the implications. Why wouldn't they take the site down after they'd raided my base? Had they simply been too lazy?

I opened another tab and ran several searches—for the base, for my name, even for Carnegie. There was nothing about the bust anywhere. No news articles, no official statement, no corny propaganda videos.

That was extremely out of character for them. The United loved to make a spectacle out of their conquests. Even the pettiest criminals were burned at the stake to reinforce the government's dominance. The fact that I wasn't mentioned at all was a bit of an insult, really; if I had thwarted a plot to cut an entire *planet* off from the United, I would at least brag about it.

What did they stand to gain by concealing the ordeal?

I kept searching. I tried the Smyrnas. There was no mention of the fictitious transit explosion that had "killed" Ephesus two years ago; according to the public records, he had worked at the same lab on Earth since getting out of college. The only thing available for Phil was her school records.

Smyrna turned up more results—apparently, there'd been a police investigation into his wife's death that had caused a brief flutter of media activity—but his profile had been quiet since then. There was no indication that he'd ever been assigned to Mars.

I tabbed back to the base's website and scrolled through the most recent updates. I suppose, with some mental gymnastics, it wasn't too hard to justify keeping Project 74 a secret. After all, the United had decided to simply pick up where I'd left off and create Red Rain for themselves. It made sense that they wouldn't want to advertise their new superweapon before it was complete.

But why leave the base's site up? Why was there no mention of Smyrna going to Mars? Those records should have been public. And what about Ephesus's transit explosion? That absolutely should have made the news. Either the explosion had never gotten reported, or someone had made the effort to go back and scrub the data after Ephesus returned from the dead. Both options raised a litany of insidious questions.

A thought pecked at the edge of my consciousness. If all the public records were untouched, some other things might be intact, too—like my login to the base's website. I was sure they'd been smart enough to change my access codes to the sensitive databases, but the base's blog might have slipped under their radar.

I navigated to the login. The site accepted my username and then prompted me to use face ID. I held the tablet up to my face, wondering if it would work in the half-light of the garage.

It did. The circle flashed green and the control panel loaded—at the same time the door behind me slammed.

"What are you doing?"

I glared over my shoulder, annoyed. Stanyard stood on the step. "Where did you get that tablet?"

"It's fine," I dismissed him, turning back to my work.

He was upon me in two steps and leering over my shoulder. "What site is that?" He rudely snatched the tablet from my hands without allowing me the dignity of answering. He scanned the screen, anger and fear burning the grogginess out of his eyes. "You hacked into the base's website?" His voice shot up an octave.

"I didn't have to hack in."

He wasn't interested in the technicalities. "And on the public wifi? You idiot!" he screamed, followed by a few more colorful words. He threw the tablet at me. I missed, and it landed on the concrete with a crack. "They're going to trace this."

I picked the tablet up and brushed off the damaged screen. "I doubt anyone's spying on the internet usage from your rat-infested pizza parlor."

"Are you deaf?" He was yelling like I was. "You literally just blew up their lab yesterday—you don't think they're watching for any activity on your accounts? Someone's definitely going to see this and trace the device back to here."

He looked like he was contemplating punching me, then wisely thought better of it. He sighed and pinched the bridge of his nose. "We need to get you out of here, now."

"If you're so worried, I'll take the tablet to the coffee shop down the road and log in again. Then they'll think I've moved on."

He wagged his head. "And let you out of my sight? Too risky."

I shrugged. "It's your funeral."

Stanyard spun on his heel and raced out of the garage. I stood up and went back to the browser, only to find that half the screen was pixelated, thanks to the kid's rage. I sighed and turned the device off.

To his credit, the kid was prepared to move. Within five minutes he had everyone awake and in the garage ready to leave.

Cea slapped me before I could even make eye contact. In retrospect, I probably should have been prepared for that.

"What were you thinking?" she hissed in a whisper that was just the right pitch to make my ears ring.

"I was phoning home," I replied, rubbing my cheek.

As usual, she wasn't listening and forged ahead. "You're going to get us all killed! Why are you always so—"

"Hey." Ephesus shoved himself between us. "Save it for when you don't have to whisper."

Cea snarled, but she obeyed on the first try—a luxury she had never afforded me. I studied Ephesus and reached the somewhat uncomfortable conclusion that he had been "busy" with more than one project over the past few months.

The door slammed, and Stanyard returned. "Everyone in. Who's volunteering to ride in the trunk?" The hatch on his dying green sedan popped open with a weak chirp.

"Nic and I will," Cea said with a glare that told me not to object, not that I had any intention of wasting energy on something as pedestrian as seating arrangements.

The others started clambering into the car. Cea slid into the trunk with an agility that was leftover from her cheerleading days. I waited until she had arranged herself, then climbed in after her. I briefly considered facing away from her, but thought better of it.

With some maneuvering of my long legs, we fit. Our knees were pressed together and our foreheads were nearly touching. One of her bedraggled curls tickled my nose. It reminded me of all the times we had hidden under the bed or buried ourselves in blanket forts as children. Her curls had been much longer then. I would have made a comment about it had I thought she was in the mood for reminiscing.

Stanyard slammed the hatch without ceremony, plunging us into stuffy darkness.

I thought Cea would use the privacy to resume her tirade, but she didn't. She was silent, her breathing eerily steady.

The car groaned to life. I hoped our commute would be short, or the vibrating of the engine would give me a migraine in short order.

The car eased down the driveway and idled at the street for a long moment—long enough that I ventured conversation. "There's no record of my arrest in the news," I declared.

"I know," she replied, voice so soft that it was difficult to hear her over the engine. Muffled chatter came from up front, and the car turned onto the road.

Clearly she had been watching my file while I was gone. "Don't you think that's odd?"

"Yeah, I—"

Her sentence was lost to the successive sounds of a gun firing, glass shattering, and Philadelphia screaming. I knew it was her; I'd heard that sniveling scream more times than I cared to count.

Cea swore. I did the same as the unwelcome realization dawned on me that I was wrong.

Stanyard had been right. They had been watching my accounts.

Very closely, apparently.

The car swerved, and then the engine revved for all it was worth—which sadly wasn't much. I tried to mentally calculate the odds of our escape, but judging by the laboring of the engine, we were starting at a disadvantage.

"They must really want you!" Cea shrieked. It wasn't accusatory.

The car jerked around a corner. I grunted as my head bounced against the roof of the trunk. *I hope this kid knows how to drive!*

"I think it's the base!" I shouted to be heard. My neurons continued to fire even as I struggled to maintain some sense of direction. "Something's going on—there's no reason why—"

My eardrums shattered as a bullet ripped into the trunk and Cea yelled.

"Laodicea!" I reached for her, just as the car took another hairpin turn and slammed me against the side.

"Nic," she wailed, voice shaky.

I scrambled towards her. I grasped her shoulder and felt blood. "Cea..."

And then we crashed.

The car whipped around and slammed into something solid. All the forward motion ricocheted back into the truck, hurling both Cea and me against the wall.

The wind left me like birds scared out of a thicket. Pain throbbed against my temples, as if the leftover inertia was still trying to escape. I forced myself to take even breaths, counting off the seconds between each inhale and exhale, even as I reached over and felt for Cea.

"Cea?"

She was silent.

"Cea!" I rolled over and found her neck. A quick examination told me both her breathing and pulse were steady; she had simply been knocked unconscious.

I gingerly felt the wound on her shoulder. It was superficial; the bullet must have just grazed her.

The trunk popped open. Instantly I was assaulted with sunlight, sirens, and the delirious shouting of the others.

I sat up and looked at Cea. She appeared to be sleeping, her angelic curls cast around her head. She was slightly pale, but I knew she'd be fine.

I clambered out of the car and scanned the area. We'd crashed into a dumpster behind a warehouse. There were two exits—we could go back to the street, where the cop cars were rapidly approaching, or we could cut down the alley and maybe lose them in the inner city.

It was feasible. I knew I could make it.

Smyrna. I whipped around. I couldn't see Phil, but the old man was bent over the passenger seat. "Smyrna!" I yelled. "This way!"

He didn't hear me. I ran to him and caught his arm. "Old man, we have to move, *now!*"

He shrugged me off; my hand left a smear of blood on his soiled lab coat. "If you want to be useful, go get help!"

"What?" I didn't understand what I was hearing, but I didn't have time to argue. I had to get him out of here. If the United caught him, it would all be over.

I grabbed his shoulders and dragged him back, betting on the fact that I was younger and stronger than him. He resisted. "Thomas, for the love of God, let's go!"

He whipped around and shoved me. It was a reaction I'd never expected from him, and I was woefully unprepared. I stumbled backward into the car.

"Don't you get it?" he panted. "I'm not going anywhere!"

"You fool—" I started, but then I glanced past him and saw Ephesus slumped over the passenger seat, face bloodied beyond recognition.

And that's when I acknowledged that I'd lost.

Smyrna would never make it. Or, more accurately, he would *refuse* to make it.

I saw flashing lights approaching out of my peripheral. I became aware of Stanyard screaming at Phil to *come on*.

I didn't move. I knew there was no point in running or panicking. I looked down at my hand and rubbed Cea's blood between my fingers.

The United had what they came for.

12

Of course I was sentenced to Rott. It was the obvious choice, and the United was, above all, predictably obvious. It was one of her worst traits.

What annoyed me was that it took them an idiotically long time to do it. Wasting three perfectly good days in solitary confinement just to be told something I already knew was an insult.

Perhaps that was their intent. If so, they were succeeding with an uncharacteristic amount of efficiency.

I suspected, however, that the delay had little to do with me. In fact, I spent the better part of those three days resigning myself to the uncomfortable reality that what happened from here on out would have next to nothing to do with me.

I had outlived my usefulness to the United. I had known that months ago, but their small minds were finally coming to terms with the prospect. Smyrna was now their primary target.

I found this new reality bothersome, but not because I minded deferring the stage to greater men. Of course it was irksome that the old man had been able to solve in a weekend what had eluded me for years, but I knew how to set aside my pride in favor of results. What perturbed me was the realization that I would now be an accessory to his life's story. I had become the accomplice, the witness, the bystander.

There was no thought more loathsome. If I was going to suffer in prison, I demanded to be the cause of my own calamity.

I correctly assumed that I was being made to wait while the bureaucracy ran Smyrna through the wringer. They were probably interrogating him right now, trying to threaten or bribe him into finishing his work.

How I longed to be in their shoes. Every fiber of my being wished it were my fingers around his daughter's throat, making him dance for me. I had been right, right about everything. Red Rain could work, and Smyrna was the man to do it.

If only I had realized how close I had been to perfection back when we were on Mars. If I had known I held the key to success in my hands, if I hadn't underestimated that brat of a girl, I could have had everything I wanted.

That was my mistake. I had underestimated them, all of them. I'd underestimated Ephesus. I'd underestimated Smyrna. And I'd let a stupid teenager in a skirt upstage me.

She had hovered in my blind spot the whole time. Why? Why had I overlooked her? Why had I underestimated her determination to live?

I knew the answer, however much I tried to conceal it with circumstantial evidence: It was because she was a Christian. I had assumed that anyone who allowed themselves to be detained in a camp was weak and unprincipled. I had expected her to buckle under pressure. I had expected her to compromise. I had expected her to be like my sister.

My own prejudice had ruined me, and I couldn't deny it. I had finally fulfilled that Proverb Cea liked to quote at me: "Pride comes before a fall." Even broken clocks are right twice a day, and this was clearly not my hour.

My suspicions were confirmed when, after three days of boredom, they stuffed me in a car with Ambrose and Phil. If I were them, I would have kept Phil close at hand, in case her father needed additional incentive, but to each his own.

I was not the least bit surprised that they sent Ambrose with us. I knew Ambrose had also outlived his usefulness, but he hadn't figured that out yet.

I spent the first part of the ride to the docks savoring the taste of the pure, well-aged hatred I had for both of them. But after a few minutes, I came to the conclusion that having feelings was a waste of energy. Ambrose was inconsequential; eventually he would take himself out with his own stupidity. Phil was annoying, but even I had to admit that my misfortune wasn't her fault. I was the one who hadn't watched my back.

As soon as our ship launched and Ambrose got bored with supervising us, I put as much distance between myself and both of them as possible. I correctly assumed that Phil would have zero desire to be crammed in the hold with a bunch of men, so that's where I intended to wait out the voyage.

I waded into the crowd, embracing the anonymity while it lasted. On Rott there would be too many people that knew me, too many people who wanted to call me either friend or enemy. There would be no rest for the wicked on Rott.

The next day, I begrudgingly surfaced for first meal. The rations could barely be considered food, but, unlike a certain someone who was noticeably absent from the line, I knew that refusing to eat only put me at a disadvantage.

Out of boredom I decided to take a lap around the deck. Might as well get a head start on my steps before we landed. That was when I saw the fight.

I'll never tell Phil that I saw the whole thing. She'll never know that I could have stopped Ambrose from tossing her reader overboard had I intervened a moment earlier. I'll keep that information to myself, although if she ever annoys me enough, I might let it slip.

I watched the whole exchange from a comfortable distance. They were both too absorbed in their emotions to notice me—Phil in her pathetic capitulations and Ambrose in his even more pathetic power trip.

I smiled when Phil punched Ambrose. It was impressive, and the shock on his face was the most entertaining thing I'd seen in weeks.

My smile faded when he punched her back.

At first, I was jealous. How many times had I longed to slap her, hit her, even kill her? It was infuriating to watch Ambrose, who was a sniveling coward of a man, do what I'd been too polite to do myself.

But when he kicked her—one, two, three times—a different emotion came over me. I thought of Cea and remembered why, against my better judgment, I had always been too kind to the Smyrnas.

"Hey!"

Ambrose stopped mid-strike to look at me.

"I'm curious: Did the United train you to hit women, or are you just that vile on your own?"

I could tell by the looks on their faces that neither of them knew what to make of that, and I loved it. I slathered on the sarcasm. "I'll admit to being a little impressed, though. I mean, you had the guts to hit a woman in front of all these men, whose protective instincts might flare up at any moment. Even I don't have the courage to do that."

Ambrose laughed, and it gave me an immense amount of pleasure to cut it off with a punch to his gut.

The resulting scuffle—I wouldn't gratify it by calling it a "fight"—was immensely therapeutic. Why hadn't I thought to start something before? This was genius. Each punch I landed released a little bit of tension, and watching the growing frustration on his face was downright delicious. He did get a few weak slaps in, but they only gave me more adrenaline.

I was so high on the drug that I forgot Phil was even there. She screamed when Ambrose caught me off-guard and knocked me back on the deck. Did she actually think I was going to get hurt? How quaint.

I was a little disappointed when the captain interrupted us. I would have loved to continue the jaunt a little longer, but all good things must come to an end.

"What is the meaning of this?" he demanded.

Even though I thought the situation was rather obvious, I decided to help him out. "Just having a friendly duel in defense of a lady. All in the good fun."

I watched the captain read the room and reach the appropriate conclusions. All I had to do was stand back and grin as he sent Ambrose to timeout and put Phil away where she wouldn't cause trouble.

Phil was a bit slow on the draw. As usual, she idiotically assumed she was in trouble. But as they lead her away, she seemed to connect the dots.

She glanced over her shoulder at me. I could tell she was crunching the numbers, trying to gauge how much goodness had been behind my actions.

Don't think too hard. You might strain a muscle.

I'm not sure what conclusion she reached—I didn't care. But she did mouth a "thank you."

I acknowledged it with a nod.

13

Tower wasn't surprised to see me back on Rott.

He seemed—well, his expression was ambiguous at best. He greeted me with a raised eyebrow, peering down from his rusty patrol perch. But that gesture could have meant anything—amusement, confusion, speculation.

But at least it wasn't disdain. There hadn't been a trial on the mainland, a somewhat unexpected mercy. But what the United had lacked in legal process, I was confident my familiars on Rott would more than make up with public scrutiny.

And if there was one thing I couldn't stand, it was judgment from lesser men. Most of the prisoners on Rott had been put away for petty crimes—theft, propaganda, smuggling. At least I had *attempted* an act of insurrection. Most of these men had no idea what it meant to truly buck the system. Most had never tried. They could never understand me.

I could only hope they would all quickly tire of the spectacle of my arrival and return to the comfort of their monotonous lives.

They put me back in my old cell, which was either an attempt at irony or sheer laziness. Judging by the way the dust had settled on the desk and bed sheets, it didn't look like the room had been occupied since I'd left.

Perhaps they had known I would need it again.

As usual, however, the locked door didn't afford me any privacy. Not ten minutes after I'd been deposited in my cell, Ambrose came knocking.

I looked up to see him eagerly sliding his hands up and down the bars of the window. He had clearly been planning this moment for a very long time, so I let him play out his fantasy, hoping it would end more quickly if I didn't interrupt.

He savored the moment until he got bored, which thankfully was only about thirty seconds. "Well, let's be going," he said, as if we'd both known this was coming all along.

Perhaps, in a way, we both did.

I followed him down a floor, where we picked up Phil. She looked annoyed but wisely said nothing.

Ambrose unhelpfully filled the silence. "I'm here to assign you to your new jobs."

They were finally going to rectify my unemployment. Being put to work might be considered an act of mercy, although I'm sure Ambrose would do everything in his power to turn it into cruel and unusual punishment.

We followed him to the factory at the center of the island. It looked like construction had been completed; all the scaffolding and building debris had been swept away, and steam churned steadily from the smokestacks into the sky. A deep rumble could be heard vibrating through the walls.

That rumble grew as we descended an elevator three floors down. The doors opened, dumping us onto a platform that overlooked a cavernous factory. It must have been at least the size of a football field, crammed to the overflowing with machines that were laboring like they were late to work.

I think, subconsciously, I knew what it was as soon as I saw it. Something about the smell, the sound, the sight of the three-story-tall storage silos at the far end of the room—I had seen it all before. In dreams, in concept sketches, in crude diagrams scribbled on the whiteboard during late-night planning sessions with Carnegie. This was my factory.

But still, I had to ask. "What is this factory making?"

He sneered, which was enough answer for me, but he had the gumption to use words anyway. "We're making Red Rain."

Phil had the decency to express the expected human emotions of horror, grief, and fear. Me, I couldn't muster up the energy to be surprised. It was inevitable. The only surprising thing was that I hadn't seen it before; my only regret was that I had made it all possible.

"Wow," I murmured, feeling the need to acknowledge my role. "I guess the old man really did have it."

Phil was livid. She threw a decent fit, insisting that they couldn't make her do this and that she'd rather die than produce an ounce of the abominable liquid.

I left Ambrose to sort out that problem. I walked up to the railing and took it all in. In spite of myself, I couldn't turn off my engineer's brain. As I scanned the factory, I mentally calculated how it all worked, traced the product flow, and estimated the output. It was a decently constructed factory. I would have made a few changes to increase efficiency, but it would suffice to win a war, no doubt.

Not that there would be any more wars after the United revealed their weapon.

I tried to explain this concept to Phil over dinner, but she wasn't having it. She'd been assigned to do literally pointless paperwork in Ambrose's office, so we hadn't seen each other since morning. I'd been sent to monitor the control panels on the side of the storage silos—a job that was only slightly less useless.

I had hoped a day of slaving as Ambrose's secretary would cool her down, but apparently I'd misjudged her yet again. If anything, she was even more fired up. She sought me out across the mess hall and, before even taking a bite, launched into a spiel about how we had to stop production.

"It's too late," I insisted, hoping to let her down quickly.

"No, it's not. They can't have had that factory operational for more than a few days. There's no way they've already shipped a boatload back to the mainland."

"Not that…" I sighed. I was far too exhausted to be engaging in this kind of moral debate. How do you explain to an optimist that the game is over? "I mean it's too late—just, how do you propose destroying something that eats metal?"

"Why are you eating metal for lunch? The rations aren't *that* bad, except on pizza day."

I looked up to see John and Dowe approaching our table and realized my night was about to get much worse.

They collectively ogled Phil. "Oh, you brought a lady friend back with you! How nice!"

"Dowe, she's too young for him. Don't be disgusting."

"You're right. She could definitely do better, John."

It was almost enough to make me believe in either God or the devil. Clearly, one of them had sent these two to torture me before my time.

Phil glanced rapidly between them, going cross-eyed. "You're John… and Dowe?" She looked back at me.

I shook my head. She was on her own with these two. "And you thought 'Tower' was a weird name."

"So how you doing, Q? I didn't expect you back so soon." John and Dowe confirmed my worst fears and sat down at the table with us.

I looked them dead in the eyes. "But you did expect me back."

They shrugged and started eating.

Phil was still studying the pair. "Are you… friends?"

I sighed. "What did I tell you about friends?"

"Whatever he told you was wrong!" Dowe jostled the table with an emphatic thump. "We are definitely your friends, so don't listen to this stick-in-the-mud."

"Yeah! We're way more fun than he is, anyway."

Well, aren't you three going to get on like a house on fire?

Phil looked to me. "Should I tell… them?"

Tell them what? I wanted to snap, but I knew. I also knew I didn't have to put up with this basal conversation. I started gathering my trash. "Pretty sure we're not the only people on the island who know what that factory is making," I droned, and then stood up and left the table.

She watched me leave. I hoped she got the message. I didn't know how to make it more obvious, short of yelling "shut up and leave me alone" to her face. I wasn't interested in her revolution.

We had lost. My greatest enemy had my life's work, all because I was a coward. I'd called on the Smyrnas to save my own skin, and the United had gotten everything they wanted. They won and would continue to win with the help of my weapon. No amount of kicking against the bars of my cage would change that.

I could only hope Phil would take the hint.

14

Phil did take the hint, at least for twenty-four hours.

John and Dowe, however, did not.

"Hey Q, you awake?" they hissed through the door of my cell at an hour when I definitely should have been.

I put the pillow over my face. "You know I can't sleep without a bedtime story."

"Well, have we got a story for you!" They snickered, and then the door to my cell popped open with a chirp.

I jerked upright. "What the—"

They sauntered in, both unashamedly clothed in pajamas. "Slumber party!"

I was too dumbstruck to object as they crammed themselves onto my tiny cot. "How did you—"

"Oh that?" John gestured his shoulder at the door. "Just a little thing I whipped up called a master key…"

I glared at him. I wasn't sure which would be more loathsome—him joking about having a master key, or him not telling me he had one.

"Actually," Dowe said, mercifully sparing me any further sarcasm, "the door wasn't locked."

"I'm sorry?"

"Tower did us a solid. The lock on your door is conveniently 'malfunctioning.' It hasn't been locked all night. You didn't notice?"

I stared at the open door. "Never thought to try." It wasn't like I had anywhere to go.

"And that," Dowe jabbed me in the shoulder, "is exactly your problem, Q. You don't try."

"First step to self-improvement is acknowledging the problem. Step one, check!"

"Spare me step two." I contemplated kicking them off the bed but wasn't sure I wanted that much physical contact.

John had no such qualms. He planted both hands on my shoulders and shoved me off my own bed. I was so startled and disgusted that I made a yelping sound I am not proud of.

I stumbled to my feet and whipped around. "Get out!"

They were both oblivious and settled in to fill the vacuum of space I had left. "The second step," John continued seamlessly, tucking my blanket over his knees, "is to get off your butt and change things."

I sighed. "You're right, there is something I need to change—my room number."

John cackled like he actually thought that was funny.

Dowe attempted to hold me in his gaze. "What happened, Q?"

Of course I knew what he was generally referring to, but the question was too vague to gratify it with a functional answer. "I lost a bet."

"No, you didn't." Dowe spoke quietly, more quietly than I'd ever heard either of them speak. "We did."

For the first time since we'd met, he stared at me with clear eyes full of intelligence. "We took a gamble on you, Q."

I returned his stare, feeling absolutely no remorse. "That was your first mistake."

"And now the entire free world has to pay out." Dowe gestured in the general direction of the factory. "We could have bailed you out, Q. All you had to do was order pizza."

"Unfortunately, the kid doesn't offer a gluten-free option."

John gagged.

Dowe wasn't fooled. "Why did you tell them about Smyrna?"

I had no desire to confess my sins to him like I'd done with Cea. "The United would have gone to Smyrna as soon as they figured out I couldn't do it—I didn't have to tell them anything."

It was a plausible explanation, but I didn't truly believe it. If the United had realized Smyrna was their man, they would have tried him first. But according to the paper trail I left on Mars, Smyrna hadn't been involved in the project at all; I hadn't even granted him full access to Wing 74 yet. Only Carnegie and I had known how qualified the old man really was.

No, I was fully aware that, had I not said anything, the Smyrnas might have slipped under the United's radar. In spite of myself, I was beginning to profoundly regret dragging the old man into it—but not for the reasons Dowe was expecting.

John, with a spurt of wisdom not belied by his facial expression, said, "Well, no use crying over spilled milk. How do we fix it?"

I rubbed the bridge of my nose. "You don't."

"I said 'we.'"

"I know, and I don't care."

"We've got, at best, a few days before they ship a load back to the mainland. We need to blow up that factory, and fast," Dowe inserted.

"Oh, you want to blow it up? Luckily for you, I know just the woman for the job. And she lives on *another floor*." I stood back and jabbed my finger at the door.

John frowned. "Phil ain't always going to be around to clean up your messes, Q."

I had no patience to dissect the moral implications of that statement, if any were intended. "We're done here."

"You're the only one who can end this, Nic."

If Dowe was hoping to foster an emotional connection by using my real name, he failed. "I just did. Leave."

"Nah." John flopped back on the pillow. "We've got all night."

I growled, my frustration reaching the boiling point. I considered using a loud volume and swift fists to make my point, but instead I opted to be as clear and precise as possible in hopes of avoiding any ambiguity. I dumbed my voice down to a five-year-old level and stated, "Get out. Leave me alone. I'm not interested in your war for independence, and I won't help you."

"That's no way to talk to your friends, Q," Dowe scolded.

"We're trying to help!"

"I don't need your help." I met their eyes. "And we're not friends."

Somewhat to my disappointment, neither man looked offended by the latter statement. "That's debatable," Dowe said with a raised eyebrow. He didn't clarify what he meant.

Thankfully, I didn't care. "Get out," I repeated, hoping the third time was the charm. "And tell Tower that he'd better get my door lock 'fixed,' or I'll report the oversight to his superiors."

John blew a raspberry. "Tell him yourself." He jumped up and sauntered out the door.

Dowe followed at a calmer pace. He paused in the doorway and glanced back.

I eyed him. "Don't."

He shrugged. "I was just gonna say—I hope you got a good seat in the peanut gallery."

"Excuse me?"

He didn't elaborate. "Just don't bring any *actual* peanuts—I'm allergic."

And with that, he left and closed the door behind him.

A few minutes later, I heard the deadbolt slide shut.

15

The worst part about my prison job was that there wasn't any actual work involved.

The entirety of my job description was to sit and watch the machines work. I monitored the controls on the side of the holding tanks, mindlessly observing while the dials and digits cataloged the ongoing production. I hadn't even been given instructions on what each display meant or what to do in case of a malfunction. I was literally supposed to just watch.

Ambrose was probably hoping it would be torturous for me to watch someone else produce my weapon, but he underestimated the totality of my resignation to failure. He also forgot that I had three PhDs; within six hours I had completely worked out how the factory operated and sketched a flow chart in my mind. I also figured out there were thirty-seven dials, buttons, and switches across the factory that I could access without any security clearance—four of which were on the holding tanks.

None of this information was in any way useful. I could have easily jammed the system and made a big mess, and I thought about doing it, just for the amusement. But causing any long-term damage to the factory would require computer access, which was something they wisely hadn't given me.

Still, mapping out the flow of the factory distracted me long enough to get me through my shift. What I was going to do tomorrow, or the day after, I had no idea, but at least I'd survived one day without my brain withering from atrophy.

Phil watched me the entire shift. I knew because every time I glanced towards the control booth, I saw her looking down at me. I could tell she hadn't given up the fight yet; her face was permanently glued into a concentrated frown, and she paced the office like a caged rabbit. I could also tell she was silently judging me, weighing whether or not she should involve me in whatever pathetic revolution she was cooking up. I desperately hoped she would decide I wasn't worth the effort.

No such luck. I knew I was in for it when she hung back in the elevator at the end of our shift.

"Meet me at Tower's place after dinner," she hissed.

I sighed loudly, but she was already scampering away, attempting to look natural.

She avoided me for the entire meal, as if that would defer suspicion. Someone probably should have told her that it was actually *more* suspicious than not, but I certainly wasn't going to volunteer the information.

John and Dowe also spared me the misery of their company. I didn't see them at all, in fact, or anyone I knew. Everyone at the nearby tables completely ignored me. I was able to eat in undisturbed peace and solitude, just like I'd always wanted.

I hope you got a good seat in the peanut gallery.

I rolled Dowe's words around in my head as I chased the last bite of gruel around the bottom of my bowl.

Then, with a dramatic grunt that was appreciated by no one at the tables around me, I slammed my spoon down and went to find Tower.

He watched me approach from across the yard. When I got closer, he gave a jerk of his head towards the shadows behind his post. Phil was there, overtly fidgeting.

Her face brightened when she saw me. *Don't get too excited, buttercup.*

She didn't wait for me to say anything and launched right into her spiel. "We need to destroy Red Rain."

I raised one eyebrow.

"I have to try. I won't just stand by and watch while they destroy the world. I can't…"

She paused. I waited.

She took a deep breath of resolve. "*We* can't let them do that."

Why did everyone think I was going to fall for that? "Why don't you just destroy it yourself? You've done it once before."

Her eyes flickered, but she kept her cool. "There aren't any tables of chemicals I can turn over. And I need your help."

For once, her voice carried a palpable amount of sarcasm. She was finally speaking my language, so I took the bait. "Why do you need my help?"

"Because I'm no good with computers," she declared humbly, as if I didn't already know that.

"You seem to do just fine hacking security systems."

"Only because I stole a device *you* invented."

"I'm impressed that you'll admit to stealing."

"We need to hack the computer in Ambrose's control room." Much to my disappointment, she dropped the sass and got back to practicality. And I had just come up with a great comeback. "From there we can wipe their data and shut down the operation."

It wasn't the worst plan—at least, it was a better plan than I would have expected from her. Regrettably, however, that wasn't how computers worked, and her naivety fell short of being adorable. "Even if... even *after* I hack into the computer, it will be incredibly difficult to erase the data such that it's irretrievable. It is almost impossible to permanently delete information from a computer."

"I know. But this will do it for you." She reached into her pocket and withdrew Ephesus's flash drive.

I hoped my surprise didn't color my facial expression. I was impressed; Ephesus had been smart enough to split his work up, and Phil had been smart enough to hide the drive. But while I'm sure Ephesus had downloaded some intriguing files, there was also something else very important stored on that drive.

I decided to tell her, just to see how she'd react. "What good will that do? That has all the Red Rain files on it too, you know."

"What?"

She sounded like she'd been slapped, and I mildly enjoyed it. "I transferred the complete research files from the lab before we escaped. I'm sure the United added a bit after we left, but I could easily figure it out from your father's notes."

She washed pure white. I decided to have some mercy and keep the conversation on track. "But how is that going to help us destroy their operation?"

Her fingers clenched around the drive. "It also contains my brother's virus."

With a flash of recognition, everything snapped into place. That's why Ephesus had been so confident he could wipe the computers at the lab. That was the mysterious program he'd run right before we broke out—he'd unleashed his data virus.

It was a virus designed to wipe all data from all devices it infected. It was also the one I had prematurely released onto the internet because I was too inept to realize the system wasn't fully secure. Through some bizarre miracle, the virus hadn't been fully functional then—Ephesus had sabotaged it. But now—

"Yes," Phil said slowly, her eyes tracking mine. "He and Cea fixed it."

The mention of Ephesus and my sister in the same sentence caused uncategorizable emotions to flare. "So the little twerp *did* know how to code it properly."

Phil's nose twitched disdainfully. "Yes, and if you upload it to the computer in the control room, it will completely wipe their systems."

The silence stretched for a beat, but not because I didn't have anything to say. No, my brain was firing rapidly, fueled by the somewhat disconcerting realization that the virus changed everything.

Phil tested the waters. "Hopefully it's a closed system so nothing else will be affected."

I shook my head. "Yes, no doubt it's a very secured private system, but if we're lucky the gates won't be too hard to crack. They must have some way they're transmitting progress reports back to the mainland. If we can find out how, hopefully we can use that access to open a two-way door."

I looked up and realized she wasn't getting it. "Wiping the control system in the factory won't be enough. The United will have copies of the research on their mainland computers. Even if we destroy the factory, they can rebuild it. If we want to stop them from producing Red Rain, we need to wipe all their systems."

As I talked it out, the implications took root in my stomach. Playing with the virus was an insane gamble, but it was a bet I was willing to take. If I could pull this off, I could still keep Red Rain out of the hands of my greatest enemy.

And I'd put anything on the line for a chance to do that.

"If we're going to do this, we have to do it right. We need to hack through the computer and upload the virus to the internet, wiping everything. We have to erase Red Rain from their systems for good!"

I hadn't realized I'd raised my voice until Tower shushed me from above. I took a deep breath and locked eyes with Phil, hoping I was getting through to her. "We have to use the virus as it was originally intended."

"But that will erase everything!" she squeaked in terror. "The Bibles—"

I groaned. *That's what you're worried about? You'd trade an ancient book for the known free world?* "Then why did your brother create the virus? He didn't have to rewrite it. Why would he code it and keep it on hand, if it wasn't for a situation like this? We have to use it."

I reached for the drive. She pulled her hand back.

I grunted and weighed my options. It would not be that hard to force the drive from her hand. Even Tower probably wouldn't stop me, if he'd been listening to our conversation.

But while I could probably accomplish this act of rebellion on my own, it would be a lot easier with a second set of hands.

I looked up into her face. And I waited.

She eyed me—judging me, weighing me. I let her.

After a moment, she held the drive out.

I nodded in recognition, then went back to business. "This still won't be enough. We have to destroy the product they've already made."

"Why?"

"For one, there's enough in there already to desecrate a small country. I did the calculations during my shift today. And two, there's a risk they can reconstruct the formula from a completed sample. We have to destroy their reserves so there's no trace left."

"How are we supposed to destroy something that can eat metal?" She threw my own words back at me; had I been in a different mood, I might have appreciated the irony.

As it was, I ignored her and mentally retraced the plans I had sketched of the factory. I followed the flow of chemicals, snatching at every dial, crank, and access point we could potentially manipulate. I calculated a dozen ways to jam the machines, but disposing of the completed product was problematic. Releasing a warehouse worth of condensable gas right next to an ocean seemed ill-fated. Even a wave of wet sea breeze could cause it to liquify and—

I blinked. "We let it burn."

"What?"

I threaded my words carefully. "We drain the vats. If we can release the acid and get it to condense, Red Rain will burn through the floor and destroy itself."

It was pure poetry. We paid it a moment of respectful silence.

"We'll need to get Ambrose out of the factory during working hours when all the systems are open and online," I continued, mentally checking off all the potential hiccups to my idea.

"How?"

How indeed? Before my analytical brain could process that problem, an inhumanly cheerful voice joined the conversation. "How about a distraction?"

John and Dowe appeared beside us. By the way they casually stepped out of the shadows, I could tell they had been standing nearby for a decent amount of time. "Tower!" I glared up at him.

He didn't gratify me with eye contact. "I didn't think they were a problem."

John repeated himself. "How about a distraction?"

"A big one," Dowe echoed.

"We could do a demonstration!"

"Those are always fun!"

"We could make it like a talent show, and Philli here can help us. I bet she can put on a real good distraction!"

In his defense, that *was* one of her better talents.

Dowe flicked him in the ear. "Don't be a fool! We don't want a woman getting tangled up in a demonstration. This could get messy."

The gears started turning, and suddenly I realized that Tower might not be wrong about these two.

"We need it to be messy," I said, stepping closer. "Really messy. 'All guards on deck' messy."

I glanced between them, hoping the expression on my face was encouraging. It wasn't an emotion I practiced very often.

My efforts were rewarded with identical grins.

In an attempt to secure our alliance, I did something I'd never dreamed I'd do: I smiled back.

Dowe winked.

"Oh, I think we and a couple dozen of our prison buddies can handle that," John sneered.

"Let's ask Art."

"And Marty. And that guy who calls himself 24… What's his real name again?"

"I think it's Cloud."

"How's that a real name? You sure the guy ain't duping us with a double-double alias?"

Phil and I collectively ignored them. "Commander Ambrose always locks the control room door when he leaves," she said. "What if he takes the time to lock it this time?"

As if locked doors had ever stopped her. "If that happens, you can figure out a way to circumvent the lock."

She wisely did not argue. "When should we do it?"

"Tomorrow." Tower's head emerged from his window. "A ship is coming at noon to transport the first batch of Red Rain. If you want to keep the reserves out of the hands of the United, you need to destroy it before that ship comes."

The implications backhanded me. "Tomorrow is my floor's 'day off,'" I groaned. "We're all forcibly confined to our quarters. For lack of a better phrase, I'll be locked in my room."

Unless the lock on my door were to conveniently "malfunction."

Tower and Phil shared a long look. She silently pleaded with him. He studied her—looking for what, I'll never know.

Then his gaze shifted to me.

Your move, friend.

He broke eye contact and retracted into his tower. "I'll make it happen." And then he slammed his window shut.

I looked down to see Dowe smirking at me.

I turned my attention back to Phil. "We have less than 18 hours. Better get back to our cells before we arouse suspicion for being up here."

I left without saying goodbye to any of them. My brain was already occupied with working out a schematic for tampering with the machines, and I didn't have the energy to waste on civility.

John and Dowe crowed bedtime wishes that I ignored. Phil said nothing, but I knew she was watching me again.

344

John and Dowe crowed bedtime wishes that I ignored. Phil said nothing, but I knew she was watching me again.

16

I was up all night working on a plan to force the factory to self-destruct.

Designing a schematic to overload the machines wasn't particularly difficult. I could think of a couple of ways to redirect the chemicals, the easiest one being to drain everything into the holding vats.

What stretched the limits of my college education was figuring out a way to explain that plan to Phil. For our sabotage to work, I would need her to monitor the gauges on the side of the storage tanks and reroute the flow when I told her to. It wasn't difficult, but if she flipped the wrong switch, we might flood the entire island with gaseous Red Rain.

Meanwhile, I would need to hack into the office computer, override the factory's automatic functions, and crack the firewall so I could upload the virus to a server on the mainland.

All of this needed to be done in about twenty minutes, or however long John and Dowe could keep Ambrose distracted. And I wasn't exactly the world's most competent hacker.

I scarfed down breakfast and then took the scenic route back to my cell, passing under Tower's lookout.

"Your lockdown starts in 2 minutes, 120518," he called down by way of warning.

I glanced at the mix of guards and prisoners milling about. "Yeah, and I'm bored. Got any coloring supplies?"

There was a pause, then a permanent marker hit me on the head. I stooped to pick it up. "Any paper?"

He snorted. "Why do you think I was using my arm to track your laps?"

I wasn't about to acknowledge that. I pocketed the marker and hurried back to my cell.

The deadbolt clicked shut right on schedule—8 AM, end of breakfast hour. I looked around the room for anything I could both write on and transport. The sheets would work, but that seemed excessive. I rooted under the bed and found my dirty shirt from yesterday.

I spread it out on the floor. Marker in hand, I closed my eyes and recalled a snapshot of the controls on the holding tanks. I waited until the image crystalized, and then I started sketching.

I was almost done when I became aware of an increase in the ambient noise. It was hard to quantify through the concrete walls of my cell, but there was definitely agitated activity going on in the yard. I scribbled faster.

Something that sounded like an explosion—or fireworks—went off. And then a heavy bass beat kicked in.

I hesitated, for a brief minute regretting that I'd left the important task of "distraction" to John and Dowe.

At that moment, the lock on my door clicked open.

Balling the shirt under my arm, I checked to make sure I had the drive in my pocket. I cracked open the door to my cell and looked around.

Mercifully, there were no guards. However, half of my floor mates were also standing in the now-open doorways of their own cells.

I guess it looked less suspicious if an entire wing went offline.

Several of the older and wiser ones gazed at me, as if subconsciously understanding that I was likely to blame.

"Wow!" I said with a glee that did not match my age. "Sounds like a party out there. Glad we've got the day off!"

That did the trick. A cheer went up. More cells opened as people called to their companions, and a consensus of inmates flowed to the stairs. I blended seamlessly with the crowd and followed them out to the yard.

As soon as the doors burst open, we were assaulted with hideous pop music. The song was at least fifty years old, which meant it was uncensored—a clever touch. Why they couldn't have gone a few more decades back and picked something worth listening to, I don't know, but beggars can't be choosers.

The atmosphere in the yard was more like a party than a riot. I couldn't see what was going on through the crowd, but some stray balloons were floating away into the sky, and I heard fireworks going off. The air also smelled sickeningly sweet. I couldn't put my finger on the taste, but when I heard a chant for "more sprinkles" rippling through the crowd, I decided I'd better not ask.

Whatever they were doing, it was working. Guards were flowing from all corners of the island, and I heard a siren from one of the towers. It synced surprisingly well with the pop music.

I slinked along the barracks until I was close enough to dart into the shadows of the factory. I waited around the corner and watched the door for one minute, two.

More guards scurried towards the commotion. A second siren joined the chase. And then, finally, Ambrose emerged from the factory.

He took one look at the mess in the yard and groaned. Muttering under his breath, he stormed towards the crowd, cocking his gun.

I slipped into the building. The guards at the first and second doors had already vacated their posts. The secretary at the elevator, however, had not.

She looked at me over her nose. I collected myself. "I'm late for work."

She groaned and paged me in. "Don't make me do this again," she said, as if pressing the button with her manicured fingernails required all the energy she had to give for the day. "Or I'll report you."

"Go right on ahead," I muttered as I stepped into the elevator.

Phil rushed to meet me as soon as the doors opened. I shoved the shirt into her hands.

"This is a diagram of the control panels on the side of the holding tanks. If you flip these switches, it will drain all the product from the factory into the two main holding tanks and seal them off." I heaved, realizing with chagrin that I was out of breath.

Phil squinted at my scribbles. I pointed as I talked. "If you move these dials to the right numbers, it will begin to chill the gas to the point of condensing. Then all we have to do is puncture the bottom of the holding tanks, and the liquid acid will drain safely out the bottom."

"Safe" was a relative term, of course.

Phil glanced across the factory, mentally calibrating the plan. "Got it."

"Wait until I give the signal. I have to shut down production first, and then the tanks have to fill completely before we can close them off and condense the gas. Don't touch anything until I tell you to."

I hoped the emphasis in my voice was enough to make my point. I didn't wait to find out. I jogged into the office; Phil had wisely left the door open for me.

I was greeted by the thrum of an ancient printer as it obliviously continued to spit out paper. I looked at the stack that was rapidly building up on the tray and shook my head. Ambrose always had been a waste of resources.

I tapped the screen in the center of the desk, and a trio of monitors glowed to life. A beautiful array of control programs was running. The biggest one, displayed on the center monitor, tracked the progress of the weapon being pumped into a special transport container on the surface. Ambrose had wisely paused this delicate process before he left the room.

They'd made the economical but daring choice to transport the weapon in liquid form, which made my job much simpler. All I had to do was reroute it back into the factory and then empty the holding vat. Because all the pipes and hoses were still connected, it took only a few clicks on the control panel to reverse the flow and drain the product back into one of the holding tanks. It was easy—too easy—and I could only hope that wasn't a premonition.

The printer hesitated in the middle of a page. With an angry chirp, it spit the rest of the paper out blank and started printing a different report.

While the acid drained back into the factory, I swiped through the other applications. The hard part would be dealing with the Red Rain that was still flowing through the factory. The weapon was produced in gaseous form, which meant I had to halt production, collect the product in the second holding tank, and condense it—a multistep process the system wasn't designed for.

That said, the software wasn't too complex—after all, they expected Ambrose to monitor it—so I quickly found the control panel that let me halt production.

I tapped on it, and it informed me that the login had timed out.

"Are you kidding me?" I yelled, in the most colorful way possible.

I had two login options. I could use face recognition, but there was no way I'd fool the camera into thinking I was Ambrose, not with my mustache and overall good looks. The other option was a passcode. I could try to hack it, but we didn't have time.

I scanned the other applications, wondering if there was a redundancy I could exploit. Red text in the corner of one screen caught my eye: EMERGENCY SHUT DOWN.

I hit it, and it asked me to confirm—no security clearance needed.

I could shut the entire factory down, but there was no telling what kind of alarms would go off when I did. I might only have minutes before Ambrose came rushing back, and in the meantime, I'd have to chill the remaining product manually. Emergency mode would no doubt lock Phil out of the control panel on the tanks.

It could be done—I knew where the right levers were—but I'd have to do it. There was no way I could explain it to Phil.

I closed my eyes and ran the numbers. I would need to find a place to upload the virus and have it ready to launch. I would wait until the product on the surface had finished draining. Then I would have Phil reroute the pipes so that the product in the factory would begin to flow into the tanks. I would engage the emergency shut-off and immediately upload the virus, before running to chill the product and drain both tanks. That way, if someone showed up before I got back to the office, the damage would already be done.

It could be done. But only if I could find a decent place to upload this virus.

I toggled through the open programs. Ambrose's email was logged in, but that wasn't good enough; even the government wouldn't be stupid enough to open a suspicious attachment from Ambrose.

I opened a browser. Uploading to a very public website might work— except I quickly found that Ambrose's computer wasn't connected to the internet. I tried several URLs, and everything was blocked. A glance at the toolbar showed that the computer was connected to something, but it was apparently a private internal network.

I cursed. I knew beyond a shadow of a doubt that wiping this terminal alone wouldn't be enough. It might set them back a few months, but it wouldn't erase the data. I needed to wipe all of their servers, or at least most of them. That should take care of Red Rain, as well as give them several more pressing problems to worry about. Even Smyrna wouldn't be able to reconstruct their empire after I wiped them clean.

I tugged on my mustache, a habit I thought I'd abandoned in college. It made no sense for Ambrose's computer to be totally offline. Not only was it out of character for the government—they liked everything to be connected at all times so they could monitor it from anywhere—but they had to be tracking the progress in the factory somehow. There's no way they were *actually* making Ambrose fax paper reports.

A glance at the other screen revealed that the shipping container was almost empty. At least five minutes had passed—I needed to figure this out, and *now.*

I opened the control panel and rapidly clicked through all available submenus. Even if this computer was only linked to an internal network, surely someone else had access to that network. Was there a shared folder or database?

Jackpot. My panicked digging was rewarded—Ambrose had access to several shared databases. I opened them all, scanning the folders to find the one with the most traffic.

The printer screeched, exactly at the right moment to cover the oath that left my lips.

These weren't just any databases. These were high-profile government databases, and the United was clearly planning a war.

Everything from Project 74 was there—all the weapons I had ever designed were in production. They'd also created dozens of other ballistics— everything from nuclear warheads to mines big enough to turn an entire city into a crater. There was even interstellar weaponry; whatever war they were planning, they weren't afraid to take it to the skies.

And, of course, there was an entire database on Red Rain.

A respectful terror seized my soul, but it also sent my gears spinning. This armory could win any war. What you didn't bomb you could melt with Red Rain. If the United got all these weapons into production, there would be nothing stopping them.

And right now, there was nothing stopping me from copying them all to the flash drive.

The printer continued to yell. I glanced at it and saw that it was out of paper. *I do not have time to deal with this!* I hit the button to turn off the wireless connection, and the device silenced.

Turning back to the computer, I pulled the drive out of my pocket. How much storage was on here? I looked around and mercifully found a port on the side of the monitor. Opening up the drive, I started copying the entire Red Rain database and a prime selection of the other folders, as much as I could fit.

While the drive synced, I checked the status and saw that the shipping container had fully drained back into the factory. I had to act fast if I wanted to make it out of here alive; a pocketful of war wouldn't do me any good if Ambrose caught me in his office and murdered me on the spot.

I leaned my head out the door. "Now, Phil!"

I saw her grab a dial and crank with vehemence. I hoped it was the right one, but honestly, I wasn't worried about the factory anymore. It would give me great joy to destroy it, but even if the United had a tankful of Red Rain, they couldn't stop me once I had all of these other delightful weapons.

I went back to the drive and found the virus. I copied it into the main folder of the most prominent-looking database, then removed the drive from the computer. I tabbed back to the emergency override panel.

Twisting the drive in my fingers, I rehearsed the steps in my head. Shut down the factory, launch the virus, drain the tanks—if I could—and then get out of here before Ambrose came. Did I even care about the tanks? If I could get away with this drive, I'd have everything I needed to cut myself off from the United. And if Ambrose didn't find me here, he'd probably blame Phil for the sabotage. It would at least buy me enough time to hide the drive somewhere I could retrieve it later.

I took a deep breath. There was no guarantee I could get off this island alive. But if I could...

It would have been worth it.

I hit the button and sent the factory into emergency shut down.

17

Instantly, the display exploded in a firework of warnings and flashing buttons. The control panels locked as a dozen popups prompted me to confirm or override the state of emergency. They all required a passcode, so there was nothing I could do but let the automatic program run its course.

I heard the factory change gears, and lights all across the cavern switched from green to red or orange. But, pleasantly, I didn't hear any sirens. I was sure anyone monitoring the factory remotely would see a warning, but hopefully they were all too far away—or too busy observing the spectacle of John and Dowe—to respond immediately.

It looked like Phil had correctly rerouted the flow, and the last of the weapon was beginning to fill the holding tank. I tabbed back to the file directory and found the virus. Setting the drive down on the desk so I could use both hands, I opened the computer's command window and typed the magic words.

I might not know how to code viruses, but I was an expert at launching them.

I felt satisfaction mold my lips into something like a smile. There was no telling how far the virus would spread. The government did love a secure database; the virus might just take a lap around whatever office Ambrose was synced to and then go no further. But even if that's all it did, it was going to create one beautiful mess. Their secret armory was about to go up in digital smoke, and I could only hope some fat, lazy politicians were sitting at their desks right now to witness it.

I closed my eyes, breathed in the moment, and hit enter.

At first, nothing happened, which was what I expected. I clicked on a random item and was greeted with an error about the file being "unavailable." I refreshed the folder, and the file list went blank.

I clicked on another folder and found the same thing. I backed out several levels, each time revealing a deeper and deeper vacuum of empty space. Soon the entire database was gone.

I rewarded myself with a cackle. "Ephesus, you dirty little genius."

I clicked on another database, but the file explorer froze. I tried going in another way and only got an angry screech.

Flashing alerted me out of my peripheral. I turned to the other monitor to see one of the control programs glitching out like it had been possessed.

Two more windows followed suit. Soon the whole display was throbbing with errors and pixelated graphics like the entire computer was being choked to death.

I jumped when Phil screamed. I ran to the window and heard rather than saw the commotion. The factory hadn't shut down—if anything, it was working harder than before. Every machine was churning at full speed while every display flickered in a panic. Raw chemicals rushed into the factory to fulfill the imaginary quota—but they had nowhere to go. The pipes we had sealed off swelled, bloated like beached whales.

I saw it coming with only enough time to mutter an appropriate oath. The pipes burst, releasing my invisible angel of death into the air.

So much for not flooding the island with Red Rain.

I raced back to the computer and tried a program, any program, but the terminal was unresponsive. The entire screen was locked up, the corrupted applications twitching in their death throes.

The virus was consuming programs as well as data files. Whether that was by design or poor programming, I'll never know.

I wasn't entirely surprised by this turn of events, but the computer didn't know what to do with itself. The only thing it could process was that the factory was in a state of emergency, and it responded appropriately.

I recognized what was happening with only seconds to spare. I raced out of the office, waving my arms to get her attention.

"Phil, get out of there!" I yelled at the top of my lungs, hoping she could hear me over the din. "The entire system is failing!"

She stood up, face pinched in confusion. Why she wasn't already running was beyond me. I tried to make myself clear with wild hand gestures. "You need to get out of there! The computer thinks the factory is on fire and it's going to—"

I needn't have bothered. The sirens and pulsing lights that ignited just then made the situation clear. The emergency sprinklers engaged, and my weapon made its debut.

Phil screamed, but she was upstaged by the symphonic hiss as the spraying water married the gases in the air and condensed into liquid fire. Red Rain showered over the factory, the drops of acid sparkling like cursed rubies, bathing the room in corrosion and death.

I took a defensive step back, but I appeared to be safe. The office and the path to the elevator were, wisely, on a different fire suppression system.

Phil was not so lucky. The alcove was sheltered enough, but the rest of the factory was covered in the downpour. The walkway leading to the holding tanks was slick and glistening, and it was only a matter of minutes before the acid ate the metal and trapped her for good.

If we could find something to cover her head, she might be able to make it before the pathway washed out. She'd get a few burns, but that would be better than dying, I assumed.

I started shouting at her to that effect, but she interrupted me. "The emergency panel by the door! Shut off the sprinklers!"

I glanced in the direction she was pointing. There was an emergency access panel in the far corner by the elevator—the elevator Ambrose would no doubt come storming out of any minute.

I abruptly remembered the drive sitting on the desk. I had to get the drive and put it somewhere Ambrose wouldn't find it. It was my only chance at freedom—and even if I couldn't get out of this alive, I definitely didn't want the United to have my copy of Red Rain *or* Ephesus's mastermind virus.

"Just hang on!" I yelled. "I need to grab the drive! Don't move!"

I darted back into the office and snatched the drive off the desk. Clenching it in my fist, I paused in the middle of the floor and weighed my options. Hiding the drive in the factory seemed unwise—I might not have access to the factory after today, if it didn't burn itself to the ground. I could hide it on my person, but I knew that, no matter how much blame I tried to bestow on Phil, Ambrose would correctly assume I had been the primary instigator. I would be receiving the brunt of the interrogation and any invasive searches.

It dawned on me that Phil was actually the safest place to store the drive. Ambrose would never assume she was carrying weapons, and at the very least, he would be too preoccupied to search her immediately.

Yes, giving the drive back to Phil was my best bet—which meant I definitely needed to get her out of here alive.

I looked out the office window in her direction—and stopped.

Despite devoting my entire adult life to the project, I had never seen my weapon in action, but now the effects of it were on full display. The entire factory was coated in blood, the emergency lights reflecting off every acid-wet surface. The factory seemed to be melting away as Red Rain chewed at the metal, stripping the finish from the machines and gnawing holes in the pipework. The smell of corroding iron and steel choked the air, even in the office.

It worked. My weapon really, truly worked, and it did everything it was supposed to. It *was* the perfect weapon. Released during a rainstorm, Red Rain could burn an entire city to the ground, and there would be no kill switch to stop it.

I glanced at the holding tanks and imagined how many cities—countries—the United could have melted with the contents. I knew exactly what the United would do with the weapon: They would rain it on every errant country that had refused to join their conglomerate. Every last holdout of individuality would be brought to its knees or burned to the ground.

And if anyone dared rebel, the United could simply wash them off the map. Primitive countries, the poor, stubborn religions—anything they didn't want or need could be scalded to death, until the entire planet was conformed to their idiosyncratic mold.

That was, of course, if I didn't shoot first.

Phil's shrieking shattered my thoughts. I turned towards the holding tanks, but she was no longer there. Had she made a run for it?

I scanned the factory, and my fears were confirmed—Red Rain had destroyed the walkway to the alcove. Several chunks were missing from the middle. Phil was nowhere to be seen.

My brain skipped a beat. Had she—? I pressed my face to the office window, searching the factory floor for her body, but saw nothing.

The flash of moving metal caught the corner of my eye. I looked up to see Phil dangling from a broken catwalk, suspended several stories in the air.

I watched in horrified admiration as she hauled herself back onto what was left of the platform. I retraced her path; she'd been smart enough to find another way out of the alcove. She'd climbed up the side of the tanks and onto a service catwalk that hung below the ceiling. She was out of range of the sprinklers but not out of harm's way; Red Rain had eaten away at the chains supporting the catwalk, and she'd nearly plunged to her death.

As it was, she'd only postponed the inevitable.

And so have you.

I looked down at the drive in my hand. If the United didn't start a war with Red Rain, I would. If Smyrna couldn't reconstruct the formula for them, they'd come after me for it. We'd chase each other in circles until one of us pulled the trigger, and then this is how humanity would end: The last holdout clinging to life while Red Rain set the world on fire.

It was just a matter of who made the first move. If it mattered at all.

You're the only one who can end this, Nic.

I scanned the office. The desktop was useless—but my eyes fell on the printer. I had taken it offline, which meant it was safe from the virus and presumably still operational.

I found the port and jammed the drive in. The screen brightened with a chirp, and the file list loaded.

The printer bemoaned its lack of paper. I tuned it out as I began to manually delete every file that didn't belong to Ephesus. It was agonizingly tedious, and the decades-old electronic ran at a snail's pace.

Clattering metal from outside the office reminded me that I needed to hurry. I wiped all the weapons files I had copied from the United's database, and then I came to Red Rain.

I stared at it, a million computations firing in my mind. Then, with a curse and a sigh, I deleted it.

18

I yanked the drive out. I assumed the printer didn't have any kind of file recovery, but for good measure I hit the button to bring the device back online.

Pocketing the drive, I raced out of the office and looked for Phil. She lay completely still on the swaying platform high above. Red Rain gushed from the broken sprinkler pipes right beneath her.

The sprinklers! I turned towards the elevator. There was a dry path to the emergency panel, the spray of the sprinklers falling just short of the wall. I could make it—but probably only because I was lanky and agile.

I flattened myself against the wall and started sliding towards the door. "Philadelphia!" I shouted to get her attention.

There was a beat, and I wondered if she hadn't heard me. Then a weak "You idiot!" came floating down.

You can do better than that, but okay. "I'm coming!"

"Ten minutes too late!"

Fair.

I made it to the panel. A swift fist shattered the protective glass, and I began rapidly flipping all the levers off, ignoring the blood that formed on my knuckles. I took the sprinklers offline, followed by the equipment and, for good measure, most of the power.

The sirens ceased as the entire factory ground to a halt. The headache-inducing whir died away, and the lights on the machines went dark. The room shuddered and sighed, as if glad to be put out of its misery.

Most importantly, the sprinklers turned off. I turned around and watched the water dry up, taking the hiss of Red Rain with it. Soon the room was shockingly silent.

I walked up to the edge of the platform, avoiding the standing puddles. I scanned what was left of the walkway and judged it to be useless. It was only a matter of time before the rest of the weakened metal snapped, and it didn't go out nearly far enough to catch Phil if she fell.

I leaned over and looked at the factory floor below. It was a deadly mess of broken pipes, scraps of metal, and pools of Red Rain. But those puddles were slowly shrinking as they ate through the concrete floor and bled into the earth below.

Eventually, the floor would be passable—but how long would that take?

"Just hang on!" I yelled up at her. "As soon as a path clears, we'll get you down!"

I scanned the factory for anything helpful—a ladder, a lift, rope—but saw nothing. After a beat, I realized Phil hadn't responded. I looked up at her. "Did you hear me, Phil?"

"I don't think we have time to wait!" The fear turned her voice into a warble. "These chains aren't going to hold!"

She pointed. Even from this distance I could see that Red Rain had weakened most of the chains supporting the catwalk. It was only a matter of time—maybe minutes—before more of them snapped and sent her plummeting to her death.

An angry yell disrupted my mental attempt to solve that problem. "What have you done?"

I turned to see Ambrose standing in the elevator, gawking at our handiwork. I groaned. I did not have time to deal with him right now, but maybe if I could keep him engaged long enough to get Phil down, we could at least make it out of the factory before he murdered us all.

"What did you expect?" I cracked with a sarcasm that, for once in my life, I didn't feel. "You left *her* alone unsupervised."

It didn't work. He charged, and I didn't have enough time to brace myself. He slammed me backward into the railing, almost flipping me over into the factory below. The corroded fence groaned and shifted but held.

I stood up—right into a punch to the face.

Colors swam before my eyes. I could barely see, but I managed to avoid the next hit. I was attempting to focus on his hands through my blurred vision and didn't see the kick until it was too late.

Pain ricocheted through my body. I involuntarily buckled over and backed up, trying to give myself space to find a better defensive position.

Ambrose gave me no such luxury. He charged at me. I sidestepped to avoid him—right onto what was left of the walkway.

I realized my mistake a moment too late. Ambrose blocked the way and continued his approach, slow and menacing this time. I stood up to meet him, even though my body was still screaming from the kick.

"I hope you enjoyed your little act of rebellion." He took another step. I backed down the walkway, feeling it creak and shudder beneath me.

"Because once you're out of the picture, we'll just rebuild and pick up right where we left off."

He jabbed my shoulder, hard. I coughed. I glanced behind me and realized there were only a few paces left between me and my doom—if I was going to enjoy my victory, I had to do it now.

I met Ambrose's eyes. "I know you will—after you finish repairing all the damage from the virus I just released onto your perfect little United internet."

He glared at me in confusion. I straightened until I towered over him. This time, the sarcasm in my voice was proud and genuine. "You really do have great upload speed, especially for being so far out in the ocean."

I'm sure he didn't fully understand what I meant, but he knew I'd done him dirty, and it infuriated him. I soaked in his anger—my last mistake. I wasn't prepared to dodge the backhanded slap he landed on my face.

I stumbled backward to the end of the walkway. Ambrose closed the gap. I scanned the shredded factory floor beneath me, trying to spy a safe place to make the jump.

I registered Phil screeching at Ambrose, begging him to spare me. He paused to cast threats in her direction—just long enough for me to predict his next move.

He lunged at me. I ducked, and his cumbersome form stumbled over me. I swung at his legs, sending him over the edge.

He landed face-first in a puddle of Red Rain with a smack and several other unpleasant sounds.

Before I could even draw a breath, Phil screamed again, this time in tune with a snapping chain. I looked up to see her scrambling at the pathway as it bucked under the strain.

"Nic!" she gasped.

The other chain broke, at the same time something in me cracked.

She fell backward into the factory below, her dark hair fanning around her like a funeral shroud. I could come up with no sound, no words, no heroic ideas—just one burst of a very cold, very heavy, and very unfamiliar emotion.

Regret.

Then I judged her trajectory, and the world restarted. She crashed to the ground—right on top of Ambrose, whose voluminous frame absorbed the brunt of her fall. She flailed like a ragdoll, and then her head fell back and cracked onto the concrete. She went limp without a sound.

I spied a piece of fallen walkway that formed a temporary island of safety. I jumped onto it, then, in the most twisted game of "the floor is lava," navigated to Phil's side. The ends of her hair grazed a puddle of acid as I lifted her. I laid her out on the piece of fallen walkway like a stretcher.

I felt her neck. Her pulse was weak but steady, her breathing even. Her leg was burned in several places, but it was superficial. She'd probably get a nice scar out of the deal, but she would recover.

I sat down on the metal next to her to wait. I was sure the rest of the guards would come running soon enough to fish us out.

I glanced at Ambrose. It looked like Red Rain would spare them the expense of a burial.

I looked around the still factory. The last drops of my weapon dripped silently from the ruined machinery. The tired fluorescents high above reflected off the pools of blood. I watched as the puddle nearest to me gurgled through the concrete and wondered, dryly, if this was the last I'd ever see of my creation.

Into the silence, I laughed.

ANDROMEDA

RED RAIN #3

RACHEL NEWHOUSE

JUNE 2076

1

"Jump, tuck, and roll," they'd said.

It was only after I took a running leap off the moving train that I realized I had no idea how to execute that.

In the split second of panic as I hurled from the train to the building, my muscles did the only thing they could think of. I curled into a ball and threw my hands over my head as the roof rushed up to catch me. My landing was more of a "splay" than a "roll" as I crashed hip-first onto the concrete.

I moaned as the inertia shuddered through my bones. The skin on my right leg screamed, reminding me that the chemical burn I'd sustained this morning was fresh and festering. At least I was wearing thick jeans and long sleeves.

I looked up and was privately gratified to find that my traveling companion hadn't nailed the landing either. Nic stared at his bloody palms and then brushed them off with a wince.

"Can you walk?" he said as he struggled to do the same.

"Yeah." I knew nothing was broken; my hip and thigh would probably just wear a bruise for the next decade. It would go nicely with the leg scars I was no doubt developing under the layers of bandages.

I grasped the ledge and hauled myself up. I glanced over the edge of the roof and nearly vomited. Not because of the height—it was only two stories—but because of the headache that was ramming into my skull like a bull beating down a gate. This was the third time this week that I'd taken a hard impact; it was a wonder I could still remember my name.

I pinched my temples and reminded myself why I had jumped off a moving train. Nic and I had just been deported from the prison island of Rott to be questioned by the United for our various and sundry acts of rebellion—except our train had been "hijacked" by friendly strangers, who, assuming everything was still going to plan, were going to take us to a safe place.

I looked up. Three men were waiting on the roof. They were dressed like maintenance crew, in jackets with a forgettable company logo on the back. If anyone had seen them on the roof prior to our dramatic arrival, I don't think they would have thought anything of it.

I could only hope the passing train had blocked our botched "jump, tuck, and roll" from any nosey passerby.

"Come on," one of the strangers approached me, "we need to get you two out of sight."

He grasped my arm. I was grateful for the guidance; my headache was blurring my sense of direction. He pulled me through the door and down the stairwell to a rear exit, where a windowless white service van was parked in the alley.

Nic followed. "They told me we'd be taking the subway."

"Change of plans." One of them rapped on the rear door of the van. "The subway's been compromised. Our connection didn't make contact. So we're going to have to slog it through rush hour."

The doors opened, and a hand reached out of the shadows in the back of the van. I accepted the offer of help and let the faceless stranger pull me up and guide me into the corner, where I sank down against the wall.

The van rocked as Nic joined us. The doors were slammed and latched without ceremony, plunging us into complete blackness.

"Hang on," an unfamiliar voice said. There was a clatter, and then a weak light flickered on. Our chaperone held a flashlight that cast his features into sharp relief.

I heard the cabin doors shut, and the engine revved to life. The diesel rumble made the whole van shake, and the shudder shot straight up my bones and into my head. I moaned as my headache roared. The whole world swayed, completely out of time with the rocking of the van as it jerked forward. Black spotted my vision.

You're going to pass out. The warning flared across my subconscious. I scooted away from the wall, buried my face in my knees, and closed my eyes. *Breathe. Breathe!* I sucked in a shuddery breath and let it out, then pulled in another. And another.

"Hey. You good?"

Against my better judgment, I lifted my head and looked up. Our escort leaned over me. He'd balanced the flashlight on a nearby crate, projecting its diffused light onto the roof of the van.

"No," I managed, my slurred tone confirming my statement.

"Here, this will help with the nausea." He held out a water bottle—the cap mercifully removed—and a small white pill.

I squinted. "How did you know I was—"

He raised an eyebrow. "You look like death."

I didn't doubt it. I accepted the offerings and gingerly sipped the water. When my stomach didn't refuse it, a took a mouthful and swallowed the pill.

Vaguely I wondered where he had gotten it—did they know I had suffered a head injury this morning and came prepared?

Did all that really happen this morning? The day's events flashed through my mind like a movie starring someone else. Nic and I had blown up a factory of dangerous chemicals and released a vicious computer virus onto the internet. We did that. We destroyed the government's superweapon. We crippled the United.

I repeated that fact over and over in my mind, hoping it would ground me in reality. On one hand, our escapades on Rott seemed like a lifetime ago. On the other hand, my body still felt trapped in that self-destructing factory. I heard the endless sirens wailing, smelled the blood-like stench of Red Rain as it burned through the metal machinery and scalded my leg, and felt myself falling, falling…

"Philadelphia." It was Nic this time. He caught me as I swooned. He took the water bottle from my hand and propped me up against a crate. "Deep breaths."

I ignored the admonition; my lungs were fluttering in tune with my heart. "Tell me what happened. Everything."

His eyebrows shot up. "Why?"

"Just do it! I need someone—anyone—to keep talking." I tipped my head back and sucked small breaths in through my nose.

He shifted uncomfortably. "Umm, okay. Where do you want me to start?"

I used my last remaining ounce of motor control to glare at him. I knew our alliance was loose, but he owed me this one. It was his fault I nearly died in that factory today.

"Okay, okay." He sat down cross-legged next to me. "The United captured us—all of us. You, me—"

"Dad. Ephesus." I wrapped my arms around my knees.

"—and Cea. Yes, that's right." He used the same tone you would with a five-year-old; it seemed to help him as much as it was helping me. "They separated us. I don't know where the others are. They sent us to Rott."

"Ambrose," I growled. My anger gave me a moment of mental clarity. "Ambrose is dead."

"Very much so."

I shuddered, remembering his body splattered on the floor of the burning factory. I tried to muster an emotion—any emotion. Commander Ambrose had overseen the unassimilated concentration camp my family had been detained in, until he'd gotten a better offer to help produce Red Rain. He had breathed down my neck for so long—surely his death should rouse some response from me, Christlike or not. Maybe it was the fog in my head, but I felt nothing, and that terrified me.

"Keep talking."

Nic chewed his lip. "They were making Red Rain on Rott."

"Because my dad finished the formula." That was why they'd chased us down and thrown us in prison: to force my father to finish what Nic had started. Presumably they'd threatened to kill me if he didn't, but I'll never know. My father hadn't explained the last time we talked, before they sentenced me to Rott. He hadn't even said goodbye.

Chaotic emotions came at me in a wave, but they were drowned out by a swell of nausea. Whatever that guy had given me, it was *not* helping. I heaved through my nose.

Nic watched me. "Yes, he did. But we destroyed the factory. We set the systems to overload."

"And you uploaded the virus."

"Nasty bugger," our escort inserted himself into the conversation for the first time. He handed Nic another water bottle. "Where in the world did you get a weapon like that?"

I let my muddled mind churn over the question for a minute. "My brother..." Ephesus had made it, along with a bunch of other programs and prototypes—and it was all on a flash drive that was currently wedged in my shoe. I reached for it.

Nic grasped my wrist. "Less talking, more listening." He pushed me back against the crate, then kept talking before I could muster up the cognitive ability to argue. "The United sent us back to the mainland for questioning, but our friends here intercepted us." He nodded at our escort, who gave a sarcastic salute. "We're going to a safe place, where we'll get our files wiped."

"I have to pick a new name," I whispered, remembering.

"That's right." Nic took a swig of his water and grimaced.

I leaned my head against the crate, questions swirling faster than the stars that were dancing in my vision. I knew it was necessary to avoid prosecution—but how? How could I pick a new name? Not only did I have absolutely *no* idea what I'd call myself, but I couldn't imagine being anyone but Philadelphia Smyrna.

Changing my name seemed like the final betrayal, the last shred of my self-autonomy being ripped from my grasp. Despite all the trauma that had happened to me over the past six years—being labeled a criminal and contained in a camp, having my family torn apart multiple times—my name had stayed with me. I was Philadelphia, and that was something not even the government could take from me.

If I'm not Philadelphia, who am I?

I wanted to cry, but the need to vomit was greater. Before I could register what was happening, I retched.

"Phil!" Nic dropped his water bottle.

"Everything hurts," I moaned, and I meant it. The feeling of pain in every joint of my body was overwhelming—and so *heavy*. I suddenly felt like I'd left Earth's gravity and was slogging through wet concrete.

"What did you do?" Nic yelled, but the question wasn't directed at me. He grabbed his now-empty water bottle and sniffed it. His voice jumped an octave. *"What did you do?"*

Black again splattered my vision, and this time it wouldn't blink away. I couldn't even see the ground as I plunged.

Someone caught me, but I wasn't sure who. They must have laid me down on the ground, because my body stopped moving, but I couldn't feel anything. Not the van floor shuddering beneath me, not the pain in my joints—nothing. For a brief moment, it was almost peaceful.

The last thing I registered before succumbing to the darkness was Nic screeching.

2

I woke up to silence.

It wasn't a scary silence—the kind where you know there should be sound but there isn't any. Instead, it was an unassuming quiet, like the rest of a predawn morning. The stillness cradled me as I slowly came to consciousness and opened my eyes.

It was dark but not black. Low security lighting near the floor sketched out the shape of a small room. I was lying on a bed in the corner, a blanket pulled tidily up to my shoulders.

I carefully pushed it away, testing my muscles. It didn't take long to register that everything still hurt, especially my head, but the pain wasn't as intense as I remembered. My leg, even though it was still bandaged, no longer burned. I was stiff more than anything, and for the first time in what felt like forever, I wasn't nauseous.

This gave me the confidence to try standing up. I was still in my old clothes—the smell gave that away—but my shoes had been removed. My socked feet touched the cold metal floor, and I panicked.

Ephesus's flash drive! I dropped to the floor and looked around, but it was pointless in the dark. I stumbled to the door and felt the wall until I found the light switch. My eyes protested the sudden brightness and my head started throbbing again, but I ignored the flashing colors and hastily searched the near-empty room.

My shoes were gone. The windowless room contained only a bed, chair, and nightstand, on top of which sat a water bottle.

I picked the water bottle up. The feel of the room-temperature plastic in my hand brought everything rushing back.

They'd drugged us. I'd taken the pill straight like a moron; Nic's water must have been contaminated. Our escort had knocked us out, which meant something was very, very wrong.

I looked at the door. There was no handle, and a piece of scrap metal had been bolted on the wall where an access panel might have been. In fact, the whole room had an unfinished air, like it had been hastily retrofitted into a cell.

My first instinct was to rage like a caged animal, but I swallowed it back. Whoever put me in here couldn't have gone far. So I tried the only thing I could think of—I knocked on the door.

To my surprise, I heard footsteps outside. There was a beep, and the door slid open, revealing two guards. At least, I assumed they were guards; they were dressed in light combat gear and carried pistols. Both had their guns holstered; I guess they correctly assumed I was in no position to jump them.

One lifted a phone to his mouth. "She's awake."

The other gave me the once-over. "How do you feel? Can you walk?"

The answer to the latter question should have been obvious, so I ignored it. To the former, I responded, "Not terrible. Where am I?"

The first slid his phone back in his pocket. "We can't answer that, but we'll take you to the person who can."

They parted, and I stepped out into the hall, which was somehow even more blindingly lit than the bedroom. I threw up an arm to shield my face.

One of the guards pinched my elbow. "This way."

I let him steer me down the hall. I looked in all directions, trying to see as much of the building as I could. But as my eyes adjusted, I realized there was nothing to look at. The entire hall was a windowless tunnel of metal in both directions, and every door we passed was shut. Most of them were unmarked, and some didn't even have access panels installed yet.

The guards opened a door and ushered me into a wing that looked slightly more civilized. There still weren't any windows, but there was a bench and a few potted plants, plus an abstract painting that might have been called art. All the doors appeared to be finished, with lit access panels to the side and shiny numbers above. The guards walked me to door number 6 and punched the doorbell.

A male voice crackled over the speaker. "Is she with you?"

I tensed. I recognized the voice, my subconscious latching onto it as familiar, but I couldn't put a face with it. What's worse, I couldn't remember if the voice belonged to friend or foe.

Although, based on all the circumstantial evidence, it was probably safe to assume he was a foe.

"Yessir," one of the guards affirmed.

"Bring her in, then go get him."

The door beeped and opened in response to an unspoken command. I took a step in and stopped, and time with me.

He sat in the same commanding pose, behind the same excessive desk, with the same ostentatious array of bookcases and soldiers behind him. If it weren't for the fact that the entire room was made out of shiny metal instead of dark mahogany, I would have sworn we were in the same office he'd interrogated me in a week ago.

It was definitely him. His precise dark hair and piercing eyes were unmistakable; he was the man who had held Cea and me hostage to coerce my father into creating Red Rain. I could only hope he had a better plan this time—better than blackmailing my father while I rotted in a cell.

"You again?" I said after an indeterminate pause. Even I wasn't sure if that was an accusation or genuine question.

He gestured to the chairs in front of his desk for an answer.

I shuffled in, suddenly reminded of my socked feet as soon as they hit the plush carpet.

"Oh, my apologies, I had them cleaned." He fetched my tennis shoes from the floor and set them on the edge of the desk.

I sat down in a chair and picked them up. To his credit, they actually did look clean—but of course my brother's flash drive was no longer inside of them. He didn't mention it, so I decided to follow suit. I knew there wasn't any point.

I shoved my shoes back on. "Do I get your name this time?" I asked.

"Thames." He didn't specify whether that was a first or last.

I stole another glance around the office while I fiddled with my shoelaces. It definitely wasn't the same office, so presumably it wasn't the same building. But we were in a high-rise somewhere; this room actually had windows, and they revealed a setting sun and nondescript cityscape. It wasn't a skyline I recognized, but the telltale glimpses of ocean peeking from between the high rises made me hope we were still on the East Coast.

Thames hadn't said anything, so I decided to initiate the questions. "Where are we?"

"My office."

I glared at him. "How did we get here?"

"Everything that comes—and goes—from Rott passes my desk first. It wasn't difficult to interrupt your 'escape.'"

"The virus didn't scramble your systems?" That had been the ace in our escape plan; the virus was designed to wipe all data from any device it infected. Nic had uploaded it to the internet from Rott, taking out the factory and several government servers with it. I had no idea how far the virus had spread, but it should have given them much bigger problems to worry about than a couple of ragtag criminals.

He looked down his nose at me. "You released a virus, not an EMP. I still got the call that you were being deported."

I wanted to be upset that I'd fallen into his trap again, but instead I just felt oddly annoyed. "Then why not just detain us on Rott? Why wait until we'd jumped off the train?"

He looked equally annoyed. "There were… delays in communication."

I closed my eyes. I hoped our real escort, whoever they were, had seen the danger and run the other way.

I took a steadying breath and released a prayer. *What do we do now, God?*

I looked up at Thames, who was patiently waiting for me to process my emotions. "What do you want?"

He reached for a tablet on the desk at the same time the door opened. Nic came in—much less willingly than I had. The guards ingloriously shoved him into the chair next to me.

He looked ready to spout off, but when he saw Thames and I were already deep in conversation, he opted for a sarcastic, "I see you two have gotten acquainted."

"We go way back," I droned, and didn't elaborate.

"Did he tell you anything?" Nic asked as if we were alone in the room.

"Absolutely nothing."

"I'm about to, if you two will let me get a word in edgewise." Thames flicked his fingers across the tablet screen. "It seems we both have a problem, Philadelphia."

He turned the tablet to face me. Soundless security footage was rolling on the screen. I watched as two blurry figures scuffled on the crumbling catwalk in the self-destructing factory on Rott. They were too far away to be identified, their faces obscured by the mess of pipes and machinery between them and the camera, but my memories supplied the screams and shouts that couldn't be heard. It was Nic and Ambrose, moments before Ambrose plunged to his death.

Suddenly, I darted into view. I fell to my knees below the camera, my bleeding hand stretched helplessly towards the men below. Even as a drop of Red Rain slid down the camera lens and stained the image, you could clearly see the terror burning in my eyes.

"I don't see a problem," I said as I tried to swallow the panic that reflexively shot through my system.

"Despite the chaos your little virus caused on the internet, social media has spread this video like the plague. Between this and the virus, you two have become accomplished and—dare I say it—popular terrorists. You should see the hashtags you have trending."

I hadn't been on social media in six years—thanks to the internet restrictions they enforced in the concentration camps—so I had no idea how trending hashtags worked, but I really didn't care. I was a little perturbed that a video of me had been seen by thousands of strangers, but I didn't see how it posed a problem. If anything, I wanted *more* people to see the damage we'd caused.

"Your point?" I prodded.

"The point is, I have a major act of terrorism and no terrorist group to take credit for it. Do you know how much of a PR nightmare that is?"

I didn't, and if he was trying to bait me into a reaction, he was failing miserably. "How is this my problem?"

Nic, who had been watching the conversation with the observant eyes of a hawk, leaned over to remind me, "He could *make* it your problem."

Thames smiled. I rolled my eyes. I knew he could—he always could. That's all the United had ever done—threaten and manipulate and coerce—and I was tired of it. I was tired of rehearsing the same song and dance and reciting the same lines. I was tired of being their puppet, and I wasn't going to play by their rules anymore.

"If you really need pain to motivate you, I can accommodate," Thames was droning, "but I'd prefer to take the easy route—for both of us. I think if you'll listen to my proposal you'll—"

"I don't care," I cut him off. "I'm not helping you. I'd rather die."

Thames blinked, although I think he was more surprised that I'd interrupted him than alarmed at the content of my outburst.

After a beat, he flicked his hand at the window. "Be my guest." Then he leaned back, all his facial muscles relaxing as if he were grateful for the break.

I glanced at the darkening skyline that punctuated the view out his—very high—office window. I swallowed, almost choking on my bubble of courage and anger as it burst.

What have I done? Oh, Jesus, I—

I heard that tiny voice deep inside of me say, *It's going to be all right.*

Sniffing indignantly—it was the most resolute sound I could muster—I scraped the chair back and marched toward the window.

Nic muttered something under his breath I dared not repeat.

I paused in front of the window and took a deep breath, inhaling a dozen prayers with it. Then I braced my feet, squared my shoulders, and grabbed the bottom of the window pane—only to find that there wasn't one to speak of.

Upon closer inspection, I realized the window had no latches and no frame. The surface was completely smooth, its too-perfect image glowing faintly.

"Would you be a gentleman," I snarled, attempting to save face, "and open the window for me?"

Thames obliged by swiping on his tablet. The image on the monitors—there were three of them spaced out across the wall—changed simultaneously to a chirping woodscape with an unseen brook babbling in the background.

"Well, things just got interesting," Nic mused, although he was looking at me, not the fake windows.

I sulked back to the desk. Thames continued seamlessly. "If you are resolute in your desire to die, a functional window will be provided to you. But while you are waiting, will you at least oblige me by hearing my offer?"

"Sure," I said, gracelessly slumping into the chair.

"Thank you," he said, for the first time condescending to match my sarcasm. "It's quite simple, really. I want you to record a few videos for me, Philadelphia. I want you to stand in front of a camera and take responsibility for these acts of terrorism. Tell them you're the face behind the attack."

I frowned at him. "Don't you already have security footage proving that I did it?"

"That *we* did it," Nic inserted.

"Of course," Thames said benevolently, "but that's not the same as you taking responsibility. I don't know how much you know about terrorism, Philadelphia—"

Nic coughed. "More than she cares to admit."

We collectively ignored him. "—but terrorists typically have an agenda. They have demands. They don't typically blow up a factory and release a mastermind-level virus onto the internet, only to vanish into obscurity."

"Why does it matter?" It was a genuine question. Maybe I truly *didn't* know how terrorism worked, but the math wasn't adding up for me. "Say I record these videos and take credit for it. What good does that do you?"

"It gives us a target to eliminate."

That's it? "So I take responsibility, and then you take me down—all through carefully staged videos, of course—so the government can save face."

"Precisely," Thames admitted without shame.

"And what if I refuse?"

He shrugged. "Then I guess I'll find another window."

There it is. There's the death threat. Even so, he wasn't lying—it *was* simple enough. And yet, it didn't seem like the most efficient solution to the problem. Why pick me when they could use—

"What about me?" Nic voiced my thoughts. "What role do I play in this?"

Thames regarded him. "With all due respect," he said in a tone that conveyed absolutely no respect at all, "you have no role in this, doctor. As far as I'm concerned, this operation doesn't involve you."

Nic huffed. "But it's my weapon!"

"It was your concept, perhaps, but you were woefully unable to complete it. Dr. Smyrna is responsible for making it operational."

I flinched, but there was no denying it.

The pathetic look in Nic's eyes said he couldn't deny it either. "I uploaded the virus…" he whined, mostly to himself, sounding like a kid who had lost a game of king of the hill.

"A representation of the younger Smyrna's coding, I understand."

Nic slouched in his chair.

"If I may be blunt, doctor…"

"Please," I answered for him.

"The only reason you're still alive is that we have observed Miss Philadelphia to be capable of extraordinary feats in defense of her family and friends. And you, through some ironic twist of fate, seem to have found yourself in the latter category."

Nic could not have been any more offended. He was flushing both red and white at the same time, and it would have been comical had I not been equally mortified.

The cruel irony that Nic—who had once imprisoned my brother and caused my family so much pain—was now being used to blackmail me was more than my fragile constitution could bear.

What made it worse was the realization that Thames was right.

"But why me?" I blurted, desperate for a topic change. "If we're awarding points based on scientific achievement, I have even less claim to fame."

Thames smiled, which was not in any way a satisfactory answer to my question.

"If you needed a poster child, couldn't you have grabbed any scruffy-looking nerfherder? Anyone could claim responsibility and say Nic and I worked for them. Aren't there plenty of people you could have bribed with money—or threatened with death, since that's more your style?"

He just kept smiling. I locked eyes with him and repeated slowly and deliberately, *"Why me?"*

"I don't like to be wasteful. You were already a loose end that needed to be tied off. Why recruit someone else when I could make a deal with you and solve both of our problems?"

Even I knew that wasn't a cost-efficient solution. Wouldn't it be so much cleaner to use one of his own? Why was he going to so much effort to negotiate with a petty criminal when he could simply order a guard to stand in front of the camera?

Thames correctly interpreted my silence as skepticism, because he continued. "Besides, I know you, Philadelphia. Everyone has a price, and yours is one I'm willing to pay."

He opened a drawer and pulled out a chunky silver object. He turned it on before sliding it across the desk towards me.

My gasp was involuntary. *My reader.*

But it couldn't be. My reader was corroding at the bottom of the sea where Ambrose had tossed it over the boat. And yet, this device looked incredibly familiar.

Nic helped me put the pieces together. "Is that one of my prototype tablets?"

I snatched it off the desk and opened the main menu. It was—it was the reader Mr. Sardis had given me back when my family had been stationed on Mars under Nic. I could tell because all of my note files were exactly where I left them.

Right under the folder labeled "Bible."

I stared at the precious name, afraid that if I blinked the file would vanish again. My last copy of the Bible had been lost when Ambrose chucked my reader into the sea. A small part of me had been worried I'd never see a Bible again—and I'd certainly never expected a government official to be the one to give it to me. It was an illegal book, after all.

I looked up at Thames, unsure which of my dozen questions to ask first.

"It was in the evidence collected from Wing 74. I thought you might like it returned."

I bit my lip.

He folded his hands tidily on the desk. "My terms are very simple, Philadelphia. Record those videos for me—help me clean up the mess you made on Rott—and you and your friend here can go free. I will wipe your files and replace them with clean identities, and you can start a new life, no questions asked."

I stared at him. He seemed completely sincere, and that was terrifying.

Reality hit me in a rush. "What about my father?"

He hesitated, and I thought I'd called his bluff. "And Ephesus? Cea?" I pressed. "What about them? Do they get to go free? How are you planning on tying off those 'loose ends'?"

He sighed. "I'd be happy to offer your father his freedom, if I knew where he was."

"What?" Nic spoke before I could formulate a thought.

Thames snarled at him. "Turns out the chaos your lovely virus caused in our systems made the perfect cover for a little jailbreak. I have no idea where your families are."

I gaped at him. I was battling too many incongruent emotions to form a coherent facial expression. Should I feel hopeful? Worried? Did I even believe him? Thames had been holding our families when we were deported to Rott— that much I knew. Had they really escaped?

Thames returned his gaze to me. "Trust me, if there's any activity on their files, you'll be the *first* to know."

He made a concerted effort to relax back in his chair. "In the meantime, if you'll play ball with me, you can earn their freedom. Do what I say, Philadelphia, and I'll give your whole family clean files."

"Really," I said, the word flat.

"Really. I can make it so that there's no record of anything—no Red Rain, no virus, no criminal charges, nothing. It will be like the last three years never happened. And," he added with an indulgent smile, "you can keep your Bible."

I tightened my fingers around the reader.

Something wasn't right. It was too easy, too painless. Why would he be willing to offer me my freedom when he could just as easily threaten me into recording these videos and then kill me? And what about my father and Ephesus? It was probably easy enough to sweep me and Cea under the rug—we were little more than collateral damage, in the grand scheme of things. But my father, Ephesus, and Nic had been too involved. There was no way the government would be willing to just release them into the wild, not after they'd collectively created several superweapons.

I didn't trust Thames, not for a minute. It felt like a trap. Worse, it felt like compromise.

I started to push the reader back across the desk, but a hand closed around my wrist.

"Maybe you should give her a day to think about it," Nic said, his eyes on mine.

"Excellent advice." Thames nodded at the guards hovering around the room.

I stared at Nic, trying to translate the unspoken message his eyes were broadcasting. After a minute, I nodded and let go of the reader.

Thames waved his hand. "Keep it. As a gesture of goodwill."

I definitely didn't trust any "gesture of goodwill" from him, but for a Bible, I was willing to risk it. I snatched the reader and clutched it to my chest, half expecting him to take it back.

Two guards approached Nic and me. "They will show you the accommodations," Thames said.

Nic and I stood up together. Thames directed his final words at me. "Please, get some rest. We'll discuss details in the morning."

I didn't gratify him with a goodbye.

3

I assumed Thames was being sarcastic by calling our cells "accommodations," but as it turned out, the arrangements were surprisingly generous. They were certainly the most luxurious prison cells I'd ever seen, and I'd been in quite a few cells recently.

In fact, calling them "cells" seemed disingenuous. In reality, Nic and I had a whole wing to ourselves. The guards ushered us through a large gate—it was labeled "B" from both sides—and told us we could go anywhere we liked beyond it.

Wing B was made up of a wide hall that doubled as a common area, off which were at least a dozen other rooms. On the left were the dorms. I had been assigned to dorm 5, which was at the far end of the hall; Nic was a few doors down in dorm 3. On the right, there were several larger doors that the guards claimed led to a cafeteria, a lounge, a computer lab, and a rec room. At the far end of the hall was another large, presumably locked gate marked "C."

Everything was sparsely furnished. There was no carpet, no cushions, no art on the walls. And yet, it felt minimalist, not harsh, as if the place truly had been designed for human consumption.

"The doors on all the common areas are set to accept you both," one of the guards explained. "But only you can unlock your personal dorms."

I assumed Thames and the guards could also unlock them, but they didn't specify.

"Breakfast will be at 08:00 tomorrow and will be available for half an hour. Don't be late," the other guard admonished, not unkindly.

Then without further ceremony, they excited Gate B and left us alone.

Mechanically, both Nic and I walked to our assigned dorms. He studied the darkened panel next to his door, then chuckled humorlessly. "I should probably warn them that you are notorious for overriding this system."

I flapped my hand over the panel next to my door, and a familiar green circle blinked into existence. These were the experimental locks Nic had developed on his Martian base; they read DNA through the hand instead of requiring a fingerprint or face ID. Thames had the same locks installed in his office building where he'd imprisoned me two weeks ago. I guess when they stole Red Rain they decided to borrow a few of Nic's other inventions, too.

Nic was right; the system was flawed, and I'd been able to exploit it to my advantage before. But unless they'd programmed the doors to accept my father or brother, my DNA wasn't going to help us this time.

I stepped inside my room. "We'll talk in half an hour," Nic called just before my door sealed shut. I locked it and didn't bother to answer.

As soon as the silence settled, all of the emotions I had glazed over during the day came rushing back, demanding to be processed. Shock, grief, fear, anger. Gulping down rage and bile, I leaned my head against the cold door and poured all my conscious effort into taking even breaths. *One step at a time. You can do this. Holy Spirit, I need you.*

Straightening, I turned to face the room and instantly lost my fragile emotional composure.

Mama's purple suitcase lay in the middle of the bed.

Suddenly crying, I ran to it and threw the flap open. A quick inventory showed me that all my belongings were there—everything I'd left behind in my cell when Cea and I had escaped from Thames the first time. I sobbed as I ruffled through the clothes and toiletries. My fingers found Mama's floral skirt and clutched it like a lifeline.

I was so grateful to have my stuff back; this suitcase contained the entirety of my worldly possessions. And yet, the whole situation seemed strangely cruel. *He planned this. Thames knew what he was doing all along. He was ready, and I wasn't.*

I blotted my tears on the skirt. *One step at a time, starting with a shower.* I gathered a few toiletries and stumbled into the bathroom.

The bathroom was small and plain, but it appeared to be fully stocked with everything from toilet paper to shampoo. They weren't the dorky single-use products like you'd get at a hotel, either; everything was name-brand and full-size.

On the counter was a clean towel with a shiny packet on top. I picked it up and examined it. It was conditioner—one of those intensive hair masque treatments labeled "for thin and frizzy hair."

I ran a hand over my lifeless, matted mane. Not only had Thames logically deduced that my scalp hadn't seen the inside of a conditioner bottle in weeks, but he'd made the effort to research what kind of hair I had and buy a (rather expensive) specialty conditioner for it.

A new emotion pervaded my already cluttered subconscious. It was that nauseous sense of unease—a clingy premonition that I was falling right into his trap.

Why? Why would he do this—any of this? Why would he be kind to me when it was fully within his power to shove me around? Why was he working with me at all? I didn't buy his flimsy excuses; I knew full well that it would be much easier for the United to dispose of me and cover up the factory incident with creative media coverage. Keeping me alive was a liability. And the fact that he was making a pretense of being nice to me while doing it made the whole situation even more sinister.

Could I trust kindness from someone who had done so much evil?

One step at a time.

I peeled the bandage off my leg and discovered that the chemical burn I'd sustained in the factory had nearly healed. For the first time since the incident, I paused to admire the damage. A splatter of white wounds ran down my shin, forming a morbid constellation. The skin around them was tight and peeling, but it was no longer oozing, and the pain was nearly gone.

Unfortunately, that also meant we'd been out for several days or more.

Swallowing a nip of panic, I cranked the shower on nearly as hot as it would go, ignoring the sting on my wounded leg. Tearing the conditioner packet open, I slathered it on my hair and let it sit for twice the recommended time. I crouched on the shower floor with the water pounding my back, breathing in lungfuls of steam and repeating the same chaotic prayers over and over.

I emerged from the bathroom to hear someone milking my doorbell. I opened the door and was greeted by a frustrated Nic. His look of anxiety melted into one of annoyance at the sight of my wet hair, but he wisely opted not to complain.

He stepped in without being invited, closing and locking the door in one practiced motion. I opened my mouth to say something but decided I'd been in far more awkward situations over the past week.

He walked to the middle of the rug and looked around. "Where's that tablet he gave you?"

"Why?" I flinched, all of my distrust coming out in one syllable.

He held his hand out.

I took a step back. My reader was, of course, where it always was—in the pouch tied around my waist. I slid my fingers, still wrinkled from the long shower, inside and gripped the cold metal.

He rolled his eyes. "Phil, if we're going to get through this, I need you to grow up fast. If you can trust me enough to blow up a factory and jump off a train, I think you can trust me to touch your phone for thirty seconds."

He was right, of course, and I did trust him, to an extent. I guess just wasn't ready to feel the weight of the empty pouch flopping against my leg again.

I gave it to him with a sigh. He flicked it on and rapidly toggled menus. "What kind of music do you like to listen to?"

"Excuse me?"

"I'm a millennial fan myself—you know, the 00s and 10s."

"Are you serious right now?" I squawked, partly because I had no idea what he was getting at, and partly because I distinctly remembered my grandpa telling me that everything produced after the 1980s was unfit to be heard.

"You got another request? Because otherwise I found a Maroon 5 album on here."

"Here where?"

He held the reader out to me, which I took as a cue to step closer. On the screen was the massive file directory for a music archive. It did appear as though he'd found a Maroon 5 album—whoever they were—but what was important was the text he'd typed in the search bar:

OUR ROOMS ARE BUGGED

"Oh—" I started to say, then caught myself. "Please, anybody but them. My grandfather would be appalled." I took the device from him and toggled menus, looking for anything I recognized. I finally found a band that was from this decade at least—some alternative rock something-or-other Ephesus had listened to in college. I picked a random album and hit play.

Nic visibly swallowed a grimace. He put on a brave face and started bopping his head like he was actually into the beat. He jammed his thumb upwards; I cranked the volume, blasting the chaotic tune as loud as my little handheld device could muster.

"Remind me to never let you be in charge of the radio," Nic said, just loud enough for me to translate him over the music. He took the device and set it on the nightstand; far enough away that he and I could manage a conversation, but presumably still loud enough to garble any audio recording.

"How did you find out our rooms are bugged?" I asked.

"I actually don't know that they are," he admitted, "but I think it's safe to assume this entire wing is bugged. There's probably cameras, too. I'll let you know if I find out exactly where they are."

The thought should have perturbed me, but with a twinge I realized that I didn't have the energy to care. For the last six years, my entire life had been under strict surveillance, to the point where I subconsciously assumed that someone was watching me, in some way, at all times.

When did I stop caring about my personal freedom?

"You need to accept Thames's offer." Nic jerked me back to the present.

"Why?" Through context clues I had reached the conclusion that Nic would probably tell me to do it, but I hadn't yet figured out how it would benefit us. Sure, it might save us some pain and bloodshed, but I hadn't exactly been walking the path of least resistance lately.

Nic didn't waste any words. "I think it's our best chance of finding our families."

I skipped my next breath.

"If he's telling the truth—and I realize that's a big 'if'—then he needs those videos to go viral. He needs *everyone* to see them."

My heart and lungs caught up with reality. "They'll know we're alive."

"If we can teach you how to wear a poker face, we can do more than that— we tell them where we are."

"Do you know where we are?"

The silent beat told me all I needed to know. "Did they knock you out too?" I asked.

"Eyup."

"My leg is nearly healed," I offered. "So I think we were out awhile."

"I agree, which unfortunately means we could be literally anywhere."

I glanced around the bare room. "Judging by the lack of functional windows in this place, I'm guessing they don't want us to know where we are."

He nodded his begrudging consent. "I'll figure it out. The computers in the lab have internet capability, and I know that tablet does. Right now everything is connected to a secure network that just has a bunch of games and books and music on it." He gestured at our makeshift radio.

"Secure?" I repeated. "Is that why it hasn't been affected by the virus?"

"Maybe. Or he's lying about how far the virus spread. If I can hack onto whatever network they're using for their communication, I'll find out."

I rolled Thames's words around in my head, trying to shift out the obvious lies. He could have easily lied about the virus, but what would that have gained him? What did any of this gain him? "Do you think he's telling the truth about the others escaping?"

Nic shrugged. "I don't know why he would lie about that. If he had them in custody, he probably would have led with that. 'Record these videos or I kill your father' would have been a much simpler solution. It's what I would have done."

I glared at him, but I knew he was right.

"If I can hack around the internet block, I'll look up their files and see if they've been updated."

"'If' you can hack it?" I echoed, noting the repetition of the word.

He blinked. "If you have any better ideas, I'm open to them."

"Fine." I took a deep breath, tidying my thoughts like a stack of paper on a desk. "What do I do?"

"Buy me time. I need you to play the terrorist as long as possible. The more videos you record—the longer you're 'on air'—the more time we have to figure out where we are and send a message to Ephesus or Cea. This can't be a one-and-done deal."

I knew exactly what he meant. I had seen a lot of government takedown propaganda in my life—they made us watch it in school so we could see what fury would await us if we stepped out of line. The procedure was always swift and tidy to the point of being comical. They showed as little of the terrorist's work as possible, using clever editing of police footage to make it look like the United had swooped in and rained down justice at the first sign of trouble.

If Thames used that script—only allowing me to record one or two statements before he had me removed—then we wouldn't get anywhere. I had to put out a lot of videos over the span of several weeks.

I really did have to play the terrorist.

"Find out how many videos he's planning, and convince him to double it," Nic was saying.

I nodded. I walked over and picked up my reader, eager to turn the volume down. My head was pounding again, this time for more reasons than one.

Nic mercifully took the cue to leave. He let himself out, then turned in the doorway.

"Thanks," he called.

"For what?" I hesitated with my finger on the volume button.

His expression flickered. "Cea is my sister, too." And then he left.

I killed the music app, then sank down on the bed as silence flooded the room. Nic's comment shuddered through me, a chilly reminder that this wasn't just about me, or even about Nic. Our stunt on Rott had affected hundreds of thousands of people. A million had seen the video of our act of defiance—millions more might see the propaganda I was about to record.

I moaned as the realization hit me. If I agreed to record these videos—if I gave the United their clean and tidy takedown—I would be admitting to the world that I was wrong. I would be reinforcing the message that there was no hope in fighting the United, that the government always won. I would be strengthening the monstrosity I had spent so many years resisting.

I flopped back on the bed, sick and tired all at once. I couldn't do it—I couldn't get caught in the same scripted cycle. I couldn't keep bargaining for life and limb while the United always came out on top, always gained a little more control over my life.

If I agreed to Thames's plan, isn't that what would happen? Wouldn't I go back to being a pawn in a game I couldn't control? Isn't that why I nearly jumped out a window today—because I couldn't go back, not ever?

I pinched my eyes shut. If I was honest with myself, I didn't care about Thames. I didn't care about the surveillance video and I didn't care what the United did with the propaganda. If I refused to do it, they'd just cover up the mess some other way. It really *wasn't* my problem.

But Nic was right. It was our best shot at contacting our families, at least for now. And wouldn't it be worth it if it meant seeing my family again?

My reader squawked in protest. I realized I was crunching buttons with my white-knuckled grip, creating a nonsense request the computer couldn't process. I relaxed my fingers and cleared all windows, then opened the file I loved most in the world.

I didn't know all the answers, but I knew someone who did.

4

I almost missed breakfast the next morning, because for the first time in my life I couldn't decide what to wear.

I was halfway through braiding my hair when it dawned on me that I would be going on TV in a few hours. I knew it probably wouldn't be live, but the idea that other people—possibly millions of them—would be seeing me made me second-guess my wardrobe. What in the world did a teenage terrorist wear?

Despite the fact that I only possessed three complete outfits, it still took me a good thirty minutes to answer that question. I ultimately settled on my well-worn linen skirt, walking boots, and gray jacket. At least this outfit didn't make me look like a secretary or something.

It was only after I walked out the door that I realized I looked exactly the same as I did every other day.

It turns out I needn't have bothered, because as soon as the guards ushered me into Thames's office, he pawned me off on a sharp, black-haired woman wielding a comb and hair dryer.

"This is your stylist," he said by way of introduction.

"Narissa," she clarified, then proceeded to size me up. I returned the favor. I wasn't sure what I expected a professional stylist to look like, but I was somewhat surprised to find that her makeup was subtle and her clothes practical. She was, however, heavily armed: A multi-pocketed black tote lay open at her feet, revealing a meticulously organized array of brushes, creams, and paints.

"This is your terrorist?" Narissa ended our mutual scrutiny to cock a sculpted eyebrow at Thames.

He gestured with his hands. "That's why I hired the best."

"You should have spent your money on a better casting choice." She sighed with palpable disdain. I would have been offended if I didn't completely agree with her.

"Well, for starters, we need to lose the skirt and that braid. You look like you're going to ask me if I've heard of our Lord and Savior Jesus Christ, not usurp the government."

The absurd truth of that made me laugh outright. It was only after the sound left my lips that I realized how long it had been since I'd found something genuinely funny.

My amusement faded when she reached into her bag and pulled out a pair of scissors.

"Is a pixie cut too brash?" she asked Thames. "I feel like going all-out punk is cliché."

Thames was about to respond when I cut him off. "Absolutely not. You are not cutting my hair."

I was impressed by how firm my voice was, and judging by the flick of her eyebrows, Narissa was too. Thames was unaffected. "You really don't have a choice in the matter."

I flinched, but I kept the fear out of my voice as I replied, "Actually, I do."

He waited.

"I don't have to record these videos for you."

"And what do you think happens if you refuse?"

I didn't hesitate. "You owe me a functioning window."

Narissa clicked her tongue in amusement.

Thames didn't rush to reply. I took advantage of the moment of silence to release a quick breath and a prayer. Nic's advice flashed across my consciousness, and I slowly organized his theory into words.

"Look, if you want this to work, it has to be convincing. If people can tell these videos are staged—if they can tell you forced some random prisoner to stand in front of a camera and claim responsibility—no one will believe it. Everyone will know that you're covering something up, and you'll have an even bigger problem on your hands."

Believability had never bothered the United before, but Thames didn't interrupt me, so I kept going.

"People have to really believe that I did it. And that's going to take a lot more than a wardrobe change. You can't just throw some eyeliner on me and expect people to believe I concocted a premeditated plan to blow up a factory."

"*Thank you,*" Narissa exclaimed.

"What are you proposing?" Thames asked, straight-faced.

I looked him dead in the eye. "We tell them the truth."

"The truth?" he said, although less incredulously than I expected.

"Yes. I go on air—as myself, no makeup, no theatrics—and tell them what really happened. I tell them the story of the poor 'unassimilated' teenager, who's been imprisoned and abused and separated from her family and just finally had *enough*. I'll tell the world why I really blew up that factory: because I didn't want to be responsible for giving you more firepower."

He shared an involuntary look with Narissa. I plowed ahead. "This will take time. I need to record a dozen videos—at least—and release them over the course of several weeks."

His eyes returned to mine. "That's a big investment for a petty terrorist."

"Petty?" I scoffed, mimicking one of Nic's snorts. "I blew up your factory. I ruined your weapon. I know Red Rain was your big project of the year. I know that virus hit several of your fancy government servers. If that were petty, you would have covered it up already." I threw his own words back at him with as much sass as I could muster. "You said yourself—terrorists don't typically come out of the woodwork, release a mastermind-level virus on the internet, and then vanish into obscurity."

He made a vague gesture of consent.

I straightened, drawing on a confidence I couldn't feel. "You can't have your tidy takedown. Not this time. I've caused far too much chaos to be swept under the rug by a carefully edited video. If you botch this, people are going to know that I did a number to the United you can't cover up and started a rebellion you can't contain."

He leaned back in his chair. "I think you're giving yourself too much credit."

"Am I? Then why are you using me at all?"

The silence was embarrassing, and he knew it.

"People are already wondering how—and why—some Mennonite-looking teenager destroyed a factory and released a deadly virus onto the internet. If this were easy to explain away, you would have done so already. But people aren't buying your press releases and official statements, are they?"

My mind began to connect the unspoken dots. Maybe that was why they were using me, why they were willing to go through all this pomp and circumstance for a couple of videos: I broke the mold, and there was no putting it back together again.

Pride rippled through my nerves and strengthened my voice. "You can't just lump me in with the usual criminal riffraff. I don't fit your profile. People are asking questions, and that's why you need them to see me on camera. You need me to explain my motives and give you a target to shoot at."

He studied me, eyes holding neither agreement nor fear.

"If you want this to go away, we have to do it right. People will believe it, because it will be the truth. Give me time to sell them on my story—at least two weeks—and then, *and only then*, can you take me down."

He lifted his eyebrows. I added one last layer of security.

"If you want your clean, one-and-done takedown—where I record a statement and you swiftly swing in and oust me—then you'll have to find another actor."

I let the threat incubate in the silence.

I'll never know how Thames would have responded to that, because Narissa answered for him by clacking her scissors together twice. "Well," she chirped, "at least let me trim your dead ends."

*

"You convinced him to do what?"

It was several hours later at lunch, and Narissa and I had finally settled our battle of the wills over how short my hair should be. Unsurprisingly, her definition of "dead ends" was far more generous than mine. We'd finally agreed to take three inches off, and while I still felt like she'd been too excited with the scissors, I had to admit that my hair looked amazing. She'd slathered my scalp with a dozen products and used a curling iron to coax some bounce into my flat locks. For the first time in years, I felt pretty, and I was more than a little miffed that Nic hadn't commented on my haircut yet.

"I convinced him to let me tell the truth," I repeated. I pulled my hair over my shoulder and pointedly ran my fingers through the loose curls. Not that Nic had noticed the last three times I'd done it.

"I don't understand." He jabbed assorted steamed vegetables with his fork. "Why?"

"Why not? It will be more convincing."

He wagged his head. "It makes absolutely no sense for them. It's suicidal."

Now I was miffed for more reasons than one. "It was *your* idea! I was just taking your advice!"

"I told you to buy us time. I didn't tell you to be honest."

I sighed and flopped back in the chair. "You're right, I should have known better. None of your plans involve honesty."

There was a beat of silence. Before I could decide whether or not I should apologize, Nic spoke again. His voice was kinder this time.

"Look at it this way. From what you've told me, you've convinced him to let you go on air and tell your whole life story. Being contained in a camp, forced labor, family separation—the works. Right?"

"Yeah, I think so."

"You've basically convinced him to let you rip the United to shreds on live TV."

I sat up.

"What happens to people like you is not something the United talks about. Concentration camps don't exactly support an aesthetic of tolerance and prosperity. Sending an underage girl to a male prison in the middle of the ocean doesn't make them look like the benevolent, caring parent they pretend to be."

"Does anyone really believe that story, though?"

The look in Nic's eyes could only be described by one word—sad. "Enough of them do." He laid his fork down in the pile of obliterated vegetables. "Look, I don't know how much TV you've watched—"

"As little as possible."

"But the United is a very talented actor. They are professionals at using editing and lies to make any situation look good. They can explain anything away with a few tweaks in vocabulary. By slapping some prepackaged labels on you, they can easily make the concentration camps look like an act of mercy—if you only see the outside."

I nodded. I'd seen it done. Years and years of gaslighting and conditioning had shown me just what expert manipulators the United could be. "So what are you getting at?"

"I'm saying it doesn't make sense for Thames to let you go online and air the United's dirty laundry. Your story is not one they want told."

I chewed that thought and a piece of chicken. "Are you sure convincing the internet that I'm telling the truth isn't the bigger problem?"

"I doubt it. They don't tend to concern themselves with pedestrian issues like truth. Like you said—there's no reason they can't just fake a video and sweep this under the rug. That's what they usually do. Besides, airing your story will create more problems than it will solve. At the very least, it's going to get some feminists riled up."

I wanted to laugh, but I suddenly realized the situation wasn't funny. The sense of unease that I'd been harboring returned to my stomach like a stale biscuit. *Something's not right. It shouldn't be this easy.* I tried to swallow the feeling with my bite of food and only barely succeeded.

"So what should I do?" I asked after I'd calmed my stomach with a gulp of water.

Nic shrugged. "If he's going to let you talk, do it. Just don't be surprised if he offers a lot of 'creative direction.'"

"Do you think he's planning on editing the footage?"

"You can only fix so much in post."

The wave of confidence I'd been riding crashed into the shore. I thought I'd cornered Thames, called a little of his bluff. But Nic reminded me that we still knew absolutely nothing. I had no idea what Thames was planning.

And until I found out, I might be playing right into his hand.

The fact that the sign was red made me stop and stare at it. So much of my life had been controlled by red signs—usually accompanied by a screech of denial—that it seemed ominously ironic that this red sign had been installed specially for me.

Thames had spared no expense on the recording studio. For some reason, I had expected to record my videos sitting in front of a laptop with some headphones—like most teenagers record videos. But Thames had procured a behemoth of a camera that looked like it cost more than a small car. It hung on a sleek robotic arm, wires snaking up to the ceiling. The elongated lens stared condescendingly down at the room.

In its line of sight was a plain metal chair. Behind that, a frame draped with a huge sheet of obnoxiously green fabric. The whole place was bleached with white light from the dozen lamps crammed into every corner.

Suddenly, I was very glad I had been assigned a stylist.

Thames was in the control booth, visible through a plexiglass window. Servers, soundboards, and monitors crowded the room, barely leaving enough space for the man himself as he hunched over a keyboard.

"Have a seat, Philadelphia," he said, his voice coming from some invisible speaker.

I did as I was told, sitting up straight with my feet flat on the floor.

Thames cast a side glance at me while he fiddled with the sliders on a soundboard. "You're not being interrogated."

"Coulda fooled me," I muttered under my breath.

"Relax," came the repeated admonition.

I sighed and tried to rearrange myself. After a few awkward attempts, I settled on crossing one leg over my knee and folding my hands in my lap.

"Better." He flicked a switch, and the playback monitor above the camera blinked to life. I couldn't help but jump when I saw myself reflected on the viewscreen.

I looked good, I had to admit. Narissa's fawning had done its job; with a curling iron and concealer, she had smoothed over my imperfections and made me look far more put together than I felt.

"All right, before we begin…" I looked up to see Thames scrolling on a tablet. "There are some rules."

I didn't bother to conceal my eyeroll. *Here we go with the 'creative direction.'*

"I want you to start by introducing yourself. Tell them your name, your age, and that you're here to share your story."

Well, that's easy enough. "Okay."

"As you're describing the events, do not name anyone else by name. Do not give any specific locations. Refer to everything in the generic."

"What?"

He kept reading. "You should not name anyone by name—including Ambrose, myself, Dr. Nic, and Cea—or give any locations. Do not tell them you were sent to Mars; simply say you were on 'a research base.' Don't call it 'Red Rain'; call it 'the weapon.'"

"Let me get this straight." My tone was laced with enough incredulity to kill a cow. "You want me to explain to the internet how I got involved with Red Rain—including blowing up a factory of it—without actually calling it 'Red Rain.'"

He tossed the tablet on the desk. "Exactly."

"Why?" I spat back.

He looked up and met my gaze. "If you want me to give your family clean files, you'll do as I say."

I glowered. That threat was the dictatorial equivalent of "because I said so," and we both knew it.

"Besides," he said in a diplomatic tone that did absolutely nothing to restore the morale in the room, "terrorists don't typically disclose their accomplices and whereabouts on live TV. There is a certain *anonymity* to this art."

I slumped back in the chair, crossing my arms. He wasn't entirely wrong; if I were a real terrorist, I wouldn't want to make it easy for the United to find me. I guess my videos would seem more realistic if I acted like I was still on the run from the officials.

But hang on… "Then why would I tell them my real name?"

He bestowed me with another one of his patronizing frowns. "It's not that hard to ID you from the security footage. Everyone already knows who you are."

He turned back to the monitor, leaving me to drown in the thunderous silence his words created in my head. He was right—you could clearly see my face in the clip, and the internet had spread that video like wildfire. That meant thousands, maybe millions, of strangers knew my name. More importantly, hundreds of government officials knew it, too.

And, according to them, I no doubt *was* a terrorist.

Thames spared me the horror of wallowing in that revelation. "Stop sulking and sit up straight, Philadelphia."

I shakily did as I was told. "Where—where should I start, then?"

"Wherever you want. Remember, it's your job to convince me—the viewer—that you're the one behind the terrorist attack on Rott. So, convince me."

Was that a threat? His voice was so controlled that I couldn't tell.

"You're on in two minutes."

The camera whirred. I looked up to see the robotic arm angling the camera closer to my face. The lens twisted back and forth as it focused on me. My glassy reflection filled the viewfinder, where all the fear and trepidation on my face were projected in unnervingly high definition.

I saw rather than felt sweat bead on my forehead. "Will it be live?"

"I don't think that's wise, do you?"

No, I definitely don't.

I swallowed, but nothing slid down my throat, not even air. All my confusion and annoyance at Thames evaporated as I collided with the reality that I had absolutely *no* idea what I was doing.

How on earth was I supposed to convince millions of strangers that I'd become the center of a war I didn't mean to start?

How even *did* this all get started? Nic had started it, of course, when he summoned Ephesus and then Dad to Mars. But I couldn't just talk about them— if this was going to work, it had to be about me.

As if noticing my discomfort—not that it wasn't blatantly obvious— Thames reached out with a suggestion. "Why don't you talk as if you're explaining it to your father?"

My last memory of my father flashed before my eyes—and it wasn't a pleasant one. "My... dad?" I croaked.

"Of course," Thames soothed. "What would you tell him if he were here?"

The words leapt to my mind before I could consciously produce them.

This is all your fault.

I flinched. How could I explain this to my dad? It was, in a very real way, his fault that I blew up the factory on Rott. I blew up that factory because he'd completed Red Rain. He'd given the United a weapon, and I couldn't live with that. I blew up that factory because I didn't want to be like him.

A weight of complex emotions I couldn't process, let alone swallow, clogged my throat. I shook my head to dissipate the visions of my father, searching instead for a neutral face. I couldn't talk to my dad right now. Who else could I explain this to?

Her name came to me like a comforting hug from a friend. *Cami.* I could talk to Cami.

I almost laughed. Cami had no idea what had happened to me after I'd been taken from camp, and if she ever found out, she would *demand* the full story. I didn't know if I'd ever see her again, but if I did, I would definitely have some explaining to do.

I took a deep breath and crystallized the memory of her face. I imagined her sliding across the bus to sit next to me, pressing her arm to mine and lowering her giggling voice as if we were about to share a great secret. I pictured her brother Aid twisting around and looking over the back of the seat in front of us, pretending to be eavesdropping and knowing we both didn't care if he heard.

A little smile crept to my lips, and with that, I knew I was ready.

I became aware of Thames counting down. "On in three, two, one..."

The *On Air* sign flickered on.

I looked straight into the camera lens.

"My name is Philadelphia Smyrna."

6

"That was too easy."

We were in my room after dinner. This time Nic was using a tablet he'd borrowed from the computer lab as a makeshift radio. He'd picked the music before he'd even knocked on my door, and, much to my surprise, he'd held true to his word and dredged up something from the 00s. Also to my surprise, the artificial music, that was somehow both too-bright and too-brooding all at once, was even worse than the noise Ephesus used to subject me to.

I held my tongue, however, partially because Nic had taken the words right out of my mouth. Once I got started, recording turned out to be way easier than I expected.

I'm not sure how long I rambled. Long enough that Thames had to cut me off and tell me that was "enough for today." I started the story with the day we were forced into a containment camp for refusing to sign the file that said we denied all religious, racial, and national identities. I talked about Mama dying, Ephesus getting sent away and reported dead, and Dad being called to work on a "special project."

I tripped when I recounted how Stanyard and Mira had abandoned their family to live with outsiders. Even though I didn't mention him by name, the memory of Stanyard turning his back on me in the schoolyard intertwined with the memory of him running away down an alley, leaving me to die. The images flickered back and forth like a glitched film, threatening to trap me in a replay of abandonment that would never end.

Thames inadvertently broke the cycle by asking a question and prodding me to continue, and I was able to pick up my sentence and keep going. I had just shared how I was forced to stay behind and be adopted by Mrs. Nolan when he cut me off, which I suppose was as good a cliffhanger as any.

I was surprised at myself, but I was even more surprised that Thames hadn't given me any further direction. He hadn't interfered at all, except to remind me once or twice with a subtle shake of his head to steer clear of proper names. Otherwise, he'd let me talk uninhibited, spewing as many of the

United's dirty secrets as I wanted, without even the slightest flicker of emotion on his face.

I had planned to tell Nic that. I'm sure he would have been as surprised as I was, but he didn't seem too interested in asking about my day. Instead, he thrust my reader at me and repeated, "That should *not* have been that easy."

I humored him. "What was too easy?"

"Hacking onto the internet."

My shock rose to match his. "What? You did it already?" I looked down at my reader and toggled to the connections menu.

"Yeah. Didn't even take an hour. I found a couple networks, but 'NCC1701D' was the easiest to hack into."

My reader confirmed his statement. The networks menu showed two options. "Wing B Guest" was the aptly, if not patronizingly, named closed network we were supposed to be on. Nic had disabled that one and switched my reader to the new network, which boasted a pleasantly strong signal.

"What can this network access?"

"Just the United internet. I haven't found any servers or clouds shared on the network yet. I might try some of the other networks to see if I can hack into their communication channels—"

"Wow," I interrupted him, partially because I didn't realize he was still talking.

His eyebrows met his hairline.

I clarified. "I can't remember the last time I was on the 'regular' internet."

His lips twitched, but I don't think it was from amusement. "Just remember, if someone asks you for sensitive information, it's a scam."

If his tone had been any drier, I would have thought he was cracking a joke. As it was, he sounded more serious than anything else.

I opened a blank browser window, mostly just to see if it worked. The choices of unrestricted internet access should have astounded me, but I knew without thinking what I wanted to search for. Unfortunately, it was also the one thing I had no idea how to find.

"Have you looked at our files?"

He nodded slowly, as if he had been waiting for me to ask.

"And?"

"Currently, I can neither confirm nor deny whether or not Thames is telling the truth about our families."

"As per usual," I consented, "but how so?"

"Well, according to their files, they're all still contained at Street 17 camp. Your father, brother, *and* Cea."

A brief shot of illogical hope raged through me, but my conscious mind quickly caught up. "There's no way that's true."

"I agree. Especially when there's no record of your reassignment to Mars."

"I'm sorry, what?" I was surprised my brain used actual words rather than stunned silence to communicate my reaction.

He nodded again, even more slowly. "I don't know what to tell you, but according to the main records, Ephesus never went to Mars, let alone died and came back to life. Your father never went to Mars either, and there's no record of him being involved in any jailbreaks or lab explosions—all of which seem pertinent."

A revolting sense of déjà vu washed over me. Wasn't it only a week or two ago that I'd had this same conversation with someone else?

It's bizarre… It's not like it's confidential. It's like Nic never existed.

I stared at him, as if studying his neglected mustache would help me put the pieces together. "Has your file changed?"

Uninhibited offense burned in his eyes. "No. According to the records, I'm still the governor of Base #9.6.11, which is doing quite swimmingly, not that you care."

That information definitely seemed like something we should both care about.

I can't find anything in the news, not even on the Martian sites, about his arrest. There's nothing linking him to the virus. His file hasn't had any new entries since he was granted governorship of the base.

I jumped to the most obvious explanation. "Are there other, less-public records?"

He twisted his hand in a "maybe, maybe not" gesture. "There could be sealed files. I'll definitely keep looking. But the records I hacked into aren't exactly the kind you can pull at a library. And besides, they made the effort to update *your* file."

He made no attempt to hide the scorn in his voice.

An instinctive shroud of fear fell on my shoulders. "What does it say?"

"Only that you had a perfect academic record and an acceptable compliance rate… until you blew up a factory on an island you weren't supposed to be on."

"I don't follow."

"Me neither," he admitted, and the coyness left his voice. "I don't know what's going on, but there's no record of you going to Mars. Nothing about turning me in." He related that fact with no malice at all. "Nothing about being used as a hostage. Nothing about escaping or being sentenced to Rott. There is literally nothing on your file except your graduation and some pending job applications, until a week ago."

"A week ago," I repeated, the underlying significance of those words not escaping me.

"Yup," he confirmed. "They had us out for six days. We really *could* be anywhere. They must have put us both in a medically induced coma—which is *not* a good sign for your mental health after sustaining multiple brain injuries."

I decided not to dwell on that last part, mostly because there was no space in my conscious thought to even process what that could mean. "So what does it say happened a week ago?"

"You were caught on camera assisting in the destruction of a factory on Rott, and that's propelled you to Public Enemy No.1."

I tried to breathe slowly through my nose and hoped he would keep talking and explain.

He did keep talking, but he didn't explain anything. Instead, the more he revealed, the less sense everything made.

"As soon as that security footage was leaked onto the internet, there's a flurry of activity on your file. All of a sudden, there's a top-level investigation into what was happening on Rott. The big boys are trying to figure out what that factory was making and who was behind it all, and you're their best lead."

I shook my head, as if I could rattle some logic into place. "Wait, they didn't know we were making Red Rain?"

"If they did, they aren't calling it by name."

Thames hadn't wanted me to mention the name "Red Rain" on air—but somehow those facts didn't seem related.

"Let me get this straight," I said, even though I knew things were anything but straight. "According to the public records, the United didn't know what was going on—on Mars, on Rott, any of it—until that video leaked."

He nodded. "Thames is telling the truth about one thing—that video gave them a PR nightmare. I'm just not entirely sure who 'they' are anymore."

"But I thought the United was making Red Rain for themselves."

"I still think that's the case," Nic said. I couldn't gauge the level of confidence in his voice. "The computers on Rott were connected to some top-level government servers, so at least *someone* from the United is involved. Plus, that factory cost millions and would have taken months to build—not exactly rouge rebels making Molotov cocktails in the garage."

He sighed. "The easiest explanation is that the project was top-secret, and when the video got leaked, some departments got their wires crossed. If that's the case, the records should sort themselves out in a few days, they'll get their tidy little social media takedown, and everything will go back to normal."

He sounded like he was trying to convince himself more than anything. It didn't sound like it was working.

I wanted to believe it too. Because if the "easy explanation" wasn't true, the alternative was far worse. If the United wasn't making Red Rain, then who was?

I grasped at our failsafe. "What about the virus? Did it—"

"The virus didn't spread very far," he said without the least bit of concern, "but it still took care of Red Rain."

"How can you be so sure?"

"I'm never sure of anything," he said, and I wondered if he actually lived by that mantra. "But the thing about the Red Rain formula is that it was new data. New data is much easier to erase, because there are fewer copies. And based on how hush-hush this whole project was, I can guarantee you they weren't uploading backups to public databases or sharing the formula in chain emails."

I had to admit that was probably a safe assumption.

"I'm not saying they won't try to reconstruct it, but they have their work cut out for them. I saw what that virus did to those servers. Whoever funded that factory, they won't be rebuilding it anytime soon."

I swallowed a prayer and hoped Nic was right. *Please, God, never again.*

"You should be proud of yourself," Nic huffed. "They're crediting you with the virus, too. It was clear it originated on Rott, so, yet again, they're assuming you're the criminal mastermind here."

He had no idea how much I would have loved to share the blame with him. "Why is my file the only one that's been updated? You were in the video too."

"You can't identify me, though. You're the obvious scapegoat."

It's not that hard to ID you from the security footage. Everyone already knows who you are.

I stared down at my reader, which felt strangely cold in my hands. My cursor still blinked in the empty "search" box.

"Look it up for yourself. I sent you a chat with instructions on how to look up the files."

"You sent me a what now?"

"Unless you want me knocking on your door at all hours of the night…"

I grimaced.

"…I need another way to contact you. So I installed a secure messaging system. Well, semi-secure."

I arched an eyebrow.

He shrugged. "Nothing's perfect. But you have to at least be *trying* if you want to spy on the chat records from this app, and as long as nobody's thinking to look, we should be safe."

He tapped the screen. "This *is* a public network. I'm guessing that's why it was so easy to get onto—it's probably a free wifi connection they didn't realize was in range. But that means anyone with administrative access to the network has the ability to monitor the activity of connected devices. But as long as they don't realize that I've hacked the blocks and connected the reader to this network, they won't be looking. But still, watch what you say."

I nodded and closed the browser window.

"I saved it in one of the folders under 'Users: Philadelphia.' I tried not to make it *too* obvious by putting a shortcut on the homepage, in case anyone else picks up your reader. But you won't have trouble finding it."

He didn't offer any more explanation. He didn't even say goodbye; he just turned to leave, taking the radio with him.

My exhausted consciousness became aware of the idiotic music again. I stifled a headache-induced moan.

He glanced back from the doorway. "I'll find out what's going on. Just keep stalling Thames. As long as possible."

I managed a nod, grateful when the door shut behind him.

7

I never did find the chat app. I spent an hour pawing around the menus on my device, opening every program I came across, and none of them had messaging capabilities. I'm sure it wasn't an actual hour, but with how badly my head hurt, it felt like a torturous eternity. Before long, my eyes started to blur, and I was having trouble concentrating on the file names.

It even felt like the folders kept changing. At first, I was sitting at the foot of my bed, but when my headache got too much to bear, I laid down on the pillow. I held my reader above my head and went back to the main menu, and I could have sworn the file list was longer and in a different order. I skimmed through it and tried to pinpoint exactly what was different, but by that point I could barely read the names of the folders.

I gave up in frustration and closed my eyes, hoping the darkness would relieve some of the pain. I ended up passing out, fully clothed on top of the blankets.

My doorbell woke me up. "Phil!" Someone yelled at me through the speaker. "Phil?" They repeated my name a few more times, long enough for me to process that it was Nic speaking.

I sat up. "What?" I yelled—more like rasped—having no idea if he could hear me or not.

"You're about to miss breakfast," he declared, and, having apparently done his friendly duty, left.

I tried to calculate what time that meant it was and failed. Food didn't sound particularly enticing, but my head still ached dully, and I figured starving myself was not a good way to avoid another migraine.

I stood up. Instantly the weight of the bad night's sleep fell on my aching joints, crushing my mood. I stumbled to the bathroom, took one look at my grotesque appearance, and decided I had zero motivation to fix it. I settled for containing my hair in a bun and changing my shirt for one that was less wrinkled. Narissa would fix the rest later.

I made my way to the cafeteria and found the buffet already swept clean, but someone had made up a plate and left it on the counter for me. Whether it was the cook or Nic I had no idea, but I took it gratefully.

I decided to take advantage of the empty room and linger over my meal, cold or not. After a few bites, I took my reader out of my pouch, opened the Bible folder, and there it was—the messaging app. At least, I assumed it was a messaging app, based on the fact that the icon was a speech bubble.

You won't have trouble finding it.

My annoyance at Nic faded just a little as a small smile tugged on my lips.

I decided to deal with the app later and opened the Bible to the chapter I had been reading last. It was one of my favorites—from the Gospel of Mark—but I didn't get more than a few verses in before I realized I couldn't concentrate.

It wasn't that the passage didn't make sense—I practically had it memorized. It was like my eyes couldn't focus on the words. I would read a sentence, and by the time I got to the next one, I would forget what I had just read. I kept losing my place and having to read simple phrases over and over. It was like the words were getting lost in translation between my eyes and my brain, and after twenty minutes of struggling, the only thing I was sure of was that my headache was back.

It was a relief when a guard interrupted me to take me to Thames. I left my reader in my room, charging.

"You look awful," was how Narissa greeted me when I walked in.

I just nodded. It was too truthful a statement to be offensive.

I sat down on the chair in front of the greenscreen, and she started tugging on my tangles. "Are you sure you want to record today?"

"She needs to." Thames appeared in the control booth. "We need to stream a video daily if we want to keep your numbers up."

Narissa grunted. "I'm gonna need more than concealer to make this work."

Thames lowered his tablet long enough to study me. "Did you not sleep well, Philadelphia?"

Like you care. "I'm fine—I just had a headache."

"How bad was it?"

"It's gone now," I lied. I had no desire to discuss my health with him. "How are—ow—my numbers?" I changed the subject, trying not to complain as the hair on my aching skull was yanked around. It was my fault for not brushing it last night.

"Acceptable," he replied, which really didn't answer the question. "But we need consistent videos over the course of several days to truly garner attention. I want you to keep today's video short—no more than fifteen minutes."

"No problem." We'd be lucky if my headache let me get out a complete sentence.

"I want you to talk about going with your father to the base, finding out your brother worked there, getting lost, and accidentally discovering Wing 74."

"Okay."

"Remember—don't tell them that the base was on Mars. Just say 'it was on the other side of the country.' Call Dr. Nic simply 'the governor.'"

"Fine."

"End when you discover Cea deleted the security footage showing you breaking into Wing 74. That should be enough—"

"Wait, Cea did what?"

He arched an eyebrow. "Don't you remember?"

I remembered watching the tapes with Cea after I'd gotten lost wandering the halls of the base. I remembered her playing dumb about Wing 74. And I *vividly* remembered watching the recordings of Ephesus and the emotions they brought.

And now I remembered the screech the terminal had made when I'd tried to replay the video of me walking into Wing 74.

Error: File not found.

"That was Cea?"

Thames nodded in time with my lagging thoughts.

Of course it was Cea. She'd deleted the record to try and keep Nic from finding out. I'd never put two and two together, but looking back, it made perfect sense.

What didn't make sense was how Thames knew all of that. Come to think of it, he seemed to have a disturbingly detailed knowledge of my movements on Mars, almost like someone had printed out a complete itinerary for him.

"How do you know all this?" I tried to make my voice sound curious, not accusatory.

Narissa told me to look up so she could slather my undereye with concealer, so I couldn't see Thames's expression as he replied, "We have all the records from the base."

They must have kept really good records. It probably didn't take a computer genius to figure out that Cea had deleted the footage; I'm sure there was a log somewhere that proved her credentials had been used to override the file. But to know that she had done it while we were in the viewing room together would have required watching the cameras in that room. To know that we were in the viewing room at all would have required reviewing a ton of security footage to track our movements. I had never told anyone except my father about watching the tapes with Cea, and, by his own admission, Thames hadn't been talking to my father or Cea recently.

Narissa finally stopped touching my eyeballs. I looked over at Thames, but he had gone back to staring at a monitor. If he'd picked up on my suspicion, he didn't seem bothered by it.

I tried to organize my thoughts around the ache in my head. Someone had done their research—and a lot of it. Someone had taken the time to scour the records from Mars and track my movements from the moment I got to the base. That seemed like a herculean effort when my involvement with Wing 74 was, at best, peripheral. If they had tracked my father or brother I would have understood, but why pay so much attention to me?

Clearly, someone was deeply invested in my time on Mars. The question was: Why?

✳

Nic had already moved on to dessert by the time I got to the cafeteria for lunch. "How was work?" he quipped without looking up from his tablet.

I ignored the sarcasm in his voice because I was relieved he was finally asking. "Creepy and weird."

He spared me a sideways glance.

I shoveled a spoonful of whatever was on the buffet onto my plate and sat down across from him. "Did you know Cea deleted the video of me breaking into Wing 74?"

He put his tablet down. "I'm going to need some context."

"Remember when I got lost on the base and accidentally broke into Wing 74?"

"The beginning of the end."

"Well, after you found me, Cea and I went to the security room and reviewed the tapes to figure out where I went."

"Smart." It wasn't sarcastic.

"She claimed she didn't know where Wing 74 was—said it was probably unfinished."

He nodded. He didn't seem very interested in my story, but to his credit, he kept his eyes on me.

"Well, after she left me alone, I tried to pull up the video to look at Wing 74 again, but it said the file couldn't be found."

"She deleted it," he surmised.

"I guess so."

"First I'm hearing about it," he answered my original question.

Wherever Thames got the information, it wasn't from Nic. I chewed a bite of the ambiguous pasta I'd slopped on my plate and tried to determine the significance of that. "How did you find out I'd broken into Wing 74?"

"Carnegie told me. And besides, I had backups of all the security footage from Wing 74 on a dedicated server. She would only have deleted the public copy on that terminal."

I twirled the pasta around my fork. Even Ephesus had mentioned seeing the tape of me getting into Wing 74. Clearly, Cea's coverup had done absolutely nothing—which made it all the stranger that Thames knew about it.

I looked up at Nic. "Thames knew Cea had deleted the video. He specifically asked me to talk about it on air."

I could tell by the way his eyes flickered and then darkened that it took Nic only a fraction of a second to reach the same conclusion I did.

"Someone went to a lot of work to analyze my every move while I was on Mars," I declared, even though I didn't want to say it out loud.

"Or they've been watching you from the beginning."

I stared at him with unfiltered horror. I hadn't considered it, but it was a much more realistic explanation. "But who?"

He shrugged and sipped his coffee. "Wasn't me. If I'd kept a closer eye on you, we wouldn't be in this mess."

My mind shifted through possible candidates. "Carnegie—?" I ventured, recalling the ancient ghost of a man that had been Nic's assistant.

Nic stared into his cup for a long moment, his face displaying something close to human emotion. "Carnegie kept impeccable records, but sadly we can't blame this one on him."

"Sadly?" I pressed.

Nic looked up. "They killed him after they busted the base—or rather, he decided it wasn't worth living."

"Oh." I shivered. "I'm sorry." I searched Nic's face, wondering if my sympathy would land.

It didn't. He brushed it off with, "He was close to retirement."

I swallowed. "So… who else could it be?"

Nic bravely held my gaze. "I have absolutely no idea."

My mind scrambled for a plausible villain. The United certainly had the power to monitor me that closely, but they hadn't known about Wing 74 until I'd alerted Commander Ambrose. There would have been no reason to watch me before then—no reason that I knew of, anyway. My file also hadn't been updated, so if one of the higher-ups had flagged me for monitoring, they hadn't made a note of it.

Something told me Thames wasn't the mastermind behind it all, either. He hadn't acted like he knew all this when we'd first met in his office a few weeks ago. He'd asked me a lot of inane questions about my involvement with Red Rain—questions he would have known the answer to if he'd followed my movements on Mars from the beginning.

No, it seemed more likely that Thames was getting his information from someone else. I thought back to the hair conditioner that had been left in my room—all the premeditated, sadistic details that had been planned for my arrival. I was now convinced that someone had been watching me closely for a very long time. But who?

And, more importantly, what did they want with me?

8

After lunch I found myself with a near-forgotten novelty: free time. Nic wandered off, and I, having literally no obligations, decided to explore the rest of Wing B.

Next to the cafeteria was a rec room with a few basic pieces of workout equipment and a ping pong table. Beyond that was a computer lab. It was a small room crowded with two computer terminals and a shelf cluttered with tablets, headphones, and other electronic paraphernalia.

At the end of the hall was the lounge. There were a few relatively comfy-looking chairs facing a TV. A rug softened the floor, and the harsh overhead fluorescents had been replaced by homey lamps.

Intriguingly, there was also a small shelf of physical books in the corner. I walked over and scanned the titles. I recognized most of them as popular releases from the last decade, which meant they were all censored media. Still, I wondered about the kind of person who would waste the luxury of real paper books on two prisoners. I ran my hand along the spines to savor the scratch of paper on my fingers, but none of the titles looked interesting, so I left them be.

Out of curiosity, I tried Gate C to see if it was actually locked.

It was. *Worth a shot.*

I retired to my room. Stripping the thin blanket from the bed, I bundled myself on the chair in the corner and took my reader off the charger. I figured now was as good a time as any to try the messaging app. If I was only going to be recording for a half hour a day, I'd have a lot of "free time," and the sooner I could master the internet, the sooner I could be useful.

I fired up the messaging app. The username and password autofilled on the login screen. I read the username Nic had picked for me and almost gagged.

"'peanutp91'?" I muttered, not realizing I had said it aloud. Where did he come up with that? It wasn't even clever.

I logged in. The app was simple enough. The homepage had a search feature and a list of my contacts, of which I had only one—"120518," presumably Nic. The left sidebar held my chat history. I had a dozen unread messages from 120518.

I opened them and saw that Nic had, indeed, left me detailed instructions for how to look up my family's files. A quick skim told me that it involved some creative searching and not a small amount of hacking.

I swallowed a gulp of inadequacy. I had no idea how to do half of what he was asking, and several words were completely foreign to me. Despite the fact that the entire world ran on digital, the internet restrictions at camp had been strict, which meant my computer literacy was limited to emails and designing digital presentations for school.

It didn't help matters that my headache was back—had it ever left?—and the words had begun their slow dance on the screen.

I sent Nic a message.

I NEED HELP WITH THIS

I pondered the words after I hit enter, wondering how he'd react to my neediness. Certain death had made us allies on Rott, but holding my hand while I learned basic computer skills might be going a step too far.

Somewhat to my surprise, he replied almost instantly.

MEET ME IN THE LOUNGE

ARE THERE CAMERAS?

YEAH BUT I FIGURED OUT WHERE THEY ARE

I got up, taking the blanket with me. Nic came out of his dorm and joined me in the lounge, where he wordlessly gestured me towards the chair closest to the TV. I tucked myself into the blanket while he fired up some pedestrian sitcom—something bland enough that we could easily tune it out. I was grateful for the monotony of talking and laugh tracks; it was much gentler on my skull than hard rock.

Nic took the chair next to me. I looked up and realized we were facing away from the room's only security camera, which was rather obviously hanging from the ceiling in the far corner. From this angle, anyone watching wouldn't be able to read our lips or see the screen of my reader.

Nic folded himself into the other chair with a casualness and agility that surprised me. "What do you need help with?"

"Everything," I admitted.

I couldn't tell whether the grimace on his face was one of amusement or annoyance.

"You have to remember, my only experience with the internet is a monitored school computer. I don't know what half these words mean." I held my reader out.

He took it. "It'll just be easier if I do it. Let me—"

"No!"

He stopped mid-keystroke.

"Sorry, I mean, I want to learn. I want you to *show* me how to do it."

Now I could clearly tell he was annoyed. "Phil—"

"Don't tell me we don't have time for that. You got places to be?"

He grunted.

"Look." I took a deep breath and struggled to make my emotions coherent. "I want to be useful. Turning over tables of chemicals and blowing up factories isn't always going to be an option. I need to be able to look this stuff up for myself."

He didn't interrupt.

"I want to learn to program," I confessed. He didn't need to know that, but spelling it out was the only way I could make sense of my own thoughts. "I want to be able to do what Ephesus does. I want to fight back. And if I don't know how to run a simple internet search, how can I learn?"

I'm sure he didn't need the whole sob story, but he didn't disagree with it. "Well," he said after a beat, "I wouldn't call this a 'simple internet search.' It's technically breaking into a government database, just not a very secure one. You can cheat the system by pretending to be an employer doing a background check on a potential candidate, and…"

He paused and rolled his eyes to the ceiling. "Three PhDs, for *this*?"

I smiled.

"Fine," he said with a courage-summoning sigh, "I'll show you." He passed the reader back into my hands. "Start by opening a browser window."

✳

It took three tries. Nic walked me through it once. Then I tried and failed twice to repeat the steps on my own. On the third attempt, I succeeded and was rewarded with the database's homepage. I was elated. Nic was simply relieved.

I looked up Ephesus's file. Nic was right; there was absolutely no record of his time on Mars, much less his death and resurrection. Instead, his file said he had been working for some generic company since getting out of college. A quick internet search revealed that company to be fake; Nic knew as soon as I opened their webpage that it was a farce. I could tell this both fascinated and concerned him—why the façade?

"Do you think the United covered up Mars because they wanted to keep Red Rain for themselves?"

Nic shrugged. "What's there to cover up? All they had to do was say my base violated 'regulations,' close it down, and send your family back to camp. No need to lie about it."

I kept reading, hoping to find a clue. The last entry in Ephesus's file was from a mere 12 hours ago. Suddenly, there was a bold warning that Ephesus was wanted as a suspect in the Rott case and his current whereabouts were unknown.

Nic muttered an oath.

My pulse jumped. "What?"

"His prints have been flagged." He gestured to some icons in the sidebar.

"What's that mean?"

"It means they're actively searching for him. If he checks in anywhere—even borrows a library book using face ID—it will alert the officials. Anyone using his ID, his name, or his fingerprints will get flagged." His eyes shifted to my face. "This is new as of this morning. I checked everyone's files yesterday."

I stared back at him. "They saw my video."

"Pull up your father."

My father's file was much longer. I could tell just by skimming the first few entries that he had been labeled as unassimilated long before there was a term for it. I rapidly scrolled to the end, where the same red-bordered message appeared.

We checked Cea and Nic, but their files remained untouched.

Nic stared at the dated mugshot that decorated his file, his finger tapping out the rhythm of his agitated thoughts. "Have you not mentioned me in your videos?"

"Thames told me to just call you 'the governor.' I'm not supposed to mention Cea either."

"But your father and brother?"

It took me a minute to explain that one. I hadn't named my father or brother on the recording—but I had given my real name. I groaned. "No, but they know my real name—it isn't a stretch for them to look up my family."

Guilt flooded my soul as the realization took hold: I did this. Because I aired my life's story online, my father and brother were now wanted men. If I hadn't agreed to record the videos, would they have gotten away?

Did I make the right choice, God?

"Well, one thing's for certain." Nic's sigh interrupted my self-flagellation. "Thames doesn't know where our families are—and apparently the United doesn't either."

I tried to decide if that was a good thing or not.

We both ruminated for several moments. Nic kept scrolling on my reader. I stared at the TV, watching the characters comically bicker over some plot device. I traced their dramatic hand motions with my eyes, feeling the same flurry of activity in my brain. It was right there—the obvious conclusion—but it ignited so many new unknowns that I could hardly see through the smoke.

"He's not with the United," I declared, desperate to bring some order to the chaos.

I turned to find Nic staring at me. "Thames isn't," I clarified.

"If that's true," Nic's voice was cautious but not doubtful, "he's still a very powerful man with an insane amount of resources."

I knew Thames was working with someone who had a creepy knowledge of my time on Mars—someone who, apparently, knew more about me than the government did. "I suppose that's not much better."

"It's not."

I curled into the chair, suddenly exhausted from the weight of unanswered questions. "What should I do?" More fear came out in my voice than I intended. "I mean, should I just keep recording videos? What if I'm right and he's not with the United? What if he's… worse somehow? Should I try and find out who he's working for?"

"I wouldn't push him," Nic replied, also with more fear than he probably intended. "This is the same man that knocked us both out for a week. Until we know more, he's holding all the cards."

I chewed my fingernail.

"On the bright side," Nic said in a tone that wasn't positive at all, "we'll know the minute your family is found. The entire government is searching for them."

"That's… helpful, I guess."

"Not if the United gets them first."

Don't let that happen, God! Protect them! Hide them!

I pulled the blanket around my shoulders. "What do you think they'd do to them?"

"At this point, I have no idea—and I don't think they do either. According to their files, your father and brother are accessories to some weapons plot the government was completely unaware of. My guess is they want information more than their heads." He handed my reader back to me.

It felt heavy in my lap. "And me?" I ventured.

Nic looked down his nose at me with an unreadable expression. "Let's just say, you might be lucky that Thames and the United aren't sharing intel."

I pinched my eyes shut. *What am I going to do, Holy Spirit?*

Nic took that as his cue to leave. I heard the chair creak as he stood up. "We'll keep digging," he said for the dozenth time. I appreciated his use of the plural. "I'll message you later."

"Yeah, about that." I opened the app. "What's the deal with this dumb username?"

He shrugged. "No deal. It's autogenerated. You can change it to anything you like."

That was a relief. I started pawing around in the settings. "Can't I just be Phil?"

"No," he said so coldly that I stopped and looked up at him. His eyes were dark. "You can't. Don't use your real name or any of your nicknames, not if you want to live."

I flinched.

"I mean it, Phil. Don't even type your name in a chat—even to me. There should be absolutely no connection to the name 'Philadelphia Smyrna' with any of your online activity."

He sighed, but if I was hoping for empathy, I didn't get any. If anything, his voice got harder as he continued. "Thames is right. Everyone knows who Philadelphia Smyrna is now. You can't go back. That girl is dead to you. For the love of God, let her die."

And without any encouraging word to bandage the wound, he left, leaving me alone with my tears.

9

I cried for an indeterminate amount of time. I wanted to pray, but any attempt at words melted into chaotic anguish. After a while, I wiped my face and opened my Bible, but I just ended up crying again because for some reason reading still *hurt* and it was confusing and everything was spinning and I had no idea what was going on.

My tears finally dried from exhaustion. I skipped dinner and went straight to bed, hoping tiredness would pull me under before my emotions returned.

Nic had already eaten and gone by the time I made it to breakfast the next morning, which suited me fine. I didn't want to see him. He was right; what he'd said to me yesterday was the truth, and I hated him for it.

I'm not sure why I'd gotten so upset. I knew I was going to have to change my name. But I guess I imagined it would only change on paper. My official file might say something else, but to my friends and family I could still be Phil.

And maybe that was true—a week ago, before Thames forced me to become "famous." Now the collective forces of the United government were looking for me, and the entire internet knew who I was. Even mentioning my nickname could be a death sentence.

My own name had become a curse to me. Philadelphia Smyrna really did have to die.

And right now, she felt like she was halfway there.

My sour mood—and headache—followed me into the recording studio. I managed to stop crying long enough for Narissa to plaster my face with makeup, but no amount of mascara could conceal how bloodshot my eyes were.

Thames was too engrossed in directing to notice at first. "I'd like to get most of the way through your time on Mars today. Talk about digging for information about your brother, getting a reader with a Bible on it..."

"What?" I grunted.

"The one Mr. Sardis gave you."

I knew what he meant, of course—it was the same reader I had now. When I first came to Mars, I didn't have a Bible, so the kindly horticulturalist had downloaded one from Nic's private server. It was my first indication that Nic wasn't all that he appeared.

"You really want me to talk about that?" My question was genuine, not that you could tell by my tone of voice. I was so used to referring to everything in the generic that I was surprised he wanted me to be explicit about all the illegal media Nic had kept.

"Religion is the lynchpin of your story, is it not?" He finally looked at me. "We're trying to sell them your authentic story, and I think... Is everything all right, Philadelphia?"

I cringed. It was an idiotic question—*You're blackmailing me into recording these videos; everything is definitely* not *all right*—but more bothersome was his use of my name. I loathed how it sounded coming from his lips, and the careless way he tossed it around only added insult to injury. *If I can't use my own name, you can't either!*

I brazenly dismissed his question with a salty, "I'm fine."

"Liar," Narissa hissed in my ear.

I brushed her away. "Stop touching my hair."

Her sculpted eyebrows twitched. She stood back and regarded me for a moment, then obeyed. She dropped her comb into her bag with a contemplative *hmm* and walked away.

"I see," was Thames's only comment. "As I was saying, let's try to get through your reunification with Ephesus, learning about 'the weapon,' and your father's refusal to do the job. I think if you end right when you realize 'the governor' has your father, that will make a great ending, and we can save your improvised escape for tomorrow."

He sounded altogether too chipper about the whole ordeal, like he imagined himself the director of an adventurous TV show. But I was in no mood to argue; I just wanted to get it over with so I could go lie down.

"Sure, whatever," I acknowledged and adjusted my position.

He gave me another sideways glance and started the countdown.

The first half of my stream went, for lack of a better word, "fine." I spoke clearly and coherently, and, with the exception of getting a bit teary-eyed while talking about Ephesus's return, I managed to keep my raw emotions in check. But that was also the problem—there was *no* emotion in my delivery. I droned on in a monotone, gaze wandering anywhere but the camera. In the viewfinder I could see that my eyes were so swollen and bloodshot that I looked drugged.

I could tell by the crease of his lips that Thames wasn't pleased, but he wasn't motivated enough to stop the recording and scold me. He tried various hand motions to get me to be more engaging, but I purposefully ignored them all.

It wasn't until I got to the part about Red Rain that I suddenly remembered I had emotions, and a lot of them.

"I didn't understand exactly what the weapon was," I narrated, "but my brother was insistent that our father not work on it."

I faltered, the competing voices coming back to me.

No! Tell him no! Tell him not to accept. He can't accept.

I remembered Ephesus's panic, the feel of his palms digging into my shoulders as he shook me. I also remembered my own resolution, my calm assurance that I knew who my father was and what he would do.

He won't.

Something hit the back of my throat.

I forced the next sentence out. "Dad… felt the same way."

I won't work on the project. Dead or alive.

My eyes burned. Was I crying again?

"He knew the project would be dangerous in anyone's hands."

Daddy, what happened?

No, my eyes were dry. Dry and on fire.

"He was going to say no. He was going to refuse the project."

I did work on it a little.

I swallowed, but it felt like my throat was cinching shut. Terror filled my lungs, like a panic attack, but deeper, from the furthest reaches of my soul.

"But then…"

Old man, you nearly had it!

Shut up!

"He…"

It was the only way.

My breath was coming hot and fast, but it felt like no air was leaving my lungs on the exhale. With every gasp I was packing my chest tighter and tighter. Full of fear. Full of pain. Full of rage.

Just go. Please. Before you get hurt.

I saw my father's face, his dry and weary eyes gazing into the distance. And then I saw Ephesus, and Nic, and Stanyard, and Ambrose, and every man who had ever betrayed me, abandoned me, lied to me and refused to apologize.

You… wrote the virus.

Nic won't have to use it.

He already did.

The voices heaped on top of each other—lie upon lie, threat upon threat—like endless shovels of sand burying me under and reminding me I wasn't worth believing, worth saving, worth protecting.

Phil, if you don't come now I'll leave you behind!

And through it all my father's last words kept echoing like a wave slapping the shore, wearing my identity down piece by piece like a rock rolled by the river.

Just go.

He never apologized. He never admitted to what he did. He never even said goodbye. And now it was too late.

Just go.

For the first time, I looked dead into the camera.

Thames, oblivious of the impending storm, gestured at me to continue. I spat out the only thing that could justify the emotions clawing at my stomach.

"You betrayed me."

There were the tears again, but they weren't the wet tears of anguish. They were hot and painful, scratching my eyes as I forced them out with all the words I had been hiding for so long.

"This is your fault! All your fault! *You* did this to me!"

I jumped up, shoving the chair out of my way. It toppled backwards into the greenscreen. I heard the stand crash against the wall.

"How could you?" I probably wasn't in frame anymore, but I continued to scream at the camera. "How could you do this to me? You let them win! You let them win!"

I registered that Thames was shouting at me. I looked up to see him pressed against the glass, saying my name over and over, straining to get my attention. Every syllable rammed into my skull, reminding me that everything was out of my control, and I was being played for the fool, and my life was over, and it was all because my father had completed Red Rain.

"Philadelphia! Sit down!"

The curse was out of me before I could stop it. I didn't want to stop it. If I didn't say it, scream it, *do something* to relieve the tension inside of my chest, I knew I would shatter.

"I hate you!"

Thames was silent for a beat—I think because he knew I wasn't yelling at him.

"Philadelphia," he said with a deep breath that fuzzed the intercom. "Sit down. Close your eyes. Breathe."

I ignored all of those admonitions. "I'm not going to do this."

He grabbed a handheld device and smashed a button. "Philadelphia, please..."

"Don't make me do this," I screeched. "Just let me go!"

I stomped to the door. I was surprised that it opened for me; it must not have been locked.

Thames met me on the other side. I tried to shove past him, but he caught my arm. I debated about where to hit him, but before I could react, he grabbed my chin and forced me to look up. He glared at me, but not in a condemning way—it was almost as if he were looking past my eyes, trying to see what was going on behind them.

"Why didn't you tell me you weren't feeling well?" he asked.

I wriggled out of his grasp. "Would you have listened?"

He frowned. "What kind of man do you think I am, Philadelphia?"

The noise I made could most accurately be called a snarl. "Why don't you tell me?"

Nic's warning flashed across my consciousness—*I wouldn't push him*—but at that point I was in so much pain, emotional and physical, that I didn't care. "I know you're not with the United. I know you're lying. Who are you?"

He ignored the question. "Are you still having headaches?"

"Just tell me who you are!"

He had the audacity to shush me. "You need to lie down."

I shrieked in frustration. Filled with utter revulsion for him, I spun away and stormed down the hall. I had no idea where I was going, and I didn't care, as long as it was putting distance between him and me.

"Let me help you, Philadelphia," he called after me, voice temptingly gentle.

"Leave me alone!" I reached the first door down the hall, but before I could see if it would open for me, a gloved hand closed around my wrist. I screamed like I'd been shot and wrenched my warm, but I was rewarded with only pain. The grip didn't give.

A strong arm wrapped around my waist. Someone tall and powerful gripped me to his chest, holding me like you would a rebellious toddler. I fought like one, even though I knew I was hitting only air and body armor.

"Let me go," I cried, more of a moan than a demand.

Thames knelt in front of me. "You're not well."

"Please stop, please stop, just stop…"

"Let me help you," he said again.

I sobbed. "No." *I don't want your help. I don't need your help!*

Thames stood up. "Take her to her room. I'm calling a doctor."

The recessed logical part of my brain acknowledged that was probably a good thing, but adrenaline still burned my nerves, and all I could remember was that he was evil, and I couldn't trust him, and I wasn't safe, and I didn't want him—any of them—to *touch* me.

I shoved, but against what, I couldn't tell. The room was spinning, and my vision was blurry from both tears and a migraine. I collapsed, losing the coordination to do anything but weep.

Let me help you.

The last thing I remembered was feeling very, very alone as big arms picked me up and carried me down the hall.

10

By some miracle, I didn't pass out. I was terrified to think what another blackout would do to my brain, and that fear gave me the motivation to hang onto my last shred of consciousness. I fought through the blinding pain and unstoppable tears to hold onto my self-awareness, narrating what was happening to keep myself grounded in reality.

A guard carried me back to my room. I counted the *whoosh* of each door as we passed through it. He set me on the bed and told me the doctor would be right there. I nodded precisely three times, counting each motion. I took my shoes off—one at a time—and removed my jacket—one sleeve at a time. I laid back mechanically on the pillow and counted off the seconds until I heard the door open again.

The doctor dutifully checked me over, looking in my eyes and throat and taking my pulse, but it didn't take a PhD to know what was wrong with me. I'd banged my head one too many times over the past few weeks, and it wasn't healing.

The doctor sat down in the chair and started typing on a tablet. "Do you know how a concussion works, Miss Smyrna?"

I was still wounded about my overused name, but the fact that he was addressing me so professionally helped me put some distance between reality and my emotions. "No."

"Essentially, the damaged part of your brain isn't getting enough oxygen, so it can't function normally. To compensate, your brain tries to use other pathways to complete the same tasks—it takes the 'scenic route,' so to speak, and that can feel very frustrating."

That's why reading hurts so much. It made me feel a little better to know that it wasn't my fault.

"The trick is to let those parts of your brain rest and then slowly exercise them until they're functioning normally, just like any injured muscle. Your problem is that you're not resting."

I turned my head to see him gazing over the tablet at me. "Talk to Thames about that."

"Oh I will be. In the meantime, you need to limit how much time you're spending on that reader."

My eyes reflexively looked to where the device was charging on my nightstand.

"At this point in your healing, I only want you using screens for twenty minutes at a time, and only two or three times a day."

You mean I can't read? The objection rippled through my body like a pinched nerve. *But my Bible… How many times do I have to go through this?* I closed my eyes.

The doctor kept droning on. "The rest of your day should be spent resting and doing light mental activities."

"Like what?" *What is there to do around here that doesn't involve screens?*

"Do you like to color?" It was said so patronizingly.

"I… don't know. Can't remember the last time I did it."

"Try it. Coloring would be good for you. Or ask that friend of yours to play some easy games with you."

"Nic?" *Of course, who else is there?* "You might have to give him a doctor's order to make him do it."

He chuckled. "I also want you to do about thirty minutes of gentle exercise a day. Slow walking on the treadmill would work."

I sighed, but there was nothing to argue with. I wanted to get better. I *needed* to get better. I didn't want reading to hurt for the rest of my life; the Bible was all I had.

"Okay," I said, opening my eyes to look at him. "And thank you."

He smiled, a genuine gesture. "I'll be sending up some pain medication. Follow the dosages on the side of the bottle. It should minimize the pain. If it doesn't work, or your symptoms change, tell them to call me."

"Yes, sir."

He patted me on the shoulder and left.

As soon as the door shut behind him, I sank back and closed my eyes again. *Now* what was I going to do all day? I couldn't read my Bible, I couldn't watch TV (not that there was anything to watch), and getting Nic to "play games" sounded like torture for both of us. And I definitely hadn't seen any coloring supplies laying around.

What's worse, if I wasn't supposed to be using the computer, I couldn't help Nic. I was back to being a useless victim.

I let out a long breath, hoping the motion would relieve my frustration, but the sound just rasped against my throat. *What do I do now, God?*

About fifteen minutes later, my doorbell chimed. "Yes?" I shouted, hoping they could hear me—because I had no intention of getting up to use the intercom.

The door slid open, and Thames stood there.

I jerked upright, every nerve in my body curling from revulsion. In principle, I knew that Thames was holding me hostage and I had no expectation of privacy. But in practice, I assumed he would have the decency not to violate what very little space I had to call my own.

"Get out," I snarled.

He ignored me and walked over. He reached into the sack he was carrying and removed a white pill bottle. He held it out like a peace offering, and I took the bait. I snatched it from his hand and wrenched the cap off, squinting at the label to see the maximum dosage.

I shook three pills into my hand and swallowed them dry. Out of the corner of my eye, I saw Thames offering me a water bottle. The sight of the clear plastic brought back unwanted memories, but I shoved them away and accepted it.

He sat down on the end of the bed while I chugged half the bottle. "I'm sorry," he said when I came up for air.

"For what?" I could think of a dozen things he should apologize to me for, but somehow I doubted any of those were on his mind.

"You should have gotten medical attention a long time ago."

"You shouldn't have kept me in a drug-induced coma for a week."

"It was necessary."

"I don't think you understand the concept of an apology." I downed the rest of the water.

"You'll understand one day."

"Yeah? When?" I glared at him until he met my eyes. "When are you going to tell me what's really going on? When are you going to start telling me the truth?"

He bravely held my gaze. "Philadelphia, the truth is…"

I steeled myself, prepared for him to tell me anything *but* the truth.

"This is all my fault."

I was so startled by the accuracy of that statement that I was speechless.

"I could have prevented all of this."

A million sarcastic replies leapt to my tongue, but I swallowed them. *Let him talk*, the Holy Spirit admonished me. I used all my willpower to make my voice sound curious instead of angry. "What do you mean?"

His eyes drifted to the wall. "I should have never let you go to Mars."

"What?" The confused exclamation ripped out of me before I could filter the emotions attached to it.

"I should have vetoed Dr. Nic's request to have you transferred to Mars with your father. I should have listened to Mrs. Nolan and insisted you stay on Earth. None of this would have happened if you hadn't gone to Mars."

I wanted to hurl. I wanted to scream. And I absolutely wanted to punch him in the face. Memories of Mrs. Nolan's buttery voice and sticky affection weren't helping my self-control in that department, either.

Stay cool, stay cool. It was a disgusting revelation, and it was even more proof that Thames was evil, manipulative, and cruel. Under what circumstances would have it been better for me to be taken from my dad and forcibly adopted by a stranger who hated my religion? But as much as I longed to spit all that in his face, I knew flying into a rage wouldn't get me anywhere. I'd proven that already once today.

Holy Spirit, help me!

"You approved that?" I questioned, after I'd taken a beat to check the temperature of my voice.

He nodded. "All transfer requests from the camps come across my desk."

So that's how you got involved in this. The pieces were starting to snap together, but I needed more. "So you were, like, Commander Ambrose's boss?"

"Regional director, yes."

"And that's your dream job?"

He chuckled dryly. "It pays."

Keep him talking. "So Nic was the one who requested my transfer?"

"Yes, although having met him, I really can't fathom why. He's not much of a family man himself."

I had never stopped to consider why Nic requested me in the first place, and looking back, I suppose it didn't make much sense. It made more sense than whatever warped logic Thames was using to justify his actions, though.

"And you are?" I prodded. "A family man, I mean."

He turned to face me again. "I'm sure this will surprise you, but I actually am. I'm very close to my family."

"Then I don't get it," I said with genuine confusion. "If you're such a big fan of family, why would you want to separate me from my dad? You knew my mom and brother were dead. He was all I had."

"Because," he said without qualm or regret, "you deserved better."

I narrowed my eyes and let him explain.

"You weren't ready for all this... all that. Mars, Wing 74, the politics, the bloodshed. You should never have been involved."

He wasn't wrong, but he also wasn't one to talk. "Then why did you drag me back into it? After we came back from Mars, you could have left my family alone in that camp. You're the one who arrested me to blackmail my father into working on the project. Weren't you?"

Grief pinched his face, but he didn't back down from my stare. "That was not my decision."

I believed him. I was right—Thames *was* working for someone else, someone else who had the final say.

I swallowed. "Then whose decision was it?" *Tell me. Tell me!*

He didn't. "All of this could have been avoided if I had denied Dr. Nic's request in the first place. Mrs. Nolan's application had already been approved—I should have pushed it through. I'm sorry, Philadelphia."

I grasped for words. Utter disgust was competing with my need for the truth. I wanted to show him the door, but I also wanted him to keep talking. I was so close—so close to finding out what was really going on.

Before I could come up with anything, he pulled something else out of the bag and laid it in my lap.

It was a coloring book and a set of colored pencils. I stared at them.

He didn't wait for a reaction. He got up and walked to the door, where he paused and glanced back.

"I'm sorry," he said again. Then, with a sigh that was almost wistful, he added, "When this is all over, I'll do my best to give you a normal life. I promise."

The door shut before I could force anything past the blockage in my throat.

11

I sat on the edge of the bed for a long time, just staring at the colored pencils in my lap. I wanted to chuck them into the wall, to get them as far away from me as possible like they were a ticking bomb about to go off. The colored pencils, the hair conditioner, Mama's suitcase—it was all these little kindnesses and gestures that made me feel threatened and unsafe.

What did Thames really want? I suspected most of what he told me was the truth—at least, it was the truth as he imagined it in his own mind—and that just made his actions all the more confusing and terrifying. He cared about me, or he told himself he did, and yet he was willing to use me and abuse me and ruin my life over and over. Either he was a very sick man, or there was something else going on, something that was bigger than him and his desires.

I suspected it was a combination of both.

One thing I did know for certain: There was someone else behind the curtain. Someone else was involved, and that someone had been the one to blackmail my father into completing Red Rain. They were probably the one with the money—and all the information about my time on Mars. And whoever they were, they must want something more than just a few PR videos. We were in too deep for this to simply be social media damage control. They had an agenda, and until I knew who they were and what they wanted, I would have no idea who my real enemies were.

Just when my grinding thoughts were starting to get painful, my doorbell buzzed again. "What?" I called, tiredly this time.

Nic let himself in.

I sighed. Even though, comparatively, he was the least repulsive person it could have been, I wasn't in the mood for more visitors. "What are you doing here?"

For an answer, he held out a white slip of paper. Even from a distance I could tell it was covered in nearly illegible handwriting—a doctor's note.

I laughed. "I didn't think he would take me seriously."

Nic took the chair across from me and reached for my reader. I didn't stop him. "What happened?"

I tried to decide where to start.

Soft music cued up, then he added, "I saw the stream."

I flinched. "They uploaded that?"

"It was live."

I gaped at him, vacillating between shock and mortification.

He studied me. "I take it he didn't tell you."

I shook my head. *That's why Thames didn't want to interrupt me.* Embarrassment warmed my cheeks. "When did it cut off?"

"Right after 'You betrayed me.'"

I let my breath out, deeply relieved that Thames had been the only one to witness my hysterics.

Nic arched one eyebrow and waited. I rubbed the back of my neck. "I was mad… and had a really bad headache."

His eyes shifted to the pill bottle on the nightstand. "Do they have you on bedrest?"

"Not exactly… but I'm not supposed to be using screens. Guess you're going to have to do all the legwork for now."

"So no reading, huh?" He tapped the screen of my reader.

"Yeah. I guess I'm supposed to color." I tossed the coloring book and pencils towards the end of the bed.

He kept typing and didn't respond. After a minute, I ventured, "Why do you think they're streaming live? That seems risky—if today was any indication."

"They don't have a choice—the United is removing your videos as soon as they're streamed."

"So no one's seeing them?" I felt a chunk of despair drop in my stomach like undigested food. Had I really been wasting all this time and emotional energy for nothing?

"Oh they're seeing them," he assuaged my fears. "You had a good 800,000 viewers on that last one. Going live is helping—it's a lot harder to censor a live video."

"Can I see?" I said, even though I wasn't entirely sure I wanted to watch a recording of myself.

"I'll see if I can find a copy. As soon as the United figured out it was you, they took down the stream. People have been reuploading the recording, but most are getting flagged and taken down within minutes. They probably set up a censorship filter for your face or something."

To think of my face as the object of censorship was both hilarious and utterly dehumanizing. Had Philadelphia become more symbol than person?

"Do you think Thames is the one reposting the video?" I wondered.

"I'm sure he's helping, but most of the uploads are from regular civilians."

I tried to imagine what kind of person would share my videos. Were they other unassimilated? Sympathizers? Were there people out there who cared about what was happening to people like me? How many people like me even were there?

My old camp had been so small, no more than 100 families at its peak, and that had been my entire universe for six years. I had no internet access, and my only connection to the outside had been domineering commanders and belittling schoolteachers. Their mission had been to constantly remind us that we were a dying race, and at some point, somewhere, I had started to believe them.

I realized with some shame that I had never imagined there were thousands—let alone nearly a million—of people like me still out there.

Yet I reserve seven thousand in Israel—all whose knees have not bowed down to Baal and whose mouths have not kissed him...

I registered that Nic was talking. "That's probably why Thames wants you to keep the videos shorter—so they can stream the whole thing before the United has time to catch them and block them. They've been streaming from a different account each time, because the United takes down every account that shares one of your videos."

"Wow," I murmured. I knew this was what we wanted—the entire point of these videos was to cause a stir. And yet, I couldn't help but be mystified that it was actually *working*—as well as be a little bit perturbed that hundreds of strangers were so invested in my story that they'd risk their accounts to share it.

"If we needed more proof that Thames and the United aren't working together, the fact that the government is nuking his videos is decent evidence," Nic mused.

I nodded. "I found out how he got involved in all this. He's a regional director for the unassimilated camps—our transfer requests to Mars had to be approved by him."

Nic knotted his eyebrows together. "How did you find this out? Did he tell you?"

I blushed as I remembered how brazenly I had ignored his advice to "be careful." "Yeah... I kind of blew up at him and demanded an explanation. He gave me half of one."

Nic waited.

"He's basically Ambrose's boss. So I'm guessing that's how he found out about Red Rain—when I reported to Commander Ambrose."

Nic nodded. I slowly put the pieces together in my own mind. "That must be when they decided to keep your research for themselves. But Thames said he wasn't the one who blackmailed my father into completing Red Rain, so someone else is in charge. But he wouldn't say who."

"Unfortunately, until we know who that person is, we really have no idea what we're dealing with."

I replayed all of Thames's words in my head, searching for clues. My mind snagged on the one question I knew Nic could answer.

"Why did you call me to Mars?"

He blinked, caught off-guard by the question.

"Thames said you were the one who requested my transfer."

"Actually, it was Carnegie who recommended it."

I gaped. Carnegie? The frail assistant had hardly given me a second glance the entire time I was on Mars, except to comment on my uncanny ability to bypass security systems.

"He thought it would make your father more compliant if you two were together. He was probably right, but looking back, I see that your father was never the problem. It's always been you."

I took that as a compliment.

The music stopped. Nic stood up and handed my reader back to me. "Here, this should help."

"Help with what?" I picked the reader up and squinted at the screen.

He pulled a pair of earbuds out of his pocket and tossed them in my lap. "Keeping you entertained. I'm not really into games."

I scanned the screen; it was open to my Bible folder. Underneath the text files was a new download—an audiobook.

"Where did you—?"

"I had several saved on my database for Cea. I guess when they scalped my servers they decided to keep my personal library—that's where that music directory came from. I figured it out today because I found some special Eminem recordings I'm pretty sure aren't in the public domain." He shrugged. "Guess you're lucky Thames doesn't seem too concerned with following United censorship laws."

I grinned, feeling the biggest burst of genuine happiness I had in weeks. *Thank you, Jesus.*

I waited until Nic had left before popping the headphones in my ear and relaxing back on the pillow. I picked a book, hit play, and closed my eyes. The lull of the narrator's posh accent pulled me in, and I felt every nerve relax as I absorbed the familiar words without frustration or pain.

I was deep into the Psalms—and probably half asleep—when an obnoxiously loud *bing* shattered my serenity.

I jumped upright. My pulse hit the ceiling and stayed there for several seconds until I realized the sound was coming from my reader.

I looked at the task bar, trying to figure out which program had made the noise. I didn't have any email or social media on this device—what would I be getting notifications from?

Then I remembered—the chat app. Nic must have messaged me.

I opened the program, and sure enough, I had an unread message.

But it wasn't from Nic.

The message—and pending friend request—was from a user named "Aurelius396." There was no profile picture.

A dozen warning bells went off in my head. *No one is supposed to know I'm on here. How did they find me?* Who *found me?*

I took a deep breath. It was probably just spam. If Thames or someone higher up had found out I'd gotten on the internet, they would have just taken my device away or changed the internet access codes—they wouldn't send me a text. There was literally no one else on planet Earth besides Nic who knew I had this device, so there was no way anyone could find me. It was probably just some creep fishing, or whatever slimy people did on the internet these days.

I should just ignore the message and block the request.

But you should at least read it first... just in case it is something bad. You might need to warn Nic.

My hand hovered over the unread icon. It wouldn't hurt to read it, right? It's not like opening the message would set off a bomb or release a virus or anything. That's not how the internet worked.

I wasn't at all confident that clicking on the message would be harmless, but I did it anyway.

The user had sent two simple words, but those words were enough to send me into a tailspin.

HEY PHIL

12

All of Nic's warnings coursed through me like an alarm.

I mean it, Phil. Don't even type your name in a chat. There should be absolutely no connection to the name 'Philadelphia Smyrna' with any of your online activity.

I could think of no good reason why anyone but Nic would know I was online. That meant this person was very, very dangerous.

What do I do? Don't panic. Stop panicking! Just delete the chat, block the user, and tell Nic. They can't hurt you if you don't respond.

I searched for an "options" menu, the device shaking in my hands. But just when I found the drop-down, typing "dots" appeared at the bottom of the screen.

YOU REALLY NEED TO TURN OFF THE SETTING THAT LETS THE SENDER KNOW YOU'VE READ THEIR MESSAGE

I froze. *Nic! Why didn't you tell me?*

I KNOW YOU'RE ONLINE

I still didn't respond. They didn't give up.

I KNOW IT'S YOU PHIL

Block them. Block them, delete your account, and start over.

YOU'RE THE ONLY PERSON ON THIS NETWORK USING AN EREADER. NO ONE ELSE I KNOW USES AN EREADER LIKE A LAPTOP

I opened the drop-down and found the "block" option. I clicked on it, and a bubble popped up asking me to confirm.

Another message came through.

I KNOW THAMES IS HOLDING YOU HOSTAGE

I hesitated. This person knew about Thames, which meant one of two things. One, they *were* Thames, or were working for him. Or, two, they knew what was going on and might be able to help me.

Was it worth the risk? I was running out of options; Thames wasn't being forthcoming, and Nic hadn't found anything out despite two days of searching.

I typed back.

WHO ARE YOU?

The response was instantaneous.

A FRIEND

That could not have been any more ominous.

HOW DID YOU FIND ME?

THROUGH A FRIEND

YOU'RE NOT DOING YOURSELF ANY FAVORS HERE

I KNOW I KNOW. UH HANG ON

I waited. About a minute later, they started typing again.

LET ME SAY IT THIS WAY: YOU'RE LUCKY CEASAR HAS TERRIBLE AIM

Ceasar—that was Cea's codename with the "underground." This person knew Cea, which was a point in their favor. But what did they mean about her aim? Cea had shot at a *lot* of people when we broke out of Thames's office, and most of them she'd hit. I don't remember her missing anyone except...

Hey, drop that gun!

Jayde. She'd shot at Jayde, my sympathetic guard, and missed, hitting the wall behind him. Looking back, I'm sure that had been intentional, all part of the theatrics so that Jayde could play the double agent and help us escape.

My anxiety dissipated as my mind connected the dots. Jayde was a friend and a member of the underground. He had worked for Thames, and assuming nothing had gone terribly wrong in the meantime, presumably still did. He would know Nic and I had been captured—and he might know a lot of other useful things.

Jayde was waiting patiently for me to respond. I took the cue and didn't use his name in chat.

GLAD YOU'VE RECOVERED. DO YOU KNOW WHERE WE ARE?

NO. THAMES'S RECORD SAYS HE CONTRACTED A VIRUS AND WAS APPROVED TO WORK FROM HOME. HE HASN'T BEEN INTO THE OFFICE FOR A WEEK

That confirmed my suspicions—Jayde still worked at Thames's main office, but Thames wasn't there, which meant we were being held somewhere else.

HOW DID YOU KNOW ABOUT THIS NETWORK, THEN?

The dots flickered for a minute while he explained.

THAMES'S GOVERNMENT-ISSUED SPYWARE LETS HIM MONITOR NETWORK ACTIVITY REMOTELY. AFTER I SAW YOUR STREAM, I ASKED AROUND AND WAS TOLD Q HAD BEEN REACHING OUT. ALL I HAD TO DO WAS FIGURE OUT WHAT NETWORK HE WAS ON, PULL IT UP ON THE MONITORING SOFTWARE, AND LOOK AT THE OTHER CONNECTED DEVICES. YOU'RE THE ONLY EREADER WITH RECENT ACTIVITY

Thames did say he was a regional director of containment camps; it didn't surprise me that the United had created some fancy program for spying on their prisoners. And Jayde, as a guard, could easily have access to that program.

It all made sense, which was highly disconcerting. Apparently all Thames had to do to see my online activity was log into an app.

As long as they don't realize that I've hacked the blocks and connected the reader to this network, they won't be looking. But still, watch what you say.

Jayde seemed to make the same inference.

IN CASE YOU'RE WONDERING, NO ONE'S FLAGGED OR PULLED A REPORT ON YOUR DEVICE YET. SO I DON'T THINK THAMES KNOWS

THAT'S THE FIRST GOOD NEWS I'VE HEARD ALL DAY

There was a pause before the dots appeared again.

I'M SORRY PHILLI

I pondered his use of the familiar. Had I ever told Jayde my nicknames? He'd asked about them when we first met.

I NEVER GOT A CHANCE TO SAY THANK YOU

His response was fast—too fast.

DON'T

I struggled to come up with a reply. He spared me the trouble.

LOOK, I'M JUST HERE TO HELP IF I CAN. I'D RATHER NOT WATCH THAMES KILL YOU ON LIVESTREAM IF IT CAN BE AVOIDED

I had to admit that was a mutual interest. Jayde continued.

THE SOONER WE GET YOU OUT OF THERE, THE BETTER. I DON'T KNOW WHAT THAMES IS UP TO, BUT IT CAN'T BE GOOD. WITHOUT YOU AND Q HE'LL HAVE LESS LEVERAGE

FAIR POINT. ANY THEORIES AS TO WHAT THAMES IS UP TO? ANY OFFICE GOSSIP?

NOT A WORD. ANYONE WHO WILL TALK KNOWS NOTHING. WHATEVER IT IS, HE'S KEPT IT COMPLETELY SEPARATE FROM HIS DAY JOB

I was disappointed but not surprised; everything we'd discovered so far led me to believe Thames was doing this under the table, outside of United surveillance. Apparently that meant even most of the people in his own office were in the dark.

TALK ABOUT A SIDE HUSTLE

HA. BUT WHATEVER IT IS—HE'S IN BIG TROUBLE WITH THE HIGHER-UPS FOR IT

A hybrid between fascination and fear gripped me.

HOW SO?

THAT VIRUS YOU GUYS RELEASED? IT HIT SOME MAJOR GOVERNMENT SERVERS

This wasn't news to me; Nic had mentioned that the computer on Rott was synced to some important government databases.

IT'S CLEAR THE VIRUS ORIGINATED ON ROTT—AND SINCE THAMES'S OFFICE WAS CONNECTED TO THE SERVERS ON ROTT...

I felt a rush of gratification.

THE VIRUS HIT THAMES'S OFFICE?

EYUP—AND IT LINKS HIM DIRECTLY TO ROTT WHEN HE HAD NO OFFICIAL REASON TO BE INVOLVED WITH THAT PRISON

The fog in my head began to settle. Thames wasn't supposed to be on Rott anymore than I was. Which could mean only one thing: It must have been *his* factory.

HE'S UNDER A LOT OF SUSPICION RIGHT NOW. THE BIG GUYS ARE LOOKING FOR BLOOD

That was Thames's PR nightmare. The virus tied him to Rott, which meant he had to find another scapegoat. That's why he needed me to take responsibility for the virus—so he could make himself look like the innocent victim of a terrorist attack.

But how was he going to explain away the factory? Someone had to fund that multimillion-dollar endeavor, and no amount of makeup and stage lighting would make anyone believe I was behind it all. My videos only solved half the problem.

For that matter, why was Thames's office synced to major government databases? If he wasn't with the United, wouldn't he have set up a private network for Rott? Were other government officials involved? If so, who?

CAN YOU FIND OUT WHAT OTHER NETWORKS WERE HIT AND WHO WORKS THERE?

WE'RE TRYING, BUT THESE NETWORKS AREN'T EXACTLY EASY TO HACK INTO FROM THE OUTSIDE. I'LL LET YOU KNOW WHAT WE FIND OUT

I drummed my fingers on the back of my reader. I was grateful to have Jayde as an ally, but we still had no idea where we were being held, who Thames worked for, or how deep this corruption ran in the United. But one thing I was confident of: Thames had been making Red Rain for himself. Our terrorist demonstration had caused a stir, and he needed to cover his tracks. But who was he hiding from? And, more importantly, what would happen if he succeeded? What came next in his plan?

Whatever it was, Jayde was right. I didn't want to be a part of it. The sooner Nic and I got out of Thames's clutches, the better.

My headache was starting to return. I'd been on the screen too long, but I needed a plan. Thames was going to expect another video tomorrow—what should I say?

I took another wild swing of hope.

DO YOU KNOW WHERE MY FAMILY IS?

NO. NONE OF THEM HAVE TRIED TO MAKE CONTACT THAT WE KNOW OF

My heart sank into my stomach, even though I hadn't really expected a different answer. I nursed my loneliness while the dots did their slow dance.

THEY WERE BEING HELD BY THAMES WHEN YOU TWO WERE DEPORTED TO ROTT. THAT VIRUS HIT ALL OF THAMES'S NETWORKS, SO WE'RE ASSUMING THEY USED THE CHAOS AS A COVER TO SLIP AWAY. WHEN EVERYTHING CAME BACK ONLINE, THEY WERE GONE, AND THE ENTIRE OFFICE HAS BEEN IN A PANIC EVER SINCE

My chest tightened at the realization: Thames had been in control the entire time. He coerced Nic into working on Red Rain, and then he held me hostage and blackmailed my father into finishing it. We tried to escape, but they caught us and dragged us right back to Thames—who deposited us on Rott without a second thought. All this, and yet Thames was pretending to care about me now?

I swallowed the feeling of disgust that rose up in my throat. There was still one person unaccounted for. I decided to ask, even though I wasn't sure I wanted the answer.

IS AUGUSTINE SAFE?

The pause was long, long enough that I feared the worst.

I HAVEN'T HEARD FROM HIM

I hoped that meant Stanyard had gotten away, not that he'd been captured and quietly disposed of.

I sighed. I had no closure, anywhere. It was like my consciousness was a sweater that had been cut down the middle, all the ends left to unravel and disintegrate.

Jayde's message interrupted my stewing.

I'LL LET YOU KNOW IF I HEAR ANYTHING

THANKS

The screen was blank for a moment while we both debated what to do next. My spine stiffened as I remembered something.

HANG ON

WHAT?

IF THE VIRUS HIT ALL OF THAMES'S NETWORKS, WHY DOES THIS PLACE SEEM TO BE RUNNING SMOOTHLY?

I thought back to all my interactions with computers over the past few days. Except for Thames mentioning it, it didn't seem like this place—wherever this place was—had been affected. Nic's music database was intact, after all.

NO IDEA. BUT I'M CONVINCED YOU'RE NOT ANYWHERE NEAR THAMES'S MAIN OFFICE

That was fast becoming the obvious conclusion.

CAN YOU USE THE SPYWARE TO SEE ALL THE ACTIVITY ON THIS NETWORK?

YEAH. SO FAR THERE'S BEEN NOTHING OF INTEREST. IT'S NOT A BUSY NETWORK—I THINK IT'S MAINLY USED FOR ENTERTAINMENT SYSTEMS. THERE'S A BUNCH OF TVS AND GAME CONSOLES HOOKED TO IT

HOPEFULLY THAT MEANS THEY'RE NOT LOOKING FOR OUR DEVICES ON IT

HOPEFULLY

I opened the network menu of my reader and considered our options. There was "Wing B Guest," but I doubted there would be anything helpful on there. Nic said he found other networks—maybe they had something.

I shot him a message. While I waited for him to respond, I flopped back on the pillow, eager to relieve some of gravity's pressure. I held my reader above my head—and remembered. While I was looking for the messaging app two nights ago, I could have sworn the file list kept changing. I thought it was my migraine warping reality, but maybe it wasn't. Maybe my reader was picking up another network.

I moved the reader around in a slow circle above my head, watching for another network to appear on the connections menu. When I didn't find any, I got to my knees and held it higher. Still nothing. I scooted to the corner of the bed and put my reader against the far wall, sliding it up and down.

I desperately hoped there weren't cameras in my room. I didn't want Thames to see this, for more reasons than one.

I stretched as far up the wall as I could reach—and there it was. A third network, in addition to NCC1701D and Wing B Guest.

I made a note of the name: ECV197. A message from Nic came through; I clicked on it and found a rather lengthy list of networks. Sinking back down on the bed, I copied it, added the network I found, and sent it to Jayde.

TRY THESE. THEY'RE OTHER NETWORKS IN RANGE

ON IT

A whisper of peace tried to find room in my crowded consciousness. It felt strangely good to have a plan—to know that someone, anyone, was making progress.

I smiled, but the good feelings were quickly washed away by a flashflood of pain. Was it too soon to take another dose of medication?

I NEED TO GO

I'LL TEXT YOU IF I FIND ANYTHING

THANKS

There was a pause, and I thought we were done. But before I closed the app, he sent one last message:

I'M SORRY PHIL. I REALLY AM

13

In spite of everything that had transpired in the last two hours, I actually obeyed the doctor's orders and rested for most of the day. I silenced and closed the messaging app, then turned the audio Bible back on. Within two chapters I was fast asleep. No one woke me for lunch. I was just coming back to consciousness when Nic rang my doorbell and let me know dinner had been served.

I dragged myself out of bed and took a small plate, enough to wash down another dose of medication. I took a shower, braided my hair, and went back to bed as the painkiller kicked in, pulling me into a dreamless sleep.

Thames woke me up in the morning. Thankfully he had the decency not to come in. He informed me that he wanted me to take the day off from recording and reminded me to do 30 minutes of light exercise, per the doctor's instructions. I mumbled some affirmative through the door, and he mercifully left without another word.

I thought about going back to sleep, but as my self-awareness warmed, I realized that I wasn't tired. For the first time in who knows how long, I felt well-rested. I was still somewhat groggy as I wandered into the cafeteria for breakfast, my joints heavy from the abundant sleep. But the pressure—both emotional and physical—had lifted from my head, raising my spirits with it. I scooped up a generous portion of food and dove in.

Nic voluntarily shared the same table in companionable silence. He scrolled through his tablet as he sipped his coffee. I watched the text flickering across his screen and abruptly remembered what had transpired yesterday.

I pulled my reader out of my pouch and fired up the messaging app. Sure enough, Jayde had sent me consistent updates all night—it looked like he had been working well into the A.M.—about what he had found on the other networks.

I skimmed to the bottom and typed a welcome message.

HEY SORRY, JUST NOW SEEING THIS

The typing dots appeared instantly.

NO PROBLEM. WANT THE SUMMARY?

I glanced at the timestamp on his previous message and compared it to the clock.

DID YOU SLEEP AT ALL?

DID YOU?

YEAH ACTUALLY

GOOD

The dots stopped. When I got tired of waiting, I typed again.

SO WHAT DID YOU FIND?

MOST OF THE NETWORKS ARE USELESS—THERMOSTATS AND AIR PURIFIERS AND WHATNOT. BUT ECV197 IS INTERESTING. I THINK IT'S AN INTERNAL NETWORK FOR SOME KIND OF RESEARCH FACILITY

My heart leapt at the sight of the phrase "research facility." My father and brother had spent so much of their lives in various research facilities that the thought of being near one was almost comforting, however irrational that emotion might be.

WHAT MAKES YOU THINK THAT?

THERE'S ALMOST NO OUTBOUND COMMUNICATION. ALMOST ALL OF THE ACTIVITY IS STUFF LIKE STATUS REPORTS AND TEST RESULTS. IT'S ALL GREEK TO ME. I'LL SEND YOU SCREENSHOTS OF SOME OF THE DATABASES ON THEIR CLOUD—SEE IF Q MAKES ANY SENSE OF IT

A few images began to load. I looked up at Nic, who had just started his second cup of coffee, and realized I had some explaining to do.

So instead of explaining, I just scrolled back to the beginning of my message history with Jayde and shoved my reader across the table at him.

Nic's mouthful of coffee ended up back in his cup (for the most part). He quickly composed himself and started reading. He held the screen close to his face so I couldn't see the expression in his eyes. I continued to eat like normal, trying to put on a good show for the cameras that were no doubt in the room.

After a few minutes, Nic handed my reader back to me. "Sorry," he said with no detectable emotion, "I thought I disabled that feature."

I ran my finger around my plate to catch the last bit of pancake syrup. "Want to watch some TV after breakfast? I have the day off."

"Aren't you supposed to be avoiding screens?"

"Just one episode," I begged in a practiced teenager whine.

Ten minutes later, we were again arranged in the lounge with a sitcom providing mundane background nose. Nic folded his legs under him, cradling his third cup of coffee in his lap. He regarded me for a solid minute before initiating conversation.

"Remember when you first got to Mars and I told you to keep your head down?"

My eyes narrowed involuntarily. "Yeah?"

He shrugged and picked my reader up. He clicked on the images Jayde had sent and studied them, his eyebrows nearly meeting in the middle as he squinted at the screen.

I gave him a minute. "Do you recognize any of the files?"

"Yup," he said, and took a morale-boosting chug of coffee. "It looks like a carbon copy of all my work from Mars—which I guarantee you is exactly what it is." He grunted. "I guess they did have a backup."

I swallowed a bubble of fear. "Does he have Red Rain?"

Nic was utterly unalarmed. "No—at least not according to these files. This database is several months out of date. In fact, it looks like it hasn't been updated hardly at all since I was governor—it's probably an old server they dragged out after the virus wiped their other networks."

I collapsed back into the chair, releasing my anxiety in a sigh that was far too dramatic for the situation.

Nic looked up at me. "Thames does not have Red Rain," he said with a confidence I wish I could emulate. "If he did, he wouldn't stoop to all these theatrics. A man with weapons doesn't need to cover his tracks."

I had to admit that was the logical conclusion. Thames was trying to cover up Rott; if he had Red Rain, there would be nothing to cover up.

"However..." It was Nic's turn to sigh. "I hate to break it to you, but if they get your father in the same room with this data, he could reconstruct the formula."

He could... and he would.

I avoided Nic's gaze. "Then I guess it's a good thing he got away."

Nic didn't comment. I eagerly changed the subject. "My friend says there's been new activity—so that means we're close to wherever they're doing their research, close enough to connect to one of their internal networks."

"Which, sadly, tells us absolutely nothing. You can build a lab anywhere. We could even be back on Rott, except I *know* Rott's databases are in shambles right now." He passed my reader back to me. "And, if this is an internal network with minimal outbound communication, I'm not sure how this will help us."

The device sank in my lap like a chunk of lead. "My friend said most of the other networks were useless—thermostats and stuff like that."

Nic swirled his coffee. "I figured as much. Sadly, looking at the activity log for the automated thermostat isn't going to tell us anything, except maybe give us an idea of how hot it is outside."

I nodded ruefully. It was a cruel irony that, in a world where every single device communicated wirelessly, we would be strapped for information. Even the locked doors fencing us in were probably controlled remotely.

An idea shot through my brain. The laugh track on the TV seemed to lag as I tried to capture the thought before it faded.

"Nic," I said slowly, giving my words time to catch up. "Do your door locks run on a wireless network?"

He blinked several times, clearly processing the same thoughts I was. "Yes…" The hope in his voice rose and fell with the inflection on that one word. "But unless they've redesigned them, you can't program a new user over wireless. You have to have the physical disc. It's a safety feature—to prevent exactly what you're thinking about doing."

The door. Yesterday. You didn't have access.

No, but you do. And I'm your sister. By blood.

"I may not have to reprogram them."

He didn't ask for more explanation. He looked at me for a moment, then leaned back in the chair and picked up his coffee. "If you tap the upper-left corner of the screen and hit 'settings,' you can see what network it's on."

I grabbed my reader and got up to do just that.

"Phil," he called when I reached the doorway. I glanced back.

"Be careful."

14

I left the lounge and strode to Gate C. I reached for the panel, then hesitated with my finger poised over the screen. Would it make a hideous noise when I touched it? Would it trigger an alert and cause Thames to look at the activity log? Was he watching me right now?

I decided it didn't matter. I steeled my nerves—and my eardrums—and tapped the corner of the screen. Mercifully, the only noise it made was an informative chirp.

Several icons glowed to life, just like Nic had said. I tapped the gear to bring up the settings menu. "Connectivity" was the last option.

I wrote the network name down on my reader and went back to my room. I locked the door for posterity, sat down on the bed, and opened the messaging app.

YOU ONLINE?

There was digital silence for one minute, two, and I began to wonder if Jayde had finally exhausted himself and logged off. For all I knew, he was at work. I had no right to expect he'd be at my beck and call at all hours of the day, but I knew I was onto something. The pressure almost made me desperate enough to try the audio call feature.

Mercifully, he started typing back.

WHAT'S UP?

CAN YOU GET ONTO THIS NETWORK?

I dropped him the name.

I'M SURE I CAN LOOK IT UP ON THE SPYWARE. HACKING INTO IT MIGHT TAKE MORE EFFORT. WHAT IS IT?

THE NETWORK FOR THE DOOR LOCKS

The word he sent back was foul, but spoken with admiration, I'm sure.

GIVE ME AN HOUR

I groaned—out loud, even. I'm sure an hour was an amazing turnaround time for expert hacking work, but it was still an hour I had to lie around and be useless.

Well, not totally useless.

I turned my notification volume up to max, cued up some millennial worship music I'd found in the archive, and paced the room. I chanted the lyrics over and over until my heart rate slowed to match the pace of the song, then slipped into prayer.

I tripped over the rug when the incoming message shattered my concentration.

GOOD NEWS BAD NEWS

I sat back down on the bed.

GOOD NEWS?

I KNOW A BIT ABOUT THE SOFTWARE THAT CONTROLS THE DOOR LOCKS. I CAN LOOK UP ALL THE DOORS ON THAT NETWORK

I was happily surprised, but maybe I shouldn't have been. Jayde was a guard, after all. Managing door access was probably part of his job.

It occurred to me then that getting arrested and meeting Jayde might not have been the worst thing that ever happened to me.

Thank you, Jesus.

Before I could celebrate over text, Jayde continued.

BAD NEWS IS YOU AND Q ARE BOTH BLACKLISTED

MEANING?

MEANING YOU'VE BEEN SPECIFICALLY BLOCKED FROM ALL DOORS ON THE NETWORK. ADDING YOU TO THE WHITELIST REQUIRES A LEVEL 1 SECURITY OVERRIDE

WHAT LEVEL DO YOU HAVE?

LIKE 4

Ouch. I chewed my lip.

CAN YOU HACK INTO LEVEL 1?

I'M SURE SOMEONE COULD

I knew the lack of further explanation meant we'd have to recruit help—and there was no telling how long that would take, if we could even find someone to do it.

But, if my theory was correct, maybe we didn't have to add *me* to the whitelist.

HOW HARD IS IT TO ADD SOMEONE TO THE WHITELIST?

I TOLD YOU—YOU'VE BEEN BLACKLISTED. I CAN'T JUST COPY AND PASTE YOU IN

I know, I know! Work with me!

OKAY BUT LIKE WHAT ABOUT A NEW USER?

BASICALLY IMPOSSIBLE. YOU HAVE TO HAVE THEIR DNA ON FILE, AND FOR THAT YOU NEED THE PROGRAMMING DISC. WE'VE YET TO FIGURE OUT HOW TO HACK THE SYSTEM REMOTELY

That's what Nic had said, but I knew there had to be a way around it. I kept mashing the idea around in my head like modeling clay, trying to force it into a useful shape.

WHAT IF YOU ALREADY HAD THEIR DNA ON FILE?

IT NEEDS TO BE IN A SPECIAL ENCRYPTED FORMAT—AND NO, I DON'T KNOW HOW TO FORGE THAT EITHER

I KNOW! BUT *IF* YOU HAD THE ENCRYPTED FILE FOR A USER, HOW HARD IS IT TO ADD THEM TO THE WHITELIST?

The typing dots cycled for a minute. I clutched my reader, begging God to help us out on this one.

OH THAT'S EASY. I CAN JUST PASTE THEM IN—IF THEY HAVEN'T ALREADY BEEN BLACKLISTED

I squealed, more to relieve internal tension than anything else. It was so simple; if we could get a copy of my father's or brother's file, we could add them to the door. And, assuming Nic hadn't spent any of his jail time improving the software, the glitch still might let me through.

But where were we going to get a copy of their files? When was the last time they were in a building that was controlled by the DNA locks?

It looks like a carbon copy of all my work from Mars—which I guarantee you is exactly what it is.

Idiotic typos peppered my text as I struggled to type fast enough.

THE DATABASE FORM THE ECV NTWORK ARE THEIR DOOR
LOCK RECORDS

He took a beat to translate that. It was a stretch—or was it? Ephesus's prints had definitely been on file in Wing 74. He'd been heavily involved in the creation of that research and had access to all the labs and computer terminals. But were the user files for the doors on the database that Thames had? Had that information been saved? If Thames had literally "copied and pasted" all the data from Mars, it just might be there.

WHO SHOULD I BE LOOKING FOR?

I figured at this point using real names was the least of my concerns.

EPHESUS

HOW'S HE GOING TO HELP?

I flexed my fingers to relax them, slowing my typing pace to a legible speed.

ON MARS, I COULD GET INTO ROOMS THAT WERE SET TO ACCEPT MY FATHER OR BROTHER, EVEN IF I HADN'T BEEN WHITELISTED. I THINK IT HAD TO DO WITH US BEING BLOOD RELATIVES AND OUR DNA BEING SIMILAR

His delayed response confirmed I was on to something

SOUNDS LIKE THEY NEED BETTER SCANNERS

LET'S HOPE THEY'VE BEEN TOO BUSY TO UPGRADE

LET ME LOOK

I flopped back on the bed and closed my eyes. I took artificially even breaths—in and out, in and out—swallowing a plead with each inhale and releasing a thanks with each exhale.
Within ten minutes Jayde responded.

GOT EPHESUS AND YOUR FATHER

I cheered into the empty room.

CAN YOU ADD THEM?

I TRIED

AND?

IT WON'T LET ME

My spirit and soul crashed to the floor.

WHAT? WHY? WERE THEY BLACKLISTED?

NO

I scrambled for an explanation, but before I could type anything out, Jayde clarified.

THEY WERE ALREADY IN THE SYSTEM

For a minute, the only movement was my cursor blinking. I certainly wasn't breathing.

Jayde didn't wait for me to formulate words, much less muster the coordination to type them.

THEY'RE ALREADY ON FILE FOR THAT WING. I'D JUST HAVE TO ADD THEM TO SPECIFIC DOORS

That should have been good news, but somehow I knew that it wasn't.

I typed and deleted several messages, struggling to clear away the smoke. Why would Thames already have Dad and Ephesus on file? He didn't know where they were, so it made no sense for him to program them into the system. Unless...

I felt sick just typing the words.

DO YOU THINK HE'S EXPECTING THEM TO COME HERE?

It was plausible, all too plausible. I thought of all the planning and preparation Thames had done to bring Nic and me here and realized nothing was out of his reach. Was he looking for Dad and Ephesus too? Was he lying about giving us all clean files? Was he planning on keeping us all imprisoned here? For what? What if—

Jayde derailed my panic train.

NO I MEAN IT'S LIKE THEY *WERE* HERE. THERE'S ACTIVITY LOGS UNDER BOTH OF THEIR NAMES FOR SEVERAL DOORS ON THIS NETWORK

Hope strangled me. *It can't be. Could they? Are they?*

WHEN WAS THE LAST ENTRY?

ABOUT SIX MONTHS AGO

I did the math. That was when we were all on—

My head spun, but for once, it wasn't because I was getting a migraine.

I scrambled to my knees, nearly falling off the bed. I grabbed my reader and held it up towards the corner of the room. There it was, the network connection that kept flickering in and out.

A wave of dizziness knocked me back on the bed. I knelt there, every muscle shaking. My reader throbbed in my hands.

Where did you get this? It's connected to Wing 74's private wifi. It can access all of the base-level data.

I started to cry, whether from fear or joy I couldn't tell.

I'm not surprised you didn't notice. I doubt the range on the wifi is very far.

I threw up. Not figuratively, but literally, the cheap rug absorbing the splatter as I retched a dozen emotions over the edge of the bed.

It can't be, I wanted to scream, but the more I considered it, the more I knew it really, truly could.

All the metal. The fake windows in Thames's office. The door panels. The data and devices magically resurrected from Wing 74.

There was a Gate B and a Gate C. It only stood to reason they'd be past Gate A.

Wiping my mouth on my sleeve, I grabbed my reader. Jayde had sent me more messages, but I didn't read them.

CAN YOU ADD EPHESUS TO GATE B OR GATE C?

YES. THEY HAVEN'T BEEN BLACKLISTED YET

I breathed roughly through my nose, praying wordlessly as I did so.

I'D RECOMMEND GATE C. BASED ON THE LOGS, THERE'S A LOT OF ACTIVITY ON THE OTHER SIDE OF GATE B. YOU'D PROBABLY RUN INTO SOMEONE. WING C ISN'T VERY BUSY

IT'S PROBABLY NOT FINISHED

I took his lack of comment as consent.

YOU SURE ABOUT THIS?

I nodded, even though he couldn't see me. I needed the motion to anchor my courage.

I HAVE TO SEE FOR MYSELF

15

I paused in my doorway and glanced both ways. Nic had disappeared back into his room, and no one else was in sight. The entire wing was silent.

I glanced towards Gate C. Was now a good time? Should I wait until after dinner when everyone was off work and the power went into energy-saving mode? Or would that just raise more suspicion?

I realized, after regurgitating the thoughts through the logical part of my brain, that it didn't really matter when I did it. If I was honest with myself, I wasn't expecting my jailbreak to go undetected. My prints—or rather, my brother's—would be on the door's activity log, and I'm sure cameras were watching me right now. Thames would find out, sooner or later, that I'd accessed that door.

The trick was to stay one step ahead of him—and that meant I needed to act fast.

I swallowed one more prayer. Then I strode up to Gate C and flashed my hand across the sensor before I could think twice about it.

It shone green and opened.

I was so blinded by the sudden onslaught of natural light that I almost let the gate close again on my foot. The hallway beyond was gorgeous. To the right, the metal wall had been polished to a mirror-like shine. Sleek benches and trendy art speckled the length of it, and the floor was boldly decorated with irregular black and white tile. To the left, an archway of solid glass stretched from floor to ceiling, revealing a stunning view of the Martian countryside.

Somehow, my feet carried me up to the glass. It was nearing midday, and a halo of robin's egg blue surrounded the keyhole of light that was the distant sun. The rest of the sky was blurry like melted butterscotch, melding seamlessly with the dusty landscape. The view went for miles until it ended in an uncut plateau. The only movement was the flickering light on top of the nearest guidepost.

I knew what I would see. I knew, as soon as Jayde pulled up the door records, that we were on Mars. I knew this was Wing 74. But seeing it, splayed before me in undeniable color, was no less overwhelming.

My stomach flipflopped, as if suddenly realizing it had left Earth's gravity and needed to catch up. I sank to the floor on my knees and waited until the world came back into focus. A few tears—gentle ones—slipped down my cheek and dampened my lap.

"What now, God?" I said aloud.

A voice answered me, but it definitely wasn't God's.

"You really are a clever girl."

I whipped around, nearly falling over, and for a moment I could have sworn I was seeing a ghost. Not only had I never expected to see him again, but he was so slight and pale, with his aged hair and bleached lab coat, that it wouldn't have taken many special effects to turn him into a wraith.

"Carnegie," I said after I put a name with the face.

He nodded and drew his hand from his pocket. The reprogram disc for the door was clutched in his wrinkled fingers. He snapped it on the panel next to Gate C and started fiddling with it.

I stood up, self-consciously straightening my skirt. "I thought you were dead."

He didn't answer. He didn't need to. "I could have sworn I fixed that glitch. But, as usual, you continue to provide invaluable product testing." He glanced at me, but he didn't seem particularly bothered.

I decided not to tell him I had help opening the door. "What are you doing here?"

"I never left."

"You work for Thames?"

He shot me an incredulous look over his shoulder. "Thames works for me."

It took only seconds for me to catch up. "It was you. It's always been you. You've been using Dr. Nic this whole time."

"He was a necessary evil. The original idea for Red Rain was his, although his execution had all the practicality of a science fiction novel." His lips twitched in a gesture too cruel to be called a smile. "His charisma was good in meetings, though. He was much better at getting sponsors than me."

He punched a button on the disc. The door beeped and whooshed shut. "There, that should be fixed now."

I sank onto a bench against the wall. Clearly, I wasn't going anywhere anytime soon. "How long have you been in charge?" I asked.

He pocketed the disc and sat down next to me, leaving a comfortable gap between us. "Long before your brother got involved. Who do you think pulled the strings to get Ephesus reassigned in the first place? Transferring unassimilated personnel is a *nightmare*. Nic never could have done it without me, not without raising huge red flags."

"So why'd you let him? Couldn't you have found another scientist?"

Carnegie shrugged. "Perhaps, but Nic had his whims, and it was to my advantage to let him think he was in charge." He gave me a conspiratorial smile, as if I were in on a secret. "That said, he was right on the money with your father. I always knew your brother couldn't do it—he was too young, too inexperienced. But your father had the best credentials of anyone I'd ever seen."

Every hair on my arms prickled. "How many scientists did you try?"

He groaned wearily. "Dozens."

"And did they all make it out alive?"

He frowned. "Child. What do you take me for? Most of them didn't get far enough to be given full access to the project. The few that did were paid off easily enough. I didn't have any trouble until your brother pulled his stunt." He chuckled, almost as if it were a fond memory. "Again, Nic is very lucky he had me to make that problem go away."

"So when I sent that email…"

He regarded me for a moment. "I underestimated you," he said without flattery or admiration. "I expected you to be too scared to do anything, or at least anything significant. I certainly didn't expect you to blow up a lab, escape, and alert the officials all within fifteen minutes."

I couldn't help but smile.

He didn't return the gesture. "Thankfully, the only person you contacted was Commander Ambrose, who was already on my payroll."

So Ambrose didn't find out about Red Rain when I alerted him; he already knew. A speck of guilt lifted from my soul and was immediately replaced by dread. Ambrose—and, by inference, Thames—had been involved all along. From the moment Ephesus was summoned to Mars, our lives had been pawns in his race to acquire Red Rain.

My whole body tightened, my hands coiling into fists at my side. Carnegie didn't notice. "After I generously granted him a 'raise,' he was very happy to forge some reports for me."

I thought about our blank files, and everything settled into place. That's why there was no record of our time on Mars. That's why they built the factory on Rott, an island in the middle of the ocean, even though it was gloriously impractical. That's why my multiple arrests and imprisonments had seemed strangely informal and involved shockingly little paperwork.

"So the United never did find out what happened up here," I said, for the first time in days feeling fully confident in my conclusion.

"They still haven't."

That's why Thames didn't want me to drop names on camera; they were trying to keep the Martian base clean. "So why involve Dr. Nic again? It seems like you finally had the opportunity to cut him from the picture. You could have left him on Rott to, well, you know."

Carnegie leaned his head against the wall. "I wanted to, believe me. But I still needed Red Rain. None of the other experimental weapons we've produced can even hold a candle to the tactical power of Red Rain."

He closed his eyes. "We tried for months to find another scientist to complete the work. No one even came close. Thames insisted we let Nic have another go at it. I knew he would be useless, but sometimes we compromise for our allies."

Realization filled my veins with ice. "Is that why you dragged my father back into it?"

He rolled his head and looked at me. "He was, quite frankly, our only hope. Nic tested him when he was up here, and the results were astonishing. I knew he could do it, given time and appropriate incentive."

Every nerve in my body flared. "So you kidnapped me and Cea to use as blackmail," I hissed, cramming as much bitterness and accusation as I could into every syllable.

He held my gaze. "You won't believe me when I say this, but I'm sorry it had to be this way."

"You're right, I don't believe you."

"I would have taken anyone else over your father. I knew he was emotionally unstable. After what he did to your mother, I knew he could be unpredictable and dangerous. But I thought that, if I had you, perhaps he could at least be controlled."

It was Carnegie who recommended it. He thought it would make your father more compliant if you two were together.

I shivered. Now I knew who had been watching me the whole time.

He laughed joylessly. "You see where that got me. First you blow up a lab and scare off my best scientists. Next, you destroy my multimillion-dollar factory and force me to drag you back up here to film a bunch of idiotic TikTok videos."

"What's TikTok?"

He shook his head. "Never mind, you're too young to remember." He rose. "We'd better be getting back now, or you'll miss lunch."

I warily stood up. "What are you going to do with me?"

He smiled benevolently. "My dear girl, you worry too much. Despite your flaws, you've proven to be very useful to me, and as long as you continue to play the part of my rising internet star, I won't let a hair on your head get hurt."

He gestured, and I reluctantly followed him back through Gate C. "Are you really going to let us go when you're done?" I prodded.

"Absolutely," he said without a moment's hesitation. "Once I've gotten everything I need, you'll be free to walk out those doors."

He walked me back to my dorm. I opened the door and stepped inside.

"But once it's all said and done, I don't think you're going to want to leave."

I turned to look at him. He laid his hand on the frame to keep the door from closing.

"No, Philadelphia, I think once this is over, you're going to realize that you're safer with me."

He smiled, a cold, vicious smile that left no room for doubt: He was in control. And despite the fact that he had so graciously answered my questions, he had, in reality, told me nothing.

He let go of the doorframe. "You should try your coloring book. Thames picked it out especially for you."

He smiled at me until the door closed.

16

I stood there, staring at the door, long enough that it opened again to reveal Nic.

"Well?" he demanded without ceremony.

Thankfully I had spent the better part of the last fifteen minutes debating how to break the news to him and had reached the revolutionary conclusion that I should just state the facts.

"You know that ECV network with all the lab activity?"

"Yeah?"

"It's one of the private networks for Wing 74." I let that revelation bake for only a half-second before I added the icing on the cake. "And Carnegie says hi."

Nic was silent. I could tell by the way his eyes flickered that he was running the numbers and reaching the appropriate conclusions—at about triple the speed it had taken me.

After his eyebrows had run their full gamut of expressions, he turned, opened the door, and walked out.

"Where are you—"

He stopped in the middle of the hall and faced the corner. Then he flashed an obscene gesture and started vomiting a stream of words that were colorful even for him.

My door drifted shut, dampening his tirade only slightly. I waited. A few minutes later, he calmed down and came back in.

"I guess I know where the security camera in the hall is now," I offered.

Nic shrugged and smoothed his hair back into place.

I let curiosity steal the moment. "Did you have any idea it was him?"

He shot me a look. "If I had, we wouldn't be in this mess." He sighed and seemed to shuffle his emotions together like a stack of cards. "Well, the good news is that I'm now completely confident Carnegie doesn't have Red Rain. If he did, I'm pretty sure he would just bomb the United instead of posting those dumb videos. As it stands, it sounds like all he has is the Wing 74 data—which is out of date."

"Because it's such a secure network," I filled in the blanks.

"For better or for worse."

"So what now?" I put the obvious question on the table.

"No idea," he responded without hesitation. "Unfortunately we can't just walk out the front door—even if we could get the front door open."

I bit my lip. I hadn't considered that.

"I hate myself for saying this, but our best bet may be for you to finish recording the videos and see if he holds true to his promise."

I searched his face. "Do you think he'll keep his word?"

He returned my stare. "At this point, I don't want to bet on anything. But I would rather buy ourselves more time than try to blast out of here, guns blazing, without a plan. I'll take patience over death."

I had to agree on that point.

A thought came to me, and I rolled it around in my brain for a minute before sharing. "Should I try to drop hints in my videos about Carnegie and Mars? Maybe someone will pick up on it and—"

"Absolutely not," he interrupted in that all-too-familiar stern tone of voice. Only this time there was no bitterness in it—just genuine fear.

"Look, I may not have known Carnegie as well as I thought, but I do know one thing about him—he will kill. I've seen him do it. He's made it clear that we are both expendable, so if you outlive your usefulness, he will kill you without a second's thought."

I had no words. There was nothing to say; I knew he was right.

"I know you don't make a habit of listening to me..."

I frowned.

"...but this time, when I say 'keep your head down,' I really mean it."

I searched his face and found only honesty there. "Okay," I said after a moment.

He didn't look relieved by my consent. He probably didn't believe me.

I wasn't sure I believed me, either.

*

Carnegie joined us in the recording studio the next day.

I couldn't tell by Thames's reaction whether or not he had heard about my little breakout. He was startled that Carnegie showed up, but I think he was more uncomfortable with his boss hovering at his elbow than anything else.

Having Carnegie in my line of sight didn't make my job any easier, either. Every time I glanced up I found him staring at me, eyes unwavering. It was a constant reminder that he was in control and that each word I breathed was for his benefit. He was using me, and every second I was on air, I was making him stronger and more powerful.

It was also a warning about what would happen if I said anything out of line.

"Good job," he commended after I'd finished recording. It sounded like a genuine compliment, which was disgusting. "Let's do another session this afternoon. We don't want to keep your fans waiting after you've given them that delicious cliffhanger."

Two videos in one day? I involuntarily glanced at Thames, who was also visibly caught off-guard. *But why?*

I asked the same question of Nic at lunch.

"It's probably a power move," he replied without looking up. "Reminding you who's boss—since you have a habit of forgetting that."

I made a face at him, not that he caught it. "Or he's getting desperate. Which could be good for us."

"Or, more likely, it could be really bad for us."

I tried not to let that comment get to me as I walked back to the recording studio.

"Desperate" definitely seemed like an accurate description of Carnegie's behavior, not that his calm demeanor revealed any urgency. During our afternoon session, he made me record no less than five videos. Every time the stream would get cut off—which happened more quickly with each successive video—he would switch to another account and tell me to start over.

I narrated the end of my time on Mars and rolled right into the events of recent weeks—getting arrested, realizing I was being used as blackmail, breaking out with Cea. Every time I thought I'd reached a good stopping point, he would level his gaze on me, and I would have to suck in my breath and find the strength to keep going.

I think he would have made me recount the whole story in one sitting if Thames hadn't gathered the courage to interrupt him.

"Take a break, Philadelphia, and drink some water. I've stopped the stream," he said to me over the intercom. I gladly obeyed. As I chugged down the water, I watched them engage in a silent battle of the wills, staring each other down with increasing amounts of male dominance.

It was clear who had been pulling the strings the entire time. It must have been Carnegie's decision to send me to Rott—with or without Thames's consent.

To my surprise, Carnegie deferred. "Yes, I suppose that is enough for today." He turned his smile to me. "Rest up, Philli." He said the nickname with extra butter. "We'll do some more in the morning."

I avoided his gaze as the guards escorted me out.

When I returned to my room after dinner, Daddy was there to greet me.

Not in the flesh, of course—although if someone had taken my pulse at that moment, they might have thought it was really him. Instead, his face gazed out at me from a digital picture frame that had been propped on my nightstand next to a small planter of red flowers.

I cautiously stepped in and gazed around the room, wondering what else had been tampered with. The sheets looked like they had been changed and the rug vacuumed. My belongings were all there, but they had clearly been "tidied"—the position tweaked just enough to let me know that someone else had touched them.

I shivered, hoping that would shake the feeling of being violated from my nerves. Thankfully my reader had been on my person all day.

I walked up to the nightstand. I avoided my dad's eyes, instead studying the flowers. I recognized them instantly—it was the plant Mr. Sardis had given me when we arrived on Mars. He'd said I needed "a little color for my room," and it had sadly gotten left behind when we returned to Earth.

But he—or someone—had taken good care of it in my absence; it was blooming prolifically. Was Mr. Sardis still here? Did he know what was going on? Did he care?

I reached out and fingered the velvety leaves. To think I could be less than a hundred feet from friends and safety, and yet a few locked doors were keeping me from reaching them. It was infuriating and made me feel even more powerless and pathetic. Was this how Ephesus felt when he was imprisoned on Mars?

I swallowed and summoned the courage to look at the picture frame. It wasn't the most flattering picture of Daddy; it was professional, if not a bit stoic, probably scalped from an employee file. But it was still him, and the sight of him ignited a dozen emotions I didn't have the energy to deal with.

I wanted to feel sad, and lonely, and homesick. Those were safe emotions. I knew what they felt like, and I knew what to do with them. Those were the emotions I was *supposed* to be feeling.

The problem was that those weren't the only emotions I was feeling.

I picked up the frame and almost dropped it when the touch of my hand made the picture change unexpectedly. A profile of Ephesus appeared—another professional photo that had clearly been downloaded from somewhere.

I sat down on the bed and cycled through the images. Most of them were dated photos from the internet, but there were a few I'd never seen before. There were several shots of Ephesus that looked fairly new; had they been taken while he was on base? There was one of Dad that was definitely recent—I could tell by the creases under his eyes as he bent over his work in a lab I didn't recognize. Where had Carnegie gotten these?

I scrolled faster. And suddenly, there was Mama.

It was an old photo, taken before Ephesus was born. I could tell by the quality that it wasn't an original; it was probably something Dad had posted on his social media before the government had blocked his accounts.

Daddy and Mama posed in the picture together. They were somewhere bright and sunny, but the photo was zoomed in too closely to tell where. Their faces filled the frame nearly to the overflowing. Mama's sunlit hair spilled over her shoulders as she leaned her head on Daddy's chest. Her face sparkled with a laugh that was frozen in time.

Daddy's eyes were closed, and his face was buried in Mama's hair so deeply that you couldn't see his expression. But I could tell. I could tell by the crow's feet in the corners of his eyes and the flush in his cheeks: He was smiling.

A tear slid down my cheek. When was the last time Daddy had smiled like that? I shifted through my recent memory, scrolling through my own mental camera roll, trying to recall a moment in time when I had seen true joy on his face. I couldn't come up with one—not since Mama died.

I flinched, as I always did when I thought about Mama's death. But this time, my mind snagged on a different memory.

I would have taken anyone else over your father. I knew he was emotionally unstable. After what he did to your mother, I knew he could be unpredictable and dangerous.

The more I repeated Carnegie's words in my head, the more uncomfortable they made me—but not in the same way his other slimy behavior did. "After what he did to your mother"? Daddy hadn't *done* anything; the United was responsible for my mother's death. The situation was rather cut-and-dry: They accused her of a crime, and then they executed her. My dad had nothing to do with it.

Or did he?

The questions seeped into my mind. I tried to shove them away, but like a persistent leak, they continued to pile up. Did my father have something to do with Mama's death? Did something happen that day that he hadn't told me? What did Carnegie know that I didn't?

My reader buzzed in my pouch, and I realized that, for the first time in my life, I had the power to answer my own questions.

Setting the picture frame back on the nightstand, I pulled out my reader. Ignoring whatever notification had caused the alert, I pulled up the personnel file database and hacked in, just like Nic had taught me. Then with a deep breath, I hit search and typed *Abigail Smyrna*. Her picture was the third result.

In the nanosecond of lag between clicking on her image and the page loading, I flirted with irrational hope. I had never actually seen my mother's body. There had been no funeral. I only knew what I had been told, so maybe...

The air left me when the page loaded and I saw the bold word "DECEASED" branded at the top of her profile.

I stuffed my grief back down my throat and scrolled to the bottom. It was tempting to read her whole file, but I didn't have the emotional composure to handle the memories right now.

The last entry in her file was a yellow-bordered message, formatted differently than anything I'd seen before. I squinted at the header of the message.

Incident Flagged for Potential Police Misconduct. Investigation Status: Acquitted

I read the words again, slowly, letting them sink in. Police misconduct? Could it be that Mama's death had been ruled an accident?

The thought filled me with such dread that I couldn't breathe for a second. I suppose it should have made me feel better to know that it was all a mistake, that the United actually *wasn't* in the habit of executing people for coping Bibles. But instead it made me feel worse. The United had murdered my mother; the least they could do was own up to it and not have the *audacity* to call it an accident.

Anger turned my knuckles white, but I kept reading.

On October 11th, 2072, an investigation into a possible account of police misconduct was opened regarding an incident that occurred on October 10th at the Street 17 Reassimilation Services Compound. Police had been dispatched with a warrant to arrest Dr. Thomas Smyrna [husband of the deceased] for the charges of transmitting illegal media.

Time stopped—or, more accurately, it stumbled. Reality seemed to dip off-kilter as I processed that sentence.

My father had said that Mama was the one charged with transmitting. But it wasn't her; it was him. He was the one they had come to arrest.

You lied, Daddy.

The universe restarted, and faster. I gripped the reader and held it a hairbreadth from my nose as I fought to read the rest of the file as quickly as possible. My eyes kept tripping over each other, and I had to reread the words over and over before my brain understood them.

Mrs. and Dr. Smyrna were home when officers arrived. Dr. Smyrna resisted arrest. Officers drew weapons in an attempt to subdue him, and Abigail Smyrna was unintentionally shot. She died of her injuries en route to the hospital.

I felt sick. All I could see was Mama, my precious, innocent Mama, bleeding out, her blood filling the grout in our entryway like a river—my beloved Mama, draped over a stretcher, sirens wailing as her life slipped away.

And Dad, kneeling on the floor, viciously attempting to scrub the blood from the tile before I got home. *Oh, Daddy...*

Officials reviewed all available evidence, including bodycam footage and Dr. Smyrna's own confession, and determined that the officers had acted appropriately. The fatal shooting was clearly caused by direct interference from Dr. Smyrna as he attempted to grab an officer's weapon.

I tried to picture the scene, but I couldn't. I couldn't imagine my placid father punching an officer in the face and going for his gun. I couldn't imagine my father using a weapon at all. My father wouldn't resist arrest. That was not the Dr. Smyrna I knew.

Or thought I knew.

All charges against the officer were dropped. In light of Dr. Smyrna's compliance with the investigation, officials rescinded the arrest warrant and issued a warning. All affected personnel files have been appropriately updated.

My reader hit the floor. I didn't bother to pick it up and instead wrapped my arms around my chest—tighter, tighter—as if by squeezing myself I could keep my world from shattering. It didn't make any sense. That's not how it happened—that's not what Daddy had told me.

And yet as my mind involuntarily replayed that day—and the weeks, months, years that followed—it tripped over all the clues I should have seen. All the signals I had missed in my delirious grief: the premeditated speeches, the resignation, the calculated tones of voice. The guilt.

Well, Dr. Smyrna, coming around, are we? You used to be the troublesome one.

And then, like a torn sweater unraveling, I watched my father regress. I saw the lines deepen under his eyes, the frown hardening on his lips. I remembered how his attitude and actions had changed—bit by bit, day by day. Here a little compromise, there a little surrender. The slow retreat.

I'm surprised your father didn't offer any objections, Phil.

We talked about it, last night. He said it wasn't worth the blood right now.

Oh the talks—we had so many talks. Always explaining, always justifying, always moving a little more out of the way to try and keep me—or himself—from getting hurt.

Philadelphia, it's the only way! There's nothing I can do... nothing!

Suddenly I was back in that alley. Stanyard's car was smashed against a dumpster, and Ephesus was bleeding in the front seat. There were sirens, and screaming—probably mine—and Stanyard yelling at me to run. And through it all cut my father's cold voice, telling me to stay put until the officers arrived.

I'm not letting either of you get hurt anymore.

He'd turned himself in. I understood that now. He'd chosen not to run—perhaps because he was afraid that if I ran down that alley, I might get shot in the back, just like Mama had.

And maybe, just maybe, that was why he had agreed to create Red Rain.

Just go.

I cried. Curled up on the bed in the tiniest ball I could manage and sobbed. The tears poured out of me, rolling off my nose and clogging my throat. Faster and faster they kept coming as I shed years of lies, manipulation, and guilt onto the blanket.

Why, Daddy, why?

Why did you do it?

Why did you lie to me?

Eventually my tears slowed enough that I could hear around the throbbing in my ears. The air in the room shifted, as if the Holy Spirit had sat down on the bed next to me. My final tears slid out silently as I strained to wrap my nerves around that feeling, as if by holding my breath I could pull Him closer.

Why, Daddy? The question wafted through my consciousness again. *Why did you do it?*

He should have—what should he have done? Should he have gone quietly? Fought harder? Been more careful? I didn't know—I couldn't even process the million alternate scenarios that were spiraling just out of reach in the realm of what-if.

But he should have told me. He should have told me the truth. He should have told me why. Why wasn't he resisting Commander Ambrose? Why did he agree to go to Mars? Why did he make Red Rain? Maybe, if he had told me the truth, we could have been fighting together—instead of against each other.

I sat up slowly. My center of balance was off, as if I'd shed part of my mass through my tears. I bent down and retrieved my reader off the floor.

I brushed the screen off and tabbed back to my Bible. It was open to Matthew.

I clutched the device to my chest. There was only one way to end this.

17

Narissa had her work cut out for her in the morning. Between the constant crying (the tears never really stopped all night) and staying up late praying, my face was a train wreck.

But for once, I didn't *feel* like a train wreck. I was scared—terrified, even. I had no idea how I was going to get the words out around the bleeding emotions that hadn't scabbed over. I didn't know if Carnegie would let me say what I needed to say. Was my dad even listening to the streams? But despite the fact that I was weak and exhausted, my heart felt strangely calm as I walked into the recording studio and arranged myself in front of the camera.

Carnegie was in the control booth again. "Pick up where you left off yesterday and just keep going," he instructed. "I'll tell you when to stop."

There was no room for argument in that statement. I just nodded and took a moment to regulate my breathing. *In, out. In, out.*

Thames glanced at both of us uneasily before starting the countdown. I closed my eyes and did my own countdown—*in, out, in, out*—praying in time with the beat.

When Thames gave the go-ahead, I opened my eyes and looked directly into the camera.

"Hey Dad. I know what happened with Mama."

I glanced at the control booth. This was it—this was their opportunity to cut me off. Thames lurched forward, finger reaching towards the button, but Carnegie laid a hand on his arm to stop him. His eyes were watching me, as they always were.

I turned away from him and focused my attention squarely on the camera lens. I tried to imagine my father's face reflected on the curved glass, channeling all my energy into getting the words out.

"I looked up her file and read the official report. I'm sure it didn't happen exactly like they said, but—I think it's close enough to the truth. And..."

I sucked in a breath. *Holy Spirit, I need you now.*

"I think I understand."

Another breath. *Don't leave me.*

"I think I know why… Why we stopped arguing with the commander. Why I started going to school without complaint. Why you didn't fight back when they sent Ephesus away, and then you. Why you told me to 'be discrete' and 'obey' and 'not cause trouble.' Why you didn't want us to run from the officials. Why you let them send me to prison. Why you worked on…"

I'll never know if Carnegie would have stopped me from saying "Red Rain," because my pain did it for him. The emotion exploded out of me in an ugly sob. I hid my face as tears swam in my eyes, making my eyeliner sting.

I took a deep breath, but there was no damming the emotions now. "I'm scared, Dad," I cried, my voice garbled with another sob. I forced myself to look back into the camera, even though I was squinting through the tears. "I feel—I feel like I don't know you anymore. You abandoned me, you really did. You left me with those men and just *walked away!*"

My voice cracked in a scream. I looked to the ceiling and gulped several lungfuls of air. "'Just go,' you said. Not 'goodbye' or 'I'll come find you' or even 'I'm sorry.' 'Just go.' How could you?" The question came out in a squeaky whisper, but I didn't repeat it. I didn't have the strength to.

"I'm scared," I said again. "I'm frightened and I feel alone and I'm questioning everything you did and I don't know if I can trust you. I don't. I really don't."

I swallowed. It was done. I had done what he—what both of us—had been unwilling to do for so long: I told the truth.

I felt the Holy Spirit stirring deep inside of me like a river. "But." I pressed the heels of my hands to my eyes; they came away smeared with mascara. I stared at them for a minute, gathering all my courage to say the hardest three words of my life.

"I forgive you."

Seventy times seven.

I looked into the camera and said it again, louder this time.

"I forgive you, Dad. I forgive you for lying, and I forgive you for what happened with Mama. Maybe it was a mistake—maybe you shouldn't have resisted. Or maybe it really was just an accident."

I winced as the word left my lips. It still stung—bitterly—to call Mama's death an accident, like I was forfeiting the one grievance I had been able to hold onto for so many years. But it felt right. It was right.

"I'll never know if you did the right thing or not. I wasn't there, and that's… that's okay. I don't have to know if it was right or not." My voice grew clearer as the revelation flowed through me. "I don't have to decide that. I don't have to judge."

The Spirit was pressing so hard against my chest that it hurt. I sat up straight.

"But I do know we're not there now. This is not that moment. Maybe it was a mistake, maybe it wasn't, but we can't keep looking back and basing all our decisions on what happened then."

I leaned forward, my eyes searching the camera. "You can't keep giving in—*we* can't keep giving in. Look where it's got us. We should have run down that alley—ran and kept running. We have to fight, Dad. Fight for our family, fight for freedom, fight for people who can't fight for themselves. We can't let them win."

I glanced at Thames and Carnegie out of the corner of my eye. Both men were still watching me in silence.

"They *can't* win. We can't surrender, not this time. I'm not going to let them keep using me."

Carnegie didn't even blink.

"Help me, Dad. Fight with me. Don't let them use you. Don't let them blackmail you. Whatever they tell you, whatever they say they're going to do to me, don't listen. Don't let them win. Don't let them have—"

The forbidden name died on my tongue as all the air evaporated from the room.

No, Philadelphia, I think once this is over, you're going to realize that you're safer with me.

I met Carnegie's gaze. He stared back, eyes like ice.

I hate to break it to you, but if they get your father in the same room with this data, he could reconstruct the formula.

I turned to the camera, where the playback screen reflected my horror in high definition.

Despite your flaws, you've proven to be very useful to me.

On the bright side, we'll know the minute your family is found. The entire government is searching for them.

They saw my video.

Pain ripped through me. "I've been leading you right to him."

It was barely a whisper, but Thames heard. I saw him scrambling in the control booth and knew I only had seconds.

"Don't do it, Dad!" I screamed, lunging towards the camera. "Don't come for me! They're using me to get—"

The last sound the world heard was my strangled scream as Carnegie's fingers closed around my throat.

18

I hit the floor, gasping. Carnegie had kept his fingers around my throat until he was sure I wasn't going to resist, then dragged me down the hall by my collar. By the time we reached whatever room he threw me into, I had convinced myself that I was going to die. I knelt there, hacking, trying to force air back into my lungs, but breathing felt like dragging a heavy dresser across the floor. It was like my throat had been crushed and no air could get through.

He was talking, but I couldn't hear him around the throbbing and flashing colors. I pressed my forehead to the floor, forcing my breaths to become smaller and slower. I waited until the burn subsided and the panic faded from the edges of my vision before I looked up at him.

"You monster," I rasped.

Whatever he had been saying apparently wasn't important enough to repeat, because he just crossed his arms and glared at me.

I carefully swallowed, trying to get some volume back into my voice. "You want Red Rain." I had to hear it from him; I had to know I was right. "That's why you're using me. That's why you needed those videos to go viral. You're trying to find my dad."

"Such a clever girl, as always. I figured if he didn't try to make contact with you, he would get picked up by the United somewhere—and I have contacts who will be happy to sell him back to me."

"It won't work." My voice still sounded like sandpaper, but it was full of confidence.

"Won't it?" He walked to the door and started fiddling with the panel. "I'm sure *you* won't be cooperative, but I have high hopes for your father. I still have his favorite incentive—and after that stunt you just pulled, I'm sure he knows exactly how much danger you're in."

I winced. He was right, but Dad—if he was watching—also heard the rest of my stream. He knew what I wanted, what I *needed* from him, and maybe, just maybe, he was listening.

Not this time, God. Give him courage!

"I'm not going to let you do this," I challenged, and I meant it.

The panel hissed at him. He glanced over his shoulder at me. "And just what are you going to do about it?"

I didn't hesitate. "I'll figure something out."

He sighed. "That's what I was afraid of." He tapped a button on the panel, and it screeched and went dark. Then he reached into his pocket and turned to face me.

A loaded syringe lay in his hand.

My heart leapt to my throat, but I swallowed it. I clenched my jaw and my fists.

"On second thought…" Carnegie rolled the syringe around in his palm for a second, then dropped it back in his pocket. "I want you to tell your sweet boyfriend that you have three days to live."

My thoughts crashed to a stop, unable to process that statement on the first try. Thankfully, he repeated himself.

"Tell him that unless your father or your brother makes contact with me in the next 72 hours, I will kill you."

The panic rolled back in. Did he really think we'd been in contact with my father? "But how—"

"Don't play dumb with me!" he shouted, for the first time his voice changing octaves. "Don't you think I know you've been chatting with that boyfriend of yours online?"

I flushed all sorts of colors as horror filled my nerves. "You've been monitoring my reader?"

"I've been monitoring everything," he snapped. He sighed and resumed his usual monotone. "And yes, I know all about the 'help' you had with the doors. Believe me, when I find out who your boyfriend is, I'll invite you to the hanging."

I swallowed rapidly to suppress the fear. I didn't have time to be scared right now—I needed to focus. Something wasn't adding up. "If you knew I was online, why didn't you pull the plug? You could have taken my reader away, or changed the access codes, or something."

He frowned at me over his nose. "Because I was hoping you'd do exactly what you did—try and make contact with your father. Why do you think I made it so easy for Nic to get onto the internet? Let me spell it out for you: If Nic can hack into it, the door wasn't locked in the first place."

I shivered.

"The doors, though… I have to give it to you on that one." He ran a hand through his bleach-white hair. "I really thought I'd fixed that glitch, but you played me for a fool yet again."

"Then why didn't you take Gate C offline or something?"

He scoffed. "It wasn't worth the effort. It was much easier just to blacklist your father and brother."

Several of my escape plans evaporated at that statement.

"But, just in case, I've disabled this panel."

I looked up at him. He gestured over his shoulder at the darkened panel. "This door will only open from the outside now. So feel free to have your friends tinker with the lock all you want—it won't help you. In fact…"

He took a step towards me. I instinctively slid back.

"Let's send a message to your friends, shall we? Pull out your reader."

I didn't.

"Don't you want to let them know you're okay? I'm sure they're worried sick about you."

It wasn't a suggestion. I slowly slid my reader from my pouch.

"I want you to send a message to both of them and tell them they have three days to find your father. You have five minutes before I cut your internet off. Use them wisely."

He stepped out into the hall and tapped the exterior panel. The door hissed shut and locked with a beep.

I waited until his footsteps retreated before opening the messaging app. I was instantly assaulted with a dozen notifications. Jayde had been texting me nonstop. Nic had texted me once.

YOU GOOD?

I typed back.

FOR NOW. CARNEGIE SAYS WE HAVE 3 DAYS TO FIND MY FATHER BEFORE HE KILLS ME

There was a beat. I steeled myself for a sarcastic "I told you so" response, but instead he sent two words I never expected to hear from him.

I'M SORRY

I pondered the screen for a moment before remembering I was running out of time. I sent a hasty "thank you" message back and hoped he could infer the rest.

I switched over to Jayde and skimmed the message history. It was clear he had been watching the stream and couldn't decide whether to be mad or worried.

A new message popped up even as I was reading.

I CAN TELL YOU'RE ONLINE. ANSWER ME

I'M SORRY. I'M FINE

He sent back a message that, run through a profanity filter, would read *"What in the world were you thinking?"*

NO TIME TO EXPLAIN. CARNEGIE IS GOING TO CUT MY INTERNET IN A FEW MINUTES

WHO?

YOU NEED TO RUN—HE'S BEEN LISTENING TO OUR CONVERSATIONS. HE'S LOOKING FOR YOU

I CAN TAKE CARE OF MYSELF. IT'S YOU I'M WORRIED ABOUT. WHAT'S HE GOING TO DO WITH YOU?

No sense in sugar-coating it.

IF MY FATHER OR BROTHER DOESN'T MAKE CONTACT WITHIN 3 DAYS, HE'S GOING TO KILL ME

The typing dots appeared immediately—and then cycled indefinitely. I waited one beat, two, before I realized the message was never going to come. Carnegie had pulled the plug.

I glanced down at the taskbar and was surprised to find I still had three bars of service.

What's wrong? I clicked on the connections menu. NCC1701D and Wing B Guest were grayed out, but ECV197 was glowing strong.

Wing 74.

I stood up and looked around the room for the first time. It looked a lot like the room Nic had thrown me into six months ago when I'd broken out of Wing 74; it could even be the same one. But wherever it was, it was deeper into the wing, which meant I could freely connect to the network.

Carnegie must not know my reader was connected to Wing 74. I replayed my conversations with Nic and Jayde and realized I'd never said my reader was connected to ECV197; I'd only mentioned it as one of the many networks in range. Carnegie had no idea I was on here.

Hope soared through my veins—and then crashed off the edge like a waterfall. Wing 74's wifi was a highly secure internal network; there was no way to access the internet through it. I knew that from experience.

I sat down on the bench bolted to the wall and toggled to the file menu. As I expected, a lengthy list of cryptically scientific folders appeared. I leaned back and studied it, for the first time fully aware of what I was holding. This was Carnegie's war: The remnants of Red Rain, plus a dozen other weapons designed to beat Earth into submission.

My fingers tensed as I fought the urge to start aggressively deleting files. Carnegie could surely recover them, and as soon as he saw that someone was tampering with the database, he would figure out my reader was connected and take me offline. Or he'd just kill me.

I sighed and leaned my head against the unforgiving metal wall. There had to be *something* I could do. I held his entire empire in my hands; surely there was some way to set it on fire.

We let it burn.

It came to me in a rush. The sirens, the coursing lights, the factory shrieking and wailing as it self-destructed, all its systems thrown into a panic.

The virus.

I instinctively looked at my shoe. Thames had taken my flash drive—which meant Carnegie had it. Surely he'd looked at it and copied over anything that was useful to him. And where else would he store his weapons but Wing 74?

I ran several searches and couldn't find it. My flash of brilliance faded as quickly as it had flared; maybe Carnegie was using a different server. Nic had said this database hadn't been updated—

Until recently. Jayde had said there was new activity.

I pulled up "recent files"—and there it was. Carnegie had renamed it, but I recognized the file extension.

I clicked on it, and my device screeched in warning. A prompt consumed the screen, asking if I wanted to allow the program to make changes to my device. I hesitated with my thumb on the "run" button.

I had seen what this virus did to the factory. Every system had gone into a tailspin as the virus consumed programs in a tidal wave of chaos. There was no telling what would happen when I released this virus onto a space station, which was an even more delicately balanced machine than a factory of lethal chemicals. For all I knew, the virus would take the habitat systems offline and suck all the oxygen out of the room.

Of course, if a system glitch didn't kill me, Carnegie would be happy to finish the job.

I pulled my hand away from the screen. This stunt wouldn't save me. There was no guarantee it would stop Carnegie, either. He'd still have the base, and he'd still have Thames and his money. He could rebuild. He could still try to find my father.

But without Wing 74's data, he'd be starting from scratch. No matter how much government funding he had, it would still take him a long time to reconstruct ten years of labor.

If he wants Red Rain, I'm going to make him work for it.

I closed my eyes and prayed. I prayed for my dad, for Ephesus, for Cea, for Nic—all the people I would never be able to tell goodbye.

And then, without even a flicker of hesitation, I opened my eyes and hit "run."

19

At first, nothing happened, and my adrenaline fizzled out like a dead firecracker when it realized it had nothing to stick to. Did I do it right? Did I miss a step? Was there an art to launching viruses?

I clicked on the program again, and my screen flashed with an all-too-familiar warning:

Error: File not found.

I smiled.

I backed out, and the whole folder vanished beneath my fingertips. I clicked on a few other directories and found the same thing.

My device started to lag. A few more clicks, and the whole screen glitched. I tapped it rapidly, but it was bricked. The virus had done its job.

I turned off the device and slid it back into my pouch, even though I realized, with some grief, that it was now a glorified paperweight.

Now what? Surely it wouldn't take Carnegie long to realize what was happening, and if he was as smart as he appeared, it would only take him a second more to conclude that I'd done it. He'd be coming for me; I had minutes, at best.

In spite of myself, my heartbeat started to escalate. At least I knew who would be waiting for me on the other side of death.

I got up and walked to the door, listening. There were no angry shouts, no footsteps—but I did hear a faint beeping.

I pressed my ear to the door. It sounded like it was coming from the other side of the access panel. I'd never heard a door make that sound before, but it was annoyed and incessant—like an error message.

I remembered the frozen dials and throbbing displays on the machines in the factory. If the virus could send a factory into overtime, maybe it could cause the door locks to malfunction.

A light of hope flickered on in my chest, and all my adrenaline clung to it.

I stepped back and regarded the door. Didn't they say you should always push on an automatic door in an emergency?

Steeling my nerves, I threw all my weight into the center of the door with my shoulder. It didn't open—I moaned as the force shuddered back through me—but it felt different. It felt loose, almost as if the hydraulics were no longer holding the panels in place.

I scraped at the seam with my fingernails, struggling to get a handhold. I felt the panels shift.

"Jesus, come on!" I screamed through gritted teeth. I hissed as my fingers slipped on the sharp metal edge. Ignoring the smears of blood across the door, I crammed my fingers into the seam and shoved. With a labored groan, the doors slid open a few inches.

I pried my shoulder in, then my knee. With a strangled cry, I pushed with everything I had. Metal scraped on metal as the doors shuddered open.

I stumbled into the hall. A quick glance showed me the hall was empty, but surely not for long.

I pressed my wounded palms against my jacket, trying to think past the pain and survival instincts. The irritated beeping of the door panels rippled down the hall, completely out of sync from one another. I could pry any one of these doors open right now, but my bloody handprints would give Carnegie a clear trail to follow. I needed to put as much distance as possible between us and then find place to hide—or find a way out of Wing 74 where maybe I could get help.

It was a fifty-fifty chance which way he'd come down the hall. I mentally cast lots and chose the left.

I ran as fast as I could without thundering. I strained to hear any sound over my footsteps and the erratic beeping. I heard a shout and nearly tripped over myself in panic, but it sounded like it was echoing from far away, so I kept going.

I rounded a corner and screeched to a stop just in time. At the far end of the hall, a door was open. The light—and agitated voices—from within spilled out into the corridor.

I spun around. I had to duck in somewhere, fast. Doubling back down the hall, I chose the biggest door; maybe if I went into a hall with more doors, I could lead them astray.

I held my breath and wedged my fingers in the door, hoping they couldn't hear my grunting. I slipped through and immediately realized I'd made a mistake.

The hall was silent; all of the access panels were lit and intact. This wing must be on a different system. It hadn't been affected by the virus, which meant I was trapped.

Was it too late to turn back? Or would it be safer to hide and wait until the coast was clear?

I scanned the hall, looking for an alcove, and a familiar red sign caught my eye:

On Air.

The recording studio. I'd been able to open the door the other day, either because it wasn't locked or because it was set to accept me. Hopefully one of those things was still true.

I ran to the door and flapped my hand over the panel. It opened agreeably.

I slipped in and waited for the door to shut behind me. The room was just as I'd left it half an hour ago. All the lights were on and the camera was still running. The viewscreen showed a crystal-clear image of the toppled chair and torn greenscreen.

I glanced towards the control booth and saw that it was mercifully empty. It, too, had been hastily abandoned; all the monitors were up and running. My last stream was paused on one screen, my terrified but determined stare ominously frozen.

My heart rate began to tick in time with a different beat. *There's one way to make sure Carnegie never rebuilds.*

I turned back to the door. I put my ear to the seam and listened. When I heard nothing, I opened it and ran to the control booth. It, too, opened without complaint.

I shoved the desk chair out of my way and approached the monitor. I took one glance and decided I didn't have time to decode the labyrinth of controls needed to run the camera. I would have to use something simpler. I searched the desk and found Thames's abandoned tablet.

I picked it up and flipped through the open apps. One was a video streaming service. I clicked on it. He'd run a search using the terms "blue fire."

What's "blue fire"? I refreshed the results, and hundreds of videos popped up—most of which had my name in the title.

Whatever "blue fire" was, it had something to do with my videos, and it was an insanely popular upload tag. Thames hadn't been lying when he said I was trending.

I clicked on Thames's profile. It was a dummy account; there was no profile picture, and all the details looked fake. There were no posted videos. But the "Go Live" button glowed welcomingly, bright and red.

I tapped it, and it prompted me to add a title and description. I put the juiciest title I could think of—"Philadelphia tells the truth about what happened on Rott"—then barfed a couple of hashtags into the description.

#REDRAIN #SMYRNA #BLUEFIRE

Satisfied, I hit "next." The tablet's camera flickered on. The screen showed me a preview of what my stream would look like, and I cringed at the sight of my own reflection. My face was a mess of mascara and blood.

I pulled down my sleeve and gave my face a quick swipe, then coughed to clear my throat. I had to talk fast to get out what I needed to say before someone found me—or the United cut off my stream.

Although, once they heard what I had to say, they would probably let me through.

I centered myself in the frame and hit "start." The player counted down— *3, 2, 1*—then glowed red. I spoke as loud as I dared into the empty room.

"My name is Philadelphia Smyrna, and I'm here to tell you what really happened on Rott."

My viewer count ticked in the corner of the screen. It started at 1 and slowly started to climb—5, 18, 33.

"That factory was making an extremely lethal weapon called Red Rain. It's like manufactured acid rain, but worse."

My count reached the low 100s, then stagnated. Had I used the right hashtags? *You've gotta do this, Jesus!*

I pressed on. "It's a gas that can turn any kind of water or precipitation into an acid strong enough to melt metal—and kill anything that breathes. They were going to use it against the United."

I hesitated. *Who's "they"?* I had to incriminate Carnegie, and concisely— which was a problem, because they probably had no idea who Carnegie was. Even Jayde hadn't known Carnegie by name. I could tell them about the Martian base, but Carnegie would be long gone before they could get here.

My viewer count tripled. I needed to tell the United exactly where to look, and fast.

And then I remembered—there was someone else involved. Someone who was already in hot water with the officials.

"Their contact is a government agent named Thames. He has an office somewhere in the Boston metropolitan area. He's the one who kidnapped me and blackmailed my father into completing the formula. He was the one monitoring Rott. If you trace the data virus, you'll find it leads straight back to him."

My viewers skyrocketed—at the same time the door hissed open.

I whipped around. Thames stood in the hall.

I gaped at him, startled but somehow unafraid. There was nowhere to run, even if my nerves had been willing to cooperate.

"What have you done?" he said, barely a whisper.

I didn't answer.

His eyes fell on the tablet in my hands, which was still streaming. "You've ruined me."

Abruptly I realized he was crying.

The big guys are looking for blood.

He stepped into the room. I stumbled back into the desk, causing a monitor to rock precariously.

"You have no idea what you've done!" he screeched.

But I did know. I knew exactly what I'd done.

I straightened. "You ruined yourself."

His eyes searched me angrily. "You don't understand. I could have *helped* you!"

"You could never help me."

He roared. He lurched forward and yanked a desk drawer open, withdrawing a gun.

I screamed. The tablet clattered to the floor.

Thames cocked the weapon. Tears were coursing down his face as he drank me in one last time. "We would have loved you!" he yelled, and leveled the gun.

I threw my hands over my head. Five seconds too late, I realized he wasn't pointing the gun at me.

20

Thames slumped over, slowly, as if he still had enough vitality left to guide his fall. His body collapsed into the desk chair, sending it crashing into the wall.

I waited until the chair had stopped spinning and my ears had stopped ringing and he had stopped breathing before I moved.

I gingerly stepped forward—right into a pool of blood.

Suddenly I could smell it, see it, almost *hear* it pouring out onto the metal floor. I tasted bile.

Against every fiber of my being, I bent over and pried the gun from his still-warm hand. I slid it in my pocket, where it thumped against my thigh like a brick. Choking on a sound between a gag and a sob, I snatched the tablet from the floor and darted out of the room.

There was no one in the corridor. I ran to the gate, marked by my bloody handprints, and glanced around the hall beyond.

No one came running. There was no sound at all except for the obnoxious beeping echoing from the broken door panels like a dying heart monitor.

Where was Carnegie? Had he made a run for it? Or had he also—

I didn't want to think about it. I needed help. I needed to find Nic.

All I had to do was retrace my steps from the recording studio—I'd walked that way enough times before. I closed my eyes, and immediately I saw everything I didn't want to see—Carnegie with a syringe in his hand, me with blood on my palms, Thames with a bullet in his...

Jesus Jesus Jesus, was all I could think to pray.

I forced myself to start walking. I found Gate B, which was still online.

I panicked. I had no way to contact Nic or Jayde; the messaging app was on my reader, which was useless. All I had was Thames's tablet.

Which no doubt had the door lock software on it. And Thames had level 1 security clearance.

It took longer than it should have. My hands were shaky and my fingers slippery with sweat. My mind was spinning and struggling to process even the simplest tasks without seeing flashing colors and imagining disembodied screams. But with no small amount of help from the Holy Spirit, I managed to find the door lock software and whitelist Nic and myself.

Nic must have heard my muttering and broken sobs, because he was waiting on the other side of the door when I finally got it opened.

"Show me," he demanded.

I led him back to the recording studio, even though every nerve in my body recoiled in horror. I swear I could smell it—him—all the way out in the hall.

Nic took one look inside the control booth and immediately assumed command. In a blink the old governor returned. He let us into a nearby office, where he commanded me to wait.

I gratefully did so. I curled up on the chair in front of the desk and numbly watched as he started making calls.

Ten minutes later, he left, telling me not to move. I had no intention of doing so. I pulled my knees to my chest and rocked back and forth. I wasn't crying—I wasn't sure if I wanted to cry—but I had to do something, execute some repetitive motion, or I was certain I was going to crack under the emotional pressure.

What were we going to do now? Where was Carnegie? Had the United seen my stream? Would they find Thames's office? What about Jayde? What would—

"Philli."

I screamed and fell out of the chair, where thick arms caught me. I panicked and fought—until I realized the hands holding me were large, black, and crusted with potting soil.

I looked up into his face. "Mr. Sardis?"

His pained eyes squinted at me, and he opened his arms for a hug. I threw myself into them. I grabbed him around the neck like an anchor and sobbed, releasing all the fear and terror in an unfiltered stream.

He let me cry until I paused to breathe again. Then he stood up and put his hand on my shoulder. "Let's get you home."

I vainly rubbed my eyes as we took the long trek back from Wing 74 to the front of the base. The sense of familiarity grew like heat rising in an oven as we neared the dorms. I couldn't tell if it made me feel more at home or further away from it.

He let me back into our old dorm. I sank down on the couch and looked around at the familiar furniture, trying to scrape together a feeling other than emptiness. I couldn't find anything.

Mr. Sardis returned a half-hour later with all my baggage, including my colored pencils. I shoved them to the bottom of my suitcase, intending to deal with them later and knowing I probably never would. I grabbed my toiletries and did the only thing I knew how to do—shower and pray. Even if the prayers didn't wash away the sense of horror, at least the water would wash away the blood.

Around six, my doorbell rang. I answered it to find a stunning black woman I only vaguely remembered—Mr. Sardis's wife.

"We want you to eat with us," she said with a gentle smile.

I didn't argue. I sat with them in the cafeteria, letting their young son entertain me with his constant jabbering. I didn't eat much, but I soaked in everything. The smell of food. The dying sunlight soaking through the windows. The bright plastic. The ambiance of people—other people. It felt like it had been so long since I'd been in community with other people. I listened to their talking, the clattering of their silverware, their laughter. I let it seep into my veins like an IV, bringing a small trickle of life back to my soul.

I wasn't quite ready to be alone for the night, but the Sardis's seemed to have thought of that. Their son dragged me back to their dorm, where we sat on their couch and watched episode after episode of his favorite TV show. We watched until he passed out on my lap and his dad carried him to bed.

Mrs. Sardis walked me back to my dorm. "Ring if you need anything—any time of night."

I thanked her with a hug.

A brand-new tablet lay on the couch. I picked it up. It was light and razor-thin, and the screen blinked to life at the sight of my face. Only three programs had been installed: the messaging app, an ereader, and a music player.

I clicked on the messaging app and saw two new texts from Nic.

I COPIED MY MEDIA ARCHIVE TO THIS DEVICE. I HOPE THAT WILL SUFFICE

I smiled, then saw the second message.

CARNEGIE IS TAKEN CARE OF. I'LL EXPLAIN IN THE MORNING

For once, I was all too grateful to accept his explanation and leave it alone. I curled up on the couch and opened a chat with Jayde.

HEY

His response was instant.

I'VE BEEN TRYING TO REACH YOU FOR HOURS

I glanced back at the message history and realized that was true.

SORRY

I started to explain, and then realized I didn't want to.

DID YOU SEE MY STREAM?

WHY DO YOU THINK I'M FREAKING OUT?

I winced.

IT'S FINE. I'M FINE. THAMES IS DEAD. NIC TOOK CARE OF CARNEGIE

I licked my lips and hoped he wouldn't ask for further explanation. He didn't. There was a long pause before he responded at all.

I THOUGHT I LOST YOU

I typed back another "I'm sorry," even though I didn't know exactly what I was apologizing for. I didn't regret any of my actions, and I would do it all again if it meant keeping Red Rain out of the hands of Thames and Carnegie.

I redirected the conversation back at him.

WHAT ARE YOU GOING TO DO? THE UNITED IS PROBABLY GOING TO BUST THAMES'S OFFICE, YOU NEED TO GET OUT OF THERE

The typing dots appeared, vanished, and reappeared again several times before a message came through.

DON'T WORRY ABOUT ME, I'M LONG GONE

WHAT ARE YOU GOING TO DO FOR WORK?

This time, there was a good minute of silence before he responded.

I'LL BE FINE. THE THING ABOUT THAMES IS THAT HE WASN'T ALL UP-AND-UP WITH THE UNITED. SINCE HE WAS IN THE HABIT OF FORGING PAPERWORK HIMSELF, IT'S A LOT EASIER FOR SOMEONE WITH FAKE CREDENTIALS—LIKE ME—TO SLIP IN HIS RANKS. I'LL HAVE MY FILE SCRUBBED BY MORNING, AND THEN I CAN JUST GET ANOTHER JOB

I smiled and thanked God.

I'M REALLY HAPPY TO HEAR THAT

GET SOME REST. WE CAN TALK TOMORROW

OKAY. THANK YOU AGAIN FOR ALL YOUR HELP. I COULDN'T HAVE DONE IT WITHOUT YOU

He didn't respond for an unusually long time. I began to wonder if he'd already signed off.

Several minutes later, he texted back.

IT'S THE LEAST I CAN DO

21

Nic met me for breakfast the next morning.

"Carnegie escaped," he announced as soon as we'd sat down with our food.

I spit my toast back onto my plate. "I thought you said not to worry about him!"

Nic seemed unruffled. I could tell he was already on his second cup of coffee and had taken some time to prepare his words. "Because I'm legitimately not worried—at least not right now."

"Why not?" I demanded.

"I'm his only alibi."

He slid a tablet across the table. Carnegie's file was displayed on the screen. "Carnegie kept himself—and this entire base—clean. That's why he never involved me in any of this. The United has no idea anything went on up here, then or now. As far as they know, Rott was the center of the action. Mars isn't even on their radar."

I scrolled through Carnegie's file. "But couldn't he turn you in?"

"Of course—at his own expense. If he blows this place up, he destroys his own alibi with it. According to his file, he still works here, and any job transfer would have to be approved by me as his last employer." Nic took the tablet back. "If the officials come snooping into me, they'll find a whole server's worth of intel on him."

"But doesn't he have connections? Couldn't he forge files or alter evidence or something?"

"He *did* have connections—but I think those connections are rotting in the morgue right now."

I gagged.

"Sorry," Nic said, and I think he was being truthful. "What I mean is, I think Thames *was* his connection. Carnegie doesn't have any power on his own. He was, and still is, just an overly ambitious chemical engineer. He doesn't have any clearance with the United. Thames was his master key—the one signing off on reports and issuing blank checks."

"What about Thames's people?"

"Those that are smart will run. We won't have to worry about those that don't."

I shuddered. I hoped Jayde meant what he said about being long gone.

"Your stream told the United exactly where to look. They've probably already razed Thames's office to the ground. They're going to scour those servers—but if Carnegie is as smart as he appears, they won't find anything linking Thames to Mars."

That seemed like a reasonable assumption. Even Jayde hadn't known Thames was involved with Mars, and he worked for him.

Nic stirred a spoon through his coffee, even though I hadn't seen him add any sugar. "He'll be looking for other allies. But the United has no doubt frozen Thames's assets, which means Carnegie is temporarily penniless and homeless. He's going to have to hold his cards close to his chest, and it will take him a long time to rebuild what he had here."

Nic glanced up at me. "He'll be back. I have no doubt of that. But until then, I have the upper hand."

"So why not rat him out first?"

"Because then I'd be throwing myself under the bus. There's millions of bites of data linking Carnegie to me. If I incriminate him, I'll be the first person they investigate." He sighed and ran a hand through his unwashed hair. "I'm going to work on scrubbing the data and distancing myself from him, but it will take time."

"So until then, stalemate."

He nodded.

I rubbed the goosebumps on my arms. Sitting around waiting for one of them to pull the trigger did not sound like my idea of a good time. "So what do we do now?"

"Well, I don't know about you, but I'm going back to work."

I just stared at him.

He gestured at the cafeteria around us. "As far as the United knows, I never left. My file is spotless. Carnegie was careful not to link anything to me, and by some miracle you didn't blow my cover in your impromptu confession. I can, quite literally, pick up where I left off."

I glanced at the people milling around. "But how can you trust these people? How do you know they aren't with Carnegie?"

"There are a few," he admitted. "But they, if anything, have the most incentive to stay quiet."

He leaned back in his chair and eyed me. "You forget, Phil, that you're not the only person here who hates the United. Everyone has a bone to pick. Some, like you, are malcontents. Some want to run experiments that don't have federal approval. Some just don't want to pay taxes."

He nodded at an Asian businessman as he passed our table. The man gave Nic a distracted wave as he continued to chatter into his phone.

"Most of these people don't even know what happened," Nic went on. "Those that do have no reason to tell. Everyone up here has a secret—and they know that if they keep mine, I'll keep theirs."

I gazed at the diverse faces around us. "So what are you going to do now that you're back in business?"

"Keep fortifying my base."

When I shot him an incriminating glare, he put his hands up. "Don't worry, I'm not about to start work on Red Rain."

"And why not?" I countered. It was a genuine question, and every fiber of my being begged him to prove me wrong.

"First of all, it doesn't work on Mars—the atmosphere is too thin. It would only be useful in a large-scale offensive strike against Earth, and thanks to all the damage Carnegie's done, I simply don't have the resources for that kind of wishful thinking right now. Not to mention you also wiped my last database with that virus."

There was a sprinkling of salt in his voice, which I ignored. "And?" I prodded, not satisfied with his explanation.

"And, frankly, I have no desire to start another game of cat-and-mouse with the United. It was fun while it lasted, but I don't want to spend the rest of my life trying to keep the formula out of their hands."

"That's it?" I sputtered. None of those were the reasons I wanted—needed—to hear.

"What do you want me to say, Phil?" he said, too loudly for the ambiance in the room. Several people glanced in our direction. He waited until their eyes drifted elsewhere before continuing.

"Do you want me to apologize? Promise that I'm never going to launch an attack on the United? Swear to never ever do anything that violates your personal moral code?"

Well, at least two of those things would be nice.

"Because I guarantee you that last one *will* happen. The United is still the enemy, and I still intend to fight back."

His eyes found mine. "Look, I don't know how you feel about it, and frankly, I don't care. But revolution has to start somewhere. You said yourself—we can't let them win. We have to fight back. And if you don't want to fight with guns, pick up some other weapon. Write a freaking pamphlet for all I care. But if you want things to change, start changing."

I turned away, churning his words over in my mind.

"But while you're figuring that out, you're welcome to stay here."

I looked back at him. He hit a button on the tablet, then held it out to me again. "There's something you should see."

I took the device and was startled to find my face staring back at me.

It was a personnel file with my picture on it. The photo had been retouched slightly—my hair was lighter, and glasses had been shopped onto my face—but it was definitely me. I squinted at the name on the file.

Andromeda Nolan.

I felt sweat collect on my palms.

"I found it on Thames's computer. Clearly, he had it made for you, and he made himself your legal guardian."

Nolan? Thames Nolan?

The horrible truth drowned me in a rush.

I should have listened to Mrs. Nolan and insisted you stay on Earth.

My husband is well spoken of with the commander; they have agreed on the terms.

When this is all over, I'll do my best to give you a normal life. I promise.

The tablet shook in my hand. I remembered the hair conditioner, Mama's suitcase, the colored pencils—all the little kindnesses that proved he had been watching me for a very long time.

We would have loved you!

"Delete it," I hissed through clenched teeth, afraid that if I opened my mouth, worse things would come out. I threw the tablet on the table, jostling our cups.

Nic watched me carefully. "You might reconsider."

"No," I said without any consideration at all.

"I'm not kidding, Phil. This is a beautiful file."

I glared at him out of the corner of my eye. He tapped the screen. "It has been masterfully forged. It's easy to fake a file—it's not easy to fake one that looks legitimate. This file has everything—perfectly constructed medical and school records that all sync flawlessly with public databases. I did some searching, and I couldn't find anything online that would contradict this file. I even called one of your old schools, and they swore up and down that you were one of their best students. It must have cost him millions to forge this."

"I don't care."

"You should," he shot back. "Your real file is a mess. You're wanted by the highest levels of government, and there's no turning back that clock. But with this—you can walk out of here scot-free. And because you're part of his family, you'll have some special privileges—including some bank accounts, it looks like."

"Won't associating with him get me incriminated?"

"He seems to have thought of that. You're not actually his daughter—you're the daughter of his deceased brother and sister-in-law. It checks out; they had a daughter who would be about your age, and they all died in a car crash, so there's no one to contradict your story. No one's going to think to investigate his dead relatives. He was going to list himself as your legal guardian—but guardianship is easy to change."

I looked up to find him staring at me.

I retched. "Don't even think about it."

He groaned. "Trust me, this doesn't give me warm-fuzzy feelings either. But I'm your best shot. Your father and brother aren't going to be able to find you based on your old file. At least, if you're associated with me, they have a chance of connecting the dots."

He had a point—a point I couldn't deny. I let my breath out.

"Let me do this for you, and we can call ourselves even on the whole saving-each-other's-lives thing."

In spite of myself, a smile tweaked my lips. "Deal."

He nodded. "All we have to do is get your fingerprints surgically altered just enough. Then we can link the new prints to your file, and you'll be a new person."

"Do you know someone who can do that?"

He rubbed his own fingertips contemplatively. "I can make some calls."

I picked the tablet up and looked at myself again. "Andromeda," I rolled the name over on my tongue.

"Nice to meet you, Andromeda," Nic repeated, then grimaced. "Why can't you pick a name with less than four syllables? I'm calling you Andi."

A laugh escaped my lips.

Andromeda. It didn't sound anything like me.

But maybe that was the point.

I set the tablet back down. "What about my father and brother?"

"Unfortunately, the United is still looking for them. If they're smart, they'll do exactly what you're doing—forge new files."

"Then how am I supposed to find them?" I cried, the hope dying in my words.

"I honestly have no idea."

I slumped in the chair, the energy draining from me as the unanswered questions returned with a vengeance.

"But I'm sure you'll figure something out."

I glanced up. He had gone back to eating and wasn't looking at me.

I straightened. "Well, there's one thing I can try. But I'll need a favor."

One eyebrow twitched to indicate he was listening.

"I need access to Wing 74."

22

The lights in the recording studio flickered on. The place had been swept clean; you couldn't tell there'd been a deadly scuffle in here only a day before. The camera had been polished and straightened, and the folding chair had been set back up in its line of sight.

On the seat was a thin black tube. I walked over and picked it up. It was mascara. Wrapped around it was a piece of masking tape with a microscopic note:

DON'T FORGET TO CONDITION YOUR HAIR -N

I turned the tube over in my hands, then slid it in my pocket.

A tech I'd only just met had volunteered to run the soundboard. He was in the control booth, spinning around in the chair and salivating over the equipment. "This is a beautiful setup. I wish I could stream my gaming with this."

"You ready in there?" I shot back.

"Let's do it!" He slid up to the desk and tapped a monitor.

I arranged myself in the chair. The viewfinder flickered on. I gazed at my reflection and took a minute to straighten my hair.

"Just give me a signal when you want me to start."

I nodded, closed my eyes, and rehearsed what I was going to say. *Hi. My name is Philadelphia Smyrna.*

The name felt almost foreign now, like it belonged to a different person. Philadelphia Smyrna was the girl who blew up labs, destroyed factories, and sabotaged the United. She resisted. She fought. She was a terrorist. That was the Philadelphia everyone knew.

But, perhaps, she wasn't so foreign to me after all.

I opened my eyes and nodded at the control booth. He gave me a thumbs up and punched a button. The *On Air* sign glowed to life.

I turned to the camera.

"Hey, Dad. It's me, Phil."

AURELIUS

RED RAIN #3.5

RACHEL NEWHOUSE

MAY 2076

1

My world ended when I saw Philadelphia in the back of the van, cuffed and unconscious.

It was noon when I got the call for two emergency pickups. This was nothing unusual—it was my job, after all. That's why I ran a takeout-only pizza shop. The frequent deliveries were the perfect cover for transporting people who had gotten themselves on the United's bad side.

Cea—or Ceasar, as I knew her—was the one to make the call. I'd been in contact with her off and on over the past few months. She'd been stirring the waters, making a name for herself and figuring out who her friends were, so I knew it was only a matter of time before she needed a pizza.

What I didn't know was that she and I had a history together.

Jayde, our mutual contact, wasn't forthcoming with this information either. Jayde was my first connection with the underground, and we'd worked together enough that we might almost call each other friends. My shop was the closest pickup and dropoff point to the office were Jayde worked. And since Jayde was a guard for a high military official, he was involved in plenty of shenanigans that required pizza delivery.

I hadn't shared a lot of my past with Jayde, but he knew enough to realize that Cea and I had come from the same unassimilated concentration camp. You'd think he would have put two and two together and had the decency to give me a head's up that I might actually *know* the people he was depositing on my doorstep.

Instead, I was wholly unprepared when he opened the back of the van and I saw Philadelphia lying there.

I recognized her instantly, even though she was blindfolded. Her long brown hair pooled around her head like spilled coffee. She wore her favorite outfit—a khaki skirt and gray jacket with leggings and combat boots. It was the same outfit she'd been wearing when I saw her last, the day I left camp for good.

Take their offer while you still can, Phil—take it and run.

The memory of her face—watery eyes begging me to turn around and change my mind—brought with it several other images I was unprepared to handle. My parents, the commander's gun pointed at my chest, Mira, the callous goodbye note taped on our bathroom mirror—everything I had spent the last several months trying to bury came rushing back with all the requisite unwelcome emotions.

You denied Him.

Jayde was unappreciative of my existential crisis. "C'mon, man, we've gotta move!" He'd already uncuffed Cea and helped her down from the van.

I nodded, sweeping the emotions back into the corner of my mind. Jayde knelt next to Philadelphia and removed the cuffs, and I picked her up.

As her dead weight settled in my arms, I saw the dried tears on her face and was slammed with two unsettling realities:

One, she had been through hell.

Two, a *lot* had gone down since I'd left camp.

Jayde helped me get the girls into the bunker, then made himself scarce. The bunker was a concrete cellar under the shop's basement and the one part of the building the government didn't know existed. It was where all my deliveries waited until they could catch a ride somewhere else.

Somehow I had the feeling I couldn't just load Philadelphia on the produce truck and ship her back out of my life.

I laid her out on a blanket in the corner of the bunker, then took care of Cea. I got her a first aid kit and water, and she gave me the rundown while she cleaned and bandaged her own wounds.

The short of it was that Philadelphia's dad, Dr. Smyrna, had been summoned to Mars to work for Cea's brother, Dr. Nic, and gotten tangled up in a weapons plot. Now the United wanted the project finished, and they had been holding Cea and Philadelphia hostage to blackmail the scientists into completing the weapon.

The long of it was that Philadelphia's brother Ephesus, whom we all thought was dead, apparently *wasn't*, and the project was a world-ending superweapon called "Red Rain," and Philadelphia had blown up a lab and turned Nic over to the authorities, and now the United wanted the weapon for themselves, and Jayde's boss, Director Thames Nolan, was overseeing the project.

Luckily for all involved, Cea knew how to order pizza.

None of this really surprised me, except maybe the part about Ephesus coming back to life and definitely the part about Philadelphia blowing up a lab by herself.

I watched her sleep from across the room and wondered if she was the same girl I had left behind.

OCTOBER 2075

2

"Mr. Dass, need we use force?"

I shifted uncomfortably. All down the street, families gathered on their doorsteps for the daily ritual of handing their kids over to armed guards to be escorted to public school. It didn't have to be dramatic, and for most families, it wasn't. They protested with frowns and tears but wisely kept their words and fists out of it.

My father, however, was not so wise.

"You will need to use a lot more than force if you expect me to move!" he snarled, spittle slurring his words. He clutched my sister Mira to his chest like some sort of sacrificial lamb. I stood behind him, back pressed against our front door, as if that was much safer.

Commander Ambrose, foot on our bottom step, issued another threat, but I glanced away and tried to tune them both out. Their tirade would continue for several minutes as they competed to be the most hateful one in the room. The commander always won, but only because he had weapons to prove his point.

My eyes roamed the street, searching for a safe place to land. My classmate Philadelphia and her father stood in front of the house across from ours. She stared at me, eyes so wide with fear that they seemed to swallow her plain face. I ignored her.

Suddenly, Mira screamed, jerking me back to the debacle in front of me. Ambrose grabbed my sister's shoulders and shoved her to the sidewalk. Before I could object, my father roared like a bull. He charged at Ambrose, but the commander swiftly clipped him across the chest.

My dad stumbled back and caught himself on the railing. "You beast! Just try and take my son."

He stepped back, crushing me against the front door. My heart leapt to my throat even as I coughed in protest. *This can't be happening.*

"Are you enjoying this? Is this some sort of game to you?" the commander scoffed.

If it is, I don't want to play.

My father didn't have a comeback. His whole body shook with ragged breaths as he stared the commander down.

Ambrose gave him a minute to comply. I nudged him. *Please just move, Dad.*

He didn't. The commander frowned and reached for his trump card: his gun.

Survival instinct kicked in. It had been six months since anyone had died because they refused to go to school, and I was not about to break that record.

I elbowed my father in the shoulder blade and shoved him out of my way. I heard his grunt and saw his hand reach for me, but I ducked under his arm, jumped the steps, and grabbed Mira. Her fingers gripped mine as I hauled her onto the bus.

We took the bench at the very back. Mira released my hand to fold hers primly in her lap. "Thanks," she murmured.

I offered her a half-smile, then leaned my head against the seat in front of me, waiting for the adrenaline to drain from my nerves. Voices erupted outside, but I didn't turn to look. I didn't want to give my father a chance to make eye contact. He could lay it on me when we got home.

A minute later, Philadelphia slid into the seat across from us, and the bus pulled away without further ado. A few of the younger kids yelled goodbyes as we passed the concrete wall and electric gate that turned our neighborhood into a prison. With an impatient blare of its horn, the bus cut into traffic, and I briefly wondered what would happen if the bus came back without me on it.

The silence in the back of the bus was tense, so I knew it was only a matter of time before someone unhelpfully broke it.

Philadelphia made the first move. "I'm sorry," she said, voice clearly directed at us.

I just nodded.

"He didn't hurt me," Mira assured her, although the tremor in her voice said otherwise.

"I'm surprised your father didn't offer any objections, Phil." Our friend Cami leaned over the back of her seat and poked Philadelphia in the knee.

"How could he, after that?" Cami's brother Aid snapped. "The commander hasn't pulled his gun in almost a month."

And it was pointed at me.

Philadelphia's voice was small as she answered. "We talked about it, last night. He said it wasn't worth the blood right now."

"Smart man," I muttered. Philadelphia's dad had learned the hard way what could happen if you resisted the commander, but at least he had taken the lesson.

I could only hope my father would do the same before he took Mira—or me—out with him.

3

The school day started the same as it always did: with our homeroom teacher lecturing us about our pathetic existence. It was supposed to be a sales pitch, where the riches and freedoms of the United—the one-world megacountry that existed outside the concentration camp walls—were paraded before us, enticing us to join.

But our teacher didn't have the patience for that. He'd long since given up the propaganda and resorted to unveiled threats and dehumanization. Each morning he dutifully reminded us that we were civil criminals, and if we didn't wise up and sign the file, we'd be facing a lifetime of imprisonment and slavery.

I couldn't blame him for his pragmatic approach. Most of us had been in his remedial class for five years, since the concentration camps were erected and being "unassimilated" had officially become a crime. He had led a rather successful career, and our class size had dwindled until there were no more than twenty of us. But those of us who had held out were blots on his academic record, and he was not shy about his displeasure.

"Your religion will kill you," he announced for the third time this week.

It almost did today.

"This faction—this false sense of identity—you so stubbornly hold to is going to tear you apart. A meaningless label and an ancient book of lore are the only things keeping you from rejoining normal society."

"Ignore him when he talks," our parents always told us. A glance around the room showed that my classmates were all trying to do just that, to varying degrees of success. I could tell Philadelphia was listening, though. Her eyes were downcast, but her face was pinched in a scowl. She always took the lectures too personally.

I preferred to take the man head-on. I'd put on my best "bored teenager" face and lock eyes with him. I'd stare, unflinching, through the entire tirade, waiting to see how frustrated he'd get before scolding me for some imaginary offense.

Today, however, I had even less patience than he did. My morning brush with death had made me irritable, and when I got irritable I resorted to sarcasm.

"All you have to do is sign the file renouncing these foolish constraints, and you can join the United with all the rights and freedoms of full citizens," he was droning.

"Oh really?" I snapped.

The room shifted to look at me. The teacher's eyebrows twitched like he'd been stung by a bee. "Did you have something you wanted to say, Stanyard?"

"Yeah." I sat up straighter. "Exactly what do you expect us to do if we sign the file and join the Outside?"

"First of all, don't call it 'the Outside.' That kind of divisive language is exactly what keeps you segregated from society. Second," he tempered his voice with a deep breath, "I expect you to become fully functional members of society. You'll have rights, employment opportunities—"

"So what, you're going to kick me out on the street and expect me to find a job?"

He hesitated. Mira glanced over her shoulder and searched me.

I held the teacher in my stare. "I'm seventeen, dude. I've lived in a concentration camp since I was twelve. I don't have any money. No car. No job skills. No friends or relatives whose couch I can crash on. If I sign the file, I get dumped on the street with nothing."

I leaned back in my chair and crossed my arms. "No thanks. I think I'll stay in the camp where at least you're legally obligated to feed me—for now."

The teacher regarded me, but for the first time in years, his gaze wasn't accusatory. "You make an excellent point, young man. And I'm pleased to inform you that the officials are aware of your unique situation and have several programs in place."

"Like what, more tax breaks?" The United was beleaguered with programs, none of which were incentive enough for me to abandon what was left of my family and join the Outside—or I might have done it already.

The displeasure returned to his expression. "There are, in fact, several new programs that have recently been approved. I will inform you as soon as applications open."

"Can't wait," I muttered, but quietly enough that he ignored the comment and turned back to the board.

"Now, class, I'm to inform you that chemistry has been canceled due to Mr. Glasgow's absence, so you will have an extra period of study hall instead. As a reminder, you are only to access approved sites while on school grounds. Any uncensored internet activity will result in detention and possible criminal prosecution..."

The room shifted back into place. Mira frowned in a way that said we would talk later, then turned her attention to her laptop. Philadelphia was the last to look away.

4

"Why did you ask?"

It was lunch hour, and Mira and I had retreated to the far end of the schoolyard. It was the one place we could talk freely without the prying ears of our classmates—or parents.

I opened my mouth to reply at the same time my tablet screeched at me. It did that frequently. I spent most of my free time trying to hack around the internet restrictions and tamper with the school's databases, so I was constantly running into errors and firewalls. The sound didn't bother me; I enjoyed pushing the limits and seeing how far I could get before someone noticed and dragged me to the principal's office. It was the one thing I could control about my life, even if it usually ended with detention.

The reprimands had been happening less frequently this semester, though, either because I was getting better at hacking or because the principal realized there was nothing she could do to hurt me. Detention was hardly a threat when I already lived in a concentration camp, and, unlike Commander Ambrose, she didn't have the clearance to shoot students. She had nothing on me.

But I hadn't run into a firewall this time. The popup claimed that the file I had been trying to access was corrupted—which it hadn't been five minutes ago. I tried opening it again and got the same error. I backed out and refreshed the folder; the file vanished entirely.

I sighed and tossed my tablet on the dry grass. It didn't matter; I was just trying to sneak a peek at the trigonometry quiz for tomorrow.

I looked up at Mira. She was waiting patiently for my reply. "It's a legitimate question. He blathers about it every day but never has a good answer. Does he really expect me to walk out that gate and find the nearest bridge to live under?"

She glanced at the tall fence that contained the schoolyard. "Are you asking because you want to leave?"

I opened my mouth to brush off the comment, then stopped. She had that telltale look in her eye—that flicker of hungry fear that said she needed her big brother to go first.

"Do *you* want to leave?" I cast the question back at her.

She was silent, and I knew I had my answer. But then again, I'd known the answer for a while. I had just been waiting for her to bring it up.

"No," she whispered after a minute.

"But?" I prodded.

"But I don't want to die." She turned to face me. "Stan, the commander could have *killed* you this morning. I saw that gun and for a minute I was sure that you or Dad was going to end up like Phil's mom…"

I nodded. I'd been having the same thoughts all day.

She shuddered. "I don't want to die for something so *stupid*. If I'm going to die, I want it to be for something important, like…"

"Refusing to deny Christ?" I suggested, because that was what we were expected to say. But hadn't we already done that?

"I mean, yeah, I guess," Mira mumbled.

That's why we were in a concentration camp, they said. Every morning our parents reminded us why we were here—not unlike our teacher and his lectures. We chose to be unassimilated, because assimilating meant signing a file revoking all religious, racial, and national identities.

That's all it was—*a piece of paper*—no different than the terms and conditions everybody acknowledged without reading. Yes, if you read between the lines, signing the file meant legally denying Christ. But people say a lot of things on paper that they don't really believe.

"But where else could we go?" Mira uprooted random blades of grass. "Like you said—we have nothing. No relatives. No way to get a job or an apartment or anything. At least here we have a house, food, Mom and Dad…"

I tried to read the emotion on her face, but there was none, less or more. I knew family was the main thing keeping her tethered, the only reason we hadn't had this conversation months ago. But judging by the fact that her eyes were blank and dry, she was beginning to become unmoored.

My ship had drifted out to sea a long time ago.

Mira stared at her handful of grass, then shoved it back into the dirt with a grunt. "But what if we *do* stay? How long before they send us to a real prison? Or try neurosurgery on us? What if they kill us anyway?"

They would. The question was when, and whether or not the death would be physical.

"I just… I don't… I'm not…" Mira struggled for a moment, then broke down in a sob.

I reached over and grabbed her hand. "If we go, we go together."
I gripped her hand. She squeezed mine back.

5

Their names were Mark and Julia Carver, and they chose us because we were close in age to their son.

It was a week later, and our teacher had forgone his usual morning lecture. Instead, he lined us up and inspected us like he was a drill sergeant in charge of boot camp. He made Cami fix her hair and Aid stand up straight. He snapped his fingers in front of Mira's face until she pretended to look alive. When he came to Philadelphia, he told her to smile. She did, but the expression was somehow worse than the tearful frown she'd been wearing before.

As for me, I hadn't bothered to wash my face that morning, and apparently that was unacceptable. After we'd tidied ourselves to his satisfaction, he herded us into the principal's office.

I was the last in line. He grabbed my shoulder as I passed by him.

"This program is a once-in-a-lifetime offer," he hissed in my ear. "I suggest you take it while you can."

Then he pushed me into the office and shut the door behind me.

The principal divided us into separate meeting rooms. Mira and I were sent to Room 1, where we met the Carvers, a blandly normal couple who informed us without ceremony that they wanted to adopt us.

The terms were simple. The family would provide everything for us—food, clothing, a place to live. They would support us while we finished school, got our first jobs, applied for college. We would have no financial obligations until we turned twenty-five.

"But even after that, you'll still be part of the family," Mrs. Carver crooned.

In the United's defense, it was a clever solution to their underage assimilated problem. It was cheap, effective, and deliciously tempting. I knew some of the younger kids would be instantly pulled in by the promise of freedom and new toys.

I was hesitant, but only because I didn't feel any safer with Mrs. Carver than I did with my dad. Mr. Carver was all right. He had a refined pragmatism, and I got the distinct impression that he'd be getting a big tax break for taking us in.

It was Mrs. Carver who made me uncomfortable, not that I could have explained why. On the surface, she was sweet and caring, and she doted on Mira like she'd known her for years. She gave Mira a pretty necklace and told her to "keep it as a gift, even if we don't see each other again."

Mira was sold. I could tell that she'd made up her mind before we left the meeting, but I gave her twenty-four hours to think about it before broaching the subject.

"Well? Are we going?" she asked when we'd found our solitude at lunch the next day.

"Do you want to go?" I knew the answer, but I wanted her to say it for herself. I would do whatever she decided, but I needed her to choose what was best for her. That was all that mattered to me now.

She stared at the grass, taking one last moment to shift through possible objections. "We won't get a better offer."

I sighed. "No, we won't."

The United had done their homework this time—this program really did solve all our problems. We would be provided for while we got adjusted to the real world, found jobs, went to college. And, in the meantime, we'd be with people who at least had a tax incentive to care about our welfare—instead of a father who would make us take a bullet while telling us we were fulfilling our destiny.

"I don't want to tell Dad. Or Mom," Mira confessed.

I looked up at her. "You don't have to."

She flinched, and all the fear and hesitation washed up in her eyes. "I just… don't want to hurt them."

It's too late for that, but they're bringing it on themselves. "I'll take care of it," I assured her. "You don't have to worry about anything. Pack what you need tonight—I'll talk to the principal."

She smiled in a way she hadn't in months, and I knew we were making the right decision.

I spoke to the principal, who spoke to the commander, and the next morning both of our parents were conveniently called into work early. Mira and I packed the essentials—most of our worldly possessions fit in our backpacks and one duffle. I wondered if our classmates would notice our extra luggage, but frankly, by the time we got on the bus it would be too late for anyone to do anything.

Mira wrote our parents a long, no doubt heartfelt letter. I didn't read it. They would get no goodbye from me.

Mr. and Mrs. Carver met us before class started. They asked us if we were sure this was what we wanted to do. I let Mira answer for both of us, which she did eagerly. Mrs. Carver hugged us and said they'd be back to pick us up after school.

There was only one piece of paperwork to sign, and it was done.

I'm sorry, I offered as I scribbled my signature. *But I can't let my sister die.*

There was no response. I wasn't expecting one.

I was distracted in class, but our teacher, who must have heard the news, was unusually permissive. I spent the day worrying about all the practical things I knew Mira hadn't thought of, problems I needed to solve because I was the big brother. Would we be changing school systems? I desperately hoped so. What would I have to do to get a job? We needed to start saving money. Would Mr. Carver teach me to drive?

We avoided our classmates until the bell rung and we all congregated in the parking lot to wait for the bus. I knew the truth was about to come out, but Cami, in her usual way, had to make a scene of it.

"Ha! You're avoiding me! *Mira.* What's up? Why did your Outsiders come see you again today?" She got up in my sister's business, hands on hips and nose wrinkled in a suspicious glare.

Mira glanced at me, and I almost stepped in to rescue her. But then, to my surprise, she answered for herself. She took a step back, lifted her chin, and announced: "We're going home with them today."

The group gasped, and my chest tightened a little too. It was suddenly more real when I heard it coming from her lips.

Mira's face held no fear. She scowled at her former friends. "We're not going to do it anymore! We're leaving! We're not going to keep living stuffed away in a little hole until they decide to kill us. We accepted their offer, Stan and I. They'll be here to pick us up any minute."

They looked to me for confirmation. I swallowed to shove the trepidation back down in my chest, then nodded. There was no turning back now. We'd already signed the file.

"Then you… denied Him," Philadelphia whispered. Her eyes tracked Mira, who avoided her gaze.

"We signed the file saying we wouldn't practice a religion anymore, yes." My sister shrugged like she didn't care, even though the glisten in her eyes told a different story. "We figure they can't stop us from thinking about it, and that's what matters, right? It's a relationship, not a religion."

"You denied Him," Philadelphia said again, this time at me, as if she expected a different answer.

I growled. This was exactly what I *didn't* want to hear. This was why we had avoided our parents and waited to tell our classmates until the last minute. I didn't want a sermon from a self-righteous martyr about how my life would be better if I threw myself on the pyre and allowed the commander to butcher me and my family—all for a piece of paper that meant nothing.

Where was *that* in the Bible?

"It's the only way," I snapped. "If you were smart, you'd do it too." Philadelphia of all people should understand why we couldn't stay. If she didn't want to end up like her mother, she would leave too.

I wasn't cruel enough to say all that out loud, but I met her gaze and repeated, "Take their offer while you still can, Phil—take it and run."

"But what about your parents?" Cami screeched.

"We didn't tell them," Mira admitted. "I left a note this morning." Cami paled and finally shut up.

"This will kill your father, I assure you," Aid declared.

I bristled, remembering the dozens of times my father had put my life on the line, never once caring that I might get shot. "He's going to kill himself! He'll come out soon enough, when he realizes the truth."

As soon as the words left my lips, I knew at least part of that statement was a lie.

A horn honked, ending the conversation. We turned to see the bus pull in, followed by the Carvers' car.

Mira drew in a sharp breath. She glanced at me. *Are we really doing this?*

I put on my bravest face for her and nodded. *If we go, we go together.*

The Carvers parked nearby and got out to greet us. "Mira? Stan?" Mrs. Carver called hopefully.

Mira shouldered her bag, found a smile, and walked towards them without a glance back at our classmates. I grabbed the duffle and followed.

Mrs. Carver showered us with hugs and kisses, most of which were thankfully planted on Mira. Mr. Carver offered me a handshake and pat on the back. "Ready to go?" he asked.

"Yes, sir," Mira replied.

"And thank you," I added for his benefit. He gave me an understanding smile.

"Come on, our son is dying to meet you." Mrs. Carver embraced Mira again and led her to the car. Mr. Carver popped the trunk and helped me load our baggage.

As if realizing the show was over, most of the kids fled for the bus. But Philadelphia stayed. I could see her reflected in the car window. I stopped, one hand on the door, and watched her silently beg with her tears.

Come back.

I turned and glared at her. "Accept their offer while you still can," I hissed.

Then I got in the car, slammed the door, and left her behind.

MAY 2076

6

I shut the trap door to the bunker and dragged a crate over it, letting it go with a thump. I wished it were that easy to shut my past in a box, but the least it—she—could do was stay down there and be quiet for a few hours.

I flopped down on my bed with a groan. Getting Philadelphia and Cea into the bunker was only half the battle. Now we had to figure out what to do with them. Unfortunately, I had a feeling it wouldn't be so simple as putting them on a bus out of town. Thames was powerful, and if this project was as big as Cea made it out to be, then he would want the girls back. He'd probably already flagged their prints, which meant they would have to go completely off the grid until they could forge new files. And falsified files were expensive.

The softness of my pillow and the gentle drone of the TV I always left running threatened to pull me in, but I forced myself to get up and go back to work. Someone had to feed us.

I emerged into the daylight of the shop and was annoyed to find that several carryout orders had processed through the online system. Apparently I'd forgotten to pause orders before taking care of the girls. I picked the stickers up from where the printer had spit them on the floor and looked at the timestamps; the oldest one was from 40 minutes ago.

I sighed. I definitely wouldn't be getting any tips or five-star reviews today.

I fired up the oven and went to work. Even with the clanging of pans and the whir of the exhaust fan, the empty store was too quiet. I kept hearing what sounded like voices—especially Philadelphia's. After glancing over my shoulder for the third time to verify that no one was there, I surrendered and turned on some rock music.

No sooner had I packed the last pizza box than another call came through on my private line.

I groaned. I really wasn't in the mood for another run today. But I put on my best self and answered the phone.

"4th Street Pizza Parlor, how may I help you."

A voice I hadn't heard in years echoed over the line.

"Hi, yeah, I'd like to order three house specialties, please. No drinks."

Ephesus. He really was alive. I dropped the box I was holding and gave him my full attention. "Carry out or dine in?"

Someone swore in the background.

Ephesus shushed them and answered my question. "Do you offer curbside?"

Normally I didn't—but for Ephesus, I'd risk it. "Sure. Address?" I grabbed my other phone and typed into the navigator as he dictated.

Ephesus thanked me and hung up, but not before I heard what sounded like Dr. Smyrna in the background.

I switched back to the register, shut down online ordering, and canceled the active orders. I'd have to do some hacking to fix the bad reviews later—the United tended to ask questions if a store had too many bad reviews—but it would be worth it if we could extract Ephesus and Dr. Smyrna.

Then at least *one* family would be together.

JANUARY 2076

7

My first indication that I'd made a mistake was when Mira stopped crying.

For several weeks after the Carters adopted us, she cried herself to sleep every night. Transitioning into our new life was hard on her, more so than for me. I had allowed my dad's anger to cauterize our bond long ago, so I had no difficulty blending in with our host family. I saw it as a business relationship, and our foster father did as well, so we got on fine. Mrs. Carver barely paid me any attention; she already had a son, so I fulfilled no particular purpose for her.

Mira was another story. Mrs. Carver had always wanted a daughter, and she had an extreme savior complex—a trait that became apparent almost immediately after we moved into their home. Mrs. Carver saw in Mira an opportunity to fulfill both fantasies, and Mira, whose emotions were still raw and bleeding, was ripe for being rescued.

At first, they seemed to bond—they spent every free moment together as Mrs. Carver took Mira to do every girly activity known to mankind—and I thought everything might turn out all right. But when Mira's tears didn't dry and her wounds didn't heal—and Mrs. Carver got increasingly possessive as she feasted on Mira's misery—I knew we had a problem.

I tried to intervene as much as I could without imploding our precarious social position. If the Carvers decided they didn't want us, we'd be kicked back into the foster care system, which was only one step above living on the street. I didn't want that for Mira, so I tried to stand up for her without offending Mrs. Carver. I interrupted arguments, volunteered as a third wheel on outings (Mrs. Carver rarely agreed), and even talked to Mr. Carver (who didn't see the problem).

But despite the fact that I repeatedly reminded her that I was there for her, my efforts weren't enough for Mira. She never said as much, but I could read between the lines. She withdrew from everyone and continued to cry herself to sleep every night.

And then, one day, about two months after we left camp, she didn't.

I heard the silence through our adjoining bedroom wall and dared to hope that she'd turned a corner. I greeted her with enthusiasm the next morning and got nothing in return. She was calmer, yes, and she seemed more sure of herself, but she couldn't have cared less about me. Her conversations were pretenses and her laughter fake. She just wasn't *there*—and she had always shown up for me.

Just like I'd always shown up for her.

I continued to show up as best I could. I complimented her hair when she chopped and dyed it. I went with her when she got her ears pierced, and then again a week later when she added a stud to her nose. For a month I helped her change the bandage on her new tattoo as she slowly drew a dragon circling up her arm. When she received money for Christmas from our new "relatives," I offered to go clothes shopping with her, but she claimed she was going with friends.

When she came home with tops and jeans that revealed curves I didn't know she had, I began to wonder if some of these "friends" weren't women.

She didn't say. She didn't say much of anything. I saw her less and less as she started going home with friends after school and not returning to the house until late. Our foster parents were unconcerned—claiming she was just being a normal teenager—so I tried to copy their nonchalance and accept the change.

But I missed her.

Finally, just after New Year's, she broached the conversation.

Someone rapped on my doorframe, and I looked up to see her standing there. "Can we talk?"

"Of course," I said, a little too eagerly. I tossed my tablet aside and made room for her on my bed.

She took it, sitting down as far away from me as possible. I resisted the urge to close the gap and waited for her to speak first.

"Stan, there's something I need to tell you."

"Yeah?" I made sure my voice was calm and approachable.

She looked anywhere but my eyes. "It's about... us. Well, mostly me. I just... I don't think I can live here anymore."

You don't really live here anymore, I thought but didn't say. "Why's that?"

She bit her lip.

I waited—one beat, two. "Is it Mrs. Carver?"

She shrugged. "I mean, kinda. She's definitely not helping."

I chuckled, and she joined in. For one final moment, everything was back to normal as we shared a sibling joke that no one else understood.

Mira composed herself. "I just think I would be happier somewhere else, that's all."

"Well, I want you to be happy." The corny answer was off my tongue before I had a chance to rephrase it, and I laughed at myself. "Wow, that sounded dumb. I promise I'm being sincere."

"I know you are." She looked up and met my eyes for the first time.

I held her gaze. "I want you to choose what's best for you. I always have. That's why we decided to go with the Carvers—and if they're not right for you anymore, we can go somewhere else."

"Thank you for understanding." Her eyes drifted, and I could tell she was shutting down again.

I tried to jam my foot in the door before it closed. "Well, I mean it. If we need to move on, we'll make it happen." I reached over and grabbed her hand. "If we go, we go together."

I smiled, a warm invitation to let me back into her life. I didn't care where we lived—we could walk out the front door right now for all I cared. I just didn't want to lose her, not after how much we'd sacrificed to get here.

She hesitated for a long moment before she turned and looked at me again. Then she smiled and squeezed my hand.

Three days later, I found the note taped to our bathroom mirror.

STAN—I'VE MET SOMEONE. DON'T WORRY ABOUT ME, HE'S A SOLDIER AND I'LL BE SAFE. I NEED TO DO THIS, FOR MYSELF. THANK YOU FOR BEING SO SUPPORTIVE. I'LL SEE YOU LATER. <3 MIRA

She was lying, at least about the last part. I didn't see her later. She sent a few emails, but they were infrequent and insincere. It took a few months before I accepted that I might never see her again.

Turns out "together" had been a one-sided proposition all along.

MAY 2076

8

My security system woke me up.

It took me too long to register that the beeping was coming from the app on my phone, and even longer to recognize that the alarm had been triggered over fifteen minutes ago.

I stared at the clock and tried to figure out why it hadn't woken me up in the first place—then remembered that the sleep aid I'd used last night had been neither organic nor legal.

I groaned. I knew better than to binge when I had refugees in my basement. The extraction of Ephesus, Dr. Smyrna, and Nic, who were being held in one of Thames's labs, had gone surprisingly smoothly. I'd almost backed out and turned around when I pulled up to the building and saw that the place was in chaos—apparently Ephesus had triggered the fire alarm and several other emergency protocols as part of their escape. But the chaos worked in our favor, and we'd gotten away scot-free.

I should have been proud of myself. But after watching the Smyrnas reunite—a tearful event I knew I'd never have—and staying up late hacking to fix the shop's bad reviews, I didn't have the energy to deal with memories or dreams, so I'd taken the easy way out.

I cursed myself and pulled my shoes on. The alarm had been tripped in the garage. Hopefully that meant it was just a mouse or something.

It wasn't. It was Nic.

He was sitting cross-legged in the middle of the garage floor. At first I thought he was meditating or whatever, and I almost let him be, even though he definitely shouldn't have been out of the bunker. But then I saw the telltale blue glow of a backlit screen on his face.

Every muscle stiffened in warning. There was no reason someone like him—a high-profile criminal hiding off the grid—should be on *any* device.

I slammed the door open. "What are you doing?"

He didn't even flinch—just cast an annoyed glare at me like I'd busted into his office without asking. "It's fine."

I didn't buy that for a second, not from a mad scientist who was wanted for developing superweapons. I strode over and snatched the tablet from his hands. A quick glance at the screen showed that he had logged in somewhere—

which was bad enough—but I almost passed out when I saw *where* he had logged in.

Of all the sites, he picked one I knew the government would be monitoring. We had an hour—tops—before they noticed they'd been hacked and tracked the signal to the shop.

That's when survival instinct kicked in, and I did the only thing I knew how to do: Run.

Whenever I revisited that day in the nightmares of my regrets, I wondered what would have happened if I'd taken a different route. Maybe I should have insisted we split up. Maybe I should have taken them on foot. Maybe I should have kicked Nic to the curb and made him deal with the United on his own.

But I didn't. Instead I cussed Nic out, woke everyone up, and packed us into my beater of a car. Despite the fact that my head was still reeling from my military-grade nightcap, I insisted on driving.

Maybe that's where I went wrong.

Cea and Nic took the trunk. Ephesus crouched in front of the passenger seat, while Philadelphia and her father laid out on the floor of the back seat. I could hear her hyperventilating before we'd even left the garage.

I drove to the end of the driveway and sat there, debating which route to take, the blinker clicking in time with my indecision. Would we have made it if I had turned out seconds earlier and gotten a few blocks ahead of them?

"Coast clear?" Ephesus asked at the exact moment I realized it wasn't.

Cop cars—three of them—were converging from the side streets. Their lights were off, which briefly deluded me into believing they weren't coming for us.

They made their intent perfectly clear when I turned onto the road and they shot at my rear window.

No lights, no siren, no chance for me to pull over and turn myself in—not that I would have taken them up on their offer. The bullet ripped through the rear window to the accompaniment of Philadelphia's scream and exited out the front windshield. They'd missed me, but I could tell by the trajectory that they hadn't intended to.

I slammed on the gas. My car dutifully tried to obey, but I wasn't sure which was working harder—my heart or the engine.

"Where are we going now?" Ephesus shouted.

"Still the rendezvous point, if we can lose them!" I yelled, not feeling confident in either half of that statement. I swerved in between lanes, trying not to give the cops a clear line of fire.

"Can you try losing them on the freeway?"

"Not enough traffic!" I argued. But maybe he had been right—maybe gunning it on the open freeway would have been a better option. Instead I ran a red light, whipped a U-turn in the intersection, and blazed back down the other side of the divided road. That gave me a few blocks' lead on them while they navigated around the median, but it wasn't enough.

I continued to swerve, but they were getting closer, which meant their aim was getting better. They took out my side mirror, then punched a hole in my trunk. I wouldn't have cared if Cea hadn't been back there.

Their superior engines continued to gain, and I knew that it was only a mile or two before they rear-ended me. I had to find somewhere to turn off, fast.

Ephesus continued to unhelpfully copilot, and I continued to bicker with him, even though I don't remember a thing I said. It was like the words were coming from someone else while I had an out-of-body experience struggling to maintain control of the car.

I couldn't think around my headache. I couldn't see around the spiderweb in my windshield. All I knew was that if I didn't get out of sight *right now*, there would be a bullet in my head—and probably everyone else's.

So when Ephesus screamed at me to *turn*, I did—and drove us right into a dumpster.

The impact knocked the wind and soul from my body, and the airbag finished the job. My head slammed backwards into the seat, and consciousness alluded me for a fraction of a second. I heard wailing and sirens and crying and couldn't figure out how much of it was in my head and how much was in reality. I saw black, then white, then the smear of blood on the deflating airbag. I tasted more of it dripping from my nose to my mouth.

Then my brain regained control of my body, and I jerked upright. I became aware of Dr. Smyrna shouting and Ephesus groaning. I turned and saw him collapsed against the passenger seat, face bloodied beyond recognition.

I swore. I tried to open my door and found it jammed against the dumpster. I pulled my knees back and kicked it with both feet. The dumpster clanged and shuddered and finally rocked a few inches—just enough for me to get out.

I jumped out and scanned the area. We'd crashed behind a cluster of buildings, which meant there were several narrow alleyways we could take on foot.

I calculated the others' survival. Ephesus wouldn't make it, but he was also the one most capable of taking care of himself. Cea and Nic were probably already dead or wounded. Dr. Smyrna was on his own.

But Philadelphia was on my side of the car, with a clear shot to the alley. We could both make it.

I yanked her door open. "Let's go! We can escape on foot through the alleys. They can't take their cars down here, so we still have a chance of losing them."

She swung one leg out of the car—then hesitated.

I panicked. *Now is not the time, Phil!* "We have to go, now!"

Her father shouted at her. She turned.

In that split second, I could see that what had killed her mother was still holding her back. *Don't be an idiot!* I held my hand out.

Take their offer while you still can!

She looked at me. I heard shouting and tires squealing and realized we had only seconds. "Phil, if you don't come now I'll leave you behind!"

Take it and run!

Her fingers closed around mine, and an unfamiliar emotion gripped my chest.

It was too late for my dad. It was too late for Mira.

But Philadelphia. Philadelphia and I could make it together.

I hauled her from the car—right into the line of fire. An electric shot ripped the air while her scream ripped my ears.

She collapsed on the concrete, yanked from my hand. I looked at the scorch mark on her pant leg and knew exactly what had happened.

She'd been stunned. Now she couldn't run.

She gaped at her leg, then turned to me. Those wide, fearful eyes looked up at me, begging for help.

Something deep inside my gut lurched, and suddenly, I wanted to help. I wanted to be the hero. I wanted to pick her up, rescue her, *protect* her.

I could do it. I could carry her. I could pick her up and escape down that alley.

But with the dead weight, could I run fast enough? If we didn't make it out of sight in time, the cops would just shoot us both. And after all I'd done to help the Smyrnas, I'd be lucky if the government just stunned me and dragged me back to prison.

I'd already lost my business and my cover today. Did I want to lose my life too?

If we go, we go together.

I saw the lights of a cop car reflecting off a store window, and I made my decision.

I turned and ran.

"Stanyard!" Her broken cry reached me, and I almost turned around. I almost went back for her. But by then the police had arrived, and I knew it was hopeless.

I ducked around a corner and wove a zigzag pattern through the back streets. I had no idea where I was going, just that I needed to put enough space between me and the scene that the cops would give up the search.

It worked. No one came after me.

I ran until the adrenaline failed me. I collapsed next to a dumpster and leaned my head against the concrete building. I drew deep, long breaths through my nose, trying to beat my heart rate back into submission. The throbbing and dizziness faded, bringing far worse feelings in their wake.

I was wrong. Philadelphia hadn't changed. She was still the same fearful girl who hesitated too long and let the bad guys walk all over her. I was a fool for thinking otherwise.

But then again, I hadn't changed either.

9

Jayde took me in.

It was a stroke of providence that I knew where his apartment was. When Mira first went missing, I turned the internet upside down looking for her. I flooded social media with posts, begged the phone company to track her devices (they denied my request), and tried hacking into every database I could find, looking for any activity on her file that might help me pinpoint where she was. I didn't get very far, but I poked around enough that I learned there were websites—and people—existing outside the surveillance of the United. There was an underground.

I made enough noise that someone reached out and tried to help. They claimed they had seen Mira with Jayde. When Jayde was unresponsive to my texts, I asked around and learned that he worked for Thames. I followed him home from the office one day and confronted him on his doorstep.

Jayde was mortified that I'd discovered his identity, but when I mentioned Mira, he decided not to shoot me and instead invited me in. He said he'd seen Mira around, hanging out with other soldiers in his regiment, but he had no idea where she was now. If Mira really had hooked up with a soldier, it wasn't anyone he knew.

That was when I finally accepted that Mira didn't want to be found.

Jayde promised to keep me updated, and through our continued contact he'd inducted me into the underground. He helped me get the job at the pizza shop, which had been recently vacated. As soon as they heard that I could support myself financially, my host family let me go without complaint. Jayde introduced me to his contacts and helped me make my first few successful runs. After that, I was in business, with Jayde's constant undermining of his boss providing me with steady work.

That, and it turned out I wasn't half bad at making pizza.

I hadn't been to Jayde's apartment since then, but I remembered how to get there. I waited until it was dark, bought some pizzas from a shop with generic-looking boxes, then rang his intercom. Thankfully I was still in my work uniform, so hopefully the spectacle looked benign to anyone watching the security cameras.

After an elongated pause, Jayde buzzed me in.

The look on his face when he opened the door told me that he'd already heard the news.

He confirmed my fears: Philadelphia and the others had been captured by Thames. They were alive, but Jayde had no idea where they were being held. The operation was apparently above his security clearance.

I begrudgingly relayed my side of the tale. Jayde accepted it without shame or condemnation; these things happened in our line of work. It wasn't my fault; it was Nic's stupidity that had blown the whole thing up.

I knew I wasn't to blame, but that didn't stop the depression from settling on my soul like a layer of dirt on a coffin.

Jayde allowed me to crash on his couch, and we waited to find out what the government would do with Philadelphia—and me. As soon as the officials figured out that it was my car totaled in the alley, they'd realize I'd gotten away and flag my file for investigation. The question was what charges they'd lay against me and what punishment they'd prescribe.

The next morning, I hacked into my personnel file to read the damages— and found it untouched. My file, though shoddy and peppered with multiple warnings about questionable behavior, contained nothing about Nic or the arrests.

I wondered if they were simply behind on their paperwork, as they often were. But several days passed, and my file still was not updated. There was no mention of a warrant against me on any government site that I could find. I even took a risk, drove by the shop, and found it standing. The only indication that anything was wrong were the deliveries that had been abandoned on the front step.

I was beginning to believe that no one was looking for me, which meant one of two things. Either the government didn't realize I was involved, or they didn't care. Neither of those things seemed plausible.

In the meantime, Philadelphia and Nic were sent to another prison. Again, Jayde couldn't find out where. The investigation must have been marked classified, because most of Thames's people were in the dark. Anyone who was willing to talk knew nothing. The most Jayde could scrounge up was that Dr. Smyrna had resumed work on Red Rain.

I didn't need a spy to tell me that. I knew what this was all about. The government wanted their superweapon, and Philadelphia and Nic, as soon as they had outlived their usefulness as collateral, had been kicked to the curb. Ephesus and Cea were no doubt soon to follow.

Jayde continued to make calls, but I knew it was hopeless. Wherever Philadelphia had been sent, she wasn't coming back.

But I knew that when I abandoned her in the alley, didn't I?

10

My world ended when I saw Philadelphia on TV.

It was about a week after the crash, and I was still languishing on Jayde's couch. He texted me from work with the news. I almost ignored his message because it came from an unknown number, and all the message said was "You are not going to believe this!!" with a link to a video. As if realizing how spammy that sounded, he followed up with his callsign and strict instructions to rip the video and start uploading it everywhere.

I clicked on the link, and at first I didn't know what I was looking at. It was security footage of a factory that had been bombed or caught on fire or something. Emergency lights washed out the image, and the sprinklers were spraying a dark liquid everywhere. A broken maintenance catwalk swung precariously below the camera. There were no people anywhere on screen.

And then she appeared.

She lurched into the frame from somewhere just below the security camera, appearing to fall into reality from another dimension. I almost dropped my phone as my heart leapt to my throat, then plummeted back down to my stomach.

She leaned over the edge of the catwalk, stretching a bloody hand towards something below. I caught sight of what looked like two men scuffling on the factory floor several stories beneath her. I couldn't see their faces, but process of elimination suggested one of them was Nic.

The men dropped out of frame. Philadelphia screamed, the motion mute on the soundless security footage.

Then, faster than I could count the seconds, the catwalk dropped from beneath her. She scrambled for a handhold even as I yelled into the void. Another chain snapped, and she plummeted out of sight. The video cut off.

I stared at the blank screen in my hands as grief and rage competed for dominance. Why would Jayde do this to me? Of course I wanted to know what had happened to her—but not like *that*. I didn't want to watch her horrific death in real time without any warning.

I texted him the worst swear word I knew, followed by:

SHE'S DEAD?

He replied immediately.

BRO I HAVE NO IDEA. YOU WON'T BELIEVE WHAT THEY DID. THAT FACTORY WAS MAKING RED RAIN, AND THEY JACKED THE WHOLE THING UP. EXPLAIN WHEN I GET HOME

I tried to piece two and two together. Evidently Dr. Smyrna had completed the weapon. Thames must have shipped Philadelphia and Nic out to the factory and put them to work instead of leaving them in prison.

I replayed the video. That dark liquid must be Red Rain. I restarted the video again, and this time I could see the acid eating away at the chains that supported the catwalk, a ticking time bomb to her demise.

I watched the video again, and again, and again, each time vainly hoping the ending would be different. That she would get out of the way, or the last chain would hold, or the camera would shift and I could see her land safely. But each time she fell out of frame, and each time my heart cracked a little more, until finally I tore the wound so wide that I could actually feel something.

She was dead. Philadelphia was dead. There was no way she survived that fall.

"Why?" I shouted to the empty room, but I didn't need an answer. I knew why. She was dead because I'd left her to die. I'd abandoned her. I'd turned and ran, just like I always did.

Take their offer while you still can, Phil—take it and run.

I didn't cry. I wanted to rage. I wanted to scream and kick and threaten and fight, just like my dad had always done, because for the first time I understood why. Anger could be directed outwards. There was nowhere for grief to go but in.

He's going to kill himself! He'll come out soon enough, when he realizes the truth.

I threw my phone to the floor, then sank down next to it. Here I was, six months later, drowning in my words because I was now living the truth. And the truth was that the United was evil, and the Outside was a prison, and I was just as bad as everyone else. I'd done exactly what all the treacherous backbiters on the street did—I'd thrown my friends and family under the bus to save my own skin. I was a coward.

If you were smart, you'd do it too.

Philadelphia was the smart one. That shy, fearful girl we'd all taken for granted had been right about everything, especially me.

You denied Him.

I did. I'd walked away, reduced Him to a line item on a contract, a contingency that could be signed away with one stroke of the pen. I told Him I could take care of myself, and I'd ended up exactly where He said I would—on the outside looking in, without a penny or a hope to my name.

I'd died. The death just hadn't been physical.

"I'm sorry," I whispered, but I didn't mean it, any more than the last time I'd said it. The sentiment felt fake, overshadowed by the other emotions competing in my head. The pride and the fear—the big, ugly fear that I'd be left defenseless and alone—fought on my insides, suffocating the light that struggled to burn in my chest.

I dug my hands in my hair, wishing I could rip the ugly out by the roots. "I'm sorry!" I roared, and again, "I'm sorry!" I slammed my head backwards into the couch, once, twice, three times, as if I could shake free the words I so desperately needed to say.

I finally heard—no, *felt*—them rise above the chaos. With one shattering breath, I shoved out the two hardest words of my life.

"Forgive me."

Everything crumbled. It was like my being collapsed from the inside out. All the self-reliance and bitterness I had been using to shore up my personality fell out from beneath me. Just like Philadelphia had fallen backwards into the factory, I disappeared into darkness—every lie, delusion, and manipulation I had used to box myself in breaking apart like that ruined catwalk.

I sagged against the couch. I didn't cry. I didn't make a sound at all. I just waited as wave after terrifying wave of the Holy Spirit washed away everything I thought I knew about myself.

When the noise faded and I felt like I'd returned to my body, I opened my eyes and stared at the peeling paint on the ceiling.

"Do I get another chance?" I asked when I'd gathered the courage to speak to Him again. There was no answer.

My phone buzzed, reminding me that there was one thing I could do. Jayde had said to copy the video and upload it everywhere, and now I understood why.

The world needed to see that video. A girl—a single unassimilated girl— had stood up against the United. She'd been beaten, humiliated, and thrown to the ground, but she'd gotten up and kicked them where it hurt. She'd taken her last breath and determined to bring the government down with her.

There were people that needed to see that—people like me. I'd show them if it was the last thing I did.

Philadelphia was dead, and the whole world was about to find out why.

11

Jayde came home giddy with excitement, as if we both hadn't just watched our friend die on live TV.

"Dude, did you *see* that?" He shed his boots and jacket on the floor. "That girl is insane."

"So I'm realizing. A trigger warning on that video would have been nice."

The nuance was lost on him. "Oh, that ain't the half of it. Just wait 'til you hear what happened at work."

I obliged. He wheeled the desk chair over and climbed into it. "Okay, so, I'm in a meeting with Nolan, and suddenly this warning goes off on his computer. He and the people with him start freaking out—and I mean *freaking out*—and they log into the security cameras and pull up that feed." He gestured at the phone in my hand.

"Of course then they kick us all out of the room, but not before I heard them mention Red Rain and Phil. Thankfully, as a guard I have access to the camera system, so I was able to copy the video before he marked it as classified."

He flexed a muscle and kissed it. I waited.

He turned back to me with a grin. "And that's when things got *really* crazy. Every computer in the office just blew up. I'm talking every monitor has the blue screen of death, the fire alarm goes off, the security systems go completely offline, everything. Here, look at my phone."

He tossed his device at me. I caught it, turned the screen on, and saw that it was glitched out like a piece of abstract art. "Is that why you texted me from a new number?"

"Yeah, I had to use a burner phone. Dude, you won't believe this, but *Phil* did that."

"What?" I barfed, although given everything that had happened, I had no trouble believing it.

"Yeah, her and Nic uploaded some kind of virus to the factory computers, and it wiped everything. And since Nolan's system was linked to the factory…" He clapped his hands together and mouthed "boom."

I looked down at the corrupted device in my hands. "She beat him."

"Oh yeah she did," Jayde crowed. "The office is on fire. It's great."

I tossed his phone on the coffee table. "Did they… confirm she's dead?" I kept the raw emotions out of my voice.

He shrugged. "I have no idea. I don't even know where that factory is."

I frowned. He put his hands up. "Bro, Nolan's got this thing under wraps tighter than a pair of spandex on Batman. Everyone I talked to had no idea that factory existed until today—most of them hadn't even heard of Red Rain or the Smyrnas. The government has this whole project locked down—you should have seen how fast they nuked the video I uploaded. Hey speaking of." He rolled the desk chair closer. "Did you share the video?"

"Yeah." I unlocked my phone and handed it to him as proof.

He refreshed the page and cackled. "Ha! You got blocked too. See? The government is losing their mind."

I took my phone back and saw what he meant—the video I uploaded had been taken down for "violating community guidelines," and my account had been put "under review."

"Make another account and do it again. I've got a bunch of dummy IPs you can use." He whirled the chair around to face the desk and fired up his computer.

"Okay but, who do we talk to about Phil? Surely someone will go out to the factory and investigate. They're going to find a body. What about Nic?"

Jayde looked over his shoulder and met my gaze for the first time. "Look, dude, I don't know anything. If it makes you feel any better, I agree with you— she's probably dead. But I'll keep poking, and if I hear anything, I promise you'll be the first to know."

I sighed. He studied me for half a beat, then turned back to his computer. "But for now, the best thing we can do is spread that video like the plague. She did the entire free world a favor—the least we can do is light it up."

He was right, so light it up we did. For a week we spammed the internet with copies of the video. We sacrificed hundreds of social media accounts and throwaway websites to share the link. We made dozens of backups and sent them to all our contacts, who repeated the process. It was normally difficult to get a bunch of rebels to agree on a cause, but most had no trouble rallying around Philadelphia—probably because the one thing we could all agree on was that we hated the United.

Jayde and his friends invented a hashtag to channel the momentum:

#BLUEFIRE

When I prompted him for an explanation, he smirked and said, "Because what's the opposite of rain? Fire. Also, it sounds cool."

That was one of the dumbest things I'd ever heard him say, and it wasn't scientifically accurate. But it was hard to argue with him when his tactics were working. The government labored tirelessly to remove our videos and block our accounts, but they weren't fast enough. Philadelphia and #bluefire were trending.

In the meantime, Thames's empire continued to go up in flames, much to Jayde's delight. Thames's computer had spread the virus to several other elite government officials, and they all came breathing down his neck for it. He apparently didn't have a good answer for them, because he vanished. He put in a note claiming he was sick and would be working from home, then dropped out of contact.

Philadelphia's family did the same. In the chaos surrounding the virus, they escaped from wherever Thames had been holding them. Jayde had no details; he only knew that they were gone, and several heads were on the chopping block for it.

We hired help and reopened the pizza shop, although I decided to stay away from the building until I was sure how things would blow over. We wanted the doors open in case Cea or one of the Smyrnas made contact. I didn't know if they still trusted me—or if they even knew I was alive—but I wanted someone to answer the phone if they called.

I asked—more like begged—God to lead them to call the shop. I still wanted another chance, so I figured the best thing I could do was not shut up about it. Our conversations were short and uncomfortably one-sided, but at least they were happening.

There was still no official confirmation of Philadelphia's death. The United razed the factory—it was on a prison island called Rott—to the ground, but her file was never marked deceased. She was flagged as a suspect in the ongoing investigation, and that remained the most recent update for a week. I checked it every day.

Jayde was hopeful, pointing out other discrepancies in Philadelphia's file, but I didn't have the gut for wishful thinking. If the United had her in custody, they wouldn't put out a search warrant for her. It was far more likely that her body hadn't been recovered.

I've never been happier to be proven wrong in my life.

This time, I was the first one to see the video. I was online forging another account to share the security footage when she popped up in my feed.

"My name is Philadelphia Smyrna."

I gaped at the screen for several minutes, expecting it to be a trick, a stunt double, a hologram. But the more she talked, the more she moved, the more confident I became—under that layer of freshly-applied makeup, it was her.

That still, small voice inside of me gave a chuckle. *I like second chances.*

My shouted prayer probably woke the neighbors. I nearly knocked Jayde's monitor off the desk as I scrambled for my phone to give him a call.

I ripped the video and watched it twenty times, searching for clues. It was clearly staged—she recited a redacted version of her life's story in front of a greenscreen—and neither Jayde nor I could figure out where she was. But we were certain Thames, who was still MIA, was involved.

Two days later, Nic made contact.

He appeared online, asking for any information on Thames. Jayde used his boss's ritzy government spyware to trace Nic's device and found out that the network he was using was indeed on Thames's system. That didn't tell us where they were—Thames's position meant he had remote access to networks all across the country—but it did give us a place to start.

It also allowed us to search the activity of other devices connected to the network—including an ereader that had been very active over the past several days.

And there was only one person I knew who used an ereader like a laptop.

"You should be the one to talk to her first." Jayde handed my phone back to me.

He'd pulled up Philadelphia's profile on a messaging app. The "add friend" button glowed green and enticing.

My fingers twitched. I wanted to slam the button and start rattling off an apology—but I knew I couldn't announce my identity online, at least not so forthrightly.

And maybe, given the circumstances, it would be better if she didn't know it was me.

I shook my head. "I don't think she trusts me right now." I held the phone back out to him.

He didn't take it. "Seriously, dude, what's the worst she could say?"

My brain autofilled several possibilities.

I hate you.

I don't trust you.

I can't forgive you.

I muted the voices. "We don't have time to go through a whole song and dance while I convince her I'm on her side. I need her to trust me *now* if we're going to figure out what's going on and get her out of there. I mean, you saw how worked up she got while talking about me leaving camp. She's clearly not ready to have this conversation."

It wasn't a total lie—anyone could see how pale-faced and teary-eyed she'd gotten while recounting that part of the story in her first video—but Jayde didn't buy it. He arched one bushy, carrot-colored eyebrow and waited.

I put my hands up. "Okay, fine. *I'm* not ready to have that conversation."

"At least you're honest." He shrugged it off. "Fine, if you want to stay out of it, tell her it's me. She trusts me."

I knew she did. Jayde had never done her wrong, unlike me.

"You're still going to have to do most of the talking—I can't be on that app at work. But sure, you can tell her it's me. I'll be the hero." He pondered that statement for a minute, then grinned.

I ignored him and went back to my phone. I navigated to my profile and changed my username from "augustine_saint" to "Aurelius397"—subtle, but clear enough that my other contacts could probably deduce that it was me.

I threw up a prayer that Philadelphia wouldn't.

I tabbed back to her profile and hesitated with my finger over the button. Jayde was right—I'd have to face her eventually. Maybe, if I proved myself first, she would buy my apology.

Or she might not. She might hate me. She might not forgive me. That's what I deserved; I wouldn't forgive myself, either.

But for Philadelphia, it was worth a try.

If we go, we go together.

I clicked the button and sent her a message.

HEY PHIL

TO BE CONTINUED...

WANT EXCLUSIVE BONUS SCENES?

Become a Patron and get access to **exclusive bonus scenes** for this series! This bonus content is not available anywhere else, and I post a new scene every month. Plus, you can get digital ARCs, signed paperbacks, collector's edition hardbacks, and merch, or read my WIP as I write it!

Become a Patron at:
patreon.com/rachelnewhouse

Or sign up for my newsletter and be the first to hear about new releases—plus get sneak peeks of upcoming books, cover art, and more!

Sign up at:
rachelnewhouse.com/subscribe

DID YOU LOVE THIS BOOK?

Please consider leaving a review on Amazon or Goodreads! It's one of the most important things you can do to support an indie author.
Thank you!

HI FROM RACHEL

Rachel Newhouse is an author, wife, secretary, and Sunday school teacher from Kansas City, Missouri. Her obsessions are sci-fi, dystopian, and kid lit. When she's not writing, she's cooking Asian food, growing chilis that are too spicy to eat, and watching wildly age-inappropriate shows like *My Little Pony* and *Gravity Falls* with her husband, Joe. She also really likes glitter. You've been warned.

Connect with Rachel:
bio.site/rachelnewhouse

DAVID ALSO SAYS HI

David Hartung is "that guy"—the one whose fanfic became canon. If you're jealous of that, you're right to be. Outside of that claim to fame, he lives in Wisconsin with his family, where his firstborn Daniel continually robs him of his aspirations to become a master of the secret art of Narco.

www.ingramcontent.com/pod-product-compliance
Lightning Source LLC
Chambersburg PA
CBHW060634310726
48982CB00003B/779